# STEP

# BY

# STEP

## CARL DAVOS

Matador
9 Priory Business Park,
Wistow Road, Kibworth Beauchamp,
Leicestershire. LE8 0RX
Tel: 0116 279 2299
Email: books@troubador.co.uk
Web: www.troubador.co.uk/matador
Twitter: @matadorbooks

ISBN 978 1838595 494

British Library Cataloguing in Publication Data.
A catalogue record for this book is available from the British Library.

Printed and bound in the UK by TJ Books Limited, Padstow, Cornwall
Typeset in 12pt Adobe Jenson Pro by Troubador Publishing Ltd, Leicester, UK

Matador is an imprint of Troubador Publishing Ltd

For a woman I met near Cathédral Notre-Dame de Paris

'I think a man is doing his reporting well only when
people start to hate him.'
V.S. Naipaul


'Truly speaking, it is not instruction, but provocation,
that I can receive from another soul.'
Ralph Waldo Emerson


'We shall not cease from exploration
And the end of all our exploring
Will be to arrive where we started
And know the place for the first time.'
T.S. Eliot


'Why does a writer write?
To relive the past and imagine the future.
To show that whatever we see could be
other than it is.
To show worlds that may exist.
And finally, to answer the question "why?"'
C.D.

*'Alle Philosophie verbirgt auch eine*
*Philosophie.*
*Jede Meinung ist auch ein Versteck*
*und jedes Wort auch eine Maske.'*
Nietzsche


'There is nothing either good or bad
but thinking makes it so.'
Shakespeare


'How one becomes what one is.'
Nietzsche

# PROLOGUE

I met him years ago and came to know him pretty well; however, I can't say we were friends, and as far as I knew, he had no friends at the time. All I knew was that he'd lived in numerous countries, was divorced and had a daughter. I have never seen him since then and don't know where he is now and what he's doing, but what he's told me will stay with me forever. I would very much like to meet him again, and hope someday I will since I enjoyed his company despite him being sometimes rather difficult, but at the same time we were in a way pretty close to each other. I mean, we were frank in whatever we discussed and we were pretty like-minded. At the time, I must say, he was the only one with whom I could talk about anything; however, I didn't learn much about his background, and I'm not sure whether he told me his real name, but I have no reason to doubt that a story he told me was untrue because in a way I was sure about his honesty, and I'm still sure that what he told me had really happened.

We frequently saw each other because we enjoyed each other's company, and because we were neighbours living in Queen's Gate in London.

His name was Ches Adarsh which was a bit unusual, and I found the meaning of it only after he had left London. Anyway, he wasn't British. He was in his fifties, tall and well built, casually dressed, neither elegant nor shabby. There was something about his eyes – they were grey marked with green and black spots, and when you looked in them longer, you felt uneasy.

How we first met? – By chance, I'd say. It was in the morning on, I can remember exactly, 20<sup>th</sup> of March. I had just come out of my house and when I approached my car I heard someone laugh, and it was a very joyful laugh. I looked around and noticed a man and woman standing close to each other and it was her laughing. Never saw them before. They saw me looking at them, and the woman greeted me with a wave of her hand and I responded likewise. They weren't far from me, and I could see that she was very attractive. Later on, when I eventually met Ches in person, I learned that she was his third wife, Beatrice, but I'd never met her before, for at the time I met him she'd been overseas. I sometimes wonder whether our acquaintance was something which is called destiny, in which I am not inclined to believe. Whatsoever, I still value knowing him then and wish I could see him again. And I sometimes have a strange feeling that our meeting might have already been prearranged by someone, and if so, it could have been that man about whom Ches told me, and what I learned about the man from Ches, it wouldn't have been difficult for him at all. I don't really believe that, but then I know that there are things you can't really explain. Anyway, I often feel as if Ches were nearby and often imagine that we are talking, travelling again and having some adventures. I do miss him, especially now that I am on my own, alone, and there is nobody to talk to. I know a few people, but they are not who I could turn to looking for a frank and truly understanding conversation, for they are far away from the way I think and feel, not like him whom I could always trust and rely on. Whenever I needed him, he was there, and first of all he helped me to see many things aright, and therefore I will always be deeply in his debt. Without his good word, I could have been lost many times over, and some things he told me I'll never forget. Whenever I look for a solution to a problem, I miss him and his words, yes, he once told me that he who lost his faith in words lost his faith in life. Now I simply cannot bear the rambling of those I know, for I know they don't give a damn about me so, the things are for me as Charles Bukowski said: 'I don't hate people, but I always feel better when they aren't around.' Thus, I've liberated myself from people in a way, but at the same time crave for intimate contact with them and still have a great eagerness for life, but not being close to anybody I'm getting stale.

All I can do now is to recollect our time together, and the stories he told me; however, he didn't say much about himself, and a story he left with me is the only story of his life I got to know. But I don't really know why he left his writings with me. Yes, I may say again we were pretty close to each other, but at the same far away from each other.

We both used to go for long walks during which we had our most significant conversations, and during one of those he quoted Nietzsche, 'A sedentary life is the real sin against the Holy Spirit. Only those thoughts that come by walking have any value.' Ches was an anxious reader of Nietzsche and I myself was drawn to his writings. And what is my life now? For hours, I'm sitting, watching films, reading and dreaming despite being able to do many other things, but I prefer fantasy, for I know that a dream is much more certain than reality, and I can rely on what I'm dreaming about. In a dream, I can have everything and achieve anything, whereas in reality I would fail to get what I really need. And I relive the past all over again – people I knew, events and places, pleasures and failures as if I had been living my past life again. Now I ask myself *What for?* I live now and can't find the answer. *I wish you were here, Ches*, I keep saying to myself, longing for the times we were together, but I know that all I can do now is to wait to meet him again, and I know I will, for I still believe in miracles.

A few weeks past our first encounter, I met him again. This time when as usual I went to Baker Street Leisure Centre and entered the swimming pool, I saw him swimming. When he got out of the pool and saw me, he came up and shook my hand. "So," he said, "you too?"

"Yes", I said. "Do you come here often?" I asked.

"Yes, almost every day, and you?"

"I'm the same," I replied.

"What about the sauna?" he asked.

"Surely, let's go there." And it was in the sauna where our first conversation took place.

That conversation wasn't long, but I immediately recognised a fellow-soul, and somehow knew we would be close to each other in a way. And we met at the Centre quite often, but we usually didn't talk much there, we tried to make the most of the place instead. Most of our talking took place either at my place or his, and at restaurants, especially a Hungarian one, for we both enjoyed their food.

What were we talking about? The usual answer is 'about everything', but actually there were some particular subjects we focussed on, and it was history, philosophy and foreign countries we both had been to. I'd been to quite a few and he himself had been pretty familiar with many more and told me things I'd never known and couldn't find in any book or on the internet afterwards.

Ches told me a few things about himself, and I told him things about myself. But he never wanted to discuss his personal affairs. No, it wasn't a taboo, he said. However, it was, he said, a sphere where nobody else might enter directly, so to speak, he said. "You could get there," he said, "through listening to what I'd be telling you, and then you might get to know something about myself." There wasn't any other way, he said, for we actually aren't able to say anything totally frank about ourselves. "'Everyone is furthest from himself,'" he quoted Nietzsche. "You know," he said, "whatever you say about what you do, what you like or dislike, then what you actually say, this way is nothing else but a pack of banalities. Thousands of other men have similar jobs and go to the same places, but it doesn't make them alike, does it?"

"No, it doesn't," I said, for I thought the same.

He had his own company that made most of its business abroad. It was called 'Phenomenon', and he said he'd chosen the name to commemorate his previous interest in phenomenology. His MA thesis had been on Husserl's phenomenology, he said, "But, you know, as a matter of fact, I should have paid more attention to a beautiful fellow-student Margarita. How stupid I was!"

Most of its business his company did in small countries such as Hungary, Slovenia, Armenia, Georgia and a couple of others, and had branches in France, Poland and Germany. He also did business in Russia, and here I want to mention his views on the country, the views which I found penetrating and not the usual pack of superficial, silly and vulgar-in-tone views present all over in the media. He said that the main aim of that obsessive anti-Russian propaganda was to depreciate and deprecate the country in order to convince people of Anglo-American superiority. To his mind, other countries, just to mention France and Germany, held a much deeper understanding of Russian culture and history, and therefore their views on the current state of affairs reflected more thoroughly the truth about the country. An average British citizen, as a matter of fact, knew nothing about Russia. That's why he was easily manipulated by that ridiculous stream of nonsense whose only aim was to find all kinds of faults with the Russians and their country. All over again, every sort of criticism was directed at the country, and all its intellectual and artistic achievement was ignored. What was emphasised all over again was nothing but abuse of power, lack of democracy, dictatorship, and the like. All in all, the usual load of censure as if there was nothing else there. But there was, Ches maintained, but it took some intelligence, knowledge and honesty to find it out. And, in reality, Ches said, Britain didn't give a damn about all that alleged evil there, and lack, as they said all over again, of democracy, and at the same time conveniently forgetting that it had been Britain that in the 1920s was the first country to recognise Bolshevik power. The same applies to the US having no other aim but to weaken Russia, and not only her for that matter, for they tried the same with China, and in both cases, they failed. All that censure of Russia is to aggrandise themselves, but paradoxically the more they tried, the less they achieved. And there was something else that was being overlooked by that harsh criticism of Russia, and it was that her people, as is the case with, for example, the French and Germans, are far better educated in humanities than British and Americans, and that's why their Weltanschauung is far broader, and consequently they can grasp, all in all, the problem of life and the world more accurately. Moreover, democracy understood as freedom of the individual is a sham, unless he is knowledgeable, for only then is he able to have ideas of his own, for only then he's the individual in the true meaning of the word. In other words, the more learned the individual, the more independent and free he becomes through ideas of his own. And there is no other way to be free. And who is truly free reading all these rags and watching the idiot-box? But, as a matter of fact, the British establishment doesn't want him to do anything else because it's obviously much easier to rule a dimwit than an educated man. Anyway, as long as you are ignorant, democracy is an illusion. And the establishment in more than one country in the West wants its people to live by illusion, which might actually be first of all their pleasures. What prevails nowadays in some countries, including Britain, Ches underlined, is collective stupidity and ignorance which, curiously enough, strengthen the self-confidence of an average citizen because the less you know, the more confident you are, for knowledge means to doubt, to question. But then you are humane in your actions, only when you doubt, as long as you question your own decisions; otherwise, you can't be considerate towards your fellow humans. But then, the question is where that overwhelming ignorance might lead men to. First, it might lead them to a society already pictured so vividly and accurately by Orwell, and then obviously to more wars, which will eventually come to end in apocalypse, and in this way, Goethe's words, 'All that doth begin should rightly to destruction run,' will come true. "Thus, paradoxically, it is Mephistopheles who warns people of the danger," Ches said.

His company had a website and I found out that it was a pretty successful enterprise, mostly dealing in green energy. The astonishing thing was that Ches had never studied anything even remotely related to business. He'd obtained his degree in the department of philosophy, so I wondered how he could manage to run the business. He told me that when it came to business practice, all he did was to put forward some ideas which were then carried out by his staff. He was well off, but you could take him for a very ordinary man judging by his clothes. He never wore, for instance, a tie, and some of his jackets were bought at charity shops which he liked to visit, saying that you could often find something unusual there.

His views in general? As far as I got to know him, I'd say he had none. I mean, he had no convictions. "Everything is relative," he used to say, "and therefore any conviction is false, a nonsense. And this is so because we express ourselves in words for there's no other way, of course. So all you can say are the facts, which are relative because they are changing, are accidental. Consequently, whatever you say is actually half-true. We may follow some principles, have a moral code, of course, but at the same time we cannot prove its absolute legitimacy."

"I have liberated myself," he used to say, "from evaluating anything. I still use words because I have to, but I don't value them as much as other people do – their constant rambling, they can't stop talking, usually nonsense, of course. They don't realise the uselessness of their mumbling, being under the illusion that in doing so, they express the highest knowledge of things with words. You know, you can't underestimate the stupidity of the general public."

Ches was somebody we may call a nihilist, that is one who says 'no', who denies, negates the existing order, but at the same time he was the one who longed for the ideal, and there was nothing strange about that, I thought. "You must have a reason for living," he once said, "otherwise you are lost." But what his ideal was he wouldn't tell me then, and I'd only found that out when I'd read his memoires.

We often dined together at various restaurants. At a couple of them we were regulars and could order something that actually wasn't on the menu. He liked simple traditional food, and his favourites were Hungarian and Italian. He adored Italy and liked Budapest very much, and had been there several times. His favourites were historic cities such as Rome, Prague, Heidelberg, Krakow and a good few others, and Paris, of course. He didn't particularly like London, but one day I found his reason for living there, but again, it'd only been when I'd read his story. As a matter of fact, he wasn't fond of England, calling it a pokey, artificial country, and agreed with Henry Miller who considered it a repressive place despite all appearances, and quoted Lawrence Durrell: 'The stultifying English culture.' Ches, like Nietzsche, believed in French culture and some aspects of German too. But he found some things in several other countries very agreeable. He was very fond of Greece, as the mentioned writers had been, and of Armenia and Georgia, and quoted a German scientist, Ritzel, who said, 'The most charming people in the world with aristocratic features are Georgians.' And Ches shared his view and went often there, always visiting the neighbouring Armenia. Of Greece he said, "Look, that country had already shown mankind the right direction, but it had been wasted and perverted by other ones. But the spirit is still there, for it is something inborn in her people, something that cannot be learned."

"Have you watched," he asked me, "Anthony Quinn's performance in *München 1995*? I mean, him dancing that masterpiece of music, *Zorba* by Mikis Theodorakis, which Anthony called music of life," as it is indeed. And the people of Greece, as those of his other favourite countries, have inherited the ability to enjoy life, to be happy, the ability the English are deprived of. That's why they talk so much about happiness because it is something they long for, and will never get. And what actually their wealth is for if they cannot feel joy, so what is good about their riches? And in relation to that, they are in fact fantasists thinking that wealth will somewhat automatically guarantee their happiness. Thus, boasting of their pragmatism, at the same time they deceive themselves by such a fantasy.

From time to time, Ches went abroad and stayed there for a couple of weeks. Whether those journeys were related to his job or not, I wouldn't know, but he talked at length about each one, but then he sometimes disappeared for a few days and upon coming back said nothing about where he'd been or what he'd done. I was a bit curious but never asked him. Only later, I found out what those escapades had been about, and not from him but again from his diary. Anyway, knowing him at our time in London, I had a vague impression that he was planning something, and once during one of our dinners asked him about his plans for the future. "Hmm," he said, "as a matter of fact, I don't plan anything. Someone else is planning for me." When I asked him to be more precise, he politely declined. "You know," he said, "the most important thing is what we are thinking of all day, and if this thinking is consistent, you say 'yes' to what happens around you. But if you say 'no' all day long to everything, then you're in trouble. Saying 'no' all the time is a feeling of being powerless and lost. Anyway, you can't force yourself to say 'yes', for it comes itself or it doesn't, that's it. Actually, we never think, as de Lamartine says, our ideas think for us. In other words, we grasp our thoughts, but how it happens is the puzzle of all puzzles. You know, my mother had always complained that I had talked in puzzles. Yes, my mother, she could have been president of the Swiss Confederation, so well organised was she. But you know, talking in puzzles is also looking for an answer, but in a different way, I mean, once you have realised there isn't any straightforward way to solve a problem. Somehow you know that there is no direct way to get there, and then you try the other way around, so to speak, to find out the answer. You know, language is a mystery. Feeling of powerlessness happens when you can't find the right word to describe something, and if it repeats all over again, you lose your faith in words. You begin to deny, doubt everything, and eventually you believe nothing. You feel yourself as if you are living in emptiness because you aren't able to find the right words, and then all around you is alien, even hostile, and this world is not yours and then you look for another one that you may never find. I think that the feeling of being happy may occur only when you have found the right words for everything you experience, and if it happens, you agree, say 'yes' to whatever you come across. Anyway, happiness cannot be shared, for it is solely yours and nobody else's. As somebody rightly observed, the world of the happy man is a different one from that of the unhappy man. And as a matter of fact, it is happiness that chooses you, not the other way around. Yes, you may take some precautions which may make you more likely to feel happy, but there's no guarantee to be happy whatever you choose. It is the same about possession – he who has nothing has everything, as an ancient Greek philosopher said, and this is very simple, for you actually cannot have everything. And the same is about happiness – you cannot have happiness, it is happiness that has you.

"Imagine you dream about, let's say, a woman you see, and you want her to be your lover, and you're sure that when it happens you'll be happy. But then when she becomes you lover… you are not happy at all, and whose fault is it? Yours? Hers? – No, nobody's because it simply isn't the matter of fault. In other words, it is as Heidegger said: 'Whatever you choose it is wrong,' and this is so because you never know in advance what actually will be good for you."

I agreed with him. *Yes*, I thought, *our illusions keep us alive…until they have proved to be wrong.*

I've already said that the conversations with Ches not only gave me something to think about, but also inspired me to do something about my own life. I was comfortable regarding material conditions, financially independent, but except for him, I actually had no meaningful contact with other people, and I told him that it might be due to my personal philosophy that was to question the obvious; I didn't take anything as it came. And because of it, I had nothing truly important to share with other people, except for strictly business matters. But at the same time, I realised that what I really needed was to recover my interest in them, enjoy their company, and so enjoy everything else. Yes, women still attracted my interest, but to be honest, I was unable to establish any intimate relationship with any of those I met. All in all, my life was humdrum, I was growing stale, tired of doing much the same thing every day, but at the same time I had a great eagerness for life. And I wondered what motivates people to carry on, to be so occupied with their banal jobs and trivial activities. There must be something about that, but it wasn't mine for the simple reason that it is always something what someone has of his own, and nobody else can have it.

From time to time, I thought of suicide but never came close to considering it a real prospect, and I came to the conclusion that losing my life wasn't actually the worst option, but then how would you know that? Anyway, much worse was the feeling of losing my reason for living. Why are we afraid of death anyway? I thought it was because we cannot imagine it, we cannot imagine ourselves non-existent, absent in this world. It is the same with infinity – we aren't able to imagine it. Yes, the most frightful thing is something we cannot imagine, that is to visualise it in any way. The Greek Stoics say that we shouldn't be afraid of death for when it comes we have already disappeared so, as a matter of fact, we don't experience it. But the problem is that this kind of 'consolation' is purely intellectual, and as such, of little help.

We often discussed problems like that, but it wasn't conversation alone that helped me to recover some optimism, stimulation to act. I didn't and still don't know what exactly it was, and I think (and thought at the time) that there is no name for it. You may experience something in the company of a man, or woman for that matter, what you can't with anybody else, and you can't really say what it is, to name that. And Ches was the one with whom I could get that stimulation, and that's why I cherished conversations with him. Besides, he was my companion in the expeditions we set up sometimes. They were different in nature and took us to various places, and on a couple of occasions, we visited exclusive brothels in London and Amsterdam.

"'Compassion is praised as the virtue of prostitutes,' it's Nietzsche again," Ches said, "and, you know, I've heard that in Belfast you can find them close to the Salvation Army."

"So, it seems they're in a right spot," I said. Before we went on one of those trips, he asked me what I thought of the so-called oldest profession in the world. "Actually nothing," I said, "I mean, I obviously don't judge these women, no, I simply don't think anything about them."

"You know," he said, "these women, when they choose to get married, they may make excellent wives, and I've always wondered why."

"Hmm," I said, "perhaps they feel the need to make up for the time they have lost, I mean, the time they had no family, nobody to look after, no true well-being, in fact, nothing but dull routine, and not much pleasure about it, and sex surely is something that may give you great pleasure, and this is exactly what it is for."

"Precisely," he said, "that's it, but you know, if you try hard, they will appreciate your effort and may even climax. In some porn films, you can see women having huge orgasms, but I think it is forced and as such might not give them much pleasure. But how would you know? Anyway, I myself always try to satisfy a woman, and she somehow knows that so. She usually reciprocates, and in the end, we both feel good."

Sex was important for both of us. The only way to enjoy it without any obligations was to meet professionals, and in London we had plenty of choice. We could have girls from all over the world: Asian, Africans or Europeans. "You know the nine reasons for reincarnation?" Ches once asked me.

"No, I don't," I said.

"'One of them is sex, and the other eight are unimportant,' according to Henry Miller," he said.

Once, we contacted an agency and booked two girls who lived at the same block of flats. We wanted them for overnight, and since they were top class it was pretty expensive – £1,000 each. Mine was very affectionate and I was really pleased, and it seemed to me that she was too, and if she just pretended to be, she must have been a very good actress, but I don't think it was the case. Before I left, we chatted a bit and Karina, as she introduced herself, told me she was from Hungary, and as I'd been a couple of times in Budapest, which I liked, we talked about some places there we knew. She was very young, twenty-two, she said, and I couldn't resist the temptation to ask her about her plans for the future. She told me she was going back to Hungary as soon as she earned enough, and once there would find the right guy, have children, and so on. I never asked her what made her work as a call girl because I thought it would be not only an improper question but stupid too.

Since I did like her, I asked if I could be of assistance while she was still in London, and was shocked a bit when she said she wanted to see me as often as I could come to see her. I didn't ask why, but then her wish might not have been for purely financial reasons, because she was an extremely attractive woman, and I was sure she couldn't complain about a shortage of clients. I just said that yes, I would see her as often as I could, and I said so not only because of her professional skills which were extraordinary, but for something else that I couldn't really put my finger on. All in all, I did want to see her often and I did. I urged her to take a course at university (she had a grammar school diploma) at a faculty of business administration and another course at a faculty of arts with the specialisation in oriental jewellery, furniture and clothing. She completed both faculties and then returned to Hungary where she set up a shop that specialised in various kinds of oriental handmade art. She still runs the shop and with a little help from me she opened a branch in Berlin. So far, she's been living on her own, no husband, no family, and we still see each other as often as we can. Her business is very successful and gained a kind of fame, and people from other countries come for they know they can always find something interesting at her place, and have a courteous and professional conversation with her or her assistants. Some even make appointments in advance to be sure they'll meet her, as they enjoy her company, her advice and goods so much. To me, she is as she was the first time we met, the same considerate, responsive woman, and I sometimes cherish the idea of getting married to her, and actually I mentioned it in general terms to her, but she politely changed the subject. So be it, anyway, we never know who our future friends will be and where and when we'll meet them.

I asked Ches about his experience that night, but he didn't want to tell me anything except to say, "It was okay," knowing perfectly that I hated the expression, and added, "you'll see in the future," and as a matter of fact I did in the manuscript he left with me. And it was there I learned the truth about his sexual explorations with those call girls – he actually had no sexual intercourse with any of them. He'd spent the night chatting with them but of course paid them, and the reason he'd accompanied me in those escapades was that he'd thought that I would have been disappointed if he hadn't agreed to go there with me.

As for this kind of experience, I once met a man, a Pole, in Germany, and he told me about his visit to a brothel. He was married with children and while visiting the country decided to have sex with a prostitute. It was his first-time experience of that kind. And he described his 'adventure' this way: "I entered the place, was shown an album with photographs, chose a girl, was given the key to her room and went to see her. When I came in, the room was hardly lit and there was no girl, so I stood like a fool in the middle of it for a couple of minutes and then the lights went on and a woman in lingerie appeared. She was slowly coming toward me, swaying. I got such a fright that I rushed out, almost fell running downstairs and out on the street was still running for some fifty metres. When I eventually came to my senses, I couldn't tell why I'd been so scared. There'd been no rational reason for my fear."

"You see, old chap," I said to him, "what do we actually know about the difference between the rational and the irrational?"

The other story I can tell is also about a Pole. I met him at a cafe in Paris. He was slightly drunk and eager to talk to anybody. "Yesterday," he said, "I went with a friend of mine to a brothel, you know, near the famous Place Pigalle. I am a travel agent and was looking after a group of Polish tourists. I had some of their cash on me for I paid for museum entries, and the like. We went to the Place on the Metro and found the right spot. It was like a café, but once we sat down at the table two women joined us. The one who sat next to me was French, and the other one who sat beside my friend a Serbian, as I found out. The Serbian girl was very pretty and I envied him a bit. A compulsory bottle of champagne appeared and we kept talking with the women. The French highly praised their professional experience, and the Serbian, as far as I could hear, was telling my friend about her life in Serbia. After a while, I went to the toilet and stood there looking in the mirror, then hurriedly washed my face and ran out onto the street, leaving my friend on his own. When my friend came back to the hotel we were staying in, he was ready to give me a punch, so I did his best to explain myself for leaving him on his own at the café. I said that I'd run away seized by dreadful panic of being robbed there. Since there was no rational…" (rationality again!) "…reason for such a danger, my friend said that I had possibly gone temporarily mad. I told him I really didn't know why I had done what I had, and apologised. Reluctantly, he accepted my apologies and told me what had happened when I left him. The manager of the café had appeared and demanded the payment for the champagne. This kind of champagne is usually of not good quality – In Germany, it's called 'whorehouse lemonade' – but still expensive. He'd had no money on him so had found himself in trouble, and who had helped him? Those girls, yes, they had somehow persuaded the manager not to take any action and he had been allowed to leave. Before he left, he profusely thanked the girls."

"You see, my friend," I said to the Pole, "you never know who's who and what they might do for you…"

As I mentioned before, Ches and I sometimes travelled together, and a couple of times to the countries he did business with. We went to Prague, Budapest and Erevan. The only gentlemen club we were members of was The Travellers, which we visited from time to time. Actually, we went there to have fun. I mean, after two or three hours of listening to travellers' stories, we moved to a pub or restaurant and recalled the stories we'd heard. Some of those travellers spent just a couple of days in a country, but they were sure they'd learnt 'everything' about it, and talked about the country with great confidence, about things and people they met. They, of course, didn't speak the language, but that didn't prevent them gaining a 'considerable' knowledge of the country they were visiting. As a matter of fact, what they 'learnt' over there, they had already known before going there. Their stories were full of adjectives, such as *amazing, astonishing* or *incredible*. But what was really amazing was that what they actually 'learnt' you can find in any travel guide. Anyway, almost everything they experienced over there was distressing, corrupt and low-grade in comparison to England, which was for them the centre of the universe. "Yes," we concluded, "there is nothing like ignorance, chauvinism and illusion which, as Voltaire says, is 'the first of all pleasures.'"

I recollect a conversation I once had with a Cambridge University geography student, a young woman. I asked her whether she knew something of Russia and its neighbouring countries. "Yes, I do a bit," she said.

"Then tell me, please, what is the capital of Lithuania?"

"Hmm... Vladivostok."

Vladivostok is in Russia, and some 12,000 kilometres east of Vilnius, Lithuania's capital.

But it could be even worse, as they say in a country situated in a remote western part of Europe.

I was living there long enough to get some really amazing information, and I mean the conversations I had in the sauna at a leisure centre. I often went there, so I really enriched my knowledge, so to speak. Here are some of those conversations:

One day, I had a chat with a young woman, a Catholic, and I must tell you that people over there are very touchy regarding religious matters, and I asked her what Catholicism means, and she said, "I am Catholic." Never heard such a 'precise' definition before. Another one said that Jesus Christ surely existed but she didn't believe it...

Once, out of curiosity, I visited a certain church. When I went in, they were just handing out a printed leaflet. I looked at it and read, *Father, forgive them, for they know what they do.*

Afterwards, I thought that such a reinterpretation of the *New Testament*'s famous passage could only have happened over there...

Danske Bank, which has branches in that country, is according to some people either Polish or Russian, and it was 'definitely' Polish, as I was told by a man who was actually its client.

A native, who was a member of a jury more than once, was sure that the UK's population was some thirty million, and British law is codified.

A woman holding the rank of baron is a lady-baron. Another man said that Freud was the father of modern sociology, and the man in fact studied the subject.

And Germany is a land-locked country, and Syria is close to Bangladesh. And so on, and so on.

And we may ask why some places in that country, all kinds of dimwits, cripples and drunkards find so attractive? The question isn't difficult to answer – the same is attractive for the same. And that's why the so-called discontented scum appreciate it, and a lot has been done to appease those quasi-rebels, many of whom claim to be socialists, that is those who are *de facto* charlatans, phonies pretending to be humane, whereas all they want is executive power on the grandest scale in order to satisfy their inferiority complex of the least and the dumbest, i.e., as Nietzsche says, those who are superficial, envious and three quarters actors, and their concept of socialism is actually a tyranny, the revenge upon those privileged in body and soul.

I was thinking of leaving England but couldn't decide where to move. I talked to Ches about that and he said that someday I would know, and it was better not to give me any advice. He said that at some stage in his life he had been offered too much 'good advice', and nothing of it had been helpful. "There had been days when I hadn't been sure of anything; or rather I thought I'd been making the right decisions while many of them had been completely wrong. And it'd been about almost everything – where to live, what profession to choose and what woman to be with. Only afterwards, when I'd already decided and done something, I realised I shouldn't have done that, and that happened many a time. Several of my choices had been so different in nature that they had contradicted each other. I had once wanted to be an officer, so I had gone to a military academy but I hadn't stayed long. Then I started to study at a faculty of philosophy and got a degree. These two places seem to be so different, don't they? But do we ever know beforehand what decision is right for us? Moreover, people rarely do what they really want, and this is because they don't really know what they should do for their own good. And then there might be so many factors which actually make a decision for you. But all that I already said is a sort of cliché, you know, and as such doesn't explain anything, isn't helpful at all. And the same is about giving advice. It might be good, that is, it might lead you in the right direction, or it might lead you astray as well. So, it's much better, I think, to have a dialogue, and I specifically mean that ancient, unsurpassed art of conversation of Plato. And let me share with you some other observations I've made. It'll help me as well since I try my best to make clear what I say to you, and in this way, I make it clear to myself. I won't tell you any personal stories, these you will come to know in due time, my friend, you know, the true philosophy of a single man is recollection, as that immortal Friedrich says, and you know who was it who called him this way? A priest I once knew: a very unusual priest for that matter. Imagine, a priest calling Nietzsche 'immortal', the philosopher who said, 'Christianity is metaphysics of the executioner; however, he says something else too, Jesus, The noblest man ever.'"

Ches said that philosophy is to question the obvious. As it is in truth about your own life. There are no facts, only interpretations. And this is so because all the facts are relative and accidental. And what about God for that matter, and all that comes with him? You know, I'm an agnostic, and as for any religion, it isn't, I believe, about a faith but about a doing, as that immortal philosopher says. You remember what I once said, people say they believe in God, but does it prove anything? Anybody may say "I believe," and so what? Those who say they believe do this to appear good, to console themselves and to be absolved of their wrongdoing. God will forgive you, priests say, and nowadays it is said by both Protestants and Catholics. In old days, they wouldn't say that, but now they do, and I think this is because they have both realised that what people really expect from religion is consolation. They have long given up looking for answers to the questions 'why?' and 'what for?', and all that is left for them is to comfort themselves in any available way. But those questions have not disappeared; they are still with them. There is a good German word to describe that kind of superficial consolation: *ersatz*, a substitute for something. But a substitute will never satisfy your desire which is *de facto* your true need. But what most people don't realise is that we can't know the solution to the problem of life beforehand. The solution is seen in the vanishing of the problem, as Wittgenstein rightly observed, and there's no other way to solve the problem. But people, of course, deceive themselves, believing that the solution may be found tomorrow, or the day after tomorrow...

You know, all in all, 'the problem with the world is that the intelligent people are full of doubts, while the stupid ones full of confidence.' Bukowski got it right.

"One of the most popular words nowadays is 'popular,'" Ches went on, "and in common opinion, it means that something is good. The word seems to be very 'democratic', and its Anglo-Latin origin, 'populus' – people – confirms that in a way. In order to keep people happy, hundreds of tricks have been invented, and all of us, depending of course to what degree, willy-nilly participate in this live, everyday show which is a religion of our time. Speech, as usual, plays an important role, as it especially did in the past in the so-called communist countries. And to describe the essence of the effects of their kind of speech, we may recollect Orwell's phrase 'new talk'. That's something which totally changes the meaning of words and consequently our view of the world. But this 'new talk' isn't, obviously, the invention of the people, but it's been invented for them by rulers in order to deprive people of ideas of their own. Accordingly, 'popular' means 'everybody's', which as a matter of fact means 'nobody's'. The aim of this linguistic game is to keep people happy, and this is achieved by keeping them in the dark, to deprive them of the ability of abstract thinking, which is the condition of intellectual and artistic achievement, which is always the achievement of an individual. But these days, for most people, the intellect is an awkward, gloomy, creaking machine that is hard to start, as Nietzsche says. And then, the seduction of words that affect the majority of people, and I wonder how long it will take to wake up from that dream... or it only takes a full-scale catastrophe to wake up...

"Yes," Ches went on, "'Man always wants to break free,' said Canetti, 'and when he doesn't know a name for the aim which he is heading, he calls it freedom.' In other words, he doesn't know the meaning of the word because he's been seduced by the very same words which, repeated all over again, have lost their meaning. And someday, man may lose his faith in words, but then he may lose his faith in life, and it might be as well the beginning of a different life... But then, what does life consist of? – it is what we are thinking day by day, I believe, for thinking always, whatever you say, comes first. And to live means to be aware, and to be aware you need passion, so in relation to what I've just said, let's recollect Kierkegaard's words: 'Let others complain that the age is wicked; my complaint is that it is paltry, for it lacks passion.'"

Once Ches had finished, he remained silent for a good couple of minutes looking into space. We were in Hyde Park, where we usually had our serious conversations. Eventually, looking at me, he said, "That's it, I have nothing more to say until…" He didn't finish the sentence.

"I'm leaving tomorrow," he eventually said, "and I don't really know when and if we see each other again."

"Where are you going to?" I asked.

"I won't tell you now, my friend, and this is because of our friendship or rather the beginning of such, that might be important for us in the future. Anyway, you'll find out someday where I've gone to. I'm leaving this country and please don't try to look for me. I know you will be worried about me, I appreciate that, but it's for your own good not to know where I'm heading for. I do hope we'll meet again, and I'll do my best to make it happen, but it's not entirely up to me what happens. You know, 'There are more things in heaven and earth than are dreamt of in your philosophy…'

"Tomorrow, you'll receive a package and what it contains may help you to understand a couple of things. It might happen that you'll never see me again, but remember, anytime you're in trouble, someone will come to your assistance. And they won't fail to help you, trust me! And now I've got to go and please don't say anything."

And off he went. And I watched him until he disappeared from my view.

*

Next day, the courier delivered the package. It contained a manuscript, and there was also a handwritten note attached to it in which Ches gave some explanation as to why his writing was in places so harsh, and even grotesque when it came to the description of some countries, particularly England and Ireland. He says he did so because some things attracted his attention, the things which as a matter of fact were absent in other places, but which are typical in those countries.

He also said that among the reasons he found to write about them was, in England anyway, a highly elevated idea of its people who have never envisaged having been wrong in their opinions about other countries, as if their own were a sort of the Delphic Oracle.

He also said that, everything considered regarding his story, the reader should be very patient and careful, and even more than that, to reach the end of it, and since there aren't too many of this kind around these days, his story could remain totally misunderstood. And this could be due to that harsh criticism of his that focusses on pointing to the faults of some peoples, whereas overrating perhaps other ones. But he does so, Ches said, because he wants the former to be on guard towards themselves, not too be so pleased with everything they do. Let's remember what Nietzsche says about his fellow countrymen: 'As far as Germany extends, it spoils culture.' But the reader, Ches said, might have some fun after all while reading his story.

Anyway, the reader should be ready for anything; he is supposed to have imagination and most importantly, distance himself; otherwise, he will never understand what is there.

"Moreover," Ches said, "the problem of language is the problem of understanding life, and you may lack capacity to understand its inner logic. In other words, you may fail to notice some essential particularities of it. And it's related to your own experience, especially when you aren't able to put in words aright the experience meaning, and that results in confusion and frustration which in turn might produce contempt for reality. Many of us are unable to explain our own emotions, for we cannot comprehend the relation between the language and facts. Besides, having often been seduced by words, especially by that superficial and primitive language of the media, and similar kind of information of a very poor quality, we can't explain to ourselves our existential problems for we are unable to see beyond that mass of words we deal with.

'A proposition is a picture of reality,' says Wittgenstein, so the totality of propositions is the way of understanding reality. But the picture is often falsely interpreted by its recipient, due to the distorted way it is presented to him. Anyway, our average citizen somehow feels something is wrong regarding the information he receives, but then he often has to accept, willy-nilly, so to say, that distorted-by-the-media presentation of reality; otherwise, he would not survive because his survival depends actually on the acceptance of reality. So, our ordinary man tends to accept what he gets, after all.

There is hardly any truly independent thinking nowadays, for the media's language commanded by corporations with the willing cooperation of governments, tries its best to cheer up, to comfort our man in the street, giving him a beautified and falsified picture of reality. And our man, tending to accept it involuntarily, as Ches observes, agrees with such a picture. Unfortunately for him, the problem, his own problem of life, is still there, and the problem in question is actually in his inner language, as Ches calls it, in which our man accepting the given picture might reject it at the same time. This way he's in between, between his acknowledgment of the actuality of his life, and the rejection of it, and this being schizophrenia of a sort, leads to his frustration that results in what Nietzsche calls nihilism, that is the existential condition in which there are no answers to the questions 'why?' and 'what for?'. And this is because they are asked in language, after all, which is the only way to understand reality in a rational way, for the only rational way to understand it lies in language, in words.

But a modern man is losing his faith in a word, for he, despite that all comforting mumbling, somehow knows he's cheated on, deceived on an everyday basis.

Now, because the principal aim, the intention of the so-called democratic rule, is to make people happy or to make them believe they are or should be, everything possible is done in the media, being it the tool of the rulers, to keep him so at any cost, for it is the only way for democracy to survive. All in all, we've got a paradoxical and in fact ridiculous situation here that reminds us of Marx's words: 'The final phase of the historical political process is comedy.'

Then, democracy, in order to make people happy, has to provide them with that beautified picture of reality, must deceive them in its effort to make them happy. But, at the same time, the daily-routine TV and broadcasting news don't seem to be the tales from *One Thousand and One Nights*; quite the opposite. However, our ordinary man would laugh hearing that, after all, for he believes that there's nothing like simply believing after all, to submit, to accept, even if he somehow knows he's being deceived by all that 'democratic' propaganda, which is another paradox because deception has always been associated with dictatorship's propaganda. But, even under democratic rule, it is still propaganda, for it is the propagation of distorted, falsified pictures of reality, which very often are nothing but lies so, curiously enough, feeling good living in democracy depends on the efficiency of the lies our man is fed.

But democratic rule seems to allow even harsh criticism, although it may be found exclusively in some selected newspapers and books read actually by a few. Anyway, the establishment knows perfectly well that modern man, educated or not, is essentially of slave morality, and as such, especially in English-speaking countries, incapable of genuine rebellion that might endanger their rule. There might be some rioting from time to time, but they wouldn't pose any danger to those in power, especially in Britain, because of its inner tendency to be pragmatic after all, which means, Ches points out, to be submissive.

But even there, an ordinary man might be eventually fed up, exhausted by that massive current of deception because by reason of his nature, he may say 'no' to it sooner or later.

And this might be the turning point for humankind, which is very much needed to prevent an apocalypse which is sure to come, unless that deception has disappeared. Anyway, man cannot live too long by deception, for it essentially disagrees with the very nature of his being. He wants truth; after all, he longs for it, even if temporarily he accepts its opposite.

That is why an ordinary man needs to be told the real value of saying 'no', for this is the only way to prevent catastrophe, the only means of humanity's survival. Therefore, to say 'no' is to do good, and not that slavish 'yes'. And that's why even grotesque pictures, all that harsh criticism of his story, says Ches, seems to be so necessary to enforce that 'no', to reveal the truth behind the deception. "And again, as for criticism that is so harsh, even as exaggerated and grotesque as mine," says Ches, "if I made my descriptions full of politeness and consideration, I wouldn't be honest because such accounts are usually fake and as a matter of fact tell nothing.

Moreover, they leave everything unclear, muddled and do nothing to unmask what is beneath the appearances. And this is the precise job of a writer to reveal as much as he can about what is hidden underneath.

Anyway, priggishness, affectation and hypocrisy are not the best traits of character a man might be endowed with.

Ches says that while 'in exile', as he put it, he had to deal with all sorts of wretchedness and hardly experienced any good living there. But, on the other hand, it did him good, and that was because he erased his wrong, naïve beliefs during his stay.

First, he tried to escape what he was going through by drinking to excess, for he had the impression that then he was 'beyond good and evil', so to say. But that 'remedy' eventually ceased to work due, among other things, to his bad health condition. And actually, only then he thought of something else to employ, and it was nothing else but his own reasoning. And from thence he realised how much in reality he needed that all dump around him. As he'd always been in search of the ideal, he tended to find good wherever it was possible, and if there wasn't any, he did his best to embellish things. But it wasn't a very wrong method, and small wonder it didn't work at all, simply because the place was the exact opposite of his ideal. But what he found ridiculous was that people living there had such a highly elevated idea of themselves, being unable to envisage falling one day, to say that again.

But eventually, his reasoning worked, and he somehow survived the misery thanks to it. After everything he'd gone through, he became aware of the benefits of his hitherto experience, for it'd taught him what he'd needed so much: that eradication of his wrong beliefs.

His situation might have been defined by these words that we find in Pink Floyd's *Hey You*.

But, despite the fame of their lyrics, there was never any fact-changing reaction to prove their worth, due to, as Ches observed, inborn indifference and apathy of their compatriots. And, as a matter of fact, all in all, the lyrics just confirm the situation, the thinking and feelings, and don't offer any option for a change, don't show the way out. Moreover, listening to their lyrics, one might have thought that the authors gain perverse pleasure from their distorted, deviant way of modern man's life. On the other hand, the lyrics might be a ladder, as Wittgenstein would say, for someone wise enough to use it to climb beyond them, and then to throw away the ladder after he has climbed up it.

But, after all, that's it! He said to himself... not without a fight. And he says, their music might be the music of the End, but at the same time it might show, curiously enough, a beginning.

On the whole, Ches says, the experience toughed up him, made him stronger. It was, as Nietzsche put it, 'what does not kill me makes me stronger.' And he needed that strength very much, for thanks to it, he became much more self-responsible, his recklessness vanished and as a result of it, he understood that in that strength he found his own freedom. For freedom, to mention Nietzsche again, means self-responsibility, the resistance to misfortunes, and the ability not to be affected by suffering.

"I," said Ches, "learned to face the music, to fight, and it was the only means to survive and finally to win, that is to become what I am now. *Veni, vidi, vici.*"

To find the truth about yourself is to find what you really are, that is to have the courage to know what you really know, and this courage usually comes late. And it is the most challenging type of courage of all, it being the most difficult task of all we may face in life, which is to find the truth about ourselves.

After all, Ches might be seen as a helpless, naïve romantic, but then is there actually something wrong about being such a man? To be romantic, I believe, is to long for truth, for only there, in truth, does the whole reside. Where else? But the truth about that doesn't appear to be widely recognised, but it is still worth, I believe, pursuing truth, however small a chance to get there it may seem to be.

Having read Ches' preface, I opened the manuscript and began to read.

# PART
# ONE

# THE FUNERAL

'No one is as they seem, and most of life
is lies and deceit.'

'There is no greater sorrow than to recall
in misery the time when we were happy.'

Dante

I watched them. I wasn't afraid they would recognise me for I could hardly recognise myself looking in the mirror. My appearance was changed by a plastic surgery operation some time ago to prepare me for that occasion.

My hair was rather long and I had a beard. All my clothes came from a charity shop I had visited the other day, carefully selecting the wardrobe. I didn't look like a beggar, rather like someone who was in some sort of straits but who remembered better days. I was attending a funeral – my own one. The people gathered there obviously didn't know that the coffin contained no body at all. It all had been arranged by some individuals I'd already met but I, myself, didn't have a clue how they had arranged that spectacle, and didn't need to know. Anyway, I had already known before that they would do it faultlessly, as they did anything for that matter. I always appreciated perfectibility and efficiency, and they were experts in everything they did.

So, I was watching the people attending the occasion, standing under a tree some distance from them. I knew most of them. There was a priest in charge of the ceremony whom I had met before on some occasions, my former friends, co-workers and my wife who, as I expected, didn't look too distressed and I could even notice she watched the spectacle with some satisfaction. My daughter wasn't there, but I knew where she was, and why she didn't come.

It was raining and all of them except one carried umbrellas, and that one was the only one who looked really distressed, genuinely sad. It was Harry, a friend of mine whom I hadn't seen for years until now, and I wondered how come he appeared there, and there was just one explanation – someone had to have let him know. I knew he was living in California, and to come just to attend the funeral in Switzerland where we were now must have been a costly excursion for him. Since knowing him, I knew he had never been on good terms with money, so to speak. But then, his journey might have been paid by those who had let him know. Remembering our old days at university, I did want to talk to him, but for understandable reasons, I couldn't. Maybe some other day, I thought.

The others gathered there were Bernard, an artist; Justin, a barrister; Simon, a priest; Jason, a banker; Graham, an academic; Shaun, a politician, MP; and James, a civil servant; they were the Magnificent Seven, as I called them. They all came here out of duty, and perhaps because they wanted to attend their last farewell to me. It gave them, I knew, a satisfaction of job-well-done. They had the upper hand again, as they were accustomed to. And I noticed a kind of relief in their faces – they were sure they had eventually managed to get rid of me. But did they? I had known them for several years, but apparently not well enough to suspect them of having been able to do what they had done. Now they were sure they could go about their business unhindered, and finish what they had planned so meticulously. I'd discovered their scheme and hadn't wanted to be part of it, as they had hoped. They'd offered me substantial profits since they'd known that to carry out the scheme without me would be more difficult, and when they'd been certain I wouldn't participate in it, they'd done what in their opinion they'd had to. The authorities had confirmed my departure from this world and my former friends hadn't a shadow of a doubt that their enterprise would now succeed. They had even managed to persuade my wife that it had all been my fault, and as everybody else had been, with the possible exception of my daughter, and of course Harry, for understandable reasons as he'd been away all the time and we hadn't been in touch at all. *I'll see you someday*, I said to myself.

So, I watched them one by one. Each of them was now giving his own speech, and the first was Simon, 'The Evangelist', as he was known, a tall, thin man in his fifties. He did look like a personification of a preacher with that solemn face of his, deep sanctimonious voice repeating "we are" all over again. How come he'd joined the conspiracy? "We are in deep sadness bidding farewell to our friend, and…" he was saying.

*You bloody hypocrite*, I said to myself, *just wait and you'll see your divine justice*. His Sunday Mass was extremely well attended; the church was packed mainly with women who stared at him with devotion and adored his every word. However, he was known for his harsh requests of repentance after hearing a confession.

Once, he ordained a woman to prostrate before the Cross for three hours. "But, Father," she said, "I am ninety."

"Age," he said, "doesn't excuse." But in his sermons, he often said, "Your sins will be forgiven," *whatever you've done*, he should have added, as it applied to him.

Next to him stood a short, obese, balding man, and it was Shaun, whose ears were so big that he was nicknamed 'The Elephant Toad'. He was well known for his endless speeches in Parliament. Once he had been about to stand up to deliver one of them but couldn't because someone had smeared his seat with glue and he had been stuck there. The attendants had had to come to free him. He'd demanded an inquiry, which was done rather superficially because nobody had really cared what had happened to him, for he had been disliked by all his fellow parliamentarians.

Now it was his turn to deliver a eulogy, and everybody present wondered, I was sure, how long it would take. He began, "I," as he always began, "will always remember him for his integrity, unselfishness and devotion to his family. He'd been the one to respect and follow."

*Oh yea*, I thought, *you will follow, but you can't even imagine where to*.

His eulogy was surprisingly short, and now it was Justin, nicknamed 'The Casanova'. His nickname wasn't due to his promiscuousness; it was rather because of his incredible ability to seduce all at a court of law. He was a rather handsome man, impeccably dressed as usual. His legal advice was highly valued and he was sought especially by those who found themselves in financial troubles, particularly due to tax evasion. During every court session, he repeatedly sipped something from a flask. Everybody thought it was water, and water it was, but enforced by a good quantity of vodka. Once, he'd drunk a bit too much of that 'water', and instead of defending his client, began accusing him of misdeeds he hadn't even been accused of. The prosecutor and the judge had looked at Justin in amazement, as had his client. Everybody present thought that Justin had taken leave of his senses, but it hadn't been the case as everybody soon found out. Justin's speech had confused the prosecutor so much that he couldn't pursue his line of indictment and had gone silent. The judge, having been bewildered as well, asked Justin what he'd been doing. "Your Honour," he began, "I came here to seek justice and expected to find a bit of sense of it in my esteemed colleague, the prosecutor, but to my great regret I found none. He accused my client of some evil deeds he never committed, so I, accusing my client of some wrongdoings the prosecutor never put forward, point to the absurdity of his accusations, which in my opinion are as groundless as mine. In other words, my colleague's proof of my client's crimes is a mere product of imagination. And now I ask my esteemed colleague to allude to the accusations I made." The prosecutor refused, saying that those accusations had not been his. "And yours are equally not mine," Justin said, "and therefore, I refuse to refer to them as long as you refuse to refer to mine. Do you follow, my dear sir?" That all resulted in an impasse in the case because the judge couldn't decide which of them had been right since nothing like that had ever happened in his career, and there was nothing in the law books either. Thus, the judge had to adjourn the case until the two came to some sort of agreement. The prosecutor agreed to withdraw some accusations, and Justin in turn agreed to accept some other ones that didn't carry a harsh sentence. All in all, the client avoided being accused of the most serious offences, and never went to prison.

After that court session, Justin told his closest friend, Jason, a banker, that while being slightly drunk during that court session he'd had a sort of revelation as to how to defend his client. "You know, my friend," he said, "you can always rely on alcohol liberating power. Anyway, you don't really expect me to deal with law when I'm sober."

And that closest friend of Justin stood next to him. He was a lanky fellow with a pencil-like moustache. Although his looks weren't even close to those of Gregory Peck, he enjoyed enormous success with women. I never knew why they found him so attractive, who would anyway, but our tastes are unpredictable. Terrible womaniser, and his wife accepted that – the same again – you never know with them. His favourite phrase was "I am not quite sure," which he used even when asked about very trivial matters, about the weather, for instance. But everybody was quite sure that he was a terrible liar. It wasn't that his lies were always, but they were often, aimed at deceiving someone, not at all. I think that lying was simply his hobby or mannerism. He was nicknamed 'The Duck', and it was because as the Army major he had been once, during a military exercise he'd ducked under the table hearing explosions. Apparently, he had thought they'd been under a real attack.

Another man who, as far as I could see, never fitted in with them was there too. It was Graham, Professor in Philosophy, Cambridge University, called 'The Terrible' by his fellow academics for, among other things, his late-night visits disrupting their sleep. Tall, athletic, a very good swimmer. I had always liked him, and he had been the only one I could have a genuine conversation with, and that was partially due to our similar education, and our views had a lot in common.

One of his fellow academics said that Graham got tired of thinking seriously, and invented a philosophy which made that unnecessary. Anyway, he was very much liked by his students, who admired the passion with which he delivered his lectures. And he always told his students that philosophy was not the solution but the challenge. At the end of a lecture on Wittgenstein's philosophy, he said: "But you shouldn't really expect me to understand him." And he told the students about a phone call he had received: "A colleague rang me saying that during the previous night he'd eventually understood the proposition 6.54 of the Tractatus. So, I asked him, 'Had you already been asleep then?'"

Graham, whatever the weather, wore wellingtons. Because of this and the fact that he never had a tie, he never sat at the university high table. As a matter of fact, he prepared his meals at his quarters at the college, where he frequently invited his students. On one occasion, they were celebrating passing some exam, and all were tipsy, including Graham, who was just talking about Kundera's *The Unbearable Lightness of Being*, and at the very moment he uttered the title, the table he was sitting on collapsed. Everybody went silent, and there was no rational explanation as to why the table fell apart. Graham hadn't danced on it; he was just sitting and talking.

He liked a drink, and sometimes one could see him having a hangover that he cured by drinking beer. And once he was spotted drinking it in the bathroom at one of the university facilities. He quoted Bukowski's poem to a person who came in: "'We are here to drink beer. We are here to kill war. We are here to unlearn the teachings of the church, state, and our educational system. We are here to laugh at the odds and live our lives so well that Death will tremble to take us.'" And that was exactly what he was after at the university and in his life. Not once was he in trouble because of that pursuit. One day, addressing a group of students, most of them female, he said, "I can see here more women than human beings." That was reported to the university authorities, who demanded an explanation and apology. He said he could explain, of course, but he was not going to apologise for he expected his students to be open-minded and accept anything that he said as a possible topic of discourse, and not his personal views. What was interesting about the complaint against him was that the person who reported the incident was a male student. All in all, the authorities could do nothing and as a matter of fact were not inclined to, especially due to the fact that Graham was a favourite lecturer of the female students. One of them said to him after one of his lectures, "Dr Duvall, while attending your previous lecture I was pretty sure you were nuts, but now I tend to think you are a very serious man." Yes, the girls did like him, and everybody knew he had a love affair with one of them, but for some reason there was no talk about that. Anyway, once she graduated, they got married and are still together.

And there was Bernard too. He was a painter and a follower of Salvadore Dali whom he admired, and that's why he was called 'The Spaniard'. He even looked a bit like him. When asked what one of his own paintings represented, he said he didn't have a clue and added, "What is easy to understand has no value." He was quite famous and exhibited his works in several countries, and the pictures reached high prices. Once, he entered a pub dressed as a house painter, carrying a bucket full of paint in one hand and a big brush in the other. He shouted to the customers: "Get out now, emergency painting!" The police arrived and took him to the station, where he was charged with disturbance of the peace, and because it wasn't his first time (in fact, he was charged no less than twenty times for similar offences) committing a comparable offence, he was sentenced to a month in prison. During the questioning at court, he stood keeping his hands in the pockets of his trousers. The judge reprimanded him for that, and Bernard said to him, "So what? Am I keeping them in your pockets?" For that he was additionally charged with contempt.

Sometime later, the judge commissioned Bernard to paint his portrait. The portrait cost the judge a lot of money. While in prison, the governor ordered his portrait to be painted as well (which was much cheaper), and before Bernard left the prison, the governor said to him, "Dear Bernard, I hope we won't see each other again."

To which Bernard replied, "And why not? Are you going to retire?"

I always thought that there was something else behind his joyful eccentricity, but what it was, I still don't know. Now he was standing there and there was no trace of the usual sneer on his face. No, there was something I'd never seen before.

And the last of them, James, medium height, receding hair, and because of his rat-like face, he was called James 'The Rat'. He was a civil servant and worked at the Foreign Office. I always marvelled how come that moron found his way there. It might have been due to his total obedience; he would do anything he was asked to do without any reservations. Once, his fellow workers played a joke on him. It was winter and it was snowing. The telephone rang and James answered it. A female voice said, "Sir Anthony will be speaking to you." And after a minute, a male voice said, "Hullo, James, hope you are fine today. This morning, I spoke to the prime minister, and he told me that he wondered, and even worried about the stamina of civil servants these days. Do they exercise and the like? So, he has decided to introduce some compulsory physical exercise in the open for all civil servants. Now, depending on where your office is and the weather, of course, the exercise will vary. Today, you and your colleagues are to remove snow from the street outside the building. So, please get a shovel which is available just outside on the left side of the main entrance, and enjoy!" James ran downstairs at the double, grabbed the shovel and began removing the snow.

When he was hard at work, a car pulled over just next to him, and the deputy foreign secretary emerged. Recognising James, he asked him, "What are you doing, old chap?"

"It's prime minister's orders, sir."

"Aha," said the deputy, "if so, carry on, my friend." And he entered the office. James never found out the truth about the prime minister's 'order', and since then he had another nickname: 'The Shovel'.

So, they were there, 'The Magnificent Seven', those who just the previous week had been my friends, and now they were my enemies. But I always suspected there was somebody else, behind the scenes, an éminence grise, and that person was the one who was in charge. So far, I'd never found out who was it.

The funeral was about to end, and now I was supposed to meet the men who had arranged it. So, I went to Zurichberg, which was a few kilometres from where I was now.

A month ago, when I'd had to go into hiding because the authorities had been after me, I accidentally (I'd thought that at the time anyway) met two individuals in Rieterpark. I'd been strolling aimlessly around and when eventually I sat down on a bench and closed my eyes, I heard a voice saying, "Good afternoon, Mr Denker." I opened my eyes and saw two men standing before me. They were of a very different appearance – one was very tall and slim, and the other stocky.

"How do you know my name?" I asked them.

"Your photos are still in almost all the papers, dear Mr Denker," said the tall one, "and you can still be recognised despite those different clothes, hair colour and glasses. But don't worry, we aren't going to denounce you, we're here to help you."

"And why would you help me?"

"This you'll find out in due time, and now we'll take you to very safe accommodation, where you'll stay for a few weeks until everything necessary will have been done to secure your well-being."

"But how can I be sure that you will really do what you say? How can I trust you?" I said.

"Bah, dear Mr Denker, trust is a very unpredictable thing, isn't it? Just a week ago, you'd trusted some people, and now..."

*He is damned right,* I said to myself. *Yes, a week ago, I did trust some people I thought to be my reliable friends, and now... yea, now they are the opposite."*

"Anyway," he continued, "trust might sometimes be a matter of imagination, and not the so-called reality that Dostoyevsky rightly called the most incredible thing ever, my dear friend. You're a very well-read man so, please recall one particular novel and it may help you to inspire your trust in us and our offer. By the way, let us introduce ourselves. This is my dearest friend Kater, and my name's Klug."

"Pleasure to meet you," I said, and then all of a sudden, the title of that one particular novel came to mind. And I knew that despite how strange it all was, I might trust them. Anyway, in my present situation I knew that all that could help me would be what is usually called a miracle.

"All right then, gentlemen, I agree to accept your kind offer."

"A very wise decision," said Kater, nodding his large head. "So, shall we go?"

We walked to Waffenplatzstasse where a black Mercedes Adenauer was parked. We got in and drove toward Hottingen.

During our ride, my mood surprisingly improved out of the blue. When we stopped at the traffic lights next to Rathaus, driven by some impulse, I looked right and saw a woman. She was an example of my ideal female looks. I had a certain weakness, I must confess. I'd always looked for the ideal woman... and never found her. The ideal consisted, so to speak, of long black hair, slim legs and these eyes... all that was there, and I could do nothing. My ideal was just passing by our car. We had the green, and the moment we pulled out she looked straight at me. *No, it can't be,* I thought, *right now, when my life is a disaster, when I'm totally broke, a fugitive with no future... now, when I have nothing to offer, I see a* woman I've never seen before but always dreamt of. You bloody stupid idealist, I said to myself, now you know, this is the destiny of every idealist, to come across your ideal and not be able to fulfil your dream. We were moving very slowly because of the heavy traffic and she was still looking at me, and at one moment she smiled, pointed to the Rathaus Clock and nodded. And I understood – we'd meet sometime in the future. Then she raised her hand in goodbye, turned right into a back street and disappeared from my sight. And I was so sure now, yes, someday…

"Did something happen?" Klug asked. "I can see you look somewhat different, my friend."

"No, no nothing," I said. "I'm fine. Where are we going?"

"You'll see yourself and I'm sure you'll like it."

And we pulled over by a substantial villa in Hottingen. We entered and Klug led me to a large bedroom where, apart from the bed, there was a big wardrobe. He pointed to it and said, "You'll find everything you need there. I'm going downstairs and soon we'll have dinner and after, we'll discuss a couple of things."

I opened the wardrobe and found several items of clothing, all my size. How did they… no, I shouldn't be surprised by anything from now on, I said to myself. I was a bit tired, so I lay down on the bed and immediately fell asleep. I hadn't had such a good sleep for a month or so. I was woken up by a telephone bell. I lifted up the receiver and heard Kater's voice. "Slept well? Please come downstairs when you're ready, my friend." I took a shower, changed clothes and went downstairs to the kitchen.

"Here you are, our dear friend," Klug said. "Now we'll have something to eat. What's your favourite dish?"

"There are a few for that matter, but now if it would be possible, I'd very much like some spaghetti with parmesan cheese, a sausage, you know, I love all things Italian."

"No problem at all," Kater said, and produced a big, deliciously smelling dish from the oven." And I'd already stopped wondering now, How would they…

"And, of course, we'll have some nice wine," Kater said, and put a bottle of white on the table. It was my favourite Riesling.

We all had the same food, and when we'd finished, Klug announced, "Now we have a couple of things to discuss, and I suggest beginning with the most urgent, and I mean your appearance. As you know, you may be easily recognised, and since we don't want to stay here all the time, we have to do something about your looks, and I mean plastic surgery. You agree, I presume?"

"Yes, I do," I said. "I think it's necessary."

"And there's something else," Klug added. "Your funeral."

"A what?" I said. "What do you mean…?"

Klug smiled, and said, "Don't you worry, I don't mean the real thing. I mean the way to convince all others that you've disappeared for good."

"Ah, I see. But how would you go about this?"

"Leave it to us and you won't be disappointed, believe me."

Yea, they'd thought of everything, I had to admit, but… And looking at them, I said, "But why are you doing all that? You don't know me, you—"

I couldn't finish the sentence for Klug interrupted me, saying, "Oh no, we do know you since we have our ways to know what we want. Trust us!"

*And so it seems*, I thought.

"What would you like to do now?" Kater asked.

"Hmm, I don't have any particular ideas, but since I'm not sleepy we may… what about watching a movie or a chess game?"

"Certainly," they said in unison.

"A movie first?" asked Kater.

I said yes, and we all sat down comfortably on the sofa in the living room. There was a large TV set which Kater had switched on, and the movie began. But I couldn't see any inscriptions; there were no usual names of who directed the movie, actors and the like. And after we'd watched it for some twenty minutes, I realised that I was seeing all the actors' faces for the first time. The film we were watching was the story of a man who was telling the story of his life. He said in the beginning that he wouldn't tell everything, for the right time hadn't come yet, but his story would be shown in episodes which wouldn't be in chronological order. So, we were watching the first episode, and the longer I watched, the more the scenes reminded me of something already familiar. I had a vague impression that I already knew the main character, and the scenes rolling by before my eyes were somewhat familiar to me. Eventually, I got there – it was me, and what I was now seeing had already happened in my life. Now there had been the university where I'd studied, meeting my first wife and all that had happened at the time. Watching all that, I didn't feel too well because I realised how many stupid things I'd done, and there were many things I wished had never happened.

Kater and Klug looked at me from time to time while we were watching, but said nothing. When the movie ended, Klug said, "Did you enjoy it, my friend?"

"Not too much," I replied, and asked, "How many episodes in all are there?"

"As many as you wish," he said, and smiled.

I wasn't sure if I wanted to watch it any longer, so I said to him, "Do we have to watch the second episode and so on until the series ends?"

"Not at all, because you actually know what Nietzsche says about memory – 'True philosophy of a single man is recollection.' Isn't it? So, in a way you can turn back the clock. You cannot change the past but you can prevent similar things happening again, provided you've understood what you've done wrong."

"And that's why we are watching the film?" I asked.

"Yes, but it's up to you whether or not you watch the following episodes. I know it's not easy to confront the past, but is there another way to try to be better? Anyway, it's a cliché but you cannot escape your memory, and the point is what to do with what you remember, and as a matter of fact, the only way to escape, so to speak, is to understand, and to understand is to return to the things which have already happened and see them as if for the first time, and it's the only way to become what you are. What you really are, that is what you really need, what you can still do, for it was all in hiding in a way, not revealed to you yet, and to reveal it, to be aware of it, you must see yourself as you have been so far. Anyway, whatever we see could be other than it is, and whatever you've done you could have done in a different way. But this travel into the past is your own travel, and what conclusions you'll come up with will affect your future. There is nothing more to say, all now is up to you."

I was inclined to agree with him since I already had similar thoughts but wasn't sure how to proceed further, not having had enough courage perhaps to confront the past. But I said yes, and from that time on we watched those films almost every day, but we never again discussed the subject.

On the third day of my stay in the villa, I eventually mustered the courage to ask them again some details as to why they'd decided to help me. We were sitting in the living room overlooking Zürichsee when I asked this question, and it was Klug who replied.

"Before I answer your question, tell me first why you have accepted our offer to help you."

"I don't really know. Yes, my situation is rather problematical and I do need help, but I can't say why I accepted the help of two strangers who came out of nowhere. At the same time, I am certain in an inexplicable way that I can accept it. That's it."

"I see," said Klug, "and I appreciate your answer. Yes, there are things we can't explain in any rational way, but still we're sure they're right for us. As for your question, why we decided to assist you, we can't answer it, either, but for a different reason. You know, we're just messengers and there's someone else who is the decision-maker and he'll answer that question in due time."

"I see," I said, "but what are we to do now?"

"Good question, and as for now we have to go ahead concerning a couple of urgent matters. *Primo*, your appearance, that has to be altered as you already agreed, and then your funeral, of course. First, the most urgent matter is your appearance."

The following day, in the early morning, we got into the car and drove south.

# THE JOURNEY BEGINS

'There is no truth. There are only perceptions.'
Gustave Flaubert

"Where exactly are we going?" I asked Kater.

"To Italy," he replied.

"Italy? But what if we are subject to some passport control or something like that?"

"No worries, even if something like that happens, they won't bother us."

"If you say so," I said. I had to admit I now trusted them and was sure they'd overcome any obstacle, whatever we did.

We were heading south, and the further we went, the more beautiful the scenery was. I've always loved the south. The spirit of it inspires imagination, stimulates people who are living there to create beautiful things. The architecture, the paintings and the food, which is art and not just chow. I've always adored Italy and its people, who know how to live, and life pays it back. The quality of life lies in the first place in its beauty, which is quality in itself, but you must first experience beauty to be aware of its meaning. Beauty is pleasure, that is an experience and not something you may learn or be taught, and there's no life without pleasure. 'The struggle for pleasure is the struggle for life' – Nietzsche got it right.

We were now close to Lugano where, as Kater said, we would stay overnight. *Hesse knew where to live*, I thought, the mountains and the lake, and all there you have to see to know that.

We pulled over at a small *pension* overlooking Lago Lugano. Each of us had our own room which was spartan but clean and comfortable, as are many such places in Switzerland. Anyway, I've never really enjoyed luxury. There's something artificial and fake about luxurious hotels, apartments, yachts, whatever.

It was evening now, and we were enjoying delicious *linguine all'aragosta o all'astice*. "What would you like to do now?" Klug asked me.

"What about a swim?" I said.

"Surely, but to be honest, I don't enjoy swimming too much, so I'll go for a stroll, but Kater will go with you. He's an excellent swimmer, and if he took part in any competition, all gold medals would be his, and I don't exaggerate, believe me. Last winter, he swam La Manche just to warm up. And you know, all navy seals and other creatures, if you know what I mean, are a joke compared to Kater."

"La Manche… in winter?" I said.

"Yes, and he did it his way, I mean, underwater, and without the oxygen mask, of course."

*What fairy stories he invents!* I thought, and said, "Yes, of course. Everything is possible without opening an umbrella in the arse, as they used to say in the army."

"You'll find it out yourself, you'll see, and he's got many other exceptional skills too," said Klug.

So, we went for a swim. There was a small pier, and once we were on it, Kater dived into the water and disappeared. I waited and waited, but he wasn't to be seen again. I dived myself, swam for twenty minutes or so and still couldn't see him. I didn't believe the La Manche story, of course, so eventually I got Klug on his mobile.

"Don't worry, my friend," he said, "nothing will happen to him. He'll be back sooner or later."

And it was rather late when Kater reappeared. I'd already been at the *pension* for two hours or so when he came in.

"What a swim I had!" he said. "What a view deep down in the water! What creatures I've seen!"

"Did you dive to the very bottom?" I asked.

"Of course, my dear friend. I always go to the very bottom, whatever the case; otherwise, how would you know about anything, if you know what I mean. How would you understand hidden truths if you didn't get there?"

I agreed with his latter comment but didn't believe a word of the former. I was sure that he had simply returned to the shore unnoticed by me and gone straight back to the place we were staying. "But, of course," I said, "and did you find anything interesting down there, by chance?"

"Oh yes, I did," said Kater.

"And what was it?" I enquired.

"When I was down there at the very bottom, as I said, I had a kind of revelation. I realised that the line between reality and fiction is very thin indeed. You know, people believe in stories which appear to be authentic, very realistic, so to speak, and then quite often it turns out that they're pure fantasies or simply lies which are invented to deceive you. So, it's our quite common naivety to believe in something which we think genuine, and the more it is the more convinced we are it must be true. But what is reality, my friend? What is reality and what is unreality? It all depends on your perception. Everything we see is so vague and so relative. Today something is real, tomorrow, hey presto! It is unreal! Or vice versa – who knows? And the so-called common sense – what is it in fact? It is something we use in order to simplify everything, to make it easier to grasp, and at the same time we make it vulgar. Don't you agree with me?"

*Hmm, that makes sense*, I said to myself. Not long ago, a certain friendship was so real, and now it no longer exists. Yes, I thought, *as a matter of fact, we don't believe in things, we believe in our interpretations of them. But then how shall I interpret what has been happening since I met these two odd characters?* I couldn't find any explanation as to why all that was happening. That was beyond my understanding. The question 'why?' found no answer. I couldn't say why I trusted them, either, after all, and relied on them, and I thought that there must be something beyond our capacity for understanding, that is something beyond all rationality. Yes, I was sure that I didn't need any explanation, any reasoning to go ahead with anything they would ask me to do.

"I can see you're deep in thought," said Klug.

"Yes, I am, but I can't come to any definite conclusion," I replied.

"Don't you worry. Sometimes it's much better not to have one. You know, one conclusion may lead to another one, and so forth. Eventually, we roll in a circle and know what we already knew before. Anyway, there's no such thing as the final conclusion. Everything is relative and accidental, on this earth anyway. Things might look different somewhere else..." and here he stopped talking for a few seconds – and then went on, "but we won't get there just by talking, my friend."

*Yes, quite often we go nowhere by talking,* I said to myself.

"And now, my dear friends," said Klug, "it's time to move. Professor Simoni is awaiting us."

And off we went, heading for Bolzano, a lovely city in the beautiful South Tyrol. I had a feeling that the further we went, the better I felt. Was it due to the magnificent landscape and the weather? Yes it was, but there was something else as well, but again I wasn't able to grasp what it was, and eventually I gave up thinking of it.

*

We reached the clinic early in the afternoon. Professor Simoni was already in the hall when we entered.

"*Buongiorno, signori.* How pleased I am to welcome you here, and let me assure you that we'll do our best to assist you, and your every wish will be satisfied. I mean that if you need something extra, so to speak, please just let me know and I'm sure we'll find a solution. By the way, my dear Mr Klug, please pass my best on to the maestro," and here he gave a deep bow, "and please assure him of my deepest respect."

"*Molte grazie, professore,* and I will undoubtedly pass on your kind words to him," replied Klug.

"Who's the maestro?" I asked Kater.

"Who is he...? Good question, my friend, but it wouldn't be easy to answer it, but as far as I know, you'll have a chance to find the answer yourself. Just please be patient, everything in due time, step by step, so to speak."

We were told that the operation would take a couple of hours, and then if everything went well, I'd stay in the clinic for a week to recuperate. I underwent a check-up and was to have the operation in two days.

\*

And it was Monday morning when she came into my room. I had never seen such a beautiful woman before, with the possible exception of that one I'd seen in Zurich. She was a nurse whose duty was to look after me during my stay there.

"My name's Beatrice Sforza," she said.

"My pleasure, Karl Denker. So, you'll look after me while I'm here. May I ask you something?"

"*Naturalmente, Signor.*"

I wish I could speak Italian since I find it so charming, musical, and small wonder that the greatest operas have been written in it.

"Now, shall I address you *signora* or *signorina*? I presume you're Italian."

"I'm single so it's *signorina*, but you may call me Beatrice. Yes, I'm Italian. Professor Simoni asked me to be your personal nurse and said I should satisfy every wish you may have."

*Oh yes, I did have a wish the moment I saw her, but...* I thought. "I appreciate that very much, and I'm sure to have a very pleasant stay, especially looked after by such a gorgeous woman as you."

"Thank you, but tell me, please," she said, "you may have some extra wishes. I'm ready to satisfy every wish you may have," she said, looking straight into my eyes.

*Bloody hell, I thought, but I can't ask her to satisfy the greatest wish I have...* I looked at her beautiful face and said, "Thank you again, but I'm sure there's no need to ask you for anything. I mean, you yourself will know what I need."

"Yes, to be honest, I actually knew what would be your prime wish the moment you looked at me."

"But... my dear Beatrice..." I stammered.

"There's no need for any 'buts'. This evening at ten, I'll come to see you again."

I didn't reply, I was just looking at her. But then a thought came to my head: *an extra wish, yes, it was Dr Simoni who first said the word, so…*

"Beatrice," I said, and looking for words at the same time, "dear Beatrice, may I…"

"I know what you want to ask me, but you don't dare. You want to know whether I'm ready to satisfy your every wish because such are Dr Simoni's orders. No, I'm on nobody's orders. This is me alone who wants to satisfy that wish of yours. Yes, Dr Simoni asked me to be your personal nurse and to do my best, but he knew perfectly well he couldn't give me any orders. However, he could somehow guess that I would… I don't really know. So, see you at ten. Ciao."

And at ten she came.

During that first night, we not only made love, but talked, which was rather an unusual experience for me. Previously whenever I'd been in bed with a woman, I'd rarely talk to her, and if I had a conversation, it had usually been limited to a few phrases about which way she'd want to make love. This time it was very different. The lovemaking was superb and the conversation was, what shall I say… genuine is the word, I think. She told me she had never been married and had no boyfriend, which was very surprising considering her beauty. She said, yes, she'd known somebody the previous year but no, it hadn't been anything which would have lasted long.

"What are your plans for the future, and in the first place, would you like to continue our acquaintance?" I asked.

"As for my plans, it's not entirely up to me to decide, and our acquaintance as you say… hmm, yes, I would."

"You are a highly qualified nurse, Beatrice, but would you consider doing something else?" I said.

"Yes, I'd like to engage in art dealing, here in Europe and other countries as well."

"Aha, but Beatrice, may I ask, do you have already some experience, and knowledge related to that?"

"Yes, I have. I studied art in France and Italy," she said.

I wanted to ask her how come she studied art and then nursing… but I restrained myself.

21

I said instead, "It would sound a wee bit strange or even deliberate… but I've always wanted – don't know why – my partner to be an art dealer." But, changing the subject, I asked, "Can you cook as well?"

She burst out laughing and said, "Oh yes, I can. I see you're a very practical man, after all."

I felt I was making a fool of myself and wanted to explain, so I said, "Bea, if I may call you this way, I—" but couldn't finish for she interrupted me, saying, "You know, Chris, I believe that everything is still open for you… how one becomes what one is…"

Now I was stupefied – just recently, somebody else had said that. Who was she then to say the same?

"Let's talk about something else now, shall we?" she said.

"Yes, certainly, whatever you want," I said, "and what is it you want to talk about?"

"Surely, we won't talk about what sex positions you would like to try now, as you did with your women before, didn't you?"

I stared at her totally dumbfounded. How for goodness' sake did she know that…?

"I see you're wondering how I could know that, aren't you, Chris?" she said. "You know, I can see that the way you behave now is somewhat new for yourself, I can feel it. You may call it intuition, whatever, but I simply know. Am I wrong?"

"No, you are not, Bea," I said, emphasising every word.

She came every night until I left the clinic, and every night was marvellous. I had to leave but because I wanted to meet her again, I needed to be sure whether she still wanted the same, so during my last night there, I asked her. "Bea, you have told me that it's not entirely up to you what you can do. Could you tell me then what you mean by that?"

"There's somebody else whose decisions I'm supposed to obey," she said.

"And who is that?" I asked.

"I'm not allowed to tell you that yet."

Since I was curious to know, I asked, "Is it official business?"

"Not in the common meaning of the word," she said.

I couldn't resist the temptation, and asked, "Is it a man?"

"Hmm, yes, you may call that person a man, but please now stop asking me, Chris."

"I see, and as a matter of fact, my plans too are up to somebody else."

"And who is that?" she asked.

"Have you ever heard of the Maestro? Professor Simoni must know him for he mentioned the name when we arrived here."

I could see she hesitated before she eventually said, "Yes, I have, but please don't keep asking me. I can't tell you anything more."

I had no choice but to comply with her wish, but we continued talking and just before the dawn we made love again. She fell asleep and I was still awake watching her and suddenly I thought, *no, it can't be, no, how... but yes, she is the same woman I saw in Zurich near the Rathaus...*

I couldn't sleep at all because of my discovery, but not knowing why. When she woke up, I didn't tell her anything about what I had found out despite being sure of my discovery.

Everything went well with the operation, and I was recuperating pretty quickly which was due not only to their excellent medical care, but mainly to Bea. Yes, without her, it wouldn't be that quick to recover. In spite of having been worried and confused, especially because of my discovery, I felt pretty well and it was now up to me whether to stay for a bit longer, and I thought I now understood Paul Getty at his time in the London Clinic, where he was so comfortable that he wanted to stay forever.

I eventually met her... that was all there was to say. And out of the blue, Pink Floyd's lyrics came to my mind: '*Nobody knows where you are, how near or how far...*' But what was next? I felt she did want to see me again, but still my thoughts were a mess – the resemblance, her being dependent... the Maestro. We exchanged telephone numbers, and she gave me her postal address as well, and since I couldn't reciprocate, I said I would give her mine as soon as I could, but she was neither surprised nor worried at all. She said, "Chris, I know we'll meet again, but can't say when, but we will... and you do know that, don't you?"

"Yes, I do," I said. And we said goodbye to each other.

I thanked Professor Simoni and all who'd looked after me, and congratulated them on their brilliant job, and together with my guardians left the clinic.

In the car that was now another Mercedes, with diplomatic plates, as I noticed, Kater said, "I can see they did a great job, but you seem to be a bit… distracted."

"To be honest, I am, and this is because…" I couldn't finish the sentence.

"Of a woman," he said. "Ah! these women," Kater went on, "they inspire in us the desire to create masterpieces and prevent us from finishing them, as that poor Oscar observed, but your case will be different, my friend, I'm sure of it."

To change the subject, I asked him, "Where were you two while I stayed in the clinic?"

"We went to Yalta to have a rest," said Klug.

"To Yalta?" I said, "but it's pretty difficult to get there, I mean, visas, you know that not everyone is welcome because of the political situation there."

"Bah, visas," Klug said. "It doesn't apply to us, anyway, we have diplomatic privileges."

"Yes, apparently you do," I said. "I've noticed diplomatic numbers on the car. May I ask, what country do they represent?"

"It depends on the circumstances," he said.

"I'm not sure what you mean."

"You know, it depends which country we are going to visit. In the case of Yalta, we had Cuban diplomatic numbers, and now we have Hungarian instead."

"And if something happens and the authorities contact the embassy?" I enquired.

"They may, but then the embassy would confirm our identities all right."

"Would they? But how come…" I began, but couldn't finish because Klug chipped in, "because we have some influence in diplomatic circles, you see, and hardly anybody would refuse, you know, for they know what might happen if they refused… my dear friend. Every authority imagines that it has power to decide the fate of its subordinates, to rule, but in fact it's not up to them to decide. They aren't even able to predict what will happen to them tomorrow, as Bulgakov so truly put it. So, if they are intelligent enough to realise that, they will comply with our request."

"And if they don't?" I asked.

"So much the worse for them. Believe me," said Klug.

I didn't know what to say further and wondered again what was going on. Maybe I was having hallucinations or was being hypnotised, I thought, but if I were, how could I have thought of having been hypnotised…? So, I made up my mind not to think more about all that, but to take everything as it came, *carpe diem*, I thought, that's it.

"Do you like your new appearance? And you know what? We could hardly recognise you when you came out of the door," said Kater.

"I, myself, had the same problem when I saw my face for the first time after the operation. I hope I'll get used to it. I still feel a wee bit uncomfortable."

"You will, and soon, you'll see," he said, "that anyway, there are much more important matters ahead of us, our dear friend."

"Where are we going now?" I asked.

"All roads led to Rome, my friend, and in a way, they still do, so we are heading for Roma. 'Quo Vadis Domine?' This question is still valid too. Yes, 'Where are you going, my lord?' Was it the right direction? Ah, a very difficult question, not for us to answer it…" Kater suspended his voice. "But for somebody else it is. All in all, it's a very sad matter, so let's drop it for now."

"And what business do we have there?" I asked.

"Ah, this is an important matter regarding which we'll meet a certain cardinal."

*A cardinal now…* I thought. *Who else…?* "And, may I ask, what is it about?"

"It is about a still unresolved matter in a certain country, and a few other matters we are concerned about."

And we arrived in the Eternal City, Roma, on Tuesday in the afternoon. Our hotel was close to the Colosseum. Ah, Italia, you're like a museum – in one city, there's more history than all over many other countries. The hotel was in a historic building, so old-fashioned but then within there was everything that you needed. After lunch, we went for a walk at a leisurely pace, popping into several small shops. I bought an old bracelet for Bea, Klug a vintage fountain pen. "I like to write in longhand," he said, "and you know what a great writer said – 'Manuscripts don't burn.'"

And Kater bought a big wallet. "What do you need such a big wallet for?" I enquired.

"Because I expect to win a large sum of money," he replied.

"And how do you know you'll win?"

"Bah, I think I'm able to predict some future events."

"Do you like Italia?" Klug asked me.

"I love it," I said. "When are we meeting the cardinal?"

"As soon as it gets dark enough," he replied.

"Why so?" I asked.

"Bah, you know, it makes us more comfortable, and the atmosphere is cosy then."

"I see," I said, "and have you ever met a cardinal before?" I asked.

"Yes, I have, and several times for that matter. But now what about a glass of wine or beer?"

We entered one of the countless cafes, which was an old, very traditional place. There was a huge range of wine on the shelves which stood at some distance from the place we were sitting, so I couldn't see the labels.

"What wine would you like?" asked Klug.

"We rely on your choice since I know you're a wine connoisseur," said Kater.

"All right then, can we have Biondi Santi Tenuta il Greppo Riserva, Klug said to a waiter who just came to our table.

"Excuse me, signor, but we don't have it anymore, I'm afraid. You know it's a very rare wine, and very expensive for that matter, but we ran out of stock. I'm really sorry, sir."

"No, you do have one bottle left," said Klug, "please look on the third shelf from the top, first bottle on the right."

The waiter said nothing and went towards the shelves. After a couple of minutes, he returned holding the bottle. Staring curiously at Klug, he said, "How did you know there was one left, sir?"

"Bah, my friend, yesterday I phoned you and enquired about the wine. They said they didn't have it, so I called a friend of mine and asked him to deliver one bottle to your cafe, you see?"

"But, sir, how come we didn't know that?" the waiter exclaimed.

"It might somehow have escaped your memory, my friend, as it happens to me all the time."

At that moment, the owner came up to our table. "Sir," he addressed Klug, "my apologies, we should have known we had this particular wine, but…"

"No need to apologise, my good man, no need at all," Klug said.

"Sir," the owner began, "I wonder if I could make a big request of you."

"Certainly, you can. What is it?"

"This wine, as you know perfectly well, is very rare and it's almost impossible to get, so I would be most obliged if you could kindly tell me where we could get a couple of bottles of it, sir."

"*Naturalmente*," and Klug continued in Italian, "my friend, tomorrow, it'll be delivered to you at 6:30 in the morning, no worries."

Only now I noticed how perfect Klug's Italian was. Kater's was good too, but he spoke it with some strange accent, as if he was purring or something.

"This is most kind of you, sir," said the owner, "and how many bottles may I expect?"

"One hundred and twelve, my friend," Klug said.

"How…" began the owner, staring at Klug, "yes, of course, thank you very much, but there's still a small problem, sir."

"What is it?" asked Klug.

"I can't afford to buy so many bottles. It costs a fortune," said the owner.

"*Gentile signor* Montalbano, it's a gift and you pay nothing."

"A gift?" said the owner, "but I can't accept such a costly gift."

"You can, you can, my dear friend, it is a recognition of your family's deeds over the generations, so I insist."

"What do you mean by my family's deeds, sir?" said Montalbano.

"All that they have done for their fellow countrymen, *gentile signor*. All that charity, even at times when your family was not too well off. Your grandmother, for instance, whom I had the privilege of knowing," Klug said.

"But signor… may I have the honour of knowing your name…?"

"My name's Klug."

"My pleasure, Signor Klug, but how could you have known my grandma? You seem to be just over forty."

"Appearances, my friend, appearances, and how often we are deceived by them, oh yes, very often indeed. Anyway, I knew her and greatly appreciated what she did. I dare say that even the Devil himself would have appreciated that, my friend, though we know so little about him for that matter. You know, he may do some good on this earth after all. Who knows? Who really knows him?"

At that moment, something dawned in my head. The Devil, the good... yes, Goethe's *Faust* and... yes, of course, *The Master and Margarita*. Here you are! But how could it be...? But then my flow of thoughts was interrupted by Kater saying, "Yes, exactly, *gentili signori*, what do we know about him...? Nothing, I'm afraid, and therefore it's much better to follow what that difficult fellow Wittgenstein says: 'What cannot be spoken of we must be silent about.' *Nicht wahr?*"

"I agree with you wholeheartedly, *mein Freund*," said Klug, "and in the first place that poor Ludwig should have applied that maxim to himself, for it was for a good reason that Dirac called him a terrible fellow because he couldn't stop talking, whereas Dirac's fellow dons invented a new unit in science of physics – 'Dirac unit', that was 'a word per hour'. You know, he wasn't too talkative."

"Ah, Wittgenstein," said Kater. "I remember him. He almost drove me mad with his constant mumbling at lunch, and he was very short-tempered, you know. When at some stage of our conversation, or rather his monologue, I disagreed with him, he grabbed a bottle of wine and smashed it against the wall. I was afraid he would hit me with another one, but fortunately he left. And I don't really understand what Keynes meant when he in such a way described Wittgenstein's return to Cambridge. 'Well, God has just arrived. I met him on the 5:15 train.' If God would have been Wittgenstein-like, oh no, I couldn't imagine a worse one, my friends, definitely not!"

*What is it...* I said to myself ...*and now lunching with Wittgenstein, what else! Am I in the company of madmen, however extremely well educated for that matter? Anyway, I remembered not to be surprised by anything that they do or say.*

"Si, gentili signori," continued Kater, "we're now in the Eternal City, Roma, sitting in this lovely restaurant and we're happy, and thanks to our joy we see the eternity because what is eternity, my dear friends? Isn't it a joy of life when we simply say 'yes' to everything that comes to us, for what else do we need? *In vino veritas*, where else for that matter? And the right wine is part of the eternal truth, provided, of course, we drink the good one because drinking the wrong one we might go astray. Oh yes, we not only wouldn't have any joy, but all we think would go in the wrong direction, and this might happen when we try English wine because, as Oscar Wilde said, 'The English have a miraculous power of turning wine into water.' So, the wrong wine could turn our mind upside down, it would turn our thoughts into water, so to speak, and then our vision would be blurred, and we wouldn't be able to see the world aright because we felt no joy, So, yes, my friends, drinking bad wine is always a very sad story and it unfortunately happens so often."

At that very moment, I felt an overwhelming desire to see Bea, and since I couldn't see her, I wanted to hear her voice at least. I dialled her number and waited. After a few minutes, I heard that the number was not available anymore. I stared at my mobile and I said to myself, *Oh no, for God's sake!*

Apparently, Klug noticed my despair and said, "Something's wrong, my friend?"

"I can't reach Beatrice for her number has been disconnected. I want to go to Bolzano immediately to find out what has happened."

"Call the hospital first," he said.

I rang the hospital and they said that she had left her job.

"She doesn't work there anymore," I said to Klug.

"Hmm, strange story," he said, "but if I were you, I wouldn't worry."

"What are you saying! I shouldn't worry when the woman I love disappeared? What are you talking about, you damned…"

"You may finish the sentence if you wish," he said, "but these are words only, but her disappearance…" He didn't finish either.

"I'm very sorry, I, you know…"

"Oh yes, I do know and therefore I say it again: if I were you, I wouldn't worry because if she loves you too, as you say, you'll see her again."

"But…" I began.

"Forget those 'buts' you say all the time. There aren't any when you're sure of something, especially in the matter of love that is a joy as our friend Kater has just said. Apparently, there was a reason for her sudden departure, and as far as I know, it is the case, dear friend."

"How would you..." I began, but then I thought, *yes, he does know, oh yes, he does.* And I said instead, "So, what do we do now?"

"Nothing, just wait, and you'll see her in due time, that's it. And now we are here to drink this lovely wine and enjoy ourselves. You remember what one of your former friends' favourite poem was, by Charles Bukowski? 'We are here to drink beer... we are here to unlearn the teachings of the church...' and so on. And we have hardly begun, if you know what I mean."

I thought that I was beginning to understand the true reason for our travel. It was to unlearn... and at the same time to learn something, so I said, "You know, Klug, only now I've begun to grasp something I've had no clue about, and I think I want to go further."

"*Bravo, bravissimo,* my dear friend, at last! I've been waiting for it! I'm extraordinarily patient, you know, provided I get my own way in the end."

"I'm sure you will," I said, and thought, *they might be the only ones ever who will for they know that it is not words we need to solve the problem of life. There must be something else. But what is it, and will I ever find it? Perhaps someday—*"

"You are busy talking while the wine is waiting," Kater interrupted. "You waste your time, dear friends, and by the way, you obviously remember that passage in Dumas' novel when D'Artagnan returns to the inn where he left Atos on his own and finds him in a very sorry state. And he says to his friend, 'Atos, are you wounded?' 'No,' says the other. 'I'm drunk.' So, cheers, but take it easy, we don't want to go that far."

And Klug and I returned to the wine and the conversation.

"This wine is so delicious," Klug said to the owner, "that even the Pope, once he learns you have it, may ask for a bottle or two, and other dignitaries might ask as well. Your restaurant will be very famous very soon, I'm sure of it, *gentile signor* Montalbano."

"*Grazie, signori,* you don't know how much I'm grateful for your kindness. To be honest, I was thinking of closing the place, the business doesn't go well, you know, but now once I have all these bottles... ah!"

"All the pleasure's ours, dear friend, don't mention it. And now it's time for opera. *La Scala*, of course. Signor Montalbano, this is not our last visit to your lovely place and we'll see each other again. In the meantime, all our best to you, and *molte grazie* for your hospitality."

And we left for Milano where we arrived at five in the evening. "This evening, there's Tchaikovsky's *Swan Lake* I love so much," said Kater. "You too, I hope."

"Yes, we too," answered Klug, not waiting for my opinion.

"But, gentlemen," he exclaimed, "for the Devil's sake, our attire! We can't go there dressed like we are now. We must find something proper for the occasion. Kater, my dearest friend, don't you happen to know a good tailor?"

"Of course I do. We'll get there in ten minutes." And we did.

"The place is…" said Kater "…you'll see yourselves."

And it was. I had never seen such a magnificent men's store before. In comparison, any of those in Savile Row looked like a shack.

We entered and a gentleman who seemed to be in charge – it was enough just to look at him to know that – said, "Signor Kater, what a pleasure! Last time I had the honour of welcoming you, was…"

"Last year, on Thursday, 30th of March, *gentile signor* Bardini," said Kater.

"What a memory!" exclaimed *Signor* Bardini.

"How could I forget, *caro amico*? And how could I forget the pleasure of meeting your wife and daughters?" said Kater.

"Give me two minutes and I'll ask her to come to welcome you, and may I have the honour of inviting you *signori* to a family dinner later on?"

"*Certamente*, we'll be delighted," Kater replied.

And indeed, Bardini's wife arrived within a couple of minutes. She was like Marie Karall, the French singer, whose beauty is, how to say, dignified. Anyway, she was very presentable and as attractive as Bea, but in a somewhat different way. Bea's beauty was… hmm, to mention another name, like Madhuri Dixit's.

"*Caro mio Signor* Kater!" she exclaimed, and kissed him on both cheeks, which went red – apparently he was very sensitive to ladies' charm. "I'm going now to look after dinner, and I'll see you again at eight."

When she had left, Signor Bardini said, "And now, gentlemen, please try your suits on, and I hope you'll be pleased."

"But, Signor Bardini, how did you know our sizes, except Kater's, of course, which you already knew?" Klug said.

"Signor Kater phoned me the other day and told me your sizes," said Bardini.

Klug looked at Kater and said, "How did you know my size?"

"I took it when you were sleeping," Kater replied.

"How dare you!" Klug exclaimed. "You should have asked me."

"I wanted to give you a surprise," answered Kater.

"Ah, if so, I forgive you," Klug said.

"And my size?" I asked.

"The same way," said Kater.

Our suits were pieces of art, and we thanked and complimented Bardini on his brilliant job. We went for a walk in our new suits and some people, especially women, looked at us approvingly. At ten to eight, we were back at the Bardinis' for dinner.

The dining room was large and very elegant, furnished by someone who must have had refined tastes, and we expressed our praise to the Bardinis. "It's my wife's job," said Bardini. "I know something about suits but nothing about furniture." So, we complimented *Signora* Bardini and sat at the table. A minute later, the Bardinis' daughters arrived. They must have been a joy for every man's eyes, so pretty were they. The youngest was fifteen and her sister two years older, we were told, so they were teenagers but had already blossomed as women; tall, with fully developed breasts, beautiful shoulders and arms, and long raven black hair.

"Ah, these Italian women," Kater whispered to me. "Ah, some of them, like these young beauties, make me feel as if I was to have a heart attack, but be careful, my friend, they are able to talk you to death, and in this respect, they are like the Irish ones, who might be even worse."

At that very moment, I remembered Bea. *How I wish you were here,* I thought. And apparently my face must have altered somewhat because Signora Bardini said, "Something's wrong, Signor Denker?"

"No, signora, everything's fine. I've just remembered somebody I miss so much," I said.

"He misses his girlfriend, signora," said Klug.

"Why she isn't with you if I may ask?" she enquired.

"I… I really don't know, I…" I stammered.

"*Mio caro* Mr Denker," she said, "as far as I know, if she loves you, you'll see her again. Does she love you?"

"I…" and I again began stammering, "I… wish I knew…"

"*Mi scusi*, Signor Denker, but as for the matter of love, nothing like 'I wish I knew' exists. Either you do or you don't, it's as simple as that. Once you're in love, you know whether a woman who you're in love with loves you or not."

"Si, signora," I said, "you're right, but she disappeared without telling me anything, and that's why I—"

I couldn't finish for Signora Bardini interrupted me. "Looking at you, I somehow know that a woman you say you love reciprocates your feelings, *signor*, so be assured that she'll find her way to be with you again."

"*Grazie, signora, grazie.* Somehow you've made me believe what I want to be sure of so much," I said.

And we continued our delicious meal without any further interruptions. After dinner, we had coffee and some homemade cake and then said our goodbyes to the Bardinis. This time, the girls, who had already met Kater, kissed him on both cheeks, which now went even redder. Signora Bardini in turn looked deep into my eyes and holding my hand, said: "Promise me you'll believe what I've just told you. Trust me. I do know you'll see her again, and then you're both welcome to our home. We'll be waiting." And then she kissed me tenderly on the cheek. I kissed her too, thanked her again and thought: *What a woman! Signor Bardini is a lucky man.* And we left.

On the street, Klug said, "What lovely people, home, food, everything! Ah, it was a real pleasure, and we must see them again. And the daughters, ah, I wish I were younger, my friends."

"Have you ever met an Italian woman?" I asked him.

"Oh yes, I have, and what a woman she was! No words could describe her," he said.

"And what happened to her?" I asked.

"Nothing," replied Klug.

"What do you mean?"

"What shall I say… she's married now, children, you know, these things."

"And why didn't you marry her if I may ask?" I said.

"I, my friend, am not allowed to marry, and don't ask me why I'm not," said Klug.

"I see, all right then, but do you see her sometimes?" I enquired.

"Oh yes, I've actually never ever left a woman whom I loved, and I see all I loved pretty often," he replied.

"And how many were you in love with?" I asked.

"Exactly fifteen," Klug said.

"Fifteen!" I said, "and you meet them all from time to time?"

"Yes, I do, and each of them is very happy about that," he said. "You know, I'm not like that man in the Italian film, who has three or four wives and visits them one by one all the time. Eventually, he dies from a heart attack at the railway station."

I thought he was joking, so I said, "I'm sure they are extremely happy, pure happiness, in a word."

"He's telling the truth," said Kater, seeing my doubtful face. "You may ask Signora Bardini. She's met them all. Every time Klug met a woman, he introduced her to Signora Bardini because he completely relies on her advice regarding women. You know, she's an expert."

*An expert…* I thought, *yes, as my mother was. I remember, yes, she knew something about her fellow women.*

It was time for La Scala. I wasn't a great admirer of ballet, preferring symphony; however, I loved *Swan Lake* and other compositions of Tchaikovsky. In operas, some singing goes on forever as if they couldn't finish it. I remembered what my father said to my mother when they attended an opera performance. The chorus was singing one phrase – 'We go'– over and over again, and my father eventually lost his patience and said, 'May they finally go, for God's sake!'

We entered the grand foyer already full of people, and again these Italian women wearing their creations were exposing their shoulders, arms and breasts – what a sight – I could hardly take my eyes off them, and the same, I noticed, was true for my companions.

"You know, my dear friends," said Kater, "I shouldn't have come, I won't be sleeping tonight, if you know what I mean."

"Knowing you, you won't," said Klug, giggling.

We reached our seats and they began. It was the Bolshoi Ballet, and their fellow country man. The composer of that piece of music would be proud of them. During one of the very challenging dances, Kater said to me in a low voice, "Yes, this is something, but nothing compared with a performance given by Count Branicki's dancer, a Cossack, who could jump very high in the air, some three metres, and then came down very slowly."

"And you watched that yourself?" I said.

"Of course I did," he said. "Don't you believe me, my friend?"

"I do, I do," I said. "Now I believe almost everything."

We kept watching the ballet, and when it ended, all applauded it enthusiastically.

"Did you enjoy it?" Klug asked.

"All in all," I said, "yes, it's one of the best anyway."

"So did I," said Kater, "but I told our friend the story of that Branicki's dancer, you knew too."

"Ah, you mean Poddubny? Oh yes, he was great, but did you know that once he'd made his incredible jump in Moscow, he vanished and reappeared again only one year later in Paris?"

"No, I didn't know that," said Kater. "Are you serious?"

"I always am," said Klug, "and you know that."

"What now, gentlemen?" I asked him.

"Now a good supper and then bed. Tomorrow morning, we have an appointment with a cardinal, the Pope's personal secretary."

"What is the meeting about?" I asked.

"You'll see," he replied.

*

Next morning, Klug and I were already having breakfast when Kater appeared. We looked in amazement at his heavily bandaged head.

"What happened to you?" exclaimed Klug.

"Oh no, you wouldn't believe it," he said, "I was dancing all night long."

"And this bandage?" I asked.

"Ah, this. I was wounded."

"Wounded? How did it happen?" asked Klug.

"I was dancing Khachaturian's *Sabre Dance*," said Kater.

"But how come? You were just dreaming, I suppose?" I said.

"Bah, you never know what may happen in your dream, my friend. A dream is a realm of imagination which may be even more dangerous than reality, believe me. You know what that English poet, what was his name... She... Sha... I always forget the name, anyway, who reads him these days, said: 'Aye, there's the rub, for what dreams may come...' and so on."

"So, you've been to hospital?" asked Klug.

"No, I haven't. I phoned an acquaintance of mine, a qualified nurse, and she came... and bandaged my head."

"Do you have any other injuries?" I asked.

"To be honest, I have, but it was the nurse You know, she was very upset seeing me in such a condition, and was so eager to help me so, she... how shall I put it... was too energetic in her efforts, you know."

"And was the nurse Italian?" I asked.

"Of course. You know, as for looking after men, whatever the case, Italian woman come first in my humble opinion."

"And which wound is worse?" enquired Klug.

"I can't tell you. It's a personal matter," Kater said.

After breakfast, we went straight to the cardinal's palace. An imposing place it was. His Excellency's secretary welcomed us and shortly afterwards the cardinal made his entry. He was short, with beetroot-coloured cheeks and well fed. He glanced uncertainly at Kater's bandaged head and said: "*Buongiorno, signori.* Just two days ago, I had a phone call from *Monsignor* O'Prig, and he asked me to meet you. I hold him in great esteem, so I agreed, of course, but was obviously curious as to the purpose of your visit, so I asked him that, but he said I, myself, would find out when I met you. Thus, gentlemen, please tell me what brings you here, and are you here regarding a personal matter or on behalf of somebody else?"

At that moment, Klug came to him and whispered something in his ear. The cardinal went pale.

"I... I..." he began, "I am honoured, but... but my powers are limited, and I certainly want to be of assistance, yes, I do, but what does your... want me to do? I beg your pardon, dear gentlemen."

"First, I'm to tell you, Excellency, that my superior isn't too pleased with the Church's approach to some matters in *Monsignor* O'Prig's country, and not only over there for that matter. Anyway, these days, he's much more pleased with the Orthodox Church or Protestant to say the truth; however, to tell the truth, he's unprejudiced and considers all religions equal. But he does have some objections with regard to your church.

"And may I ask why it is so?" asked the cardinal.

"Of course, and that's why we've come to see you. *Primo*, you're still inclined to approach some issues in a very conservative and outdated way, and this is about sex, which you still consider sinful, whereas you should remember that 'there is no life without pleasure', as that immortal philosopher Nietzsche says. Consequently, what the philosopher said about Christianity is still valid. I mean, 'Christianity is metaphysics of the executioner', and I mean your teachings. And by the way, let me tell you that *mon maître* decided to grant the philosopher his long-time earned peace.

*Secondo*, you're still convinced you're infallible in every matter as regards human affairs, and wouldn't it be better to be more modest and humble here? Look at the two other mentioned churches – don't you think that they're more Christian regarding the matter in question? Yes, dear Excellency, they seem to be closer to what Spinoza in his wisdom says: 'Non ridere, non lugere, neque detestari, sed intelligere.'

So, Excellency, it's a very disturbing and dangerous case to grant yourself the power of omnipotence of judgement in such matters, very hazardous indeed, and fallacious, of course, especially in the long run. I'm not as *au courant* as my master in these matters, but as far as I know, omnipotence may be attributed to God alone, and the master is not content at all with you apparently usurping that power. Isn't it a blasphemy?" And here Klug looked at the cardinal significantly, and the dignitary went even paler. "Yes, your Excellence, and to go further, don't you think that if it wasn't for His omnipotence, we wouldn't be here talking to you…?"

"But…" the cardinal began, to which Klug said, "There aren't any 'buts', Excellency, *enten eller*, as that wise Dane Kierkegaard said, 'either or'. That is, either you follow His Commandments which are about a doing, for all in all, it is not about faith but about a doing. A great many people say, 'I have faith, I believe' and… what does it means? Does it prove anything? No, this alone proves nothing at all. You agree with me, of course, *mon Eminence*." The cardinal just nodded, still looking pale. He had aged. Black rings encircled his eyes.

"*And tertium*, cardinal," said Klug, "is about a certain phrase, one of your favourites, I mean, 'God will forgive you', you know, I can see a certain inconsistency about that. If God were to forgive you everything then there wouldn't be any god. What were a god be then for? We wouldn't need any god. In my humble opinion, the God the Christians have is the one whose commandments you are supposed to observe; otherwise, you are not Christian, and if you don't follow them, you have no chance of being forgiven. There is no more to say. The rest is silence, as a poet you surely know, Shakespeare, says.

"That's all for now, and we are most obliged to you for being so kind as to grant the opportunity to talk to you, your Excellency, and please pass our warm regards on to the Holy Father."

"I certainly will," said the cardinal, "and let me say that I've found our conversation very didactic and I can now see some matters more distinctly. Yes, it was all very informative. I'm most grateful."

"All the pleasure's ours, dear cardinal. There's no need to worry. Everything can still be fixed. Take it easy and all the best."

Then we all shook the cardinal's hand and left.

"Yes," Kater said, once we were outside, "it was a very valuable and promising meeting."

"And who is Monsignor O'Prig whom the cardinal mentioned?" I asked.

"Ah, he's an old friend of mine," said Klug, "a very reliable friend for that matter. I've met him countless times to discuss some rather disturbing issues which I've happened to come across in his country."

38

"And what was the nature of those disturbing matters, as you say?"

"Huh, huh, there have been so many that I don't really recollect them all, but anyway, some of them are strictly related to our conversation with his Excellency. You know, the monsignor's country has been experiencing very particular sorts of troubles for many years now, and to find a solution to them is, I assure you, not an easy task."

"Could you give us a few examples?"

"Yes, I can if you insist, but then once you hear them, you might be disturbed yourself, for they're really peculiar. Let's begin with those on the subject of religion. This matter is extremely confused over there, so confused that even my superior has been slightly bewildered. I've had a couple of discussions with people living up there, and after almost each one, my intellect has been exhausted, even close to collapse. The problem is that under particular circumstances, the intellect, as a certain philosopher, Nietzsche, says, is an awkward, gloomy, creaking machine that is hard to start, and the scenarios over there are very likely to make it happen. So, one day, feeling a bit tired, I went to the sauna to rest. You know, the sauna is a good place to relax, but on that occasion, I left it very fatigued. And it was due to a chat I had with a young local woman—"

At that moment, Kater butted in as usual: "But whatever you say about that country, my dear friend, you must admit that its women are very attractive and charming, aren't they?"

"Yes, yes, I admit, but please don't interrupt me anymore; for I may get confused again just relating the story, to say nothing about the other ones. And you are, I know that, a world- class expert on female beauty but this is not the issue now. Anyway, she wasn't too pretty for that matter. So," continued Klug, "the matter in question appeared when a conversation somehow turned to religious matters, exactly Protestantism, and I asked her who was the father of that denomination. 'You obviously know the name,' I said. There was a silence – she said nothing, so I said, 'Martin Luther, of course, I'm sure you recollect the name now.' 'Ah, Martin Luther King!' she exclaimed.

"You know, my friends, there are countless interpretations of Protestantism but until then, I'd never come across such a daring one, so to speak. You see how far we can go in these matters. There are simply no limits to our interpretations. It all might be the Devil's work."

To this, Kater replied: "I wouldn't be so sure for we actually don't really know what his job is, do we?"

"I think you're right," said Klug, "my dearest friend, we know nothing about that." And he continued, "All in all, that puzzling experience of mine reminds me of the following dilemma: 'What's the difference between genius and stupidity?' And the answer is: 'The difference is that genius has its limits.' And that's it, my friends. And to summarise the subject of religion, let me quote a reply to my other question to somebody else: 'May I ask why you have joined this particular church?' – 'Because God told me so.'

"You know, living over there, you encounter numerous challenges as regards other examples of their view of the world, their so-imaginative interpretations regarding almost every matter under the sun. Among them, Liechtenstein is a former Soviet Republic. And small wonder that the authorities do their best to improve the standard of education there, and they now claim that their two universities are among the leading ones in the world. And their media too do everything possible to broaden the knowledge of the citizens, organising various competitions and radio quizzes such the one I learnt about listening to the radio. The question was, 'Which city is the capital of France? Is it Paris, Dublin or Melbourne?' I wonder how many people gave the correct answer, for you never know what might happen over there.

"And now, since I see you seem to be a bit tired of listening to these stories, I'll make a short resume. I was bewildered so many times while visiting the country that I asked myself 'Why?' Why they know not what to think of some apparently obvious matters and in the end, they know not what they do. And eventually I found the answer, and it was thanks to a graduate of one of their illustrious universities. I once wrote a paper on our unforgettable Friedrich's philosophy, who tells us that 'Sometime in the future we will need new values.' I fully agree, yes, we certainly will. But not all of us, because over there they have so many different opinions regarding this particular statement, which in the graduate's view was wrongly translated, and therefore it should be: 'We sometime need values.' And that's it, my friends, aye, there's the rub, I mean 'sometime', for if it is the case then there aren't any values, but just in case that there are some after all, we sometime need them. And now in order to simplify the matter in question, we may say that those in favour of the aforementioned interpretation tend to deprecate, and deprecate everything so, *summa summarum*, their views of the world may be shortened just to 'he, he, he', and believe me, I don't know any other one being so self-consistent, so to speak.

"All in all, I think that in order to make things better in that country, especially considering the problem of the duality there of a sort, I mean the place being divided, I'd agree with you, my dear friend, that we should leave women in peace, for the first thing to do there would be to resettle some, let's say, fifty thousand men to Alaska. They might even be happy about that, for they love all things American.

"Ah! my dear friends, what more shall I say! Nothing... but these words of a poet, Shakespeare: 'The rest is silence.' Indeed, there is nothing more to say, for our reasoning and patience, of course, have their limits.

"Why do you say nothing, my friends?" asked Klug.

"For there's nothing to say. Everything's clear. The rest is silence, as you said," said Kater.

"Yes, indeed," Klug carried on, "but let me just tell you what eventually happened to me. To be honest, I hardly survived all those intellectual adventures, and at some stage I even sought medical assistance. I visited a doctor who asked me how he could help. I told him I was almost totally exhausted, couldn't sleep and it was because of, I told him, everything I was going through, and I told him a couple of these stories. He said there was no need to worry, just take it easy, but at the same time he wanted to know every detail of my experience, asked me additional questions, was very curious indeed. And you know what happened to him? On the same day I visited him, but later on, one of his nurses found him totally plastered, half-conscious in his cabinet. She immediately called a friend of his, a psychiatrist, who came at once and during a rather difficult conversation (difficult because of the doctor's condition) learnt of the cause of his friend's condition who told him, 'You... you can't imagine, no,

41

you wouldn't believe what I heard today, here in our beloved country, such things, no, unbelievable! I've told you just a bit of what the patient told me, but you wouldn't believe the rest, for even as a psychiatrist you don't encounter such difficult cases.' 'Oh, no, I do,' said his friend, 'and even more difficult,' replied the psychiatrist.

"Eventually," continued Klug, "I followed a well-known author's advice, George Bernard Shaw: 'I showed my appreciation of my native land by getting out of it as soon as I possibly could,' and believe me, I did that to my great relief. But now, my friends, it's time to resume our travel."

And we returned to Zurich. It was already late when we arrived at the same house we'd stayed at before. After supper, Klug said to me, "It's time for you to meet somebody, and this meeting, I dare say, might be the most significant meeting of your life. Tomorrow, you'll go to Rieterpark where you'll meet somebody, and I believe that you already know who they are."

And I did.

# THE TALK IN RIETERPARK

'Nothing is hard for me to do...
as you well know.'
Mikhail Bulgakov, *The Master and Margarita*

I had somehow always known that I would eventually meet him. All what had been happening to me until that day made the meeting inevitable, and somehow, I'd even longed for it, but it hadn't had been up to me when and where it would happen. Now the day had come, but I wasn't too sure about myself and whether I was actually ready to cope with the challenge, for how could anyone be sure of this kind of meeting, during which one has to see oneself, that is, the one what you really are? When you confront yourself, when the curtain that separated you from seeing yourself has been drawn wide? There's no more difficult challenge than that, and sometimes you won't manage to do that on your own; you need somebody else who won't have mercy on you revealing your true self, but at the same time he would be full of sympathy towards you. You never know when the day may come, for it comes all of a sudden, without any forewarning.

Klug had told me to go to Rieterpark in the afternoon and wait, and when I'd asked him what time I'd meet the person and exactly where, he'd just smiled. So, I went there and for a good hour was walking aimlessly without meeting anybody. I could see some people from a distance, but the park was exceptionally empty on that day. Eventually, I got tired and sat down on a bench. It was already nine o'clock, but it was summer, so it wasn't dark yet. *And what if he doesn't come*, I thought, *what if he's changed his mind…?* And when I was still submerged in my thoughts, I saw somebody coming towards the bench I was sitting on. When he came closer, I could see what he looked like. He was tall, grey hair but black eyebrows, grey piercing eyes and crooked sort of mouth. I immediately knew it was him. He approached me and said, "Have you been here long?"

"No sir, one hour or so."

"My name's Wahrburg and you've already met my assistants, Klug and Kater."

"Yes, I have. Pleasure to meet you, sir."

"Hmm…" he began, "it might a pleasure, we'll see. How do you find my assistants? Are they helpful?"

"Oh yes, they are brilliant at anything they do."

"Yes, they're very efficient, and I agree with a certain writer, George Bernard Shaw, who says that essentially there are only two kinds of people: the efficient and the inefficient."

"I would agree too," I said, "and will they stay with me long?"

"As long as will be necessary."

"I appreciate that, for there's still a lot to be done, and without them I won't manage."

"Do you believe in God?" Mr Wahrburg asked, changing the subject.

"I'm an agnostic, you know, so I do and at the same time I don't, something like that."

"Something like that," repeated Wahrburg, "a very interesting expression. And who rules the life of man and keeps the world in order? Actually, I already asked the question visiting Moscow some time ago and received a rather stupid answer."

"And what was the answer?" I enquired.

"Somebody said it was man himself. And what do you think?"

"I wouldn't be so sure, considering all that happens," I replied.

"That's a better answer. And by the way, wouldn't it be much better not to pose the question at all, and simply to take for granted that it is not man who rules the world? What do you think?"

"Maybe, I don't know."

"You seem to be very uncertain in your opinions, Mr Denker," said Wahrburg.

"So I am, I know that."

"And wouldn't you like to be more certain? You know, it helps."

"As a matter of fact, yes, I would, but I don't know yet how to get there," I said.

"There is a way, believe me," said Wahrburg.

"How do you mean, sir?" I enquired.

"To be certain about anything under the sun, you must first find out what you are, that is to know your true desires and needs, and only then you can find the ways to satisfy them. But in the first place, you mustn't be a follower. You know what that immortal philosopher says: 'Only when you have all denied me will I return to you. You must seek yourselves first, you should not be believers.' In other words, you shouldn't imitate anyone, whatever they are. Only then you're on the way to yourself, but this task requires courage, but it is the only way to freedom, which is always the matter of a single man. And this freedom means self-responsibility, the ability no to be affected by suffering, the resistance to misfortunes and the readiness to sacrifice oneself and others. And here I again fully agree with that philosopher, 'The Steppenwolf', as I call him. But such freedom belongs to the task, not to the solution. And by the way, remember that people's morality which is, anyway, usually a mask, pretence, shouldn't be of your concern. You should care about yourself in this respect, as a professor I knew did. Once, he was asked how he, as a lecturer on ethics, managed to coincide his behaviour with the subject he taught, and he replied: 'And does the ornithologist have to fly?' Anyway, the professor, Henryk Jankowski was his name, was a man of integrity, and I mean the way he helped the students in the so called 'difficult times'.

"Yes, dear Mr Denker, integrity means sympathy, pride, courage and insight, which are all virtues of the free spirit, a truly independent man, but to become one, you always have a long way to go—"

"But, Mr Wahrburg, if I may interrupt," I asked, "then what about this kind of integrity and other people? Isn't it a bit selfish, egocentric?"

"Bah, egocentric. This is exactly the way each of you are, but only a few have the will and courage to admit that. You know, that mumbling about equal rights and democracy is just the way to placate and console the weak. People aren't equal, and to say that is a mere cliché, for everybody knows that but hardly anybody says this aloud. Or socialism, for that matter. When it's introduced in practice, it's the terror of the dumbest, those who seek revenge to compensate for their own inferiority. That's it."

"So, all these democratic ideals—" I began, but he interrupted me.

"That's all rubbish, good for nothing in the long run."

"But they somehow function, don't they?"

"Somehow yes, they do. But it's not about somehow doing something in this life, for to live is to be aware, that is to be honest towards yourself which isn't the attribute of hypocrites and their cover-ups for their ignorance and incompetence."

"And what about justice, Mr Wahrburg?" I asked.

"Another bleached word, so to speak. Justice and morality are the inventions of rulers, whoever they may be, and they are to console the majority and to justify a punishment at the same time."

"But there is freedom of will," I said.

"To my despair, I can see that your reasoning is a mess, Mr Denker. There's no such thing as freedom of will. It is an illusion, a superstition, a misunderstanding, my dear sir, for we identify the phrase with a 'free choice', which doesn't exist because all of our actions are determined by the will of preservation of life, and we can't separate the will from life which governs us, and not vice versa. Are you with me?"

"Yes, I think I begin to grasp what you say."

"Good, I'm glad to hear that. But you, I presume, have other doubts, and I appreciate that. You know what that joyous fellow Charles B. said – 'The problem of the world is that the intelligent people are full of doubts, while the stupid ones full of confidence.'

"Now, if these stupid ones have no doubts, then they perfectly deserve what happens to them because they think they live in the best of all possible worlds, as a wise man, Leibnitz, once said. I obviously don't agree with that, and this is because we simply wouldn't know what the best of worlds looked like, would we? There is someone who knows, but who is it? But let's leave this question unanswered for the time being. Anyway, the problem is that people don't really know what they think, or rather, they aren't fully aware of their thinking because as a matter of fact they never think, their thoughts think for them, but they can't grasp them clearly enough when they eventually realise them. Only from time to time they manage to grasp what they think, are aware of what their inner thoughts are, and one has only late in life the courage to grasp what one really knows. And only when you have the courage, you can become what you really are, and to find out what you are, you have to travel back into the past, and this is what you are doing now. When you arrive where you started, you'll know yourself as if for the first time and only then aright, and only then also the world."

"Yes, I think I know what you mean, but how long will it take?"

"This is a rather stupid question because it's totally up to you how long it takes to see the past, and in a way, the future too, aright. And to do that, you must undertake a very long travel.

"But then, to see the past honestly is a very demanding task, for honestly here means to see your own faults; and not many a man wants to see them. Today's world is packed with swindlers who paradoxically like to be swindled themselves. What a strange creature is that man? All in all, it seems he deserves what happens to him."

"And I myself have to?"

"Yes, you have to if you want to say eventually 'yes' to all around you, for only then you'll say 'yes' to yourself. It won't be easy, dear sir, oh no, not at all, but it is worth doing it, believe me.

"As you can see, we talk philosophy now, and as far as I know, you know something about the subject. Some people consider philosophy, as you know, a waste of time. And it is simply because they don't have a clue what philosophy is. They think philosophy is to keep your head up in the clouds, something that has nothing to do with reality, the real life. Those who say so do that as if thinking wasn't a part of our lives, and yes, quite often it isn't for some. And this reminds me of a conversation I once had with a good friend of mine, Franz. He told me about a chat he had with his nephew, who asked him, 'Uncle, what do you actually do? – 'I,' replied Franz, 'occupy myself with metaphysics.' – 'And what do those metaphysicians do, Uncle?' – 'What sort of question is that? They do nothing.' – 'But, Uncle, if all the others were doing nothing...' – 'From all the others, you cannot demand such a difficult thing, my boy.'

"And, dear Mr Denker, that's it, you cannot expect everybody to understand philosophy. But there are some who are convinced they're pretty close to wisdom. And again, Franz talked to a would-be writer, who said to him, 'I'm just one step from fame.' – 'Yes, you are,' said Franz, 'but backwards.'

"All in all, as you know perfectly well,, you can't underestimate the stupidity of the general public."

"No, you can't," I said. "However, the so-called general public matters, you know…"

"Yes, it matters as regards its own matter, so to speak, if you know what I mean, but it doesn't have to be your matter. Anyway, you don't choose your destiny, it chooses you. Life itself isn't something you can think of. And whether you're a lone wolf or a very sociable fellow doesn't depend on your free choice, for as a matter of fact, you don't have a choice, you're who you are. And as for the majority, our dear fellow beer drinker says, 'I don't hate people, but I feel better when they aren't around.' For they don't really care about each other, *homo homini lupus est*, aren't they? And therefore, all that doth begin may rightly to destruction run."

"I don't agree with you at all, Mr Wahrburg."

My co-conversationalist gave an eerie peal of laughter, and said, "Of course you don't. How could you? You are a humanist, aren't you?"

"Yes, I consider myself a humanist."

"And what do you actually mean by that, my dear contestant?"

"Being compassionate, actively friendly and helpful toward my fellow men. These are the virtues of a humanist, as you know, Mr Wahrburg."

"Splendid pack of trivialities, dear Mr Denker, but totally useless in the reality of human affairs. They are just for show, to cover up the true character of your beloved human beings, whose actual needs are to exploit their fellow man, to rule in order to satisfy their own desires. Am I right?"

"You might be, sir. Humanists are in the minority, as it is with everything of quality not quantity. Still, they represent the good on this earth, I believe."

"The good, you say? But what actually is the good? Isn't it actually a pleasure that is looked for by each of you? And it would be rather difficult to get it following your splendid humanistic virtues. Don't you think so?" said Wahrburg.

"Yes, I agree, but in the end what you are, what values you respect, is your own business, isn't it?"

"Ah yes, here I agree with you, dear Mr Denker. Yes, the way you are towards others is exclusively yours, and nobody else's. And this is what we were just talking about – to find out what you are – step by step... And then to act according to what you have found out, and only then you may be satisfied, which is to say 'yes' first to yourself and then to everything around you. Once you know who you are, you see the world and life aright. But to get there might take long, Mr Denker, it is actually always a very long journey, and you never know before whether it takes you in the right direction, but some have to take a risk, simply because they are seekers all their lives. This is their true nature, so they cannot give up searching. And it seems to me that you're one of them, and despite your hitherto side paths and wrong turnings, the delays and blunders, I am somehow convinced you will eventually reach your aim. You don't quite realise it yet. You will resume your journey tomorrow, dear Mr Denker. And there's one another thing – my assistants say you're in love."

"I think I am."

"You think... love is nothing to think of. Either you are or you aren't."

"Yes, sir, a slip of the tongue. Yes, I certainly am in love."

"Love, ah, I envy you. I've always been alone."

"May I ask why?"

"Bah, good question, my dear sir. Hmm, it's due to who I am, and you obviously have some ideas who I might be. So, you know, a good many people suspect me of being responsible for all evil that happens on this earth. But I find it very unjustifiable, undeserved, for in fact I do some good. It may sound strange but I'm very just because I'm the only one who is absolutely impartial, for I don't judge anybody, so I don't take sides, and being so, I am actually beyond good and evil, for to judge is to be unjust. But people, poor things, don't appreciate that. They always want you to appraise them for what they do, but how could I? They know not what they do. Anyway, not to appraise them means being honest towards them, that's impartial. There's somebody else, as you know, who's willing, they say, to forgive them their ignorance, but I don't. That's the point. But not forgiving them, I manifest their wrongdoings, and they hate me for that. Ah, a day may come when they'll see how wrong they've been, sometime in the future they may eventually have their new values and then they'll praise me for what I've done for them. But it'll be a long journey! Now they just sometimes need values, yes, only sometimes..."

"I feel like I finally understand your point, sir. Yes, there might be a long journey ahead of us. You know, most of my life I've spent in my imagination, so to speak, and now the time's come to see the real value of my dreams. I have to do what a truly good writer does, that is to relive the past and in doing so imagine the future. To show that whatever we see could be other than it is. To show worlds that may exist. And first of all, to answer the question, 'Why?'"

"You got it right. Bravo. You seem to be ready to resume your journey. Good luck to you! We'll meet again at the end of your journey, and then we'll discuss a couple of things which you may see then in a different light. We'll see. And remember what that immortal Friedrich says: 'What doesn't kill me makes me stronger.' Doesn't it?"

And our conversation ended then. Mr Wahrburg shook my hand and left. I returned to the villa on foot, thinking of what we'd been talking about, and somehow I felt more confident about myself and was awaiting my journey with greater certainty than before. He had raised my confidence despite contradicting me almost all of the time. Yes, I now remembered that phrase: 'I am the spirit that forever denies...' and I thought... *Yes, it might be due to his denials that he actually does some good...*

I was passing by Schweiz Landesmuseum when I saw her. Yes, it was Beatrice. I was sure it was her walking on the other side of the street. What was she doing here and why hadn't she contacted me before? There was heavy traffic so I couldn't cross the street until I reached the street lights, but fortunately I could still see her. The lights changed to green and I ran to the other side and looked for her, but she had already disappeared.

I was so upset that I was shaking, and trying to calm down, I drank a couple of beers and some schnapps at the nearest pub, but that didn't help much and when I came to the villa I was still very distressed. Kater immediately noticed that something was wrong and said, "What's wrong, my friend?"

"Yes, something's very wrong and I… I don't know why it must be so…" I stammered.

"Did something happen on your way back from the park? Maybe you saw somebody you recognised?"

"Yes, I did, and it was Bea," I said.

"And couldn't you talk to her?"

"No, by the time I crossed the street, she was on the opposite side, you know, she had already disappeared."

"I see, and I, myself, am upset now, but you know how things are with these women. They're totally unpredictable, so you never know what to expect from them."

"Thank you very much for such encouraging words, dear friend," I said.

"Oh, my dear friend, there's no need to be sarcastic."

"I'm not trying to be sarcastic. I… I am… bloody hell! I've found her at last, I was so sure, I…" I was so beside myself that I couldn't finish the sentence.

"I do understand, believe me, but sometimes you have to go through, what shall I say, a trial test, you know, to see something you're so sure about afresh, so to speak."

"How many more tests will I have to go through? Haven't I already gone through enough?"

"Apparently, you haven't. Otherwise, there wouldn't be any left."

"And how do you know that?"

"Bah, how do I know…? Hmm, I can see it in my mind's eye, my dear friend."

"Stop talking in puzzles. I'm already tired of them."

"Are you? Don't you think that your life isn't one of them? Do you think you have already solved this one and all others?"

I was silent for a good while, asking myself, *Have I actually solved anything?*

"You see, dear friend, you begin to understand, don't you?"

"Yes, I think I do, and—"

"And Mr Wahrburg," Kater interrupted me, "didn't he tell you anything that might help you to see aright a couple of things?"

I could recollect my recent conversation in the park almost word by word, so I said, "Yes, he did."

"Then there's no need to worry, for he does know what he's doing, believe me."

"Yes, now I know he does."

"Good, so stop worrying and leave the matter in question with him. Anyway, as regards this matter, and a couple of others, of course, it's up to him, and I kindly suggest you rely on him."

As a matter of fact, I already knew that, but having been so upset at seeing Bea without a chance to speak to her, I'd somehow forgotten about that. *Yes,* I said to myself, *I know now I have no choice for it's up to him. However, it still matters, I know that, what I myself do, and what I think of the matters that I've actually never solved yet, never even tried to solve, for that matter, up to now—*

"So, my friend," Kater interrupted the flow of my thoughts, "I'm happy to see you've calmed down a bit, and please be patient, and it's never too late, but it might be for some… but fortunately not for you, so take it easy."

*How…* I thought, *how does he know? No,* I said to myself, *this would again be a stupid question.*

"This having been sorted, we can now discuss something else," said Kater.

"What do you mean?"

"I mean our upcoming travel to Moscow."

"To Moscow, why Moscow?"

"The question 'why?' finds no answer until it's been answered, so we have to go there to find answers to some questions."

"But why Moscow? I've never been there and know nobody who has."

"You're mistaken, my friend, you know them, but you don't know they've already have been there."

"And who do you mean?"

"Your former friends, 'The Magnificent Seven', of course."

*They have been to Moscow…* I said to myself. *What for…?*

"That's it, what for?" Kater said.

*Can he read my thoughts?* I thought.

"Yes, they've been to Moscow, and not only once for that matter. They visit the city quite regularly. You remember that they disappeared from time to time from Zurich, and when you asked them where they had been, they said something about some urgent meetings and the like."

"Yes, I do remember, but how come you know anything about that?"

"Bah, my friend, how I can know is a very different matter, and some day you'll find the answer to that, but not now," said Kater.

"All right, but then tell me what has brought them to Moscow."

"And why did you have to go into hiding? Wasn't it because you were accused of embezzling the money that vanished without a trace?"

"Yes, it was the case, and now I know it was them who stole the money, which is now in Moscow, I presume?" I said.

"Precisely! The money is now there, and they are still visiting the city because of it."

"But what can we do about that, especially in Moscow?"

"Ah, my dear chap, there are things we can do, oh yes, there are, believe me."

"Could you be more specific?"

"Not now, once we get there, you'll find out. Anyway, it's not me but Klug for whom money has no secrets, and believe me, in comparison to his skills, even such a money wizard as George is a dilettante."

"And did our friend Klug study finance at some prestigious university?"

"Oh yes, he did, but this university is not registered, so to speak. And please don't ask any further questions. You know, some things are still strictly classified, but you may have the privilege of finding out a couple of things in due time."

"If you say so, but you know, Kater, I'm still puzzled by all that. I—"

"Take it easy, and let us deal with some difficult issues," Kater interrupted me. "In due time, you will come to know, as I say, and now Moscow, my friend. Tomorrow, we'll visit the Russian Embassy to arrange visas."

"And by the way, where's Klug? I haven't seen him since I came back."

"Klug's busy with some other things and I actually have no clue what is it. You know, he has his secrets."

"You say visas, and how long do you think it will take to get them? I heard that you may never get one."

"Yes, it's true, you may never get one, for the Russians are allergic, so to speak, to some individuals, and for good reason, but as for ourselves, I don't expect any serious obstacles."

*Are there any obstacles for them…?* I thought, and said, "I see, tomorrow you say, and if we get the visas then when are we to go to Moscow?"

"Soon, very soon, my friend."

*

The next day, we drove to Bern to visit the Embassy of the Russian Federation. It was a very pleasant, even cosy mansion, and when we came to the reception desk, Kater said, "*Zdravstvuyte, my zdes' o nashikh vizakh.*"

*How come he speaks such good Russian?* I thought, but then remembered not to ask any more unnecessary questions.

"And when, may I ask, did you apply for them?" asked the receptionist.

"I'm not sure, you know. As a matter of fact, it was our friend who deals with such matters," said Kater.

"*Ponimayu,*" said the receptionist, "*kak vas zovut, gospodin?*"

"My name's Kater and my companion's Adarsh," replied Kater.

*Adarsh…* I thought, *where has that come from… what's…?* But couldn't finish my thinking because the receptionist, after hearing the names, jumped to his feet and said, "Mr Kater, I'm honoured, I'm so pleased… Svetlana," he shouted in the direction of the open doors behind him, "come here at once." A very pretty girl appeared and the receptionist said, "Take these gentlemen straight to the office of the first secretary, and please arrange tea, coffee and everything else, you know."

We were led by Svetlana, a real joy to the eyes, to the first secretary's office. On our way there, Kater said to her, "May I ask how long you have been staying in Bern?"

"Just a month, sir," replied the woman.

"Oh, just a month, and have you already visited some places, I mean, Munster and the like?"

"No, sir, not yet."

"Aha, and what about if I take you to see them, and then we may drop into a restaurant and have a nice meal, what do you think?"

"It'd be a pleasure, but I'm so busy here, I don't really know."

"Eh, *ma chérie*, everything can be arranged. Anyway, I don't expect any obstacles here," said Kater.

*Surely*, I thought, *there won't be any obstacles…*

"I'll have a word with the secretary, provided you would like to accompany me. It'd be a great pleasure to show you the city," said Kater.

"Yes," replied Svetlana, "if he agrees, I'd like it very much."

"Great, and thank you, mademoiselle."

We entered the first secretary's premises, and once he saw us, he exclaimed, "Dear Mr Kater, the receptionist has just informed me I'd have the honour of seeing you. Please have a seat, gentlemen. Svetlana," he turned to the girl, "please arrange everything. You know what I mean."

"*Apropos*, if I may, sir," Kater said, "I wonder if I could have the pleasure of inviting that charming lady on an excursion. You know, she says she hasn't seen the city yet."

"But of course, dear Mr Kater, certainly you can, and for how long would you like her to accompany you, if I may enquire?"

"It's up to her. I won't impose myself on her. I'll do whatever she likes."

"Yes, of course, I understand. Anyway, she may accompany you as long as you wish, no problems here," said the secretary.

"Thank you so much, sir, and I won't forget it."

"All the pleasure's mine, dear Mr Kater. And now, it's about visas, isn't it?"

"Yes, dear sir, it is. And I wonder how long—"

"But, Mr Kater, if I may interrupt, they are ready to collect. All those in Moscow were so happy, you wouldn't imagine how they were, once they heard you'd be coming."

"I'm most obliged for your kindness, and I will obviously let them know how efficient you are."

"Not at all, it was a pleasure, and thank you, and yes, if you'd be so kind as to have a few words…"

"Rest assured I will."

"Excuse me, gentlemen," said the secretary, and lifted the phone receiver. "Igor Stepanovych, please bring the gentlemen's passports."

And in two minutes, our passports were brought up to the secretary's office.

"Here you are, gentlemen," said the consul, "and I'm so glad I could be of assistance, and now let me invite you to some modest treat."

The treat wasn't too modest; we had pickled fish, sardines, caviar, pâté de fois gras, cheese and of course vodka. It was Svetlana who was serving us, and I admired her long legs and every other detail of hers.

"Svetlana," said the secretary, "Mr Kater wants to have the pleasure of your company, and I've, of course, agreed, so from now on you aren't needed at the Embassy, you can accompany him for as long as you wish, provided, of course, you want to. Mr Kater says it's up to you. So, what do you say?"

"Yes, of course, sir, I'd be more than happy to accompany Mr Kater, thank you so much."

"Pleasure, and I hope you won't disappoint him. Mr Kater's our most welcomed friend and soon he's going to Moscow where he's awaited with great expectations by everybody, and in the first place by our esteemed..." At that moment, the telephone rang.

"Excuse me," and the secretary said to the receiver, "yes, ah, it's you, dear Bogdan Nikolayich... Yes, they've arrived and we are now having a small meal... Yes, excuse me, what do you say? Aha, the president... Yes, of course... No, no, tell him please that... No, no problems at all. Everything's ready... Yes, no delay... How could I fail him? Yes, please inform him immediately, and thank you for calling me."

*What the hell,* I thought, *so now the president...?*

"*Moi dorogiye druz'ya,*" said the secretary, "everybody in Moscow can't wait to see you, Everything is being prepared to make your stay as pleasant as possible. I dare suggest, dear Mr Kater, asking Svetlana to be your guide during your tour. You know, she's from Moscow, so she knows the city."

"Oh yes," said Kater, "of course. This is an excellent idea and thank you very much."

"Is there anything else I can do for you, gentlemen?"

"No, thank you, and it was a great pleasure to meet you, *moy dorogoy drug*, and I won't forget your kind and helpful assistance."

"All the pleasure's mine, *dorogiye druz'ya*, and I wish you both a very enjoyable stay in our capital."

"I'm sure it'll be so. *Vsego horochevo!*"

With this, we shook hands with the secretary, and accompanied by Svetlana left the Embassy. Once outside, Kater said to her, "So, my dear, I'll see you this evening at eight at Casa Novo Restaurante where we'll have a nice dinner, and then we'll see."

"Thank you, sir, and see you later."

Kater kissed the girl on both cheeks, which went a bit red. Apparently, Svetlana wasn't accustomed to being kissed by men.

In the car, Kater said to me, "Ah, what a lovely girl, and it seems to me she's still very innocent if you know what I mean. I love mature but still innocent women, you know. It go perfectly well together. And thanks to it, they're so sweet."

"I'm sure they are," I said. "What do we do now?"

"Hmm, you know, I planned an excursion to the Matterhorn for tomorrow. I wanted to climb the mountain again but I don't think I will manage because of my rendezvous. I expect to be a wee bit tired after it, so maybe another time."

"I didn't know you were an Alpinist too. Have you ascended other summits?"

"Oh yes, all the highest on this planet, and not only on this, for that matter."

"Where else?"

"Here and there. I'll tell you someday. Now, as we have our visas, we may peacefully plan our journey, which begins tomorrow."

"And what about air tickets?" I asked.

"They're waiting for us at the airport."

"But how did you know we'd get the visas in time?"

"Somehow, I was sure about that, my friend, and I am seldom mistaken."

*I'm sure about that,* I thought, and said, "So, *what about our plans whilst in Moscow?*"

"Yes, that's it," said Kater, "let's think about that as soon as we get home."

"And where's Klug?" I asked.

"I still don't have a clue, but I'm sure he'll join us in time before we leave."

"Where did you manage to pick up such good Russian?"

"Oh, I'm something of a polyglot. I know a great number of languages."

"And tell me, where has my new name, Adarsh, come from?"

"Ah, we thought that for practical reasons it might be a good idea for you to use a different name. You know, you're a wanted man so… you understand why you need a new one."

"Yes, I do, but what about documents? I need some ID."

"Here you are," and Kater produced some papers out of his jacket pocket.

It was a Swiss passport and a driving licence with my new name on – Ches Adarsh.

"Thank you," I said, "but how did you manage to get these? And I can't remember giving you any photos of myself."

"Dear friend, we have our ways, believe me, and you shouldn't be worried about such trivial matters as documents, or anything else, for that matter."

"Yes, now I'm pretty sure that trivial matters don't pose any serious difficulties for you. But what about my new name – why this particular one?"

"Because it has a meaning that suits you, dear Ches, as you'll find out in the near future."

"If you say so."

"Yes, I say so, and tomorrow, we're going back to Zurich."

"You have a date this evening."

"Ah yes, indeed, and I can't wait to see her. Ah, I'm sure I'll have a very pleasant evening and, who knows, maybe a night too…"

At this moment, I remembered Beatrice, and there must have been a change in my face because Kater said, "There is no need to worry. You'll see her pretty soon, and I think it'll take place in Moscow."

"How…" I began, but immediately realised again that to ask any questions would be a ridiculous idea, so I just said, "I do hope I meet her soon, for I can't imagine…" I didn't know what to say further.

"Yes, imagination is a very mysterious thing, and actually we know nothing about it. You agree with me, of course?"

"Yes, I do, and I'm even a bit afraid of mine, you know. Sometimes it seems to go too far."

"Oh yes, I know what you mean, as does my own. Ah, my friend, if you knew what sometimes goes on in my head… but the point is to grasp the meaning of what your imagination tells you about yourself. Why you have these particular images of your own… and the better you understand them, the better you understand yourself. But this is your task, a challenge you must deal with yourself – nobody else would be of help here."

"You put it well, I think, yes, nobody else…" I said.

"It's now already past seven, so I have to get ready for my date," said Kater, "and what are you going to do while I'm away?"

"I don't really know," I said. "I may go for a stroll, some sightseeing perhaps."

"A very good idea. You know, walking calms you down, and what is even more important is to remember that the sedentary life is the very sin against the Holy Spirit. Only thoughts reached by walking have value, as my good friend Friedrich says."

"Well spoken," I said. "He must be a wise man, that Friedrich."

"Oh yes, he is indeed, one of the wisest ever, but then of course, and this is because of his deep wisdom, he's misunderstood by many, for as he himself says, for most people the intellect is an awkward, gloomy, creaking machine that is hard to start."

"I think I've already heard that, but who told me that…?"

"I'm sure you have. Moreover, you will have many opportunities to find it so true in the so-called real life. Oh yes, you will. And now if you excuse me, I must change. You know, I need something elegant to put on."

And Kater went to his room in the hotel where we were staying. After a while, he appeared again, dressed in Mr Bardini's suit. He had also put on a pair of spectacles with thick black rims which made him look even more imposing.

"What do you think," he asked, "do I look presentable enough?"

"You look great. I'd say you look like a Swiss bank manager now."

"Thank you, my friend, but you know what some of my friends say about my looks? They say that my appearance is cat-like."

"No… maybe a little," I said, "but if I were you, I wouldn't care what they say."

"That's it! I don't care. And now, see you later. I'm not sure how everything will go, but we may see each other only tomorrow morning. I don't really know what time, for, you know, I sometimes like to stay in bed late provided the circumstances are right…"

"I think I know, and have a good time."

"I'm pretty sure I will, and have a good time yourself," he said, and left.

*

Next morning at about eleven, Kater came back. I noticed that he looked somewhat exhausted, and I asked him, "How did it go?"

"Ah, no words can describe it. No, as another friend says, I mean, Ludwig, what cannot be spoken of we must be silent about. Saying this, he didn't actually mean an experience like mine. Anyway, the things I went through last night surpassed my expectations and nearly finished me off, but I did my best to stand up to the challenge, and I hope I did, for as far as I could see, Svetlana wouldn't let me go. What a sweet girl she is, and what an imagination she has! But now it's time to go about a few different matters before we leave."

"What do you mean?" I asked.

"You obviously need a bank account, and we're in the right place to arrange that, aren't we?"

"You mean Confoederatio Helvetica? Yes, of course we are, but I have no money, as you know."

"This is another trivial matter you shouldn't worry about, either. So, we now go back to Zurich to arrange this."

We left Bern in the early afternoon, and this time, Kater asked me to drive our car which was now a Porsche. He said that he loved driving, but because he was still a bit tired, he preferred me to drive.

"You're changing cars like gloves," I said.

"I like a change, you know. It stimulates you, gives you a new perspective."

60

After a couple of hours, we arrived in Zurich. In our villa, everything was as we left it, and there was no sign of Klug, so I asked Kater again what he might be doing.

"He phoned me and said he's attending an important appointment with our superior regarding our upcoming visit to Moscow. Our boss has already been in Washington to talk to somebody, but I don't really know who he talked to. You know, Klug is sometimes very secretive. He seems to be obsessed by confidentiality."

We had lunch and then went, on foot this time, to a bank. The weather was fine, so we enjoyed the walk, and I always like walking, especially in old historic cities such as Zurich.

"This is us," said Kater once we had stopped at an old, solid building, but I couldn't see any sign on it.

"Is it our bank? But I can't see any sign whatsoever."

"Ah, this is because this bank is a very discreet institution, known to not too many people since their clientele is very carefully selected. Not everyone, even the rich, may have an account here."

"But it must have a name."

"Yes, of course, and it's Katz & Kluger Bank."

"Never heard of it."

"And small wonder! As I've just said, it's a very discreet, even secretive institution. And now let's go in."

We entered the building through an unpretentious door, and into a not-too-large reception room. I looked around, and what I saw was very modest: a couple of chairs round a coffee table, just one cashier counter and a rather big palm tree in a pot, that was all. We sat in the chairs, which might have been modest-looking but they were very comfortable. Five minutes had passed already and nobody had come to greet us, so I said to Kater, "Are we to wait here forever?"

"Not at all. Anyway, are you in a hurry?"

I wasn't, but we'd already been waiting for fifteen minutes. Then, out of nowhere, a tall, slim patrician-looking man in his sixties appeared. "Dear Mr Kater, I do apologise, but there was a burglary attempt last night, and we're still busy dealing with it."

"A what," said Kater, "a robbery attempt here... at our bank? Unbelievable!"

"Yes, indeed it is, but the burglars were trapped for they'd been deceived by appearances. You know, of course, what I mean," said the man.

"Oh yes, I do. You mean that special room for the likes of them."

"Exactly, so they had already dug a tunnel leading to our bank's wall, drilled their way through it and found themselves in that room, where they were stuck because all of their equipment, the drills, torches, everything, stopped working."

"Ah yes, now I remember, that new security measure. You are the only ones in the world to have it."

"That's it, Mr Kater, the new infallible apparatus totally unknown to any other bank. Deception through appearances, which is a quite ordinary way of obtaining something, but it's something very different to have a machine that can deceive, and the machine being invisible, as it is. Other institutions have their computers, spaceships, the so-called stealth airplanes, but all of them are still visible after all, aren't they? And what is visible may always fail because they're visible, that's it. This visibility makes them so. These so-called real things are so unreliable. People in their naivety believe in what they can see, and they call it reality, and if something doesn't agree with reality, it's good for nothing. What erroneous thinking, for if something doesn't agree with reality, as our old friend Georg says, so much the worse for reality, *nicht wahr?* Anyway, reality almost never satisfies our expectations, does it? The point is to have something which cannot be seen by anybody but ourselves, and we alone have it. Other banks have heard of our equipment, you know, gossip, and not only banks for that matter, and they've asked us countless times about it, but we've never told them a word. Confidentiality as always, we never tell anybody what we're doing."

"And, Herr von Zauberberg," Kater said to the man, "what happened to the burglars? Did you hand them over to the police?"

"Oh no," said Herr von Zauberberg, "we always tend to keep things quiet, you know, privacy first, so we're still negotiating with them, and we've made some progress so far. And as a matter of fact, we never contact the police whatever happens, or any other authorities for that matter. If we have a problem, we always deal with it ourselves, always."

"I see, and I unreservedly support that. Negotiations! That's the way to do almost anything, and as you know, they try it all over the world, not having much success, and it seems to me that we're the only ones who always succeed. And why? This is very simple – because we always keep our promise, and we always manage to persuade the other side, except the very narrow-minded. The other side we negotiate with is sooner or later assured that our promise extends beyond this world. Our promises are *sub specie aeterni*, so to speak, and only such promises have value. Promises which are confined to the here and now, to a temporal, imperfect life, are worth nothing. So, dear Herr Zauberberg, I wish fruitful negotiations, and now let's talk about our small private business."

"Certainly, as you wish, sir. What can I do for you, gentlemen?"

"Yes, Mr Adarsh here wants to open a bank account, so would you please arrange everything?"

"Absolutely, it'd be a pleasure to do that. Please come to my office, and we'll deal with it straightaway."

We followed von Zauberberg to the office, which was on the first floor. In comparison to the rather shabby premises downstairs, his office was a very large, tastefully furnished room. Kater and I sat down in two leather armchairs, and the host produced some papers from the drawer of his desk.

"May I offer something to drink, gentlemen? Cognac perhaps?"

"The same I had last time?" enquired Kater.

"Yes, the same, and I'm glad you liked it. I get a few bottles every month from a certain place in France, and must say I'm very lucky to have it since they don't produce many, and the demand for it is really huge. Some time ago, two British aristocrats visited me about some financial matter, and one of them said he'd heard about the cognac and wanted to buy a bottle or two, but to no avail. They simply refused, those French. So, he asked me whether I might have a spare bottle, and if so, he'd gladly have it, and he'd pay any money to have it, he said. At that moment, his companion said he'd like a bottle for himself as well. I said that unfortunately I had just one. Then a terrible row started which ended with a boxing match between them. Fortunately, there were no serious injuries, and I somehow persuaded them to share that bottle here and now in my office, and so they drank the cognac and left in a much better mood. Yes, dear gentlemen, alcohol may turn people into, you know that story, Dr Jekyll and Mr Hyde, that's it."

The cognac was really good, and after drinking it, I signed some papers, and Herr von Zauberberg handed me a cheque book and said, "I'm very glad to be of assistance, and anytime you need to contact me I'm at your service, Mr Adarsh."

We thanked him and left the bank. "I forgot to ask von Zauberberg how much I have in my account," I said to Kater.

"I think there is some three million francs, but if you need more in the future it can be arranged," he said.

"Three million! But I won't manage to pay you back that kind of money."

"There is no need to do that, my dear chap, not at all. This is a non-refundable loan, so to speak. However, you will return the favour someday but not in terms of money."

"I see, and what shall I give in return?"

"You'll find out in due time."

I said nothing, and we continued our walk through the city centre.

"What about a couple of beers at some cosy place?" said Kater.

"A great idea," I said, "and you know what an American writer said about beer?"

"No, tell me."

"You know, that writer who said he frankly didn't deserve the Nobel Prize said that there's nothing in the world like that first taste of beer."

"Well said! Oh yes, and now I know who you mean. I've forgotten his name, but he wrote a book, something called *Tortilla*… you know, that Mexican bread."

"*Tortilla Flat*, it was, and it wasn't much about bread, but rather about wine."

"Ah yes! Now I remember, and he himself never refused it. Yes, a great writer, and he did deserve the Prize, don't you think?"

"He did indeed," I said.

"And now," said Kater, "I remember something else about beer in relation to the proof of the existence of God. Many philosophers have been driven to despair trying to prove His existence and none of them have really succeeded. But then a man, an American, curiously enough, who knew nothing about philosophy, made a great discovery. Benjamin was his first name, and he said: 'Beer is proof that God loves us and wants us to be happy.' A man of genius, that Benjamin was, and we actually don't need any other proof since that is convincing enough.

"And to say something else about those proofs," Kater went on, when we were sitting comfortably in Zeughauskeller and had ordered two Pilsners, "there had been a lot of misunderstandings about the matter in question until a great but difficult Immanuel completely demolished those five well-known proofs and then, as though to deride his own efforts, he formulated a sixth proof of his own. But now I remember a different story not directly associated with these proofs. Once, I happened to be in Edinburgh, a rather gloomy place – there's nothing like Rome, dear friend – and went to a library where I wanted a copy of Immanuel's extremely difficult book, I mean *The Critic of Pure Reason*. So difficult that once when I asked a woman what the book was about, she said that in his book Kant criticised pure reason. Upon hearing that, I almost fell off the chair because as you know, the book is really difficult and may confuse everybody, but not to this extent anyway. It may be clever, as a Russian writer says, but it's horribly incomprehensible, and people might think that Kant was mad. And his name may be incomprehensible too, in a way, as it was the case of a librarian in Edinburgh who, upon hearing my request, said to me that she found my request very inappropriate, and it was so, I think, because she thought I meant a different 'kant', if you know what I mean. Ah, this literature! It may have an even worse effect on the human mind than alcohol. Yes, sometimes much worse, as history tells us.

"Anyway, perhaps we shouldn't worry too much about literature after all. I remember watching a movie, *Educating...* I don't really remember the full title, in which an actor, an Englishman as far as I remember, a very good one anyway, plays a college professor, and during his lecture a student says something about William Blake, you know, the poet. And the professor says: 'Who is he anyway? He's just a dead poet, that's all.' The student protests, praising Blake, but the professor doesn't pay much attention to him, looking out of the window instead and swaying in his chair as if he was drunk. The student, apparently annoyed by the professor's disrespect of Blake, says: 'Sir, are you drunk?' to which the professor replies: 'Drunk? Of course I'm drunk. You don't really expect me to teach this when I'm sober.' And that's it, my friend, we can't really appreciate literature when we're sober. One of the eminent poets, Idefons was his name, once went too far as happens often with writers as regards the liberating power of alcohol so, on his wife's request, whenever their friends invited them, there was no alcohol available. Once, at one of those visits, he sat there being very sad, but suddenly he stood up and went to the bathroom. When he returned, his mood had improved incredibly, and he said to his host: 'I'm terribly sorry but I've just drunk your Yardley. But I'll give it back to you, I promise.'

"And the host said: 'Fair enough, but please not here and now...'"

At that moment, Klug entered the restaurant. "Welcome back, we missed you," said Kater. "Where have you been, dear friend, and what have you been doing?"

"I was very busy, my dear friends, busy indeed. I was in Washington."

"Washington? And what brought you to Dollaria?" enquired Kater.

"I went over there to see their president."

"The president? He's rather difficult to talk to, I'd say."

"He usually is," said Klug, "and the beginning of our meeting was indeed a bit difficult, but the longer we talked, the better understanding we had. Our meeting was arranged by a certain senator who is very well disposed towards our case, and on his request, the president agreed to meet me. You know him, he's a big fellow, very confident of himself, even imperious, so to speak, and the beginning of our meeting was a bit strenuous. As a matter of fact, he looked down on me and was very patronising until he asked me, 'I hold Senator Thunderbaum in great esteem, and that's why I agreed to meet you, but the senator didn't actually tell me why you had insisted on meeting me, and who you represented, so please be more specific in this respect.' So, I told him who had been the person who'd wanted me to meet him.

"Once the president heard the name, he staggered a wee bit – we were still standing – and then fell in the chair. He was silent for a good while and then said, 'I see, to be honest, I knew that sooner or later I'd have such a visit, but until now I'd tried to convince myself that it had been just... what shall I say, a fantasy, and illusion. I don't really know, but now I know that we should take our imagination more seriously.'

"'I appreciate that, Mr President,' I said to him, 'and indeed I agree that yes, we should take imagination much more seriously. You know, what you just imagine today might be reality tomorrow. You never know.' And from then on, our conversation went smoothly, my friends. It was very fruitful and promising, and actually we agreed on every subject we discussed, so I don't really expect any problems in the future. I told the president about our upcoming visit to Moscow, and he asked me to pass his best wishes on to the president of Russia. All in all, I'm very pleased with my visit and so is our maître."

"My congratulations," said Kater, "and I'm sure now that our visit to Moscow will be more rewarding, no doubt about that.

"So, now," he continued, "I'm certain that our stay in Moscow will also be a very pleasant adventure, and we can plan it now at a leisurely pace."

"And could you tell me more about what we'll be doing over there?" I asked.

"Ah, our visit will be full of surprises, you'll see, dear friend," said Klug, "and you, yourself, will be happy about everything you'll find there, especially with meeting a person in a very nice, historic part of the capital, called Arbat. Since I know you like historic places, that rendezvous has already been arranged."

"And who will it be I'm going to meet?" I enquired.

"Ah, this is a secret I won't reveal now, but rest assured you'll be very pleased," said Klug.

"If you say so."

"So, tomorrow after ten in the evening is our flight, and now since I've already been over there, let me tell you a few words about the country we're going to visit," said Klug.

"Over the years, an incredible great number of stories have been amassed about Russia, and almost all of them are nonsensical because they have failed to grasp the spirit of the country, its soul, as the Russian people say. And most of these stories' purpose is in fact an attempt to downgrade the country by showing its inferiority in comparison to the western world. And comparison, dear friends, is not something that would catch the essence of anything, because as our dear Ludwig says, it is always relative and accidental, as it is, as a matter of fact, with any description based on facts. Yes, the facts, but you agree of course that it's always about what lies underneath these facts, for once we try to interpret them we run into trouble. Our interpretations are in flux, so to say, all the time, aren't they? This subject had already been mentioned by somebody else," and here Klug gave me a quick look, "but we return to it again for it's of importance regarding our upcoming journey. Yes, all those stories, descriptions, definitions, whatever… most of them good for nothing, and the worst are those intellectually pretentious ones, as it is about this one, I mean, a politician who once said of Russia: 'a riddle, wrapped in a mystery inside an enigma.' You know, my friends, this description itself is an enigma for actually it says nothing. It's nonsensical for it fails to give any meaning to what it says, and we learn nothing from it. It's something that is a crafty but actually petty word game. And in so-called practical terms, I mean, the intellectual struggle between intelligence services, no wonder that the Russians have always duped the other side, haven't they? And it's been the case, probably due, among other things, to them being very good at chess. And very like their chess game, efficiency is related to the other one. Anyway, whatever we say about that, compared with our own, it is a joke, a Sunday school, so to speak."

"Of course, they're very good at chess," said Kater. "I was once almost defeated by one of them, and as you know, my friend, I'm not bad at chess. They are very good indeed."

"That's it," Klug said, "and back to the country and its history, at times difficult indeed. We must remember that its people have always shown great courage, the spirit which has always prevailed in the end, and of course we mustn't forget that it is them, not somebody else, who has suffered most.

"But now, my friends, to brighten up our conversation, I'll tell you some different things which are rather amusing. So, in a neighbouring country during the time when the Russians were under the red flag, people used to tell jokes about their mutual relationship. The first one referred to the symbol in use at the time when the country had a different name. And their neighbours described the symbol in this way: 'The sickle cuts your throat, the hammer bangs over your head, and you see the star in your eyes.' You agree that this description is pretty accurate remembering the old days, isn't it?

"Or another story about the benefits of the trade between them: 'We' (refers to this neighbouring country) 'deliver them fifteen ships every year, and in return we get 200,000 shoes… for fixing the soles.' As for the wealth of the country at the time, another joke went: 'A Russian woman calls a radio station and asks: "Is it true that there aren't any floods in our country?" And they replied, "No, we have no floods, for even the rivers never overflow." They used the phrase 'to overflow' to indicate the abundance of wealth. And another one: 'Is it true that wheat in our country is as tall as telegraph poles?' And they answered: 'Yes, it is, and even taller.' And the last two about the size of bees and the educational level of the nation. 'A man who guards sheep in our country is called a shepherd,' says the neighbour. 'What is he called in your country?' – 'He's called an engineer-observer,' was the reply. And there was an exchange of opinion with regard to beehives. A Russian says: 'In our country, a bee is as big as a fist.' To this, the neighbour says, 'If so, how does it gets into a beehive?' The answer: 'It squeaks but goes in.' But in order to understand some of these jokes, you have to speak the language. You know what our unforgettable Ludwig says: 'The limits of my language mean the limits of my world.'

"No wonder that jokes and proverbs are considered the wisdom of people, my dear fellows, and we should always study an ordinary man, for in this way, we study society. Anyway, there is no other way to understand it, and for sure not through quasi-sophisticated long-winded pretentious accounts which only blur the subject. Thus, once we get there, we'll do what we customarily do – we'll meet a man in the street – the salt of the earth, as our master always does. I must tell you, dear Mr Adarsh, that he's already been in Russia, but secretly, incognito, so to speak. And various bodies tried to contact him, but in vain. You know, you may see him only if he wishes so, otherwise, no chance. But he visited the place a while ago, and since then things have obviously changed. Oh yes, they have – no doubt about that. So, we'll try our best to see the country as it is now, and not, we must remember, through all the accumulated prejudice that inevitably obscures everything. As far as I know, your friend Harry had once been under the charm of Russia, its people, literature and a particular woman, hadn't he?"

"How do you…" I began, but immediately realised the foolishness of such a question again, so instead I said, "yes, indeed he had."

"And what is he doing now?" asked Klug, as if he didn't know…

"I saw him at my funeral, you know, but I don't have a clue what he does these days because we lost contact a long time ago."

"Aha, but I think that you'll meet him again in the near future."

"And I," Kater chipped in, "will challenge their best at chess, of course, so I've got to get ready in order not to bring shame on us all, my friends."

"Oh yes," said Klug, "do that now, for there's not much time left, and if you lose more than two matches, we'll leave you over there so that you can improve your skills."

"I don't think I will lose even once," said Kater with his customary modesty.

"Yes, the country," continued Klug, "has space, and that makes their minds boundless. I mean, their emotions, imagination, and that is to be seen in everything they do. They've obviously, during their difficult history, crossed the limits of what is expected from a decent human being, but in the end, it is not an individual to blame but the regime, my friends, and we must always remember that. All in all, it is as Mr Mencken rightly noticed: 'All in all, every decent man is ashamed of the government he lives under.' But then, please don't take me for an anarchist. Anyway, as our far-sighted Friedrich says, society has never regarded virtue as anything but a means to strength, power and order. And to be frank regarding crossing the limits of decency, the others haven't been any better in this respect. You know, atrocities happen everywhere and every time, and countries which claim to be fair as regards their own people and other nations' too, have committed terrible things as well, haven't they? But apparently their memory suffers whenever it's convenient for them, or we may say there's nothing like being a hypocrite. The collective will, as usual, is manipulated by those in power, and all it takes to turn people into monsters is the fear of being an outsider. Thus, for instance, war itself, whoever wages it, is the only culprit. But, of course, in some countries, the boundless hypocrisy allows them to claim moral superiority, which is obviously not the case. Yes, hypocrisy – the escape of the self-righteous scoundrels. We, in turn, are very impartial for we don't judge, and our superior always reminds us not to judge anybody else, and why? – because actually, everybody and no one is to blame. It is a paradox that someday you'll comprehend, our dear friend," Klug said to me.

"And how long are we going to stay over there?" I asked.

"It depends, but not too long, for we have other matters on our mind," said Klug, "but long enough to sort out some of your problems."

"Can we expect any assistance from the authorities?"

"Oh yes, they will surely assist us in everything, as they always do. They may have some objections at the start, but then all things will go smoothly, I dare say. You know, they realise that to be stubborn with us would lead to… what shall I say, rather unpleasant consequences for somebody, don't you think so?"

"Having been with you for some time now, I can easily imagine that," I replied.

"I appreciate that, and believe me, as regards your own problems, I mean, what your former friends did, we'll do our best to assist you, and I'm pretty sure we'll succeed. But, my dear friend, we expect your cooperation, for there are things that depend on yourself alone. Don't forget that."

"But I don't really know if I recognise what exactly depends on me alone."

"Bah, I encourage you to do your best, my friend," said Klug.

"I'll try. Could you tell me something more about the conspiracy they made up?"

"Once we get there, I obviously will, but not here and now, and to see the details and how they work in practice, you must be on the spot. But afterwards, as I've just said, you'll be mostly on your own, but not in Moscow, in another country."

"Where exactly?"

"In England. Have you been there?"

"Yes, once. I stayed with a friend of mine in his apartment in Queen's Gate, pretty close to the place where that comedian I like used to live."

"Ah yes, him! I like him too," said Klug.

"Are we going to meet some actors and other artists in Russia? I've just remembered that my friend Harry liked Wysotski, you know, that singer and actor," I asked.

"Oh yes, a great singer he was, and what a passion he had. We will indeed meet some artists in Moscow and perhaps a few other people of art, and will honour one of them who sadly isn't with us anymore. I mean the author of a novel in which everything starts in Patriarch's Pond, we'll visit of course. Our superior has decided to create a prize to commemorate his achievement."

"It's a great idea and I'd like very much to take part in everything that is needed to make it happen."

"Your involvement is very welcome, my friend. And now let's drink to our adventures in Moscow, my friends. *Na zdorovie!*"

And we did, and then we returned to our villa to get ready for the journey which I was very curious about. What we'd find out over there, and in the first place – would I see Beatrice again, as I'd been promised?

# THE FLIGHT

'Convictions are more dangerous
enemies of truth than lies.'
Nietzsche

At ten past nine in the evening, we entered the building of Zurich Airport. I had just a small suitcase, but both Klug and Kater were carrying a lot of luggage. Kater, as well as a big rucksack, had two big bags, and Klug a huge chest.

"May I ask why you need so much luggage?" I said.

"Ah," said Kater, "we have some gifts for our friends in Moscow."

"And what are they?" I asked.

"You'll see when we get there," he replied.

"The Russians are very generous people," said Klug, "so, it would be a *faux pas* if we didn't have anything in return for their hospitality."

"That's it," Kater said. "Last time we visited them, Klug received a giant babushka filled with bottles of vodka, and I got an enormous teddy bear full of cans of caviar."

"You know," said Klug, "they aren't like those English misers."

"You seem to be of the same opinion as my father," I said. "He called them the 'bloody shopkeepers.'"

"A very accurate description," said Kater.

We approached the departure desk, and I put my suitcase on the scales. Just ten kilos it was. Then Kater placed all of his luggage; seventy-two kilos, and Klug's eighty-one.

"Your luggage is too heavy," said the attendant, a pretty young woman.

"*Unmoglich, mein Schatz*," Kater said. "Please check again."

And she did, and this time Klug's was just thirty-one, and Kater's twenty-two.

"Something must be wrong with the scales," the woman said. "Never happened before."

"You can't trust any machines these days," Kater said to her. "They're all very unpredictable, so to speak."

Thus, we were done with our luggage and moved to the departure area. There, quite a lot of people were waiting for the flight to Moscow, and we could hear different languages spoken: French, German, Russian, English and a few others I couldn't identify.

Our flight was announced and it didn't take long to board the plane. Once we were seated, Kater said, "I hate flying, and this is because in here I feel as if I was in a fish cane, and if something happened, we'd have hardly any chance of survival. Klug," he said, "have you forgotten our parachutes?"

"No, of course not. They're here and there's another one for Ches. By the way, do you remember a story about a parachutist instructor who was pushed out of the plane while training a group of novices?"

"Oh yes," said Kater, "I do remember, and he didn't have his parachute on but he landed unhurt."

"Landed unhurt?" I said. "How come?"

"Bah," said Kater, "he was carried by a bird, a very big one, for that matter. You know, he studied ornithology before he became a parachutist, so he spoke bird language, as do I, my friend."

"You know, Kater," I said, "this time you exaggerate a bit."

"Not at all," he said, and began making loud, strange noises which were heard all over the plane.

A stewardess arrived and said to him, "Sir, please, this noise makes the passengers anxious."

Kater stopped his performance and said to her, "You know, love, I've just asked them, I mean, the birds, to escort us all the way to our next stop."

"Yes, of course, sir, we are most grateful, but please don't ask them again," said the woman.

"There's no need to call them again. Anyway, they should be here in a minute. Please look out of the window, Liebling."

So, she did, and we could all see a large flock of very big birds that just approached the plane. The stewardess opened her eyes wide and in a trembling voice said to Kater, "I… I am very sorry, sir, I… " She couldn't finish the sentence.

"There's no need to apologise. However, if you were so nice and agreed to have a glass of wine in my company when we land in Moscow, I would appreciate it very, very much."

"Yes, of course, sir, it'd be a pleasure."

"Wunderbar! Then tomorrow at 10 am at the café in the Metropol Hotel," said Kater.

"I'll be there, sir," she said and smiled.

"You know," Klug said to me, "our Casanova here wouldn't miss a chance to pick up a girl. If he did, he would fall ill, I think."

The birds were still flying close to the plane and everybody was watching. The leader of the flock came very near to our window and blinked at Kater, who responded the same way. Since many passengers could hear his conversation with the woman and see the birds, a few of them were giving him strange glances. Then we could all hear a male voice say, "Apparently, we have a magician among us, ladies and gentlemen."

"Is it you, Professor Jerkins?" said Klug.

"Yes, it is, and how do you know?" replied the man.

"Ah, dear professor, I had a chance to listen to your lecture at Oxford, and as far as I remember, it was something about the importance of being realistic, common sense and the like. But as a matter of fact, dear Professor Jerkins, in the first place, common sense is not so common as the great Voltaire says, and secondly, it might be completely useless under some circumstances."

"What do you mean?" asked the professor.

"I mean, for instance, the question of imagination, which is the power of predictability or, if you like, the ability to see hidden truths, that is to have second sight."

"And you claim to have such an ability, and could you give us a practical example of it?" said Jerkins.

"With pleasure, dear professor. For example, I can say why you received the summons to appear in court, and a letter about that you have in the left upper pocket of your jacket."

Professor Jerkins, who was sitting in the armchair right next to us, turned red, and all the passengers sitting nearby were staring at him now.

"So, my dear professor, this is one example of the practical use of second sight you demanded. And regarding the nature of the summons, I don't really know why this kind of summons is so popular in your country. Maybe you, as an academic, would be so kind as to enlighten us poor ignoramuses."

Jerkins said nothing. He was just sitting still, and his face turned pale for a change.

"The summons, dear ladies and gentlemen, if you forgive me my indiscreetness, is about the so-common, in the professor's country, accusation of sexual assault. And because Professor Jerkins, as a highly esteemed researcher, surely wanting to know why this particular offence takes place so often, tried of course to research the issue in practice. But in his passionate eagerness to find the truth, he might have gone too far, and that's why the summons. Apparently, the law representatives took a different view of the problem, which might now end the way that dark genius Dostoyevsky described in his novel *Crime and Punishment*. And by the way, could you tell us what the reason is for your travel to Moscow, dear professor?" said Klug.

Jerkins was still silent. He was just sitting with his eyes closed.

"I can see you don't feel particularly well, dear sir," said Klug, "so I'll take the liberty of helping everybody present to understand the nature of the problem in question. Imagination is, in my humble opinion, closely related to what we call magic. Professor Jerkins has written numerous papers in which he strongly denied the existence of any supernatural powers, using every possible argument. And then, one day, when he felt sufficiently satisfied with all he'd done so far, something happened. Do I recollect the story accurately so far, Professor?" Klug said to Jerkins. But the professor didn't reply. He was just sitting there still and silent as if he were in a coma.

"So," continued Klug, "one year ago, sitting in his university office on a lovely, sunny Thursday afternoon, he heard a knock on the door.

He said, 'Come in, please.' The door opened and a stunningly beautiful young woman entered. The professor immediately forgot what he'd been thinking about, sitting there like a mummy, his mouth open wide.

"'What… can… can I do for you?' he said in a trembling voice.

"'I'm a first year philosophy student,' said the woman, 'and I wonder if I could attend your lecture. I've already joined a couple of others but heard that yours is pretty interesting.'

"'I… I'm flattered… and delighted, miss…' stammered the professor. 'What's your name, miss?'

"'My name's Margarita Blagodarodnaya,' said the woman.

"'May I… I ask you where you are from?' he said, still stammering.

"'I'm from Russia,' she replied.

"'Aha, aha, very good, yes. I'm honoured. Yes, of course, I'll be more than happy to agree. You can join my lecture any time it suits you. And… and what is it, may I enquire, you're particularly interested in?'

"'I'm interested in black magic, Doctor Jerkins.'

"'Eh… then… I, dear Miss Bla… Blado, I'm terribly sorry, forgive me.' *What's happening to me?* he thought, *never happened before.*

"'No need to apologise,' said the woman. 'I understand you have had neither a chance nor need to familiarise yourself with the Russian language.'

"'To tell the truth, no, I haven't, but now under the circumstances, I… I may consider learning it, you know…'

"'Excuse me, what circumstances do you mean?' she said.

"'I don't really know. I had a feeling as, hmm, I've just seen, I don't really know. Something's been revealed to me, no, I'm sorry, I don't know what to say.'

"'I understand, yes, something's been revealed to you, sir, yes, and what was it, if I may ask?' the Russian beauty said.

"'I can't really put into words what I mean. I'm sorry,' said Jerkins.

"'Do you mean that what you can't put into words, you dismiss as worthless?' said Miss Blagodarodnaya.

"'Yes, something like that,' replied Jerkins.

"'But don't you think that everything that is thought and expressed in words is one-sided, only half the truth, and it lacks totality, completeness and unity? You know, our ideas are changing all the time, and what was true yesterday isn't today anymore, don't you think so?'

"'Yes, you're right, but you know, there's no other way to keep going,' said Jerkins.

"'Keep going, you say. Where to?'

"'As a matter of fact, nobody knows that,' he said.

"'Nobody, you say, and how do you know that?'

"'I… I just assume that.'

"'But truth, dear Dr Jerkins, cannot be based on assumptions,' said Margarita.

"'Yes, I agree, but I don't really know whether there would be another option to carry on, you know, to communicate, to pursue research, simply to keep on living.'

"'Keep on living, you say, but what for, what is the ultimate aim of doing so, Professor?'

"'I don't know, I can't answer the question,' said Jerkins.

"'If you can't then you are in trouble, I mean, your own life. Am I right?'

"'I have some, what shall I say, problems, yes, I do, but I don't really know what I can do about them except doing what I've always been doing.'

"'There might be a way to find out that aim, to answer the question 'Why?', and let me tell you what I mean. You won't find the answer in reality because it is changing, as that Greek philosopher Heraclitus described it, I mean, his 'panta rhei' so, in other words, reality is incredible, untrustworthy. Therefore, you must look for the answer regarding the question in a different place, which I believe is imagination. Yes, imagination is the realm of ideas which are changing too, but then you may find your very own ideas which you may find reliable and unalterable and as such they will support you in life. And thus, these ideas will make your life worth living by telling you what tasks you should undertake to achieve what you really need.

"'Imagination is magic, and as such makes wonders, and he who doesn't believe in it is simply stupid, and sooner or later he'll pay for his stupidity. Your future actually depends on your imagination, which is your own under any circumstances, and as such it is a supernatural power because of its independence from reality, a kind of black magic if you like. Imagination is the ability to see the future, whereas reality put the chains on your mind, and as long as you live only in reality, your mind is in a dungeon. Paradoxically, and curiously enough, dear Dr Jerkins, we know nothing of reality, and this is exactly because it is in flux and that's why we cannot grasp it as a whole, a unity. But then strangely enough again, it is thanks to imagination that we can view reality as a whole, and only then we're able to understand reality, and not vice versa. You agree of course that through reality alone you cannot view it as a whole, for because of what has already been said, it would be contradictory to assume so. Anyway, what is reality? Material objects, events? They themselves have no sense of their own, and it's our imagination alone that gives them meaning, and without the meaning, they would be nothing but material objects. If you lack imagination, you are deprived of the ability to think abstractly, and consequently of the ability to understand reality, and imagine its future. But you already know that all, Dr Jerkins, in theory of course, so why don't you put it into practice?'

"'I don't really know, dear Miss Blagodarodnaya,' said Jerkins.

"'Oh, you've eventually pronounced my name correctly. I appreciate that.'

"'My pleasure, and as for practical use of the aforementioned ideas, you know, I wouldn't have the strength, because to tell the truth, I, what shall I say, hmm, have never been pleased with anything. I say no to everything too often, yes, so I do.'

"'And have you ever been in love?'

"'No, never experienced the feeling that others call love, but now after our conversation, I might be able to see some things differently.'

"'All the pleasure's mine, dear professor, but now excuse me. I've got to go.' And she left.

"After the conversation, Dr Jerkins went for a long walk, thinking all the time about what she'd told him. He was anxious to do something but couldn't grasp exactly what it might be. Eventually, he decided to find relief from his troubled thinking by going to a pub and drinking some vodka. But it was much more than some, and later at night he woke up in a place completely unknown to him. He looked around but could see nothing in the total darkness, and in an effort to find out where he was, he decided to get up, which he did with some difficulty, and stretching his hands forward he made a few steps, but then he stumbled and hitting his head against the wall, fell. At that moment, the light went on, and still lying down he saw a young woman staring at him. She was completely naked, and Jerkins lay there gaping at her with his mouth open, but couldn't help admiring her magnificent body, those long legs and full, firm breasts.

'"What are you doing here, and who are you?' the woman asked in a surprisingly calm voice.

'"I… I'm very sorry, I don't know how come I'm here. I… I was drinking in a pub, and then… don't know what happened afterwards and why I'm here. My name's Dr Jerkins. I—'

"He couldn't finish for she interrupted. 'Ah yes, Dr Jerkins, I know who you are. A friend of mine, Margarita, told me about you.'

'"Isn't your friend's surname Blago…?'

'"Yes, it's Margarita Blagodarodnaya,' said the woman, and went on, 'she says you're a very confused man. She feels sorry for you.'

'"I… I do appreciate that. She's lovely, and a very intelligent young woman.'

'"Oh yes, she is indeed. And now I suggest you get up and come with me to the kitchen and drink a cup of coffee.' And the woman, totally unashamed of her nakedness, led him downstairs. They sat down at the kitchen table, and the woman made some coffee and they drank it.

'"My name's Sophia Marlini,' she said.

'"Pleased to meet you despite that awkward situation, Miss Marlini.'

'"Don't you worry. It could happen to anybody, stress and such things.'

'"You're living here on your own, if I may ask?'

'"Yes, I am. I'm a university student as Margarita is,' she said.

'"And what is it you study?'

'"Demonology,' said Sophia.

'"A what? But we don't have such a subject on our university curriculum here at Oxford.'

'"No, you're right, you don't, but I study it somewhere else.'

'"And what's that, if I may enquire?' asked Jerkins.

"'This is a society, based at a private house where we meet once a week having discussions and something else too.'

"'And what is that something else?' enquired Jerkins.

"'We have sex sessions, and you're welcome to join,' said Sophia.

"'I… I don't know, and you mean group sex, do you?'

"'Yes, indeed it is, and you'll enjoy it, but if you prefer to have an individual partner, no problem, it can be arranged. You may start right now if you wish.'

"'What, you mean, right now?' he asked.

"'I mean my bedroom, of course.'

"Jerkins still couldn't help looking at her naked body which promised so much, so he eventually said, 'Well, yes, I want, I do want if you…'

"'So, come with me,' said Sophia, and they went upstairs.

"'And now don't say anything but just undress and lie down on the bed,' she said.

"And so he did. What she did to him that night, he would never forget. He'd never had such sex in his life. She instructed him on what to do to her, and she did all imaginable things to him. They went along with almost everything the *Kamasutra* recommends, and afterwards Jerkins lay down completely exhausted but happy.

"'Have you enjoyed it?' asked Sophia.

"'Have I… that was… I can hardly find any words. It was… magnificent. You're wonderful,' he said.

"'All the pleasure's mine,' she said. 'Anytime you wish, you can call me, and if I'm not busy, we'll do it again.'

"'Thank you, you're… don't really know what to say… I am so happy.'

"And they did meet from time to time, and Jerkins, for the first time in his life, enjoyed so close a relationship with a woman. She introduced him to her lady friends and encouraged him to have sex with them too. She in turn did the same with other men. Some of their now-mutual partners were bisexual, so they both enjoyed threesomes or more at the same time. Some of those women Jerkins had, were very young, and they gave him the greatest pleasure. He especially liked deep throat, and his favourite was Cecilia, who preferred to be fucked in the mouth than into somewhere else. He loved doing it, particularly early in the morning before his university duties, and she called it don's breakfast. She often sucked his dick for an hour or longer, enjoying his every ejaculation in her mouth all over again. She had a big mouth, so she could take his whole dick in, held it in, sucking, and when he came, she swallowed.

"He and Sophia sometimes made love to one girl, doing with her everything possible; some of those young girls were hard to satisfy, and they wanted to experiment all the time and didn't object to anything what was done to them, including tying up, slapping or dildos of every kind. One of the youngest, by the name of Karen, especially enjoyed being fucked by several men and women at the same time, and she often begged for double and triple penetration. Once she asked for double penetration in the cunt, another man put his dick into her anus, and another one in the mouth, and since then she wanted it every time they had a session. And she had such a stamina that she could fuck all day long. She also loved to swallow, doing blow jobs to several men at a time or doing cunnilingus to another woman. All in all, everything went very well, all participants rejoiced in their sexual games until Jerkins made a mistake. He began bragging about his sexual life which now became known to almost all university staff, and one day he was invited to the vice-chancellor's office.

"'Dr Jerkins,' the vice-chancellor said to him. 'Some disturbing rumours have come to my attention, and I'm sure you know what I mean.'

"'Yes, I know what you mean, sir, but I believe it to be my personal matter what I do outside the university.'

"'Not exactly, Dr Jerkins,' said the vice-chancellor, 'this is also about the reputation of our institution, and reputation is as important as our intellectual achievement, or might matter even more. Therefore, I ask you to refrain from those personal activities which have now have become public knowledge and as a consequence of which, our reputation has been damaged.'

"Jerkins refused to comply with the vice-chancellor's request and, as a result, to cut a long story short, by agreement with the Foreign Office, he was offered a job as Consul for Culture at British Embassies either in the Democratic Republic of Congo or the Russian Federation. He chose the latter, and that's why he is now on his way to Moscow.

"Have I related the story correctly?" Klug asked Jerkins, while other passengers were curiously watching them.

"Yes, you have, but how come you know it so well?"

"Bah, dear professor, we have our ways, oh, we do, and only short-sighted people cannot appreciate that, and that's why they eventually pay the price. Anyway, you didn't back off, I mean, the vice-chancellor's request, and I respect that. And now, you know, the Russians aren't prudish at all in contrast to your fellow countrymen, so you will be able to carry on what you like so much. Anyway, you may visit other countries as well, seeking willing women. I especially mean Thailand, where, in Chinatown, you can have a girl as young as nine and sex with her may rejuvenate you."

"Are you sure about that?" asked Jerkins.

"Oh yes, I am. You'll have a great time in Moscow, and I encourage you to renounce your British citizenship and apply for Russian citizenship. You will find many willing girls there, as you actually did in Oxford, but the difference is that in Russia nobody cares what somebody else is doing, within limits, of course, which are much wider over there than in your country. Anyway, you may try women in other countries as well – China, Thailand, Vietnam, anywhere, and believe me, the Asian girls are sweet, ah, so sweet and so good."

Upon hearing that, Jerkins somehow brightened up and said, "Thank you. You've made me believe that not everything is lost, and I'll enjoy life again. You know, I thought I would be going into exile where I could expect nothing but misery, and now you've managed to make me think differently, as I'm sure you know something about the country we're about to arrive in."

"Oh yes, I do," said Klug, "and about a few others too, as a matter of fact. You are an Englishman, Dr Jerkins, but to be one doesn't suit you, so to speak. I mean your temperament, preferences and non-slave morality, and I mean your fellow countrymen's faked self-satisfaction, hypocrisy, self-righteousness and compliance with everything the Government tells you to do. You obviously know what George Bernard said: 'Englishmen never will be slaves: they are free to do whatever the Government and public opinion allow them to do.' And in this respect, and a few others, your country is a very provincial, godforsaken backwater which used to rule many parts of the world, having always remained such a bloody parish pump. A famous Russian writer, Solzhenitsyn, a man of extraordinary courage and independent mind, having once visited England, said to your former fellow dons: 'You say I fought Communism. Communism came from the like of you, you self-righteous bastards.' That's it, dear professor; it wasn't the invention of the working class, not at all."

"Yes, you're right," said Jerkins. "I begin to see that all the more clearly now, and you know who helped me to broaden my mind? It was Sophia, that's it. She showed me what I really needed, what was and still is good for me. But now, you know, I've lost her."

"No, you haven't, and I mean other women too, for you can, if you so wish, invite them to your new home," said Klug.

"Goodness, I was so confused and upset that I didn't think of it! Yes, you're right, they may come to see me anytime they want to. I especially miss Cecilia, but Sophia too. Ah, ah, she's so great in bed."

"Yes, my friends, sex is very important," Kater butted in, "and I don't know anybody who could emphasise its importance better than our dear Henry, who some time ago asked me the question: 'What are the nine reasons for reincarnation?' 'I wouldn't know,' I said, a bit ashamed of my ignorance. 'So, I'll tell you,' he said, 'one of them is sex, and the other eight are unimportant.'

"You see," he continued, "and in which religion does reincarnation play such a primordial role? Ha, Hinduism, of course, and small wonder that the *Kamasutra* was written in a country which has such beautiful women, and one of them, I mean the stunning Madhuri, looks like some other lady, doesn't she?" and Kater gave me a glimpse.

I said nothing but looked back at him and just nodded.

"And our dear Ches is going to meet her soon, and I'm very happy for him, for she's not only beautiful but very wise as well, and I envy him a wee bit. Ah, if I were so lucky!"

"You are lucky enough," said Klug, "you don't miss any chance whenever you see a nice ass, and if you could, you would have a harem, wouldn't you?"

"You exaggerate, my friend," said Kater.

"I don't at all. I can't even remember how many of them you have met so far."

"It doesn't surprise me. You've always been very bad at mathematics," Kater shot back.

"I, how dare you, and who helped that poor Albert, I ask? No one but me. He was very good at physics, I must admit that, but his mathematical skills weren't too great, as were those of, let's say, Poincare."

"All right, I'm very sorry, my friend, I've forgotten. Yes, without your assistance, he would have got lost. Ah, anyway, his theory, that relativity is in truth so simple, even obvious, so to speak, that I don't really know why it has been so difficult to understand it. And yes, Albert all in all was a nice fellow, and look, his great theory was invented when he was still a very young man, and in later years, especially after moving to Dollaria, he did nothing but sign some useless letters. What was it? Aha, they were about nuclear bombs or something like that. But you know, I believe that it was his stay in Dollaria that deprived him of his intellectual powers. Yes, I'm quite sure about that. Anyway, that United States of Loonies, as a certain great poet used to call it, agreed with me on that point when we had a wonderful chat in a country of the sun and such beauties."

"And here he goes again," Klug chipped in, "physics, mathematics and women of course, at the same time. But then, women always come first."

"Don't start again," exclaimed Kater. "You envy me my success with them, jealous prig!"

"What did you say? Jealous prig, you… you…" Klug apparently was losing his temper when suddenly we heard someone say, 'And what do you mean by Dollaria or the United States of Loonies?'

The three of us turned in the direction where the voice came from, and we saw a man wearing a Texas hat on his head.

"Howdy," said Klug, "and here we go again, I mean, another obvious matter. Are you a native of Texas?" he asked the man.

"No, I'm not. I'm from New York City," replied the man.

"Oh no, I've been there, no, never again. What a fraught time. And why do you wear a Texas hat then?"

"Cause I like it," said the man.

"As for your question, don't you have a feeling that something's rotten in the state of America, as that English poet would say. And I'm afraid that it's much rotten in yours than in a country which he had in mind."

"I don't know what you mean," said the New Yorker. "America is great again, as our president says."

"Again, and again, so how many times has it been great if I may enquire?" said Klug.

"My country has always been great, no doubt about that!" said the man.

"If you say so, but then why to say great all over again?"

"I think this is just a semantic matter."

"Yes, you have a great number of semantic matters over there, but actually, this semantics isn't just semantics. I mean that it doesn't translate into what things really are, doesn't correspond with reality. In other words, it doesn't depict correctly what things really look like. Let's take, for instance, democracy and freedom – are they in your country, as their meaning is? I'm afraid they aren't, they are nothing but slogans. On the other hand, other words such as crap or junk correspond perfectly with reality, don't they? But all this semantic confusion might have in the future some unpleasant consequences for your fellow countrymen. Oh yes, not only might but has already. Half of all hospital beds are used for mental patients, so I think your eminent poet was right in saying that all of America is an insane asylum. And now we're going to a country which I find much saner, and that might be due to its religion, among other things, which, as the country's great film director says, is the main force which opposes cultural and intellectual McDonald's. And by the way, you know what, in the neighbouring country, I mean Poland, people are endowed with some prophetic power. Years ago, I was there and having a stroll in a park…," at that moment Klug looked at me, "…and must say that some very interesting things often happen in public parks, and I noticed an inscription on the wall protecting some religious facility. The inscription read: 'Donald Duck for President'. You see, the prophecy has come true, hasn't it?" And he smiled at the American.

"I am not quite sure what you mean," the man said.

"Ah yes, of course you're not, and it might be due again to that semantic confusion. "Bah, these words, what a trouble they might be. There is a passage that begins 'What do you read, my lord?' Are you familiar with it? 'Words, words, words…' And then what happens, all that is left is 'the rest is silence', that's it.

"But to change the subject, what's your business in Russia? Oil, precious metals?"

"No," the American replied, "ladies' garments."

"Ah, this is something where our dear friend," and Klug looked at Kater, "may be of great assistance, especially with regards to underwear, which is his area of expertise."

"Really?" said the American.

"Not the slightest doubt about that," said Klug, and turning to Kater, asked, "will you be willing to share your experience with our American friend?"

"Certainly, anytime," said Kater.

"And now, after such an interesting conversation," he went on, "we may relax a bit, so I suggest we drink some champagne before we land at Sheremetyevo where we'll be in ten minutes and five seconds," he said.

I didn't realise that we were approaching Moscow right now, and I began to wonder again what awaited me there. One thing seemed certain: I could still rely on my two companions. Yes, they were trustworthy, and I knew that as long as I was in their company I was safe.

Our plane eventually landed, came to a stop at some distance from the main airport building, and the captain announced: "Thank you, ladies and gentlemen, for flying with us, and I wish you a pleasant stay in our capital."

*Why didn't we come closer to the buildings?* I thought, and apparently, I wasn't the only one who asked the question, for the passengers were all looking out of the windows. Ten minutes had already passed and we were still standing, and no vehicle came to take us to the airport. Then I heard a noise, a siren or something like that, coming closer to where we were. And indeed, I saw a cavalcade of several cars approaching our plane. The sight caused some excitement among the passengers, and one of them shouted, "Anti-terrorist forces, Alpha regiment. There must be terrorists in here, my God!"

Fortunately, the voice of the captain came again: "Stay calm, ladies and gentlemen, no need to worry, no danger whatsoever. They've just come to collect some VIPs that are with us."

And then the door opened, and a tall, well-built man in a uniform entered and said, "*Zdrastvuyie, ne volnuysya pozhalnysta,*" and his words were immediately translated into several languages by the stewardess. "May I ask *Messieurs* Klug, Kater and Adarsh to accompany me to the car please," said the man, and it was Klug who replied.

"*Privet,* let's go, my friends," he said to us. And we followed the officer out of the plane towards the waiting vehicles. We came to a Mercedes Pullman, in front of which another officer was standing, and when we came closer he saluted and opened the door. We got in, and the car pulled out.

"Quite a welcome we received," I said.

"Ah yes, they're very hospitable," said Kater.

"But not everyone receives such a welcome," I said.

"No, of course not. But then not everyone deserves that," Klug said.

In the car, very comfortable indeed, we were offered champagne and caviar. The officer in charge asked us, "*Uvazhayemyye gospoda,* do you want to go straight to your hotel or shall I show you a bit of Moscow first?"

"Yes, please give us a tour first, and then we'll go the hotel," said Kater.

# MOSCOW

'Ty po strane idesh. I net takoy pregrady,
chtoby tebya ostanovit' mogla.'
Mikhail Isakovsky

Moscow has for sure a lot of space. Wide streets and pavements and of course large squares, of which the Red Square is the most prominent. I liked the city, it seemed to be open-ended, the opposite of London, which seems to be stuffy. Paris and Berlin are also spacious and give the atmosphere of freedom and perspective.

"How do you like our capital?" asked the officer.

"I'm as impressed as my master was," said Klug.

"I'm very glad to hear that, and am especially happy about your master's opinion whom we always heartily welcome here," replied the officer.

"All the pleasure's mine," answered Klug. "Tomorrow, we'll take a long stroll all over the city, and now please take us to the hotel."

"At you command, sir, and our cars are available for you all the time, day and night, whenever and wherever you wish to go," said the officer.

"That's very kind of you, thank you," said Klug.

"And gentlemen, tomorrow you are invited to a banquet at six in the evening. Our driver will get you there, of course," said the officer, "and here we are, the Metropol, have a nice stay. Aha, somebody is waiting for you in the reception hall. See you tomorrow, *dorogiye gospoda*," said the officer.

We entered the hotel, looked around and there was no living soul in the large reception hall.

"What's going on in here?" said Kater. "Did they run away once they heard we'd be coming?"

Then we heard a sound of music which was *Piano Concerto No 1* by Tchaikovsky. The large doors in front of us opened by some invisible force from inside, and a woman appeared with a pretty large crowd of people behind her. It was none other than Svetlana.

"*Moya krasavitsa!*" exclaimed Kater, "how happy I am. I missed you so much, and you're the best of what the city may offer me."

"Here he goes again," Klug said to me.

"*Zdrastvuityie uvazhayemyye gospoda,*" Svetlana greeted us, and came up to us holding a platter on which there was a round loaf of bread and salt in a small saucer. We kissed the bread, and each of us had a bit of it with a pinch of salt.

We all kissed her on both cheeks, and I had to admit she was something to look at. Tall, slim, with long beautiful legs and a gorgeous bosom like that of Madame Kokriatskaya, a Russian actress. Then the manager of the hotel and his staff shook hands with us, wishing us a pleasant stay in Moscow. Among the crowd there were several foreigners, and some of them were diplomatic representatives of their countries. The first to greet us was Polish consul, Mr Czartoryski. "He's a prince," Kater whispered in my ear, "one of his ancestors was Katherine the Great's Minister of Foreign Affairs."

"But both countries were at war countless times," I said.

"So what!" said Kater. "It's history, let bygones be bygones, *carpe diem,* as our maître always says."

Then the French Ambassador shook our hands, saying, "*Bonjour, Messieurs,* and I do hope you visit us pretty soon."

To which Klug replied, "*Bien sûr,* Monsieur Ambassadeur, we will. We wouldn't miss your delightful country. *Vive la France!*"

Next came the American consul. "Howdy, dear fellas, warm greetings from the president."

To which Klug replied, "How do you do, sir, and thank you very much." We were also introduced to several other people, and then the party began. There were a lot of different dishes for which the Russians are famous, and I enjoyed the food and so did my companions.

"You know, my friend," Kater said to me, "I love their food. It's simple, I mean truly organic, and so tasty, not like that American junk which is good for nobody but pigs, those hamburgers and hotdogs of theirs. And small wonder that obesity is a national illness there, and their vassals, the British, are the same. Subconsciously, eating that crap and drinking slops, they punish themselves, so there's a kind of logic in all that. I mean, they punish themselves for their stupidity. And this is obviously related to the way they think and act. Look, they constantly advertise, so to speak, human virtues, and you know why they do so? Because they are deprived of them. Therefore, they have to create a façade to deceive others. Putting it all philosophically, '*Jede Meinung ist auch ein Versteck und jedes Wort auch eine Maske,*' as our dear Friedrich says. Yes, nothing but appearances, which show the great eagerness for love, sympathy and benevolence that they don't possess, so they ask for them in their sentimental lyrics and other writings or movies, creating the impression of being able to experience and enjoy these feelings. But then, they're actually prigs, two-faced, treacherous people. Anyway, what are these current standards? Crap, that's it. In fact, there aren't any ethical principles these days, are they? Of course not, what's left is deceiving word games of hypocrites. Anyway, which ethical criteria are the best, and why are they superior to others? Ah, all that circus makes our master very displeased with the current state of affairs, and if people don't come to their senses, I really don't know what steps he may take…

"But now, dear friends, let's enjoy the party and forget all those distressing subjects for a while."

And so, we did. It was a very pleasant evening, but I wasn't entirely happy for all the time. One thought never left my mind: *Will I really see Beatrice here? What business might she have in this city, after all?*

"You look somewhat unhappy," said Kater.

"I enjoyed the evening," I replied, "but, you know, Beatrice…"

"But we've already told you you'll meet her here. Don't you believe us?"

"I believe you, but…"

"Another of your 'buts'! Haven't we told you recently to get rid of them?" he said.

"Yes, I was," I said. *How could I forget that conversation in Rieterpark?* I thought, and then said to him, "You're right, Kater. I should forget all those 'buts', but, you know, they still persecute me out of habit, so to speak."

"I see, but soon we'll be very busy, especially our friend Klug since he's in charge of our financial affairs. Tomorrow, there'll be another party, then we're going to meet several people, but fortunately not all of them will be financiers. Ah, how I dislike this profession! Money is a crime, my friend."

"What about going outside to get some fresh air?" I suggested to him.

"Great idea," said Kater, "let's go."

"I just now remembered a rather funny story," he said, once we were outside the hotel, smoking cigarettes.

"A long time ago, a school friend of mine, not feeling well, also went outside during a matriculation party, and the police, who were patrolling the area, asked him for documents. He reached into his pocket to get them and pulled out a knife and a fork instead, which had been placed in his pocket by some malicious friends of his. You see, those rascals took advantage of him being drunk. The police were about to arrest him, you know, they took him for a thief, when fortunately for him, his girlfriend arrived at the scene and told them he wasn't a thief but a student, a school director's son, in fact, celebrating passing final exams. The police believed her and let him go. You see how helpful women can be when you're in trouble."

"So, I wouldn't know you attended a grammar school," I said.

"Of course, I did. What haven't I attended!" he replied.

"I can easily imagine that," I said, and reached into my inner pocket as his friend did, not to get documents but tissues, for it was a very hot evening and my forehead was sweating profusely. But instead of a packet of tissues, or a knife and a fork, for that matter, I pulled out an envelope. I looked at it and said to Kater, "How did that get into my pocket, and what is it, anyway?"

"Open it and you'll see," he said.

So, I did, and pulled out a sheet of paper on which was written: *Tomorrow, Sadovaya Street, 12:00.*

And below there was a capital 'B'. I looked at the writing in amazement and thought, *Who's that...?* but then immediately, *it must be her, Beatrice, who else?*

"You know, Kater, I'm pretty sure it's a message from Beatrice."

"May I see?" he said, so I handed him the message.

"Yes, certainly. It's her handwriting, and her favourite ink too," he said.

"How do you…?" I began, but once again realised how stupid the question may be, so I said instead, "but how happened…?"

I couldn't finish for Kater chipped in, "A miracle, perhaps. You know, I strongly believe in miracles, don't you?"

"The longer I'm with you both, the more I believe too," I replied.

"Most obliged, and all the pleasure's ours, dear Ches," he said.

"What time does tomorrow's banquet start?" I asked him.

"At 5.30 pm, and it takes place not far from Bolshaya Sadovaya Street, so you'll have plenty of time to talk to her."

"Good, and who are the people we're going to meet there?"

"All kinds. It'll be, I'm sure of it, a very interesting event. We'll meet people from the very bottom up to the very top, so to speak. However, sometimes this order may be rearranged, if you know what I mean. Anyway, we must be ready for every sort of intellectual struggle which sometimes, as we know, may lead to violence, but I don't think it'll happen at our banquet. Some top officials will be there. Even the president may come, so violence is out of the question. He is, after all, a peaceful person, the opposite of Mr 'Fire and Fury'. Russia, of course, may use her strength if there's a need, which is the obligation of any country when it has to protect its interests. 'Sei stark!' but sympathetic and understanding too, as our unforgettable Friedrich says."

We returned to the ballroom where the party was still in full swing. Klug came to us and asked, "Where have you been, aren't you enjoying the party?"

"No," I said, "we are. We just went outside to breathe some fresh air, and you know, I got a message from Bea."

"I told you she wouldn't leave you, and what does she say?" asked Klug.

"I'm to meet her tomorrow in Sadovaya Street at 12:00," I answered.

"Ah, Sadovaya, hmm, what a coincidence. Some very significant events happened there some time ago," he said.

"What do you mean?"

"Our master himself stayed in an apartment there, and long after he left, some people still remembered and even commemorated those inexplicable things which had taken place in Moscow at the time," said Klug.

"And what exactly happened then?"

"As a matter of fact, just a few people understood what really took place and the significance of what happened."

"I see, but could you tell me something more about that?" I said.

"I could, but it'd be much better for you to find out yourself, and you will in due time," Klug said.

"I see, if you say so."

At that moment, Svetlana came to us and said, "My dear friends, why don't you enjoy the party? You neither dance nor drink, what's up?"

"No, no, *moya liubimaya*," said Kater, "we do enjoy, but Ches just received a message from his girlfriend, and we discussed some other things by the way."

"Ah, I see, and I'm happy for you," she said to me, "but now," she continued, "my two favourite dances are coming, I mean Monti's *Czardas* and Theodorakis' *Zorba*, and I want you," she turned to Klug, "to dance with me the first, and you," she looked at me, "the second."

"And what about me?" said Kater.

"You're a very poor dancer, you know that yourself. You're much better at other things, *moi lumibij kot*," she said.

"I protest," said Kater. "I'm one of the best, and even great Nijinsky admired my dancing, and I'll prove it in a minute." And he went up to a tall, athletic woman who stood nearby, bowed and said, "May I have the pleasure?"

She smiled and said, "Certainly, my friend," and they walked towards the middle of the floor.

Once they got there, Kater shouted to the conductor, "Maestro, Hopak, please." And he took the lady in his arms and they began to dance. At some stage of their dance, the woman got hold of his hands and started revolving him at tremendous speed, and then she suddenly lost the grip of his hands and Kater flew out of the open window. All who were gathered there froze, and the orchestra stopped playing and everybody present rushed to the window, but there was no sign of Kater.

"*Gospodi pomiluy*," Svetlana screamed, "he has surely been killed. It's a good ten metres to the ground."

"There's no need to worry," we heard Klug say. "Nothing bad can happen to this rascal. He'll be back shortly. This is nothing. He once jumped from a plane ten thousand metres high in the air, and his parachute didn't open. That happened during a military exercise during which he was the parachute instructor. Everybody on the ground waited for him to fall, but he didn't, so a massive search for him was mounted, but there was no trace of him. A general in charge asked for an emergency number for his master, and I reluctantly gave it to him. He dialled the number with a shaking hand and in a trembling voice told the master what had happened. The master laughed and asked him to calm down and wait patiently. The general thanked him profusely, apologised for disturbing him and calmed down a bit.

"We waited three days for Kater to return, and he did indeed, unhurt and in good condition. He told us that he'd been rescued from falling down to the ground by a very large bird which had taken him to his nest, where he'd a very nice stay with the bird's family. Nobody believed the story, but they restrained themselves from further questions. Anyway, he was a great instructor and several parachute regiments asked him to be their commander-in-chief, GSG 9, Russian Alpha, SAS, Green Berets and more, but Kater politely refused because of his neutrality and inborn modesty. But actually, he did train all of them, and in this country his advice was so valued that he was awarded the highest military distinction: the Order of Behemoth the Invincible. So, you see; no need to worry."

And at that very moment, Kater entered the ballroom and said, "Privet, *dorogoye druzya*, what a flight I had! There's nothing like seeing and contemplating the city from with a bird's eye view. I actually met an old friend of mine, the same bird, Patronus is its name, that rescued me before, and we had a very nice chat again and it told me things which you may see only from the sky. Yes, you must have your head up in the clouds to see them, and not down in the crowds."

At that moment, a man in general's uniform entered, came to Kater and gave him a hug, saying, "*Moi dorogoy drug, kak diela?*" to which Kater said, "*Gospodin general, rad videt' vas snova, vse v poryadke.*"

"We have a problem, and I'd be most grateful," the general said, "if you would be so kind as to assist us again."

"But of course I will, and what's the matter?" asked Kater.

95

"That I can tell you only in private, and must tell you that none other than the president insisted on asking you to help us," said the general.

"What about meeting you tomorrow at the banquet and discussing the matter in question?" Kater replied.

"Splendid! See you tomorrow then, and it's very likely that the president himself will have a word with you too. Thank you very much, my dear friend." And he left.

We continued to enjoy the party until the small hours next morning. I didn't sleep well for I couldn't stop thinking about my meeting with Beatrice, so I was up at five, drank two cups of strong coffee in my room, smoked several cigarettes, read a bit and at seven went downstairs to have breakfast. Klug and Kater were already in the dining room.

"So," Klug said to me, "you're seeing your lady today, my friend, but why are you so sad? Is something bothering you?"

"You know, I'm not quite sure what's going on. I couldn't contact her and now out of the blue I'm to meet her again, so I don't really know what to think of the situation."

"Apparently, she had a good reason to be away for a while, and if I were you, I wouldn't worry at all. Don't you remember what our charming Signora Bardini said?"

"Yes, I do remember what she said, and perhaps should believe it for she seemed to be a very wise woman."

"She is indeed, and therefore take it easy. Everything will be fine."

"I do hope so, but you know, I'm not accustomed to take anything easy as you may know by now."

"I do, I do, but it's high time to think positive, don't you think?"

"I'll try."

"That's it," Kater chipped in, "think positive, and you'll see the world aright. However, restrain yourself from being too positive about certain matters, for it may blur your understanding, I mean that we shouldn't embellish anything we experience, for in doing so, we cover up the truth."

"I can see," said Klug, "that particular seminar you attended once made you a philosopher."

"I've always been in philosophy's service, but I hardly ever say anything philosophical, being an ardent disciple of Wittgenstein," Kater shot back.

"Yes, I know you are, but I suggest you leave philosophy for the time being and concentrate on current matters. You, Ches, are seeing Bea only at midday, so we have plenty of time till then, and we can go for a walk to have the first glimpse of the city," said Klug.

"Good idea," I said, "let's go."

And off we went. First, we had a stroll through Red Square, and I was impressed by the Kremlin and St Basil's Cathedral. "That's something," I said, "the view is exceptional, unique and not to be seen anywhere else in the world. And this is what Russia is. This shows the soul of the country."

"What about seeing the inside?" said Klug.

"Oh yes, I'd very much like to see it," I said.

So, we went inside, bought candles, lit them and looked around. Silence, that was it, I felt the sound of silence as I never had in any other church I'd visited before. I was an agnostic, but now I felt that silence inside me, getting hold of myself, and I enjoyed peace that I hadn't had for a long time. I closed my eyes and stood there motionless as if in a trance, feeling no need to say or think anything. When I opened my eyes, I noticed Klug and Kater were looking at me, and one of them, I didn't realise which one it was, said to me, "You left time and space for a while, didn't you? In other words, you experienced eternity, and you needed no words to understand something you couldn't even utter. Am I right?" Only then did I realise it was Klug who asked me the question.

"Yes, you are," I said. And we left the cathedral.

"We'll come here again when mass is celebrated, and you'll listen to their music and singing, which is the most magnificent of all the other churches, *sui generis*," said Klug.

"I'd very much like to come here again," I said.

"We don't have time to visit the Kremlin now," said Kater, "but we will in a couple of days. And now let's go to Patriarch's Pond, my friends."

As soon as we got there, now walking under the limes, Klug said, "Yes, it all began right there, and the weather today is the same as it was on that day."

"Exactly the same," said Kater. "I remember the day, every detail of it."

"What are you talking about?" I asked.

"What about, my friend?" Klug asked in a very surprised voice. "You haven't read *The Master and Margarita*?"

"No, never heard of it," I replied.

"I'm sorry to say, but you should be ashamed of yourself," said Klug.

"Is the book so important?"

"Important, you say? Much more than important, my friend. It is a revelation, and it is our master's favourite novel. He says that no other is better than that, and we agree of course. How couldn't we, anyway? The book proves how wrong some people are in their opinions about what they call the evil. They're inclined to blame some mysterious power for their own wrongdoings, whereas they know nothing about what they're talking. As a matter of fact, that power is utterly impartial and equally sympathetic to the people fighting on either side. Consequently, the outcome is always the same for both sides. The evil is to be found nowhere but in themselves, and if they don't admit this in time, I'll be sorry for them. Oh, here we are, this is the same bench. Let's take a pew."

"What you mean the same bench?" I asked.

"We're now sitting where a very important conversation took place some time ago, this is what I mean, and you'll understand the meaning of it as soon as you read the novel," said Klug.

"I see, but could you tell me something about that conversation now?"

"Hmm, I can, but just a bit because I want you to come to the conclusions yourself so that they will be your own, and not mine or anybody else's for that matter. So, all I can tell you is that the conversation proved how overconfident man is regarding his own power, his exaggerated belief in himself, his conviction that he's the measure of all things. He even believes that he has power over his own future, whereas in fact he can be certain of nothing, and this is exactly his destiny. The trouble is that his powerlessness is proved to him so unexpectedly and suddenly, he cannot even say actually what he will be doing in one hour, to say nothing of tomorrow. That's it, my friend."

"Yes, I appreciate what you've just told me, and surely I'll read the novel." I said.

"Do it, and the sooner the better, for it'll help you to grasp your own problems and to see the way to deal with them. But as for now, you're going to see your lady, and remember, don't repeat your previous mistakes, and you know what I mean, don't you?" said Klug.

"Be assured, I won't. So, see you later, my friends."

And I left them heading for Bolshaya Sadovaya Street, where I was to meet Beatrice. When I was a good fifty metres from the bench, I heard Kater call, "Greet her from us, and don't forget that all your future depends on her." I turned around but they were nowhere to be seen.

*Yes*, I said to myself, *Klug's right, she's my destiny, and now I am on my own. They can assist me everywhere but not now, where there are just two of us, Beatrice and me.*

I still had plenty of time to get to where we were to meet, so I decided to get there on foot. It was a sunny, bright day and the city was crowded with people, and I usually liked to watch the faces, women's clothes and the way they walk but not now. I was preoccupied with asking myself one question: *Is she still mine, the only one I want and need?* I was just crossing Malaya Bronnaya Street when a huge black cat which appeared from nowhere ran my way, and I thought, *Uh-oh, a bad omen?* The cat then ran onto the pavement and sat down as if it was waiting for somebody or something.

When I reached the place where it was sitting, the cat looked at me, rose and joined my stride. *Why is it walking with me? Does it want something from me?* I thought. Suddenly the cat stopped walking, looked at me and pointed with his paw in the direction of a small shop on the right-hand side, and it was a flower shop. I looked at the animal in amazement, standing petrified, unable to move. *What's going on?* I thought. *Am I hallucinating, or what?* Then the cat came to the shop, and its door opened as if by itself, and the animal made a gesture, inviting me inside. Eventually, gathering all my strength, I moved and came into the shop with the cat on my side. Looking around, I was astonished to find in such a small place so many various kinds of flowers, and spotted a beautiful bunch of yellow ones. I came up to have a closer look at them, but then something got hold of my trouser leg, and it was him. The cat was pulling it and shaking his head, and I heard a woman's voice: "She won't like them."

I turned around and saw a very good-looking woman whose appearance was somehow familiar. *Yes*, I thought, *what's her name? That actress, yea.* I remembered now. *Natalya Antonova, a beautiful Russian actress.*

"How do you mean?" I asked the woman.

"I somehow know what kind of woman she is, and her taste, so she won't like them," she said.

I saw that the cat was nodding his head as if he was agreeing with her. I was bewildered by the situation and couldn't utter a word. "Please put it back, and take the orchids instead," said the woman. "She'll love them."

Being still astounded, I just took the orchids and, *Yes*, I said to myself, *she's right, these are Beatrice's flowers.*

I looked at the woman, who smiled and said, "Remember to give a woman what she really appreciates. Otherwise, she will never be truly yours. The point is to know what it is she loves, and you never know that unless you love her."

*Now I may know at last*, I thought, *what a woman I love expects from me She wants me to know what she loves, and then she will love me.*

I looked at the woman and thanked her but said nothing else because I knew that saying anything here and now wouldn't be appropriate, so I just took out my wallet, intending to pay for the flowers, but she said, "It's a gift, and pass my best on to her. You're a lucky man to know such a woman."

I thanked her again and said to myself, *At last you know that any questions are useless in situations like that.* And I left the shop with the cat still by my side.

When we reached Bolshaya Sadovaya, the cat came to a halt and handed me a small pouch. I looked inside it and found a bunch of keys. The cat looked at me, giving me a sort of smile then he stood on his hind legs and, stretching out his paw, shook my hand and left me. Having already had some inexplicable experiences, I wasn't now much surprised and continued walking towards my destination. It was one minute to my meeting time, and when I turned into Bolshaya Sadovaya, the bell somewhere struck twelve, and I saw her.

She was even more beautiful than before, or it was due to my longing for her I thought she was so. She stood there waiting, with that usual knowing smile on her sensual mouth. I came to her, and for a good while neither of us said anything but just smiled, looking into each other's eyes, and she was the first to speak.

"How have you been?" she said.

"Why…" I began, but immediately realised the stupidity of the question and instead said, "I've just been waiting for you," and said, "Here you are," handing her the bunch of flowers. "I've heard you don't like yellow."

"Who told you that?"

"A lady at the flower shop where I got these."

"Ah yes, Natalya."

"Do you know her?" I asked.

"Yes, I do. She's a very good friend of mine."

"I see, and I made a rather strange acquaintance with a cat that gave me this," I said, showing her the pouch.

"Ah yes, the keys, let's go there," said Beatrice.

"How did you—" I began, but she interrupted.

"You should have guessed by now, shouldn't you, darling?"

"Yes, of course, a stupid question."

"That's it, so it's not far, shall we?"

And we went there and soon came to a big block of flats built in the nineteenth century, I thought. She led me up to an apartment on the fourth floor, and we entered. It was a tastefully furnished very large flat, and we went straight to the bedroom where there was a big divan. Bea slowly undressed and I saw again how beautiful every part of her body was, those long slim legs and full, firm breasts. I undressed too, and we began lovemaking, and soon I was in a different world where there was neither space nor time. We already knew each other's preferences, and each of us knew how to satisfy them. I loved to caress and kiss her breasts, and she did the same to my penis and wanted to have it in every spot of her body, and enjoyed to suck and swallow. She could delay ejaculation, giving me great pleasure all the same, and when I came she still held my dick in her mouth until she sucked it dry. She in turn liked cunnilingus, and she was the first woman I was happy to do it to. Beatrice had already told me before she'd had several orgasms during our lovemaking, and that's why she wanted to carry it on as long as possible. I'd had many women before her but with none of them had I had such pleasure as with Bea, and I knew she was happy as well. However, we never talked about our former partners. Anyway, there was no need to say a word about our other affairs.

When we finished our lovemaking, we lay on the divan for a while looking at each other, saying nothing. Eventually, it was Bea who was first to get up and went to the kitchen to make some coffee. We were drinking it and I was asking myself, *Shall I enquire about what she has been doing until now?*

I still hadn't made up my mind when she said, "Do you want to know what happened to me, and why I haven't contacted you, do you?"

I began, "I... I am obviously curious about that, but apparently you had a reason—"

I couldn't finish, for she chipped in, saying, "Yes, there was a reason... but I'm not allowed to tell you anything now. You'll find it out in due time, my love."

"Bea," I said, "you know I have no doubts about you. I just, you know, I've been very worried. I thought I might have lost you, I—"

"Enough," she said, "you will never lose me," and she said that with such conviction that I was stunned, and I was just looking at her, and neither of us said anything for several minutes.

I realised that everything had been said, and I felt peace of mind and body for there was no need for any words, and I saw everything aright.

"Bea," I said, "do you know I am to attend a banquet this evening?"

"Yes, I do. Do you want me to come along?"

"I wouldn't imagine going without you," I said.

"I know you wouldn't, and there isn't much time left, and I still need something to put on."

"Shall we go to the place you're staying to get what you need, or...?"

"I'm staying with friends in their *dacha* on the outskirts of Moscow pretty far from here. Anyway, I don't have anything suitable there for the banquet, so let's go to the shops. There's one nearby I know."

"All right then, let's go."

We left the apartment and went to a rather small ladies' clothes shop, but as soon as we went in, I saw they had a large collection of everything a woman would need to look presentable, but I couldn't see any shop assistants. Then I heard a familiar voice coming from somewhere in the back. *No,* I thought, *is it him?* But it was, and we saw Kater coming to us with a big smile on his face.

"My princess is here. How I missed you!" he exclaimed and kissed both of Bea's hands.

"What are you doing here?" I asked him.

"I'm a part-time assistant. You know, ladies' clothes are one of my fields of expertise," Kater replied.

"Surely they are, especially when they don't have them on," I said.

"This is very untactful of you, my friend. I appreciate women under any circumstances, and now I'll assist your lady if you don't mind," he said.

I looked at Bea, who smiled, giving me a wink. "Certainly, my naughty animal, you may assist me," she said to Kater.

"All the pleasure's mine," he said. "I invite you to a changing room, and I'll fetch a couple of dresses for you to try on."

Bea went there, and I saw Kater running up and down picking several dresses, bras and some other stuff. Then he disappeared into the room.

*No,* I said to myself, *what a cheeky fellow,* and heard them laughing and talking in excited voices, and after a few minutes Bea reappeared dressed in a full-length red ballgown so regal that I just looked at her and wasn't able to find the proper words to express my admiration. Yes, she was a princess, that rascal Kater got it right. I came to her and still saying nothing just kissed her hand. She smiled and said, "And…?"

"You know," I eventually recovered my voice, "don't leave me for a second during the banquet if you know what I mean."

She laughed and said, "I do, I do, but there's no need to worry. Nobody there would dare to try anything, and if they did, I wouldn't like to be in their shoes," and she gave Kater a glance.

"Oh yes," he said, "I, myself, can't even imagine what would happen to somebody who would dare to attempt even the slightest impertinence towards our princess, to say nothing of our master's wrath. I just shiver at the thought alone. No, it just transcends my imagination."

"It's time to go," I said, "and how are we to get there?"

"In this dress, I wouldn't feel comfortable walking, so shall we call a taxi?" said Bea.

"No need for that, my princess. A car is already waiting for us outside," Kater said.

And indeed, there was a large car of a make unknown to me in the street when we came out. "What make is it?" I asked Kater.

"Ah, this is an old Russian ZIL, once used by dignitaries in this country," he said.

When we came closer, the door of the car opened, and the same officer whom we'd already met at the airport emerged, saluted and, taking his cap off, kissed Bea's hand. "*Ochen' rad videt' snova, vashe blogodaroye,*" he said, holding the door for her.

"*Sposibo, ya tozhe rada,*" said Bea, and got in.

Inside the car sat Klug who, upon seeing her, said, "Your Highness, may I have the honour of being the first to have a dance with you?"

Bea gave me a questioning look, and I said, "I don't mind if you wish."

We pulled out, and soon we arrived outside a very nice baroque mansion. A lot of cars were already there. We got out of the car and walked towards the main door of the house at which stood two soldiers in historic uniforms. When we approached the door, they saluted and opened it for us. We came in and saw a rather large crowd of people in a very spacious ballroom. Almost every man there, upon seeing Bea, rushed towards us, and soon a long queue of them formed, wanting to be introduced. The first man was a tall, slim, patrician-looking gentleman in his sixties. "May I introduce myself," he said, kissing Bea's hand, "Nikolay Vladimirovich Romanov."

"I am delighted, your Highness," said Bea. "I've already had the pleasure of meeting your cousin, Alexander Nikolayevich."

"Ah, him. I presume it took place at Monte Carlo Casino."

"Yes, indeed. How would you know that?" she asked.

"Bah, I'm familiar with his certain weakness. I mean gambling, of course. He's a very nice chap but totally irresponsible. He's already lost a fortune at casinos all over the world and keeps borrowing money from everybody, and I'm afraid he might have asked even you, Madame."

"Yes, indeed, he asked me and I lent him 50,000 euros," replied Bea.

"Oh no!" exclaimed Prince Romanov, and said, "And he obviously hasn't paid it back, and if not, I'll refund it immediately."

"No, thank you, your Highness, there's no need. He already paid it back the same evening."

"How come? He usually always loses."

"But that time, he won, and it was two hundred thousand."

"Did he? I can hardly believe it," said the prince, "and didn't he bet it again and eventually lose?"

"Yes, actually he was about to do that, but I forbade him to do so."

"And he obeyed you, incredible!" exclaimed the prince.

"Yes, he did, and immediately after winning, he gave me back what he borrowed and invited me to a supper at which we had a lovely conversation. You know, he's a very charming man indeed."

"Oh yes, he is, and so charming that there are husbands who are eager to lay their hands on him all over Europe and other parts of the world. Anyway, I'm very glad that for once at least he behaved like a true gentleman. And now allow me to wish you a very pleasant evening, and I do hope to meet you again, Madame."

"It would be a pleasure for me too, your Highness. Goodbye."

I listened to the conversation and was thinking, *I still know nothing about her. Now Monte Carlo. Where else has she been, and what actually does she do? And her acquaintance with Wahrburg, and her job as a nurse at the Bolzano Clinic? Questions, questions – will I ever have the* answers…?

"You seem to be immersed in thought, *mon cheri*," said Bea, giving me a questioning look.

"Yes, I am, because so many unanswered questions remain."

"You mean myself, I presume, so you doubt in the truthfulness of our relationship. You think there must be another reason behind it," she said.

"No, I don't doubt the sincerity of us being together. Just feeling a bit unsure, darling."

"I can understand that, but at the moment I can't tell you everything, for you aren't ready for that yet, but once you are, you will get answers to what bothers you now. Be patient, trust me, darling, and wait until the right time comes. Will you?"

I realised I had no choice but to agree, so I simply said, "Yes, I will, my love."

We were introduced to several people by Kater who apparently knew them all, and then at nine, a strong voice heard all over the ballroom announced, "Ladies and gentlemen, the President!" And the man whom I had seen many times on the screen entered and walked straight in the direction where Bea, Kater and I were standing.

"*Dorogoi* Mikhail Vladimirovich," exclaimed Kater, "*ochen' rad videt' vas snovo.*"

"*Mne tozhe, moi dorogoi drug,*" said the president, and then turning to Bea, "it's a great pleasure and honour to welcome you to our country, Madame," he said, kissing her hand.

"*Bolshoye sposibo,* Mikhail Vladimirovich," said Bea.

"Please tell me, what should I do to make your visit as pleasant as possible?" he asked her.

"I feel here much at home, but thank you for your consideration, but there might be something I would like to happen."

"Tell me what it is, and be assured I'll make it happen."

"As a matter of fact, I'm just a messenger, and it's my master who has asked me to pass it over to you."

I could see the president immediately straighten his back, and then bow, saying, "It's a privilege to do what he asks me to do, Madame."

"Thank you, *dorogoi* Mikhail Vladimirovich. I'm happy to hear that, and it's about an author whose novel they refused to publish. The master says it's very well written, a masterpiece, and he doesn't really understand why it's been rejected all over again."

"Please tell me the author's name and what this book is about," said the president.

"His name's Pobog, and the story is about a man who strives to achieve his ideals here, on this earth, longing for peace of mind at the same time. As you can see, it's slightly contradictory stuff."

"It is indeed, but if the master himself likes the story, I am sure it must be very good, and please tell the writer that I personally will see to it that his book is published with no delay."

"I'm very grateful and will inform the master straightaway."

"All the pleasure's mine, and please tell him it's always a pleasure to do what he asks, Madame. And now, if you'll excuse me, I'd like to have a word with Mr Kater."

"But of course, *dorogoi* Mikhail Vladimirovich," said Bea.

And Kater said, "At your service, sir."

"I suggest we move to a place where we'll have more privacy, dear friend," said the president.

And they walked to a room upstairs, and once there the president said, "I need your kind advice regarding some disturbing matter."

"I'm all ears," Kater said.

"It's about our rather strained relationship with the West at the moment, and I don't really know how to deal with it."

"Yes, I'm aware of the current state of affairs and will try to be of assistance here. However, I think we should invite here my dear friend Klug, for he's much better informed than me."

"Certainly, I always highly value his advice."

And exactly at that moment, Klug entered the room and said, "I've just heard that you need me to discuss some urgent matters."

"Yes, my dear friend, we do," said the president, "and how come you've found that out?"

"I somehow always know whenever somebody needs me, you know, I can see it in my mind's eye. So, what's the problem?"

"I wish I had the same capacity," said the president. "It would greatly enhance my abilities."

"I, in turn," said Klug, "sometimes wish I didn't have that skill, for then I would have more peace of mind, but what can I do? It's been given to me, so I must obey it."

"The problem nowadays is," said the president, "that Dollaria especially treats us as an enemy, for it needs one in order to keep its status, and I presume it wants direct confrontation which might trigger an open war."

"Yes," said Klug, "you might be right. Yes, they may strive for a war subconsciously, so to speak. I don't know what decision has been made regarding it," and here Klug looked at the skies, "but I have been instructed to prevent any calamity that might be in sight. Anyway, we are determined to keep the peace, and we have the means to achieve that."

"Undoubtedly, you have," said the president, "and I'll follow any advice you give me, my dear friend."

"I appreciate that, and I'll do anything to improve your country's relations with Dollaria and other countries too, dear Mikhail Vladimirovich, and I'll present you with a few options soon."

"Thank you, and I can't wait. And now I must leave you, dear friends. Enjoy Moscow, and if there is anything I can do, please don't hesitate to contact me anytime. I and my people are at your service."

The president shook hands with us all, and left.

"So," said Kater, "let's go back downstairs. They may wonder what has happened to us, and I feel like dancing very much."

"And what dance will it be this time?" I asked.

"Waltz, and with Beatrice, if you don't mind."

"No, I don't, but no excesses. Behave yourself, promise?"

"*Noblesse oblige*, my dear friend. I swear I will."

We went back downstairs where the banquet was still in full swing. Bea and Kater began to dance and I had to admit he was a very good dancer, and she apparently enjoyed the waltz. When they finished, she said to me: "He is really good, much better than you, but dancing and any other skills for that matter are not everything, for there's something else that a wise woman appreciates more, much more."

"And what is it?" I asked.

"She wants a man she can make happy. She wants to satisfy his every desire, and if he is able to appreciate that, and reciprocate, she is in turn fulfilled, and her life is complete."

"I see, and am I that man for you?"

"Yes, you are," said Bea.

There was nothing else to say, but now the rest was silence, and we just looked at each other and stood there as if there was nobody else around, only us and silence. And we would have stayed like that forever if it wasn't for somebody's voice: "I'm terribly sorry for disturbing you, but there's an urgent matter, and…"

And we saw a tall, pretty brunette we had never seen before. She smiled, but there was no joy in her smile. I immediately knew that it must be something very serious, for she seemed to be exhausted, and I could see that she must have been crying because her beautiful eyes were puffy, and there was deep sadness in them. And I somehow knew I would do my best to help her, so I said, "No need to apologise, madam, what can I do for you?" And at the same time, I glanced at Bea, who just nodded, so I knew that she understood the situation too.

"I would never," the woman said, "dare to spoil your evening, but I don't have any other option but to ask you, Mr Adarsh…"

"How do you know my name, madam? As far as I remember, we have never been introduced."

"No, we haven't, but…" She stopped, as if she wasn't sure how to proceed, "but I too was living in Switzerland where I met a woman who had known you, and…"

"And who was it?"

"Your wife."

"My wife…? Then you didn't hear anything good about me, I presume."

"No, as a matter of fact, she did say some good things about you. And sorry, I haven't introduced myself. My name's Emilia, and I am German."

"Pleased to meet you," I said, and there was something in her I liked, but I couldn't say exactly what it was. Was it her voice, the way she looked at me? Anyway, I knew I would help her if I could, so I said, "What can I do for you, Emilia, if I may…"

"Yes, surely you may, and it's about a man I met in Zurich, and he's Russian and we came here to visit his family who live in Novgorod, then we returned to Moscow and the day before yesterday he disappeared. His mobile is silent, so I rang all the hospitals and went to the police, but no trace of him."

"And what's his name?" I enquired.

"Cyril Pobog."

*Pobog,* I thought, *just a… yes…* and I looked at Bea who joined us now, and upon hearing the name, she exclaimed, "That's him, I just talked about him with the president, and it was the master himself who was interested in him, and now I can hardly imagine what might happen if something bad happened to Cyril, how the master would… no!"

"Calm down, darling, calm down," I said. "I'll immediately have a word with Kater and Klug." And I looked around and saw Kater who as usual was busy talking to a very good-looking woman, and Svetlana, who stood nearby, had a dangerous flame in her eyes. I came straight to him and said, "Excuse me, we have an emergency, my friend."

"A what, emergency, what…?"

"Yes, a man by the name of Pobog has disappeared. His partner just told me that, and it was the master on whose behalf Bea asked the president…"

I couldn't finish for Kater interrupted, saying, "Thank you, my friend, for telling me. The master himself, my… we'll sort it out, don't you worry."

And pulling a mobile out of his pocket, he said to me, "Come outside with me."

We went over to a large terrace and once there, he dialled a number and immediately somebody answered it, asking, "Who's that?"

"It's Kater. Can I speak to Mikhail Vladimirovich, please?"

"Mr Kater, yes, of course, I'll put you through to him."

Two seconds later, I heard the president ask, "Yes, my dear friend, what can I do for you?"

"Dear Mikhail Vladimirovich, we have a serious problem. Mr Pobog has vanished without a trace, the man about whom Miss Sforza spoke to you a few hours ago, and the master himself…"

"Yes, I understand. No need to worry. I'll take care of the problem myself right now."

"Shall I inform my master that we'll see Mr Pobog soon or…?"

"Yes, be assured, my friend, that he'll be back in a couple of hours, I guarantee that, and please pass my best on to the master, and tell him I would very much like the honour of seeing him again."

"Thank you again, and we're waiting anxiously for Mr Pobog here, and I'll tell the master there's no need to worry. However, I must tell you that once he heard about Mr Pobog's disappearance, I had the impression that he may… you can imagine, dear Mikhail Vladimirovich, what he might…"

"Oh yes, I can, and that is something we would have never wished for, dear friend, never ever. Be sure of it!"

"I am pretty certain you wouldn't, my friend. So, we are waiting here for good news. Good bye for now." Then he said to me, "I take him for a man who is imaginative enough to understand that it would be a very bad idea to upset the master, who may not have any panzer divisions at his disposal, but he has something incomparably stronger, and no other power on this earth can match it. Nothing is hard for him to do, and you know that by now, don't you?"

"I do," I replied curtly, "so, we're waiting, and I'll tell Emilia not to worry, then."

I went to look for her and found her talking to Beatrice. She looked at me with so much despair in her eyes, such as I had never ever seen in any person I'd met.

"We have been promised," I said to her, "that your partner will be back with us, and I'm certain he will, so please don't you worry."

"Do you really believe their promises?" asked Emilia.

"All in all, not too much, but now when the master himself... you know, they wouldn't dare to disappoint him. Especially now, when the president himself knows what it is about."

"But why has he engaged personally? For him, my partner's disappearance must be a trivial matter."

"I wouldn't know, but he must have a reason about which we may find out sometime in the future. Anyway, all we can do now is to wait."

And we were waiting, but not too long. One hour later, we heard some commotion at the front door, and a group of men entered. In the middle of them, there was a rather tall man looking a bit distressed, looking uneasily around, and all others in the ballroom were looking at him. Then, I heard Emilia scream, "It's him!" And she rushed to him. He stood there as if he couldn't believe his eyes, and eventually a smile appeared on his face and he took hold of her hands, said nothing but just looked at her for a good few minutes until Kater, who now came to him, said, "Welcome back, my friend, how are you?"

"I'm fine now, but a while ago..." here he stopped "...yes, a while ago it was a different matter, but if you excuse me, I don't want to talk about that now, maybe later."

"Certainly, my friend, now Emilia will go with you. You need a rest, and then whenever you are ready, we can have a chat about your experience."

Emilia and Mr Pobog said their thanks and went upstairs, where a room had already been arranged for them by Kater, who had apparently been sure enough that it all would come to a happy end.

Now, he looked at the men who brought Mr Pobog, and one of them, evidently a leader, said, "Sir, please accept our apologies on behalf of the president, who himself was very distressed by that unfortunate incident."

Kater said nothing for a good while, just stared at them all. Eventually, he said, "Apologies accepted. Please thank the president, and tell him I will contact the master who... what shall I say, was a bit disappointed too, so to speak."

I and all gathered there were looking at the scene and could see the leader's face went pale, while all his companions' eyes fixed to the floor.

"I... I..." the leader began, "I did my best, sir, believe me, and the president, after hearing about the incident, never went to bed, stayed awake to supervise personally the search for Mr Pobog. As it turned out, some people detained Mr Pobog, and his detention, I assure you, was not authorised by the authorities."

"I appreciate that," said Kater, "and luckily, all that ended well, for if it hadn't... Anyway, thank you again, and please pass my best on to Mikhail Vladimirovich."

All the men stood to attention as long as it took him to leave the ballroom. I could see how relieved they were now, and they surely didn't belong to those who easily lose their self-confidence. Apparently, they had been told who they would be dealing with if their operation failed, and I could easily imagine how eager they were to accomplish their task. Despite all their power, they were sufficiently imaginative to understand their own weakness. Yes, it's a paradox how power and strength may at the same time be its own opposite – a weakness, in fact. The saying *vive gladio peri gladio* has always been very true wherever you are, so be it here in Russia or Dollaria, yes, wherever. But most of the time the realisation comes too late because of the hyperbolic naïveté of man positing himself as the meaning and measure of the value of things, that monstrous stupidity that he is judge of the world, as that immortal German philosopher Nietzsche says.

There was only one business left here, in Russia: the business of the Magnificent Seven, who also thought of themselves as the rulers of their own destiny, as untouchable. And I now understood how to take advantage of their confidence, which may turn into their weakness, whatever their scheme was.

"It seems to me you're thinking hard about something," I heard Klug say.

"Yes, I am, and to be honest, I think hard too often, and no wonder I cannot come to any conclusion, if you know what I mean."

"Yes, I've noticed that thinking hard is your destiny. And then you don't allow yourself to judge, for you know that every judgement is false because it's always a temporary and therefore relative solution, and you've always been looking for the final solution, haven't you?"

"Yes, I cannot do otherwise, and this is as you rightly say my destiny. Yes, I can't help it because I have subdued myself, so to speak, to my inner thinking, where there might be no words after all, and that's why I can't say much. There is no language which could grasp the meaning of what is going on over there, that realm we call the soul or the mind, whatsoever."

"I see," said Klug, "but so far, man has found no means to express himself but in words, with the exception of some arts, but yes, you cannot communicate through them but just contemplate, so the only means of communication left is language."

"But don't we," I replied, "recollect whatever we have done through pictures? But then again sooner or later come words. I mean, propositions, for a proposition is a picture of reality as Ludwig says."

"Ah, Ludwig," said Klug, and smiled, "but then that poor fellow finally turned everything upside down later on. However, what he'd said previously still matters. But the question is what is it we are actually looking for in the philosophy of life, if I may put it this way. What would you say?"

"The answer to the question 'why?' I think," I said, "but quite often without being aware of it. Yes, this is our innate eternal question we can never dismiss because of reason of our nature. But where does it originate? Isn't it the perennial difference between that inner thinking and what we are able to put into words? To get to know yourself is to answer the question 'why?', and I believe that in order to answer it, we need to erase the difference between our inner thinking and that what we are aware of, and to be aware is to live, and to live a good life is to say 'yes', and then you don't need any words as a matter of fact."

"You've got it right, my friend," said Klug, "and anyway, words may lead you astray, and it has been going on forever for that matter. But you know, I think the real problem is that playing those word games, you cannot restrain yourself from judging. You judge everyone and everything every day, that's it. And what happens then is you eventually know nothing about yourself because of that constant judging of yours. You live the lives of others instead, having views on everything but yourself. But at the same time, you may pretend to be understanding, full of empathy and the like, so in a word you're a hypocrite. You know, I believe that to be sympathetic towards other fellow men, you first have to be sympathetic, empathic towards yourself. You can even pity yourself if you need so, but pity shouldn't be the motto of your life. What should be is courage, pride, sympathy and insight, and only then are you your own man, and only then is your life worth living, and only then will you be respected by others and may truly respect them."

Our conversation was interrupted by Emilia who upon approaching us said, "I'm sorry about interrupting you, gentlemen, but my partner says he would very much like to reciprocate as far as he can your kind assistance, and told me to ask you what he in turn could do for you before we return to Switzerland."

"Hmm," Klug cleared his throat, "we appreciate that but what is it that he would actually like to do for us?"

"He's rather familiar with the finance business. In fact, he's an expert, and the way Russian banks operate is his area of expertise."

"Ah, that's good to know, for we are actually in need of somebody like him. But you said you would be returning home soon?"

"Yes, said Emilia, "we want to, but we decided not to go back before we could return your favour if it would be possible."

"That's very kind of you, and we gladly accept your kind offer, and we'll talk about the details tomorrow, and now please thank your partner, and I wish you both good night, Frau Englert."

Emilia looked at him in surprise, wondering of course how came he knew her surname, and it looked like she was going to ask him but thought better of it and said instead, "Then see you tomorrow, gentlemen."

"Nice woman," I said, "and actually I used to know somebody who resembled her a lot, and strangely enough her name was Emilia too, and she was the only one I never quarrelled with. And she was very good in bed, eager to comply with my every wish. Yea, she was a good girl, and sometimes I think it would have been much better for me to marry her, for I still think she would make a good wife. You know, my greatest mistakes were those concerning women, and I have never forgotten that, and this time, I mean, Beatrice, I will not repeat the previous blunders."

"Yea," Klug said to me, "you'd better not. You've made enough mistakes, and there's always a limit, I mean, incorporating your previous blunders all over again until you don't have a way back, and when you can change nothing in your life. But I hope you're imaginative enough to understand that yourself. Yes, my dear friend, imagination is a mysterious word, but only imagination may allow you to travel back, to arrive where you started and know the places for the first time. But this is exclusively personal travel, during which you may become what you are, and during that journey the blunders of your life have their own meaning and value. And this is so because there is no other way to find out what value your personal values really have, and to see whether you may need, sometime, new values. All in all, that travel is the only way to say 'yes' to your own existence, for only then can you say yes to everything that exists in the world.

"But now let's get back to the issues which are here and now, and they're related to that travel in a way. Yes, everything is related to something else. Nothing is on its own except… but let's forget it for now. So, what do you think of our Mr Pobog?"

"I don't really know," I said, "we have just met him, and we don't really know him so, hmm, let's see what he is to tell us."

"I believe," said Klug, "that we can rely on him. I presume he's a trustworthy fellow, and you know, I'm almost never mistaken as to who is who."

"Yes, I'm sure you aren't, so let's have a word with him. Shall I ask him to join us?"

"Yes, go ahead."

I went looking for Mr Pobog, who after having some rest was back, and found him engaged in a conversation with all the others: Bea, Kater, of course, Emilia and Svetlana.

"Sorry for interrupting you, but I'd like to have a word with Mr Pobog here," and turning to him, I said, "tomorrow we would like to discuss a few things with you which you kindly offered to help us with. Would you be available at, let's say, nine at the Metropol Café, and then depending how our things go on, we can move somewhere else?"

"Certainly, I'm at your service. I'll be there."

"Done," I said to Klug, "he'll be at the Metropol Café at 9 am."

"Tomorrow we have a lot to do, and I'm going to bed now. It's already two o'clock and me being an early bird, there's just three hours left to have some sleep. What about you?" Klug asked.

"Yes, me too. I'll ask the others what their plans are for tomorrow. Anyway, Kater is going with us, I presume?"

"I'm not sure, you know. He finds financial matters rather boring. Besides, he has made an appointment to see the president to present him with a gift."

"Ah, and what is it?"

"A very interesting device, "said Klug, "he invented himself in his spare time. It's a mirror in which you can see things as they really are, but because most people don't want to know the truth, this device is not for everybody because not everyone would have the courage to find out the truth about themselves, for that matter."

"And why has he decided to give this to the president?" I asked him.

"No, it wasn't his decision but the master's, and we don't really know why. You know, we ourselves don't know everything, but we obviously follow his every order, no questions asked."

"I see, but don't you have an idea why he's chosen the president as the recipient of that mirror?"

"Hmm, I dare say I do have some ideas, but I won't share them with you now. You'll be present when Kater hands it to the president, and then you yourself will have a chance to have an idea what might have been behind the master's decision."

"I'm a bit tired, my friends," said Kater, who accompanied by Svetlana came to us at that very moment," and tomorrow's a very busy day, so we're leaving now."

"Don't forget we're meeting Mr Pobog tomorrow at nine, which is rather early for you, especially when you aren't alone," Klug said to him.

"Oh no, I won't. Anyway. I'm so exhausted that I will be sleeping like a log, so I'm sorry, my love," he said to Svetlana, 'please don't expect anything.'

"This time you are granted a dispensation, but you'll have to make up for it next time," she replied.

"I swear, I will. See you later, my friends. Have a good night," said Kater and they left.

"And you," Bea said to me, "want to be excused too?"

"No, not at all, duty comes first."

"Aha, so it's just about a duty."

"It may be about something else too, darling," I said, smiling, "and you know that."

"Yes, I do," said Bea, kissing me on the cheek.

She was the first woman I'd ever known for whom there was 'something else' I could offer, and what had been hidden, inaccessible for me to give to somebody else. A man may have thoughts and feelings to offer provided he's able to get them out from within himself, but he cannot share them with any woman. No, there is always only one, and he may never meet her, but if he's lucky enough to find that woman then it is what is called love, which means having everything, that is, not wanting anything else. Meeting Beatrice was like waking from a long sleep. All my best feelings, those which could make you joyous, had been asleep for many years, and she was the one to wake them up. You may call such a woman your 'ideal', and this is because meeting her gives you absolute fulfilment and satiability. And being with her, there was no past and no future but present, that is to live forever. Yes, *carpe diem*, that is what we really want and need to be satisfied, to say 'yes', and not being the one who forever denies, as I had been before meeting Bea. I've always needed ideals to reveal my innermost feelings and thoughts which otherwise would have never been unveiled, and I needed them to live, that is to be aware, and I needed another person to be aware of them, and to share them with that person who could understand them and so doing understand me. And that person must have been a woman, and now she was, and it was Beatrice. A woman may have a much better understanding of that ulterior mysterious domain of a man, and whatever we call her ability, be it intuition or instinct, it is her innate capacity and she too needs a man to implement it in order to reveal in turn her own hidden feelings, her intimate world, and to do so, she needs no words either. They both in the end find mutual understanding without any reasoning, they communicate almost without words, and how it happens they do not know themselves. And this mutual understanding is what we may call love, which is a kind of sensual form of perception, when no words are needed – the limits of language have been crossed – they have both achieved the ultimate aim of philosophy.

I wasn't ready yet, but somehow knew I would soon answer the questions 'Why?' and 'What for?' and then I would be silent, that is at peace at last, for the only way to express truth is to be silent, and peace can be achieved only in silence.

"What are you thinking about?" asked Bea.

"We never think. Our ideas think for us, you know that. And now I can grasp some of them, and they make me aware of how long I haven't been living. I have just been dreaming. And you have interrupted that dream waking me up, and now I live. Thank you, Bea, for being there."

"We haven't met by chance, Ches, but I thank you too, all the same."

"Let's go to bed now, darling. Tomorrow's a busy day. Are you going to take part in all these banking negotiations?" I asked.

"No, banking is not my cup of tea, but I may come along to see the president."

We said goodbye to everybody and went to our room at the Metropol, and after a shower went to bed but couldn't sleep. Bea was exceptionally affectionate to me, and seeing that I was rather tired, took the initiative, making love to me while I was lying on my back. She did everything to please me, first, fellatio, delaying my climax as long as possible, and then riding me, changing the positions, and in the end asking me to come in her mouth. Never ever before had I had such an orgasm as that night, and I could see she was satisfied too.

We slept just a few hours but were very well rested due to our passionate lovemaking. When we went downstairs to a brasserie for breakfast, Klug and Kater were already there.

"Here you are," said the latter, "did you have a good sleep?"

"Oh yes," I said, smiling at Bea, "we did have a very good sleep."

"Good, for a busy day is awaiting us," said Klug and turning to Kater, asked, "your present for the president ready?"

"Of course it is. I didn't sleep at all. First, Svetlana kept me busy and was so demanding that I could hardly meet her expectations. You know, she's insatiable and I thought I would have a heart attack or something like that."

"And what about your present?" I asked. "You never told me what it was."

"Ah, wait until we meet the president, who, I hope, will be pleased with it."

"We are going to see Mr Pobog at nine, as you know, and it's already eight, so let's finish breakfast before he comes."

The breakfast was very good. The bread especially was excellent, *vollkorn*, which was my favourite. While we were drinking our coffee, Pobog came to our table.

"Good morning, everybody," he said.

"Please have a seat," said Klug, "and you," he said to Kater, "fetch your present."

"So, dear friend, what is it you want to tell us?" Klug asked Pobog.

"First, I want to say it won't be easy to get information about the bank you mean. Yesterday, your friend Kater told me that the bank has some dealings in Switzerland and England. You would need to have inside info to get to know anything, and I may know somebody who could help us."

"And who is it?" asked Klug.

"A former friend of mine who owes me one, but I haven't seen him for a good couple of years, so I'm not sure about him. You know, people tend to change."

"Oh yes, yes," said Klug, "they do. However, you may always try."

"Okay, I still have his phone number, and provided he hasn't changed it, I'll give him a bell right now."

Pobog dialled the number, which was answered after just one ring. "Hello," he said, "am I speaking to Boris Nikolayevich?"

"Yes, you are. And who is enquiring?"

"It's Cyril Cheslavovich," said Pobog.

"Oh, what a nice surprise. I haven't heard from you for ages. Are you in Moscow?"

"Yes, I am, and would very much like to see you regarding something."

"Certainly, my friend. I don't complain about my memory if you know what I mean," said Boris.

"Yes, I do, and appreciate that. Where and when can we see each other?"

"What about today at our once favourite den, let's say, at five?"

"Perfect, thanks a lot, and see you there."

"Done," said Pobog, "and, you know, I wasn't at all sure it would be just like that."

"When we are finished with this bank business, are you going back to Switzerland?" asked Klug.

"Yes, we are, you know, because of Emilia's job and I, after so many years, got accustomed to living there, but if everything goes well, we'll come up here from time to time."

"Where is he? Why is it taking him so long?" said Klug.

"You know, Kater might be having one of his usual adventures," I suggested.

At that moment, we saw our adventurer carrying his huge suitcase. He put it down by the table where we were sitting and plunged himself into the chair.

"So," he said, "shall we go now to meet our dear president?"

"Yes," said Klug, "the officer we've already met twice should be here in a minute."

And we saw him coming, accompanied by two other officers. "At your service, gentlemen," he said.

"Pleasure to see you again," Klug said.

"Would you be so kind as to help me with this suitcase?" Kater asked the officer.

"Certainly," said the officer and grabbed the thing but couldn't lift it up an inch. Terribly ashamed of himself, he said, "I don't understand. I mean, I'm a weights champion but this is so heavy that... I'm so sorry."

"Bah," Klug said, "there is nothing to be ashamed of, my friend. You know, it's not the physical weight of this thing but its intellectual value that makes it so heavy. It's not that I underestimate your power of intellect, but hardly anybody would be able to lift it, to say nothing of carrying it. You know, many a man overestimates their strength, and this results in very unpleasant consequences for many others and also for themselves. Would you believe that even the great Einstein could lift it just a few centimetres off the floor?"

"Did you know him, sir? You don't look… I apologise," said the officer.

"Oh yes, I did. Who haven't I known, for that matter? And no need to apologise. I know I don't look old enough to know him, but I am very old in a way, so to speak, my dear friend."

And Klug stood up, got hold of the suitcase and effortlessly lifted it high up.

"*Bravo, bravissimo*, my friend, you seem to be very strong indeed. I, myself, don't complain about my strength, but you're even stronger," exclaimed Kater.

Klug put the suitcase back on the ground and said, "Let's go then, my friends, and who will be carrying it?"

"May I try?" I asked.

"Surely, give it a try," said Kater.

I grabbed the suitcase, stretched my muscles and nothing happened. The thing didn't even move.

"No, no, not like that," said Klug. "First, try to think of something you desire most on this earth, just one thing, and only then try."

I said to myself, *What do I need most of all things here and there? Yes, most of all, I want to…* I hesitated. *What is this only one thing? Is it… something or somebody? No, not something, all things are unimportant in the end, for the only solution of the problem of life is somebody, another human being, and yes, it is Beatrice.* And I got hold of the suitcase again, and this time I lifted it with ease.

"That's it," said Klug, "now you know the meaning of your life. My congratulations. And now it's time to go," he said, taking the suitcase in one hand, and we all came out of the café onto the street and got into the waiting car.

"Tell me," Bea said, "what did you think of when you made the second attempt to lift the suitcase?"

"It was somebody I thought of."

"And who was it, if I may ask?"

I looked at her and said, "You know that, my love."

"I do, and as a matter of fact, I have always known that."

"How would you have known…?" I began.

"Someday you'll find out, not here and now, and please don't ask any more questions."

After a ten-minute drive, we arrived at the president's residence. We entered and were asked to wait for him in a spacious reception room furnished with 19th century antiques. Some might have been even older, and I wondered whether they were originals or imitations. We didn't wait long for the president, who was accompanied by his main advisor and a few other men, who judging by their appearance must have been scientists of some sort.

"Pleasure to see you again, my friends," he said. "I've been told you have a gift for me for which I want to thank you, and I'm sure it's something of great value as is anything that comes from the master."

"All the pleasure's ours," said Klug, "and now my friend Kater, who's our chief engineer in a way, will make a presentation, but first he needs some privacy to assemble the machine, so would you be so kind as to provide him with a separate room to go ahead with it?"

"Certainly," said the president, and turning to his assistant, "Ivan Borysovich, please take Mr Kater to the adjacent room."

The assistant and Kater, carrying the suitcase, moved to the room, where the latter was left on his own. We waited rather impatiently for the presentation, and when the clock struck eleven we heard a bang and found ourselves in complete darkness. Total chaos ensued. People were shouting and bumping into each other. We heard someone cry, "Protect the President," in a word, a terrifying mess.

"There's nothing to worry about," I heard Klug say. "That's usually Kater's tricks, you know. He's a showman." But, after just a few minutes, the light was back and Kater, his face covered in soot, his overalls half-burned, emerged.

"I'm very sorry," he said, "but some unexpected problem occurred. I'll fix it in no time. And having said that, he left us again. Then, after a minute, a blinding light encompassed the room we were in, so intense we could see almost nothing except a blurred picture of a fogged park.

The image began to clear up slowly and eventually we saw Mr Wahrburg sitting on a bench under a big lime.

"Good day, everybody," he said. "You, dear Mikhail Vladimirovich, will be in possession of my gift which may be very useful provided you handle it reasonably. This instrument will allow you to know what the schemes are of any other country. This machine will reveal any information you need, and if you use it wisely, you will benefit from the knowledge you have acquired. So, it's up to you to decide how to use the thing, but please remember that it'll be up to somebody else to evaluate your usage of it. You, in fact, will bear great and actually burdensome responsibility, so think carefully, for metaphorically speaking, you'll be playing a very difficult game of chess. Are you with me, *dorogoy* Mikhail Vladimirovich?"

"Yes, I am, and I'll do my best. You have my word, sir."

"That's it for now," said Wahrburg, and looking at me, added, "I will see you again in due time, Mr Adarsh."

And then the picture disappeared, and everything was as it had been before. However, I could see that the president was deep in thought, very pensive. Apparently, he took to heart what Wahrburg had just told him.

"This apparatus," said Klug, "is called *Zauberspiegel*, and you, dear Mikhail Vladimirovich, have been chosen to receive it for a couple of reasons which will become clear to you in due time, and now all I can reveal is just one of them. Your country is still treated as inferior and backward by some other powers who consider themselves superior. But then, they seem to conveniently forget that this backwardness of a sort was due, with the notable exception of Peter the Great, to the hundreds of years of autocratic rule of the tsars. Anyway, we may ask what their superiority actually means. What are the criteria of being superior? And, what were they actually doing in the old days? In fact, all they did was to exploit your country, making capital out of it. that's it, nothing else. And some of them claim they have always been Christian countries, that is those respecting the Christian principles, 'Jesus commands', but as far as I know, there was only one Christian, and he died on the Cross. So, all in all, it might be the superiority of a hypocrite who has achieved some comfortable standards of well-being, but what's next? I mean, that by having achieved what they are so proud of, they have not answered the questions 'Why?' and 'What for?' yet. And these questions are the most fundamental, eternal questions asked by a human being who doesn't want to live a worthless life which is shared by millions in those 'superior' countries of superiorly vulgar, primitive entertainment culture. Moreover, what makes everything much worse is that they do not bother to seek the answer anymore. And to answer the questions is the *sine qua non* for the survival of humankind, and they are inborn questions which nobody can get rid of. They are the questions asked without even being aware of what you are doing. You ask them in silence, so to speak. Anyway, you'll get a chance to answer these questions, for only then some unpleasant, even disastrous events can be prevented, and making good use of this apparatus you'll have a chance to do so. Anyway, Mr Wahrburg believes you won't fail his expectations, so try your best not to disappoint him. Good luck!"

"I certainly won't," said the president, "and I do appreciate his trust in me."

"That's it for now, dear Mikhail Vladimirovich," said Klug, "we're leaving you now, but I'm sure we'll see each other again."

"You're always welcome, and if there's anything I could do for you, please don't hesitate to ask."

"Actually, there's something we could sort out ourselves, but if you're so kind as to offer us your assistance, we may gladly use it."

"Then please tell me what is it," said the President.

"It's about a certain bank which is involved in world-wide operations, and a man who's one of the main shareholders of it did something very wrong to our friend Ches Adarsh some time ago. A man whom you were so kind to help, Mr Pobog, has a friend who works in banking here in Moscow and has promised to assist us regarding the bank in question's operations, but as you know, it won't be too easy to obtain data. We need to do justice to our dear Ches. Of course, we could use, as you may guess, our own methods to sort out the problem but now for a certain reason we don't want to. Anyway, we're meeting that friend of Mr Pobog – his name's Boris Nikolayevich Ponyryov – today at five and, hmm, we'll see what he can do for us."

"And what's the name of the bank?"

124

"Cheats & Partners, and it's a British bank with branches in Switzerland, here and some other countries."

"Dear Mr Klug," said the president, "before meeting that Boris Nikolayevich, you'll have all the information about the bank in question, and I'm very glad to be of assistance, my friend."

"I'm most obliged, dear Mikhail Vladimirovich, and we won't forget it. Goodbye now, and *bsego horoschevo, dosvidanya.*"

"Now, my friends," said Klug, coming to us, "beer time, and I know a good place to enjoy it. Let's go."

We all – Bea, Kater, Svetlana, Pobog and me – happily agreed to Klug's proposal and after saying our goodbyes to the president, left his residence.

"The place I mean, it's not far from here," said Klug. "We can take a stroll."

And it wasn't, we got there in ten minutes, and it really was a cosy, charming bar. Once we were seated and had ordered beer, Klug said, "For a very long time now, the most distinguished thinkers have been trying to find proof of God's goodwill toward humankind. And, yes, they did find some, but none of it as convincing as this: 'Beer is proof that God loves us and wants us to be happy.' That's it, my friends."

"I agree, and he who said that is a man of genius," said Kater, "let's drink to it."

We were drinking and chatting about this and that, when suddenly there was a commotion at the front door. We heard somebody say, "Let me in or you'll regret it, *proklatye duraki.*"

"Kater," said Klug, "let have a look at what's going on over there."

Kater rose to his feet, but at the same moment a tall, powerfully built man entered, accompanied by two waiters, and one of them said, "So, where's your friend?"

"Oh my, that's none other than our dear Aleksey Pavlovich," cried Kater and, turning to the waiters, he said, "I know the gentleman. You may leave now."

We looked at the man and seeing the way he was dressed weren't surprised they didn't want to let him in. His attire seemed to come from a charity shop that must have been itself on the edge of bankruptcy. A large black beret with several holes in it, on his head. A jacket with no buttons, one sleeve missing, checked trousers of unidentified colour and dirty, worn shoes – in a word – a perfect beggar.

"Let me introduce," Kater said, "Prince Aleksey Pavlovich Golitsyn of one of the oldest aristocratic families in Russia. He's a bit eccentric, as you may have noticed, and he says that being eccentric makes him free. Moreover, it allows him to study an ordinary man, for in this way, he studies society."

"My dear friend," said Klug, addressing Aleksey, "how did you know you would find us here? Were you watching us?"

"I'm not that stupid," replied the other. "Since I know it is Kater's favourite bar, I popped in in the hope of meeting you. Anyway, Mikhail Vladimirovich has told me about your arrival in Moscow, and he's told me he's extremely pleased by your visit."

"I see," Klug said, "and I'm happy to see you. Now tell me, please, have you heard of a certain bank, I mean Cheats & Partners?"

Aleksey Pavlovich burst out laughing. "Have I heard of them? Who doesn't know those swindlers, my friend?"

"If they are, as you say, crooks, how come they are still doing business here, and other places too for that matter?"

"Bah, good question, but easy to answer. Bribes, profit for other banks involved in shady affairs, and connections in high places."

"High places, you say," said Klug. "Here too?"

"Oh yes, and I know exactly who it is."

"Then tell me please who they are."

"But you already…" began Aleksey.

"Yes, I already… as you say, but I still value your own expertise."

"I appreciate that, and as far as I know, they are those members of the government and Duma who oppose any further political changes which would result in transforming this country into a truly open society. They're very old-fashioned, so to speak. You know, old habits die hard, and the leader of them is Ivan Likhodeyev, *byvshiy chinovnik*, who is now the president's chief advisor, and who follows two somewhat contradictory maxims, which are profit before people, and rule by profit, at the same time. In other words, autocracy through kleptocracy, so to speak."

"And the president approves of that?" asked Klug.

"Hmm, good question. It seems he does but then it would be hard to get rid of all those scoundrels at one go."

"Yes, you're right, it would. However, we may help Mikhail Vladimirovich. What do you think, Kater, shall we?"

"Certainly, we may. What about paying him a visit? I mean that Likhodeyev character."

"An excellent idea, yes, go and see him and try to persuade him in your own way, and I don't think that after you have left, he'll be the same man. Go to see him right now."

Kater left us, but before he went, he said, "It won't take long, I suppose. I'll be back in two hours or so."

"He's very efficient, believe me," said Klug. "His powers of persuasion are incredible."

"I can easily imagine that," said Aleksey. "I, myself, wouldn't like to be his adversary."

"Who would?" said Klug. "I wish nobody to be his adversary. While we're waiting for Kater to come back, let's have a drink, my friends," he said. "What would you like to have, Aleksey?"

"A bottle of Stolichnaya if you'd be so kind."

A waiter brought the bottle and one small glass since all the others preferred another beer. Aleksey looked at the glass with contempt and said, "Are you joking? Fetch me a big beer mug."

The waiter was back with the mug, and Aleksey poured the whole bottle of Stolichnaya into it. "*Zdorov'ye, dorogiye gospoga!*" he said, and drank it in a gulp.

Everybody except Klug stared at him in amazement, and Bea said to me, "Fortunately, your habits in this respect are different now."

"Yes, they are, but how would you know what my habits used to be?"

"I'll tell you that another time, darling."

It was five o'clock now and I said to Cyril Pobog, "Where's your friend Boris Nikolayevich?"

"He should be here any moment. He's never late," he replied.

And indeed, his friend entered the restaurant room at that very moment. He was a tall, handsome man, and our ladies looked at him with interest.

"Good afternoon, everybody," he said, kissing the ladies' hands first and shaking the men's.

"Thank you for coming," said Klug. "We have just been talking about a man by the name of Likhodeyev. Have you heard of him?"

"Oh yes, I have," said Boris. "He's unfortunately one of the most influential men in this country now."

"Is he? But he may not be soon," Klug said.

"What do you mean?" asked Boris Nikolayevich.

"Somebody will pay him a visit this evening, and then we'll see what happens."

And that somebody was Kater, of course. When Ivan Likhodeyev entered his house that evening after a long, tiresome meeting with the president and some members of his cabinet, he noticed that mysteriously nobody was there, neither his domestic help nor bodyguards. *Where are they?* he asked himself. *Has something happened, but then what?*

He rushed to his studio to make some phone calls to find out, and once he'd opened the door, came to a halt, petrified. At his desk sat some unknown-to-him individual who said, "Welcome back, dear Ivan Ivanovich. How was the meeting? You must be tired, I suppose. Have a seat and drink some of this excellent cognac of yours."

Ivan Ivanovich stared at the man in amazement, and when he eventually came to his senses, he shouted, "What are you doing in here, and how did you get in here, and who are you?"

"There is no need to be upset, my dear friend. Who I am doesn't really matter, but what does is that I came here to make you an offer, and as for coming here, you know, just some ten minutes ago, your security men were recalled on the president's orders."

"What... what are you talking about? I've just talked to him, and..."

"Yes, you might have talked to him, but you will never talk again, that's the point."

"I won't, you say, let's see," he said, and grabbed the telephone receiver. "Likhodeyev speaking. May I talk to the president? What do you say? I'm barred from... how come...?" But apparently whoever answered his call had already hung up.

*What's going on?* he thought, totally devastated by the news, *and why...?*

"I will gladly tell you why," said the mysterious visitor.

"How would you…?" said Ivan.

"Let's say that somehow I can tell you why. You see, apparently you were with the wrong people, I mean a certain bank you dealt with, particularly an Englishman by the name of Jason Goodman who so far has done no good at all, as a matter of fact. And then we know you believe in nothing higher, and by the way, let me ask you, is there no Devil, either?"

"Of course there isn't any Devil. All these stories are pure nonsense," said Ivan Ivanovich.

"Nonsense, you say," said Kater, "and why do you consider that a nonsense, my dear fellow?"

"Because there's no proof whatsoever that would convince me there's anything else but man, and he alone is in charge of his own affairs."

"You think so, hmm, and what if I gave you some proof that might prove something different, my dear friend?"

"You may try after all," said Ivan Ivanovich.

"You see, first of all you cannot prove there isn't anything higher than man. Secondly, man finds out all the time, all over again, how wrong he was just a while ago, convinced that now he's right, and then the same story repeats again, a vicious circle so to speak. All in all, he finds out all over again that his truth is always provisional. He always wants to discover the ultimate answer, and when he doesn't know a name for it, he calls it truth. In fact, he never finds out truth, but another interpretation of what he takes for truth, and so on *ad infinitum*. At the same time, he's sure that this ultimate truth must exist but never finds it. And the story goes on forever, doesn't it?"

"Yes, I agree," reluctantly agreed Ivan Ivanovich. "However…"

"However," chipped in Kater, "we can do nothing about that, you wanted to say, didn't you?"

"Yes, we can do nothing, therefore—"

"Therefore," Kater interrupted again, "man in his upside-down logic thinks he may always excuse himself for all his wrongdoing. This is what you were going to say. Hmm, I wouldn't be so sure about that. You see, ultimately, it's up to you to decide and that's why you alone bear responsibility for what you have done, and this responsibility cannot be shifted to anything or anyone else, for it's called self-responsibility, the only one that is actually valid and true, and no other one exists. But then, let me tell you there's actually a power which judges your deeds according to what you do, and that power isn't as forgiving as you wish it to be. And now to the point: you want proof, certainly a material one to begin with, that some higher power exists," and here Kater produced a bundle of sheets of paper out of his pocket. "Yes," he said, "What do we have here? Hmm, I see some strictly confidential bank documents, aha, numbered bank accounts but in the names of their holders, some transactions, all in all, some very interesting things."

Ivan Ivanovich was sitting there pale as a sheet with opened mouth, saying nothing but staring uncomprehendingly at his interlocutor.

"Yea," Kater went on, "judging by all that, and these are originals, of course, anyway, never ever are any copies made of such stuff, and I wouldn't like to be in your shoes if Mikhail Vladimirovich gets hold of these papers. It would result, I presume, in at least ten years in some very remote place, don't you think so?"

Ivan Ivanovich said nothing. He just sat there as if turned into a stone.

"So, my dear friend, tell me, what am I to do with all this?" asked Kater.

With an almost super-human strength overcoming his weakness, the other man eventually managed to utter, "But that was all in the bank's vault to which only the director and his vice have access."

"Apparently," Kater said, "there was somebody else who could get possession of it, and if I were you, I wouldn't doubt his ability to do whatsoever he wants to do, so I suggest you kindly agree to whatever he tells you to do."

"I… I agree," said Ivan in a barely audible voice.

"Good, you're a wise man after all. I appreciate that." said Kater. "So, now," continued Kater, "tell me everything you know about that Jason Goodman."

"He… what shall I say," began Ivan, "represents a group of businessmen from England who transferred quite a lot of money up here—"

"Strange," interrupted Kater, "usually the money goes the other way around."

"Yes, it does, but in the matter in question it arrived here because local businessmen wanted to invest it in some very profitable businesses. And then the money goes through several other banks to end up God knows where."

"Not only God may know," said Kater, "and we'll find it out anyway. And in the meantime, so to speak, please kindly call Mr Goodman and arrange a meeting with him for me. Tell him also that a friend of mine is coming along."

"And what shall I tell him?"

"Use your imagination, my dear friend, for you've got some whatever the others may say about you."

Ivan took his mobile and dialled a number. "Good evening, Jason, it's me," he said. "Somebody would like to meet you to discuss a matter which is of great concern to me and some other people."

"And who might it be?" asked Jason Goodman.

"I don't think you know them. It's a gentleman by the name of Kater and his friend Klug."

"Never heard of them."

"Neither have I until this evening, but I assure you it would be very wise to meet them."

"If you say so. Okay then, tomorrow in the afternoon, let's say at five."

Ivan looked at Kater who heard everything, and nodded.

"Yes, perfect, at five at our usual place," said Ivan.

"Good," said Kater, "and this usual place isn't by chance a club called 'U Mojego Podruga'?"

"Yes, it is," said Ivan, "and how do you know that?"

"Bah, how I know that, and a couple of other things for that matter, would be hard to explain. But now you know that we know something, don't you?"

"Yes, I do," reluctantly agreed Ivan.

"I appreciate that, and I'm sure that our cooperation will progress smoothly from now on."

Ivan just nodded upon hearing that.

"Better had, otherwise..." said Ivan's guest, and left Ivan on his own.

Later on, Kater phoned me, saying, "We're going to meet your former friend, Jason, so, get ready, my friend."

"And when and where is the meeting?"

"U Mojego Podruga" restaurant, at 5 pm tomorrow," he said.

"I'll be there. At last, things are going their way."

"As they should, *Ordnung muss sein*, as it always is when we do something, my dear friend," said Kater.

After Kater had left, Ivan tried to grasp what had actually happened but couldn't, and still a stubborn man, he asked himself, *And what if I warn Jason, and try to contact the president after all?*

At that moment, the telephone rang and when Ivan answered it, he heard Kater's voice say, "If I were you, I wouldn't do anything stupid if you know what I mean."

"No, no, of course not, I just..." and thought, *Bloody hell, how could he...?* but couldn't finish his thought for Kater said, 'How could we, bah, good question, my friend. Yes, we can as you should know by now, and I strongly advise you never to forget that again.'

"Yes, of course I won't, and as for now... I just accidentally... but no, of course not. I won't do anything stupid."

He wanted to say something else but didn't manage because Kater said, "Good, and never forget that we always can." And having said that, hung up.

Long after that conversation, Ivan had difficulty pulling himself together. He was thinking, *What does all that mean, and what shall I do?'* But not being able to come to any reasonable conclusion, he gave up thinking and decided not to do anything at all. He was after all a clever man, and knew now that those people... *Were they actually people?* he thought... *Chert eto vosmi*, he said to himself. *I can do nothing but comply.* And we must agree with him that it was a very wise decision.

U Moyego Podruga was a very cosy place, and the next day at five in the afternoon was, as usual, full of people. They were mainly of some artistic profession – poets, writers, painters and actors.

"Yes, a very nice spot," said Klug.

"Isn't he, that man over there in the corner... wasn't he a chef in that TV series, *Kitchen?* A very good TV series, loved watching it, and he's very good, and sympathetic too," said Kater.

"Yes, it's him," said Klug, "and next to him that nasty character Dima. Do you recognise him?"

"Yea," said Kater, "it's him, and at the table next to theirs, Irina Tarannik with Karina Andolenko. Ah, what beautiful women they are, and what about if I…"

"I know what you mean, my Casanova," said Bea. "I may introduce you to them if you want, provided," she turned to Svetlana, "you don't mind."

"No, no, thank you," Kater hurried to say. "Just admiring them, platonically, so to speak."

"Platonically," said Svetlana, "you may do whatever you want."

"That means nothing at all," Kater replied.

"Am I not enough…?" Svetlana said, looking straight in his eye.

"You're more than enough, and you know that," he replied.

Svetlana said nothing but smiled.

"And you?" Bea asked me.

"What do you mean? Ah, if I admire them too? Platonically, of course."

"No, not that. I mean, whether I, myself, am enough too?" I just looked at her, saying nothing. She smiled and said, "We don't need any words, do we?"

"No, we don't," I said, "and you," I turned to Svetlana and Kater, "you two seem to be like us."

"*Konechno*," said Kater, "*ah, ya uzhe propal.*"

Svetlana burst out laughing and said, "But you enjoy it after all, don't you?"

"As a matter of fact, I do," he said. "I can't live without it, and you're the first to get me, so to speak. It's hopeless. Before, I thought I could do whatever… but now I don't need anything else."

"It's him," I said.

"What do you mean?" asked Bea.

"Jason Goodman has come. Look over there," and I pointed in the direction of the entrance where 'the Duck' now stood.

Bea looked and said, "What appalling looks he has. You can see straight away he's a bastard."

"Yes, he is," I said, "but you wouldn't believe his success with women."

"What!" she said. "They like him? Unbelievable."

"Kater," I said, "Mr Goodman's arrived along with Ivan, over there." I pointed with my head to the place where they stood looking around the café.

"I'll meet them," said Kater, "and then you, Klug and me will talk to them at a separate table."

He went to welcome them, and after a short introduction led them to an unoccupied table in the corner where they sat down.

Klug said, "So, that's him, Jason 'the Duck'. Ay, ay, as the French say. One glance and you know he's a prick who deserves a lesson he'll never forget. So, let's join them."

In the meantime, Kater led them to the table, and when Klug and I got there, we were introduced by Kater. Jason looked at me and apparently didn't recognise his former friend at all. "So, gentleman," he said, "we're here to discuss some matters, and I agreed to the meeting on the insistence of Mr Likhodeyev." And turning to Klug, he said, "Would you please tell me what is actually the purpose of this meeting?"

"The purpose is," Klug replied, "to make some financial agreements between you and us, that is Mr Adarsh, Kater and me. We represent a company called Phenomenon which intends to make business in the UK."

"Sorry," said Jason, "but I've never heard of such a company."

"Ah, you know, we're very small, almost invisible so to speak, but believe me, we're very efficient."

"I don't doubt it," said Jason, "but what actually is your business about, if I may enquire?"

"We specialise," Klug replied, "in recovering money which has been obtained by illegal financial operations, namely laundering, tax evasion and the like."

"Hmm," said Jason, "it's a very virtuous activity indeed, but it must be at the same time extremely demanding…" and here he interrupted himself, and I could see a sparkle of mocking irony in his eye.

"Oh yes," said Klug, "it's very difficult, but we're never discouraged, and as a matter of fact, nothing is hard for us to do."

"Aha, I see," said Jason. "I appreciate that, but what might your honourable enterprise have to do with the bank I represent?"

"Bah," exclaimed Klug, "a lot. Ay, ay, believe me. Just take your recent operation here in Moscow." And out of nowhere, a pile of papers appeared in Klug's hand, and he continued, "What we have here, let me have a look. Ah yes, here we are, I can see a transfer of 150 million pounds from London to Russia to finance a Russian company called 'Zvezda', a very legal operation, but then the money was transferred furtively, of course, to Panama, then to Singapore, then to Macao, where it is now. But you're planning another operation, and a much bigger one for that matter. Taking advantage of very low corporative tax in Switzerland, you're going to set up a company in Zurich which will in fact do nothing but invest, let's see, aha, 500 million, in some rather shadowy business in the Democratic Republic of Kongo, Nigeria and Zimbabwe. And what else have we here? Aha, numbered accounts, yes, in Luxembourg, the Caymans, Liechtenstein and some other countries. All in all, a pretty sophisticated operation. Am I right? No mistakes so far, dear Mr Goodman?"

Mr Goodman said nothing. He sat there as if paralysed. Eventually, after a good five minutes, he cleared his throat and said, "No, your information is very accurate, Mr Klug."

"Thank you, sir," said the other, "so now, would you consider cooperating with us, or would you prefer, you know..." He didn't finish the sentence. There was no need. Jason immediately understood what the other man meant and said, "Yes, of course, we would be delighted, Mr Klug."

"We appreciate that, sir, and our representative in London will be Mr Adarsh," said Klug, nodding in my direction.

"Yes, of course, it would be a pleasure. When may I expect you to arrive in London, Mr Adarsh?"

"Very soon, sir," I said, "and I'd certainly like to meet all of your friends that are *Messieurs* Prigstone, Scornbash, Bragly, Witmore, Serfield and Mockingham."

"And how come, may I ask, you know my friends' names?"

"Dear Mr Goodman," Klug chipped in, "believe me, we know much more than that."

"Yes, I see," said Jason, who was still sitting as if welded to the chair, and there was nothing left of his usual arrogance and self-confidence.

"So," continued Klug, "we have arrived at a very satisfying agreement, and I'm convinced that our cooperation will develop smoothly and be beneficial to us all. Mr Adarsh will see you and your friends soon in

London. And now, would you excuse us, but we have another meeting, so all my best and goodbye."

We returned to our company, and Bea asked me, "How did it go with that prick?"

"As you might have expected. He agreed to everything we suggested to him, but Klug says that he'll try something after all, which will, of course, have very unpleasant consequences for him. But let me ask you something much more important. Are you coming with me to London?"

"Yes, I am," she said curtly, "but I may leave you there on your own for a while."

"For what reason might that be?"

"I expect the master will assign me a task, but don't you worry, my love. I'll be back, always."

"I know that," I said, "I've been longing all my life to know, to be sure that someday there'll be somebody like you, and I wondered what was wrong with me as I couldn't meet that somebody for a long time. But then everything was wrong, and it was so because of the way I was thinking, saying 'no' to everything and everybody. Why did I think that way? I don't really know. There is actually no answer to the question, anyway, now I know that if there was any then it would be in words. Now I know that the solution to my problems has always been beyond words, that is, in a way, beyond the world, that is the facts, but curiously enough, at the same time here and now."

"Ah, here you are," said Kater, "as usual," he continued, "so occupied with yourselves that the rest of the world doesn't seem to exist, eh? We are leaving tomorrow, so we bid farewell to our friends here today, for we're leaving very early. You, Beatrice, are going with Ches, but Klug and I aren't, that is, we're going too, but we'll leave you on your own at some stage of our journey to London, for we have something to do in Germany and France. But don't you worry, we'll always be close. Distance doesn't matter, anyway, as that stubborn Immanuel rightly observed, space and time are just our pure forms of intuition, and I agree with him."

So, we rejoined our friends, who were engaged in a very animated conversation, and when I asked what it was about, Klug said, "We're talking about our impressions of Russia, and so far, we haven't reached any final conclusions. Our opinions are rather different."

"Precisely," said Aleksy, "so, let's try again to summarise our views. You go first, Emilia."

"Considering my personal experience, I mean Cyril's trouble, and my overall impression, I can say nothing good about this country. I think that what the Marquis de Custine said is still valid, that everything in Russia is deceit, and it's a dumb nation which has been turned into automata, a nation lacking nothing… except freedom… that is, life, and by reason of his nature, man can't be happy unless he is free. This is a nation of slaves which, as Voltaire or Diderot said, has gone rotten without even ripening."

"Very harsh opinion," said Aleksy, "but yes, it's still valid as you say, but to a degree, I mean, it's much less true than used to be under the tsars and the communists. By the way, as a matter of fact, there has never been such a system as communism on this earth, and the only place it might exist is heaven or hell, for that matter."

"That's it," Klug chipped in, "and as far as I know, it does exist in the latter, believe me."

"I can confirm that," said Kater, "and, by the way, I wonder if you know what the final phase of the historical political system is according to the father of communism, Karl Marx." And he looked around, waiting for an answer, but none of us said anything. "It is comedy," he said, "and I fully agree with him, and it proves that Marx was a man of genius after all."

"That's it, and that was my own impression of him," Klug said. "After we had a conversation at dinner in London, I said to him, 'My dear chap, it took you a long time to arrive at some reasonable conclusion after wasting so much time, and if you'll excuse me, writing rubbish that people were laughing at wherever they were.' And you know what? He admitted he had been totally wrong and said that the only way left for him to save his soul would be a conversion to Catholicism, and then a full honest confession."

"And did he convert?" asked Cyril.

"As far as I know, he didn't manage, for shortly after our conversation, he found himself in a place where no Catholic would like to be, if you know what I mean."

"Oh yes, I know what you mean," said Cyril's friend, Boris Nikolayevich, "and I'll tell you in confidence," and he looked around, lowering his voice, "a friend of mine is an Orthodox Church priest, and he told me he knew from a very reliable source where Marx ended up, and it was the right place for him, the place he had always belonged to, my friends."

"That's it," said Aleksy, "and let's drink to it, Mesdames et Messieurs!"

"Let me tell you," said Kater, joining the conversation, "that the place at which Marx arrived is commonly called Hell, but the word is rather confusing, and therefore hardly anyone knows what he's talking about. Yes, my friends, the seduction of words, this is where all the problems begin, and which is the very source of evil.

"And, by the way, I just remembered a story about Prince de Talleyrand who, on his arrival in Hell, was paid the highest honour by Satan who yet hastened to point out: 'Prince, you exceeded my instructions.' Another story goes that the prince, after tricking everyone, in the end managed to trick God as well. Yes, it would be something, to trick God, bah, and in truth, this is another word people misuse, and abuse for that matter. Anyway, the prince did deserve the honour, but the followers of Marx received no honours. Oh no, it was something very different they received, but I'm not allowed to talk about that, you know. It's classified so, hash, hash, the rest is silence."

"So, my friends," said Klug, "our journey to Russia is coming to an end, and I, myself, would like to say a few words to conclude my observations. And, as my best friend just rightly noticed, the problem is that the logic of our language is misunderstood. Language creates illusions by which many a man lives, and it is still the case in Russia, I mean, the illusion of power which people believe can replace reality, be a substitute of what they really need and want. This power is an anonymous force that still deceives the people of this country as to their true desires and needs. And those who are in power forget that their rule may end unexpectedly, that they don't have power over their lives, they actually don't know what will happen to them the next day. Anyway, power for power's sake, hmm, this is sheer madness. Sometimes I have the impression that the whole world is a psychiatric asylum where, of course, some wards are more comfortable and others not so much, and some simply terrible. In this country, the recent past still exerts, obviously, an enormous impact on everything and everyone. In the first place, people here think in terms of quantity, and this isn't the invention of those 'heroes' whom many Russians still glorify, dwelling now who knows where. It started much, much earlier, and it did for many reasons, and they can't just throw away their heritage. It takes time, and it may take a lot of time for that matter. But the obvious question always present is: What is the ultimate criterion of human deeds wherever and whenever they live? Yes, a man can pose this question, and does so obviously in whatever language he speaks, but the point is whether it can be answered in language, and the question is the puzzle of all puzzles."

"We cannot," I said, "answer the question, for an answer would have to be in language, and the question transcends the limits of language. In other words, we humans are not able to think what cannot be thought, as Ludwig pointed out."

"That's it," Klug said, "so, are they, people, able to formulate an absolute moral criterion of their actions?"

"Yes," I said, "we can, but we can never be sure with regard to what we have just observed, if such a criterion would be absolute, for our capability as humans is limited in this respect, and that's why we never know the ultimate answer."

"All in all, you say," Klug continued asking me, "you are able to formulate criteria after all. So would you tell us what it might be?"

"Hmm," I was thinking hard, but at the same time very reluctant to say anything, for I didn't want to come up with something ridiculous and make a fool of myself. Eventually, I summoned up courage and said, "To my mind, the only criterion I may think of is this. Only that which enhances independence, self-responsibility and awareness of the individual has value, and only society which aims at achieving it may be approved of by all and each one of its members at the same time."

"Yes, I see," said Klug, who seemed to be pondering my definition. "Not bad, but what or who would be the supreme judge of this or any other definition for that matter?"

"I have no idea," I said.

"But I have one. What if there was someone, somewhere, who could judge everything and everyone, wherever and whatever they might be?"

"We cannot exclude that, who knows, such power might exist."

"That's it, it might, but I think it would be better now if we didn't bother ourselves with the question. Let's accept Ludwig's advice: 'What cannot be spoken of we must be silent about.' For the time being at least," said Klug.

"May I ask you something?" asked Aleksy.

"Surely, go ahead," said Klug.

"What is your final opinion of my country?"

"I don't have any final opinions, my friend."

"Okay then, so your temporary opinion, so to speak."

"Hmm, temporary, you say," began Klug, "you know this sort of opinion always comes from a comparison, and I'll tell you what in comparison to other countries yours looks like. And my view will be only to satisfy your and your fellow countrymen's temporal curiosity. But first, please keep in mind that for me there's nothing either good or bad, as it is for you people, for your thinking makes it so. And this thinking is based on comparison which is the criterion of good and bad, whereas everything that exists is beyond good and evil, but you aren't ready yet to perceive that. So, comparison will have to be sufficient for the time being. Yes, some of you may experience revelation and see life and the world *sub specie aeternitatis*, but this isn't communicable. By comparison then. When a most distinguished poet of Dollaria was asked by a journalist when he had been released from the psychiatric hospital, he replied: 'I never was. When I was released, I was still in Dollaria and all Dollaria is a psychiatric asylum.'

"You see. And as far as it extends, it spoils culture. This is an insane country. Some say that alcohol, drugs and the illusion of grandeur keep its going, but the question is for how long…? Not forever, as they believe in their naivety, for decadence cannot last forever. Or that wretched little island, inhabited by self-righteous bastards, as an eminent Russian writer put it, Dollaria's vasal across the ocean, isn't much better for that matter, and some say that all evils of civilisation originated there, and its capital is the money-laundering capital of the world. The aforementioned comrade Marx said that religion is the opium for people, and now it is the other way around. Opium is the religion in those places, and many wouldn't keep going without it. Anyway, it is the best investment available. No other gives such high revenue – *pecunia no olet* is truer nowadays than it has ever been.

"So, where's the truth? Nowhere in this world, my friends, and comparison doesn't establish any truth. And consequently, Russia isn't worse than the aforementioned places. Yes, some things are worse, but some others, and I mean some spiritual things, seem to be better, for where is the spirit today in the world, anyway? For sure, it isn't among shopkeepers."

There was a silence when Klug was finished. What was left to say? Nothing, for the time being, at any rate. The only way to express the truth is to be silent. That's it, for the facts, that is reality, belong only to setting the problem, not to its solution...

I couldn't carry on this way, for Klug chipped in, "I know what you want to say, but the time for saying that hasn't come yet. You'll have a chance to say that much later, and not to us, for those who will listen to you will understand you. All of us here, including myself, wouldn't, to be honest."

"I," Aleksy said, "am very grateful to you for coming to my country, and not only me, believe me. And I'll be waiting to see you again. Thank you, my friends. *Bon voyage et au revoir*!"

"Svetlana," said Kater, "are you coming with me, or...?"

"I wouldn't dream of letting you go alone, you monster."

"Am I a...?"

"Yes, you are, but a very nice one for that matter."

We could see how flattered Kater was after hearing that; his cheeks even went slightly red, which had never happened before, maybe with the exception of one or two occasions in Italia.

"We're going back to Switzerland," said Emilia. "Cyril, like me, is missing that beautiful, orderly and rich country. You, I mean everybody present here, are very welcome to visit us anytime it suits you, and you can stay with us. We have a villa in Ascona which is spacious enough to accommodate all of you."

"Thank you very much," said Klug, "and we for sure will visit you, and very soon, for that matter. Anyway, we have some business to attend to in der Schweiz."

"I, too," said Boris Nikolayevich, "thank you and will be happy to see you again in Russia. *Vsyego horoshyego, dorogoye druzya i do svidanya.*"

And he and Aleksy left. Klug, Kater and I remained at the table, and for a good ten minutes none of us said anything.

"Yes," Klug eventually said, "we'll come here again. I expect some things to happen, or rather our master expects them, and I've already been instructed by him to visit the country pretty soon."

"May I ask," I said, "what you mean by some things are to happen?"

"You'll get to know in due time. I can't tell you that now. All I can tell you is that nobody would have ever expected them to happen."

"Oh no, nobody indeed," Kater said, "but as usual, there are more things in heaven and on earth than are dreamed of in your philosophy. They themselves here wouldn't think of them, to say nothing of other countries."

"So, tomorrow, my friends," said Klug, "we're leaving, and the question is what means of transport would you prefer?"

"I'm for a submarine," said Kater. "You know, I have a weakness for those deeps where a total silence reigns, where there's no news, where nothing happens at all and where you can experience eternity on its own. What do you think? Is there a chance of hiring one?"

"Anything is possible," Klug replied, "as you know perfectly well, but I suggest a train, and then a plane, and I have a good reason for choosing that means of transport, so, agreed?"

"As you wish, my friend. As you know, I'm a very agreeable man," Kater replied.

"A man you are not, and an agreeable one even less," Klug said. "And what about you, Ches?"

"For me, it doesn't matter. Any means of transport will do."

"All right then, let's go for a stroll now so as to have a glance at the city again before we leave," said Klug.

"*Si, signor, andiamo,* and we may see something we have failed to notice before," Kater exclaimed.

"You miss Italia, don't you?" I said.

"*Il dio mio in paradiso,* oh yes, I do, especially those..." but he reflected in time, noticing Svetlana's gaze on him.

142

"I mean those magnificent views, architecture and everything else, of course."

"Yes, and especially everything else," said Klug, clearing his throat.

Beatrice burst out laughing. I joined her, and eventually everybody did, including Svetlana.

"Well," said Klug, "sometime in the future, someone may describe our adventures, and it will be a good account of everything that we have been doing, provided the readers will start to hate a man who has described it. But his description will be good only when he first understands one main thing: that is that what we were actually doing was to question the obvious. This is our philosophy, and only when you follow it will you grasp the heart of the matter of reality. Ah, that reality, it's nothing but trouble. Agree, Ches?"

"Yes, I think that I eventually understand what in point of fact we've been doing so far. Now I know that all the rambling about the so-called 'world affairs', conspiracies and the like, is a mere theatre that means nothing, has no value, and will vanish into nothingness, and the sooner the better, I believe. In other words, all that doth begin should rightly to destruction run, and start again from scratch."

"You've got it, my friend, and I'm sure now you know what to do when you get to London, or anywhere else for that matter. Kater and I will accompany you there, and then you will be left on your own. However, be sure that if you need assistance, someone will come to give you a hand. You know perfectly well now that you can rely on us whatever happens.

"And now, yes, the train for a change. Much more interesting and we'll see more, and who knows whom we'll meet during our journey."

"Excellent," said Kater. "I hate flying. I love trains for anything is possible there."

"So do I," said Bea, "and we can do some things which we won't be able to do in a plane."

"What do you mean, darling?" I asked her.

"You'll see, don't be so impatient."

"I, myself," said Klug, "also prefer trains to airplanes, so if everybody agrees we'll go on the train."

Everybody did, and now we decided to take a stroll and have a last glance at Moscow before we left. We left the hotel and began walking towards Red Square. As we approached it, we saw a large crowd of people gathered there.

"What is it about?" Kater enquired of a passer-by.

"This is an anti-government demonstration," said a man.

"And what is this protest about?" asked Kater.

"You know, as it is what all demonstrations in the world are about. People there express their dissatisfaction with the government's policy, and in this case, it's about the very typical matter in our country, namely the authoritarian powers of *our vlast*, too much executive power, and the courts aren't as independent as they are in other countries."

"Yes, I see, but the history of your country is very different from other countries in Europe where you have always wanted to belong. You have always imported as much as you could of western culture up here and mixed it with all of your heritage that already existed. This is still a half-civilised country by western standards, or so they say. And this is due mainly to all those years of tsarist and soviet rule which rejected all western values, and in the first place rejected God and all moral principles which follow Christian beliefs. There used to be, and still is, too much admiration for power for power's sake, and that prevails in all your actions. Human life as such is of little importance, and it has value only as long as it is useful to the rulers, and in consequence, your people have paid dearly. But during the previous rulers' time, the tsars, things in this respect had not been much different. Anyway, as for strength in this respect, the state is never strong and prosperous unless its citizens are.

"Have I got it right, my dear friend?" Kater asked Klug.

"Oh yes, absolutely. And you know what? I never expected from you such an accurate opinion on the matter in question, or on any other for that matter. No, no, I am saying it isn't that I doubt your intellectual powers, not at all. What I mean is that you have never been interested in politics, history and the like. You always told me these are passing matters of no value, and the further a man strays from them the better for him. A man, you have always said, should be preoccupied with his own life first and only then with the public one. I agree, and all those possessed thinkers like Marx, Engels and many others, succeeded because they seduced millions of people by words. It's been naive of man to think that his personal matters can be solved by those in power. Yes, the seduction of words – not for the first time we mention this, and we'll return to it again. Ah, that mumbling and rambling of a human being is his worst enemy ever. If he only knew. But, as our dear Friedrich says, 'One has only late the courage to this what one really knows.' That's it, my friends. But I'm afraid that man actually deserves what he gets. You know, ignorance and stupidity do not excuse… and it might even be that man is born already stupid, and wicked too. And what does he actually know for that matter?"

"May I say something?" I said.

"You're very welcome," said Klug.

"I'm not interested too much in politics, but since it's always related to history, I'm interested in this country's transformation to democracy, and I think it is a matter of a remote future, and this is because Russia in her history never experienced any truly democratic government, and as a matter of fact isn't ready for democracy yet. Anyway, it cannot be introduced at one go. This country has been ruled so long by autocrats that its people's mentality is still in the past, I mean, so influenced by it that they wouldn't even grasp the meaning of those freedoms associated with democratic rule. But then, my friends, those freedoms aren't freedom itself."

"You've got the point, my friend," said Klug. "They aren't ready yet since their minds aren't, and this is all about that."

"Can we talk about something else, dear gentlemen?" Bea chipped in.

"But of course, *mia bellissima*," said Kater, "and what would you suggest?"

"First, let's leave these people to their own devices, and let's find some cosy café to discuss our upcoming journey."

"An excellent idea," said Klug, "let's go, and I actually know a place nearby."

And indeed, the place we got to in just a ten-minute walk was a quiet, nice small bistro where we sat in comfortable chairs, and when a waitress arrived we ordered coffee and cakes.

"And you, my dear," Kater addressed Svetlana, "why don't you say anything?"

"I wouldn't dare to interrupt your learned conversation, gentlemen, since I'm a simple provincial girl who knows nothing about what you talked about."

"But, my love, we would love to hear your opinion, and as for learned conversations and people in general, let me tell you what one of your country's great writers, Solzhenitsyn, said at an English university where he was greeted with great honours. 'Communism,' he said, addressing the gathered dons, 'came from self-rightness bastards like you.' You see, *mia donna*, that's why we value the opinions of ordinary people. As our dear friend Prince de Talleyrand said, 'No politician can be wiser than the whole nation.' You see, and he did know something about politics, believe me."

"Then, I'll say something," said Svetlana. "I agree with what you've just said, but my approach to people wherever I am is always personal. I mean, whenever I deal with a person, I treat he or she as an individual, whoever and wherever they are."

"Bravo," said Klug, "this is the right attitude that I admire."

"I wonder," said Kater, "why this personal approach is so rare whenever and whatever people do, and I am inclined to think that this is because they don't have any ideas of their own. And in relation to just mentioned western freedoms, this one would be freedom of stupidity, I mean, people there believing what they're told by all the rags they read and the idiot box, and they are happy to do so, that's the point. So, how then can I take them seriously and treat them accordingly?"

"Tell me then," I asked, "what would prevent them from being stupid?"

"Hmm, I don't really know, but there's someone who does and they're still in need of him whoever he is, but all their conceptions about whom this really is are ridiculous, good for nothing, useless, and our master has always been amused by them. These ideas of a something higher, as people say, were actually born in the human mind and the question is: what is the reason for the existence of such a being? The master, of course, knows the answer, and my dear friend here, Klug, is much better suited to tell you something more about the matter in question, for philosophy and psychology aren't my areas of expertise."

"Don't underestimate yourself, my dear chap, you do know a thing or two," said Klug, "but as always, you being extremely lazy except for activities of a different kind, you pretend not to know anything and burden me with all that tiresome intellectual business.

So be it, let me try to explain a couple of things related to the matter our friend Kater started to consider. The so-called higher power? There isn't, obviously, any convincing proof that such a power really exists, and paradoxically, that's it, my friends. Since if there were, people wouldn't believe it. They would question it forever. That's why they believe in something whose existence cannot be proved, and this is the heart of the matter of any faith. You know, the fact is that man actually realises his limitations, his weaknesses regarding his own intellectual powers, and therefore imagines a being which is omnipotent, almighty, and which makes up for man's weaknesses and all his shortcomings. A being which will save him from any oppression and disaster, whatever it is, and thanks to the idea of such a being, man is left with the hope that he always needs, for if he lost it, he wouldn't be able to live. That hope is like a dream, and in this dread, the idea of a god was born. Anyway, people have created the image of their gods according to their own image, and not vice versa as they say. And God of Christianity is the idealised representation of man himself, which is not the case in other religions. Moreover, the Christians established their God as an absolute arbiter of all earthly matters, in the first place, moral principles which according to them should be obeyed by all humankind. They don't tolerate any other religions, and this is an arrogance that contradicts the teachings of the father of their faith. However, as a matter of fact, no human is able to grasp the mystery of his own imagination, for paradoxically he invented a being that is beyond the ability of his understanding, and that was done deliberately in order to make it the supreme judge of everything and everyone on earth. I presume that it was done on purpose by the Apostles and doctors of the Church in order to subdue people by telling them that they had to submit to God because of their ignorance, their inability to comprehend Him. But by the reason of his nature, man eventually dismisses what he doesn't comprehend, for everything that exists must be of his own measure, and in this way, he began to doubt and reject that supreme being of his own invention. Anyway, the question as to whether God exists is nonsensical because any answer is kept within

147

the limits of language that is with man himself, who cannot claim the infallibility of his reason."

Every one of us was listening carefully to what Klug was saying, and once he had finished, nobody said anything. Eventually, it was me who said, "Yes, I agree with what you have just told us, but the problem which is still there is whether we humans still need any gods, or may we get rid of them for good, for they are useless beings that only confuse people?"

"Bah," Klug said, "good question, but in the first place, how come such a being or beings have always been, let's say, obligatory in human history? You see, man has always wanted a god or gods because he has been well aware, as we just mentioned, of his limited powers, so man needed a higher being to act on his behalf, and what's more to legitimise his earthly rule. If a sovereign's subjects were not willing to subordinate to him, they were forced to do so facing the power of a god, and there was no excuse not to obey him. But in the first place, it's about the arrangement of society, its laws, administration, etc. God of Christianity and Islam personifies absolute power, which is not the case, for instance, in Buddhism, and a ruler who represents Him on the earth may therefore claim such a power for Himself so that every subject has to obey, including the ruler, but he as God's representative *per* se enjoys a supreme position.

"Now, when it comes to atheists, things look very different. Since they cannot rely on God to legitimise their rule, they must rule by terror. That's why I say that communism is the tyranny of riff-raff that usurps the power of God. Moreover, people in communist regimes, having been deprived of God, could not appeal to any ethics because the system itself does not base its rule on any moral principles, for the only principle that is valid and compulsory is obedience to the system. The communists rejected tradition and everything that follows, that is, all religious and moral values, and there aren't any absolute standards governing people's lives. People aren't even supposed to think, to have any ideas of their own, and therefore their behaviour shouldn't be based on the faculty of making value judgements on the basis of reason, and deciding between good and evil, and acting upon the decision. As we noticed before, even an absolute monarch has to obey God's moral commandments and to justify his laws on them, whereas the communist ruler doesn't answer to any other power but his own.

"So, my dear friends, on the whole, it seems that a god, whatever he is, might still be needed for the common good. Anyway, he may exist after all. Who knows…?"

"Eh, my dear learned friend," Kater chipped in, "somebody surely knows that."

"And who do you mean?" I enquired.

"You'll find out yourself in due time, believe me."

"It's time to go, my friends," said Klug. "Our train is leaving at 8 pm today. Have you forgotten?"

"Trains," said Kater, "there's nothing like them. You can meet some interesting people, engage in a conversation. Ah, I love the trains."

"Oh yes, you do," said Klug. "I know some of your adventures on the trains. Tell the others the one you had in England."

"Ah, that one, you mean that one when I was on the train smoking a cigar?"

"That's it, for it says something about Albion."

"Yes, it does. Some time ago, I was on the train from Liverpool to London. Once I'd sat down, I lit a cigar, but as you may know nowadays, over there, smoking is not allowed on the trains and my fellow travellers looked at me in surprise and objected to that. I pretended not to understand English and kept smoking. Eventually, a conductor appeared and said, "Sir, smoking is not allowed here."

To which I replied, "But I'm smoking in silence, not aloud."

"Please extinguish your cigar, sir," he said.

"Once I finish it, I will," I said.

"No, please do it right now," he said.

"No, I won't, since I have special permission to smoke wherever I want to."

"Can I see it?" the conductor said.

I reached into my jacket pocket and handed him a small red book which he opened and read what was inside.

"Yes, I see, it seems you actually may smoke not only here but even at Buckingham Palace."

Then he left, and the passengers were giving me strange looks but said nothing.

"And what was written in that small red book?" enquired Svetlana.

"It was given to me by Her Majesty the Queen and it stated, *Whatever Mr Kater does, he does so on my royal prerogative.*

"And did you really obtain that from the queen?"

"Of course I did, and it was just after my conversation with her during which I mentioned to her an evening I spent at Balmoral on the invitation of Queen Victoria, during which we were both very concerned about the future of the country because of the progressing decline of royal authority. Anyway, deep at heart, I'm a monarchist."

"Queen Victoria, you say," said Svetlana, "how come? It was a long time ago, and you…"

"Time doesn't really matter here, my love, believe me."

"If you say so, but tell us anyway why you are a monarchist."

"You see, a sovereign is supposed to be apolitical. He or she personifies a country's history and unity, stays above all political games, and above everything which is just temporary, passing, so to speak, in a country. And since I hate politics with all its bitchiness, I'm for monarchy. You know what von Metternich himself said, 'Politics is like a whore, she gives to those who pay more.'"

"I like it, it's the best definition of politics I've ever heard," said Klug.

We were just passing by the Kremlin when Klug said, "Politics, ladies and gentlemen, is not for us. Yes, we sometimes engage in it out of, let's say, curiosity, but as a matter of fact we consider it something which is an illusion of grandeur for those who believe they can do anything, have the power to decide the fate of others, whereas those poor sods don't in truth know what may happen to them the very next day. But mankind has been unable to create anything else to replace politics, for in fact people love to quarrel, to deceive because only then they're stimulated to carry on living, and that's why I feel sorry for them. They, up there," and he turned his head towards the fortress, "were so sure they outwitted the Devil himself, even trickled God, but *de facto* they deceived themselves. It's a paradox. People invent beings they believe in, and then out of the blue, so to speak, stop believing in them, and then the story might go the other way around and so it goes on *ad infinitum*.

"Their revolution we mentioned before was a revolt of the serfs but organised not by themselves, but by those who came to the conclusion that men should still live in slavery, although of a different kind, much worse than the former one for that matter, for they imagined that that was the way to save people from suffering in future. Moreover, once Russia became the Soviet Union, its poor oppressed people compensated for their wretched lives by the illusion of the power of their country, as if by some magic their delusions could replace real well-being and happiness. But, of course, it couldn't last forever, as history had taught us so many times. The so-called October Revolution, a *coup d'état* in fact, was another crazy idea of a few intellectuals who are so often a curse of mankind. Ah, I can imagine how tired our master is, dealing with all that madness—"

"Excuse me," I interrupted, "but I can see something inconsistent here."

"And what is it, my friend?" asked Klug.

"I mean that if everything is as you described and it is so wretched, then why would all that have been allowed to happen after all?"

"Ah yes, good question. Hmm, let's say it was allowed deliberately. It may sound strange, so let me explain. It is an experiment, a sort of check-up of man as such. By allowing him to believe that he is the measure of the universe, of everything that happens, which is of course an illusion, it had been decided to allow him to live as he wished, and to have any ideas he wanted, but he failed. It had been known, of course, for those who adopted the experiment, that mankind *en masse* would fail with the exception of a few, so the experiment's aim was to find out, to select these very few. But you know, I'm not privy to know everything about it, but you will learn more about that in the near future."

"And who will reveal more about that?" I asked.

"But, my dear friend, you know already who it will be, don't you?"

*Yes, of course, a stupid question*, I said to myself. I did know the person.

"It's 7 o'clock," said Bea. "Isn't it time to go to the railway station, my dear philosophers?"

"Yes, *ma chérie*, it is," said Kater. "Fortunately, we are in the company of ladies who are always much more practical, and without them we would miss not only the train but who knows what else, once we men started our philosophical enquires."

So, we began to walk towards the Bialorusskyi Voksal from where we would take our train to Paris. When we got there, I noticed that Kater was no longer with us, so I said to Klug, "Kater's missing."

"Don't you worry about him. Apparently, some ideas came to his mind."

We went up to the platform, where our luggage had been delivered by the hotel car, and the manager himself was guarding it and once he saw us, he said, "It was a rare privilege to be your host, and I do hope I'll see you again."

"Certainly, you will, and we appreciate very much your hospitality, and in recognition, please accept a small gift, my dear friend," said Klug, handing him a small parcel. "Open it," he encouraged him.

The manager opened the parcel, and his eyes bulged in astonishment and he said nothing, standing there open-mouthed for a good few minutes. At last, he managed to mumble, "But, sir, I don't know, I don't deserve it. I…"

"You do, I know you do and that's that. Don't make a fuss. Take it, for actually this is something that is yours."

I looked at what the manager held in his hands and saw a beautiful necklace with diamonds and other precious stones, apparently worth a fortune.

"What do you mean, sir, saying it's mine?" said the manager.

"Aren't you a descendant of Prince Konstantin Trubeckoyi?"

"And how do you know that, sir?"

"Bah, how do I know? You know, as a matter of fact, I often wish I knew less. And by the way, do you know who got hold of this in the happy days of the rabble, so to speak?"

"No idea, sir," said the manager.

"What was the name of that scoundrel? Something like that small fruit that can be found in your woods – jaguda… jugoda, something like that."

"Jagoda, sir."

"Oh yes, that's it. Jagoda, and that Jagoda, which of course wasn't his true name. Anyway, hardly any name at the time was true. All those bandits were in disguise, so to speak. So, that Jagoda being a chief of the executioners, accumulated as much as he could manage to steal, including the necklace. He too thought in his naivety that he was all-powerful, untouchable, and… and he ended up as his victims did. People say that there's justice after all. Yes, there is, but they don't actually have a clue whose justice it is, my friend, that's it. They don't know and this is the rub."

At that moment, I remembered something, the machine we presented to the president, so I said to Klug, "Tell me, for I have a feeling that that machine we left at the Kremlin is somehow, what shall I say, related to what you have just told the manager, and I mean justice people still believe in."

"Justice, said Klug, "hmm, a very elusive concept, my friend, even mysterious."

"What do you mean?"

"Bah, what do I mean, you say? You see, justice as any other grand concept depends on the criteria we choose to denote its meaning. Usually, people don't have a clue what they're talking about, especially while they use all those words, you know, freedom, truth and the like. They're confused, victims of the seduction of words, as our good friend Friedrich says. Using them, they actually beg for a miracle, salvation from the suffering, but in fact they don't have any precise meaning in mind. With regards to the machine you mention, and everything else we do, it is about something very different, but somebody else will explain that to you in due course."

"You mean Mr Wahrburg?"

"Yes."

"Yes, I knew there would eventually come a day when I'd get my questions answered, and as a matter of fact, not knowing why, I was afraid of that day." We were all standing on the platform waiting for the train that was about to arrive when I saw a commotion some fifty metres away. A couple of the station's uniformed officers were talking loudly and gesticulating wildly. But we had no idea what it was about since they were too far away from us. Suddenly a dark object emerged from the place where the officers stood and began moving towards us with them in chase after it. When it got closer, we saw a big black cat which came to Klug and sat on its hind legs.

At the same moment, the officers arrived, and the older one of them said, "Cats aren't allowed on their own in the station, and this one is a very suspicious one for that matter."

"What do you mean by that, Officer?" asked Klug.

"This cat," said the officer, "seems to understand human speech, you know. Once we spotted it, we said, 'Stop, you're forbidden to be here, back outside.' And it did stop, looked at us, sort of smiled and then sprang to its paws and here it is. But you know, why we actually talked to it, we don't really know. I've never ever before talked to a cat."

"I'm not surprised, Officers. The point is that this one is a very special cat and is allowed to be not only here, but wherever he chooses to be, for that matter."

"Just a moment. How come he may? Who for God's sake gave him that privilege?"

"I strongly suggest you leave God alone, Officer. Anyway, somebody else gave him that permission."

"And who might it have been?"

Klug reached into his jacket's inner pocket and produced a sheet of paper that he handed to the officer, who took it, put his glasses on and began reading. After just a few seconds, completely bewildered, looking at the cat with terror in his eyes, he gave the paper back to Klug and said, "I see, sir, and please accept our sincere apologies. We didn't know, you understand."

"I do," Klug said, "apologies accepted. Don't you worry, you were just doing your duty, and now goodbye, *i vsego horoschego, gospoda.*"

And then the cat spoke up in a human voice. "I don't feel insulted, gentlemen. You may carry on your duties, and all my best for the future."

The officers went pale and stood to attention, listening to what the cat was saying. "You are free to go, Officers," said the cat, and they saluted and left us.

When they were still close to us, I overheard one of them saying, "*Gospodi pomiluj,* what is it, or rather who is it? The president's decree for a cat? What's going on in this country? Anyway, we are lucky the creature accepted our apologies. I dread to even think what would happen to us if he hadn't."

The cat looked at me and said, "And you, my dear friend, don't you think that cats deserve much more respect, being such ancient creatures which nobody has ever actually understood?"

"Yes," I said, "they obviously do since really nobody knows who they really are. I mean, what might be behind their appearance? Yes, they're very mysterious creatures."

"And you're not surprised I can speak the human language?"

"Maybe a bit, however, not that much, for you actually remind me of somebody I know."

"And who might that be?"

"A certain gentleman by the name of Kater."

"You're very observant, my congratulations. You have a good eye for spotting appearances. You already know how much may be hidden behind them, behind all these games which take place all over the world that are actually not what we see, living an ordinary life. The world, where the ideas of ordinary people,' as Arthur said, 'count for nothing as a matter of fact. However, a philosopher should study an ordinary man, for in this way he studies society as his fellow philosopher says. The world they live in is a big theatre where they just play their roles, being better or worse actors, and this is happening especially in these vast countries which made exclusive claims regarding their superiority, demanding respect from other small ones. Moreover, they demand the absolute obedience of their citizens, pretending at the same time to be democratic. Ah, what a useless, bleached word it has become, and we'll return to it again in due time.

"Now, I presume I remind you more of Mr Kater, don't I?" said the cat.

"Yes, you do, the way you talk, and the faces you make, which despite cat-like features are very much like those of Kater's."

"So, you wouldn't be surprised if I actually were him?"

"No, I wouldn't be at all."

"Good for you, my friend, you have just passed another test. Hasn't he?" the cat said, turning to Klug.

"Yes, he has, and what about you? Are you going to remain a cat for the rest of our journey?"

"I'm not sure," said the cat-Kater. "I'll think about it and decide later."

"As you wish," said Klug.

At that moment, our train arrived and we began looking for our carriage. We soon found it and at its door stood a stocky woman in a uniform. We presented our tickets to her and were about to embark but she, looking suspiciously at the cat-Kater, said, "Cats need to have a medical certificate to travel on trains, so do you have one for that one?"

It was Kater who answered her. "And what about yourself, darling? You need it as well and the one you have with you expired a long time ago."

The woman's eyes bulged and her mouth opened but no words escaped through it. She just stared at Kater, petrified.

"I strongly advise you to visit your doctor very soon. your back problem may get much worse if you don't get the right treatment soon. And, as you know yourself, the problem you have is the result of too much rough sex you're having. Am I right?"

The woman's cheeks went red and she staggered, but eventually she managed to utter, "Yes, sir, I will. *Sposibo vashe blogodarodyie, bon voyage, vashe vielichestvo.*"

With the tickets' problem sorted out, and having found our compartment, we were eventually able to sit down. "What about something to eat and drink, ladies and gentlemen?" said Klug.

"An excellent idea, "said Bea, "I'm starving."

"I'll find the train's restaurant, and order whatever you wish," offered cat-Kater.

"You stay here," said Klug, "we've had enough of your adventures for now. I will go."

Kater seemed to be very insulted and said, "I would have never expected such an offensive remark from my best friend. You have betrayed our friendship, you traitor."

"Spare us your dramatics, leave them for The Globe when we get to London. But if you insist, you can go with me."

Kater seemed to immediately forgive 'the traitor' and jumped to his paws, saying, "Then, let's go, my friend."

In the train's restaurant, all the staff seemed to have heard about the mysterious cat, and both friends were welcomed with great respect, and as soon as they sat down at the table, the train's manager in gala uniform came to them, saluted and said, "It's a great honour for us to welcome such esteemed passengers, gentlemen. I do hope you'll have a pleasant journey, and please don't hesitate to tell me if there's anything I could do to make your voyage comfortable."

"Thank you very much, sir," said Kater, "and we are most obliged for your kind words, and if there's anything we need, we'll let you know. Thank you again."

"All the pleasure's mine, gentlemen," said the manager, saluted again and left.

Later, when we discussed the events on the platform and the train, we came to the conclusion that cat-Kater was taken for a superagent of the president himself, travelling on a top-secret mission abroad, so we never encountered any more problems during our journey, and when we reached the Russian-Belorussian border, neither customs officers nor border guards bothered us with checking our documents. Apparently, word had reached the Belorussian authorities as well, so there were no problems whatsoever.

During our journey through Russia and Belorussia, we discussed some of our experiences in the former and came to a few conclusions.

"In the first place, whatever we would say about the country," said Klug, "would be temporary, in passing so to speak, in respect of the future. And, it would be a prejudiced opinion, of course. What I'm going to say is that in any opinion we shouldn't limit ourselves only to what we see and consequently judge as it is now, which is exactly what stupid people do, the idiot-box being their Delphic Oracle. You know, I can't help thinking that all that doth begin is founded on human stupidity, the stupidity of the so-called majority for which the intellect, as our unforgettable Friedrich says, is an awkward, creaking machine that is hard to start.

"It is a mere cliché to say that ordinary people's ideas count for nothing, for history is made by great men, or especially nowadays by the system itself which decides what the masses should know, feel and think. And, as a matter of fact, they enjoy being led like sheep, manipulated, for it would be too hard for them to find their own way. Now, the future of a country mainly depends, among other things, on how educated the majority is, and of course what kind of education it is. For instance, British education on humanities is good for nothing; therefore, they will always be slaves of their tradition, which is a dogma of those narrow-minded, obedient shopkeepers, which gives them the feeling of self-confidence and security. Thus, Britain is an artificial, stultifying place in which there's no place for free-thinking spirit, but as they too need to liberate themselves from their oppressive system, they do that by drinking hard, taking drugs and being degenerate in their sexual desires. And, obviously, this time the Channel won't help them. No, that scrap of water that more than once saved them from severe French and German beatings won't be of any use in the future, and common sense neither, for it is actually their enemy regarding the future. But then, history is being distorted by other nations too. Russia, for instance, claims to have defeated single-handedly Germany, whereas if it wasn't for British and American weapons and all kinds of other supplies, she would have been finished.

"The point is that man has to liberate himself, I mean, to break the chains imposed on him by any system in which he lives, that is by its laws, public opinion, customs and morals. And as long as he is able to do so, he has a future, and apart from Russia and her difficult history, there are other countries which have a future ahead of them, but not Britain, for it is already finished, and so is its neighbour where there aren't any banana trees but still it looks as if they were there, if you know what I mean. They should be there, anyway, because of this their favourite quasi questions, since the problem is they don't have a clue what 'quasi' means.

"Now, my friends, as far as I can see, Russia, as regards the spirit of her people, is a country of the future, whatever else we would say about her. She is the country of the potential, of the perspective, as her citizens believe. However, in their praise of their country, they're inclined to exaggerate a bit. At any rate, the future belongs to where it has not already been suppressed by the past."

"And what about Dollaria?" I asked.

"Ah, them, hmm... I asked the master, but he said he hadn't decided yet. He said he still couldn't forgive them for what they had done to Ezra and tried to do to their genius chess player, Bobby, and of course, a couple of other things too, so they pay for that themselves from time to time if you know what I mean."

"Yes, I do, *vive gladio peri gladio*, they exercise justice toward themselves, so to speak. And what about France and Germany or Poland, for instance?"

"France is arguably the most delightful country in the world. You know what Henry said: 'I prefer to be a beggar in Paris than a millionaire in New York.' And the master told Maurice that he shouldn't worry at all, for his country had always been dear to him and he will always look favourably upon her.

" As for Germany, the master says that she is considering her great minds of the past and shouldn't worry either.

"Poland, hmm, the master has a lot of sympathy towards her, and he says there's always something underneath over there, something with the promise of the future, but he's still worried about their 'hay-fire', you know, they're often over-eager to do something, but when they actually do, it doesn't last long, as it doesn't take long to burn hay, that's it. And they have an inclination to brag, '*puszenia sie*' as their Frei Geist Witkacy put it, and a very unfortunate disposition to celebrate defeats. Moreover, they're so self-absorbed, and to give a picture of it, let me tell you a joke.

"The students at a Polish primary school were asked to describe the habits of elephant, and when they were ready, the teacher asked a little Jas or John what he had written down. Jas stood up and read aloud, 'The elephant and the Polish question.' And by the way, it was their great national hero, Marshal Pilsudski, who said about his own country, 'A great nation, only the people are cunts.' And then there's always been the problem with politicians there, you know, the country has hardly ever any clever ones, and nowadays the typical thing in politics in Poland seems to haunt them, a political party which vows to be just does the opposite, and therefore is called the lawless and injustice party.

"You see, another paradox so common for that brave nation. There's also a poem by their own poet, in which he addresses God: 'You did not make me blind/Thank you for this Lord/You did not make me hunchback/Thank you for this Lord/You did not make me an alcoholic child/Thank you for this Lord/You did not make me hydrocarbon/Thank you for this lord/ But why, oh my Lord, did you make me a Pole?' Ah, one can laugh and cry at the same time, and I think the Poles would need to have from time to time another Pilsudski, who, by the way, once spoke to an aristocrat, who asked the marshal, 'Sir, and what is the programme of this party?' /The party the marshal thought to be the most needed at the time/ And the marshal said, 'The simplest of all: beat cunts and thieves, dear count.' That's it, my friends, it seems they do need another marshal like him now and then.

"As for the present time and their foreign relationships, which have always been a problem, fortunately they have very good relations with Germania, so it will help them, paradoxically perhaps, to keep on burning their fire. Anyway, whatever we would say about Poland, she is a country rich in very talented people, great minds of art and science, and if only her people had more luck with politicians, things would be much better.

"I must also say that the master likes their poetry, especially that of that notorious joker Idefons who, the master says, was a very serious man after all. And, of course, Witkacy is close to his heart, and they quite recently had a chat while the master's portrait was being painted, the so-called psychological study of character, and the master was full of praise for Witkacy's masterly job, but he asked him not to show the portrait to anybody else because it was too accurate, and most people weren't yet ready to know him that well. They chatted all night long, mainly about concepts implicated by the concept of existence."

"And what conclusion did they arrive at?" I enquired.

"None, of course. How could they anyway? They were talking about existence after all."

"We're heading for England," I said. "Shall we visit her neighbour across the water too?"

"Hmm, there's no need, I think. What for anyway? It's a clumsy imitation of England, even vulgarised as an English historian, Michael Butleigh, says. But you know what, there's something incredible about it. Some of the people over there are more English than the English themselves, but at the same time they say they hate England. The main problem is that most of them can't read English, and that's it. And as for their famous rebellions, you know, it is typical for slaves to rebel, slave morality as Friedrich says. And by the way, let me tell you what stupidity means. So it is an inner force to act towards someone's own destruction."

Our train was soon to arrive at the Belarus-Polish border, and until now there had been neither customs nor passport control, so I turned to Kater, who had meanwhile turned back into his human-like representation, asking him, "Why has no official bothered us so far?"

"What for?" he replied. "We have nothing to declare except our genius, as an Irish writer, Oscar Wilde, said about himself. A poor guy, for him and his fellow writers, their own country was not for them. They showed their appreciation of their native land by getting out of it as soon as they possibly could, as one of them said."

Our train was now entering Poland and we heard Polish customs officers checking the compartments. Then two of them entered ours, saluted and asked for our passports. "*Prosze uprzejmie,*" said Klug and handed them his and each of us followed.

"*O ktorej godzinie bedziemy we Warszawa?,*" asked Kater.

"*Okolo pierwszej,*" said one of the officers and added, "*panowie swietnie mowia po polsku.*"

"*Ah, moi drodzy panowie,*" said Klug, "*my mowimy wieloma jezykami jesli o to chodzi, a wasz jezyk nalezy bezwglednie znac, aby uchwycic ducha jego kraju.*"

"*Swietnie powiedziane, szanowny panie. Zyczymy milej podrozy i zapraszamy do Polski,*" said the officer.

"*Dziekujemy bardzo i oczywiscie odwiedzimy wasz kraj, szczegolnie jego piekne gory, jeziora a takze wasze piekne historyczne miasta.*"

"*Jeszcze raz serdecznie zapraszamy, wszystkiego dobrego i do widzenia,*" said the officers and left.

"Yes," said Kater, "we'll certainly visit Poland. I have a certain sentiment towards the country; and what about you, my friend?" He turned to Klug.

"So do I, and now that we are here, I'll tell you why I do like this country too.

Poland is a land of dreamers, yes. I mean, they never want to be who they are and very good for them, for it means they aren't merely self-serving, perfidious, calculating bloody shopkeepers as the English are with their pretence, those hypocrites and prigs. You know what they are most afraid of? Scandals, my friends, for a scandal may reveal who they really are. The Poles are one of the very few nations who still believe in chivalry, while the others only pretend to honour this virtue. And they have always been very good soldiers, and war, my friends, is the ultimate test of man's strength; that is his will, courage and loyalty."

"This is exactly what I think myself," said Kater. "And what about you?" He turned to the rest of us.

"I must admit I know nothing about the country," said Bea, "but now, after what I've heard, I may visit Poland." And then she turned to me. "If you still plan to visit the country, I'll join you, for I find what Klug and Kater have just said very captivating. What about you, Svetlana?"

"I know nothing about Poland, but I do know that it was once under Russian control, and not only ours for that matter, and that my country committed terrible atrocities there, but where hasn't it for that matter? And in fact the worst happened in Russia itself."

"Let bygones be bygones," said Klug, "this is the essence of our ethic, whereas in some countries where there is neither honour nor courage, nor insight, nor pride but pure self-interest, they will pay dearly in the future. And why, you may ask. Because the time will come when humans understand at last the utmost essence of their own nature as my master says, but when I asked him for more details he refused to tell me, saying that even those who are so close to him aren't privy to know everything. And I, of course, didn't dare to ask him why it's so."

"And what, according to you," I asked, "might be the most superior attribute of a human?"

"Courage," said Klug, "whatever your affiliation may be, whoever you are, courage is the superior virtue of a human being. For courage proves man's strength and there's no better trait of character a man might possess."

"Yes, I agree, and I believe the master himself is of the same opinion," said Kater.

"Oh yes, indeed," said Klug, "for him, courage and truth are one and the same, for you need courage to seek truth."

Our train kept moving towards Germany where I used to live for over one year, and liked it there, and surely the Germans are not short of courage, like their neighbours the Poles. As for the former one's attributes, such as orderliness, they are envied and even hated by some who lack them, and this is what is called an inferiority complex of those who must hate, despise somebody else to be able to appreciate themselves. Ah, it so often seems to me that humankind's history has been first and foremost the history of utmost stupidity."

*Yes*, I thought, *human life is a paradox, so in consequence, whatever we say about it must be shown through paradox too.* Language cannot be separated from life. Life, as Friedrich observes, is a journey during which we have incorporated only our errors, and all our consciousness refers to errors. And that hyperbolic naivety of man positing himself as the meaning and measure of the value of things, man as judge of the world, such monstrous stupidity of this attitude has finally dawned on man and bred pessimism – the contempt for that existence. And all this seems to be a paradox. Friedrich is right here.

*I, myself, am a very good example of the paradox of life, but of a different kind, having lived so incoherently, at random, so to speak.* My inconsistent, even nonsensical behaviour is proof of it, but as a matter of fact, who may say that he has always been in the right and never committed any foolish things? Anyone might be a saint or a criminal.

*And now*, I thought, *now, when I undertake that journey, am I wiser and better than I was before? I don't know yet*, I thought, *and all that has been said until now, and all that has been happening so far, shows that I have not arrived at my destination yet, for I am still not sure. I feel I still know nothing. But life being a paradox, small wonder that much of what I say seems to be paradoxical. Otherwise, it wouldn't depict life truthfully. Anyway, whatever we say about life – in every truth about it, the opposite is equally true.*

"What are you thinking of, my friend?" asked Kater.

"I never think. My ideas think for me," I answered.

"Oh yes, that's it, and what's next?"

"I don't have a clue."

"And very good, you aren't supposed to know that yet."

*We are doomed*, I thought. We contradict ourselves all our lives, and start doing everything all over again, and our lives are never-ending tautologies. All our conclusions are temporary and relative and good only for the time being, and it seems we'll never know the final answers, and if we don't know someday we may lose the will to carry on living. Yes, in our lives, we long for the absolute, the final solution to the problem of life which is to comprehend its meaning, but the problem is that we cannot formulate the problem in language, and that's why we cannot solve it. That's why people have always needed a god who would solve the problem for them. But we have made our gods useful for our everyday lives, simplified them, and if there is just one god, the only one we would like to believe in, then only he himself would know what he is like, and any attempt to define his existence would be ridiculous, for we would not be able to comprehend him in language, and even what I am saying now seems to be futile and even nonsensical, but it might at least hint at what errors we make in reasoning.

"Ah, my dear friend, the problem of God, I mean that only one," said Kater, as if he could read my thoughts. "The eternal mystery it is, and not once I asked my master to enlighten me as regards the question, but he said that it would be better for me not to know too much. And I strongly advise you to give up any attempts to solve the mystery. Take it easy, mind you, you may either believe in God or you may not. If you find His existence helpful, then believe in Him, but if you don't, forget the problem. Either way, you would have no influence on the matter in question whatsoever."

"You might be right, my friend, but–" I said, but Kater didn't allow me to finish.

"You've been reminded not once that there aren't any buts. Follow that wise Soren – *Enten* – *Eller* or *Either* – *Or*, and nothing in between. And if you insist, you will find the same advice, but differently formulated, somewhere else, and it says: Be hot or cold; otherwise, I will spit you out. You see?"

Yes, I began now to understand the problem here more clearly, but wasn't really ready yet to understand clearly enough to put it into practice in my life. Kater said nothing more and I was still thinking when Bea said to me, "What are we going to do when we get to London?"

"I'm not sure yet, but I may set up a small company, but I want to start writing again as well."

"Writing? You've never told me about that."

"Well, it somehow escaped my memory, but yes, I did write a few pieces."

"And what was it?"

"Philosophy."

"Philosophy? And what exactly was it about?"

"First, it was Husserl, then Nietzsche and Wittgenstein."

"Ah, them, I've myself read something by them."

"And what conclusions did you arrive at?"

"I believe that for both of them philosophy is a task, which is to question the obvious."

"This is exactly what I think. What a coincidence!"

"It might not be a coincidence, darling, it may be destiny."

"Yes, it may, but then what cannot be spoken of we must be silent about."

"That's it, so leave it for now, and we'll return to that sometime in the future."

"You're right, now it's not time for that. And you, Svetlana," I addressed Kater's partner, "have you any interest in philosophy?"

"Hmm, actually yes, I have."

"And what is it?"

"The philosophy of love, in other words, the Kamasutra."

"Oh yes, I can confirm that," Kater chipped in. "She deserves a PhD in this field, and in comparison, I, myself, feel as if I were just her student."

"Don't be so modest," said Svetlana, "you know something about that too."

"Just a little bit but it helps, for that matter."

"We're approaching the German-Polish border," said Klug.

And yes, we heard German and Polish border and customs officers' voices, and the door to our compartment opened and a German officer said, "*Guten Morgen, Pass Kontrolle bitte.*"

"*Guten Morgen liebe Sorgen, sind sie shoen alle da?*" said Klug.

"The officer burst out laughing and said, "It depends what you mean, sir.""

"Nothing in particular, I just like the expression."

"*Sie sprehen Deutsch ganz gut,*" said the officer.

"*Nicht schlecht, so zu sagen,*" replied Klug.

"Anything to declare, ladies and gentlemen?" asked the officer.

"Nothing except my genius," said Klug.

"Genius is free from any customs duties, quite the opposite – it's welcome here all the time."

"Yes, indeed it is, and therefore I always feel good in your country."

"*Danke schoen meine Damen und Herren, und haben sie eine gute Reise, aufwiederschauen.*"

When the officers left, Klug said, "I've been to Germany countless times and always felt good here."

"So have I," said Kater.

"And what about you?" Klug asked me.

"Oh yes, I like the country and the people. You can rely on them, they're generous and helpful and it's a beautiful and orderly land, and whatever you may say about it, its people are neither hypocritical nor perfidious nor deceitful as some other nations are."

"*Genau!*" said Kater, "and I wish them well."

*I, myself,* I thought, *would like to spend some time here again, to reciprocate the generous help I once received while living here.* Yes, my countless journeys have led me among other countries to Germany, and in spite of my rather uncomfortable situation, I still remember their hospitability and recollect the time spent there with sympathy.

Yes, I carried on thinking, those countless journeys – where was I actually heading for, or was I running away from something… but from what? From my then constant denial, from saying 'no' to everything and everyone? As a matter of fact, I didn't actually know where I was going to. And now I recollected those places and people I had left behind, and began to appreciate them, not all of them, but enough to remember them with sympathy and nostalgia. Had it always been my fault not to be able to be aware of them at the time, that is, to comprehend, to cherish? No, it had not been my fault. It had been my inability, my inner incapacity to be aware of them, that is, to appreciate. At the time, I had felt and thought as I had, and I had not been able to think and act differently, for my ideas, as is always the case, had been thinking for me. But now, what should I do? Should I return to those people and places to see them as if for the first time? Perhaps I should – some of them anyway, many of them at least. So, my future steps in life will move me forwards and backwards. And all my hitherto blunders, side paths, wrong turnings in doing and thinking might have been necessary. They had their own meaning and value on my way to becoming what I am. It seems that we have to commit blunders and errors to understand and appreciate the value of some things; otherwise, we will never see them aright. It seems that there is no other way to get there, and those who think otherwise are mistaken, for it is very human to be in the wrong, and no one is wise enough when one starts his journey through life. I, myself, even had to hate some places in order to appreciate other ones I'd left. I had a feeling that the only way to find out the right direction in life was to esteem some things through denial, so that, in the end, we say yes to them. But even now when I am writing this, I know that I have already made some errors in my reasoning, but at the same time I have the feeling I am eventually on the right path, but the question is that I still don't know where exactly this path will lead me to. But, all in all, I am now sure that we actually never know whether our thinking and the decisions we undertake are the right ones. However, there are people, and plenty of them for that matter, who, being endowed with some knowledge, might be right as regards specific matter, but who are also convinced they can claim to be universally and 'eternally' right regarding anything under the sun, as if they were a Delphic Oracle whatever they judge.

And then, there are those who actually have nothing to say, and because of knowing nothing, paradoxically, claim to be supreme judges whatever the case, and this is precisely because they have nothing to say, but words like rubbish, nonsense, absurd, and the like. On the whole, people might be right temporarily, but even then, how would I know that for sure?

Anyway, at the same time, there seems to be another problem. A man who lives by reason alone is on his own and eventually lives in eternal silence and sadness, for man is made for society, for the joy of life, and not for living for himself. I was under the illusion I was living to achieve an ideal, having not realised that I would never get there, for we actually do not know what ideal means, so we wouldn't know what we were looking for. Yes, our belief in words and their magic which seduces us in our daily lives and all other spheres and still has a fearsome power to lead us astray all over again. So, back to reality, as they say, but how?

I might have been sleeping while thinking, for now when I opened my eyes, I realised I was alone in the compartment. *Where are they?* I thought, and for a moment I was afraid they had left me for good. Had they gone to the train's restaurant, if there was one? I decided to check and came out of the compartment. A conductor was just walking through the corridor, so I asked him where I could find the restaurant.

"I am going there, so please come with me, sir," he said.

We got there in a couple of minutes. I thanked him and looked around, looking for my friends. No, there was no trace of them, and I began to worry. On my way back to the compartment, I heard a loud conversation in a compartment I was passing and recognised Klug's high tenor. Since the compartment's curtains were drawn, I knocked on the door, opened it, and yes, they all were there.

"Have you had a good sleep, my friend?" asked Klug, smiling at me.

"You know," I said, "as a matter of fact, I don't know how it happened, I fell asleep. Anyway, you could have let me know before you left."

"Oh no, my friend, we wouldn't dare disturb your dream, especially the one you were having," and he smiled again.

"What do you mean?" I asked.

"Bah, you know actually what I mean, my friend, don't you?"

Klug's insight into my personal, inner thinking began getting on my nerves, so I said to him, "Would you be so kind as to leave my private, intimate meditations alone, sometimes at least?"

"I'm very sorry, friend, but you know it's a professional mannerism I can't help, but I'll try, I promise."

I just nodded, not believing what he said, and only then did I notice the other people sitting in the compartment. There was a handsome man in his fifties and a stunningly beautiful woman around forty. Bea was beautiful indeed, but I had never ever seen such beauty like that woman, so I couldn't help staring at her for a minute or so. She too was looking at me, slightly smiling. I was sure she must have been accustomed to men's reactions to her awesome looks.

Bea, of course, didn't miss my own, and anticipating future events, she and I would be seeing her quite frequently. The woman was bisexual, and Bea wouldn't mind a threesome from time to time.

"Let me introduce," said Klug, "Madame de Rohan and Herr zu Schwarzenberg."

"My pleasure," I said and bowed slightly.

"*Et voila!*" began Klug, "we were just discussing something that might interest you."

"And what's that?" I said.

Klug exclaimed his favourite "Bah!" and said, "we were talking about reality as opposed to our self-deceptive, dreamlike ideals."

*Here we go*, I said to myself.

"So," said Klug, "let's take music – is it reality or a dream, or both? Anyway, can we actually say something about it in words? No, whatever we say, it wouldn't describe the meaning of music. And to ask whether music is real is a ridiculous question. All in all, we shouldn't talk about music, but just listen to it. This is so obvious that… however, to question the obvious is a given task and destiny of man. Thus, man questions everything and spares nothing and that is where the rub is, this is his beginning and the end. Music, I mean of course great classical music, expresses truth, and music is the only way to convey, reveal it. So, because truth cannot be defined, it is like a dream, a sort of illusion. And whatever those practical people say, man is unable to cease dreaming. By reason of his nature, he is a dreamer.

"But now, I have a feeling that I'm a bit vague here, hmm, words… You know the words of Hamlet, who when asked 'What are you reading, my lord?' said: 'Words, words…' The problem is that people have no other means of communication, but as you know, there are of course different ways to communicate, but not now and here, if you know what I mean.

"And this reminds me of a story about a great poet Konstanty Idefons, for whom (and for many of his fellow writers, of course) a drink was

169

sometimes a necessary, so to speak, companion. So, his wife and friends decided not to serve alcohol whenever they were meeting together. During one of those, Konstanty was very gloomy and hardly said anything, but then he jumped to his feet and went to the bathroom. He was shortly back and in a much better mood, and said to his host, 'I'm terribly sorry but I drank your Yardley, but I swear I'll give it back to you.' And the host said, 'no problem at all, but please not now and not here.'

"You see? That is the rub with the here and now. So often, my friends, we can do nothing here and now, but it doesn't mean anything, in fact, for this here and now actually never exists, I mean, we never do anything just because of the here and now. Moreover, wherever we are, at the same time, we are in our dreams, expectations, and the like. And in this way, we are part of eternity.

"And back to Beethoven and other great composers, their music is eternal for it gives you not only great pleasure, you might be even in a state of ecstasy listening to it, but it is an insight into truth and as such cannot be put into words, cannot be spoken of, and when you listen to it the rest is silence… And in this trance, so to speak, you don't need any words, you have no need to say anything for everything is clear and you see the world aright. It is a state of revelation in which you know, and that's it.

"You know what, my friends, words in fact are the way to escape the truth, and all the facts, the so-called reality, are the means of getting away from it."

I was listening carefully to what Klug was saying and thought, *Yes, he says something that reminds of Plotinus, his Enneads, I once read and was under its spell. We humans need sometimes to be in a trance to live our lives in full. But then, it is always the task of a single man to live his or her* life, and this experience cannot be shared with anybody else. And a man alone is able or not to understand the sense of his life, but afterwards is unable to say what constituted the sense of his life. And, I thought, we can actually paraphrase the well-known Marx's statement, and say, 'Reality is opium for people.' And this is because living only in reality, our lives are merely tautologies. We do almost everything *idem per idem*, and our understanding lacks totality, completeness, unity and how we can then solve the problem of life that is seen only in the vanishing of the problem, that is, in silence. And yes, no one is immune to the problem, whatever one's status in this world…

What is it all about, anyway? Is it about achieving peace of mind, so-called happiness, pleasure, freedom from suffering, or something else? As long as we ask these questions, 'Why?' and 'What for?' are there, and we have no answers yet, and we are still nihilists, that is, we doubt, we deny, we say 'no' to our own and others' lives.

I must have been sleeping again, and this tended to happen more frequently now whenever I was deep in thought, but I did not understand how come I could still remember exactly what I had thought of, once I was back from my dream.

And now, it was Madame de Rohan who woke me up, touching my hand.

"Monsieur Adarsh," she said, "we're soon arriving in France, so I wonder what you would say about my country."

"Hmm, to be honest, I've been there only twice, and each time not long enough to experience anything more than a fleeting impression, but what I have noticed is enough to say that I'm pretty sure I'd like very much to know much more, for I've liked what I've seen."

"I appreciate that, monsieur, and you're very welcome to visit me" (she gave me her address and phone number) "when you happen to be there again."

"Merci beaucoup, madame. I certainly will, and you're welcome at my place in London anytime. When I get there, I'll ring you and tell you my details, for now I don't know yet where exactly I'll be staying."

"Please do, monsieur, I'll be waiting, and in the meantime, so to speak, tell me please what is your sexual preference."

I was taken aback by her straightforward question, especially as we'd known each other for just one hour or so. Anyway, I said to her, "I'm straight, madame."

"Aha, good, but have you ever slept with two or more women at the same time?"

"No, never, but why not? I would if it were by mutual consent," I said, and immediately envisaged her and Bea in bed with me.

"If so, it may be arranged in due time," she said, and turning to Bea, said, "and you, madame, what would you say?"

Bea looked and me, smiled and said, "Well, I wouldn't mind being with such a beautiful woman and my partner together."

"I'm happy to hear that," said Madame de Rohan, "and let's keep in touch then."

Klug and Kater didn't miss a word of our conversation, of course, and it was the latter who eventually said, "Oh yes, I strongly recommend this kind of experience, and if I only could—" but he didn't finish the sentence for he suddenly jumped in his seat. Apparently, Svetlana nudged him in the side.

"I, myself," said Herr von Schwarzenberg, "know something about that, having had pleasure in the company of several open-minded men and women. I've tried almost everything in this respect and always enjoyed it enormously. You all, *meine Damen und Herren sind willkommen* at my place," and he handed us his visiting card, "which is pretty spacious, so it will ensure your privacy when needed." I later checked his address, and it was 'pretty spacious' indeed – a big castle surrounded by a huge park and woodland.

"And, you know," he carried on, "there's nothing worse than prudery. Prudish people always have something to hide, I mean, some evil. They actually hate people, envying them qualities they lack themselves. They suppress their feelings and desires, not being able to satisfy them, and this suppression often results in either depression or aggression, or both."

"Oh yes, *mein* Lieber Herr Schwarzenberg," said Klug, "you're right, that's it. Moreover, he who believes in morality condemns life, as a dear friend of my grandfather said. And he, Friedrich, was in fact the man who embodied the saying, '*Homo sum, et nihil humane a me alienism put.*' And those prudish misanthropic meek prigs, who talk so much of moral principles, are unimaginative cowards, in fact, deprived of the will of life, but who still want to have the upper hand after all, so they condemn those who have qualities they lack themselves. Morality is for them an *ersatz* of will to power, and they're a danger for the future of mankind, because wanting what they call decency, they prevail over everything. They aim at wiping out all joy of this planet. They suffer from *schadenfreude*, not being able to find joy in anything, and we know that there's no life without pleasure. The struggle for pleasure is the struggle for life, as our wise Friedrich observed."

Pleasure, yes, and our struggle for it, I thought, I used to be deprived of it for years and did know something about the desire to get it, and I knew that there were no substitutes for it, no substitutes for having sex with a woman, nor for true friendship, no substitutes for anything genuine. Alcohol, which I used to abuse, is a deceiver, another kind of substitute, and its liberating power deceives us as long as we are under the influence of it, but sooner or later this comes to an end, which brings huge disappointment, to say nothing of physical suffering. The problem is in finding what we really need, and it isn't easy to find it, for we usually don't know what we really need. Many a time, we want something that we actually don't need, that is, it will not give us the joy we expected to get from it. So often I dreamt I wanted something and then came to realise that it wasn't that that I needed. But then, all I was able to do about my desires was to dream about them, for I couldn't fulfil them under the circumstances. I was travelling every day in my thoughts, and all I could do was arrive at a conclusion that resulted in nothing real. With my head up in the clouds, I used to say, but I wasn't with my feet down on the ground, that is, I still wasn't satisfied, and as a matter of fact I couldn't even try to find satisfaction under those circumstances, in reality, but in my dreams, which were substitutes again. And I dreamt how it would be good to be able to have a chance to experience what I dreamt of, but no, I couldn't because I didn't have a chance, having been a total outsider living in a foreign, even hostile milieu which I found rough, petty and stupid. So, how could I be one of them, for only having being one of them would I be able to find satisfaction, and the number of substitutes were limited too, and eventually even those few that gave me some pleasure ceased to work. And then I thought what's next, and I could see nothing. Thus, all I could do was wish for a miracle, that is, something that couldn't and wouldn't be a rational outcome of the course of events, but something that would come out of the blue, so to speak, and then I'd find satisfaction at last. And that thought was my only reason for living.

"We are in France," said Klug, "and we are here to have a beer, which they like too, don't you, madame?"

"Oh *oui*, we do, *cher monsieur*," said Mme de Rohan. "Shall we get some when the train comes to a stop?"

"*Bien sûr, madame*, I'll take care of it," he said, and at that very moment the train came to a halt. We were at a tiny station, where I supposed trains like ours never stop, but ours for some strange reason did. Klug went in search of beer and Herr Schwarzenberg, Katter and I went outside for a smoke. I offered them my Geologises, my favourite cigarettes along with Gitanes. Almost all others I find to be sawdust.

"Are you going to stay in Paris for a while?" Katter asked Herr Schwarzenberg.

"Yes, indeed, I have an apartment in Rue de Hugo."

"Ah yes, a very nice street. A friend of mine lives there too, and he's very pleased with the location."

"I may know him by chance. May I know his or her name?" enquired Schwarzenberg.

"Surely, his name's Auguste Fort," said Kater.

"My dear sir," exclaimed zu Schwarzenberg, "I do know him, he's a great chap, a very good companion indeed but a bit hot-tempered, I must say. You know him anyway."

"Oh yes, I do, but he's a very reliable fellow. You can always count on him. He would never leave you alone if you happened to be in need," Kater praised his friend.

"That's him," said Schwarzenberg, "and actually he's proved that more than once. Let me tell you a story. Once, I was talking a stroll in Boulogne Forest and was approached by two nasty fellows who demanded money from me. I'm not a coward and can defend myself when necessary, but on that occasion, I would have been in trouble anyway for they were big and fit. So, in order to avoid escalation, I offered them some money, which only encouraged them to demand more, but I refused. I could see they were ready to attack me, when suddenly out of nowhere your friend appeared. 'Ah,' he said, 'pleasure to see you, sir, and these gentlemen are your friends?'

"'Actually, they aren't,' I said, 'this is about, let's say, a loan they approached me about.'

"'A loan,' said Auguste, smiling, 'wouldn't it be better to visit a bank, gentlemen?'

"They apparently took him for a bourgeois gullible moron and began laughing. 'I appreciate your sense of humour,' said Auguste, 'but if I were you, I would leave the gentleman alone, apologise for disturbing him and leave at once.'

"Now they were laughing even louder, at which Auguste sighed deeply and said, 'It was your last chance for a peaceful solution to the loan problem, but it seems you are still dissatisfied, aren't you?'

"'Yes, we are,' said one of them and discharged a powerful blow directed at Auguste's face. And then everything happened so fast that I didn't even notice how it happened that they were both lying unconscious on the ground. 'Ah,' said Auguste, 'I hate violence, and always look for a peaceful solution, but you know, quite often people aren't interested in peace. They want war instead and then war they have. At the same time, they are incorrigible fantasists dreaming of paradise where they would like to get to... by force, can you believe it? To paradise by force... I still don't grasp the logic of their thinking, and can't forgive them either because stupidity doesn't excuse. Moreover, it is a curse of our times, a *signum temporis*, my dear sir, and so it is indeed.'

"I," said Herr Schwarzenberg, "thanked Auguste for coming to my rescue. He called an ambulance, and the police arrived too. The officer asked what happened to those guys, to which Auguste replied, 'The gentleman here,' he slightly bowed in my direction, 'was considering a loan for them under certain terms which weren't satisfactory for them, and then, I happened to come here and join the discussion, which eventually ended in disagreement due to one of them attempting to strengthen his application for a loan, so to speak, and these are the consequences.'

"The officer smiled upon hearing such an elaborate explanation and said, 'I see, monsieur, and I actually know these applicants pretty well, and have told them more than once that their day would come, but apparently they didn't believe me, and good for them, they deserved it. I accept your explanation, gentlemen, and you can go. *Au revoir.'*

"Then we went to the Dome to celebrate the victory of reason over brute force, and once there, Auguste said, 'Yes, my dear sir, it doesn't make sense to talk to the stupid, and whenever you approach them, don't forget your whip. Some of them are in such a hopeless state of mind that even psychoanalysis wouldn't help them. Once I happened to talk to Sigmund at dinner and said to him, 'You know, esteemed professor, the world today has gone to the dogs, and only terror might save humanity from total annihilation,' to which the deeply humane thinker responded, 'I still believe in humankind having a compassion deep in its heart which will eventually prevail. The time will come when those basic primitive instincts will vanish, for deep inside, man wants peace, tranquillity and love.'

"'Do you think so, professor?' I said, 'and on what basis do you claim this?'

"'Hmm, actually, I'm not sure, to be honest, it's just my… well, good intention.'

"'Don't you know that hell is paved with good intentions?'

"'You mean of course they are good for nothing in this world.'

"'Yes and no, as usual it depends. Anyway, we have crowds of people over there who intended to do their best, and it paradoxically resulted in their downfall.'

"'Excuse me, Mr Fort, but what do you mean by 'over there'?'

"'I mean hell, of course.'

"'I… I am not quite sure… do you mean that place described in the *Bible*?'

"'Yes, exactly, dear professor. That's what I mean. However, I assure you it looks very different to that of the *Bible*.'

"'But, you know, I would prefer not to discuss what the *Bible* says at the moment. I'm rather in favour of a purely rational conversation based on purely scientific psychological research.'

"'You say psychology, professor, and what is scientific about psychology and science itself for that matter? What science and psychology say is nothing but assumptions, shooting in the dark. You know what Ludwig says? 'The whole modern conception of the world is founded on the illusion that the so-called laws of nature are the explanations of natural phenomena.' Yes, my dear professor, 'the illusion' or just an attempt to simplify, to schematise everything, nothing more than that, that's it, and not the truth about what the world is really like. Moreover, says Ludwig, 'even when all possible scientific questions have been answered, the problems of life remain completely untouched,' you see, dear professor?'

"'Yes, yes, hmm, what shall I say,' the professor cleared his throat, 'but there are still questions left.'

"'Oh yes, there are, and how many of them for that matter? And we're always surprised over there by the numbers of them, I mean, the more scientific discoveries have been done, the more unanswered questions there are.'

"'Yes, yes, I must agree, but I still don't catch something, and please don't take offence, I mean, you just mentioned hell, and we over there so, I'm not quite sure what you mean, if you forgive my ignorance.'

"'Oh no, don't mention that. I'm not offended, my dear professor, and actually it's my own fault for I should have been more exact, but first let me tell you that your description, image, whatever you mean by hell is, I'm sorry to say, ridiculous.'

"'Yes, yes, it might be, but you know, actually I'm not interested in religion, but you have just mentioned terror as the means of saving mankind from destruction.'

"'Yes, and this is the only way left to you, humans. Now, dear professor, you may have read a certain book in which a highly educated man, while in a sanatorium in Switzerland, says that during his conversation with another educated Italian, a great advocate of democracy. Now, professor, first what is democracy today? Hardly anyone knows. The majority mumble some banalities and clichés which have long lost their meaning. What's left are mere tautologies, and what most people are interested in is chow and drink. They have no ideas of their own, and that's why they're manipulated, and as a matter of fact they have to be for they don't recognise the common good.

"'Now, the less interference into the individual's life by a State, the more democratic the State is, and this is not the case these days as you must admit, dear professor. The terror of law prevails and will only increase in time. The power of the system is a terrifying machine within which you may be outspoken, but as you actually have nothing to say, you are commanded, you listen and obey. And even if some have something to say, it changes nothing. There's an illusion of freedom of speech today, for yes, you may say almost anything, so you are under the illusion of living a free life, whereas you are the victim of a trick, that is, you are free to express your opinions but they have no influence whatsoever. *Pust' govaryat'*, as Vladimir, a great Russian singer says. Let them talk, yes, and they may talk themselves to death.'

"'The professor was sitting there with his head down, and you could see how distressed he was, so unhappy that he himself might have been in need of psychoanalysis. Eventually, in a very weak, hardly audible voice, he said, 'Yes, I agree with you, Mr Fort, but I still don't catch where you are heading to telling me all this.'

"'Bah!' exclaimed Auguste, 'I want to deprive you of these few illusions you still have about humankind, and of course, about the effectiveness of the famous treatment you invented. You're still convinced that mankind may be cured by peaceful, compassionate methods. Not at all, dear professor, the opposite is true, for this has all gone too far. I mean the degradation of people *en masse*, their decadence. They're nothing but a slave-morality herd of animals.'

"'Excuse me,' said the professor, 'but you've just said that only terror may save humankind from annihilation.'

"'Yes, indeed, I have, but I mean a very different terror than you usually mean.'

"'And, what is it you mean?"

"'Hmm, I'm not sure if you're ready to hear that, but I'll take a chance anyway.

So, what man needs in fact is order, and it has to be because this is what it is for, full stop. And order paradoxically makes him free, for the order, I mean imposed on him self-discipline, self-responsibility which in turn enable man to exercise his will to power, whoever he is, and there is no greater freedom than this. Thus, freedom and order are the same, but nowadays people *en masse* think the opposite, identifying order with obedience, slavery, indeed, but they don't know yet how wrong they are, so they must be taught to think differently.'

"'And what do you mean by teaching?' asked Sigmund.

"'What I mean is that you are in need of a different system, one in which the current system of values will be reversed. As a matter of fact, the values I mean are already there, but they're in hiding, so to speak. They have to come to light, be made known as those to respect and to follow. For a very long time now, compassion, humility and modesty have been advertised, so to speak, as those to value and respect, but in fact the very opposite ones have ruled mankind due to the monstrous hypocrisy of the rulers to satisfy the weak and meek, in accordance with that famous sermon on the mountain. But, paradoxically, he who gave the sermon was a man of strength and courage, so why he chose to teach the opposite is a mystery.'

"'Yes, yes, I perfectly understand what you mean,' said Sigmund, 'but, you know, I think that people actually enjoy being deceived. I mean, they appreciate illusion so much that—'

"'Oh yea, they do,' butted in Auguste, 'the problem is that their illusions are hopeless, simply ridiculous. Anyway, dear professor, that's all I have to say for now because it's not yet the right time to say anything more. You know, some things are still classified and will be revealed only later. I don't really know when, for it's not up to me to decide.'

"'And who are those decision-makers?'

"'You don't really want to know, Professor, not yet, anyway.'"

"And that was the end of my discourse with the famous Sigmund," said Auguste to Herr Schwarzenberg, who now looked at Kater and said, "An amazing fellow, that friend of yours, so strong in body and mind."

"Oh yes, he is, for he follows an ancient Greek maxim that in the strong body, strong spirit resides.

"And," Kater went on, "nowadays, the opposite is true. Neither is real, in fact. Appearances have replaced reality, and I especially mean these lamentably stupid shows of strength which take place in Dollaria. But the day will come when all these façades will disappear, but my master is extraordinarily patient, as he says himself, provided he gets his own way in the end, and rest assured he will."

"And who is your master, *Mein Lieber Herr?*" asked Schwarzenberg.

"You will find that out pretty soon, but not now."

"It might be better not to know that yet," said Schwarzenberg. "Anyway, let's now join our lovely ladies. We've already made a *faux pas* leaving them alone for too long. And by the way, where's Mr Klug?"

"Bah!" said Kater, "him? I think that sometimes he himself hardly knows where he is, you know, his favourite part of a certain lyric he seems to follow is '*nobody knows where you are, how near or how far.*'"

They rejoined the ladies and me, but Klug still wasn't there.

"I wonder what happened to him," said Madame de Rohan.

"He'll be back sooner or later, you know, madame. He's unpredictable, especially when he catches somebody with whom he can engage in a discourse for then he may talk forever. He might be even worse than Socrates, and actually he once talked to him and, oh, what a conversation it was."

"To Socrates? But he lived…"

"Oh yes, he did, but for Klug, anything's possible, believe me, simply black magic, that's it."

"Black magic?" said Madame de Rohan, "and what is it, monsieur?"

"Uh, uh, this is in truth something very real, madame, but people are so narrow-minded they have rejected it as a superstition, a nonsense, and laugh at those who believe it."

"Would you mind explaining what you mean by black magic being so real?"

"Certainly, madame, all the pleasure's mine. So, people believe they are in charge of their lives, that they rule the world and are in full control of earthy affairs, but nothing, believe me, is more ridiculous than that. They think that the only real existence is that which they can grasp by reason, but their minds have very limited power, believe me, there are more things in heaven and earth than are dreamt of in your philosophy, as an Englishman, Shakespeare, said. But people believe they are the measure of all things, whereas they are the measure of nothing at all. For them, black magic is nothing but nonsense, for they cannot comprehend one thing that they actually know to be temporary, short-lived and relative. And by the way, they used to believe that what Newton discovered would be valid forever, and then that rascal Albert came and turned everything upside-down, didn't he?"

"I see, monsieur, and now I seem to grasp what you call black magic, that is, to believe in the unexpectable, isn't it?"

"*Bravo*, madame, *bravissimo*! That's it. And this belief will open your mind and you'll be rewarded. We'll take care of it soon."

"Merci, monsieur, I'll be waiting, because now I'm sure you are part of that magic, aren't you?"

"Hmm, I don't want to brag, but yes, I have a small share in it, *ma chère madame.*"

At that moment, Klug made his appearance and said, "You'll hardly believe it but I was about to be arrested by plain flics."

"You, arrested?" exclaimed Kater. "How come?"

"Bah, I eventually found the beer I was looking for, Weihenstephaner, that is, and remembering happy old days, I mean, my university time. I sat down on a bench to drink a bottle or two. The sun was shining, memories were floating in my head, I became very nostalgic, and then a bit tired, even sad, and fell asleep. I don't know how long I was sleeping and woke up only when someone stroked my shoulder. When I opened my eyes, two men in suits were standing beside the bench, and one of them said, '*Police. Excusez-moi, monsieur,* but you aren't allowed to sleep here.'

"'But,' I said, 'I wasn't sleeping, I was dreaming, *mes chers messieurs,* and it was a beautiful dream. In that dream, I was back at the Sorbonne where I studied sociology under Professor Durkheim.' They looked at each other curiously. 'And then I moved to Heidelberg, next was Warsaw. Ah! *Mes messieurs,* what a dream it was!'

"One of them asked me then, 'Are you sure you were taught by Durkheim?'

"'Of course I am,' I said.

"'And how are you feeling, *Monsieur?*'

"'*Très bien!*'

"'We aren't sure you are, so we ask you to go with us.'

"'And what for, *messieurs?*'

"'We want to clarify some things, and it won't take long.'

"'Am I under arrest?'

"'No, not yet anyway.'

"So, we went to the police station where I was handed over to a higher-ranking older officer who boasted an enormous moustache, and upon seeing me, he said, 'My colleagues say you said you had studied under Durkheim, and dreaming of those happy days, fell asleep.'

"'*Oui, Monsieur Inspecteur,* I did.'

"'And you say you're well?'

"'Never been better. Anyway, whenever I am in France, I feel much better. *Vive la France!* And let me tell you that at my time at the Sorbonne, my best friend was your esteemed grandfather.'

The inspector's eyes bulged, he cleared his throat and said, 'My grandfather, you say, then tell me something about him, please.'

"'With pleasure, he was a lovely fellow. Ah, those were happy days, our escapades, you know, Place Pigalle, and the like. His name was Maurice, tall, with a moustache like yours, strong guy, but a bit shy with girls. And his beloved Adriane he married at Notre-Dame, I was his best man then.'

The inspector was listening, wide-mouthed, and eventually said, 'And what's your name, monsieur?'

"'My name's Klug, *cher inspecteur*, and yours Maurice after your beloved grandpa, and the second Duchamp.'

The inspector went pale and uttered, '*Oui*, actually, my dear grandpa mentioned your name, and not just once, for that matter. He said that Klug was his best friend, and was very sorry when he heard about your disappearance. Klug was never seen again, and nobody knew what happened to him.'

"'You see, monsieur, I moved to places which are inaccessible for the majority, so to speak.'

"'I see, but is it indeed you? You are still a bit too young to have known my grandpa, if you know what I mean.'

"'Ah, *mon cher monsieur inspecteur*, age, ah, strange thing it is, very strange indeed.'

"'My last question to you then, monsieur, my grandpa received a wedding present from his best friend. Tell me, please, what was it?'

"'It was a Longines watch with my name engraved and the date, 12th August 1913.'

The inspector said nothing. He sat there just looking at Klug with his face changed, and eventually said, 'Yes, there are more things… you're free to go, monsieur. I actually don't know why but I believe it is you who knew my beloved grandfather. *Bonne chance!*' And with some nostalgic look in his eyes, the inspector shook Klug's hand.

"And I left the police station in a car driven by one of the officers I had met first, to the railway station, and here I am."

"I like the story," said Kater, "and especially that inspector. What an imaginative fellow! We must reward him with something, my dear friend."

"Oh yes, we certainly will, and very soon for that matter. He deserves our gratitude," said Klug.

"You know what," said Kater, "we'll support his promotion, and because we know that his wife is unwell, we'll arrange treatment for her at Bad Ragaz."

"An excellent idea, I'll contact our friend Karl in Paris to go about that."

"And you," I asked Klug, "did you really study at those universities?"

Klug seemed to be offended by my question, looked deeply into my eyes, and said, "I wouldn't expect such a question from you, my friend, Do you still doubt that whatever I say is true?"

I went slightly red, having realised what a gaffe I'd made, and said, "Forgive me, my friend, don't know where that stupid question came from."

"It's all right, anybody may forget himself. Humans are very forgetful creatures."

We were still in France, delightful scenery was flowing outside our train's window, and I, myself, began remembering my university days. Yes, I thought, it had been the best time of my life so far, how much I would like to be there again, in the same places, walking the same streets, drinking at the same pubs and talking to the people I knew at the time. Why did I want those times to be back so much, to live the past once again? I knew why – because my life was still so incomplete, despite being with Bea and going through all these adventures. What was missing then? I thought. What was it that I had not completed yet? Was it a sorrow of conscience which reminded me of the blunders, my silly decisions? Yes, I thought, that's it. It was that. So, what should I do then? To make apologies in my conscience wasn't apparently enough. Could I do something more, but what? I was still carrying on the examination of my conscience. I had expiated my wrongdoings but that still wasn't enough. I had to do more so that those people I had let down, disappointed, could be rewarded somehow, for it was up to them to forgive me, not just me making amends. But what could I do? I kept asking myself. Yes, I thought, there is only one way left – to return to those places, men and women, to revisit them so they themselves could forgive me, for my own expiation alone wasn't enough to have peace of mind. So, how could I go about that? I couldn't go over there straight away, just leaving behind what I now have. No, for it would be another blunder, the same I had committed more than once back then. No, first I had to carry on what was expected of me here, now and in the near future, and only then could I think how to arrange my travel back. But it wasn't an easy task because first of all, it wouldn't be possible to see all those people because too much time had passed since then, and I wouldn't be able to locate them all. The places? Yes, but I suspected and actually knew that some of them had disappeared or changed very much to be the same. But despite all that, I still knew I had to return.

*Yes, I will*, I thought, *for if I don't, I will persecute myself with my own recollection of all those faults.* But not only them, for there had been happy days too, and I wanted them back too. Yes, I had to go back.

"You seem to be sad, my friend," Klug said to me.

"Sad? Hmm, yes, you know, memory."

"Yea, memory is the only way to expiate sins, to remember is to have a chance to be better. However, we can't actually mend anything what we have already spoilt, but then thanks to memory we can become what we are, in other words, to see for ourselves what we are, and then what we really need, that is what we want. And then we may avoid making the same mistakes. And now the question is, and in fact the question is always at the very beginning of a man's life story, what actually you, yourself, mean by wrongdoing? Is it doing evil to others or actually not being able to do that, meaning to be forgiving, compassionate, all in all, a good Christian? But then, the absolute majority of those Christians in their actions aren't Christians at all. The faith they claim and proclaim serves them often as the means to pull the wool over others' eyes, cheat them, and at the same time to justify by the very faith their own wrongdoing. And religion perfectly suits the task. Anyway, the main question is what is it all about? In other words, what values are supreme for man to make them his own and to make his own life worth living? Anyway, memory allows you to go much deeper in your consciousness, and not just skate over it. You know, as a matter of fact, those faults of ours give us, curiously enough, the upper hand while we try to understand ourselves. There aren't any saints on this earth, everybody's guilty, and those who think otherwise, considering themselves sinless, are simply hypocrites and prigs. They're the worst part of humankind. But due to your own faults, you have a chance to know yourself better, that is, to understand that everyone else is equally selfish. Those who think of themselves as unselfish and blameless are, paradoxically, the worst sort of selfishness incarnate, and to hell with them where they actually belong, if you know what I mean."

"I think I begin to understand that only now, but slowly," I said.

"And very good, *festina lente*, my friend."

"You two seem to be misogynists," Bea chopped in, "all your mumbling apparently concerns mostly men."

"Yes, it does, we leave women alone," said Klug, "for no woman is a genius. Women are an attractive sex, as our poor Oscar says. But the point is that women know much more by instinct, of which men are very much deprived. Therefore, I sometimes wish I were a woman; however, only sometimes… Anyway, I do appreciate women, and my friend here, Kater, even more."

"He seems to," said Bea, "but you are being cheeky, my friend, I mean, your opinion of us women."

"Not at all, *mia cara* Beatrice," Klug protested. "What I've just said of you is proof you're generally better than us men, and that's why I often leave you alone whenever I discuss humans' bad traits."

"If so, sorry, I beg your pardon," said Bea.

"Apologies accepted, *signora*."

"As my friend rightly observed, yes, I do cherish women," said Kater.

"Yes, you do," said Klug. "I must admit that, and you might even be a hen-picked husband sometime in the future. What do you think, Svetlana, is he on his way?"

"No, he isn't, and in fact I wish he weren't."

"Thank you, my love. You alone understand me," and Kater kissed her on the cheek.

"We are now entering Paris," said Klug. "*Ma chère madame,*" he turned to Madame de Rohan, "so, you're leaving us here but we'll see each other in the near future."

"*Mon cher monsieur,* it was an amazing experience to travel with you and your friends. *Merci beaucoup, monsieur,* and we both," she turned to Schwarzenberg, "are awaiting you at our homes as soon as you can come."

At that moment, the train pulled up at Saint-Denis Station, and we all disembarked from the train. On the platform, Klug, Kater and I kissed Madame de Rohan's hand and shook Schwarzenberg's. When they were about to leave the platform, they turned around and waved.

"Lovely people," said Klug, "and yes, we certainly will see them again."

"So, now to de Gaulle Airport," said Kater, "where we'll say our goodbyes and give you some last piece of advice before you leave."

We took a taxi, and on our way to the airport, Kater handed us the plane tickets and keys to our apartment in London. "You will find it comfortable, I hope. It's in Queen's Gate, so a short distance to everything you may want, including a swimming pool in Baker Street. As for financial matters, you'll visit Baer and LGT Banks where you're expected. Tomorrow, you'll meet a man who will assist you with everything you need arrange. I know him and he's a very reliable chap, and discreet for that matter. So, you won't be left on your own despite us not coming with you. However, in a sense, we will never be too far away, and whenever you are in need, we'll know that, so don't you worry. And now my, friends," and Kater looked at Bea and me, smiling, "I believe you're ready to carry on, and you yourselves know you are. But there is one thing I have to say," and Kater looked significantly at me, "I beg you to remember, my friend, knowing your previous experience with women…" He suspended his voice, looking at me attentively.

"Yes, I know what you mean," I said to him, and then to myself, "*he even knows that, yea, my treatment of women I used to be with wasn't too good, and he expects me to be better now.*

"That's all, everyone. Our play is done, for now, anyway," said Klug. "*Bon voyage* and take care, my friends."

Bea and I stood there, on the platform, watching them leave until they disappeared from view.

# LONDON

---

'Corruptisima re publica plurimae leges.'

Tacitus

That morning, the prime minister, John Oddhouse, woke up much earlier than usual. He didn't actually know what had been disturbing him since he had gone to bed last night. There was something he couldn't put his finger on, and he wasn't well rested, and still felt uneasy. He decided to have breakfast straight away in the hope his good mood would return. *But first*, he thought, *a cup of very strong coffee*. So, he went down to the kitchen, came in there and froze. On the kitchen chair sat a huge, black cat, staring at him with wistful squinting eyes. *How has he got in here, with all this state-of-the-art security system?* thought the prime minister, *nobody's safe these days*.

*Maybe I should call security*, he thought, but for some reason he thought better of it. *I'll speak to them later on*, he thought, *and in the meantime, hmm, he might be hungry. Shall I give* him *some food and milk?* The truth was that he wasn't accustomed to animals, had never had any, and he was surprised by himself now feeling somewhat sympathetic towards the cat. He opened the fridge and got a bottle of milk and poured some of it into a small bowl. But the cat wasn't interested in drinking it at all. *Hmm*, thought John, *apparently he's neither hungry nor thirsty. Strange, but why did he come here after all in the first place?* But it was still a very early hour, and hours before the scheduled Joint Intelligence's meeting regarding

187

some urgent security measures. *But I, of course, won't mention the cat's problem there*, he said to himself. *However, I'm curious as to what their reaction would be if I did*, and he chuckled at the thought of it.

*Let's do some work then*, he decided, and went to his studio, and the cat followed him there. He sat down at the desk, took some documents out of his briefcase, put them on the table and began looking through them, finding eventually what he was looking for. It was a very confidential letter he had recently received from the president of the USA. In his long-winded letter, the president expressed his extreme worries concerning the usual, their countries' strained relations with Russia. The prime minister began to read the letter, and the cat was apparently interested in it as well, for sitting next to him on the sofa, he followed every page of the letter with his eyes. And only when the PM reached the last page did he notice the cat's interest. *A very strange creature*, he thought, *wasn't interested in milk but very much so in politics.*

"Ah," he sighed, *how tired I am of the same all over again. Perhaps I should step down. I'm fed up with all that shambles. How it would be nice to leave it all and go fishing in Alaska.* "Ah," he sighed again, *it'd be liberation*, but what would they say if he left them right now, out of the blue, so to speak? *No, I can't do that*, he thought, *my integrity and public opinion, and a couple of other things. No, I can't right now, maybe next year.* He was so preoccupied with his thoughts that he completely forgot about the letter, and it was only now he noticed to his astonishment that the cat was holding the letter in his paws and seemed to be reading it. *No, it can't be, such things don't happen*, he thought. *I must be dreaming, haven't woken properly yet*, and he closed his eyes, but when he opened them again, the cat wasn't reading the letter any longer. He seemed to be asleep as he lay down on the sofa. *Yes, of course, I must have been dreaming*, John said to himself, *and fortunately everything's back to normal.*

What we must stress here is the fact that the prime minister didn't believe in any witchcraft, supernatural forces or magic whatsoever, and we may reveal also that he didn't believe in God, either, privately that is; he never announced that publicly. The general public considered him a believer, Anglican Church obviously, a very modest man, and the only doubt left was that he had been a bachelor all his life, but not gay, at least.

All things considered, the public thought him a good chap, to a degree of course, as had always been the case with anybody holding his position.

*What's next?* he thought now. *It's only 8 am, the meeting starts at eleven o'clock, so plenty of time left. I'll take a bath, shave and have breakfast then.* He went back to the kitchen, and this time the cat didn't follow him. He had his favourite soft-boiled eggs – he always makes his breakfast himself, we must notice – then a cup of chamomile tea, and afterwards went back to the studio and lit a cigarette. Yes, he smoked, and too much for that matter. When he was smoking, the cat was still asleep.

*What about a swim?* he thought. *A good idea before the meeting, but what shall I do with him?* he asked himself. *Should I leave him here? But then, when the cleaning woman comes, she might be surprised finding the cat and will call the security men, for she knows perfectly well that I have never kept any animals here. Hmm, no, I'll take him with me,* he decided. He went downstairs, put his swimming stuff in a bag, called for a car, put a coat on and went to the front door and the cat was already there. *As if he already knew,* he thought, *but how come? Impossible!* he thought. Anyway, his life was so arranged that he was not used to supernatural phenomena; he was a very sober-thinking man. So, he let the cat out, following him to the waiting car outside.

His chauffeur and his bodyguard said, "Good morning, sir," in unison, and after noticing the cat, the latter said, "What a beautiful creature, never before have I seen such a huge one." The cat apparently was very pleased by the bodyguard's comment for he came up to him and rubbed himself against the leg of his pants. "And how nice it is, anyway, I must say I love cats."

When they got to the swimming pool, all the staff there were a bit surprised seeing the prime minister in the company of the cat, but said nothing. They went to the changing room, and then to the Olympic-sized swimming pool where the PM immediately dived into the water and the cat sat down on the chair by the pool. We must notice here that the cat never sat on the floor, always on a kind of seat. John Oddhouse was a pretty good swimmer, often praised for his stamina, and he swam as often as he could, and no other member of the Cabinet could match his skills in the water. John forgot about the cat for a while, fully enjoying his swim, which was usually crawl, and now when he switched to backstroke, at which he was good too, something attracted his attention. A black object was moving at tremendous speed next to him, and John, stupefied, recognising the cat, choked on water and struggled with his breathing. *No, it can't be true*, he thought, *cats do not swim*. But apparently the one here could, and how for that matter since now all the lifeguards and John's fellow swimmers were admiring his speed and technique. And when John got out of the pool, everybody who had watched the cat's performance congratulated him on his outstanding coaching skills. Some of them, especially cat owners, even wanted to know his exact training syllabus. But John, now eager to get out of the place, excused himself, saying, "Sorry, maybe next time. I've got to go now," and rushed to the changing room.

Once there, he sat down and began thinking, *There's something odd about this cat, something I don't comprehend at all which has never happened to me before. What does it* all *mean?* And then suddenly a thought passed through his head: *And maybe that famous William was right after all.* Yes, now he remembered that verse, 'There are more things in heaven and earth...' We must remark here that our dear John didn't admire Shakespeare, and he even suspected that it actually wasn't him who wrote all that stuff. Of course, he kept that opinion to himself, for if his supporters knew his opinion, it might even be the end of his career.

*Yes*, he thought again, *what does it all mean?* But he decided not to ponder the thought further, and his thoughts strangely went back to the cat. *But where is he, is he still swimming?* He went back to the pool, but no, the cat wasn't there. He asked the attendants, but they said the cat had left the pool just after him. John was slightly upset on hearing that. Moreover, strangely enough, he began missing the cat. *But where's he gone, what's happened to him?* He took a shower, changed, and the cat still wasn't back, so he went to the reception and said he would be very much obliged if they could look for the cat and contact him immediately about their results of the search. Then John left the Magic Leisure Centre (that was the name of that facility), still very distressed.

In the car, his men enquired about the cat, and John said he would be coming later in the afternoon. Once back in Downing Street, not waiting for a call from the pool reception, he rang them first. "No," they said, "we are very sorry, but we couldn't find him anywhere." John thanked them and hung up, now even more worried.

*And what about contacting Scotland Yard?* he thought, but dismissed the idea for he realised they would laugh at him. Moreover, because some of the officers there were known for their contacts with the media, it wouldn't take long and half of London would know his extreme fondness for cats. Then his telephone rang, and when he answered, he heard a woman's voice saying, "Can I speak to the prime minister, please?"

"Yes, it's me, madam, how can I help you?"

"It's about your cat, sir."

John felt a tremor in his chest and hurriedly asked, "Something wrong with him?"

"No, sir, not at all, it's fine. We're just having tea."

*What is she rambling on about? Tea with a cat?* he thought, and she continued.

"And your lovely cat is such a good companion, believe me, sir."

"Yes, madam, I appreciate that, but please tell me, how did you find out my listed telephone number?"

"Ah, your cat gave it to me," said the woman.

"Eh what?" he exclaimed, forgetting his manners, sure he had misheard that.

"But yes, sir, he did that by pointing to my apparatus and to your photo in the open newspaper. Then he tapped the numbers on the table with his paw. What an intelligent cat he is, sir!"

The prime minister was totally bewildered but somehow managed to say, "Yes, he certainly is, madam, but what's next?"

"Ah, he also imitated a steering wheel with his paws, sir."

The prime minister being a very intelligent man understood immediately, and said, "Aha, so I assume he wants a lift, madam."

"I think so, and I'll be waiting, sir. My address is…" but by then, an automatic system identified the lady's number along with her address, and he already knew that, so he said, "Yes, thank you, madam, a car has already been sent to collect him, but please tell me how he found his way to your house."

"He simply knocked on my door, sir," said the lady.

Now John thought of nothing. He just looked out of the window at the sky for a good minute, and then said, "Thank you very much again for looking after my cat, and I allow myself to make you a small gift in recognition of your kindness, madam, and my driver will leave it with you, madam."

"Oh, thank you, sir, but really it isn't necessary."

"No, no, it is, madam, and thank you again, goodbye, and if there's anything I can do to be of assistance, please don't hesitate to contact me, but please do not pass my number on to anybody else. All my best," and he hung up.

*What's going on?* he thought now. For the first time in his life, he could understood nothing of the situation. He tried to find a rational (couldn't think of anything other than that) explanation, but obviously failed, and eventually gave up thinking at all, his mind completely blank now.

Another ten minutes passed, and there was a knock on his living room door. He said, "Come in, please." The door opened and the cat came in.

The prime minister noticed with some surprise that he was relieved, and even glad at seeing him again. He looked at the cat and he too was staring at him with a flash of amusement in his eyes that now seemed to be human-like. And at that very moment, John decided to give him a name, so he began looking in his head for a proper one, and for some reason he preferred it to start with a 'B'. So, he started, "'Be', 'Ba', 'Bu.'" *Hmm, yes, but what's then?* he thought, and made another attempt. "'Bib', 'Bob.'" No, and then yes, he got it at last. "'Bulky', that's it," and saying it aloud, noticed it was as if the cat smiled at him.

*From now on,* he said to himself, *I will never leave him on his own,* and true to his word, Bulky accompanied him everywhere he went. Visits to his friends, the Cabinet and Parliament sessions, official foreign travels, but he noticed that the Joint Intelligence Committee meetings were Bulky's favourite.

Anyway, during any kind of meeting, Bulky always sat on the chair next to John. At first, everybody was surprised at the cat's presence at those gatherings, but in time they somehow got used to it. It seemed to them that the cat was listening attentively to every word said during the meetings, especially the Joint Intelligence's, whose chairman strongly disapproved of Bulky's presence, underlining its strictly confidential character; and we must notice here that the chairman was inclined to distrust everyone, including the prime minister himself, because, as he declared, it was his job. The other participants of the Committee were suspicious too, and there were some who were even afraid of Bulky, for some unknown reason. Some others even suspected him of not being a cat at all. But the prime minister himself not only put his confidence in Bulky, but even felt more confident in his presence, which encouraged him to be bolder in his proposals on every matter, and his position was, he felt, strengthened when accompanied by the cat.

At the same time, he was still amazed by Bulky's peculiar habits, him being a cat. For instance, he never drank milk or water, but only beer or on special occasions champagne or vodka, but never whisky. As for food, only salmon or caviar. That all cost John quite a lot of money considering it was the salary of the UK's prime minister, but he didn't care, for he always wanted to please Bulky's extravagant tastes, and apparently the cat appreciated that. He was always very nice towards John, often close to him and comforted him with his lovely purring and the sympathetic look in his eyes.

But one of Bulky's habits was of great consternation to John. From time to time, Bulky disappeared for a couple of days, not telling John anything – how could he, anyway? – when he was back. And how he could always come in and out unnoticed was a complete mystery. The security service of its own accord tried its best to find out but failed. Anyway, Bulky always came back and that was enough for John.

We must notice something else which at first came as a shock to John. At some especially important meetings, when some of the proposed resolutions were being presented by the members of the Cabinet, Bulky showed his approval by nodding his head or disapproved of others by shaking it, and he was always right when John thought it over afterwards, so after a while closely watching Bulky's reaction, he acted according to it, and it invariably brought good results.

Considering all that, John Oddhouse was devastated when one day Bulky disappeared for good. The prime minister's distress was so serious that he began seeing a psychiatrist, and once even visited a fortune-teller, but all that was good for nothing. His gloomy mood affected all those close to him. He even, which had never happened before, shouted at people, even threatened them. In a word, he was not the same man. But now, his decisions, following Bulky's advice we mentioned, benefited the country, and he became one of the most efficient and popular prime ministers ever, and his approval ratings reached an astonishing 92%.

But the prime minister's gloomy mood continued until the day he found a letter on the desk in his study. How it was delivered was a mystery, and John's enquiries brought no results, but when he eventually read it, his mood changed for the better, for the letter was from Bulky. John was so pleased reading it, and so nostalgic at the same time, that for the first time in his life, his eyes became wet with tears. His entourage was happy too, for John was from now on the personification of politeness and kindness. And his cleaning woman especially was overjoyed upon hearing from John about the letter, because she loved Bulky, who apparently reciprocated her feelings. But John had known nothing of it until now and seeing her joy, he showed his appreciation of her by significantly raising her wages.

But there was one man who wasn't happy at all once the news reached him. We must notice here that the man in question, Boris Dumblodge, was the Chairman of the Joint Intelligence Committee. Boris hated Bulky because of his influence on John, for until Bulky's arrival, it had been Boris who had almost always been able to persuade the prime minister to agree to his schemes.

We should mention here that Boris was a close friend of Mr Jason Goodman, whom we already met earlier when Ches, Beatrice and their friends visited Moscow. And because of Boris and his friendship with Jason, the Magnificent Seven was privy to many of Boris' extraordinary intrigues which, to tell the truth, usually ended up in disaster. Anyway, those grand designs of Boris should never have been made privy to any unauthorised persons, but as he thought himself to be the ablest and the cleverest of them all, he granted himself almost limitless freedom of action. He would pay for his exaggerated opinion of himself when his dealings eventually reached the public due to the investigation of a rather unknown newspaper The *Daily Mysteries*, which was contacted by a man who (we noted that he spoke with a Russian accent) provided the paper with very reliable documents which sufficiently proved Boris' suspicious activities.

So, what then was in Bulky's letter? We are obliged here to warn the reader that it's still classified information under the Official Secrets Act, and therefore we ask him not to divulge any of what he will be told here to a third party. However, on the other hand, considering the very enigmatic character of the letter, there is very little danger of any harm to public and national security, even if its full contents were to be revealed. Anyway, what happened after the prime minister read the letter is still not known to the public. For the obvious reason that you cannot underestimate its stupidity, its greed for sensationalism, obsession with celebrity and the like. But, certainly, there are some who will understand the letter's true value and to them we address its revelations.

So, in his letter, Bulky warns John that a conspiracy is under way to force his resignation, and if it happens, his successor would likely be Boris Dumblodge. We can easily imagine what a catastrophe it would be for the country if it had happened. Accordingly, John undertook immediate steps to prevent it happening. First of all, following Bulky's advice, he contacted a certain Lord Hellbridge (however, we are still not sure whether it was his real name) who could be, said Bulky in his letter, of great assistance to John in the matter in question, and any other for that matter. The lord enjoyed the strange reputation of being an ardent supporter of

unconventional ways of dealing with urgent problems whatever they might be; as he himself stated, the only way to tackle a serious issue was a sort of spiritual approach to the problem. As we may imagine, he obviously had neither many followers in the House of Lords or among the general public, considering their mutual allergy to any of the so-called supernatural phenomena. John himself had little or no confidence in it, either, but as he trusted Bulky, and not just once acting on his advice had achieved good results, he agreed to his proposal and agreed to see the lord. So, as it was, Lord Hellbridge arrived at Downing Street on a certain Friday during a very hot day of May at sunset.

The lord was a tall man in his fifties, with dark hair and piercing black eyes. He was ushered to the living room where John was already awaiting him. They shook hands, sat down on the sofa next to each other (afterwards, John couldn't understand how it happened, for he had never ever sat next to anybody before) and got down to business straightaway.

"It's come to my attention, sir," began the lord, "that you may require my assistance since some nasty characters don't wish you well."

"Yes, indeed," said the prime minister, "they're doing their best to force me to step down, and I don't really know what their motives are for doing so."

"Bah," said Hellbridge, "small wonder since they're the masters of deception, but they aren't actually as clever as they think they are, so don't you worry too much. Anyway, there's a certain coterie which is called the Magnificent Seven, and I know a man who used to know them, and I'll introduce the man to you soon."

"And who is that, sir?"

"His name's Ches Adarsh, and I met him in Switzerland where, due to the aforementioned coterie's machinations, he found himself in dire straits and, as it happens, his problems came to my attention. And as I'm always willing to help people in trouble, those who deserve it, of course, my assistants came to his rescue."

"I see, but is he really a person to rely on, to be trusted?"

"Yes, he is, I can assure you of that as I know something about men."

"Aha," said John, "and may I ask what it is about him that makes you so sure he's the right man for the job?"

"Bah," Hellbridge exclaimed again, "you see, *primo*, he isn't stupid, but still a bit naïve, I mean, his idealism, which despite its flaws I find attractive after all, and this is because those idealists are mostly honest people, people who still appreciate honour in this rotten, decadent world, and that's why not all, of course, but some can be trusted. They are still, let's say, innocent, my dear sir, that's it, for they are dreamers, who dream of a perfect world and at the same time they know that there's only one perfect one, but far, far away for that matter. And in that world, you can meet the most interesting men who have ever lived on earth, and yes, it's true that some of them have done rather nasty things here, but they expiated their wrongdoings, so they've been forgiven."

"Excuse me, sir," said John, "but I'm not quite sure. Is that perfect world you mean what Christians call heaven?"

Hellbridge looked at the prime minister as if he was trying to make sure he was still of sound mind and said, "I assure you that their heaven is very different from the one they imagine. You see, the Christian imagination of heaven is not simply naive but silly, for their limitless hypocrisy makes them believe that their faith alone makes them worthy of deserving what they call eternal life. Thus, they think that whatever they have done, they will go to heaven. Consequently, they aren't capable of being truly sorry for their wrongdoings, and therefore of genuine penance. Their interpretation of the *Bible* is totally perverted. It is a blasphemy, in fact."

John was listening to all of that in great amazement, not saying a word, being so astonished by what he heard and feeling very uncomfortable, even feeble, but eventually overcoming his weakness, he said, "This is a very unusual theory, sir—"

But Hellbridge interrupted him, saying, "No, dear sir, it's not a theory, but practice."

"Practice? Would you please bother to explain?"

"Certainly, my dear sir. By practice, I mean that I actually know somebody whose job is to decide where your life henceforth will eventually lead you, and this is because he doesn't judge people for what are called sins, but for what they actually are, that is, according to the attributes he values most, and these are courage, pride, sympathy and insight, which are the only ones recognised as *sub specie aeternitatis*, he says."

Now the prime minister simply didn't know what to say. He felt as if he were drowning in a whirlpool and it continued until Hellbridge said, "I perfectly understand your confusion, but believe me, some of the most eminent theologians he'd met felt even worse, even after a not- too-long conversation with him," and here the lord chuckled.

"I'm sorry, but we have to continue our chat until you understand where the rub is, which is your conviction that everything that happens can be explained by natural phenomena. In other words, that there must always be some rational explanation of everything that happens, but, my dear sir, wouldn't we have to explain first what this rationality means? Rationality is just a premise from which you conclude something else, but doing so, you might have already made a mistake at the very beginning, that is, your premise was false, and so your reasoning may continue in a vicious circle *ad infinitum*, and end in nothing.

"Now, here in this country you are endlessly talking about evil things which usually happen somewhere else, assuming you're the arbiter of ethics, that you alone can tell good from evil. In other words, you assume, this is a premise in your reasoning, that here everything's fine and you're the model to follow. Yes, your country is not a bad place after all, but, my dear Mr Oddhouse, do you really think that there's nothing to make it better?"

"Oh, there is, and quite a lot for that matter," said the prime minister, "and I see that clearly now in our current situation, I mean that conspiracy and a few other things."

"That conspiracy, my dear sir, hasn't appeared out of nowhere, for long ago there had already been the right circumstances to make it happen. I especially mean the City of London with its banking empire. I perfectly understand your country's need for that, but pretty often it's out of control. They behave as if they were a state within the state, don't they?"

The prime minister cleared his throat and said in a rather weak voice, "Yes, indeed, they are quite often too bold and even impertinent."

"That's it, they are, and this time it is, among other things, that conspiracy they're going to carry out. Believe me, they would go very far to achieve their goals."

"But can we prevent that, for, as you may know, our special services might be of little help. They are actually often good for nothing, useless. With them, everything goes smoothly in novels and movies, and they have great successes, but upside-down, so to speak, I mean those spies who worked for the opposite side. Ah, what a shame. And now, when that rascal Dumblodge is involved, things don't look well."

"No, they don't," said Hellbridge, "but something can be done after all, believe me. But first I would like to tell you a couple of things that at first glance you may see as totally irrelevant to the matter in question, but as things are in this world, everything is related to everything else.

"So, good and evil, do you think you can really always differentiate between them? Do you think you can tell heaven from hell?"

"Hmm, you may try, after all," said John, but there wasn't much conviction in his voice now.

"Oh yes, you may, but I assure you that it very often ends in error."

"What do you mean exactly?"

"Let me explain, and it is in strong relation to the conspiracy which is of our prime interest, and to make everything more real to you, so to speak, let me tell you the story of Ches, the man I've just mentioned.

"He used to live on his own, completely alone, no friends and no woman, in a place not that far away from England, every day saying 'no' to everything around him, and there was a good reason for that. You yourself know the place and would agree with him. Ches compared the place to a kind of zoo, considering its many people's mentality in comparison to other countries in Europe. And the only country where violence was the obvious solution to their problems, the duty of a patriot who, however, for whatever he needed, didn't go to his fatherland, but to his alleged enemy – England. Their patriotism was therefore a pretence, a mask they wore to find recognition, but underneath there was pure opportunism. In a word, the place was an intellectual wasteland, a parasite country too, and small wonder that there was nobody to talk to with the exception of some women. Quite a few of them were pretty and charming, and he often wondered how they could stand those redneck men.

So, all considered, Ches was usually talking to himself, and if occasionally he spoke to someone, it was often disappointment and disgust he experienced. But thanks to that conversation with himself, he found out a lot of things about himself and others that he wouldn't have living in a cultured, pleasant country such as France. Ches found out that he in fact needed to be in such a godforsaken backwater; otherwise, he would have never discovered about himself what he needed to so that he could become what he was. And he found it, curiously enough, through saying that 'no'. And now, on the whole, I mean Ches' experience, we may recall Friedrich's words, 'What doesn't kill me makes me stronger.' And that's it. Ches became stronger and, due to that newfound strength, he learned how to say 'yes' and how to strike back, that is, how to deal with those who insulted him. You see, sometimes you need to be in an alien, hostile place to toughen up and to erase your false beliefs which made you weak.

"In the end, he asked himself a question: 'Why have I come to this place?' And the answer was: 'To experience the very opposite of what I appreciate and need, and through that, to become what I am.'

"But I recommend Ches for our task in question for another reason as well. I mean, he remains still innocent in a certain sense of the word, that is, he has retained his integrity, his frankness towards other people, and he is still looking in them for reciprocation of these feelings, for in fact you are looking for it all your life if you have some honesty left.

But Ches hasn't found himself yet. He is still on his way. As I have already said, he has found what he needs, but he has not fulfilled his needs, and this is because he still thinks he can find the final answer to his problem of life in words alone. Yes, words may help you to find it, they may show you the direction, but alone they are insufficient to complete the task, to achieve the goal. And this is only when you have found the solution to the problem of life, you say 'yes' to your life, and once you have said 'yes', you don't need any more words, for you've found the truth which can be expressed only in silence. You know, for instance, when you are happy, you don't talk about happiness anymore.

"When you are happy, you say nothing about your feelings, for happiness and silence are one and the same. You can't explain why you are happy, for there are no words to describe the feeling. You actually don't know why you say 'yes'. And you may look for that silence, that peace of mind, using different ways. One of Ches' own ways, apart from his linguistic enquiries, was, but he fortunately doesn't do it anymore, drinking hard, not every day, but once he began he stopped only when his health condition was really bad. And he kept on drinking, for he was still thinking he could find the final solution to his life problems in words, but he couldn't of course. So, actually, drinking was an escape, but you actually do not run away far while drinking, and especially when you're back in reality and you're sober, everything is much worse than it was before.

"One day, he gave up drinking, but he couldn't say why he did so. As you now see, not everything can be put into words, and by the way, I often wonder why you mumble so much in this country of yours. You do, don't you?"

"Hmm," the prime minister cleared his throat, "yes, in truth we do, but you know, there are a lot of things to discuss, and democracy—"

He couldn't finish because Hellbridge chipped in. "Democracy, you say the word all over again as if it were a magic phrase which allows you to open a locked door to happiness, whereas it's nothing but a cliché.

"But leave it for now, and let me say more why I find Ches the right person for the job. He knows the conspirators very well, having previously worked with them, but no worries. Now they wouldn't recognise him, and his contact with them, M7 as it is called, was already arranged during his stay in Moscow."

"So, I presume you have some means at your disposal."

"Yes, I do have, and I say that for I'm not in favour of the false modesty of a man who at the same time thinks himself the meaning and measure of the value of things, man as judge of the world. Such monstrous stupidity always makes me laugh. And the most ridiculous trait in him is his longing for salvation after all. As far as I know, just a few are eligible for that, and that is those who have understood that the only way to salvation leads through themselves, that is through their own actions and willingness to admit their nothingness and what follows powerlessness towards the world and life. And this admission is paradoxically proof of the highest degree of courage, yes, that a man admits his weakness, and only then his creator will save him. But, as happens all over again on this earth, the creator's words have been misunderstood, even perverted for convenience, my dear sir, if you know what I mean. And there's no need to explain why that convenience is the main obstacle to admission to paradise.

"Now, the reason I tell you about Mr Adarsh is that we have confidence in him despite him still being in search of himself, that he hasn't found yet what he is. We trust him because we already know what he is, but what he eventually becomes depends very much on himself. Anyway, because he'll be living in this country, I urge you to accept his assistance, which will be of course enhanced by our assistance. So what do you say?"

The prime minister, being a bit confused by all that he was told, wasn't sure whether he should accept Hellbridge's offer, but then, remembering Bulky's great help, something unexpectedly persuaded him, and he said, "Yes, sir, I will."

"Very wise of you, dear sir, so now, because you've accepted my offer, let me tell you even more about him and the reasons he has been chosen for the job.

"His job, as I already mentioned, will be to infiltrate the Magnificent Seven. It won't be an easy task, considering their ruthlessness, cleverness and influence, but I'm pretty sure he will accomplish his mission after all. Anyway, we'll guide and supervise him all the time as we decided some time ago, having found him in trouble. Believe me, he was then hopeless, good for nothing, but as I possess some, let's say, second sight, I already knew he would overcome his weakness and wouldn't give up. And remembering the one who loved the weak and suffering and decided to lead them, you must acknowledge that he himself did not lack that will, and that's why he was the noblest and bravest man, as Friedrich says, who ever lived. We, obviously, don't agree with him on certain issues. However, we still admire him after all.

"For Mr Adarsh, the job in question is a test he has to undergo, but we'll help him to find his way, first by remembering the past, for only then he'll be able to enter the future, so to speak, that is to be aware and self-responsible in order to find his own sense of life. We know that he had to experience humiliation and insult, but he did so to learn how to fight, to overcome his weakness that, among other weaknesses, was his eagerness to please, to be agreeable, even to submit. And his recklessness, his zeal for euphoria – especially that fuelled by alcohol – its liberating power made everything even worse. And perhaps worst of all was his naïve belief that man *per se* is good, that he is a benevolent creature – what a naivety, for he only might learn to be such.

"So, dear sir, I've just preliminarily introduced Mr Adarsh to you, and now the question is whether you trust my introduction," and here Lord Hellbridge glanced questioningly at the prime minister.

John Oddhouse hesitated. He'd already said yes, but now he wasn't that sure, but then he thought, *That Hellbridge is undoubtedly a strange fellow, and why my predecessor decided to award him a lordship is a mystery…* but he couldn't finish his thought, for Hellbridge, as if he was able to read his thoughts, said, "Yes, my dear sir, the world is full of mysteries. Everything's strange for that matter, and to be honest with you, strangeness is my business," and he glanced at John again.

Then something happened to the usual sober-thinking prime minister, and much later on, he still couldn't tell why it was that he suddenly trusted that eccentric character, and he said, "Yes, I accept Mr Adarsh' help."

"Very well, sir, I appreciate this, and from now on, Mr Adarsh will keep in touch with you to inform you how things are, but then for obvious reasons it won't be open contact, and as we have some means at our disposal, you shouldn't worry too much about the outcome of the matter in question. Anyway, you may set your mind at peace, for we'll always be nearby. Goodbye, sir."

"Goodbye, and thank you."

"All the pleasure's mine," said Hellbridge, and left 10 Downing Street.

# SHAUN

'Politics is like a whore, she gives to those who pay more.'
Ascribed to Prince Metternich

'The final phase of a historical political system is comedy.'
Karl Marx

Shaun Swindley's – alias 'The Elephant Toad'– career had been very peculiar indeed. He was born in Dublin, where he attended primary school and at the age of twelve moved to London with his parents. The family was Irish through and through, and remained such while there, so Shaun was brought up in a very patriotic atmosphere. However, as he said in his adult life, he had never been sure what that patriotism actually meant. Anyway, he always emphasised his Irish origins of which he was very proud, but some malicious characters claimed that when he was in his second year at Cambridge University, he was already more English than the English themselves.

He married an English woman – not actually a pretty thing – he never loved, and he did so because of her family's connections, which greatly helped him in his career, and the same nasty people said that career was always his sole aim in life. Shaun had always been very obliging, but at the same time pushy, even impertinent, but towards his superiors always eager to please, and willing to agree with anything they said. That too, of course, enhanced his career, which wasn't too illustrious, to tell the truth, but seemed assured enough.

We should also mention Shaun's superb ability at identifying people who could be of assistance to him, and here he would stop at nothing once he sensed the opportunity of charming his way into their grace. In this respect, he mastered in practice the saying, 'When they throw you out of the door, you should come back through the window,' and on more than one occasion, he succeeded in doing so. But, as always, there were some who regarded these considerable skills with great suspicion, calling him a two-faced opportunist, or even a liar and trickster. But his superiors were always happy having him at their beck and call, for accustomed to comfort, they were in constant need of a chauffeur and gofer and he was perfectly skilled there.

His views, especially him being an Irishman, were unorthodox indeed. For instance, in an interview with an *Irish Times* journalist, he said that the Republic is a coarse place where the natives are obsessed by money; a banana republic, where if there is any culture, it is of English origin. As regards Northern Ireland, he called it a godforsaken backwater, parasite land, and recommended no special privileges at all, for in his opinion that special treatment only emboldened them to increase demands and keep everything as it is. He even advised the opposite; they should be left on their own so that they solve their problems themselves. More than once he said that the so-called patriots there are lunatics and fantasists. "'For them,'" he said, quoting Samuel Johnson, "'patriotism is the last refuge of a scoundrel.'"

He also said that the weather over there largely contributed to their gross stupidity, for it forced them to stay indoors most of the time, and the lack of fresh air significantly limited their ability to think. But not once did he say that he was actually in favour of a united Ireland, saying that as a matter of fact Great Britain always wanted that. Moreover, he said, it was only thanks to the English that the Irish State was established, which would never have happened if those savage warlords had been left on their own. All this, obviously, made him a lot of enemies and he received numerous threats, but we must say to his credit that he never backed off.

Now, the question is how he found his way to becoming a member of M7. It was a very conservative society, however, in some aspects, very democratic, since formally no one of the members was superior to the others. There was no chairman, and all decisions were made by vote and had to be unanimous for that matter. However, since being a kind of gentlemen's club, it was very selective as regards choosing its members, and Shaun was the only non-English ever admitted. The society was a secret organisation, had no website and wasn't housed at any specific address. Its meetings took place at the members' private residences, except that of Shaun, for his was totally unsuitable for that since he lived in a rather modest abode. So, how come he was granted the honour of being admitted to such an exclusive club? As a matter of fact, when his name was mentioned for the first time, and it was Simon who did so, the other members were strongly against taking him into their ranks. They considered him an unrefined foreigner, bumpkin, plebeian, who should know his place and stay where he belonged. So, what was it that made them change their mind and eventually consider his candidature?

Simon's arguments in Shaun's favour were his cunning, connections as an MP and his enormous appetite for money, to say nothing of his hopes for knighthood or even something higher, and his greed to belong to high society, as we know, is rather common for those like him, and Shaun himself ridiculed those of his background who still wanted to sing the International, calling them incorrigible silly fantasists. He also laughed at those who still believed in the prophecy of the Sermon on the Mountain, who were convinced that the meek are blessed and will inherit the earth. He said of them that they believed in God and carried the Devil under their shirts. But deep in his heart, Shaun was pretty certain that some metaphysical power existed; otherwise, who had prevented that irresponsible, scatterbrain humankind from having already vanished from the face of the earth a long time ago? Anyway, it could not have been the dissolute and venal Church. And he was also an Irish patriot too after all; however, not one of those imposters who pretend to be while shamelessly aping and, in fact, admiring their allegedly mortal enemies, the English.

And now we may ask again, what was it that persuaded the Society to eventually accept him? It was, as we've already mentioned before, Simon who supported him, and thanks to his arguments, the other members said yes to Shaun's membership.

Simon in his expose during the vote meeting said that they needed Shaun because of his incredible knack for finance, and since *pecunia non olet*, and because of their urgent need of funds, they agreed. Shaun wasn't rich yet because he hadn't had the opportunity to make money, for he lacked capital. How Simon, being a parish priest, managed to notice Shaun's skills was a mystery. Anyway, the others were somehow persuaded by his confidence in that particular talent of Shaun's which later on proved to be true indeed. His candidacy before the final vote was also, not surprisingly, enforced by Jason, the banker, persuaded too by Simon's expose.

After the meeting that took place at Jason's apartment, Shaun was invited in (he had awaited the decision at a café nearby) and there was a short ceremony, at which he was sworn to absolute secrecy and unreserved allegiance to the Society for life. Afterwards, they all went to Bellamy's to celebrate the occasion. None of them was a heavy drinker; however, during the celebration, Shaun drank more than usual, being so happy to fulfil his dream at last.

He'd always dreamed of that day when he would sit down in a place like this as an equal to the privileged, the establishment. On the other hand, he felt uneasy. *Do I really belong to this company?* he kept asking himself. *They will never really treat me as their equal*, he thought. *I'm only here because they need me.* Anyway, whatever we might say of Shaun, he was rather honest with himself and had no illusions about his newfound friends. *Let's wait and see*, he said to himself. He looked around and caught sight of a middle-aged lady sitting at the table next to theirs. *She's surely one of them*, he thought, *these airs and graces, and all the rest.* And at that moment, the lady in question, as if she knew she was under his scrutiny, looked at him briefly, and Shaun, being observant, didn't fail to notice something else in the way she looked at him. *Hmm*, he thought, *she might be something more, after all*, but what it was, he couldn't yet tell.

Now, it was Justin's turn to say something, and every one of the others, being aware of his amazing rhetorical skills, expected something really impressive.

"My dear friends," he began, "I am very happy to be here because for the first time in my life I have the opportunity to be in the company of an Irishman I can trust. Shaun is now our friend, and we're delighted to have him among us as we need people like him, and we put a lot of hope in him and know we won't be disappointed. Each of us has a specific task according to his abilities, and his most spectacular is to sneak in anywhere he wants to. Moreover, hardly anybody can resist the power of his charm, his willingness to please and his ease.

"Comrades!" loudly announced Justin, "let's drink to his health and welcome Shaun!" Everybody stood up, raised his glass of champagne and drank, and they were about to sit down when the lady that had attracted Shaun's interest came up to them and said, "Excuse me, gentlemen," and every one of them looked at her in amazement when she came close to Shaun and said, "you're Mr Swindley, aren't you?"

"Yes, I am," he said, totally confounded now.

"You don't know me, but I've actually heard of you, and by the way, let me introduce myself. Fiona Titsbrook."

"My pleasure," said Shaun, still feeling uneasy. "Would you mind telling me how come you know who I am?"

"A good friend of mine, Suzan Boobsham, told me about you," and she smiled at him.

"Ah, Suzan," said John, and for an unknown reason went red in his face. "Yes, yes, of course," he stammered, "and how is she these days, madam?"

"She's fine but, you know…" and looking at him significantly, added, "she's slightly disappointed not to have seen you for a while, if you know what I mean."

"Yes, yes, of course," mumbled Shaun. "Tell her, please, that I'm very sorry and will see her at the first convenient opportunity."

"Make sure you do, dear Mr Swindley. She's expecting you to visit her soon."

Now, every one of his new friends looked at him curiously but said nothing, and it was only when they had sat down again that Justin said, "Aye, aye, my dear friend," looking at Shaun. "I wouldn't expect you to be such a good friend of Mrs Boobsham. She's is, hmm, a delightful lady, my congratulations."

Shaun, still red in the face, muttered, "She certainly is, and—"

But Justin chipped in, "Yes, very delightful, and blessed by nature for that matter." And he smiled knowingly at Shaun.

Let us say here that indeed Mrs Boobsham was richly endowed by nature in one particular respect, that is, her magnificent breasts, which attracted the attention of every man, and those who were lucky enough to know her closer said she was especially skilled at pleasing a man using that charm of hers, and not only that one for that matter. She enjoyed having two or more men at the same time, and they could do with her anything they wanted, and she even encouraged them to do so and was very inventive telling them how they should proceed. She even used male escorts to satisfy her insatiable appetite for sex, and they said afterwards she had been better than the pros. Justin himself used to be her lover and knew perfectly well how efficient she was.

"So, if I were you, dear friend, I wouldn't wait long to see her again," he said now. "You know what I mean, and besides," here he looked at the others, "she's very well connected. She is a baroness, however, one of those fake aristocrats created by Tony, who being fed up with the House of Lords, demolished it to create the one that would have no say whatsoever. Still, because appearances are often more important than reality in England, you know, tradition, this new breed enjoy some influence in the game."

*Hmm*, Shaun thought, *yes, I may see her again, and indeed she has a lot to offer, but the problem is my wife who suspects something, but fortunately hasn't found out anything to prove her suspicion. What shall I do?* He remembered the delights of what Suzan had to offer, and her unrestrained sexual appetite. And another reason for seeing her again was his wife's prudery and certain coldness in sex, which for her was just a tiresome marital duty. And after some hesitation, he made up his mind and decided to see her the next day. And then he said to Justin, "You're right, I'll see her."

"Good man," said Justin, "and pass my best on to her."

"Certainly, I will," and looking questioningly at his friend, said, "have you had…?"

"Yes, I had the pleasure a few years back, and still remember it because it was something to remember. She's a very ingenious woman, and you know what I mean."

"Oh yes, I do," replied Shaun.

None of the others had paid much attention to the conversation between Shaun and Justin because they were discussing a certain ethical problem which had appeared out of the blue and out of place, in fact, for you don't discuss such matters on such an occasion. Whatever, the problem was there and was about the relationship between moral principles and the world of finance.

"In my view," said Jason, after all, an expert in the subject, "there's no relationship at all. These two cannot be reconciled, in other words, neither money nor morality. Only when you're a hypocrite do you claim to have moral principles while dealing with money, and politics is the same for that matter, but these days, hypocrisy is everywhere, and it's been *signum temporis* for a long time now. And the question is why we still need hypocrisy."

"I disagree," said Simon, and of course everybody expected him to do so, him being a priest. "Christian values are still there, and we respect them as far as we can."

"It's true, my friend," chipped in Graham who, being a philosopher, said 'no' to almost everything, "but the other way around, for as far as you can, you don't respect them, for if you did, you wouldn't make any money, and in politics you would be a naïve, gullible fantasist who would achieve nothing. People are so accustomed to lies, which being disguised by hypocrisy are eventually accepted, and they would be even surprised to hear the truth, especially in this country of ours."

"No, no, no!" exclaimed Simon, "I strongly disapprove of your opinion. You are a cynic, deprived of any moral principles, a nihilist, pleasure being all you care about. All in all, you're an antichrist, shame on you!"

"Ha ha ha." Graham burst out laughing so hard that he eventually got a hiccup. "No, no, my friend. Now you have surpassed yourself. You think I know nothing of what you do when you aren't at your church, my friend."

Simon went red in the face and seemed to be deeply offended by Graham's words, and after a spell of silence said to him, "I forgive what you say, my friend, for our Lord expects us to do so, and as for your accusations, I remind you of what the Holy Scripture says: *Father, forgive them, for they know not what they do.* And so, I do."

"Thank you, my friend, and don't forget to ask that for your parishioners—"

"Calm down, calm down, my friends," hastily chipped in Bernard, who as an artist was obviously a very open-minded chap who forgave his fellow men all their transgressions. "I suggest," he continued, "forgetting all about that dispute and getting down to business straightaway."

"That's it," said Justin, "and I'm nicely surprised to hear this from a man who very seldom does anything straightaway in his life."

"Appearances deceive," replied Bernard. "There could be a method in every madness, as our great dramatist Shakespeare said."

"Surely, it could be so, but it's very often very hard to see that," said Justin.

"Let me say something," said James, with his usual modesty, "I, as a civil servant, am obviously in favour of civility, and that's why I say let's forget our personal views and agree on the course of action in our planned enterprise."

"Bravo, my friend, fortunately you are the one who has retained common sense here, and yes, let's now discuss our business."

"First of all," James carried on, "we must now consider the Government's willingness to assist the new ideas we have with regard to our already running enterprise, and don't forget we were close to disaster due to the excessive honesty of our then friend Mr Denker. By the way, I wonder what happened to him. The European warrant of arrest was issued but they couldn't manage to locate him anywhere."

"I tried my best," said Justin, "to help them to find him, but nothing came of the search. He disappeared as if the earth had swallowed him."

"Anyway," continued James, "I don't think he'll reappear, for the warrant is still in force, so we can sleep soundly. Now, I've an idea how to make our business even more profitable and wonder what your opinion would be."

"What's on your mind, James?" asked Jason.

"You're all aware of the Government's extreme sensitivity to social matters, the welfare of those unlucky ones, and here is a chance for us, gentlemen."

"What do you mean, old chap?" asked Jason again.

"We'll establish a charity on a grand scale, I mean, a charity which will be active not only in this country but also abroad, as far as we can get, mind you, even in faraway godforsaken backwaters. We'll cooperate closely with UNESCO to make it truly international, and to make our business even more legitimate and trustworthy. Our enterprise will achieve an impeccable ethical status, and all this will please the Government, so it will be eager to support us unreservedly in anything we'll be doing. They, I'm sure, will provide us with some grants for a venture of such scale, and as its noble aims will enhance this country's international standing, they'll be proud of us. So, what do you say?"

"This is something you can be proud of yourself," said Simon, "and I, obviously, will seek support of the Church, which undoubtedly will be interested in such a respectable initiative."

"Aye, aye, what an excellent idea. Who would think you could come up with something like that? *Bravo, bravissimo!*" said Bernard to the amazement of all the others, for it was uncommon for him to participate in any business talk. He attended the meetings out of necessity only, as it was his duty to take part as a member of M7.

"And," James continued, "we have an important ally, gentlemen. I've spoken to Mr Dumblodge, you know, that intelligence fellow, and he's very much interested in the idea. He said that our planned organisation would allow him to make his operations more successful. You know, he thinks in his naivety that other countries' secret services wouldn't suspect such a respectable organisation of any improper activity."

"I've always known he's a moron," said Graham, who almost always, under the influence of Wittgenstein, expressed his ideas in a word and to the point.

"Now," said Simon, "the important thing is to choose a proper name for our new enterprise, you know, such an organisation's name must contain a message to the public, its noble intentions, and it should be catchy as well. Perhaps some of these organisations' names are too captivating, over-virtuous, so to speak, and I would be in favour of a much more modest name but which also tells everyone our respectable intentions. The name I suggest is 'Be Aware' for its meaning says a lot without being pretentious. What do you think?"

"Perfect, Simon," said Shaun. "I find it simply ideal. How did it come to your mind?"

"Ah, thanks to what Henry Miller said: 'The aim of life is to live, and to live is to be aware.' It's really good, isn't it?"

"Oh yes, it is indeed. Henry was a clever boy, after all. But I wouldn't know you read him."

"Oh, you underestimate me. I not only read his stuff, if you know what I mean."

"I do, I do, my friend, and am even more impressed now. And has Henry been helpful?"

"Yes, he has, and I'm very grateful for that," said Simon. "But please tell me, what do you mean by after all?" asked Simon.

"You know," said Shaun, "to be honest, in my opinion, his books deserved to be banned, and perhaps still should be, because of their terrible obscenity and his crusade against the Holy Church, against all things Christian, and I wish the Grand Inquisition were back."

"I think you exaggerate, my friend, and I tell you this as a priest. Hold back the Grand Inquisition. No, no, you go too far."

"Maybe I've overblown that," said Shaun, "for some others are even worse for that matter."

"Who do you mean?" enquired Simon.

"That sex maniac Bukowski, of course."

"My dear well-read friends," chipped in Graham, the biggest advocate of unrestricted freedom of them all. "To my mind, prudery leads either to aggression or depression, or both, and therefore should be fought by all means available. And let me tell you some linguistic curiosity, even a paradox. I mean, there are people, I mean your fellow countrymen, Shaun, who don't have a clue what the word means, but are still the personifications of it. This would be something worth investigating, and here Ludwig and Friedrich's unmasking psychology could be of help—"

"Gentlemen, gentlemen, please forget all these intellectual considerations for a while. We're here to discuss a serious business matter and not to engage in empty, fruitless word games," Jason interrupted his friends' senseless, indeed, discourse.

"Let's get to the point, let's talk business. We must have a detailed plan to carry on with our enterprise, so I suggest discussing it point by point before we carry it out.

"So, I suggest we contribute our own money to the project, not all of it, of course, to show our generosity and seriousness. Then we advertise our action in the media, but not in a too aggressive way, if you know what I mean, rather moderate appeals for support, I suggest. Then, we appeal to the Government for funds, but very gently, so to speak. And we'll begin our action in the Province, for the Government for many years now has always been overwhelmingly generous to them. But the truth is that they almost never reciprocate it. On the contrary, they usually make everything difficult for Westminster. All they want in fact is money, and the more the better. And the money is always ready for the suffering North-West. And there is no prejudice against it at all. Even the most stubborn patriots accept it, you know, the same again, *pecunia non olet*. And they still love to despair, and in this respect, they have mustered it to perfection and I believe it to be a theatre of a kind, a way of wheedling out as much money as possible. And we'll obviously follow that mood of them getting in touch with their press which will welcome us with open arms. For those rags it will be a feast they'll embark on with their usual eagerness to relieve the martyrdom of their compatriots. And by the way, I wonder what they would write about if there wasn't so much to complain about. And the same goes for their broadcasting. Every one of their radio stations mumbles the same crap, and plays the same shitty pop all over again. And I wonder whether it is done on purpose to make the listeners and readers stupid or whether those in charge of both have already found themselves in the lunatic asylum.

"One of the former prime ministers said you can't trust them for they are all liars, and you know what, they know that they are, but they aren't ashamed of it at all. No, actually they're proud of it. We, the English, in turn, know we're a perfidious nation, and so what, are we embarrassed by that? No, we regard that as our advantage, don't we?"

"And now, we of course need an intermediary to approach the Government as directly as possible, and I mean the prime minister himself, and here fortunately I know the right fellow, gentlemen."

"And who's that?" enquired Justin.

"It's a man by the name of Adarsh, Ches Adarsh, whom I met in Moscow where he was highly recommended by my friends over there," said Jason.

"And can we trust him?" asked Justin, a man who valued reliability and trust as the most respectable human virtues, and found them even in those tough ruffians he defended.

"Yes, I think so. Anyway, he was introduced to me by a man we had been working with in Moscow for a good couple of years. You know him, it's Ivan Ivanovich Likhodeyev."

"Ah, that fellow," said Justin, "a rather shady character, isn't he?"

"Yes, he is, but we can rely on him after all because he makes money working with us," said Jason.

"Yea, he does, and not only him for that matter. So, it seems that we may have access to John Oddhouse, our dear prime minister, and rely on his proverbial credulity," said Justin.

"Death to the suckers, gentlemen. We follow that maxim of ours again," said Jason, "and yes, as soon as we have a chance to talk to the PM, the first item on our agenda will be the Province. As you know, they both, the Government and those over there, play a kind of game. The latter pretend to suffer injustice, poverty, and the like, and the former pretends to believe it, so it's a sort of mutual admiration society based on well-founded mutual deception. You know, there are quite a few serious and honest people over there, but they are intimidated by mutual distrust, suspicion and by those who still fight, but actually nobody knows, including those fighters, what their fight is for. It seems to be mere lunacy, for the proclaimed fight's objectives are unattainable by fighting. So, in a word, a vicious circle, but they enjoy it, being convinced that the demented are blessed."

"Shaun," said Simon, "I'm sorry to say but I find your compatriots rough, their sense of humour mean-spirited, and their fight for freedom founded on the incredible assumption that it is a synonym of shambles and bungling."

"Unfortunately, I must agree, and I would call the northern part a cuckoo's nest. Yes, many of them are deranged."

"You know," said Simon, "what our former friend Denker said, having lived there for a while. He said they are convinced they live close to the centre of the universe."

"Yea, they do, but upside-down, so to speak," replied Shaun.

"You know what, I'm certain this is something to do with genetics. And all in all, they seem to be deprived of the ability of abstract thinking which is, as we know, the condition of culture understood as intellectual and artistic achievement."

"It could be, and therefore their faith too," said Simon, "is dubious, I would even go so far as to say they carry the Devil under their shirts, to put it metaphorically."

"Excellent description. They do indeed," agreed Shaun.

"But that fellow Denker wasn't too happy living among us, either. He called us pink rabbits because, he said, so many of us have protruding teeth and like pink, especially pink shirts and ties," said Simon.

"Ha ha, it's good. I like it. Anyway, he wasn't that stupid," replied Shaun.

"No, he wasn't, I agree, and you know what? Sometimes I wish he were still with us," said Simon.

"Are you kidding?" Shaun was now really surprised.

"No, I am serious, you know, he brought some freshness to our rather stultifying atmosphere. Without him, we are growing stale," replied Simon.

"Hmm, yes, there's something about that," said Shaun. "Sadly it's very true."

The conversation continued in the same manner for another hour or so, and later on all of them agreed to go ahead with the Province business. "And someday," Jason said to his friends, "we'll flourish there for, thank God, they are obsessed by money, those avaricious Irish. But it'll take them some time to understand that money isn't everything. But it won't be soon because they are rather slow thinkers."

The prime minister did his best to assist them for he knew perfectly well how things were in the Province, and his policy towards it was pretty much the same as it had been with his former colleagues, but not all of them obviously. A female PM would have been very different in that respect; and she might have been right, after all.

In the end, Jason commented on the situation as follows: "They think they are clever, and yes, but the point is that it is a petty, short-sighted cleverness, and consequently sometime in the future, they'll wake up to something very disappointing, but in the meantime, let them sleep, so to speak, for the longer they do, the better for us."

Simon, being a priest, was a bit concerned about the ethical side of the matter in question. "They are being duped," he was saying, "and we take advantage of their lack of imagination."

"So what?" replied Jason. "Death to the suckers, I say it again, and they deserve it."

"But wait a second," Simon said, "it's still very unfair to treat them all like that, for the Church is concerned about the situation, and not only for the sake of it. However, to be honest, the Church will always support authority, which anyway recognises its importance in pulling the wool over your eyes. The Church cannot exist without the power of the state, and the words, 'Render unto Caesar the things that are Caesars; and unto God the things that are God's,' are valid anywhere in this world. And of course, we remember what is said in Romans 13, "Let every person be in subjection to the governing authorities. For there is no authority except from God and those which exist are established by God.'"

"Yes, I see your point. We must keep up appearances after all, even when we know perfectly well that the ideas of ordinary people, as Arthur says, count for nothing," said Jason.

To make the story short, their business over there went smoothly and no one complained, and the M7 was thinking about expanding it even further.

Ches Adarsh was very helpful and they found his assistance indispensable, and accordingly rewarded him with substantial sums of money. And everything was fine until one day when John Oddhouse received another letter from Bulky.

We now take the liberty of reminding those doubters – of which England is full – those who consider the so-called supernatural phenomena, also known as black magic, nothing but fairy tales, that the Queen herself says there are some black forces in her country.

The PM was very glad to hear from him again, but at the same time, the letter wasn't amusing in its content at all. Bulky warned John about the future consequences of his unreserved support of M7 in the long run. Bulky also pointed out that Mr Adarsh was actually an honest person, and it would highly advisable to see him in person. *Then you'll have a chance*, he said, *of understanding what the M7 business is like, and who they really are.*

Since John trusted Bulky, he contacted Lord Hellbridge, asking him to invite Mr Adarsh to Downing Street. And on a sunny day in March, Ches Adarsh arrived.

John welcomed him warmly and after they were seated in the living room, came straight to business.

"You've been recommended by Lord Hellbridge, and since I much rely on his opinion, I've decided to invite you to discuss some matters in privacy. No one else will be privy to what will be said here, so please feel free to say whatever you want to, dear Mr Adarsh."

"Thank you, sir, for the invitation, and yes, I will be very frank with you during our conversation because His Lordship encouraged me to be so. So, the lord says you're very much concerned about a certain group of people, a kind of organisation which appears to be very respectable, being in fact a pack of very skilled fraudsters. I share his opinion and since I am not a stranger to their affairs, I'll do my best to assist you."

"Thank you, I'd be most obliged if you could help me because it is indeed a very complicated and at the same time embarrassing matter," said John.

"Yes, it is, but then since I myself have been asked by them to persuade you to support their scheme, it won't be too difficult, paradoxically, to sort out the problem," said Ches.

"You, yourself, have...?" John stammered, being totally stupefied at hearing that, but somehow managing to say, "but how come you want to fight them after all?"

"It's a personal matter, sir, and I don't want to discuss the reasons for doing this. Anyway, their business as you know is flourishing, especially thanks to your help..." and here Ches looked at John significantly "...and since I've been involved for some time now helping them to influence you to support the project, I'm privy to everything they do, and it'll make it easier of course to strike them when the opportunity arises."

Now John was speechless. His thoughts were a total mess, but he somehow managed to pull himself together and said, "I don't understand.

They asked you to influence me, but now when I'm meeting you, things look…" He didn't manage to finish, feeling suddenly too weak to continue that charade-like conspiracy, which now perplexed him so much that almost all of his powers of rational reasoning left him.

"Yes, I've persuaded you," said Ches, "but I suggest we leave it for now since, I'm sorry to say, you wouldn't understand my motives for doing so. What matters now is that you know I want to help you to sort out the mess, getting you out of it at the same time, so do you trust me enough to follow my advice?"

John, still being very much confused, found it hard to think, but eventually was able at least to make out one thing clearly – *but then*, he said to himself, *it was none other than Lord Hellbridge who recommended Mr Adarsh. Moreover, Bulky himself vouched for them both, so, all in all, I have no choice left but to trust that fellow.*

And yes, he had to trust Ches, even if he understood nothing of that at all now. And small wonder, for then who in England would understand black magic-like stories? Out of the question! It might be easier, we may presume, for an Irishman to understand them better. We don't mean that John was stupid. No, he wasn't, but his typical English inclination to simplify things complicated everything regarding the matter in question, making him unable to understand anything of what was happening now.

That very English phlegm and congenital disposition to mock and dismiss the irrational wasn't helpful here, either. So, John, one of those good Englishmen, was anyway lost here, and the only hope of making things clear was the man he was talking to now, and he reluctantly had to admit to himself that without the man's help, he would have no chance of confronting the conspirators. What made everything even worse was that endorsing them publicly made him their accomplice, and in the case of the conspiracy being made public, he would be finished as a politician, and, who knows, he could even face criminal charges. He faced such perfidious machinations of which, in truth, many of his fellow politicians would be proud. All in all, a terrible perspective, and John knew perfectly well that he needed all the help he could get, even from the Devil himself, provided, of course, he was available.

When John eventually came to his senses after that silent meditation, the likes of which he had never experienced before, for being an Englishman he considered it a completely useless activity, he said, "Mr Adarsh, I have made up my mind and accept your offer, but please understand my rather obvious hesitation after hearing from you some things I've only now become aware of. Especially, you used to be close to that M7 business, and now you want to challenge them. You say this is so because of some personal matter which you wish not to reveal, and I appreciate that. Anyway, what's your plan, Mr Adarsh?"

"My plan has actually been drawn up by somebody else, and I can tell you the name of this person, that's Mr Wissend, but nothing else," said Ches.

"Nothing else? And am I supposed to go ahead after all?"

"It's up to you, sir, but if I were you, I would, for his skills are rather impressive," said Ches.

John said nothing to that, feeling confounded again. He couldn't comprehend such mystifying things for he obviously had never read a single verse of the *Tractatus*. But we may forgive him his ignorance since even such a wise man as Bertrand couldn't understand much of it. And, so it is, you may read something, but to understand it might be a very different matter.

But under the circumstances, John somehow managed to overcome his inborn distrust of all things mystical and said, "I see, hmm, and you have a plan, I presume?"

"Oh yes, I do, and actually Lord Hellbridge has found it impeccable," confirmed Ches.

"Ah, if the lord appreciates it, I feel compelled to agree with him." Now, John felt much more assured.

We must emphasise here a certain disposition of the prime minister which was a bit unusual concerning his upbringing and educational curriculum. Until he met the lord, he would have never paid the slightness attention to, let's say, cryptic happenings, but now he was somehow forced to admit that they have some value after all and shouldn't be so swiftly dismissed. And he himself was amazed now, discovering his new predisposition.

"I'm very glad to hear that, sir, and now let me outline the most important details of the plan," said Ches.

"Please do, I'm all ears," John encouraged him.

"They believed I would persuade you to champion their project, and then you in turn will encourage relevant government bodies to promote it. The main project's aim was, and still is, as you know, to provide accommodation and food for the homeless and unemployed, and also to deal with some other welfare issues. Moreover, a large-scale apprenticeship programme has already been set up all over the country. People in charge of it expect to receive substantial government grants and donations from the public as well. All in all, the supposed benefits of the project, considering its scale, seem to be very positive indeed, and will very likely have an impact on the election results in favour of your party. So, you can see how ambitious the project is, and how corrupt at the same time, for the bulk of the money they receive doesn't go on the project, but in their own pockets. Taking into account its huge scale, you can imagine the money they get."

"But," said John, "they were supposed to keep a detailed account of their financial operations."

"Oh yes, they do, and it was and will be impeccable. Anyway, even if you or anybody else, for instance, HMRC, became suspicious, it would be ignored in favour of the greater good. You know what I mean, that very basis of the English utilitarian ethic. That blockhead John Stuart, as Friedrich calls him."

John said nothing to that. He knew perfectly well what Ches was talking about, and now he was thinking hard. *What shall I do?* he asked himself. *The project seems to be a sham on a grand scale, but who cares, when it's all about the common good, and it is good also for us, our party. Who would blame us, anyway, even if they had some doubts? Nobody in fact, not in this country.*

"I do understand you hesitate, sir. Under the circumstances, it's not easy to make a decision," said Ches.

"But why did you get involved in the first place and now want to fight them?" asked John again.

"I've told you, sir, I can't reveal my reasons for doing this. Anyway, do you trust Lord Hellbridge's recommendation after all?" replied Ches.

"Hmm, yes, of course I do," replied John, "but, you know, only now I remember something else as well, I mean the letter I received…" (it was Bulky's letter, but John obviously wouldn't tell Ches that) "…the other day, and the author of the letter, let's say, a special kind of friend, recommended his close friend by the name of Mr Wissend, a renewed expert on finance, who as such may be of assistance to me supposing I have any enquiries regarding the matter in question."

"That's it, I've already mentioned the name to you, sir," said Ches.

"Ah yes, indeed, you have. But now, there's something else to worry about, and I mean the public opinion which admires those who help the poor and abandoned, so people may get angry with us persecuting M7."

"I see, yes, we have to take it into consideration, but if I were you, I would even in this matter trust the lord, you know, there's hardly nothing he could not deal with." Ches said that with emphasis. And then Lord Hellbridge will help you to become the one who fought those who pretend to do good, yet will forever do evil."

"Bah, it might be so, but I'm still not sure," said John, who didn't put much trust in the wisdom of public opinion.

"I perfectly understand," said Ches, "your doubts, but then, in my humble opinion, the majority of people, here in England, love to admire a public figure who fights for the common good on behalf of them, even if he or she happens to go astray. They believe that the salvation of man means his salvation from himself, that is, from being a politician in this case."

"Hmm, this is something new for me," said John.

"Bah, we learn something new every day as you say in this country. However, as far as I can see, it doesn't change anything for the better," said Ches, and smiled.

"Ah yes, it actually doesn't," John sadly agreed.

"But now, *zu dem Sachen selbst*, as Edmund recommended," said Ches, "that is the point. Our plan will be closely related, curiously enough, to something which is called the problem of life." John now felt that something strange to him was going to be discussed, as he was now listening to Ches, who went on, "I mean, each of the members of the M7 has such a problem, and we can exploit it to achieve our goal, that is, to dismantle their conspiracy. As far as I can see, this is another way to deal with them apart from the Government's action. You, of course, will cooperate with Mr Wissend, that finance maverick in this respect, but their life problems will be dealt with by somebody else. But please remember, sir, to be very careful, for the M7 spies are everywhere. In the first place, it is Mr Dumblodge, chief of your secret service, whom they have on the lead. You know, he's proof of what Russian Intelligence says about yours, namely that at yours everything goes smoothly only in novels and on the screen. However, he might be of some help to them after all. I, in turn, will be working closely with some of Lord Hellbridge's assistants.

"That's all for now, sir. I've got to go now. Goodbye, and remember, who dares wins." And Ches left Downing Street.

*

The next day, Mr Wissend came to see the prime minister, but this time it was Chequers where they met.

In his telephone call to John, Mr Wissend insisted meeting early in the morning, saying that it was only in the early hours they can meet, for at this time his mind is at its best. He suggested five o'clock, which was a bit too early for John, but considering the importance of the situation, he agreed.

Mr Wissend arrived at five minutes to five at Chequers, on a rather odd-looking bicycle, in the company of a huge black cat who sat in a large basket in front of him. It was strange and inexplicable that nobody, including Special Branch officers, had noticed him until he appeared at the main entrance to the mansion. Later on, the officers informed John about that strange incident, but he ignored them, saying there was nothing to worry about. As a matter of fact, he was rather pleased to hear that since it proved Mr Wissend's ability to avoid detection, to sneak in even here where the head of the British Government was supposed to be so well protected. Afterwards, a special independent commission investigated the matter in question, but as often happens with something independent, it could find out nothing. We may notice here that Mr Dumblodge somehow got wind of the incident and got seriously worried.

Mr Wissend was dressed in black, which the PM found rather inappropriate, for at this time of day, no gentleman would be dressed like that. But he chose to ignore it since more important matters were at stake.

The visitors entered the mansion, and once John saw the cat, he felt a great void, for it looked very much like Bulky. Everybody sat down, including the cat, which chose a large antique armchair, and that also reminded John of Bulky's peculiar habits.

"It's come to my attention," began Mr Wissend, "that presently you are experiencing some difficulties and may need my assistance."

"That's correct," replied the PM, "and yes, I'd be most obliged if you could assist me, because the matter in question is so, hmm, let's say, sensitive, that it'd be much more advisable to obtain help from someone from outside."

"Yes, I understand perfectly, and I'm already pretty familiar with the case since Lord Hellbridge gave me a rather detailed picture of it."

"Yes, of course. He is of invaluable help here, and without him I can't really imagine how I would manage to deal with the problem," said John.

"The lord, I can assure you, Mr Oddhouse, is always of great help whenever he chooses to attend to anything, for that matter. He's a very busy person and intervenes only when a case is interesting enough, and yours really is."

"Hmm, I..." John cleared his throat, "...find it interesting too, but much more troublesome, you know, is that the consequences would be catastrophic if everything was to come to light."

"Yes, of course, I can imagine that, but don't you worry too much in advance, for I'm pretty sure you'll be all right after all, Mr Oddhouse, especially as we have the lord on our side. You know, if he were on the other one..." Mr Wissend suspended here his voice, shaking his head "...you would find yourself in a much more difficult situation."

"Yes, I'm now certain that without him, I and my party would be in possibly not only a difficult but even a hopeless position, and therefore, I'm so grateful to him. But as a matter of fact, I've forgotten to enquire as to how I would repay his priceless cooperation."

"As far as I know, the only repayment His Lordship is interested in is his satisfaction at a job well done, and hardly ever, be sure of it, does he fails, in truth, never, Mr Oddhouse."

"Yes, I'm pretty sure of it, and since I had some difficulty trying to reach him on the phone to thank him again, if you happen to see him, could you kindly pass on to him my gratitude? I'd be very obliged."

"I certainly will, Prime Minister, and now, with your kind permission, let's get to the heart of the darkness, as a famous writer would say."

"Oh yes, a very appropriate expression here," said the PM, "very relevant indeed. Yea, Joseph had a knack for all those gloomy sayings. But, you know, that Graham's writing is *de facto* much more confusing, don't you think so?"

"Oh yes, it is, one hardly ever knows what it is actually about, what his point is. The reader is lost. Perhaps your Graham wanted to tell us something but he himself didn't know what it was actually about, given his own very vague considerations. But others have been even worse, and the best description of their muddling we find at Charles's, 'It seems to me they just play word-tricks, that those who say almost nothing at all are considered excellent writers.' And I, myself, would describe the writings that prevail nowadays as crafty crap, and there's nothing more to say about that."

"I hardly have time to read anything but what is related to my job," said John.

"Bah, of course you don't, and that's it. Look, to be absolutely frank with you, I don't really know why you want to fight that M7 conspiracy, because, as a matter of fact, what they do stays within the limits of your own thinking, doesn't it? Their evil is also yours, and you might not really consider the conspiracy devious, so you are willing to destroy it because of nothing else but your self-interest, dear Mr Oddhouse. But then, if it were the case, why would Lord Hellbridge and I, his faithful servant, be helping you? We wouldn't do it out of pure sympathy, so to speak. We do what we do to maintain the balance between evil and good in the world, for this balance is based on an agreement between what you, in your very imprecise language, call the light and the dark. In other words, *Ordnung muss sein* in order to keep this planet going, but you may ask why we do so after all. St John's Gospel tells you about the end of the world, but you don't really believe it, but as a Christian you wouldn't dare say it aloud, would you? Anyway, Christianity and Jesus Christ himself are very different matters indeed, and our mentioned agreement is there because we in fact admire him. We appreciate His courage and His willpower.

Now, why do we keep the world going? I mean, why do we intend preserving it until the unavoidable cataclysm that will wipe out humankind on this earth? It isn't obviously out of our sympathy for man as such, for the majority of people do not deserve any sympathy at all. And this oncoming cataclysm is because of them. You know of course what I mean. You may remember a few verses of the New Testament, do you?

"So, I ask again, why? Why prolong the existence of mankind? And the question is obviously related to that unavoidable catastrophe. And I tell you why. It is because the life of man is nothing else but the test, the test of him as a human being, and because it is not about just one man, but a multitude of them, the test must last long enough to find out who eventually deserves salvation. And that's why we have the agreement, for it is up to us to test man and for somebody else to decide when the disaster strikes. And that's why we are part of that power that wills forever evil yet does forever good, for due to our test, the good men will enter... you know what I mean, don't you?

"I know that all sounds very vague and confusing, but it is as it is, as Ludwig would say, and as a matter of fact, it isn't our fault after all, as some short-sighted people like to say."

John Oddhouse was sitting there as if struck by lightning. All of his capacity for rational thinking had just vanished. He was about to object to what had just been said, asking Mr Wissend how Lord Hellbridge and him would know so precisely God's intentions. *And that test? What shall I now say to him? Shall I simply ignore all that? I don't really know what to do.*

He could have been deliberating like that forever if Mr Wissend hadn't interrupted his thoughts by saying, "At any rate, dear sir, *enten eller* or either or, as that troubled but great Soren said. Anyway, in the end, you are free to choose what side you are with, and it might be that whatever you choose, it is wrong."

"I am on yours," said John, not really knowing why he said so.

"Bravo!" exclaimed Mr Wissend. "I've always known you were a clever man. And now we can move to another issue that is closely related to what we've been discussing.

"I mentioned the balance between evil and good in the world which we are eager to keep, but as we know, it won't last forever. This balance is supposed to last for a long time, long enough to find out who is worthy of being admitted there, you know what I mean, and now the question is, who makes the decision?

"And let me ask you, have you ever thought of it?"

"To be honest, no, I've never contemplated the question," said John, still very much confused by all this stuff.

"I thought you haven't," said Wissend, "but don't you worry, and now I would like to tell you something that might eventually help you.

"So, in relation to what we have just concluded, partially at least, one of your predecessors said that this country had always been Christian. The person I mean was Daniel 'The Preacher', as we call him. Now, I don't think that what he said was just a question of semantics, for that very much confused man did actually mean that. However, he just expressed his inbred conviction that he actually couldn't prove. In fact, the conviction that he and his like-minded fellow countrymen are never at fault, whatever they say or do, consequently, those who don't actually believe in heaven, because if they did, they wouldn't have any convictions as regards the matter in question, for God, as a matter of fact, forbids any convictions, especially those of His area of expertise, so to speak. You know, if you claim to be a Christian you must acknowledge your fallibility, for only then you're Christian."

"Excuse me for interrupting you, Mr Wissend," said John, "but it's said that all our sins will be forgiven."

"Yea, you say so for your own convenience, that is to console yourself, even the wicked do, believing they deserve heaven despite what they've done. But if it were the case then the Ten Commandments wouldn't have any sense, and everything that is said in the Scriptures for that matter either, and there would be no God."

John was very disturbed by listening to all that and was just about to say, *But you deny what all Christian denominations say…* but didn't manage it because Wissend said, "Yes, they say so, but again, for the same reason, that is to make people happy, to cheer them up.

"And that misinterpretation of the Scriptures is done deliberately, and the reason for doing so is to give meaning to people's lives, to give people the sense of life that otherwise they wouldn't have under the circumstances. For surely, you cannot be really happy having that sort of life, but you may pretend you are. Appearances are more important than reality, in other words, façade is everything. But, dear Mr Oddhouse, deep inside, you aren't happy at all, for you cannot be when your happiness is a sham.

"I know you're surprised by all I'm telling you, and even unsettled, but I have to tell you that because it's closely related to what we're going to do regarding the M7 business."

"Yes," said John, who now couldn't think of anything else to say.

"*Voilà*, dear Prime Minister," Wissend continued his lecture-like presentation, "where are we now? Ah yes, man and the universe. Yes, it is a pretty complicated matter, but you English are inclined to simplify this and other things, and I'm sorry to say, make it vulgar, but it may cheer you up a bit to know that your neighbours across the water, up north, might be even worse in this respect. However, there's another matter you should be ashamed of, I mean your inclination to *schadenfreude*, especially towards France and Germany. Is it supposed to compensate for your own shortcomings or it is proof of your inferiority complex, or both?

"Now, let's reflect on the following. As far as I know, the Last Judgement is passed according to what an individual has done. And there are no exceptions, you know, God doesn't change His mind, as the teachings of the Christian Church might suggest. I'd say that everyone is sinful, and the only ones who deserve salvation are those who have managed to become what they are, and this is, as you would imagine, a very complicated matter. For how the hell would one think of being himself or herself as something other than they are? But actually, it is the most difficult thing in the world, for to become what you are is to know yourself. For only then, as a matter of fact, do you acknowledge your sins and may expiate. And only then are you allowed entry to heaven, for only those who are honest with themselves may get there. And once they have become what they are, it doesn't really matter what they've done in their lives. They might have been good or bad, it doesn't matter. What matters is their honesty towards themselves. Anyway, Jesus says, 'Be cold or hot, otherwise I will spit you out,' meaning, if you aren't, you will be denied entry to heaven."

Now, the prime minister looked almost ghost-like, apparently the Wissend lecture had shaken him to the core, and good for him, because it proved his deep concern about man and his fate. Mr Wissend noticed John's mood and said to him, "I'm sorry for this a-bit-too-long exposé, but I allow myself to bother you because I know you're worried about the state of affairs in your country, and I appreciate that, and now I'd be obliged if you could allow me to continue."

"Yes, of course, please do," said John, somewhat reinforced by Wissend's kind disposition towards him.

"Thank you," said Wissend, and carried on. "Now, since the M7 business is connected to a similar one in Dollaria, your country being so well disposed towards all things their government does, you may be reluctant to do anything, because whatever they do, you are with them. Your country is actually Dollaria's vassal and you accept that, because you believe it guarantees your own interest. But if I were you, I wouldn't be so sure about that, for as a certain French general, de Gaulle, said, 'They will commit every imaginable stupidity, and even the ones you cannot imagine.' Thus, they would sacrifice your country if it were in their own interest, but you wouldn't consider this, would you? Let it be, anyway, let's wait and see, or do you think you can foresee the future? But quite a few of your prophecies haven't come true, have they?

"But back to the M7 business, they have quite substantial interests in Dollaria, and it's the usual, a hedge fund, shell and sister companies, and the like. But I wouldn't be surprised if you were tempted to disregard that for the sake of your great friendship."

John was thinking hard but couldn't really make up his mind. *What shall I do?* he asked himself. *I was inclined to fight the conspiracy in the name of the common good, but now I can hardly see any good coming out of taking action against them. But what about the ethical aspect of all this? Shall I ignore it, as several of my predecessors did? I don't really know, for the Devil's sake!*

"Yes, if I were you, I would consider the ethical issues of the matter in question," said Wissend, and John looked at him and asked himself, *What the hell, is he reading my thoughts?*

"Hell might have something to do with it, after all," said Wissend. "Anyway, I would be careful choosing words in this respect, for as they say, 'Do you think you can tell heaven from hell, blue sky from pain?' You certainly know who says so, don't you?

"You see, actually those abodes are situated in eternity, thus, whoever dwells in either of them views the world *sub specie aeternitatis*, and man here, on earth, actually knows nothing about those places, does he? All he can think of are merely his own projections. Thus, all he can do is just choose what is good or bad for him, here on earth, something that may make his life joyful or miserable. Mind you, actually, God or Satan have nothing to do with it, for man is fully independent whatever he does here on earth, and bears all responsibility for what he does. Therefore, any ethic you choose is your own ethic, which will be judged by your fellow men, and whether it is reviewed by somebody above you, you will never know, for that 'somebody' is beyond your thinking. You may, of course, as many a man has been doing, reinforce your position by calling God's name, claiming to act in His name, but again, you never know whether he approves or not of anything you do.

"What your famous dramatist Shakespeare says, 'There is nothing either good or bad, but thinking makes it so,' is something esoteric for an ordinary man who in fact doesn't give a damn about such questions.

Anyway, as Napoleon said, 'The masses should be directed without their being aware of it,' and as a matter of fact they need and want to be directed, but at the same time want to keep an illusion of having their say in the Government's decisions, for illusion is the first of all pleasures, as another great Frenchman, Voltaire, said. You see, what I say is, in a way, the best example of the concord between England and France."

"Excuse me," interrupted John, "but how does all this you are telling me now have to do with our business, I mean, our action against the M7?"

"Bah," exclaimed Wissend, "it does, oh, it does indeed, dear Mr Oddhouse. For each of them, the members of M7, has a weakness, that is, a penchant for something which he cannot resist, and this is where we'll strike. Believe me, there's no other way to deal with them. Legal means are useless here, for their machinations are too well concealed, and a trial, if it would ever take place, would cause a huge scandal which would do terrible damage to your reputation."

Yes, a scandal was something that John had always been most terrified of in his life as a politician, so he said, "You're right here. A trial is out of the question."

"That's it, and that's why we'll proceed as follows," Mr Wissend went on. "Mr Adarsh will become an acquaintance of each of the M7 members without arousing any suspicion of his real task. You know, just a friendly chap with whom they can have a drink, talk, and the like. He'll be introduced to them by Lord Hellbridge, so they won't be able to reject the introduction. Since Mr Adarsh has already known them all, he is familiar with their soft spots."

"Excuse me, Mr Wissend, you say that Mr Adarsh had met them before and got familiar with them? How come? And if so, they'll be on guard. He won't be able to do anything."

"Don't you worry, dear Mr Oddhouse, for these days, Mr Adarsh doesn't look as he used to. His appearance is very different and there's no chance of them recognising him."

"I see, and at any rate, I've got full confidence in Lord Hellbridge, and in you as his confidant."

"And rightly so, sir, very wise of you. Now, their so-called soft spots are actually their vices, and strangely enough, these are the seven deadly sins, and each of them, or even more than one, corresponds to each of the M7 members. You, of course, know what the seven sins are, don't you?"

"Yes, I do. However, these days, there might be even more transgressions."

"Very accurate observation, dear Mr Oddhouse. There are many more of them, for we live in interesting times. And you know what, in China, they've a saying which in fact is a curse, and it is wishing someone to live in interesting times, that is, to experience hardship and misfortunes.

"Let's take, for instance, the so-called open society Karl admired so much, that is democracy. But what is there to admire as a matter of fact? Lord Byron might be right here saying, 'Civilisation, what benefits for you? – hunger, war and despots' persecution.'

I, myself, am a rather peaceful, introspective chap of contemplative nature, but when I see all that wickedness, that filth everywhere, I sometimes think that maybe we need terror to teach those scoundrels to behave, for what does the word freedom actually mean for them? It is now nothing but to satisfy the most primitive instincts of that riff-raff that have spread everywhere. And that's why you need so many laws to prevent evil happening, but actually it doesn't do any good in the long run, does it?"

"But is there a better solution?" enquired the prime minister.

"There might be, oh yes, and someday in the future we will require new values because these you pretend to respect have in fact lost their value. God is dead, Mr Oddhouse, but He may return, who knows? Or somebody else will take charge instead. You never know what may happen to you the next day, do you?

So, in the meantime, so to speak, you create more and more regulations, forgetting to teach people the right principles. And all this legislation of yours is actually growing, so in fact you gradually and furtively establish a police state you seem to condemn so much. All in all, your democracy is a façade, and its representatives pull the wool over people's eyes. And what does their freedom actually mean when they have no ideas of their own, that is, no self-responsibility? Your fellow countrymen are merely a herd of sheep, a rabble of slave morality that suffer from the illusion of being free. Either you will make an effort to set up new values or all that doth begin should rightly to destruction run, remember, either or, dear Prime Minister."

John was very distressed now, and he kept telling himself, *No, I can't stand it anymore, I'll step down. I've had enough.* For he knew now that that fellow was right, and he himself had very similar views, but until now he had never admitted that.

But that terrible fellow, Mr Wissend, didn't allow the prime minister to brood for too long and said, "No, dear Mr Oddhouse, resignation isn't an option, for if you step down you will always feel guilty, blaming himself forever. You must fight, *sei stark!*"

*He's right,* thought John, *whoever he is, and it might be good after all that he came to see me and told me all that. Otherwise, I'd be sitting here pretending that everything's fine, being duped by these hypocrites as has actually happened more than once.* Yes, only now John became aware of how often he'd been cheated, and wondered why he'd been so stupid as to not notice that. *Yes, he's right. Si vis pacem, para bellum.*

"And now back to the M7 and its members and their vices, which as you know are greed, wrath, sloth, gluttony, envy, lust and pride. Mr Adarsh will exploit them against themselves to demolish their conspiracy. In my opinion, he's now ready to accomplish this task since we have done our best to prepare him for it. Some time ago, he would have been totally incapable of doing anything of the sort, but now, yes, he's ready."

"And would he be able to accomplish that on his own?" asked John.

"Hmm, not exactly, we'll give him a hand," said Wissend.

"If so, I'm pretty sure he'll succeed," said John.

"Oh yes, he will. I mean, his, let's say, mission, will also be a test for him, and we'll be watching him closely."

"I think I now follow your reasoning, dear Mr Wissend," said the prime minister, somewhat astonishing himself by saying 'dear', which he had never ever said before when addressing someone. Apparently, something had changed in his attitude to people, not all of them, of course, but still it was something of an improvement, so to speak. Until recently, John had been very much reserved, aloof and even arrogant, some people had said.

"And what am I, myself, supposed to do?" he now asked Wissend.

"Nothing, you'll be doing your job as before, and what Mr Adarsh will be doing won't be your concern at all."

"I see, so I'll just be doing my job as if nothing was happening."

"Precisely, dear John," said Wissend.

Mr Oddhouse was a bit taken aback by Wissend's sudden over-familiarity, but chose to ignore that for the sake of their cooperation.

"And I'm at liberty to tell you this," continued Wissend, "they, those M7 fellas will be trashed by their own weapon, *vive gladio, peri gladio*, dear John, that's it. That's it for now, dear John. I'm leaving you now, and please carry on as if nothing has happened."

"May I," enquired John, "ask you something?"

"And what would that be, dear friend?"

"I presume you've heard of a cat, I mean, Bulky, that used to be my companion, so to speak, and I wonder if I'll ever have a chance," said John, a bit embarrassed now by what he was going to ask, "to see him again."

We must notice here that John missed the cat very much, for the cat's

233

absence deprived him of that strange, unfamiliar to him hitherto feeling of sympathy, even intimacy that he had never experienced before.

"Yes, dear friend, you will, in due time of course," said Wissend, and left 10 Downing Street.

# PART
# TWO

# SIMON

'I think that God in creating man
somewhat overestimated His ability.'
Oscar Wide

Beatrice and I had been living in Queen's Gate for a couple of months now and found our abode pretty comfortable and its location convenient. As soon as we'd settled down, we were contacted by some people who introduced themselves as friends of Klug and Kater. And due to these new acquaintances, it was been relatively easy to set up my own investment firm. It was a rather modest enterprise, but I actually made some promising arrangements with a few businesses in Armenia, Georgia, Hungary and Poland, and some other countries were also in sight. My aim from the very beginning was to do business not in big, economically powerful countries but those of medium economies, and offers I made there were very welcome, and I didn't encounter any serious obstacles for that matter. Even before I went to the Caucasus, I was sure I would like it, and wasn't disappointed when I eventually got there. Their people's pride and courage, food and mountains are the things I adore, to say nothing of their women of stunning beauty. If I weren't already bound to Bea, I would surely look for a woman over there. In Poland too, I found beautiful places; its mountains, forests, lakes, lovely historic cities and again lots of pretty women of my type. By the way, I can mention Ireland, where despite its shortcomings, you can't complain about a shortage of beauties.

All in all, I was sure I would have a long-standing relationship with the countries and visit them often.

Now, my assignment related to the M7 business was due to begin and I decided to start with Simon Prigstone, "The Evangelist". He was first on my list for no particular reason, or I perhaps chose him because of my recent visit to his superior, a bishop, whom I found to be a well-read man with whom during my visit I discussed some matters relating to my planned donations to the charities under his supervision. As I found out, the bishop wasn't too fond of Simon, barely tolerating him for the good of the Church as a community. I decided to make a substantial donation, for their projects seemed to benefit quite a large number of people. Those in charge of the projects were very efficient and not known for corruption, which was rather typical for enterprises of this kind. Anyway, since Simon himself was involved in one or two of these projects, the bishop contacted him saying that a gentleman by the name of Adarsh would soon see him. The bishop gave me Simon's telephone number and I rang him to make an appointment, and one Monday morning, I came to see him. He lived in an apartment in a house where other priests lived, and it was a rather large building situated in a quiet area close to a park.

Apart from woodlands, parks were always my favourite places and those where curiously some significant encounters of my life had happened.

I rang his apartment's bell at eleven, was let in, and once I saw Simon I noticed he hadn't changed much. He looked at me as if he was trying to associate my appearance with somebody he'd already met, but I was sure he wouldn't recognise me.

His place was nicely furnished and didn't give the impression of been inhabited by a churchman. We sat down on a large, comfortable sofa. The pricey looking coffee pot was already on the table, and after Simon had filled the cups and we had taken our first sips, a conversation began.

"You actually remind me of somebody I used to know, Mr Adarsh," Simon began. "There is a certain resemblance but, of course, you can't be him," and he gave a little laugh.

"Whoever it was," I said, "it surely wasn't me, for it is only now I have the pleasure of meeting you."

"Yes, of course," said Simon. "Please forgive me."

"Don't mention it, but excuse me my curiosity and tell me, did you know that person well?"

"Oh yes, pretty well, but it was a while ago."

"Was he a priest like yourself?"

"No, not at all, he was an accountant working for a bank, but his main interests were very untypical for a bank employee."

"And what were those interests if you don't mind telling me?" I enquired.

"Ah, his prime interest, even passion, was philosophy, then history and geography."

"Hmm, yes, that was really strange for a banker."

"Anyway," Simon went on, "he left the bank in disgrace due to a rather unpleasant scandal he was involved in. I mean the embezzlement of large sums of money."

"*Ooh la la*, that's pretty bad, and what happened to him?"

"An international warrant of arrest was issued. Police of all countries were looking for him, but he vanished without a trace."

"It seems somebody must have helped him, maybe a fellow philosopher," I suggested jokingly.

Simon gave a laugh and said, "Could be, you never know with those philosophers." Then he asked, "Now, the bishop told me your visit would be about a charity I'm in charge of."

"Yes, indeed, about a charity under your supervision, and I mean the one which takes care of the so-called fallen women," I said.

"Ah yes," said Simon, "this project is my special interest, and we've been looking after these poor ladies for a long time now. We provide free board and accommodation for those of them who can't afford to pay. Moreover, they're under medical and psychological care, and we also try to find jobs for them, and sometimes succeed."

"This is very noble of you," I said, "and must keep you busy."

"Oh yes, he said, "I'm very busy indeed."

We must notice here a certain soft spot in Simon with regard to women in general, but especially the so-called fallen ones. A fallen woman, as we know, usually means one who's known for her easy virtue, but not necessarily one who is paid for her sexual generosity. And women of this kind have been Simon's area of expertise, so to speak, for years, meaning not only providing care for them, but also them taking care of him. In other words, one good turn deserves another. He has an insatiable passion for sex with the weak, and these women provided a great opportunity to fulfil that.

Very young girls were another of his interests, and the younger the better. He liked to teach them everything. Sometimes, he had sex with two, one very young and the other older, who was supposed to make love to the young one during the sessions they had. He especially liked watching the older doing cunnilingus to the young one, and them both doing blow jobs to him at the same time. He loved coming into their mouths and called that a charity breakfast. He also liked to have a young boy along, whom he instructed what to do to them and to himself. For instance, the boy fucked one of them from behind while Simon gave him anal.

Anyway, they tried everything, and orgies too took place, with his fellow churchmen who had the same likings. On the hole, he could satisfy himself only when he was fully in charge of the opposite sex; he treated them like nothing but an object of his sexual satisfaction, and this could satisfy his utmost appetite for sex. But in those countries, he also had a few long-term relationships with mature women and their daughters, and that was he liked best. Those women were told to instruct their daughters what he liked most, and then he had them both in every way imaginable. Since he was generous with money, and they appreciated his sexual prowess, everybody was happy. But then, of course, that passion of his had to be keep secret for obvious reasons, since his supervisors would tolerate a minor transgression of that kind, but never a one of that proportion which in fact was here out of any proportion. And that argument was what I had up my sleeve for him if other ways wouldn't work.

"This is a very honourable activity indeed," I said, "and I'm sure it gives you great satisfaction to help those poor women."

"Oh yes," said Simon, "and the joy of doing that overcomes my tiredness, believe me."

"I do believe you," I said to him and to myself, *for fucking two or three of them at the same time is a tiresome business, but the pleasure might triumph over the fatigue.*

240

I'd been made aware of that passion of Simon's by Mr Wissend, who told me that his superiors would be informed of Simon's passion only when he wouldn't agree to cooperate with us. Thus, I casually said to him, "But, Father, may I ask you a personal question?"

"Certainly," he said smiling, "provided it's not too personal."

"I wonder," I began, "you know, dealing constantly with so many women, among whom there are some good-looking ones, must be a specific challenge for you, I mean, to restrain yourself from temptation, if you know what I mean."

"To be honest, yes, it is a great challenge, a test of my moral strength to resist the temptation you mention."

"But you always succeed in restraining yourself, I suppose."

"Yes, indeed, I do, but it's a real struggle sometimes, to be frank."

"I'm sorry to say, but I've been told that more than once you haven't been able to resist, Father."

Simon went red in the face and looked at me in horror, saying, "That's a slander. I've always... I..." He began gasping and couldn't finish the sentence.

"Hmm," I said, "do forgive me. My information is rather well founded," and I produced some photos from my pocket that Wissend had given me the other day. "Please have a look, Father," I encouraged him. He did, and now for a change he went white as a sheet.

"I... I..." he started again, but not wanting to prolong his suffering, I didn't wait for his reply if it was ever to come, and said, "I've got an offer you can't refuse, I'm afraid."

He somehow managed to overcome his weakness and said in a hardly audible voice, "And what is it, Mr Adarsh?"

"It is about an organisation of which you are a member, Father."

"Yes, I know what you mean," said Simon, who by then, being a rather strong man after all, had regained his composure.

"Your organisation makes some financial deals which are actually illegal, I mean, laundering vast sums of money whose origins are highly suspicious. So far, you've managed to avoid any serious scrutiny due to very clever operations, and being a respectable charity has helped too, but this may come to an end sooner or later and then you can imagine what happens, can't you?"

"Yes, I can," said Simon, and closed his eyes as if he was about to start praying.

"So, I presume you would like to avoid the consequences, which in your case would be surely disastrous."

"What do you expect me to do?" he asked curtly.

"As far as I know, you don't have access to documents related to the organisation's financial transactions, do you?"

"No, I don't, I know nothing of it."

"I suppose you don't, but you attend meetings during which these transactions are being discussed, don't you? So, if you had the right equipment, you could record all that is said during the meetings."

"No, I wouldn't be able to do that," said Simon.

"And why not?" I asked him.

"Because the place where a meeting takes place is always checked for any electronic surveillance."

*Careful and suspicious bastards*, I thought, *they don't even trust their own.*

"And who's in charge of that?" I asked him.

"Jason Goodman," Simon replied.

*That's convenient*, I thought, *because Wissend has already told me that Jason would cooperate with us.*

"Okay, Father," I said, "don't worry about that. Do what you've been doing until now, and no word to anybody what we've been talking about, promise?"

"Yes, I swear, I won't say a word, but what about, you know, my private affairs?"

"As a matter of fact, what you do in private isn't of our interest," I said, "so, you may carry on. I don't care."

"And you won't denounce me to my superiors or anybody else?" he asked.

"No, we won't, for as regards your passion, we share your view that he who believes in morality condemns life."

Simon looked at me in amazement, apparently thinking I was joking, but to assure him I was being serious, I said, "We do share your belief, so take it easy, *carpe diem.*"

"Thank you," he said. "I'm sorry I can't be of any assistance, but If I could do something after all…"

"Then we'll let you know, Father."

And I meant what I told him. Let him enjoy himself. Anyway, he wasn't doing any harm to those women and girls after all. They might too have pleasure, after all, and most importantly, an extra income, which they needed, and Simon was actually quite generous to them, so let him carry on.

*So, it's Jason who's their commander-in-chief,* I thought, *and small wonder, for he's in fact the only one of them who knows how money works. But it can't be just him,* I thought, *he wouldn't be able to manage everything on his own,* so I asked Simon, "Who are his closest associates?"

"James and Shaun," he said.

"I imagine so," I said. "I'm leaving you now, but please remember we have a deal. I won't say anything to your superiors, and you in turn won't say anything to your friends about what we've been discussing, okay?"

"Agreed, I swear I won't," said Simon.

"Better not to swear. Just imagine what may happen to you if you talk to them," I said to him, and left.

Yes, I was still thinking when I came out of his apartment onto the street and began walking towards Hyde Park that Shaun, James and Jason have something in common. They represent those in this country who consider it virtuous to be able to outwit others by lies, swindles and the like. They reversed the criteria of morality. And to excuse themselves, they used a plethora of quasi-clever word tricks, so typical for self-serving, egocentric prigs and bigots of which this country was full. Those, who kept the façade of being full of praise for selflessness, honesty and generosity, doing the opposite but surprisingly held in esteem by the tele watchers and the rags readers, who seemed to believe all that circus. And it might be due to the fact that all Jason-like characters have been always considered the *crème de la crème* in Albion.

*It won't be easy to trash them,* I thought. *However, it's still possible when their own weapons can be used against them.* But then how to go about that? That Jason, yes, he promised to cooperate with us, but now, that swine might try to sneak out of it. *Apparently, he believes himself to be smarter than us. Ah*, I said to myself, *I wish you were here*, and as soon as I said that, I noticed a huge black cat at my side, and I'd never before seen such a behemoth. I was now heading for Hyde Park and there were plenty of dogs being walked by their owners, and some of them passing us seemed to be frightened of the cat. I looked at the cat from time to time, and when he looked back, I had the strange impression he was smiling at me. There was something familiar about the cat, but I couldn't put my finger on it.

Anyway, its behaviour wasn't cat-like, for cats, as far as I knew, never ever accompany strangers on such long walks, and it was now a good mile since the cat had joined me. *Yes*, I thought, *it's very strange indeed, and why has he joined me, after all? Does he want something from me, but what it might be, for that matter?"*

Once we'd left the park, I decided to have a beer and a bite to eat, and since the cat was still there, and strangely enough I didn't want to get rid of him, I thought of buying him something too.

I knew cats like milk and fish, so I ordered some when we sat down at the table that was outside a pub we arrived at. The cat sitting on the chair attracted curious looks from other customers, especially that now sitting on the chair, it seemed to be even bigger. The cat looked around as if he were a lord surveying his estate, and when the waiter arrived with the menu carte he took it from him and began studying it as if he could read. Now, almost all of those present were watching us, apparently not being sure what to make of it. They might be thinking, I guessed, that the cat was from a Russian circus that had just arrived in London. I, myself, was surprised too, but somehow wasn't disturbed by the cat's extraordinary behaviour. Actually, I was even pleased with the situation, which strangely enough much improved my mood.

When the cat had finished reading the menu carte, he pointed with his right paw to something in it and looked at the waiter, who now with his eyes opened wide was standing almost to attention. I looked at the item chosen by the cat, and it turned out to be a very special piece of salmon. *Ay, ay*, I thought, *he has very good but rather extravagant taste.*

Using a fork, the cat was eating the salmon and drinking the beer he had ordered as well. The people around us weren't now interested in their own food and drink at all, watching the cat instead in a curious disbelief. *Now,* I thought, *they eventually have proof of something almost unreal happening there, and something to talk about later.*

Once we had both finished our food and drinks, I produced a pack of Gauloises from my pocket and offered one to the cat, but he refused, shaking his head. I lit a cigarette and as always enjoyed the good taste of that excellent French tobacco. *Now,* I was thinking, *it's time to visit those other scoundrels, Jason, James and Shaun, but how to go about that and which one of them should I see first?*

After short consideration, I decided that Jason would be first, for having already met him in Moscow could make it easier.

I had enjoyed my visit to the Russian capital and the country itself, finding it more appealing than Dollaria with its obsession with money which had became a god for its people. And in their pursuit of money, they had reversed the scale of ethical values as previously Bolshevik Russia had, with the exception that in the Soviet Union, money wasn't the ultimate aim. In Dollaria, people actually no longer believed (but they still claim they did) in Christian selflessness, compassion and humility as the most esteemed virtues of man, but in their opposite, that is ruthless, egocentric self-interest, in 'catch as you can catch'. Moreover, those traditionally respected values were now the object of ridicule and rejected as a characteristic of the weak. And again, by comparison, the people of Russia were different in that respect.

Jason, I'd been told during my stay in Moscow, in Russia, had some interests in Dollaria. Anyway, he was the leading force of the M7 and it was up to him where they were to carry on their business. He was also interested in antiques, not so much in the art itself but as a source of investment. And since Beatrice now ran an antique shop and travelled all over the world in search of furniture, paintings and other stuff, I thought that there might be a chance to approach him.

I knew, and had actually already been warned by Klug, that Jason was a tough nut, and it wouldn't be easy to deal with him, and I immediately thought of Fabiana, that Hungarian woman I met. She was a high-class hooker but an educated one for that matter, and therefore was sought after by those rich men, who appreciated not only her gorgeous looks but also her intelligence. As far as I knew, she was one of the highest paid escorts in London and always received extra money in recognition of both her assets. I had met her before, having become attached to Bea, and greatly enjoyed her company. The sex and conversation were extraordinary, and if I hadn't met Bea, I could have considered a serious relationship with Fabiana.

She, in fact, wouldn't go with every man, and she was very choosy in that matter. Once, she turned down a man who promised a very handsome payment for her service and made him furious, but she didn't care, for there were so many of them and not only in England for that matter since she often got invitations from abroad with all her travel expenses paid. She travelled as far as Latin America, Australia and Japan, having been recommended by men she met in London, and then by those she met overseas.

Knowing her, I knew she wouldn't appreciate Jason's company, but since she owned me something – I had paid her university tuition fees and rejected her offer to pay the money back – she would possibly do me a favour. Anyway, being so skilled in dealing with men, she would wrap him easily round her finger, for he might have been a clever financier, but compared with her knowledge of men, his familiarity with women was good for nothing. So, all in all, it should work, and I was going to talk to her before I was to meet him.

I phoned Fabiana one Monday morning at eight o'clock, and she was very happy to hear from me. However, she first gave me a dressing-down for not contacting her for so long. "I was very angry at you," she said. "You should have at least let me know what you were doing, for you know perfectly well how much I care about you!"

I apologised profoundly and told her that it had been due to extraordinary circumstances that I couldn't get in touch, and promised to tell her what it was that had prevented me from contacting her, not now on the phone, but in person, considering the seriousness of the matter.

As I hoped, she understood and we arranged to see each other the same day three hours later at her apartment, the same I'd already been to.

I wasn't sure what to do with the cat, who actually seemed to be listening to my conversation with Fabiana. After I finished my conversation, I looked at him, and I had the strange impression that he'd understood what I was talking about with her and now had an amusing look in his eyes, but of course all that must have been an illusion. Anyway, I didn't have to make a decision what to do with him, for when after taking a bath, I came into the living room, he wasn't there. I looked for him everywhere but in vain, and how he managed to get out, for the door was locked, and my apartment was on the fourth floor, I didn't have a clue, but to be honest, it was now roughly one year since I had made up my mind not to be surprised by some extraordinary phenomena.

So, after dressing, I went to see that gorgeous woman. She didn't live far from my place, so I went on foot, especially as the weather was very fine. On my way, I was thinking what to do if she offered me a more intimate reception, which considering our previous experience was very likely. I wasn't sure what Bea would say, or more importantly how she'd react if she found out, and in truth I was to find out pretty soon.

Once I entered Fabiana's apartment, she kissed me tenderly on the lips, pressing her magnificent breasts against my body, and I immediately remembered all the delights I had previously experienced. We sat down close to each other on the sofa and began talking. I said I was sorry for not letting her know my whereabouts for such a long time, but couldn't tell everything right now as to why I hadn't been in touch with her for so long, but I would as soon as it was possible. To my great relief, she understood, and again I had a chance to admire her intellectual faculties. The she told me something I wasn't aware of and which took me by surprise. Fabiana said she had met Bea on the previous day and learned she was my woman. Moreover, Bea had already known about my previous affection for her and wouldn't mind if I wanted to renew my relationship with her. Hearing that, I was flabbergasted. It seemed that she would always be able to surprise me. Then Fabiana surprised me even more by telling me that she knew about my current challenge, and I wondered why Bea had told her all that, just having met her, but couldn't fathom that out at all. *I will talk to her about that later on*, I decided. Now the question was how to persuade Fabiana to agree to my plan of entrapping Jason. But before I had a chance to tell her that, Fabiana got hold of my hand and began kissing me affectionately on my lips and then unbuttoning my shirt, she began to stroke my chest.

I couldn't resist the temptation and soon after undressing each other, we began making love. She knew perfectly well what I liked most and so she took my cock in her mouth and started to suck it gently, and after a good ten minutes of that delight, she drove it into herself, wrapping her legs round my body. She was superb as always, and I had a climax that was comparable to those I had with Bea. Then we lay down, saying nothing for a while until she eventually said, "You know now how I missed you. I've been, as you know, with several men, but none of them have ever given me such pleasure as you always did, and I wanted it again and again when you were away. Would you come to see me from time to time, darling?" she asked. I promised I would, and now after this wonderful hour of our lovemaking, I wasn't in the mood to start a conversation about anything related to my business with the M7. But then it was Fabiana who first mentioned it, saying, "Bea told me you had a problem with some people, and wondered whether I could be of help. Is that the reason you came to see me?"

I wanted to be honest with her, for she deserved the truth, so I said, "Yes, Fabia, the business was the reason for my visit, but once I saw you, I forgot everything about that, and, you know…"

Fabiana burst out laughing, "Ay, ay, here we go, but this is why I love you, anyway, I have always known you would never make a good businessman."

"Yes," I said, "you're right, I wouldn't, but now willy-nilly I have to."

"I see, and I'm not going to ask you why it is so, but if you want me to help you, I'll do whatever you ask me."

I looked at her and said to myself, *She would be my woman if I hadn't met Bea,* and I said to her, "To be honest, I'm not happy about you helping me, but…"

"No buts, I will do what I can," she said.

"Okay then, and thank you, and as for that business, let me tell you why I need you. There's a kind of organisation which not long ago almost succeeded in sending me to prison because I wasn't willing to take part in their conspiracy, and now I don't want them to get away with what they did and want to strike back. You, considering your potential, will be able to seduce one of them, a man by the name of Jason Goodman, gain his confidence and get some information out of him that I need, but I don't really want you to go too far, if you know what I mean."

"Yes," she said, "I know what you mean, and I wouldn't, because I'm not eager to share a bed with a man who put you in trouble. You know my principles, don't you?"

"Yes, I do, and I appreciate it, so am I to arrange your rendezvous with him?"

"Go ahead, and don't you worry, I'll manage him."

I actually already knew she would say yes, but still didn't like the idea, and I said to her, "But be careful. He's bloody cunning, that scoundrel."

"I say no worries," and kissing me, she said, "let's make it again."

And we began lovemaking once more, but this time she wanted to be in charge, first fondling my dick with her mouth and tongue, and then taking it between her firm and big boobs, holding it and moving them up and down. Then she asked me to fuck her from behind, and then come in her mouth. I did what she said, and came again, and now we were resting, holding each other in our arms. Sex with her had always been pure delight, and yes, only Bea could match her in the art of love. Making love to both of them was as if you were in a different world, where ecstasy makes you forget the misery of reality.

*

While Fabiana and I were enjoying our own company, Jason was having a rather unpleasant day, and it all began when he went for a walk early in the morning as usual in a park close to his apartment.

When he was passing by a park bench, he noticed a huge black cat sitting on it and watching him with interest. *What is that monstrous creature doing here on its own?* he asked himself, and at that very moment, the creature jumped from the bench and landed in front of him, blocking his way. Jason abruptly came to a halt and thought, *What a cheeky thing he is. One can't take a peaceful stroll these days.* We must say here that Jason to his shame hated animals, and especially cats, which in his opinion were particularly devious. But that sly creature seemed to be undisturbed by Jason's views and sat there, still watching him. So, he chose to ignore the cat and to continue his walk, but when he was just walking around the cat, he slipped, lurching forward, and his head hit the very bench the cat had been sitting on a minute earlier. Since the collision with the bench was rather hard, Jason immediately passed out and was now lying helplessly on the path, absent to the world. We must say here that very unusually on this particular day, there was nobody in the park's avenue who could come to Jason's rescue.

When he eventually regained consciousness, he realised to his horror that he was no longer in the park but in an unknown-to-him flat, but at least that monster of a cat wasn't there. *At last I managed to get rid of that beast*, thought Jason. But the most disturbing questions now were how had he happened to land in this flat, and who, for hell's sake, had brought him here? But obviously he couldn't fathom out any answer, and the mystery of his unexplained transition in time and space was really distressing.

But he didn't have time to ponder these questions for long because now somebody had just come into the room, and once Jason saw the man, he was immediately possessed with fear because of the man's ghostly, almost white face and very dark glasses he was wearing. *My God*, he thought, *he is like a black colonel, like one of those Latin American junta members*, and a tremendous shiver ran through his body. God, of course, wouldn't come to his rescue, but Jason couldn't think now of anybody else. He just stared at the man, and when he spoke, Jason was even more frightened by the man's voice, which was as if a long, sharp nail was driving into his brain.

The man said, "I'm not too pleased with your presence here, but I had to follow an order, and that's why you're now my guest. You're here to understand a couple of things you have failed to comprehend so far, dear Mr Goodman. And, as a matter of fact, small wonder that you haven't, because you're an English bloody shopkeeper who lacks the ability of abstract thinking. Yes, it's true, you people made some scientific discoveries but they have been used to enslave other people, and not for the well-being of anybody but yourselves, but not for all of your fellow countrymen for that matter. So, now, you have to pay the price, for you have refused to believe that there's a power beyond the reality, and that power is the true hegemon of this earth. You're nothing but a depraved degenerate for whom the world's limits extend to what you manage to steal from it, and every thief should obviously be prosecuted.

Now Jason was half-conscious from the fear that overcame not only his mind but the whole of his body, and was desperately looking for a chance to save himself, and for the first time in his life, he fully understood that he was in a situation he could do nothing but obey, and that his only chance was to agree to whatever he would be asked to do. And that chance came when that frightening man said, "Now you realise, I presume, it'll be much wiser to agree with us, don't you?"

"Yes, of course, I do, and—"

He couldn't finish for the man interrupted him, saying, "I knew you would agree. You're not that stupid after all. You know, we in fact need people like you, for without them we wouldn't be able to show the others the difference between truth and falsity, and good and evil. However, to tell the truth, this difference is very vague, confusing many so much that they actually have no clue as to who they are or what they're supposed to do. So as it happens, some of them become politicians, and then… but let's leave that subject for now. And going back to our main topic of conversation, we have an offer we hope you won't refuse," said the man, and looked Jason in the eye.

Another shiver of panic ran through his body but he managed somehow to repress it and said, "Yes, I will, whatever it is."

"You may remember that you made an agreement in Moscow, dear Mr Goodman, didn't you? But now you don't intend to keep your word, do you?"

"I, I—" began Jason.

But the man didn't wait for his answer and said, "But now I certainly will. This is what you were going to say, isn't it?"

"Yes, sir," agreed Jason.

"Good. You will soon meet a woman, a beautiful woman for that matter. Ah, pure delight, if I only could, ah, forget it, maybe another time. So, you'll make her acquaintance and of course you may try to go further, if you know what I mean… anyway, you'll be doing what she says as if she were your boss. Understood?"

Now Jason was so happy seeing a chance to save his ass that he was about to jump to his feet and salute, but somehow managed to restrain himself and said instead, "I'll do what she says."

"Yes, you will," said the man. "And if you don't obey her," he added, "we'll transfer you at the double to that country from where no traveller returns, as your famous writer Shakespeare said."

"No... no... no need. I will," Jason hastened to say.

"Very wise of you, so you're free to go now, but remember that we're always nearby, and what you call black magic really exists. But you can try to understand one thing at least, that when a writer introduces that black magic in his novel, as our dear Mikhail did, he does this, among others reasons, in order to emphasise the stupidity of the people he writes about and the absurdity of the time they live in. But even this seems to be incomprehensible to you, I'm afraid, so leave me this instant, for I've already got tired of talking to you."

Jason was now sure at last that he had been spared something even worse, and was so overwhelmed by the man's magnanimity that he sprang to his feet, bowed to him three times and began walking backwards towards the door, and once outside, he took a deep breath of relief and began descending the staircase, and when he reached the ground floor, he saw again that monstrous cat, which now seemed to be even bigger, standing on his hind legs.

The cat smiled at him, or so it seemed so Jason, and opened the exit door to let him out, and when at last the poor fellow was outside, he began to run so fast, despite his age, that he possibly set a new world record for two hundred metres. Tired now and still in shock after all he had undergone, Jason eventually slumped on the first bench he reached in the street where he was running, and partially regaining his reasoning faculties, he began to think of what he was now supposed to do. He knew perfectly well that they, that is, the gang that had just abducted him, wouldn't leave him alone if he didn't do what he'd been told.

*And now*, he thought, *that unknown woman who would be my boss, my God, that's a catastrophe! I'd better go now to my place and have a rest and then see what happens.* So, with some effort he got up and began walking towards his apartment, and when he was passing by a coffee shop, he noticed a very attractive woman sitting at the table outside. *What a gal, and her boobs, ay, ay, it'd be nice to play with them*, he thought, and at that very moment the woman smiled at him and made an inviting gesture with her hand. Bewildered, Jason stopped abruptly, not sure what that meant, but gathering the remnants of his courage of which not much was left after all that terrible experience, he came to her table and slightly bowing politely, said, "How do you do, madam? I don't think I've had the pleasure."

"I haven't, either, dear Mr Goodman, but we may have it now."

"How come you know my name, madam?"

"Ah, a friend of mine actually knows you and described your appearance to me just this morning, so, recognising you, I decided to have a chat."

"I see, and who's that friend of yours if I may enquire?"

"Mr Adarsh," the lady said.

"Ah, him, yes, of course, I know him," he said, and thought, *what a bloody coincidence!* And then said, "And what did he tell you about me?"

"He said you've been charged with an assignment, dear sir, and asked me to talk about it."

*Aha,* Jason thought, so, it must be her that white monster told me about. And clearing his throat said, "Yes, I'm supposed to do something for him and his friends, and—"

He couldn't finish, for the lady – that is Fabiana, as the reader may have guessed – said to him, "Exactly, dear Mr Goodman, so please sit down and we'll discuss some points of your forthcoming cooperation."

He already knew he should fully cooperate and said, "Yes, certainly," and sat down next to her.

"We need some privacy, so we'll go now to my apartment, which is not far from here, and once there, we'll talk about it. Shall we?" said Fabiana, rising from the chair.

"All the pleasure's mine," said Jason, always a gentleman.

And during their walk, Jason was thinking, *And what if I somehow manage to persuade her to—* but Fabiana interrupted his trace of thought, saying, "I've been told you're a very clever man, but somewhat stubborn, if you know what I mean."

"I'm not sure what you're aiming at, madam."

"Mr Adarsh says you might try to do your best not to cooperate with him and his friends, and if so, they'll be forced to use, you know, other means of… you know…"

*Damn it,* Jason said to himself, *they know everything, and who are they, for hell's sake, to know that much?*

"To be honest," he said, "I had some doubts, madam, but now I'm ready to do for him whatever it takes."

"Very kind of you, sir, and that's us," she said, pointing at a terraced house they were approaching, "that's us," and they came to the front door, which was flung open by a porter who apparently saw them coming.

"Good morning, madam," the porter said, holding the door for them.

"Good morning, George," said Fabiana, "and thank you."

They got in the lift which took them to the top floor, Fabiana's apartment. Once they entered, she said to Jason, "Please make yourself comfortable. Whisky and everything else is over there in the corner. Help yourself, and give me a minute. I must change, you know, it's been a hot day." And she disappeared. Jason helped himself to a very decent portion of whisky, which he hoped would improve his mood after what he'd been through since the evening before.

It didn't take long, and Fabiana was back in the reception room wearing just a transparent robe that concealed hardly anything. "You must excuse me my attire, but I always put something on like that in my place, you know, it makes me feel at ease."

"No need to apologise, madam," he said, and there was indeed nothing to be ashamed of, for we've already described Fabiana's magnificent looks, which were now displayed to Jason, who could hardly take his eyes off her.

"So, Mr Goodman, as far as I know, you're supposed to do something for a friend of mine, Mr Adarsh, aren't you?"

"Yes, madam, I am, and I will, so help me God."

"I suggest you leave God alone. He may have something more important to do these days."

We must note here that Jason was an atheist, and God or any gods for that matter, weren't of interest to him. He called His name just in that American movies way, and because he hoped to have a more intimate relationship with that gorgeous woman and was displaying his substantial linguistic skills to impress her, but Fabiana wouldn't have any of it, being not only a beautiful but also a very intelligent woman. She knew by heart those polite, quasi-clever word games so appreciated in this country, word tricks which were recognised here as proof of refined intelligence, being in fact a mere ridiculous rambling to impress or deceive those stupid enough to be impressed by them. Fabiana wasn't one of them, and that's why she said, "Dear Mr Goodman, let's get to the point. I know what's on your mind, but forget it, and as a substitute, so to speak, I'll introduce you to a woman who will, I'm very sure of it, satisfy your secret desires. Her name's Karina, and you'll meet her later on this evening."

Jason was rather disappointed with the outcome of that preliminary acquaintance with Fabiana, hoping for much more, but now realising he wouldn't stand a chance, so that Karina might be good enough for him after all. Thus, he said, "I understand, madam, and thank you for your generous offer. I'm sure your friend Karina is a gorgeous woman and will make me happy."

"Oh yes, she certainly will," said Fabiana, who knew his true desires, which he had to hide and managed to satisfy in secret but, unfortunately for him, nothing could be hidden from the formidable Mr Wissend's intelligence service, even Mossad and all others were a joke, a Sunday school compared to his intelligence effectiveness. And now Fabiana knew of Jason's most intimate inclination to be intimidated by a woman, his masochism, which nobody would suspect in such a self-assertive, ruthless and successful banker. It was decided that the right woman should be found to provide him with what he wanted so much, and accidentally it was Fabiana who knew such a girl, and accordingly everything had already been arranged. And since Jason could not be trusted despite his apparent willingness to cooperate (for how could a banker be trusted, after all?), Mr Wissend had met Fabiana's friend before telling her what kind of information he needed, and asked her to get it out of Jason during their sessions.

"I've already made an appointment for you, dear sir," said Fabiana, "and you'll meet Karina at nine this evening. Here's her address, and don't be late, for she disapproves of unpunctuality."

"Thank you, madam," politely acknowledged Jason, whose manners prevailed his disappointment at not being able to go any further with Fabiana. And so, he went to meet Karina at the agreed time.

Let us now introduce her before their meeting.

She was a tall, slim lady about forty. Long black hair covered her very pale face adorned by very large black eyes, and this was all complemented by long, shapely legs. Those who knew her said she was a bit witch-like. And Karina didn't complain about the shortage of clients; London (and other cities, of course) was full of those distressed, wretched rascals who under the mask of superiority hide sick, very much unhappy, tormented souls that need consolation. And to get it wasn't cheap, so only the wealthy could afford it. Just the induction was £5,000, and then each session or interview (sort of a psychoanalysis) four thousand, and because there were so many who were in need of Karina's service, she was already pretty well off.

And she was very good at what she did. She even received complimentary letters, some of them from celebrities, public personages and aristocrats, who somehow especially needed her help and were subjected to the most refined treatment. All in all, Karina was a star on that firmament of human despair, and Jason was just ringing her flat's bell.

The door was opened without any questions, and he went upstairs to her apartment. Its door was ajar, so he pushed it gently and entered. The apartment he found himself in was very spacious, over 200 square metres, he thought, and when he was trying to find his way through it he became more and more impressed, not only by its size but also by how tastefully it was furnished. All of the furniture was antique and must have cost a fortune. Jason had previously visited the homes of the rich, but he had never seen so many beautiful things in one place. Let us mention here that almost all of those beauties were provided by Beatrice. And much of that furniture was very dear indeed, but some was found in very remote parts of France and Italy, and were bought relatively cheaply, but now on the free market, at Sotheby's and the like, their prices were surely exorbitant.

Jason eventually saw his host half-lying on a Louis XV sofa. Once he looked at her, he immediately knew she was his woman, and she would give him what he wanted so much. Just by looking at her, he felt a shiver running through his body and could hardly restrain himself from prostrating himself before her here and now. *A goddess*, he thought, *the personification of a deity. She will make me happy. I am happy right now just seeing her.*

And that goddess stood up from the sofa, came up to him and gave him a terrible slap on the face. Jason fell on his knees and began weeping, not from the pain but from the happiness he felt.

Karina ordered him to stay on his knees, and she herself sat down back on the sofa and said, "Do you still want to undergo the treatment?"

"Oh yes, I do," Jason answered, still weeping.

"Are you prepared to pay for it? As you may know, it's rather expensive."

"Yes, madam, whatever it is."

"Good, then you'll pay me upfront for the next month, and it's £37, 000 altogether. Five for the induction and eight for two sessions a week."

Jason immediately pulled a cheque book out of his jacket pocket, wrote down the demanded amount and handed the cheque to Karina.

"So, now you go home, and we'll start tomorrow at 5 am," she ordered him.

*

Jason had never ever in his life risen so early but was now eager to see her again anytime she wanted, and when he came on the agreed day, the sessions began in earnest. They were very different in nature, that is, never the same, which made them more attractive.

During the first one, he met Karina's assistant Pablo, a very good-looking fellow, probably of Spanish or Latin-American ancestry, who played an active part in the session which took place in a soundproof room so that nobody could hear Jason's screams.

Karina made Jason do cunnilingus on her while Pablo fucked him from behind. Then gave him deep throat, during which Jason had to swallow every drop of Pablo's sperm. Then Karina fastened on her a very big artificial cock and fucked Jason herself from behind while strangling him with the silk rope, and Pablo fucked him in the mouth. There were many other compilations, for they both, Karina and Pablo, were very imaginative, but never ever did Jason have a chance to fuck either of them. However, he could watch them fucking and was masturbating himself, but nothing else. He was also regularly flogged and made to confess to everything he'd done wrong in his life. All the sessions were recorded on cameras and CD recorder, but both Karina and Pablo were wearing masks so it would be impossible to identify them, whereas Jason's face was seen clearly in every movie.

The sessions lasted one year and made Jason very happy, so he would have liked to have more, but Karina said that was enough, and they parted as good friends. Jason would have never thought he was so tough anyway, and he was very proud of himself. He also learned about himself things he had never known before, as he had known nothing of sex with a man, which he found now very gratifying, and knew he would continue his newfound pleasure.

All in all, he enjoyed himself, and what's wrong about the way he got there? There is no life without pleasure, and nothing human is alien to those in charge of human affairs with the exception of betrayal. But, as usual, there are people who would always envy you your contentment because they themselves aren't able to have any. And someday in the future such people, being envious of his happiness, would take advantage of it and drive him to serious mental disorder, which would force him to seek refuge in a psychiatric hospital. And, of course, he'd lose all the money trying to fight his accusers in courts, but in vain, for they would have all the proof needed to support their accusations. We must emphasise here that we don't blame Jason for his specific preferences, but we do so for something really sinister, that is, his willingness to conspire against his once good friend, Karl Denker, now Ches Adarsh.

Karina, in turn, would be honoured with a private audience with Lord Hellbridge, who appreciated her achievements very much, and in the first place her generosity. From her own purse, she had founded a charity for abused women which was run by her and women like her. And she was awarded several distinctions, the most esteemed of them being Baroness of Sorcerhill.

We'll return to Jason (and all the others too, of course) later again, for his story is obviously connected to his friends' stories. Anyway, we haven't finished with him yet, for the reader may find a couple of his future adventures interesting too, and we wouldn't deprive him of the pleasure of knowing about them.

And now the time has come to meet somebody else.

# GRAHAM

'If you want to be an honest and serious man, you should
never work at university.'
Ludwig Wittgenstein

Graham Witmore, nicknamed 'The Terrible' or 'The Unbearable', was
certainly the most sympathetic of them all. And he was the only one with
whom I had a relationship close to friendship, and we both actually spent
a lot of time together.

Our favourite venue for having drinks was the Boathouse pub situated
by the River Cam in Cambridge. And Graham was like me, very fond of
water sports, and here he was a precursor of a very new and particular
one called the 'Revival March', which he recommended as the best cure
for recovering your strength while drinking. The march's rules were very
simple but demanding at the same time, and the first time he put them to
the test happened by accident.

After enjoying several drinks with his friends, he came out onto the
Boathouse's terrace, where they were drinking, and saw a very pretty girl
wearing just a swimsuit in a kayak passing close to the terrace. He was so
excited by the sight of her that he bent over to have a closer look, and losing
his balance, fell into the water. The girl came to his rescue and invited him
to join her in the kayak, but Graham out of pride kindly declined but said
he would accompany her on foot in whichever direction she was heading.
She agreed, and as it turned out later, she was one of his new students

that Graham was to meet later the same day. Her seminar was to take place on Sidgwick Site, but first she needed to get to King's College, where she lived, to change. So, they both made their way in the direction of the college, the girl paddling in the kayak and Graham marching bravely next to her in the water.

Initially, he found it difficult because it was his first attempt of this kind, and obviously because of the alcohol he had drunk. But after some hundred metres, things improved, and the further he went, the better he felt, and when eventually they reached the college, much of his strength was restored. Graham thanked the girl profusely for the company and kissed her hand, which slightly shocked her because of not being accustomed to such a foreign courtesy, and they parted. Once in her room in the college, the girl told her best friend of her recent experience and admitted enjoying it very much. Having changed, she went to attend the seminar, and once she entered the classroom, she was bewildered to see the companion of her water journey. Graham, seeing her, smiled and didn't fail to notice that even fully dressed, she was still very pretty indeed.

Their water adventure turned later into something much more intimate, as Graham had told me at the time, and he'd praised not only her looks but her intellect too, and said that even during their lovemaking, they discussed philosophy. Anyway, she was the one he married shortly after their first encounter, and for the first time in his life, Graham had met a woman who could satisfy both his body and soul, as it was with Bea and me.

She was now very busy, and often I didn't see her for a week or so, but when she was eventually back, we made up for lost time. Bea had just returned from India where she attended a Kamasutra course, and now she was even more refined than ever.

But back to Graham; we want here to tell the reader more about his very unusual – as most of his colleagues said – views, which became a serious consternation in the intellectual milieu of Cambridge.

He claimed, for instance, that a man deprived of passion is incapable of faith, which is equal to selflessness unattainable to such a man, and he meant, of course, religious faith, falsely claimed by so many. Graham said, among other things, that selflessness, honour and chivalry are now absent in this world because God is dead for people, as the great Friedrich had already observed.

Ethics for him was inseparable from reason, so for the ability to believe, to have faith in the true meaning of the word, one must possess the capacity of abstract, transcendental reasoning, for only then is he able to make value judgements on the basis of reason, that is, to decide between good and evil and to act upon the decision. And what was exceptional here in Graham's view of the matter in question, was his conviction (rather strange, as his colleagues said) that both passion and reason are indispensable conditions of being able to believe in God. Graham himself was an agnostic and, as such, he was a kind of mediator whenever he happened to be in the company of believers and their adversaries. One day, having lunch at the Travellers' Club in London, Graham was introduced to Mr Wissend, and they quickly became close friends because of being themselves very much like-minded. The latter in turn introduced him to Lord Hellbridge, who impressed Graham like nobody else, emphasizing his amazing powers of observation and almost second sight (as he put it) as regards all matters related to faith, world religions, politics, finance and whatever else they were both discussing. During one of their conversations, the lord claimed that every man by reason of his nature is a believer, even if he denies the existence of God. However, this kind of man is unaware of his belief and as such he is incapable of telling good from evil. Moreover, the lord claimed that in order to follow the Ten Commandments, one must have the ability of thinking *a priori*, that is to transcend the reality. And they were both convinced that only an intelligent man may call himself a Christian. However, they both agreed that in fact there was only one Christian and he died on the Cross.

Graham was happy to find out that the lord was very fond of gambling and dealing in shares at the Stock Exchange, for he himself was a committed gambler, and more than once he lost all the money he had.

So, when one day the lord (Mr Wissend was present too) invited Graham to accompany him to the Ritz Casino, he was more than happy.

Graham once had a good friend, Andrew, who gambled, among other places, at casinos in Warsaw, where he lived, and there, watching his friend and other gamblers, Graham learned that a true gambler never wins, because for him the game alone matters, not the money. And that friend of his did win occasionally, but more frequently lost, and gambling never made him rich. But their friendship had nothing to do with gambling; rather, it was about an encounter of two like-minded men.

One day, when Graham learnt about his friend's death, he was very upset, and as a matter of fact, never came to terms with it, remembering the good times they'd had together. And now when he together with the lord and Wissend entered the casino, the memories returned, and Hellbridge didn't fail to notice Graham's change of mood.

"Are you now remembering that good friend of yours, Professor Witmore?" he said.

"Yes, sir, I am," said Graham, slightly shocked by the lord's question.

"I, myself, was sad hearing about his death, and now we are at the right place to commemorate him. I mean, the liberating power of betting money on the unknown, and you being a philosopher. Know what I mean?"

"So, did you know him too?" asked Graham.

"Oh yes, and on more than one occasion we discussed some topics, for instance, anarchism, of which Andrew was fond. And rightly so, I believe, however, it would be just a beginning," said the lord.

Graham wasn't sure what the lord meant and let it go, saying instead, "I don't claim to be a philosopher. I'm just in philosophy's service."

"That's good enough, and as a matter of fact, there have been just a few who might be called philosophers, don't you think so?" the lord said.

"Indeed, just a few, and the same, strangely enough, is true for those who call themselves Christians."

"That's it, and now in this place we have the opportunity not only to test our ability to liberate ourselves from the prudence of that calculating mind of a shopkeeper, but also to test our capability of resistance to a very likely misfortune, that is, to test our strength of character. Since only then when we go beyond our self-preserving nature may we become a strong, really independent individual being, the *Frei Geist*, as our dear Friedrich says. For only he who isn't afraid of the unknown, who is ready to face it, may call himself brave. And now let's play, dear Mr Witmore."

And they began to play, but before we tell the story of the game, we're obliged to say a few words about the casino and the way its staff treated the lord.

In short, they were all very anxious whenever the lord came to play. And that was because every time he played, the casino lost a substantial amount of money, so they prayed (but nobody knew, including themselves, where actually their prayers were going to) not to see him too often. And now cold shivers went up the spines of the staff. The casino manager appeared himself, politely welcomed the lord, but he too wasn't now in the best of his moods, predicting another disaster. But what could they all do? Nothing. Yes, in theory, they might forbid entrance to anybody, not being obliged to explain the decision, but they wouldn't dare to forbid Lord Hellbridge from visiting them. He was too powerful to be barred from entering the casino, or any other place for that matter. Moreover, as he was Chairman of the Gambling Commission, among his many other responsibilities, it was up to him (for his colleagues in every commission of which he was a member always agreed with him) to grant gambling licences. So, now the manager was just hopelessly watching the lord and his companions, hoping they wouldn't stay too long, for he didn't share the lord's belief in the liberating power of the unknown.

It was roulette they started to play, and the lord said to Graham, "Do you often come here?"

"Oh no, I can't afford it."

"I see, but tell me, what are your favourite numbers and colours, if you have any, of course?"

"Hmm, I have a few... four, six and fifteen, and the colours black and green."

"Aha, and you're going to bet on them today?"

"Yes, I'll try them."

"As you wish, but do you know that numbers are one of the greatest mysteries ever?"

"No, I've never thought of it."

"But they are, I mean, they put the world in order, dear Mr Witmore, and they're in fact from another world, for everything that is here, on this earth, is relative and accidental and as such wouldn't establish any effective

263

arrangement of things. The problem is to find out the mathematical formulas which put existence in order, but this in turn cannot be done just by applying mathematics, for these formulas may be envisioned only in revelation, and just a few people are blessed with that capacity. Some say that it is a gift from God and, as such, accessible only to the chosen, and as a matter of fact I agree with them, for how can a man who is a vulnerable, imperfect being invent such a perfect and absolute order of mathematical formulas? No, he wouldn't."

"It might be true that somebody else is in charge of the matter in question, sir, but it would be difficult to prove."

"Eh, dear Mr Witmore, not as difficult as you assume," said the lord.

"As you know, all those proofs of God's existence are unconvincing and cannot withstand logical criticism," said Witmore.

"Ah, logic, but as you know, it says nothing about the world, as Ludwig observed."

"Yes, it may not, but it does say something about our thinking, doesn't it?"

"Your thinking, you say, hmm, this is something that might always be faulty," said Hellbridge.

"Yes, it might, but it is the only one we have, sir, and we can't help it."

"That's it, and now please consider the following, I mean, those formulas I've just mentioned. They, you agree, come to us out of nowhere, so to speak, but they have to come from somewhere, anyway, haven't they?"

"Hmm, yes, but it would be again difficult to find out their source," said Graham.

"Bah, difficult, you say, but you have to assume the existence of a source, don't you?" said the Lord.

"Logically, yes, I would have to," said Graham.

"Precisely, and can you think illogically?" enquired Hellbridge.

"No, provided we aren't at a loony bin."

"Huh, huh, how many outstanding minds have found their way there, and how many of them are still waiting to be admitted?" said the lord. "But let's consider something," he carried on, "in relation to what we have just observed. Can you think, logically of course, of how these formulas come to your mind?" said Hellbridge.

264

"I may try," Graham replied, "but I know I wouldn't reach any satisfying conclusion."

"And how come you know that *a priori*, dear Mr Witmore?"

"I don't really know," said Graham, who by now felt he was short of any clever ideas.

"That's it, you don't know, and this is the answer."

"What do you mean, sir?"

"I mean, dear Mr Witmore, that the fact you don't know proves, indirectly of course, that there has to be some other power which might have planted these formulas in your mind."

"Yes, it might be so, but we can know nothing about it," said Graham.

"Of course, but it seems the only option, I mean, your ideas regarding life, the so-called existential dilemmas, the existence of God, are only suppositions, and none of them can be proved, for logic is of no use here."

Graham was already exhausted, which was unusual for him as a man in philosophy's service who had always previously enjoyed that sort of dialogue, but now for some reason he didn't. But overcoming his weakness, he managed to utter, "I must confess, sir, I'm not too bright today, and I find it difficult to carry on our discourse. I am sorry."

"No need to apologise, dear professor. Anybody has the right to be in no mood for such a discussion. But let me finish my train of thought. We're now in the casino, so let me carry out my considerations in a practical way.

"You're going to bet on certain numbers, aren't you? But my advice is not to think about any numbers. Try to distance yourself from any thinking, for that matter, and then you'll see numbers coming to your mind. They will appear out of the blue, believe me. Are you ready, dear professor?"

Graham, not being fully convinced, tried his best to follow the lord's instructions after all, and after a while, he said to the croupier, "Fifteen and thirty, black, please."

And the wheel began to move. Everybody was watching it anxiously, and when it stopped, Graham to his amazement saw his numbers win, and because on that particular game there was a lot of money bet, he won almost £50,000. He was bewildered and looked at Hellbridge, who just smiled at him but said nothing.

Graham had never had so much money in his life for, to put it frankly, he was rather reckless with it, and quite often, despite his good salary, he had to borrow from his friends. And he never knew where his money had gone. And because he was a generous man, he would give it away but hardly ever remembered whom he gave it to, for he often did that, having been in a sort of euphoria induced almost always by alcohol. Now he was thinking what this money should be spent on but couldn't finish his deliberations because Lord Hellbridge said, "And here we are, dear Mr Witmore, my congratulations. You successfully followed my advice, and now you see it has worked to your benefit. Now, the point is that we never know what comes next. All you can do is just assume, to suppose, but the final result will never be certain beforehand. You can't predict the future, and that's it. In other words, you aren't aware of your mind's limits, and so about decisions concerning anything in this world. Man tends to think he is in charge of everything that happens on this earth, but wouldn't it be better if he wasn't so sure about that? Anyway, if truth is accessible for him, it cannot be found in rational thinking, for it might be always faulty because it refers to facts which are relative and accidental. Therefore, truth may come to him only in revelation, envisioned, not thought of. In other words, you cannot discover truth in your thoughts. All the facts, as our Ludwig rightly observed, contribute only to the setting of the problem, and not to its solution. That's why truth, which is the way to see the world aright, can be found only beyond it, and it is the greatest paradox of human life. In other words, to reach the truth of the world and life, you must refrain from thinking."

Now, they both heard a commotion at the casino entrance, and as it turned out, it was about new visitors, or rather one of them: a huge black cat that was denied entrance to the establishment. It was in the company of Messieurs Adarsh and Wissend, who arrived a bit later.

"No," the porter said, "cats aren't allowed here."

"Why not?" said Wissend. "It's discrimination. Don't you know that animals have their rights and should be treated the same way as people? They're both equal before the law."

"Sorry," the porter said," but I have my instructions."

"Then, please call the manager," said Wissend.

An elegantly dressed man arrived, introduced himself and greeted the newcomers politely, and then said to Mr Wissend, "I'm terribly sorry, but I can't let your companion in. You know, sir, this is a special place and an animal could distract our guests' activities here."

"But I assure you the cat has perfect manners and won't cause any problems," replied Wissend.

To prove his impeccable demeanour, the cat stood on his hind legs and bowed to the manager, whose manners were apparently as good as the cat's, for he bowed too and smiled at him, but said, "I don't doubt it, sir, but I can't let him in. I'm very sorry about that."

"But he's been invited here," said Wissend.

"By whom, if I may enquire?"

"Lord Hellbridge, Mr Cameron."

"Lord…" the manager stuttered, "invited the cat…?"

"Yes, he did," said Wissend, "and what's wrong with that? The lord is an active supporter of equal rights for all animals, and the great advocate of their right to vote in national elections."

"Eh…" Mr Cameron was stupefied now, "national elections…?"

"Yes, of course, and it surely would improve the well-being of our citizens, for animals are known for being unprejudiced, very fair."

"Yes, of course, they are, and if the cat," and now the manager bowed to him again, "is a guest of the lord, then I think we may make an exception and let him in, sir."

"It's very kind of you, and I won't fail to mention it to the lord," said Wissend.

"Thank you very much, sir, and you're very welcome here. You'll see the lord and his companion at the roulette table. Have a very nice evening, sir."

Wissend and Adarsh thanked him profusely, and after entering, they soon saw the lord and Professor Witmore.

"Ah, here you are," said Hellbridge. "I wouldn't know you gambled," he addressed Ches Adarsh.

"I actually don't, but since Mr Wissend insisted…"

"Oh yes, he can be very persuasive," said the lord, and gave Wissend an amusing glance.

"Ah," and you are here too," he said, addressing the cat, who this time did a very graceful bow to the lord, who smiled nicely and said, "cats, especially black ones, gentlemen, contrary to common opinion, bring luck. Anyway, the cat is the personification of wisdom, and wisdom and luck complement each other. However, the majority of people hardly know anything about that, as it is about anything else with them, for that matter. And now, gentlemen, he" – pointing to the cat and raising his forefinger significantly – "will prove it."

And then, the lord looked at the cat and said, "What numbers would you advise us to choose?"

The cat looked at the numbers, closed his eyes, and then opening them, looked at the lord, who nodded and said, "I'm sure you're right, so we'll follow your advice, my friend," and turning to the croupier, announced, "ten and thirteen, please."

And when the other players made their bets too, the croupier put the roulette wheel in motion and everybody waited anxiously, looking as it was spinning. When it stopped, the winning numbers were nine and fourteen.

"Hmm, something went wrong, said Hellbridge. "He's never mistaken, so something must be wrong here, and I wonder what," he said, looking at the manager, who came to their table to watch them play.

"I assure you, sir, the device is in perfect order. It's checked every day by a very experienced engineer so…"

"It might be so," the lord said, "but still I'm sure there's a technical problem after all. You know, our dear friend is never ever wrong, so please check everything."

"As you wish, sir, I'll call him straightaway." And he went to make a call. He told the engineer about the problem and stressed the presence of Lord Hellbridge. When the man asked who had complained about the roulette's mechanics, Mr Cameron hesitantly mentioned a cat. The engineer was stunned upon hearing that, and even thought that this evening apparently there must be something wrong not only with the roulette, but with the state of mind of the manager too, but having no choice, arrived at the casino, and once there, went straight to the roulette table.

When, at last, he emerged from under the table, he said, shaking his head in disbelief, "Yes, there was a mechanical fault, but now it's fixed. You may continue to play," and then looking at the cat, he added, "there are some great engineer geniuses I would never think of." And he smiled at him, and the cat, such was the impression of many of the other evening's guests, smiled too.

Everything sorted now, the game was renewed, and because it was the cat who was the last to play, the opening bet was offered to him.

This time, the cat chose different numbers: four and six. The wheel began to whirl, and everybody held his breath. When it stopped, all present could see the winning numbers, that is, the ones chosen by the cat.

"Haven't I told you he's never mistaken?" said Hellbridge, looking around.

This time, even a larger amount of money was in the bank, some £80,000, but now the croupier wasn't sure to whom he should hand the chips, so Hellbridge made the decision and pointing to the cat, said, "Please hand them to our friend. They are his."

The croupier put all the tokens before the cat, who then generously gave the croupier a couple of the chips, putting the rest of them into a small rucksack. We failed to mention that when he appeared at the casino, he already had it on his back. Now, he received spontaneous applause from all the other roulette players.

"Now, *mesdames et messieurs*," the lord announced, "knowing our friend well, I know he'll donate the money to a charity, as he always does, being an exceptionally generous and humble individual whose personal needs are very modest." And that prompted all present to award the cat loud applause.

"So, my friends, that's all for now, our play is done. For now, anyway," said Hellbridge. "Let me invite you now," he said, looking at his companions, "to a dinner at one of my favourite restaurants, which is not far from here, and it's Russian, Rebyata. I'm sure," he said, looking at me, "that Mr Adarsh will be happy to have some Russian food he likes so much."

I thanked him but at the same time was thinking, *How come he knows I like Russian cuisine?* but of course I wouldn't dare to ask him. "*And then,*"

269

I was still thinking, *that guy Wissend too, reminded me of somebody I'd already met, and even the cat being a cat was somewhat, strangely enough, similar to a man. Hmm, that's all puzzling."*

But I didn't have time to ponder these questions for long, because we'd just arrived at Rebyata restaurant. It was an elegant and spacious place, and as soon as we sat down, a pretty waitress came to our table, greeted us in perfect English and gave us the menu.

"I'll have *blini*," said Lord Hellbridge. "I highly recommend them, they're delicious."

So, all of us ordered them too, for we already knew the lord's refined tastes, and we also had a bottle of Stolichnaya with them.

Every one of us enjoyed the food and vodka, and then we ordered cognac, *bashta* cakes and coffee, and then a conversation began. There was just us in the restaurant, so we could speak at ease. The cat was sitting on the chair enjoying a piece of salmon and some caviar with a big glass of beer, and I noticed that no one among the staff was surprised by his presence, as if it was quite common for a cat to come here, and it would be eating and drinking at the table. *What imaginative people they are,* I thought, and reflected that I had already noticed that while in Moscow.

"Gentlemen," said Lord Hellbridge, "the other day, I was thinking of something that still puzzles me, and it's that I haven't been able to answer the question as to why this country went to the dogs. I mean, why there is so much riff-raff, and consequently so many crimes are being committed."

"I, myself, sir," Graham said, "have deliberated the same question more than once."

"Aha, that's interesting," said the lord, "and I appreciate that, for I wouldn't like to be the only one to complain about the matter in question. And what conclusion have you reached, professor?"

"I have found, it seems to me, the cause of the current situation. I mean, why such a great number of violent young people are committing hideous crimes. And not only them, for there are plenty of adults who do the same. In short, this country is full of the rabble.

"Now, in the first place, we can blame ourselves. I mean that we, the English, are inclined to ignore this appalling situation, which we merely consider something temporal, an aberration which will go away in time, for our national spirit is sound after all. But, unfortunately, it isn't the case, for I find it in decline, and the question is why is it so?"

"Very accurate observation," replied the lord, "and here I think we may both share some answers as to the possible explanation of the question. What I mean is that we're still a class society, that is, we favour the rich, who have now replaced old aristocracy, and don't care much about the education of our nation as a whole. An ordinary man is supposed to serve the privileged, respect and admire them and have them as a model to respect and follow. And all this is in our long-standing tradition, which has constituted for generations our mentality, and any attempt to change it would be considered dangerous, for it could shatter the public order."

"That's it, milord," said Graham, "this is also my conclusion. I mean that those in power fear any changes, for it may threaten their status. The Government's also afraid, and to prevent any dangers, strengthens its own power by increasing the number of laws and its own executive authority. And this all contributes to establishing a furtive police state – one where democracy exists in fact on the surface, on paper, and the Government enjoys extensive powers which are unthinkable in other countries in Europe. But in the long run it won't work. bearing in mind the well-being of the majority, and I foresee serious troubles in the future, for someday many a man will have had enough of those appearances, that is, this deceitful propaganda which has literally persecuted him everywhere, watching the idiot-box, reading rags and other quasi-Delphic oracles, which this country is full of these days. Man, by reason of his nature, is a rebel, and in order to prevent him rebelling, the Government tries to appease him by appearances, trying its best at the same time to make him an automaton deprived of having ideas of his own, and that is all done to maintain the present status quo.

"All in all, it may last in this country longer than in other ones because pretence and a stiff upper lip are still very much appreciated, but what's the good of them, anyway, when they in fact make a man greedy, petty and stupid? The system's implicit aim is to deprive its member of his very individual courage, sympathy, insight and pride, pretending at the same time to value pity, compassion, selflessness and generosity, but in fact is doing everything to unteach him respect for these virtues.

"And in my opinion, milord, all that doth begin should rightly to destruction run."

"Hmm, it may happen, and actually it is very likely to happen, dear professor," said the lord, "and I appreciate your incredible insight, so untypical for an Englishman. Yes, you're one of the very few who have that power. Your grasp of the true character of this country is really remarkable, but let me add something to what you have already said."

"Please do, milord. I highly value your views," Graham said.

"There's another matter that concerns me these days, and it is bureaucracy, that has been raised to an enormous degree in the UK. It has become leviathan. It rules on its own and can no longer be controlled by anybody, and even the Government isn't in full charge of it. I wonder why this country needs so much ink, and what is even more important, why do the British so willingly submit themselves to that monstrous paper trail? But, of course, there are a couple of reasons why that plague has found such widespread acclaim among so many.

Bureaucracy is, as we know, an invention of the establishment, which in any other country is as equally well protected as it is here. But in this country, it is hidden behind countless subservient bodies, so that a citizen's way through them resembles a situation similar to that in Kafka's novels. In addition, the uncodified British law and lack of constitution creates large room for interpretation and manipulation by the rulers. But in the view of an uninvolved spectator, an ordinary British citizen is a lucky man. So many organisations are willing to take care of him that his choice of getting help seems to be limitless, and there lies the rub.

"British bureaucratic manipulation is a masterpiece, for it manages to convince many that appearances, as we have already mentioned, are the reality. The majority of the population believes almost every word of bureaucratic propaganda, and if they don't, they pretend to do so. And those appearances, the pretence of impartiality, understanding and gentleness can be so deceitful.

"This bureaucratic manipulation is a jewel in the crown, as it is able to persuade almost all that appearances are the reality."

"Excuse me, sir, may I say something?" said Graham.

"But of course, I'm being too talkative this evening, anyway," said the lord.

"Thank you, sir. We all are listening to you with great interest, but if you forgive me, I wonder why you, sir, being English yourself, are so critical towards your country and its people."

"Dear Professor Witmore, who else but you would know that only a fool is uncritical of his country and his compatriots? To be critical means to be honest, for he who criticises his fatherland and his fellow countrymen proves he cares about them. He wants the best for his country, and there is and always will be something to disagree with, to find fault with, and your criticism proves your patriotism if you are in need of the word. Those who don't find anything wrong with his land are simply opportunistic, mean-minded, bigoted and selfish morons."

"Yes, of course, sir. I don't really know why I asked that stupid question," replied Graham, ashamed of himself; he notoriously never admitted being in the wrong.

"Don't you worry, it could happen to anybody. Even I, myself, feel disoriented, lost, you know that these days we might be so easily distracted, distressed. Ah that modernity," and the lord sighed at the very moment.

"But," he carried on, "as for my Englishness, dear professor, it is in fact a rather complicated matter. I, myself, am not quite sure where my ancestors originally came from. Anyway, as you know, the word English and its derivatives come from the word Angles, you know, the land of Angles in today's Schleswig-Holstein in Germany. And my family might have come from there too and also, as far as I know, from Switzerland, but nobody knows for sure, and there's nobody to consult, for sadly I have no family of my own, no relatives. I am alone, always have been alone," Hellbridge declared with sadness.

"I'm very sorry. I wouldn't know, sir," said Graham, "but now, if you'll kindly permit me, I would like to add a word or two in relation to what you are telling us."

"But of course, please do, we will all be very glad to hear your opinion," said the lord.

"Bureaucracy, yes, I hate the word," Graham began, "but fortunately, or not, it is a necessity these days. However, it depends how far it goes, and the same for hypocrisy, which might bring this country to ruin sooner or later. A hypocrite is my enemy number one! Let me give you an example. This country has always proclaimed that it puts the well-being of its citizens above anything else. Now, our dear Karl once said that 'The police state is the state where a policeman earns more than a teacher.' It is as we can see, a kind of metaphor, but translated into what's happening these days, we might say, 'The police state is the state where more money is spent on security services than on healthcare.' And as for the latter, nothing is ever done but rambling, as if words could replace the reality.

"And the same goes for many other things, starting with so-cherished English politeness, which is so advertised, so to speak, and of which British people are so proud. But if you take a closer look then you may find out that this politeness is very often a means of concealing the truth, to deceive others, so almost always it is nothing but unfeeling routine.

"And back to bureaucracy, curiously enough, it was an American historian, Kendall, who called the rule of today's bureaucratic system, 'an organized rape of incredible strength and efficiency.'"

"May I say something?" Wissend chipped in.

"But of course, old man," agreed the lord, addressing his assistant so uniquely.

"I, by reason of my nature, am an anarchist so understandably advocate the abolishment of any authority."

I noticed just now that the cat apparently was of the same opinion, for he nodded right now. Anyway, it seemed to me as if he understood what we were talking about, but of course it might have been just an illusion. However, I noticed again that the cat was treated by the waiters with great respect, and if I hadn't misheard, one of them addressed him as *vashe blagorodiye*.

"Yes," continued Wissend. "Down with all governments now!" he said, raising his voice.

"I think you exaggerate, dear chap," said Lord Hellbridge. "Can you imagine the consequences if it were to happen, that chaos around, my dear friend? It would be an apocalypse."

"So what?" Apparently unperturbed by that vision, Wissend carried on. "But what freedom would we enjoy, but the freedom of the strong, of course, anyway, the only genuine one."

I, myself, held some ideas of anarchism. Namely, I was in not in favour of too great an intrusion of the laws into our lives, but to abolish all of them would, I was sure, cause mayhem. So, I said, "Yes, a few, I mean the strong and ruthless would enjoy the freedom to satisfy their desires, but the weak would suffer terribly."

"I don't give a damn about these bigots and prigs," said Wissend. "They deserve it, because they make up for their weakness by cheating and swindling, which they wouldn't do under anarchism because it presupposes honesty and honour. For me, a strong man is an honest and reliable one. In democracy, as under a dictatorship, there is no place for an honest, trustworthy man, for such a man is possible only under anarchism, which is a true kingdom of heaven. And as for those suffering, yes, they would suffer not being able to deceive and lie. Anarchism, my friends, means justice. That's the freedom to be just, and that's it."

"I know what you mean," said the lord, smiling, "and yes, I fully agree with you. You got it right."

I was looking at Hellbridge while he was saying all that, and I was pretty sure he'd deliberately provoked Wissend to express his opinion, knowing all the time what he would say. And now my impression was confirmed by him saying, "My dear friends, yes, that's it, and this is exactly what I aim to achieve in my life, or it would be much more proper to say, this is my job, that is my responsibility to establish the rule of anarchism on earth."

"I'm very glad to hear that," said Wissend. "Anyway, somehow, I've always known that, sire."

The lord smiled at him again and said, "Gentlemen, long live anarchism! Let's now drink to it." And we all raised our glasses to toast to the future victory of justice and truthfulness.

I wondered why Wissend addressed the lord by using the word, sire, which had always been reserved for a sovereign, but I didn't have time to ponder it because the chef approached our table and whispered something in the cat's ear. I noticed the chef's striking resemblance to a Russian actor Dmitri Nazarov, famous for his role in the film *Kuhnia*. Now, the cat jumped from the chair and followed the chef in the direction of the kitchen. Graham shot a passing glance at them, but neither Hellbridge nor

Wissend paid the smallest attention to the fact. *Hmm*, I thought, *this cat is a really peculiar individuum, for normally cats don't behave like that.* But as I didn't want to bother my companions with my observation, I let it pass.

Now it was Wissend who started a discussion on some other subject which apparently had no connection to the present situation, and it was about the beauty of expressing grief. Graham himself was stunned by Wissend's choice of words, but I wasn't because I had become used to his bizarre word games.

"There are people who have a particular skill," began Wissend, "of turning evil into good, and they do that by finding in it something to appreciate. In colloquial language, they attempt to make honey of shit. This is a very weird logic that seems to reverse the accepted way of thinking. Those people's view of the world is somewhat upside-down compared to sober, reasoning men, who normally strictly separate these two concepts. If I were you, I would beware of these people, never ever trust them, as they are an example of man being capable of doing anything, and that's why humankind's future is totally unpredictable."

"You've got it right," said Lord Hellbridge. "I, myself, am of the same opinion and plan my actions accordingly. The number of such people varies depending on a country, and not that far away from where we are now, there are quite a lot of them. And it'll be part of your mission, dear Mr Adarsh, to investigate them."

And yes, I knew what he meant. Now, I felt I was ready to accomplish my task, and understood why I should do it. First for myself, because it was about my righteous egoism of doing it, and then it may benefit a few other people too.

Lord Hellbridge interrupted my train of thought, saying, "The point is why we're so critical regarding some countries and their people, and some would say it's because we're so prejudiced, but no, with us, it's not the case. Let me elaborate. For instance, a hypocrite would say he is critical for he wants to make things better, but the same could be said of an honest person, and the problem is how to distinguish between these two, namely who's who. And this is, as you are perfectly aware, a very delicate problem, especially due to its relation to something being widespread all over the world.

"And this, gentlemen, is stupidity, and those who are naïve enough to believe that it might be cured, but no, it can't be, for it has no limits, being congenital. And it is exactly because of its limitlessness that some peoples, those living somewhere in the north-west, would never accept you because they are afraid of accepting any other ideas, and recognise none but their own. Consequently, they will never trust you, and it works vice versa of course, for you should always remember not to trust them at all. Moreover, as a person who lives close to Russia would say, those north-easterners say they believe in God but carry the Devil under their shirts. And it is the number one enemy of mankind, so the only way remaining to make the world a better place is to wipe it out. The means used of doing it might of course be different, and as for ourselves, we don't choose the external way, so to speak, to deal with the problem in question, but exclusively internally, that is, to organise the lives of the stupid in such a way that their cretinism will turn against themselves and destroy them. Those people might be clever in some particular areas, and successful for that matter, but actually they aren't in charge of their lives, for it is somebody else who is."

When Hellbridge had finished his short exposé, I wanted him to be more precise, so I asked him, "Sir, but do you mind telling us who you mean?"

"Mr Adarsh, you'll will find it out yourself in due time, for now it is too early for that."

I understood his point and said, "Yes, I see, and I'll be waiting."

"Don't you worry, you won't be waiting too long," said the lord.

Now we all saw the cat coming back from the kitchen looking very satisfied, and Hellbridge said, smiling, "Apparently, people here appreciate cats' company very much and gave him something special. And they're imaginative enough to know that appearances deceive, if you know what I mean."

I thought I knew what he meant. A cat could sometimes be much more than a mere cat.

"What you have just told us, sir," said Graham," I, as a man in philosophy's service, find very interesting, but also enigmatic. I wholly agree with what you said about stupidity and the way to get rid of it, but

I'm sorry to say, so far, you've failed to tell us what human life is about in your opinion. I mean, its destiny, mission and aims, all in all, what makes life worth living."

"My dear friend," replied Hellbridge, "the value of life can't be estimated, but a single man may judge his own life if he wishes so, but not the lives of others. And all that pseudo, quasi- humanistic mumbling has therefore no value, being just a pack of clichés and trivialities."

Graham chuckled and said, "Yes, precisely, and this is my view as well."

"As it should be, dear professor, you're an intelligent man after all," said Hellbridge, smiling.

"I, myself," chipped in Wissend, "agree too, especially as regards the unpredictability of man's ideas, and will tell you what I learnt the other day about a certain proposal made by a defence expert. He suggested that Great Britain should disarm itself, and in a case of attack, the only military equipment at her disposal would be a telephone number which would automatically repeatedly announce to an attacker, *We surrender, we surrender…*"

"It wouldn't be," said Graham, "a bad idea after all, for a country being an island. Where would its people escape to, and armed forces regroup when the country is attacked? Into the sea? And then, other countries might follow its example and also disarm themselves."

"I, myself," said Hellbridge, "like the idea, you know, all these weapons turn in the end against their own owners, *vive gladio peri gladio*, gentlemen, and nothing has been learnt from the wisdom of the saying so far. Anyway, 'So far, humankind has incorporated only its errors, and that all its consciousness refers to errors,' as Friedrich rightly observed, so man seems to be an incorrigible creature and *de facto* hasn't learned anything yet."

I now realised that I had heard that saying more than once, and wondered why Hellbridge and his assistants were using it so often in our conversations. Did they want to suggest something to me, but then what was it? And when I was still looking for an answer, the lord said, "Don't you think it's time to go ahead with the next stage of our operation, Mr Adarsh? The prime minister is getting impatient, and of course we don't want to disappoint him. Professor Witmore here is not familiar with that business of ours, but I believe we can discuss it in his presence after all, What do you think?"

"I agree," I said, convinced that Graham's honesty would prevail over his rather questionable friendship, or rather, mere acquaintance, with other members of the M7, and he wouldn't tell them anything that was being said now. However, to be sure of that, I said to him, 'Do you remember a certain man by the name of Denker whom you used to know and like, as far as I know?'

"Oh yes, I do remember him. I often wonder what's become of him. And yes again, I liked him very much."

"Don't you worry, he's fine, and he also remembers you with sympathy."

"And would you know by chance how I could contact him?"

"Actually, I would, dear professor, but not now, but will when the right time comes."

"I see, but could you pass my best on to him?"

"I certainly will. And now," I carried on, "you will hear a story which might be of interest to you, and with the kind permission of the lord, you'll hear a few stories involving the society you're a member of, that's the M7 as I call them, and what you'll learn may persuade you to consider your own involvement. And I believe that your former friend would be glad if you do."

"I'm not actually a true friend of any of them," said Graham, "and yes, I will listen carefully to what you are going to tell me, and if there is a reason to consider my membership, I certainly will think it through."

"Your former friend, Denker, was betrayed by them, that is, accused by them of a conspiracy he never committed," said Hellbridge.

"I would know nothing of that," said Graham, "and if I did, I wouldn't believe it because he wasn't a man to conspire against anybody."

"I knew you wouldn't believe the accusations and you would oppose any action against him, therefore you're now with us in more than just literally meaning, if you know what I mean," Hellbridge said to him.

"I think I know what you mean, sir, and appreciate it. But would you mind telling me how come you know so much about my opinion of Denker, and my likely reaction if I had been aware of what the others had been up to?" asked Graham.

"Dear Professor Witmore, you might be an eccentric character, but you're a man of principles, one of them being your faithfulness in friendship, and to answer your question how I would know..." here Hellbridge stopped shortly and looked Graham in the eye, "you, as an imaginative man, have, I'm sure, some assumption about who I really am, don't you?"

"Yes, sir, I do," said Graham in a very serious tone, so unusual for a man who much preferred sarcastic, ironical or mocking comments in his conversations at and outside the academy. But now, yes, Graham somehow knew that Hellbridge wasn't an ordinary man, that he was something more than a man, so to speak, and talking to the lord made him feel as if he was talking to a certain character in one of his favourite novels. Strange it was, but Graham found it very appealing and felt stimulated by the situation. Moreover, he knew it would be a very bad idea to ignore the lord.

And what Graham was saying now proved his well-hidden seriousness, his self-responsibility and integrity that almost all who knew him would never attribute to him.

"Yes, sir," he carried on, "I guess I know who I am talking to now, and I am very pleased to have a chance to have this conversation and hope this is not just one I will be honoured with, and knowing of your interest in the matter in question, I don't doubt that Denker's name will be cleared, all accusations dropped, and those responsible for them punished."

"Hmm, yes, it's rather likely to happen, dear professor," said Hellbridge, "and what you've just said proves again the favourable opinion about you that I've always actually had."

"Thank you, sir, and I am at your command," said Graham. And that was it, Graham could hardly recognise himself; he had never ever in his life said anything like that. He despised modern authorities, mocking them at every opportunity, and if there were any in which he would believe, it would be a power not from this earth.

"So, dear Professor Witmore," continued Hellbridge, "that's it for now. Thank you for keeping me company, which I'm pretty sure we will have a chance to enjoy again. Now, it's up to you what to do about your relationship with those people, and Mr Adarsh here will assist you whenever you need him, and I, myself, would like very much to keep in touch with you. Goodbye for now, but please remember not to ignore them, they aren't that stupid after all."

"I thank you, sir, and it's been a great honour to meet you," said Graham, and left the pub.

Lord Hellbridge and I left shortly after him, and once outside, the lord, looking me in the eye, said, "Witmore is a man you can trust, and I am not surprised by the fact you can also trust some women," he said, and smiled.

"Now, I'm leaving you, dear Mr Adarsh. Pass my best on to all the ladies, and *au revoir!*"

I was very pleased that Hellbridge liked Graham for I still liked him too, and he proved again to be a man of integrity, despite all that silly gossip around. My next move was to meet that meek, two-faced scoundrel James, 'The Rat', who in turn could not be trusted at all. But before I had a chance to face him man to man, he had a rather unpleasant experience on the same day, while we ourselves were having the above conversation.

But first, let's introduce him once again.

# JAMES

'In antiquity slaves were, in all honesty
called slaves. In the middle ages, they
took the name of serfs. Nowadays they
are called wage earners.'
Mikhail Bakunin

All that was now happening affected me so much I could hardly recognise myself, and I somewhat knew I would never think and act the same way I used to in the old days. All in all, I was not the same man, and the question was what would I become? And pondering the question, I remembered Nietzsche's words: 'How one becomes what one is', but what did his words actually mean? And I could not answer that question yet. All I knew was that I was aware step by step of becoming someone else or myself.

Since my meeting with Wahrburg in Zurich, I'd been making notes, a sort of a diary, but still I wasn't sure whether everything I had written reflected exactly everything I'd experienced and thought. I was still lost, that is to say not sure what to think of what was going on around me, why all that was happening and where I was heading for.

I could, I thought, tell the difference between right and wrong and good and evil, especially as regards my former friends' actions, but there was something else I couldn't put my finger on because I wasn't able to find any words to describe what I thought. To put it a different way, I wasn't able to explain my feelings and thoughts in any rational way, but I was still making notes, as I was doing now, but actually what for? I kept asking myself. To explain something for myself, to leave a testimony for others? I didn't have a clue why I was actually writing, but somewhat I had to do it, as if I'd been forced by an invisible power I couldn't resist. As a matter of fact, even now when I am telling you this, I am not sure whether what I am saying is what I really mean, and this feeling of uncertainty has been with me since my adventure began in Zurich. One day, everything was clear, but the day after, I was again confused, not sure of anything, and so it had been until now, and I couldn't do anything about that, for what could I actually do? Run away from all that, from those who were now helping me, and forget the people who did harm to me? I knew that if I ran away and hid in some remote part of the world, I wouldn't really escape, for how can one escape his own thoughts? And saying this is a cliché, but behind the triviality of that, there is something not trivial at all, for it is our life, our own 'to be or not to be', which even if we tried, we wouldn't be able to ignore, to say nothing of running away from it.

But then I thought, *What did I find out, having said all that? Nothing at all, for what were all these 'truths' for? Did they contribute to my well-being? Was I better now? No, the same as I had been before. Anyway, could all these words bring a change to my life? No, they wouldn't, so what would they do then?*"

And when I was pondering those and other questions, and eventually fell asleep, I had a dream.

I stood on a bridge – where it was I couldn't tell. The bridge spanned a very deep abyss at the bottom of which flowed a river. I was roughly in the middle of the bridge when it began to crack, and I thought it was the end of my journey, but then I saw somebody coming towards me from the direction in which I was heading, and when that man came close to me, I recognised myself. Yes, it was me, or my double, and whoever it might have been, the person extended his hand saying, "Don't you worry, for actually you're not here, you're just imagining things which don't exist," and I understood what he meant. When we think we are at the end of our journey, it may be just a beginning, for we never know for sure what we are. It is a paradox of our life – we only know something for sure when we no longer ask any questions, only when we have realised that we cannot know the truth by asking them. We must just wait and the answer will come to us, and it will be on its own, and when it happens, we don't have to say anything anymore. And only then will we be at peace, when there is no need for any words, neither questions nor answers. And once I had grasped the truth of all that, my dream ended.

It was three o'clock in the morning, and I'd been getting up so early for a long time now. And once I was alert enough to think, I asked myself the same question I'd been asking for almost one year now. Why are people so obsessed with their own well-being? Even when they have enough money to live well, they want more, but at the same time, they think they are very rational. But they aren't because they contradict themselves. For them, the ultimate aim of life is to be happy, but happiness comes only when you are satisfied with what you actually have, and don't want more, because you can't have less or more happiness; you have it or you don't. So, it seems that their thinking and consequently their behaviour isn't rational at all. Moreover, they will never be happy.

They say they want to protect their children, their families, and they do that by depriving other families of the means of protection. Thus, nobody's happy, and that vicious circle never ends. Does it all mean that man is in fact an irrational being? He seems to be, for thinking and acting this way, he's readying his own demise.

When I had stopped pondering, the telephone rang. It was Mr Wissend, and he began by saying, "Not a very promising way to start the day, Mr Adarsh, is it?"

"What do you mean?" I asked.

"I mean questioning the obvious. Isn't that what you're doing now?"

"How would you know, Mr Wissend?"

"I was just passing by your house and saw the lights on, and because it's so early, I wondered what a man is doing at that unholy hour, and thought it had to be a philosopher investigating some business of his."

"Yes, you're right, it is, indeed, and I was thinking how come so much stupidity is possible on this earth," I said.

"What do you have on your mind exactly, my friend?" asked Wissend.

"I mean, how come people are so little worried by their own stupidity? You know, they don't care even when it causes them trouble. Moreover, there are some who think that being stupid makes them superior to others," I said.

"Could you put it in a wider perspective, my friend?" asked Wissend.

"I'll try. So, I believe that to doubt is the duty of a humanist, that is, a man who is concerned not only about his own well-being, but also about what happens to his fellow humans. And the question is why doubting is so important for our own good. To doubt is to question the obvious, and this is the only way to find out what would make us achieve peace of the soul, which is the only true happiness. Peace of the soul comes when we finally cease to question our own and others' lives, that is the sense of life as such. To question is an attempt to find the solution to the problem of life, which itself is to ask what its sense is, that is, to ask whether life is or is not worth living. And this inborn question we humans ask, not even being aware of it. I mean, we ask the question subconsciously, in our inner language. We don't think of asking that question, our thoughts think for us.

"You see, this is a paradox of life, I mean that the only way to stop questioning the sense of life, that is, to solve the problem of life, begins with the doubt as regards its worth."

"My dear friend," said Wissend, "this is exactly what I, myself, think, so I'm very pleased to say we are very like-minded. But would you please carry on, I have the feeling that this isn't all you want to tell me."

"No, it isn't, and I can continue if you wish."

"Oh yes, I am very eager to hear more," said Wissend.

"So, back to having doubts, I'd say that in order to become what you are, you have to start with the questions 'Why?' and 'What for?' and, as we noticed before, to become what you are is not to question the sense, the worth of your own life. Any doubts about that can be put into words but the answer cannot be. It means, once we have answered the question, we say nothing."

"Bravo, my friend, that's something, and I'm sure the lord himself would be impressed if he could hear what you've just said. Anyway, knowing him a bit, I'm inclined to think he may somehow find out the topic of our conversation," said Wissend, smiling.

*Hmm,* I thought, *Lord Hellbridge is a peculiar individuum, yes, definitely there's something about him I have actually already experienced before, during my conversation with Mr Wahrburg in the park in Zurich."*

"I'd like very much to have a word with the lord again," I said now.

"Oh, don't you worry," said Wissend, "you will, and pretty soon for that matter."

"So, if I may say a few words more," I said, "I would stress one problem, that is that whatever we say about the sense of life is always accompanied by the questions, 'What is good, and what is the difference between good and bad and right and wrong?' And I, myself, am still not sure how to answer these questions. Yes, I've just said something closely related to the questions, and already before we discussed the problem, but as I say, I haven't arrived at the final conclusion regarding the matter in question."

"Bah," exclaimed Wissend, "who actually has, for the Devil's sake, my friend, because he, himself, I mean, the Devil, may have doubts too. Who knows?"

*Yea,* I thought, *how would we know anything about that?*

But you know, my friend, you, yourself, might have a chance to ask him someday since nobody knows where he is, how near or how far..." said Wissend, almost in a whisper. "But," he continued after a short break, "all these questions are innate in nature."

"I think that they cannot be answered by a human," I said.

"That's it, my friend, because these questions can be answered only *sub specie aeternitatis* or from the perspective of the eternal. So, humans cannot answer the question, 'What is good?' for the answer lies outside the world in which everything is relative and accidental, and to judge the value of human actions would be therefore impossible, so the judgement must be decided somewhere else."

"But where does it take place?" I enquired.

"Bah, this is the puzzle of all puzzles in human life, my friend, and you may someday find the solution to this puzzle, provided that you deserve it."

"But who will make the decision as to whether I'm worthy of the answer?" I asked.

"There's somebody, and you'll meet him in due time."

"And who's that?"

"You'll find it out yourself. And now, my friend, let's take care of our present affairs, and I mean your former friends who now, one by one, will be looked after, so to speak. And now Mr James Serfield's turn has come. Not a very nice character, is he?"

"Not at all. I've never liked him, that meek servile scoundrel," I said.

"That's it, and I'm of the same opinion, so let's take care of him according to his character traits. You see, each of the M7 members has a specific one, and all can be identified as one of the seven deadly sins. Thus, Shaun is a glutton, Simon's is pride, Bernard's is lust, Jason's is greed, Graham's is laziness, Justin's is wrath and James' is envy. And they will be punished accordingly, each one for his particular sin, and this way we put some things in order in this world.

"We've already dealt with a few of them, preliminarily so to speak, and now James' turn has come. So, what do you suggest?" asked Wissend.

"Hmm, let me think," I said, pondering the question. After a few minutes, I made my mind up and said, "Let's take advantage of his particular trait and put him in a situation to exploit it."

"A very good idea, my friend, and I suggest the following. He's a civil servant and as such, he's obliged to behave properly, and if he doesn't, he will bear the consequences. What his kind are most afraid of is a scandal, so we'll arrange things so that he'll do something for which his superiors won't forgive him. And I'm thinking of a sort of love affair he'll be tempted to pursue."

"Gosh, him and a love affair. He's an automaton, and love is the furthest of all his interests if he has any, apart from his own career," I said.

"No, you're wrong, my friend. He'll go for that and I'll tell you why. Look, he's a bachelor, and in respect of his sexuality, quite normal, so he longs for a closer relationship with a woman after all, doesn't he?" said Wissend.

"You might be right, and what would be your plan?"

"I think we'll put him in a situation, I mean, to start a relationship with a woman who will make him an offer he won't be able to refuse. This woman will, obviously, know what we intend to do, and I'm sure our dear Fabiana knows the right lady who, encouraged by our handsome reward, will be willing to go ahead with what we suggest to her. Does it sound good for you?" asked Wissend.

"Yes," I said, "it does. He may go for it, and I'll have a word with Fabiana about that."

"Splendid! Let's do it, my friend. And now, I'll leave you and see you again tomorrow evening at the Robbers' Haven, where you'll meet Lord Hellbridge again and a few others, all right?"

"I'll be there, and I'm sure I'll sort everything out with Fabiana, who likes me and therefore won't refuse to help."

"I know she does, and very much for that matter," said Wissend, and smiled.

"You know what," I said to Wissend, "all this mess we're facing now is very similar to that of a certain part of the UK I visited once. People living there call it, among other names, the North-West, and this is the place where lying, cheating, swindling and the like is the norm, and paradoxically for a neutral observer they are proud of it. Moreover, they would be surprised to deal with somebody who isn't skilled in those fields. They simply cannot help it, you know, because it is their nature, innate traits of character, to be spiteful and evil-minded. Therefore, the best thing to do is not to have anything to do with them at all, and if you do, then only from a position of strength. They might be relatively strong in their godforsaken shithole, but outside it, they are worthless, they are nobodies. They would protest of course, hearing such accusations, but there is nothing to worry about, for even their protest is false, as they are themselves perfectly aware. I would even go further and say that what Dzerzynsky and Stalin and Trevelyan once said, that man is wicked and evil by nature, is perfectly true. They have developed a certain deviousness and insidiousness of which they brag, still being Christians of course. But then, if you have noticed all of these pleasant attributes of theirs in time, it's easy to deal with them, for they are stupid enough after all. However, I would strongly advise you not to go there at all, for feeling sick might be very unpleasant after all. "Anyway, if you wanted me to summarise the experience, I'd say the following. For them, values, good ones of course, are only sometimes needed, not always as it happens, to be with truly civilised people. And this I came to know when an educated local person was displeased with Friedrich saying, 'We require, sometime, new values,' and changed it to 'We sometimes need values.' And this is exactly the change that tells you everything about the way they think, a totally different way to other European peoples, who value honesty more as the prime value, which is not the case with them in the North-West and the neighbourhood. And this is not only about the way of thinking, the way that you can never rely upon and trust them , the way that always aims at cheating you, lying and the like, for this is their always-present, that is, inner trait of character. And that way of thinking and consequent behaviour is not something deliberately chosen, that happens sometimes, but something permanent, innate, as I just said, and something that cannot be changed, something that is always present in them, not only sometimes. There are, of course, exceptions living there, and I wonder how come they survive. Anyway, exceptions just confirm the rule, as we know. And back to the M7's actions, their two-facedness, slyness, of which they aren't ashamed at all. On the contrary, they're proud of it, as the people living in that province are. And in this respect, they are both almost one and the same. But the M7 being English is still much more attractive, so to speak."

"I'm with you. I know what part you have on your mind, that one which is and isn't at the same time part of the UK, is that right?" said Wissend.

"That's it, you got it right, it is and it isn't, and it agrees with their mentality. I mean that for them, there's nothing like mess, and bungling and shambles are the synonyms of freedom. However, they've overlooked something. I mean that the stupid are always ruled by those who are able to see and appreciate the right relationship between the meaning of words and things. In other words, a proposition is a picture of reality or it isn't. When it is, it describes the right order of things, and if it isn't, it puts everything upside-down. And I wonder how come such thinking is possible."

"Bah," exclaimed Wissend, "everything's possible on this earth, and as for stupidity, I believe it is an inborn flaw, something like original sin, and people who are affected by it can't help it. You cannot cure stupidity, it is always there."

"Yes, it seems you're right. But I suggest we go back to the things in question, and I mean James."

"Oh, he's a perfect example not only of stupidity but of a couple of other things, and consequently will have a few adventures soon, but they won't make him happy," said Wissend, "and I'm glad to hear you're inspired now to act instead of your never-ending introspection."

*How would he know that?* I asked myself. *We haven't known each other too long.* But yes, I was eager now to do something and this way to prove the value of my ideas, my philosophy of life, yea, not only a critic of pure reason, but a doing. And at the same time, I came to realise that the very human question 'What is good?' is asked even by those who do evil to others. It seems to be an inborn question that stays with us whatever we do. That and a couple of other things were becoming clear to me, and I had the impression of seeing things aright and hoped that this time I would be able to reconcile myself with reality to some degree at least.

I realised at last I had been so preoccupied with pure reasoning that I had considered any other doing a waste of time. I'd been under the illusion I could sort out my life problems just by thinking, and now I eventually knew I had been wrong. And the worst outcome of my endless reasoning had been my denial of what had been happening around me. In my attitude to reality, I'd been like Goethe's Mephistopheles, saying, 'I am the spirit that forever denies! And rightly too; for all that doth begin should rightly to destruction run.' And yes, very often I meant that.

And now I was to fight people who embodied evil, but their evil wasn't the sublime one of Goethe's *Faust* or that of a certain great Russian novel.

Now, since Bea was still abroad, I could embark on the crusade against the M7 full time, and was anxious to end it before long because I had some very different aims which I was eager to carry out.

Among others aims, I wanted to find a quiet place to live in the country, but not in England, for it lacks space and is therefore a stuffy and stultifying place where no fresh ideas may appear. But some others were even worse and, for instance, I would never live in Ireland, which is a coarse place where the natives are obsessed by money, and if there is any culture there, it is the English one. Anyway, more than a few of the Irish try to be more English than the English themselves, and the country isn't truly autonomous, for they're the only nation that doesn't speak its own language. The Irish, speaking English, think English, but only to some degree, so their thinking isn't exactly the same as that of the English. However, they're still within the language and its limits mean the limits of their world. They want to be a part of Anglo-Saxon culture after all, despite not having forgotten to have been ruled mercilessly by the English for six centuries which had been the only way for them to be on some level of civilisation, but they still think Irish, and their inability to do abstract reasoning is ingenious. At the same time, we may ask why they emphasise their own importance so much, and I tend to think this is because they have none.

And I talk about them here as I did before because they're a perfect example of a socio-linguistic phenomenon which was once my interest. All in all, I did understand a man who after leaving that country said, 'I showed my appreciation of my native land by getting out of it as soon as I possibly could.' Now I was due to visit a fortress of Englishness, a very old-fashioned pub, a quintessence of Englishness, and despite my dislike of many things English, I liked it because of its cosy atmosphere. When I got there the next day, Lord Hellbridge was already there, in the company of two other men.

"Let me introduce," he said, "*messieurs* Fatum and Fortis, who are my trusted assistants whom I didn't have a chance to introduce before since they travel a lot and I, myself, see them not too often."

Mr Fatum was a tall, lean man with a very pale complexion which seemed to be even whiter because of a pair of very dark glasses he wore. Mr Fortis in turn was a short but powerfully built man, and I thought he must have been a former weightlifter or a wrestler. During my stay with them, neither of them ever smiled. Apparently, they lacked any sense of humour. However, they were very well mannered and behaved impeccably during my whole stay there.

"My assistants," said the lord, "have just returned from Moscow and have told me a couple of interesting things they found out there. It seems that our friends' business over there is flourishing after all, so the authorities did nothing about all that financial scam they have been engaged in for years now. I've heard that during your stay there you were in the company of some men who had some influence, and even met in passing, so to speak, the president of Russia, who was eager to help, but apparently nothing came of that. Either he didn't care or was misled by those who were supposed to investigate the matters in which our friends, M7, were engaged. Therefore, I'm going to get in touch with him and ask whether something can be done after all, and I'm pretty sure he will be of assistance to us for he owes me one, after all."

At that moment, I thought, *The president of Russia owes him something? Who else, in that case, owes him something?* As I was to find out later, there were several powerful men in different parts of the world who owed him 'something', and only then did I realise his influence, which seemed to have no limits. How come he was so powerful, and who was he then? And someday I was to get to know, but at the time of my stay in London, I had no idea. However, the lord reminded me of somebody I had already met in a park in Zurich. *Could they have something in common?* I asked myself, but I didn't dare, of course, to ask him whether he might know the other man.

We discussed a few other topics, and one of them was the case of James, and the lord said that he would be taken care of very soon, and when the time came to talk to him again, he would be very willing to cooperate. I shouldn't worry about that, said the lord, for my conversation with James would be very short and to the point, and again I was to find out why when it came to it we wasted no time at all. James was very happy to help. He had no objections whatever I asked him to do.

"But now," said the lord, "there's something else I want to discuss with you before you go further in your dealings with the M7, and this is about the reason why you're so determined to punish them. Why wouldn't you simply forget what they had done to you and carry on with your life, which is now pretty pleasant since you are with a woman you love, and you do what you like doing?"

"I myself," I began, "have posed this question to myself many a time, and am still not sure why I want them to be punished. However, I'm determined to carry on with them being punished, after all."

"Hmm, so are you not sure about your motives or the justification of your willingness to take arms against them, or both?" asked the lord.

"Both," I said, "but the main reason is that you should never let anyone who has insulted you get away with it. You should bide your time and strike back when you're in a position of strength even if you no longer need to strike back."

"Yes, it makes sense, and let me tell you why I think it does. First of all, it's about your feelings, which wouldn't be good if you have forgotten the injustice they've done to you. But this is in fact about something much deeper. I mean that the main reason for punishing them is your morality code, which is inseparable from reason. What they did to you abused that code and this way destroyed the order of a world you believe in. And to restore the order you feel you have to avenge yourself, don't you?"

"Yes," I said, "this is exactly the reason I have to fight them. My world, as you've just said, collapsed, and to rebuild it I have to destroy the cause of the destruction. Otherwise, my world will never be restored. In other words, thinking isn't everything. You have to act."

"I agree," said the lord, "for just to say no isn't enough to put everything in order. And you know what? This is exactly what a certain character in Goethe's *Faust* does."

I knew whom he meant; it was Mephistopheles, and now I began to realise something that had occurred to me before, the strange resemblance of them, both Wahrburg and Hellbridge, to Goethe's character, and to be honest, I was a bit terrified, thinking, *And there's no Devil, either?, But then who is he really?*

"'Who art thou then?' Good question, isn't it?" said Hellbridge.

*Does he read my thoughts?* I asked myself. *Who am I talking to in fact?* But I didn't have time to ponder the question because the lord said, "Have you ever thought about who he really is?"

"Yes, I have, but so far, I haven't arrived at any conclusion," I said.

"There might not be any," said Hellbridge, and smiled.

"That's it, and I worry a bit about that."

"And why so?" he asked.

"Hmm, you see, in the past, I didn't care much about answering such questions. I simply ignored them or I thought I could do so, when in fact they didn't disappear, and now when I feel as if I were not the same as I was before, those questions are back, and I know I have to answer them."

"Bah, it may be high time to do so," said the lord, and smiled again.

"Yes, in fact, I'm pretty sure it is the time to answer them. And let me explain why I think so."

"Please do, I can't wait, for what you say is very interesting, and because I wish you well," said Hellbridge.

"Thank you, milord," I said, "and if you find it engaging, let me continue. So, as I have just said, I used to ignore some, in fact, important questions, but now I can't help but answer them because of this feeling of becoming somebody else. In other words, I feel as if I were on my way to becoming…" I hesitated for a while, looking for words, and then continued, "…what I really am, that is, in fact, to have the courage for what I really know."

"And what do you mean by that?" asked the lord.

"I'm not sure yet because I think I can only know that when I become what I am," I said.

"But don't you think that all you're saying now is a kind of word game, dear Mr Adarsh?"

"Yes, very often I have that feeling, and it makes me very anxious. On the other hand, I don't really know by what other means I may get any answers to the problem of life, my life."

"Hmm, yes, this is a very human problem, I mean, not to be able to find answers in words alone, and this is because man doesn't actually pose the problem in language, for words are of no use here. Perhaps you shouldn't try too hard to find the answer, I mean, with words, or they may come to you someday out of the blue, so to speak. Anyway, in my opinion, there's no answer to the problem of life in words," said Hellbridge.

"I'm inclined to agree with you, but on the other hand, I can't wait to find the answer, you know what I mean?"

"Oh yes, I do, my dear fellow, but I strongly advise you to be patient and wait, and I'm sure you'll get your answer."

"And how, if I may ask, would you know that, milord?" I asked him.

"Bah, *there are more things in heaven and earth…* you know that, I suppose?"

"Yes, it's *Hamlet*, and yes, the author might have been right there. We never know what will happen to us tomorrow, or what words may come, either," I said.

"That's it, so there's nothing to do but to wait, as often happens on this earth, dear Mr Adarsh."

"It seems so, but what still worries me is we have to look for answers in words after all. We can't help it."

"Oh yes, you can't. Humankind as a whole can't help it, and that's the rub. People put too much trust in words, and that's why they can't get any answers to their so-called existential questions. This was a problem for those poor fellows Martin and Jean-Paul too. They both eventually got nowhere, and you know why, because to these questions there aren't answers in language, no language spoken on earth, for that matter, for these questions are asked *sub specie aeternitatis* where no words exist. You ask them as if you were dreaming, for you can't formulate your questions in words, but they are still there, aren't they?"

"Yes," I said, "they are, and sometimes we know the answer, but again it doesn't come in the language we speak. But it doesn't mean we shouldn't ask questions, especially those which question the obvious, for what is obvious today might not be so tomorrow. Whatever we see could be other than it is, as that stubborn Ludwig said. In other words, the sense of life consists of the questions 'Why?' and 'What for?', and we can't help but ask them even if we aren't aware of it. And this is a paradox, I mean, we can't stop asking questions we can't answer, that is, we can't do so in language, but someday the answers may come, but they won't be in words, as you've just said.

"But I wonder why, anyway, we ask these questions, and methinks the reason we ask them is to tell the difference between truth and falsity, that is, in fact, between good and evil. The order of the world depends on the right establishment of this difference, as well as the order of our life, that is, to know what to do in order to do good. Ethics, that is, our moral principles, are inseparable from reason, and they aren't given to us, they aren't congenital, but we have to learn them.

"Now, there are quite a few moral philosophies around the world, and the question is, 'Which one is superior, the best for man?' And this question presupposes another one, that is, 'What is good?' And here we are in trouble, for we can't really say which one of them all is the best for man to respect—"

"Excuse me," Hellbridge broke in, "I think that you can eventually say which one is the best, for the answer is none."

Now I was totally baffled, and it took me a good few minutes to regain my composure, and I eventually asked the lord, "But there must be one moral code which we'd be able to consider the best."

"Do you think so? Then tell me, please, what you mean by 'the best'. You know," the lord continued, "people often use words which actually have no precise denotation at all. They're slogan-like, and using them, you in truth have nothing in mind, and it's true especially about your religious beliefs. For what, in point of fact, does it mean to say, 'I believe in God'? As a matter of fact, it means nothing and proves nothing, being nothing but a cliché. For the only actual proof of your faith is a doing, not an empty declaration of faith. The same goes for some words such as 'best'."

*Yes*, I thought, *he's right*, and now, when he asked me to explain the meaning of 'best', I hesitated, for I wanted to say something of value, that is, to give a precise meaning of the word, so I began, "I'm not sure if I can manage to clarify the meaning of the word because there is always a problem with such a word's denotation, I mean, the words that refer to everything that we consider good. Strangely enough, it's much easier to give a precise meaning of what is 'bad'. But I'll try, anyway, and begin with saying that whenever we say 'good', we mean something that benefits us, that is, something which is relative and accidental, and the same goes for its superlative, 'best'. Thus, we don't mean either of the words as such, for the meaning of 'good' as such cannot be defined, either, as it cannot be in the case of the word 'truth'."

"That's it," said Hellbridge, "and what you in fact have said describes the situation of man on this earth, who never knows more than what is just temporary and therefore only valid at the time of his actual experience. In other words, something is 'true' when he considers it to be 'true', so within the limits of a given situation. But he longs for more. He wants to grasp the world as a whole, and because of the limits of his understanding, he has to refer to a power outside his limited perception, and then he invokes a being that he calls God. And this way, man relieves himself from responsibility for the world he lives in. He gives up his self-responsibility and does not accept blame for anything. Moreover, he shifts his responsibility to someone else, thus becoming a sort of a vasal where he's dwelling. But the paradox of his view of himself is that he still, after all, considers himself a judge and master of the world. And that's where the rub is."

"As far as I can see, you don't hold man in high esteem, milord." And once I'd asked the question, I realised I'd addressed him as if he weren't a human being at all, but then, 'Who was he?'

"Hmm, no, I don't, and I have every reason not to have a high opinion of him. You know, man wants to be respected whatever he does. Moreover, he believes he's allowed to be respected, for in fact he does not recognise any higher power above him, and his religions are merely a justification for what he does.

"But that's all for now. Someday in the future, we'll have a chance to return to the subject, and now you have something else to do, don't you?"

"Yes, sir, I do, and it's James and the others with whom I haven't finished yet."

"No, I know, you haven't but you will, but be careful and don't treat each of them the same way, for not all of them deserve the same fate."

"I know they're different, and I, myself, was not that innocent."

"It's good you admit that, and I appreciate it. Anyway, in dealing with that M7 business, you'll receive all the help you need. Goodbye for now, Mr Adarsh."

"Goodbye."

So, I was supposed to finish my business here in London, and knew that those who were now my allies would be very disappointed if I didn't. Thus, I had no choice but to start thinking of how to proceed with James Serfield, 'The Rat'. But what was disturbing me now was the feeling of uselessness of my previous and present actions. Why now, I asked myself, when I still had something to do, something that was so vital for me to finish, that is, the M7 business, did I begin to doubt the sense of doing it? What change would it bring to my life? What good would come of it? I kept asking myself, and why now when everything was going pretty smoothly was I beginning to be sceptical about the whole business, and was already tired of it? I was looking for an answer and came to the conclusion that the problem was that I was looking for it in words, and came to realise there was no answer in them.

Yes, words again posed the problem. Thus, where the answer was, I thought, was in action alone, I said to myself, but no, because every action should at least be somehow justified by a reason, and I couldn't find any reason to carry on, so why should I after all? I asked myself. Because it was my duty? Rubbish, it wasn't any duty of mine. Because of…? I kept asking myself, but no answer came, and then I realised the chaos, the confusion of all of my life which had been in a mess, and even my feelings for Bea weren't of any comfort or an excuse for any further actions. I just said 'no' to everything, and in the first place to the senseless search for answers in words, and the only one that remained was actually 'no'… But then, I suddenly realised that the life problem, all that doubting, and that 'no' come once man asks nobody but himself the question 'Why?', and then no answer may ever come… But the answer always lies in words since we are humans, and for us there is no other way but words to understand, to believe in the sense of life, that is, to carry on living. Therefore, I still had to look for answers in words I had run out of, and the only hope was that they would come to me again, and only then would I recover my faith in life.

But now, when I was considering all that, I had a feeling of the inconsistency of everything I had done so far, and of what I was talking about, as if logic was missing there. On the other hand, I thought, life very often lacks logic, which we try to find afterwards, and then our life stories seem to be artificially arranged, schematised, whereas in real life they're full of contradictions and have nothing to do with logic. I realised that while making those notes, I tried to grasp things as they were, that is, apparently illogical, but then I was aware that my story seemed to be chaotic, inconsistent and the reader would have a hard time following it. But then how many stories had been very craftily and beautifully told with no truth in them at all, for they were invented for no other reason than to please the reader? And they say nothing true for they have been artificially arranged in often pretentious language, crafty crap, as I call that sort of stuff. Whereas my aim of telling all that was not to please the reader, but in the first place to understand myself what had been happening, but to understand… what does it actually mean? I asked myself, and thought I might be able to know that someday, but now when I was writing about all that, I couldn't.

And when I was still lost in my thoughts, the M7 business somehow continued on its own, apparently. Someone else was anxious to carry it on and, as had been decided before now, it was James' turn to answer for his wrongdoing.

He was a man who was extremely envious of others' better fortune, and would do anything to enjoy what those others were lucky enough to possess. The only chance he had to achieve anything and rise in status was his job and, performing his duties, he did his best to please his superiors, being always on their call. Even in his free time, he was constantly thinking what he could do to please them, and especially on his way to work he was thinking intensely about what he should do that day to receive their grace, as he was on that memorable day, Friday, the 13th of July.

As usual, he entered the building where he always arrived well before time, and there were no other co-workers yet. The only person to greet him was a porter, who handed James his office keys and wished him a good day.

James unlocked the office door and immediately came to a halt seeing a huge black cat sitting behind his desk. He closed his eyes, thinking he had suffered a stroke or a hallucination, but when he opened them again the cat was still there.

He wasn't sure how to proceed with that unexpected visitor, and the first thought that came to his mind was that his superiors had placed the cat there in order to test his attitude towards animals. That's why James decided not to rush things and to see how the situation would develop, so for a good while, he was just staring at the cat and waited. That impasse was broken by the animal who, in a human voice, said to him, "Please have a seat."

James was so perplexed that he just fell in the chair that fortunately for him was close, and at the same moment, the cat looked at some sheets of papers which were on the desk and then shook his head a few times, and eventually looking straight at James, said, "So, you imagine you do your job well, dear Mr Serfield, don't you?"

James, still shocked by this unexpected encounter, just managed to mumble a few inaudible words.

"Well," said the cat, "I can see you've just written a memorandum in which you've made some proposals regarding foreign policy, and one of them concerns the arguments for and against Britain being in Europe. You emphasise the exceptional character of this country, and on this basis, you say that it should leave Europe and rely more on Dollaria in future economic and political affairs. Dollaria, you claim, will welcome you with open arms and do everything to keep you happy. Whatsoever, all in all, I'm certain you're out of your mind or are being totally naïve, or both, believing in Dollaria's generosity. Surely, it will welcome you as a handy vassal, and if this is what you mean, then you're right. So, tell me, what benefits do you expect for your country after leaving the European Community?"

Still traumatised, it took James a superhuman effort to utter, "I… I want what's best for my country."

"But of course, you've always wanted what's best…" the cat paused and then continued, "for yourself, and perhaps for your gang members."

James didn't know how to address the cat, which might not be a cat after all, he thought, but then who did for that matter? He eventually said in a mouse-like voice, "I beg your pardon, but we're patriotic, law-abiding citizens."

"Hmm, in a way you are, for it's typical for an Englishman, whatever he does, to put his own interest before that of his own country, and then to claim he has done his best for the latter, even if he lives abroad for tax evasion purposes. In other words, there's nothing like hypocrisy and priggishness, and perfidy, of course. But this time you've gone too far, dear Mr Serfield, and you're going to pay for that."

James opened his mouth to say something, but the cat banged his paw on the desk and shouted, "Quiet!" And then, he continued, "In spite of your two-facedness, we've decided to give you a chance after all."

James was thinking intensely and decided to comply with whatever the strange animal said to him, so he just whispered, "Thank you, I'm most obliged, sir." He chose to call the cat 'sir' just in case it wasn't a cat, for he thought he might have been hypnotised and was in fact talking to a high-ranking civil servant, or perhaps an MI5 officer who was testing him now. Anyway, even being horrified by that out-of-the-blue encounter, he didn't believe even for a second that he was talking to a real cat. No, ladies and gentlemen, James was convinced despite his initial fright that such things never happen. And those MI5 people could have hired a high-class hypnotist and staged all that to find out whether he was a loyal, devoted servant before, James now was close to believe it, appointing him to some special classified job. Thus, James made his mind to play along to pass the test.

"So, he began, "may I say something, sir?"

"What's that?" asked the cat curtly.

"I admit that I could have made a few mistakes, but I have never ever betrayed my country, I swear."

The cat gave him an amusing glance and said, "Well, as a matter of fact, no, in a way you haven't, and I mean that in relation to what I have just said about the patriotism of people like you. So, now tell me, please, what are you going to do with the rest of your life, dear Mr Serfield?"

"I haven't thought about it yet," admitted James.

"Aha, you haven't, and wouldn't it be wiser to start thinking about it?" asked the cat.

"If you want me to do so, I will," said James, who decided to do anything to please the cat.

"You know, we would very much like you to do that..."and the cat stopped here, and James was now quite sure that he was talking to somebody who represented an authority with almost supernatural powers, for otherwise how would they have at their disposal a cat with such incredible abilities? James had never believed in any supernatural powers or whatever they are called and, for instance, so-called black magic was for him something invented by swindlers who wanted to manipulate the naïve, using it for their own very pragmatic aims. *But now*, he thought, *what I am witnessing isn't any black magic. It is*, and he was sure of it, *a very sophisticated spectacle staged by high-class psychologists who have hypnotised me to check out my usefulness for a job which apparently must be very demanding. So, it seems*, James said to himself, *they consider me a suitable candidate for that surely classified assignment*, and now James began to feel proud of himself and hoped to pass the test. *I underestimated myself*, he thought, *and now it's somebody else who will help me to recover my faith in myself, and of course to raise my status in society*. And since his biggest dream was knighthood, of course, and then perhaps something even higher, James decided to do anything that the representative, namely the cat, without doubt from some government organisation, wanted him to do.

And now the cat, after a few minutes' break, continued, "Yes, we'd very much like you to not only rethink your life, but also to do something for us." And what the cat just said confirmed James' suspicions and hope at the same time that he'd been chosen for some important job. He listened attentively to what the cat was saying to him and was ready to agree to anything he would be offered.

"We know," said the cat, "you and your friends have set up a society which gains substantial financial benefits from laundering money in some parts of the world under the cover of charity. You're protected at the same time by the intelligence community, namely Boris Dumblodge and his people. Until now, the prime minister, Mr Oddhouse, has been unaware of the true character of your activities, but since Lord Hellbridge had a word with him, the PM doesn't approve of your activities and wants to disband your organisation. It's come to our knowledge that Dumblodge is a double agent, but since there isn't any proof of that, he's untouchable at the moment, He may, of course, be dismissed from his job as a boss of secret intelligence, but it wouldn't be of any benefit since he would continue what he's doing now. All in all, the matter in question is of a very delicate nature and must be dealt with accordingly. Now, you, in fact, deep at heart, are a man of integrity, aren't you?"

James felt very proud of himself hearing that, and said, "I highly appreciate that, and indeed I am, and will do everything I can to assist you in your action against that traitor."

"I've always known," said the cat, "we could rely on you after all, and we'll prove our recognition in due time, and now seeing you're ready to help us, this is what you're supposed to do. You're going to meet somebody who will supervise your activities, and this will be a woman of exceptional abilities as you'll find out yourself. You'll get a call from her today very soon. That's it for now, and of course not a word about what we've been talking about to anybody, understood?"

"But of course, and thank you, sir, for everything."

"Don't mention it," said the cat with a hint of irony in his voice, "and you'll thank us by accomplishing your task."

"Yes, certainly, I'm very grateful indeed, and ready to do whatever you ask of me."

"I'm sure of that," said the cat, and rose from the chair he was sitting on and came out of James' office.

James felt dizzy and it took him a good few minutes to recover the strength to think, and the first thing he thought of was how the cat would now get out of the building unnoticed, for it was already eleven o'clock and there were a lot of people around. So, he ran out of the door and looked around, but of course there was no trace of the cat but to be sure he asked security downstairs if they'd noticed anything suspicious, but they said no, nothing out of the usual, and what might that be? they asked.

"Ah," said James, "I might be mistaken but it seems to me I spotted a cat on my floor, but apparently it was… don't know, I'm tired, you know, a bit overworked."

"We perfectly understand, sir," the officer hastened to assure him, "and there's nothing to worry about. Everything's under control. Anyway, cats aren't allowed here."

Once James was back in his office, he began to think hard. *Maybe I dreamt all that*, he said to himself, *and there hasn't been any cat in here*. But he realised there could have been after all, for the experience was still so vivid in his memory, and he remembered exactly what they had been talking about. He decided to check if there was any evidence of the cat's visit, so he looked at the chair the cat had been sitting on, under the desk, and he even went around the room on all fours examining every inch of it, but found nothing, not even a single hair of the cat's fur.

*Hmm, strange*, he thought, *there should have been at least a hair or two left by that nasty creature*. Eventually, he sat at his desk and pulled out the drawer, and noticed something that wasn't there before: a photograph which had been taken apparently a few years back and showed himself and another man, and it was Karl Denker, his former friend whom he hadn't seen for some time now. *How did it get in here?* James asked himself. *Who might have left it in my drawer?* And why him? The man he hadn't seen since the latter's funeral, in fact, in Switzerland, that he attended. Anyway, whoever left it for him did it deliberately, but for what purpose? thought James, but he couldn't find any reasonable explanation.

He was still staring at the photograph when his telephone rang. James answered it and a female voice asked, "You wonder what happened to your former friend, don't you?"

James was so surprised by the question he almost fell off the chair he was sitting on, and it took him a good few minutes to ask in a weak, stuttering voice, "Who… who am I talking to?"

"I'm a friend of Karl, dear Mr Serfield."

"Aha." That was all James managed to utter.

"And he asked me to pass his best on to you," said the unknown woman.

James was flabbergasted, and still stuttering, asked, "Ah… ah, thank you… but as far I know, he's dead."

"In a way he is," said the woman, "however, not exactly, so to speak."

James felt his hairs on the back of his neck rise, and all he could say was, "Aha, I…"

"And you'll see him soon, and me too as has already been arranged," added the woman.

Now James felt he was about to faint, and having no idea what to say, just stammered, "Yes, yes, I understand."

"You don't understand yet, but you will, dear Mr Serfield. It's high time for you to understand a couple of things," said the woman with her terrifying self-assurance.

Now James was petrified for good, and his whole body began to shake, and he wasn't able to say a word, and the woman who was apparently somehow aware of his condition now said, "Pull yourself together, and don't even think of doing anything stupid. Otherwise, you'll regret it. Understood?"

James was so eager to please the woman that he partially regained the strength to speak, and hastened to say, "No, I swear I won't do anything, believe me."

"Believe you?" she said, and laughing, asked him, "and do you believe yourself, or your friends for that matter?"

"I… I don't know what to say," he admitted.

"That's better, and now, you've just been told by your visitor to see a certain woman, and it's me you are to see, so on the back of the photograph you'll find the address, and I await you at ten tonight," she said, and hung up.

James was staring at the telephone long after the conversation ended, and now he was sure the cat had indeed visited him.

And now James didn't really know what to think about all that, for there was no rational explanation to anything he had gone through over the last couple of hours. It all seemed to be something totally out of order in the world he lived in, something unreal indeed, but now after the telephone conversation, he knew that it had indeed happened. We depreciate and deprecate things, he thought. We often don't understand them and dismiss them, thinking they are mere fantasies, and then we even mock them, but in truth we know nothing for sure since we have just simplified everything for handy use, for practicality in life.

We even simplified our God so that He could suit our needs, but do we actually know anything about Him? No, we know nothing. As we know nothing either about His opposite, Satan, whom we made the personification of evil, whereas we don't know the true reason for his being. We consider God omnipotent and the personification of good, so why does He allow Satan to be there? And we aren't able to answer the question, for it transcends the limits of our understanding. Thus, wouldn't it be better for us to admit ignorance as for our eternal destiny? For only then, James thought, would we be in a position to follow God's commandments, the principles He orders us to observe, and to lead the Christian way of life. Otherwise, how could we be good in the sense of His meaning of goodness?

That feat of reflection was very unusual for James, and as it had never happened before, he asked himself, *Why only now do I have such ideas?* But he couldn't answer this question, either.

Instead, he began thinking of the past and especially his former friend Karl Denker of whom that unknown woman had reminded him. *What we did to him wasn't fair,* James thought. *It was outrageous, and now what shall I do to atone for that? And why only now am I beginning to think about it?* he asked himself. Was it because of the cat's visit, of that totally out-of-this-world experience? *Yes, if it wasn't for his visit, I would never have had the thoughts I have now, thus that unreal, incredible experience taught me something about the very real matter which I now have to deal with.* But then, what about all the others who, as he knew, except Graham and Bernard, were equally guilty? *They won't allow me,* James was sure about that, *to make amends for what they did to Karl.* Especially Jason, who was the brains of that conspiracy, and the same could be said perhaps of the others, again with the exception of those two who had done nothing. They had actually known nothing about the matter in question.

*So, tonight, I'll learn more,* he said to himself, *and I know I can't afford to not go there, for that incredible, black magic-like experience has taught me something about very real things.* Moreover, James now had the impression of being somebody else, perhaps somebody he had always been deep down, and now felt as if his true ego had been revealed and he would act accordingly.

But now, James had a problem of an ethical nature that he had never had before. It was about the so-called Christian values, such as pity, humility and compassion, and their opposite ones, that is pride, courage, the liberty of spirit, sympathy and insight which one may put into one phrase: the will to power. But there was a problem James noticed now, to his surprise: do they all actually exclude each other? No, James thought, not every one of the former was the opposite of each of the latter ones. *Strange...* He asked himself, *Why?* It was due to the traditional prejudiced way of thinking to make them opposites, but it seemed that it was not the case, and he was sure of that, but the problem was how should he proceed to prove it? First, he thought, make it clear for himself and then perhaps try to put it into practice. *Anyway,* James thought, *how come that only now, out of the blue, so to speak, I have a dilemma of this sort?* At the same time, he realised that he couldn't disregard the question, for he found himself, and to be honest, to his big surprise, even horror, a very different man now, and that difference lay of course in his way of thinking.

So, he said to himself, let's take, for instance, insight, without which one wouldn't believe in God, would he? Without having that ability, a man would be immersed in material goods up to his ears, wouldn't he? And what about courage? Apparently the same, for he who doesn't possess this virtue wouldn't be able to adhere to the principles so different from all those followed by the majority. To say nothing of Jesus' exceptional behaviour during his trial and crucifixion. And what about compassion? Now it took James a while to consider, but eventually he said to himself, no, a man who is strong and courageous is magnanimous, that is, nobly generous, not petty in feelings and conduct as Jesus himself was, and that's why Nietzsche calls him the noblest human ever.

All in all, it is due to our linguistic misinterpretations, James was sure now, that we regard all those Christian values as the very opposite to those which characterise a man endowed with the will to power. And these linguistic blunders have far-reaching consequences, for they affect not only pure academic disputes, but in the first place, our actions, our attitude to others. The reason why the problems of life are posed, it became clear to James now, is that the logic of our language is misunderstood. But why, he asked himself, can men not understand their own language, the language they speak? Apparently, there must be something wrong with their way of thinking, or... that's it, or what? Or, he thought, it might be that they take for granted that they are in charge of their thoughts, whereas they aren't. And that's the rub, for if they were, they would know what they would be thinking tomorrow or the day after tomorrow, but they obviously don't. All they are able to think and be aware of is temporary, relative and accidental, but at the same time they long for the eternal, and that's why they invented their gods. They represent eternity, that which is absolute, universal, without any reference to or dependence upon reality. Thus, man as such lives in two worlds at the same time, the absolute and the temporary, a passing existence that is relative and in which there is no truth, for truth belongs to the eternal. So, what's the solution to the problem of man's double-thinking? Is it a critique of language as some philosophers have said? And if so, then man should question the obvious, that is what is here and now, and tomorrow isn't any more, or it still might be but we would never know. That's all a vicious circle, a kind of schizophrenia, James thought, and having been exhausted by all those considerations, decided to give it up and have a rest.

James left his office a bit earlier than usual and went straight home. There was still plenty of time until his meeting with Karl and the woman, so he decided to first have a nap and then prepare for the meeting. However, he couldn't sleep at all for he was too occupied thinking about the meeting, and had no clue how he should react once he saw his former friend, what to say to him, how to explain what had happened.

James almost never drank alcohol but this time, being still so confused and nervous, decided to have some. He found a bottle of gin, poured a good measure into a glass and mixed it with tonic and gulped it. Not being accustomed to drinking, he got almost immediately drunk but cheered up at the same time and looked to the upcoming meeting in a more positive way.

The address of the place he was to reach wasn't too far from his flat, so he chose to get there on foot. He changed into his best suit and went outside. The weather was fine and his mood was now pretty good under the circumstances, but he couldn't stop thinking about what he should say to Karl. James knew that there was no excuse for what they had done to him and felt that it would be best to admit it, apologise and ask for forgiveness. It was very strange for him to think like that, and he could hardly recognise his former self and kept asking himself why he had changed so much since meeting the cat, but he couldn't answer the question.

At ten minutes to ten he was at his destination, which was an old Victorian house, and beside the door where James stood, there was a bell which he pressed. Almost immediately, the door was opened and closed itself once James was in, but he couldn't see anybody and wondered how to find the flat in question, for he couldn't see any flat number on the door to his right or the other to his left. He was still unsure as to what to do when he heard a woman's voice from somewhere upstairs calling his name, so he went up.

I, myself, before I was due to see James at Fabiana's flat, for it was her who invited him, had certain doubts about meeting him since I'd never liked him and, as a matter of fact, the other members of the M7 hadn't, either. And if it hadn't been for Lord Hellbridge's suggestion to meet him, I wouldn't think of meeting James. But the lord had stressed one thing in relation to the meeting, and it was been that I, in his opinion, was beginning to understand my life backwards but was supposed to live it forwards, and that's why meeting James was necessary. I must say that at the time I hadn't quite understood what Hellbridge had meant by what he said, and only later did I grasp the meaning of it. He also said that in order to gain peace in life, one had to get satisfaction, not just a passing, temporary pleasure but a long-lasting, permanent one, and to achieve it, one mustn't judge people just by what they've done, but also by what they are capable of in the future. But obviously it isn't easy to foresee a man's capacity beforehand as it isn't easy to understand him afterwards, for our understanding of others, and also of ourselves, is never complete, that is, never sufficient but always limited by what we think at a given time, our prejudices and the like.

And, yes, the lord, as it turned out later, had been right, for at the time when I was to meet James, despite being happy with Bea, I wasn't fully satisfied. Something was still missing and I didn't know what it was. And Hellbridge had also said something in relation to us both being together, that to make our relationship lasting, just to be satisfied temporarily wasn't enough. I had to get that long-lasting satisfaction, that is, actually to say existentially 'yes' instead of 'no' in my life. And since I valued his advice very much, I decided to try my best to follow it. Thus, before seeing James, I kept in mind what the lord had told me.

James himself was obviously very nervous before he was to enter Fabiana's flat, and what helped him a bit was that he was still under the influence of the alcohol he had drunk before. So, once he heard the woman calling him, he was quite determined to face the music after all. When he reached the next floor, he saw the door open for him and he went in, and immediately fell on the floor. He had no idea why it happened, and it couldn't have been because of his drinking. He wasn't that drunk. It had to be something else. And when he scrambled to his feet, he saw it, and it was a package that for an unknown reason was in the middle of the flat's corridor.

*Why, for God's sake*, he thought, is it here of all places? He looked more closely at it and to his amazement he saw that the package was addressed to him. "Hallo," he called, but nobody came. *Where's the woman who called me?* he thought. *Is she playing a joke on me or what?*

I, in the meantime, was already in Fabiana's flat waiting for him, and it was she who had placed the package in the corridor, and as it turned out later, a special courier had brought it before, despite it being addressed to

James, and he had done so on the specific orders of the Royal Mail CEO, who had been asked that favour by somebody else.

Then James heard the woman's voice again. "Open it," and he did open the parcel and found inside a pile of what seemed to be documents of a sort. To his amazement, it turned out to be the history of his life.

*Who, for God's sake,* he asked himself, *could have made such a detailed CV of mine?*

At that moment, he heard her say, "God has nothing to do with it. It is about somebody else. Anyway, you don't believe in God, do you?" And then before him appeared Fabiana, who said, "So, who could have done that, what do you think?"

"I don't really know. It might be the security service. Do you work for them, madam?"

"No, I don't, and they have nothing to do with it. However, you yourself have some relationship with a man, I mean Mr Dumblodge, don't you?"

"Yes, I have, but not that close. Anyway, I still don't understand why I have been invited here, and what you want from me."

"This morning, you met somebody, and then it was me calling you and inviting you to come here, and the invitation and the package are for you to understand that we have some means at our disposal, and that we want you to work for us. That somebody else has told us to invite you here since he thinks you're ready to cooperate. I don't actually know how he knows that, and it's not my business. I simply follow his orders, as your visitor did this morning."

"And who's that, and why has he staged all that theatrical spectacle?"

"What you call a spectacle is actually something very different in its very nature," said Fabiana, "for, as a matter of fact, what people consider reality is in fact a spectacle in which participants play their roles according to a script written by somebody else. You are beginning to understand that, and that's why you've been chosen to play an active role in preparation for the next stage of this spectacle, for now a part of it will concern your closest associates. I don't know how those in charge of it know you're capable of doing that because I myself would never think of you being fit to do it, but be sure they know better. And I presume that all that has been happening since this morning – the cat's visit, the package with your CV – is to make you fully understand that there are more things on this earth than man can see, and that what is believed to be an illusion, a fantasy, or black magic as some call it, is in fact an integral part of what people call reality, that is, reality of the way they think. In other words, they know nothing about what they are so sure about. They only claim to know, and this is their claim, their conviction, that is a fantasy."

I was listening to Fabiana and was surprised by her eloquence, for never before had I heard her say such things. Now she turned to me and said, "Ches, darling, would you explain to the gentleman what we expect him to do?"

The gentleman in question, James, didn't of course recognise me because of the plastic surgery I had undergone in Italy. So, I said to him, "You're talking now to your former friend Karl Denker, Mr Serfield."

He looked at me in shock and couldn't utter a word for a good few minutes, and then eventually said, "Is it really you? I… I would never have expected to meet you again, you know, I…" He couldn't finish the sentence.

"Yes," I said, "I know what you mean, and there's no need to say more about what happened then, for now the situation is very different as you can see, so let bygones be bygones. I've been asked by Lord Hellbridge not to look for revenge towards you as regards the past, and to be honest, I don't know why he asked me to forget what you and the others did at the time. Anyway, he told me that you had been rather passive, simply complying with the wish of Jason Goodman, who had organised that scheme that forced me to go into hiding. And all the others too, due to their own indifference and laziness, let him to be in charge, and as a matter of fact they knew nothing about the details of the conspiracy and its consequences. I didn't have a clue about all that until the lord told me all the details, and when I asked him whether he was convinced that the information was correct, he smiled and said, "My dear friend, my source of information is the most reliable in this world, because I always know beforehand what is going to happen, and I let it happen and only act afterwards if I decide so, and only when I'm interested in a case."

"But, forgive me, sir," I asked, "but how would you know in advance…?" He didn't allow me to finish, saying, "I'm not sure if you really want to know, for when you hear it, you might be a bit disturbed, my friend."

"I'll try not to be, so please tell me, sir."

"You see, I know in advance what will happen because I, myself, orchestrate some events and then watch people who are then like actors in a play I have written and then direct."

I said nothing to that for I had already suspected something, and knew that if I asked for an explanation I would make a fool of myself.

So, now confronting James, I remembered what Hellbridge had told me and therefore I said to James, "You'll be attending a meeting with your friends sooner or later, and if you're on our side, you'll tell them what you have thought until now of what you have all done, and then you'll see how each of them will respond to that. But remember, either or, and I suppose you know what I mean."

"Yes, I do," said James, "and I know how I'll proceed."

"All right then, I'll wait and see. Goodbye for now."

At that moment, Fabiana entered and said to him, "We had different plans for you, but Lord Hellbridge decided to take a different approach and we'll follow his decision, and let me tell you, you're a lucky man if you know what I mean."

"Yes, I do, for now I know perfectly well that there's nothing difficult for the lord to do. And having said that, James left.

I was pretty sure that James would do what he was asked to. I was also convinced that neither Graham nor Bernard would be our enemies in the upcoming struggle with the M7.

So, I said to myself, *let's wait and see what the outcome of their meeting will be, what each of them will say during it and what they will eventually decide if they come to any conclusions, anyway. But why, I asked myself, is it is important for me, that M7 business anyway? Wouldn't it be better to forget it, to say, let bygones be bygones? Why shall I not forget the past?* But then I remembered a certain maxim, 'Never let anyone who has insulted you get away with it. Bide your time and strike back when you're in a position of strength.' Otherwise, you will never find peace, and it's not true that we humans are actually able to forgive the evil done to us by others. No, all in all, we're incapable of true forgiveness. And there's no explanation to it because it is done so by reason of our nature to look for retaliation, and we can't help it. There might be some exceptions but, as usual, exceptions confirm the rule. And actually why does not only the Christian ethic but others demand us to say no to our inborn inclinations and desires? What's wrong with them in fact? But at that moment, I couldn't find the answer to these questions, but knew I would have to look for it but may never be able to come up with the answer.

And why had all that business with the M7 got complicated, when earlier it seemed to be much easier to deal with? But now it wasn't and it was due to the fact that its members' personalities seemed to be not so easy to define. They weren't as definite and see-through as before. And now, the way I perceived them had apparently changed, and consequently the way I'd deal with them should be different from that I had in mind before. Anyway, I shouldn't now live in the past, remembering what had happened all over again, but how should I go about it? And it seemed to me that the only way would be to know the past as if I was seeing it for the first time, but at the same time I knew it couldn't be done in one go. And I realised that I still wasn't too pleased with myself, not too happy and, as a matter of fact, I hated the word happiness, which seemed to me deprived of meaning mainly because it was overused. I had come to think as well that perhaps only by being a content man could you be good for your fellow human beings, whereas those who are repressed and intimidated cannot be such. Those who suffer want others to suffer as well, and it is again by reason of human nature.

Yes, not only did the M7 business not seem as simple as it had seemed before, but also my thoughts I was putting down weren't, either, for to say life's not easy isn't a mere cliché after all, and it goes smoothly only in the novels full of trivialities.

And, I asked myself, what if I said it all doesn't matter, forget it and just move forwards? Yes, you may try but you'll fail because no one can live without recollection before we go ahead with our lives. And in that sense, it's possible, even necessary, to turn back the clock.

And how little I knew, I thought, about why I had done many things that way and not the other way for, after all, you may always act differently. But can we really answer this question? Perhaps not, and if we may, it would be only by living in a very different way, and that's it, living, not just thinking of what kind of life to live.

And now, what should I actually do with my life? I asked myself. Yes, I was happy with Beatrice, my business was doing well, I lived comfortably, but still there was something missing there, but I couldn't grasp what it actually was. By accepted standards I should be pleased with everything I had, but then in truth, what did these standards have to do with the way I thought and felt? No, here, they didn't matter at all. And when those thoughts were still spinning in my mind, my telephone rang.

I answered the call, and an unknown-to-me male voice said, "Good morning, Mr Adarsh. It's about Miss Beatrice Sforza, and I—"

I didn't let him finish for immediately I got the impression that something was wrong, so I said, "What is it? Has something happened?"

"Hmm," said the man, "we don't actually know…" he said, as if he wasn't sure what to say, and then continued, "but you know, she was supposed to come to our place—"

I again didn't allow him to finish the sentence, and almost shouted, "Where is it, and what's your name?"

"Please calm down, Mr Adarsh, and let me finish what I want to tell you. So my name's Pobog, and we, as you may remember, actually met before in Moscow, and I'm calling from Switzerland."

And yes, I immediately remembered him and his problem over there, in Moscow, and Mr Wahrburg's intervention, so I said, "I'm sorry, Mr Pobog. I do remember you and your wife, Emilia."

"I appreciate that," he said, and carried on, "so, we expected her to come to see us yesterday evening, but she hasn't come yet and we've had no word from her. That's why we're worried that something might have happened, you know, and since she gave us your telephone number, I allowed myself to call you."

"I see," I said to him, "and thank you for telling me, and please keep in touch and let me know at once as soon as you have new information."

"I certainly will, Mr Adarsh, and we'll stay in touch. We, ourselves, I mean Emilia and myself, don't really know what to do, you know…"

"Yes, I see. Thank you again, and please tell me your address now."

He gave me that. I thanked him again and hung up.

*And now*, I asked myself, *bloody hell, what shall I do now?* And then immediately I remembered what I had been thinking just minutes before the telephone call, and now all of a sudden, I answered at least one question I'd asked myself then, which had been 'What should I do with my life?', and now I realised what kind of fool I was, asking such an idiotic question. She was my life, for without her, I wouldn't have any! Whatever we say about love, what I, myself, could say now, was that without Bea I wouldn't have any eagerness for life, and that's it. So, she in fact was my life, and this was my definition of life, and to hell with those who would consider my definition a cliché!

Now what really mattered was to find her, but what could I do about that? Call the police? But who knew where she was, which country she was in? No, the police wouldn't help here. But then who?

I was still pondering those questions, feeling hopeless, when the telephone rang again. I grabbed the receiver, thinking it was Pobog calling again, but no, this time it was Lord Hellbridge, and I immediately had the answer to my question, 'What can I do?', and it was him, yes, only he could do something. And he said to me, "I know about Beatrice, and rest assured you will see her again pretty soon."

And once I heard that, I became as if by magic instantly calm, and thought, *If he knows, then whoever has done anything against her will bitterly regret it, and in the first place she'll be safe.*

So, now I could only wait and I did. I wasn't able to do anything but think of Bea, our affair until now, all we had lived through and I asked myself, *Am I the right man for her?* But then if I wasn't, why would she stay with me? And why was I now beginning to be uncertain about us being together? And why had she spent so much time away from me, travelling all over Europe and all over the world? And being unable to find answers to any of those questions, I began to doubt myself, the very sense of my life, but at the same time asking myself, *But where has all that uncertainty came from, and why right now?* And I hoped I would be able to answer all those questions later, for now I could do nothing but wait.

When I was anxiously waiting for news as to Bea's fate, Lord Hellbridge summoned his two assistants, Fortis and Fatum, ordering them to bring back Beatrice.

"She's being kept against her will at a villa in Forch, which is just outside Zurich. Here's the address. You'll go there immediately and bring her back to Mr Adarsh, but not before you have punished those responsible for her abduction. Is it understood?"

"Yes, milord, we have understood," they both said in unison.

And they went there on a private plane that arrived at Zurich Airport on the same day. A car was already waiting for them and just one hour later they both arrived outside the villa the lord had told them about.

Fortis looked like Wilfried Dietrich, a German heavyweight wrestler famous for his strength, but was probably even stronger, and it was him who rang the bell at the villa's outside gate.

"Yes, what's your business?" a male voice asked.

"We're from the police," said Fortis, "and we'd like to have a word with you, Mr Dummrecht."

"What is it about?" the man enquired.

"Please let us in and we'll tell you," said Fortis.

The man opened the gate and they went towards the front door, which was opened by the man called Dummrecht, who said, "Can I see some ID of yours?"

"Certainly," said a wrestler-like Fortis, and grabbed him by his throat with his hand and lifted him up in the air. When he put him back on the ground, the man just managed to utter, "But... but you say you're the police."

"Oh yes, we are, but not from this earth. And now tell us, where's Miss Sforza?"

Mr Dummrecht wasn't so stupid as to not realise that his visitors' sense of humour had its limits, and it'd be much better to be honest with them, so he said, "She was here but this morning was taken to another place, and I don't know where it is."

The two men looked at him, and Fatum said, "Hmm, you don't know... and who does, my dear chap?"

"My boss does," said the man.

"Aha, and who's that?" asked Fortis.

Mr Dummrecht didn't feel like testing Fortis' strength again, and hastened to say, "I get orders from London, but I don't know the man's name, you know, I was just to keep Miss Sforza here for a couple of days in a locked room and wait for further instructions. The London man hired me to do so, paid upfront for that, and I never saw him because everything had been arranged over the phone."

"And who came to move her to a different place?" asked Fatum.

"I don't know who they were, either. The man from London told me to let them take Miss Sforza with them. That's all, I swear."

Fatum looked him straight in the eye, and the man could see, as others had before him, that his fate was in Fatum's hands and that he could do nothing but comply if he wanted to stay on this earth a bit longer. There were, of course, some incorrigible fantasists who in their naivety believed they had their destiny in their own hands. There were even some who believed they not only ruled their own lives but also that the others until they met Fatum, and then they realised how wrong they had been. And only then could they see that their rule had been a mere temporary illusion. And because Mr Dummrecht still had some appetite for life, they knew that to cooperate would be the only solution. And Fatum knew that himself in his piercing eyes and decided to spare the poor fellow for the time being, and said, "You will tell no one about our visit, and if you do…"

He stopped here, and Mr Dummrecht was quick to say, "No, sir, I swear to God, I won't tell anybody, believe me."

"Yes, I believe you," said Fatum, "but not because you swear to God in whom you don't really believe, but because you believe your life is more precious than anything in heaven and earth.

"Let's go, my friend," he said to Fortis, "let this clever man after all enjoy his life for a while." And they both left the villa.

These two men had been travelling a lot, and their task was to make people aware of how stupid many of them were. They had been Lord Hellbridge's trusted assistants, who had never failed to accomplish any of the assignments he'd given them. However, the final results of their missions had often been rather disappointing because their teaching hardly ever brought positive results, and this was due to the fact that people as a matter of fact are resistant, so to speak, to any knowledge, for they almost never have ideas of their own, for all their ideas come from those who rule them.

Now, they were to find Beatrice's whereabouts, and the first question to answer was who was responsible for her abduction and why? To answer the question, they contacted Emilia and her partner, Cyril Pobog, who, as they knew, was a computer wizard. And Fatum and Fortis met the couple on the same day in the afternoon.

"Dear Mr Pobog," enquired Fatum, "would it be possible to find out by whom the villa was rented?"

"It shouldn't be difficult," said Cyril, and he got to work. A mere five minutes later, he announced, "It was rented by a company called Svoboda, based in Russia."

"Very interesting," said Fatum, "and who is its Chief Executive?"

"A man by the name of Likhodeyev."

"Even more interesting, for we've actually heard of him, and apparently that *skatina*, as they call such individuals over there, is still doing his best to annoy us. You know what, my dear friend," he said to his companion, "maybe you should pay him a visit."

"But, of course, I'd love to, I mean, these kind of people, these *skatinas*, are my area of expertise."

"Yes, I know that," said Fatum, "but then, I mean, after you've visited them, they usually have some serious health problems."

"Bah, it's not my fault, you know, if some of them were still enjoying good health then they would never understand the lesson I taught them."

"I agree, you're perfectly right," Fatum hastened to agree with his best friend, "they never ever would. Ah, I don't envy your job, and often feel sorry for you, but what can we do? Our milord knows what he's doing, and that well-known historic quotation, 'Father, forgive them for they do not know what they are doing,' never applies to him, does it?"

"Oh no," said Fortis, "the quote is of no significance to our lord, for his ways are very different, with the consent of the other side, after all."

"Yes, that's it, here we have an example of perfect, fruitful cooperation, and I'm happy about that."

"So, apparently, *gospodin* Likhodeyev, *former tovarishch* Ivan Ivanovich, needs another lesson, and I already feel sorry for him, my friend," Fatum said to his companion.

"Our job, dear friend, is obviously unappreciated but necessary," said Fortis, "otherwise, there would be no order in this world."

"That's it, so let's do it," said Fatum, "and I suggest you pay him a visit while I stay here, and once you've let me know what to do, I'll get to work."

318

They thanked Cyril for his help, and now the question was how to get to Moscow as quickly as possible, and Fortis had no choice but to fly over there, which he seldom did because he was afraid of flying. He didn't trust those flying objects at all, but now he knew he had to use one of them.

When he appeared at Zurich Airport, he checked the flights to Moscow and found out that on that day there was just one flight and all the seats had already been booked.

*Hmm*, he thought, *what shall I do to get on the plane after all?* And then he heard the Russian language spoken somewhere behind him, so he turned around and saw two men whose appearance suggested they might be businessmen or diplomats.

Fortis came to them and said in Russian, which he spoke fluently without a trace of accent, "*Izvinitie gospoda*, are you flying to Moscow?"

They looked at him in surprise, and said, "*Da, konechno, my letim v Moskvu.*"

Fortis looked around discreetly and said in a low voice, "*Ya iz organov* and I've just received information concerning your flight, and that's why I'm here."

They were apparently old soviet school boys, for once they heard Fortis say that magic formula, '*Iz organov*', they took it for granted that he was either SVR or FSB, formerly known as the KGB, and one of them asked, "And what is it about?"

Fortis looked around again and in an even lower voice said, "Your plane will be subjected to a terrorist attack, and if you board it, you will never reach our dear Moscow."

"Is this information certain?" one of the men dared to ask after all.

Fortis looked at him and said, "Has my organisation ever had any uncertain information?"

"No, no," they hasted to deny, "of course not. Everything you have ever said has been true, and we certainly believe you, so you don't want us to take this flight?"

"The flight is out of the question, and that's why I'm here, to ask all Russian nationals to cancel the flight. My orders came directly from Moscow, *moi dorogyie gospoda.*"

"*Da konechno*, and we'll cancel the flight immediately," they said in unison, but the younger of them, who was apparently bolder than his companion, had after all the courage to ask, "And are you going to warn the Swiss authorities about the oncoming attack?"

"No, with big regret, I am not. You know, if we told them, then they would know something we want to keep confidential, I mean, our source of information, which we have to keep secret for obvious reasons," said Fortis in a stern voice, adding, "and I hope you understand that!"

"Yes, of course we do," quickly confirmed the older of them, but the other one who was younger and therefore not so soviet-style meekly obedient, ventured to ask after all, "and what about those who lose their lives in the attack?"

Fortis looked at him as if he was half-witted, and said, "My dear chap, have you never heard of the principle of the greater good, of utilitarianism, Bentham and Mill, those English philosophers? We too share their views on the matter in question. However, we may interpret the doctrine in a slightly different way. Anyway, hash, hash, if you are..." He didn't finish the sentence but just looked fixedly at them, especially at the younger of them.

"Yes, we understand it is strictly confidential information, and our beloved fatherland requires us to respect what you say, and we will, *tovarisch* officer."

"I was in no doubt that you would, and thank you in the name of our great country," said Fortis authoritatively, and shook their hands.

When the men left the airport, he immediately went back to the ticket desk and said, "There has apparently been a cancellation, so could I have a ticket to Moscow, please?"

"Ah yes, indeed," said a very pretty woman at the desk, smiling. "Yes, of course, here you are, and it's 350 francs, sir."

"*Vielen Dank, mein Schatz*," he said, for the woman was exactly his type. Anyway, Fortis was famous for his gallantry and it seemed the woman liked the way he addressed her because she was all smiles, and when he said, "I'll be back in a couple of days, *ma chérie*, and it would be a pleasure to see you again, so if you could tell me your telephone—"

He didn't need to finish, for the woman was quick to say, "But of course, here you are, and see you soon."

"The pleasure's all mine, and see you soon," Fortis said, bowing, always a gentleman and a great connoisseur of women's beauty.

And on his way to the departure longue, being very pleased with himself, he thought, *Bah, what a lucky day! Two things sorted out in one go, mesdames et messieurs.*

Once on the plane, Fortis began to think about whom he should contact first to get to the bottom of Bea's kidnapping. Who would conspire against her and why? he thought. She was Ches Adarsh's partner and had nothing to do with the M7 business whatsoever, so what was the reason for her abduction? Questions and questions, he thought, but no answers to any of them.

But then, what if she was somehow involved in the M7 affair and was something more than just Ches' lover? *But then again, the lord told me nothing about that, but he was obviously upset by what had happened to her, and maybe he didn't tell me anything more because he wanted me to find out everything on my own, but then why? Yea,* he said to himself, *it's possible for you to never know with him. Anyway, I can't fail his expectations because if I do, no, better not to think about what would happen to me.*

And when he was still deep in thought, his telephone rang, and to speak of the Devil, it was the lord himself.

"You are just wondering who organised Beatrice's abduction and why, aren't you?" said Hellbridge.

"Yes, milord, I am, and can't work it out," said Fortis.

"You can't, you say? Perhaps you spend too much time at the gym and other facilities like that, don't you, my dear chap?"

"But, milord, yes, I do, but that's not everything I do as you know—"

But the lord interrupted him, saying, "Yes, I know, and that's why I forgive you your temporary, I hope, blockade of mind, which might be related to what you were just recently reading, I mean, the Critique of Pure Reason."

"Yes, milord, that Kant seems to have been an impossible fellow, and I admit I still don't have a clue what he is talking about," Fortis admitted sincerely.

"Don't you worry, you aren't alone here. Hardly anyone does. Even I, myself, encountered some problems I couldn't grasp and it was only when

I talked to him that I began to see the light, but not too brightly for that matter, if you know what I mean."

"But, milord, I'm sure you warned him not to write in such a confused, vague way again," said Fortis.

"Yes, I did, but you know he's a very stubborn, disobedient fellow, so to speak, so you never know with him. But now, *zu dem Sachen selbst*, my trusted servant, forgiving you this temporary sort of amnesia for which obviously Immanuel is blamed, I'll tell you what you're supposed to do when you get to Moscow.

"So, you'll have a word with the president's assistant, who will be waiting for you at the airport, but be careful, he's a bit of a devious fellow, and you can't really trust him. Once he even tried to trick me, but then the president told him that it would be the craziest idea ever even to think of it. You see, luckily, the president is a reasonable chap, after all. Anyway, the assistant, his name's Andrei Kropotkin, has been ordered to assist you in everything you might need to do, and if he fails to do so, he won't be an assistant anymore, but somebody very different, and there won't be anything, I assure you, to be envious of. That's it for now, and keep in mind that Beatrice means a lot to me," said Hellbridge.

"Yes, milord, I perfectly understand and I will not fail your expectations."

"I do hope you won't," said the lord, ending the conversation.

When Fortis arrived at Sheremetyevo Airport, *gospodin* Kropotkin met him in the VIP longue, and without any customs formalities, they both came out of the building and got into a car that was already waiting for them.

"Have you been to our capital before?" asked Kropotkin.

"No, never, it's my first visit," replied Fortis.

They were now in the city centre and he looked with curiosity at the houses and people they were passing, and said to Kropotkin, "Are you a native of Moscow?"

"No, I was born in Tula and arrived in Moscow only when I was eighteen years old," said Kropotkin.

"I see, and you came here to study, I presume."

"Yes, I was studying languages and politics at Moscow University and after graduation was offered a job at the Ministry of Foreign Affairs, and after two years was offered the job I do now."

"And do you enjoy working for the president?"

"Oh yes, very much so," said Kropotkin with great emphasis.

"Aha," said Fortis, "and tell me, was Prince Kropotkin one of your predecessors?"

"Yes, he was, I mean, on my mother's side. I'm pleased to learn you know the name, for hardly any foreigners know anything about Russia."

"Oh yes, they know nothing. They're full-time ignorant for that matter. Their opinions about your country are prejudiced and very narrow-minded. Anyway, they don't even bother to know something more, those morons. And then, of course, their views can be totally manipulated by their governments and the media."

"A very unusual opinion for a foreigner, and I appreciate it," said Andrei Kropotkin.

"Bah, I'm a bit unusual myself, you know, and as for Prince Kropotkin, let me tell you I found him an honest man, and so passionate about people's well-being in a future he dreamt of. And, of course, he didn't agree with Lenin who, in my opinion, was ruthless, a cruel technocrat, in fact, deprived of any sympathy and compassion towards not only his fellow countrymen, but humanity as such. And, I must tell you that the prince shared that opinion of mine," said Fortis, "and I'm still proud of that."

"But I'm not quite sure what you mean by saying that Prince Kropotkin shared your opinion, you know, he died a long time ago…" the prince's relative said, with some embarrassment.

"Bah, time, my dear chap, what actually does it means? That impossible old Immanuel has already proved that time doesn't exist, so we shouldn't worry about that, should we? And for that matter, I, myself, am in full agreement with him. Moreover, my boss promised to introduce me to him at the first opportunity, and I can't wait to meet him."

Now Andrei Kropotkin didn't really know what to say. He was just staring at Fortis with a worried look, and some disturbing thoughts crossed his mind. *Is he nuts? And who is he, after all, and what is he doing here?*

"I know that what I say," Fortis continued, unperturbed by Andrei's anxious gaze, "must seem to you a bit strange, but you know, there are

323

even stranger things happening on this earth. Anyway, strangeness, my dear fellow, is my business."

Now, Kropotkin was really worrying, and at the same time thinking hard what to do, and his first duty he thought of was of course to contact the president and tell him about the problem with the visitor. So, he ordered the driver to pull over and said to his travel companion, "Excuse me, I just remembered I have to see somebody for a couple of minutes concerning a very important matter."

"No problem at all. I am not in a hurry, and *festina lente*, my dear friend,"said Fortis, who always liked to add some Latin to what he was saying.

Andrei Kropotkin rushed to the nearby building, which happened to be some government body's, and showing his ID to a security man, who jumped to attention once he saw it, said, "I immediately need a room of my own to make an emergency call to the president."

"*Tak tochno*," exclaimed the security man, and led Andrei to an empty meeting room, saluted, and left him there on his own.

Andrei dialled the president's number, and when he answered it, said, "Mr President, I'm terribly sorry for disturbing you, but I have some disturbing news regarding our guest, and…"

But the president didn't allow him to finish, saying, "And what's the matter?"

"Mr President, he said he had met Prince Kropotkin, and now he's waiting to meet Immanuel Kant, so I'm not sure, you know—"

The president interrupted. "Of course, you aren't sure, but if you met his boss, then you wouldn't be sure at all, and you could end up at a psychiatric hospital for that matter. Now, do whatever is needed to keep Mr Fortis happy, because if he isn't, I wouldn't want to be in your shoes. Understood?"

"Yes, Mr President, at your command. I'll do my best to keep him happy," said Andrei, but the president didn't hear him for he had already hung up.

*Tschiort eto vosmi*, thought Andrei, *who's that fellow that the president himself is so anxious about being happy? Who is he, for the Devil's sake?* And he decided to be extremely courteous to Fortis and now literally ran back to the waiting car, and once in, said, "I'm terribly sorry for keeping you waiting, *vashe blogorodye*, but I did have to—"

But Fortis interrupted him. "Not at all, my dear friend, I perfectly understand you're a very busy man, being the president's assistant, and by the way, how is he doing these days?"

"He...he's fine," stuttered Andrei, "I just—"

"Yes," Fortis chipped in. "You've just had to ring him, and I do understand, you aren't accustomed yet, so to speak, to the sort of visitors the president has, but you'll work it out in due time, believe me, and remember, patience, understanding, and don't be surprised by anything."

"Yes, yes, of course, whatever you say," said a now very-eager-to-please Kropotkin, for he realised it would be a very bad idea to mess with Fortis.

"Good," said Fortis, "and now, have you ever heard of a man by the name of Likhodeyev?"

"Yes, I know the name," confirmed Andrei.

"And what do you think of him?" asked Fortis.

"Hmm, he's a somewhat shady character who used to have some influence, was pretty close to the president, but not anymore. However, as far as I know, he still has some friends who support him, and he ran an investment company or something like that."

"We know that, and we know also that he looked after, so to speak, those British defectors who arrived in Moscow, and I always wondered how those men, being intelligent fellows after all, were so stupid nevertheless. Or were they not after all?"

"I wouldn't know that. I'm not old enough but he is, so he might have been involved in such matters."

"Yea," muttered Fortis, "old habits die hard. And would you be able to arrange a meeting with him, my dear chap?"

"Yes, it shouldn't be a problem," said Andrei, who was now willing to cooperate in full.

"Good, so do it please, and I want to see him very soon. And now please get me to the Metropol Hotel, where I'll be expecting your call this evening. And please remember, if some strange ideas come to your head then..." and he looked at Andrei, who saw in Fortis' eyes something which his grandmother once described to him as a vision of that eternal

325

power humans are subjected to whoever they are, and even those who once held absolute power could do nothing against, and a cold shiver ran through Andrei's spine, and at the same time he finally understood who was the true ruler on this earth, and remembered suddenly a story told to him by her about their so intelligent predecessor, Prince Kropotkin, who allegedly said, "It seems to us we can establish a paradise here and now, and this is something I, myself, once believed in until that evening during my usual walk in Patriarch's Pond where I met somebody and we had a conversation, and since then I know that whenever we try to make heaven ourselves, we end up in hell."

The vision Andrei experienced would now stay with him through all of his life, and would help him to face the problems of life he would encounter, and already now, speaking to Fortis, he understood he would always prevail, provided he never forgot what he had seen in Fortis' eyes.

And at the same time, he decided to do his best to assist Fortis in everything he would ask him to do. Thus, when Fortis said to him, "Can you contact Likhodeyev and tell him I want to have a word with him?" Andrei replied, "Yes, I'll do it now, straightaway," and he dialled a number and said, "Igor, it's Andrei. I need Ivan Ivanovich Likhodeyev's phone number if you'd be so kind, my friend. It shouldn't be a problem for you, I hope."

A man called Igor replied, "But of course, my friend," and in just two minutes Andrei got it. He thanked Igor for his help and said to Fortis, "Here you are," giving him the number.

"*Bravo, bravissimo,* my friend, you're very efficient and I appreciate nothing more than efficiency, and as a matter of fact, as an Irish writer, G. B. Shaw, said, 'There are only two kinds of people: the efficient and the inefficient.' But at the same time, he knew perfectly well that efficiency didn't apply to his fellow countrymen, and probably because of it, he also said, 'I showed my appreciation of my native land by getting out of it as soon as I possibly could.'

"So, now, I'll contact that chap, but tell me, that friend of yours, Igor, is he an efficient man too?"

"Oh yes, he is indeed and he's supposed to be for he works for an organisation whose task is to ensure the efficiency of our nation, if you know what I mean."

"Certainly, I do, my dear chap," said Fortis, "and yes, whoever is in power, efficiency comes first. And now let's give Likhodeyev a ring," and he dialled the number Andrei gave him.

And after just one ring, somebody said, "Yes, who am I talking to?"

"Is this Mr Likhodeyev?" asked Fortis.

"Yes, speaking," said Ivan Ivanovich.

"My name's Fortis, and some time ago you met some friends of mine, among them Mr Kater, with whom you had a *tête-à-tête* meeting."

And Likhodeyev did remember it, and a cold shiver ran through his spine, and he stammered, "Yes… sir… I do remember. Is there something wrong?"

"Oh yes, there is indeed, for it seems you didn't keep your word you gave to my friend, who is now very upset about that, and it was him who asked me to come here and sort out the problem."

"I'm sorry, but I don't really know what you mean," said Ivan.

"You were supposed to cooperate with us, but you didn't and still don't. Moreover, a company you ran, Svoboda, seems to be involved in the abduction of our dear friend, Miss Forza, in Switzerland."

"But I don't really know anything about that, I swear," exclaimed Ivan.

"You don't say, hmm, then tell me, who might be in it?"

"We still do some business with that British company, Cheats & Partners, and they're registered in Switzerland, so it might be them, I guess."

"Ah yes, we know them, and their boss, Jason Goodman. What a stubborn and unimaginative fellow he is, for he should have realised the dangers he might encounter if he didn't stop messing with us. Apparently, he isn't wise enough and doesn't believe in our rather wide competence and ability. And, of course, he doesn't believe in God, and even worse for himself, in the Devil. What a narrow-minded fellow he is! Ah, I don't envy him."

Ivan listened to all that and congratulated himself on being smart enough not to do anything to upset Kater and his friends because despite his Marxist upbringing he still retained his belief in an unidentified power somewhere out there which no human can comprehend, and now he thanked his dear babushka in his soul who had done her best when he'd been a child to make him believe in that all-powerful authority, and to obey it unquestioningly.

"So," Fortis continued, "it seems he's behind the matter in question, and I wonder why he's done that. What do you think?"

"I don't really know," said Ivan, "but I may try to find out something regarding the matter, and I understand it's a very urgent business."

"Yes, it is indeed, and as soon as you know something, let me know immediately. I'm staying at the Metropol Hotel."

"I certainly will," said Ivan, "you have my word of honour."

"Your word of honour, you say? Hmm, who knows what may happen to words during your lifelong career? Under their influence, you might be anything," Fortis remarked philosophically. "Ah, politics, it could turn a man into someone he would never imagine himself to be. One day he's red or white, and another he's holier than the Pope, or the other way around."

"All right, my dear chap, I can see that your beloved *babushka*'s teaching hasn't been lost after all, and I'm very glad to know that. I'm waiting for your call, and remember that colours don't really matter for those who see this earth from the perspective of the eternal, for in the end, everything that exists will be of the same colour, that is, neutral, meaning that all men will be equal at last."

This was something Ivan didn't now understand at all, for it was far beyond his powers of comprehension, but a day would come when he would, and then he'd see the world aright, that is, as something as it is, where everything is as it is, and happens as it does happen. And his revelation, his eureka, would be confirmed by a certain book he would come across by chance, looking for something very different. But we aren't convinced that he found the book by chance, we believe that to find it was his destiny. And the book in question was a story of love which was appreciated by a seemingly impossible recognition of a power which was a personification of evil. But what people actually think of evil doesn't grasp its essence, for that power actually serves people to understand their own wrongdoing. They blame something or somebody else for the evil they do themselves.

And Ivan apparently understood that and, being a Russian, it was hard for him to do so because in his country, evil was and still is thought to be an indispensable attribute of those who are in power, and people recognise it as justified because in fact the country had been beyond good and evil once and rejected all moral principles since the so-called Reds established their own power. But they and their vlast had failed to notice that what they'd been thinking and doing may turn against themselves, for if there is a supreme sovereignty somewhere out there, it is impartial. It is impartial because this is the only power that is beyond good and evil.

Since Ivan understood that, he was left alone, for such were the orders Fortis received from Lord Hellbridge.

He himself asked Ches to come to see him, and when he arrived, the lord said to him, "Tomorrow, I'll bring Beatrice back to you. As a matter of fact, I knew she would be kidnapped, and allowed that to happen to eventually find out what kind of people those Magnificent Seven, as you call them, really are, and as you can see for yourself, not all of them are that bad. But, of course, all that they have done will be scrutinised again. All in all, my actions might seem strange to you, but you'll understand me in due time. Moreover, I know you're still confused by all that has been happening until now. However, there has been no other option for you than to go through all that step by step, so to speak. Anyway, life as such isn't a one-time action, but a process, during which you see how everything that happens changes, and you're thinking about that too. That's why you have no right to judge, for your every judgement is temporary and relative depending on the circumstances and your reasoning and feelings accordingly. Man's life can be compared to certain lyrics of a band you liked and still appreciate much, and they are, 'Nobody knows where you are, how near or how far. Shine on you crazy diamond.'

"And the same could be said about myself. You may meet me again and again but you'll never find out who I really am because I can be whoever I want to, and nothing is difficult for me to do. I am like truth itself that cannot be defined, for every attempt to do so ends in contradictions. But I must say you're close to understanding the reasons for my existence because in the first place you no longer believe in that nonsense that has been said about me, and not only me for that matter, but also about my apparent adversary, and vice versa. And it is in relation to what people call good, evil and right and wrong, and they will never know the true meaning of these words, for they still don't understand the meaning of life as such. In other words, the truth of life as truth itself cannot be defined. And, as a certain philosopher says, I mean the strongest of the strong, that's Friedrich, the greatest error that mankind has ever committed is that people believed in possessing a criterion of reality, and I would add a criterion of truth as well, in the forms of reason – while, in fact, one possessed them in order to become a master of reality, in order to misunderstand reality in a shrewd manner, that is, to use it, to transform it for practical use, to exploit it. And whenever something doesn't agree with reality then, as one of his fellow philosophers said, it is much the worse for reality. All humans may know are facts, and no statement of a fact can be a statement of absolute value. And life as such isn't a fact but is like a river and as such, it is never the same, *panta rei*, isn't it? Therefore, he who wants to grasp life's meaning in words will never find it, and when he eventually understands that, he may eventually get the answer. Yes, the puzzle of life isn't one you can explain, and you may understand it only when you have ceased to try to understand it. Yes, my friend, this is the puzzle of all puzzles, a paradox, as is life itself.

"As regards other matters related in a way to your visit to Russia, the English-speaking countries, mind you, I don't say French or German, for strictly speaking their governments and media are eager to spread a ridiculous assumption that the Russian Federation's intention is to attack the West. This is a pure nonsense, and they know that, but advertising that, so to speak, has a purpose, which is to have support of their fellow countrymen with regard to their policies concerning abroad and internal spending on arms, especially in the United States, to enrich those views in charge of the armament industry. As a matter of fact, this is them. The US and the UK are aggressors these days and not Russia.

But an ordinary man there is stupid enough to believe in that nonsense because of his limitless ignorance typical to those living there. Their stupidity has no limits. They are ready to believe anything they are told through the media, especially the idiot-box, which they cannot live without. And one day, they will pay for that overwhelming stupidity of theirs.

Moreover, in their everyday life, they are cheated by their own people, the big companies, and knowing that, and now it is the summit of their idiocy, they are still allow themselves to be cheated. So, all in all, we have a society there, I call it a mutual admiration society, of cheats, for both sides must cooperate to make it happen, as it does happen. The same thing goes for the Banana Republic being *de fact* neutral. I mean of course Erie, where greed surpasses every inch of common sense left there.

But what I find most laughable of all that circus is that they in those countries, despite having so much, are never satisfied, so they want more, and then they are even more dissatisfied, in a word, a vicious circle, but one which will result, if it still goes on like that, in their own demise. When and how, they obviously don't know. Anyway, they tend to believe it will never happen, and accordingly being Christians, in fact the very opposite ones, they deny the truth of the last book of the New Testament, thus disbelieving God's words. Anyway, I'm convinced that in the end, all that will bring them a calamity of unspeakable terror which *de facto* they deserve, for foolishness, imbecility and lunacy do not excuse and must end in an apocalypse, which is a very logical consequence of that way of thinking.

They are in fact working willy-nilly on their own demise and consider themselves very clever. This is the paradox of all paradoxes typical to man's dwelling on earth, and so be it. If you want war then war you will have. But this is a war you're going to lose, and this will be your last struggle on this earth."

I'd been listening to Hellbridge and had begun to understand something I'd overlooked until then – that I'd actually met him before. And as he, himself, had just said, he could be whoever he wanted to be, but still he was the same, so who art thou then? And yes, what is the meaning of good and evil, and right and wrong? We never actually know, for there is no absolute definition of any of them. To comprehend the meaning of each one is a never-ending story which has accompanied humans for thousands of years, and the meaning is still as elusive as it has always been.

"As I've just told you," said Hellbridge, "Beatrice is coming back, as once her abductors heard of my interest in their conspiracy, they came to a very reasonable conclusion to release her immediately. And yes, it was Jason Goodman who organised her kidnapping, and it's now up to you what to do with him."

"Thank you, milord, I'm most obliged and at the same time wonder, because one good turn deserves another, what I could do for you."

Hellbridge smiled at me and said, "What you can do for me? you ask. Yes, actually there's something, my dear friend, you could do, namely, do your best not to make the same mistake as you did in the past."

"What do you mean, sir?"

"You're asking me? After all, you know what I mean, don't you?"

Of course I did, I thought, what a stupid question I'd asked. Obviously, he meant the way I treated my women, who were nothing to me but instruments of pleasure, but now with Bea it was something much more than that, and asking me not to make the same error, he was wondering whether I considered myself ready to appreciate a different partnership with a woman than before. Would it be love? But I despised the word, for it was overused and therefore abused, and that's why it meant nothing. Anyway, there is something more, so to speak, when you're in love.

But the lord interrupted my thinking, saying, "It's hard for some to find out what it is, isn't it? So, let me help you to solve the matter in question. Something more, my friend, means in fact that you don't want and need anything more than you actually have, being in love with a woman. Are you with me, my friend?"

"Yes, milord, I began to understand that some time ago, and it seems to be so simple."

"Oh yes, it seems to be, but it's a paradox that simple things are the most difficult to understand and achieve for that matter, for you people tend to make things difficult for yourselves and everybody else, don't you?"

"It appears we do, sir," I said, as I myself had recently started to wonder why we do so.

"Bah, it is about to be or not to be, in human reasoning, and this is because you don't have the courage to do what you really know, and you take your superficial thinking for truth. You're being convinced that facts are the solution to your problems, and that you're the masters of your thinking and your lives, and it is only late you find out you aren't."

When Hellbridge paused for a moment, I asked, "May I say something, sir?"

"Certainly, go ahead."

"I've been of the same opinion recently, and it began when I was forced to revise my hitherto life and all I had been thinking then, having been forced, I mean, by my life in a country which was and still is an intellectual wasteland, a perfect example of a godforsaken backwater, where there was nobody to talk to. And that revision started for good in a place they call Festival City, and yes, it is indeed a festival of stupidity, cheating, pettiness, ignorance and violence, and that backwoods was named the city of culture, but living over there long enough I dare say it would be much more proper to call it the city of subculture, for their main interest is chow and drink. Anyway, as they and their neighbours are deprived of the ability of abstract thinking, they can't have any culture understood as intellectual and artistic achievement.

"It was a very hard time for me since I had no friends, no job, no woman, and my health wasn't good. But then I remembered Nietzsche's, 'What doesn't kill me makes me stronger,' and I overcame my weakness, gained the ability not to be affected by suffering, to some degree, of course, for no one is fully able to not be affected, and managed to resist misfortunes and carried on after all. And only then did I understand what self-responsibility means, and it is to take responsibility for all you do and not to blame others for your own mistakes, and not to shift your responsibility to someone else. And only when one is able to be such can he be free in the true sense of the word."

"Hmm, I must say," the lord began, "that as a matter of fact, you already had some unusual experience long before that, didn't you?"

"How come you know that, sir?"

"How do I know? you ask. I am supposed to know, but very often I wish I knew nothing, you know, the liberating power of ignorance due to which you have the feeling you're free not being bothered by knowledge that can be, and frequently is, a heavy burden in your life."

"Excuse me, sir, but what do you mean by saying you're supposed to know?" I asked.

"You see, I never asked for that privilege. It was given to me a long, long time ago, my dear friend, and it's better for you not to know how and why I was awarded it."

"I understand, sir, and won't ask you any more questions. But you apparently have a certain aim you strive to achieve, if I may suppose so."

"Yes, I have indeed, and it is to make some people aware of the fact that their knowledge isn't and never will be sufficient to know what exists beyond the world they live in. In other words, the limits of their world mean the limits of their knowledge."

"But, sir—" I began, but Hellbridge interrupted me.

"My friend, asking questions won't help you to know the truth. Either you can see it in just a split second, have a revelation in which you understand but then you can say nothing afterwards, or you can never see truth at all, but merely shadows of it.

"Now, in relation to what I've just said, all that Magnificent Seven business you're dealing with is just a stage in your life which may help you to see the world aright. Thus, it has no significance as such at all, for it's just a passing event you're to live through to move further in order to understand what is beyond it, that is, out there where the sense of everything that happens in the world lies. For all that happens here, in this world, is of equal value because it is accidental, and what is accidental cannot be the basis of ethics in which the true value of life exists. And that value is eternal and lives on when you have passed away, for it lives in other people, so the only true value, the only truth in this world, is ethical life that is a life seen from the perspective of the eternal, and as such is without any reference to or dependence upon the temporal portions of reality. Everything is in flux, as a Greek philosopher, Heraclitus, rightly noticed, and only he who is able to reach the source of that flow may have a life worth living. But that source is beyond this world, inaccessible for many a man but only for a chosen few who are lucky enough to get there."

Hellbridge halted here, and I took the chance and said, "Sir, but who has chosen these few?"

"Good question, my friend, and the answer is that they've chosen, as a matter of fact, themselves by living a life which is then scrutinised by someone else."

"And who's that?"

"'What cannot be spoken of we must be silent about,' and as long as you observe that principle, you'll answer your question."

And for the first time in my life, I realised how little we say, talking about something that isn't actually something we encounter living in reality, how often we fall under the spell of words and their deceiving power. We have built our ethical code on facts which are relative and accidental, and at the same time we claim to believe in God, who is beyond them and as such cannot be defined.

And I asked myself, *have we been deceiving ourselves since God first appeared in our world of words?*

But Hellbridge interrupted my thinking, saying, "Now, dear Mr Adarsh, back to so-called reality. You're to meet another two of them, that's messieurs Mockingham and Scornbash. And then you may be able to summarise the M7 business and its members, which should help you to understand more about your own life. But now, of course, you'll meet your Beatrice who, I suppose, has something to tell you.

"See you again, and remember to pass my best on to her."

"I will, sir, thank you and goodbye for now."

But before I was to meet Bea, I wanted to rethink a couple of things to have a clearer picture of where I stood now. And it wasn't actually about the situation as such, but rather about the way I understood what was happening. There was something underneath I couldn't grasp yet, for I wasn't able to answer the question as to why it was happening, and to find the answer to it was crucial. But as a matter of fact, I couldn't formulate the right question, that is, a precise one that would imply an answer. And that was gnawing at me, for all I could think at that moment was asking all over again the question, 'Why?' which wasn't enough to identify the source of the problem. In other words, I couldn't identify the reason for which I asked the question, 'Why?'

All in all, it seemed as if too many thoughts were disturbing my mind at the same time, and I had to pursue them willy-nilly. Apart from the M7 business, I somehow still felt compelled (due to my previous conversations with Herr Wahrburg, and now with Lord Hellbridge) to occupy my mind with theological matters as well. And first to come was the question of Christian humanism, its pity, compassion and humility, which were shortly summarised by Friedrich as metaphysics of the executioner. Don't they, I ask myself, champion stupidity, meanness and wickedness at the same time? And it seemed to me they actually do, for they promote cunning of the weak and meek who, lacking courage and pride, will resort to swindling, hypocrisy and perfidy to achieve their aims which *de facto* are the same of the strong, those in a position of strength. But true humanism, not that of Christian pity, I thought, is in fact to advocate the intellect which through its power is able to make value judgements of which the stupid aren't capable. And since ethics in the Greco-Judeo-Christian tradition are inseparable from reason, it is necessary to possess intellect to distinguish between good and evil and to act upon the decision. And here Friedrich was right; it is not about a faith, for anyone can say I believe in God, but about a doing, as actually Jesus himself said. And who in reality is able to follow His moral code? That is why Friedrich says: there was only one Christian and he died on the Cross.

At the same time, I was thinking about evil, the one embodied by Satan, and came to the conclusion that he, whoever he actually is, may do good by punishing the stupid and wicked who in point of fact should also be punished according to the Christian ethic which teaches fairness and tolerance, but in practice does not tolerate the bad who are in any of the Christian denominations, and not only them, evil incarnate. So, it appeared to me that the Christian teachings are as a matter of fact rather ambiguous.

Anyway, the question is how come the concept of God has appeared at all, or any other gods for that matter amidst humankind? Why did people feel at some stage that they would need a superior power which would command them from out of nowhere? Thousands of treatises have been written and yet man knows as much as he knew before, and the only option to sustain God's existence was and still is a dogma. Has man realised his actually limited power despite being an autocratic sovereign on earth, or does he need Him to rule those inferior to the rulers, to legitimise their right to rule until the Communists ruled Him out in some parts of the world? But even they couldn't eradicate Him for good, with the exception of China, where in fact He has never existed in the Chinese people's ethic. Or did man need and still need Him to legitimise his own existence on this earth, facing the infinity of the universe which he cannot comprehend? All in all, I thought, there is no definite answer to these questions, and there probably never will be and therefore He may exist as long as mankind does. But another question is whether His existence is of any good to man. But here again there isn't any absolute answer to that question, and as before, thousands of elaborate, perceptive writings available aren't of any help. They are all in the end more or less clever linguistic games after all.

But then, there's also something else which may come to our consciousness, and this is the question of the ideal. These days, especially in English-speaking countries for some reason, particularly those of British sanctimonious hypocrisy, the ideal has been vulgarised and exists now in the shape of the so-called celebrities who in fact are as far from any ideal as one can imagine, and surely God would still be a much better option because of the moral code He wants people to observe. Once He is missing, what is left are perfidy, deceit and moral decline, which all together represent the freedom of the mob, rabble, that is, freedom to satisfy man's vulgar, primitive instincts, as if he had become a Neanderthal again despite all of his intellectual achievement. Or maybe it is due to technology that man is back in the Palaeolithic age with regard to his desires, which have become automatised, having made himself a robot despite his outward sophistication.

I was still thinking hard, and at some stage I realised that it would get me nowhere, so why should I bother myself with all that reasoning? But then, immediately, a question came to my mind, and it was the question of what I called inner language, which had occupied my mind for a pretty long time. And as a matter of fact, my concept of such a language was similar in its difficulty to the question of the existence of God, or even more difficult to pursue, for no dogma can be established here. And instantly, another question appeared in my mind, and it was the problem of truth. And again, as it was with God, nobody had ever managed to define thoroughly the concept of truth, which still remains an enigma and may only be solved with the help of theology, which obviously wouldn't be satisfactory for all.

But why, I asked myself, have all these concepts, such as God, truth, freedom and love, and all these ideals, been problems for man, and why have they all never been definitely resolved?

And this had been the case, I thought, because man isn't capable of solving the mysteries he himself invented. And the reason for his inability to solve them is that his mind is incapable of solving them because of the limits of his language, which mean the limits of his world. Yes, Ludwig might be right here after all – man is able to think reasonably only about facts, and nothing else. But what about inner language? The same, I thought, here Friedrich in turn might be right in what he says about the phenomenality of the inner world, and here he is very close to Ludwig, stating that everything of which we become conscious is arranged, simplified, schematised, interpreted through and through, and the actual process of inner 'perception', that is, of inner language of ours, the casual connection between thoughts, feelings, desires, between subject and object, are absolutely hidden from us – and are perhaps purely imaginary. In other words, thinking does not occur: it is a quite arbitrary fiction, an artificial arrangement for the purpose of intelligibility. All in all, 'I never think,' says de Lamartine, 'my ideas think for me.'

*Wonderful, I thought, it seems I got there. But why, damn it, are all these questions still there, and when will I be able finally to answer them, if I ever have a chance to do that?*

Eventually, I got tired of those troubling questions which so far had led me nowhere, and thought of my meeting with Bea and later with Bernard and Justin, but then something happened which afterwards attracted a lot of attention in the media. And it was a break-in at MI6 headquarters which, it was assumed, were impregnable. This imposing building in the centre of London was erected to let everybody know that this country's guardians never sleep protecting its security, but apparently this time they failed to secure themselves. Moreover, the break-in didn't take place at night as usually happens on such occasions, but during the day at lunchtime, after which a very important meeting, on security, of course, was due to begin. And when some of the spooks went out to enjoy their well-deserved meal, on returning to their bunker, they found their offices emptied of many highly secret documents. Even some computers were gone too, and in one room a very heavy and, of course, secure safe had vanished without trace.

In consequence, the mentioned meeting was cancelled, and an investigation began with the help of MI5 colleagues and Special Branch as well. In the first place, CCTV recordings were checked, and indeed they showed something very suspicious, namely a big black cat who was wandering around unperturbed even by those officers who were passing by him on the corridors. The cat was so impertinent as to enter the director general's, that is, Mr Dumblodge's office, which was always locked when he was away, where it sat at the director's imposing antique desk, put on big spectacles and began reading some documents which afterwards disappeared too. The officers watching that spectacle had the impression that all that they saw was a science fiction movie, but unfortunately it wasn't, it was the real thing. However, some whispered gossip spread that it was all black magic, employed by the sworn enemies of the United Kingdom, the Russian Intelligence famous for its sophisticated operations.

It was suggested issuing a warrant arrest for the cat by a Special Branch officer, publishing his image in papers and on TV, but the idea was eventually dismissed by the Met Commissioner, who himself had a cat that was very like that shown on the cameras, and was naturally afraid that his own might be arrested and interrogated. Besides, to be honest, the British police had no experience in interrogating cats. Moreover, the Commissioner's – Sir David Bullyngton's – grandmother was Russian and he was afraid that when it became known, he himself might fall under suspicion.

What made everything even worse was that after recently paying a visit to the headquarters, the CIA handed over some extremely sensitive documents which vanished too. And when the US President was informed of the disaster, he came near to apoplexy and shouted, "And here they come again…" (meaning those British who spied for Russia in Washington) "…we should have never ever trusted them, those bloody perfidious Limeys. They say you can't trust the Irish because they're all liars, and they're what? They're all traitors," and immediately ordered the cessation of cooperation with the British.

All in all, there was chaos and calamity, and the press somehow got wind of the break-in and provided the public with stories that exceeded in imagination the best spy novels. In one article, for instance, a journalist said he had spoken to a man who claimed that while walking his own cat close to MI6 headquarters on that eventful day, he had seen a bird-like drone landing on its roof and then flying away with an enormous load hanging below it. The journalist immediately shared the story with the RAF, but they ridiculed it, saying that the witness must have suffered from a hallucination, for no flying object would avoid their marvellous air surveillance. However, after double-checking, they did notice something suspicious, that is, blackhole-like in their cameras, images that were moving, according to the experts, faster than the speed of light. Unfortunately, no expert could explain how it had been possible, for his esteemed colleague, the only one who could solve the mystery, namely Albert Einstein, was regrettably dwelling now in places with which they had no contact whatsoever.

In the meantime, amid all that turmoil, Lord Hellbridge was calmly sitting in his mansion, which wasn't in fact too far from Chequers, and was listening attentively to his guest, who was none other than the one hunted now by all of the security services of the United Kingdom.

"Good job," the lord said, once the cat had related to him in detail all that had happened on that day. The cat was extremely pleased and proud with himself, having been congratulated by the lord.

"So, now we've got them," he said. "Those spooks think too much of themselves, don't they?"

"Oh yes, definitely," agreed the black monster. "The only place where they're efficient is in fiction."

"That's it," said the lord, who had already read the documents brought by the cat. "So now we have proof of what they really did, those cheeky twits. How they dared to conspire behind the prime minister's back. And that dummy boss of them, that Dumblodge, is the worst, isn't he?"

"Oh yes, he is indeed," said the cat, "and I suggest Fortis has a word with him."

"Hmm, actually not a bad idea. Yes, ask your mate to have a chat with that pompous clown."

What was in the documents obtained from MI6 Headquarters that made the establishment so anxious and determined to get them back before they became known to the public and/or used by people who would take advantage of their content? As a matter of fact, there was enough in them to cause a political earthquake, a scandal of enormous proportions. In the first place, two former prime ministers seemed to be involved in what seemed to be a conspiracy on a grand scale. And apart from them, several other former and current politicians, such as Igor Jobber, known as 'The Piggy' because of his looks or 'The Boomerang' because of his incredible capability for any government job. He could be anything, the mayor of London, the prime minister, or any minister for that matter, provided any of these jobs wouldn't last for too long, for he was in constant favour of a change.

Another one was an ex-PM, Tobias Bubble, famous for his ever-present smile due to which he was called 'The Grin'. He possessed an astonishing ability of balancing socialism agree with his fondness for expensive properties. His colleague in turn was a very different man. It was Daniel Camelot, nicknamed 'The Preacher' because of his predisposition to deliver long moralising speeches which he was sure would show the nation its ultimate ethical aspects. However, not being a Catholic, he was inclined after all to employ some of the ecclesiastical tribunal's methods to suppress any dissident movements, and during the recent riots in several cities, the only thing he could think of was to threaten people with punishment. Apparently, at the time, he ceased temporarily to be the Christian he claimed to be. He didn't bother to find out what was beneath that widespread discontent. And the actual cause of public upheaval was the stuffy air of this country, that is, its pretence to be democratic and just but actually to be under the rule of a self-serving, calculating establishment whose main aim had always been to preserve its power. And the UK had already been in fact for many years a covert police state whose foremost end was to assure that power survival.

And another gentleman who joined those mentioned was ex-PM John Snoberry, Baron of Prigstone, alias 'The Duck', a name given to him after a mortar attack on 10 Downing Street during which he and his colleagues, after hearing shells exploding in the rear garden, ducked under the table they were sitting at during a cabinet meeting.

So, what Hellbridge discovered was a grand-scale conspiracy whose organisers were those ex- PMs, the boss of the spooks, Dumblodge, and of course our old friends of the Magnificent Seven, but in truth not all of them.

Now, why did they decide to conspire, that is, what was the reason for their scheme? The reason was that they found Mr Oddhouse a threat to the dominance of the establishment to which many a man wanted to belong. And to keep up the appearance of *Liberté, Egalité et Fraternité*, Tobias 'The Grin', decided to create a brand-new aristocracy, for the genuine one he didn't find trustworthy anymore. In fact, such a thing had been going on for many years, but he was the first to make a few decisive steps. Among others, he deprived the members of the House of Lords of their right to inherit the seats. Besides, his reforms in Justice and other institutions were to assure that they would all be obedient tools of the Government. As for Parliament, *pust govoriat'* as Vysotsky said, let them talk. The more they do, the better for appearances.

Hellbridge, after reading the papers, actually smiled and said to himself, *Aha, it seems those poor rascals are sure they can trick the Devil himself, as if there were the likes of Prince Talleyrand among them, but actually none of them is even close to him, for in reality they are a bunch of bodgers. Yes, it's true that Mr Oddhouse, the current prime minister, is somewhat naïve but de facto an honest chap, a bit like Clement. Hmm, anyway, he won't manage to crush them on his own. After all, he needs assistance, and I, who does forever good, will give him a hand.*

When Lord Hellbridge was busy with the documents, I was sitting in a café waiting for Bea. She had rung me the previous day when she had been on her way to London and instead of coming straight to our place decided to meet me at that cosy little coffee house.

It was ten in the morning when I saw her enter the place, and immediately noticed she was not her usual self. She kissed me and sat down at my table but not next to me as she usually did, but on the chair opposite mine.

"What's wrong darling," I asked straightaway.

"I was advised not to meet you at our apartment until we've discussed a couple of matters," she said.

"And who was it told you that?"

"Mr Wissend on behalf of Lord Hellbridge," she replied.

"And did he say why not to meet at the apartment?"

"Yes, he did, and what he said unsettled me."

"What was that?" I asked her.

"He said our apartment is bugged, and so are our telephones."

"Hmm," I said, "it seems they've got wind we are after the M7, and their friends of MI6 are helping them. But how come they found it out?"

"Someone must have informed them and the question is who was it?" I said.

"The only one who comes to my mind is Jason Goodman because since we met him in Moscow, he's the only one who knows what we are after," said Bea.

"Yes, you're right, and I'll have a word with the lord about that. But now, darling, tell me where you've been that long?"

"I'm sorry, Ches, but I can't tell you now," she said.

"I don't understand. You can't tell me! But we are..."

"Yes, I know, we are together and we are very close to each other, and this is exactly why I can't tell you," she said.

I was totally confused by her reply but didn't want to leave the subject, so I kept on enquiring. "But could you give me one reason at least why you can't tell me?"

And Bea, going straight to the point, said, "Because you aren't ready yet for it."

I was speechless, and it took me a while to say, "Bea, darling, we've been in love for some time now, and love as such isn't enough for you to be honest with me?"

"That's it, love is the reason I can't tell you."

"But how love..." I began, but she didn't let me finish and said, "Because love and truth are the same, and you aren't ready for truth yet."

"So, in other words, you're saying I'm not ready for love yet, yes?" I exclaimed.

"No, you are not," she said with emphasis.

"How come?"

"For truth is not what you want to have, not something you desire from a woman, but something that comes to you as an understanding of the whole world which has been understood once it has become your own world, and this way, the world and you are one and the same. And you haven't understood that yet. You are still living in two worlds, in reality and in a world of your imagination, and only when these two become one will you understand the truth I'm telling you. You are on the right path to getting there, but you haven't finished your journey yet. You must keep on going. You still, at the same time, live in the past and future, and only when you are living entirely in the present will you see the world aright, will you finally understand it.

"You desire me. I'm the only one you want, and without me you won't have so much happiness and pleasure. I mean, you're being contented and sexually satisfied, which you identify with love, but that in fact is something more than that."

I was totally perplexed. We had previously had some conversations which touched, so to speak, on philosophical issues, but now it came as a shock to hear Bea's exposé. Until now, I wouldn't have believed her to be capable of such subtle, refined analysis. And now when I came to recognise that, I still wasn't sure of my own philosophical powers of reasoning, so I said to her, "Bea, I… I don't really know what to say, but please tell me, do you doubt I love you?"

"No, not at all, darling. You just haven't reached the full dimension of what love is, which is what I've just told you. Yes, I too want to be with you. I love you in the same way you love me, but we're still living in separate worlds, and only when we are in the same one will our love be complete."

"But, I still…" I began, but she interrupted me saying, "Yes, you still don't understand, and that's it, but you will as I've been told."

"And who told you that?"

"You'll find out in due time, but as a matter of fact, you've already had a preliminary conversation regarding the matter in question, haven't you?"

And yes, I had, and realised what she meant; it had been my conversation with Mr Wahrburg in Zurich. And since that conversation with him, a lot of my previous ideas had been transformed, and not only ideas, but I could see a change in my personality. But now for the first time, the matter of love was put forward with such emphasis by a woman I was in love with, or I thought it to be love, but now as Bea pointed out, that love wasn't complete yet. So, what was still wrong about it? But apparently, I was to discover that myself, on my own, and here no one could help me but that man by the name of Wahrburg. But why him?

All in all, at that moment, nothing had been fully clarified. The M7 business was still an open matter. Moreover, my feelings to Bea weren't that certain anymore according to her. In a word, I was still living in a sort of mess, with incertitude, doubts, suspicion, and there was no clear hope to put everything right and to end all that chaos. But first, I had to clear up my own thoughts and examine my feelings as I had just been told. But I still found it difficult to put everything that was happening into words while occasionally making notes when some ideas came to my mind and I found them worthy enough to write down. And then who, anyway, would understand them? I, myself, found it hard to comprehend fully what I was writing, and suddenly realised with all clarity that I wouldn't manage to put in order my thoughts and my own life in words alone. I needed reality to carry on. So far, I thought it, curiously enough, almost useless. I imagined that I could sort out my life problems by the critique of pure reason, as Immanuel Kant would say. But apparently the method wasn't enough to solve the problems which were still there, and in the first place, it was the lack of an answer to the questions 'Why?' and 'What for?' that I kept asking.

But then a lot was happening around me, so what did I actually mean by reality? Wasn't the present reality good enough to find the answer to these questions?

Eventually, being already tired of asking the same questions all over again, I said to myself, *Enough for now, I need peace and quiet...* and to have the sexual satisfaction that I needed, which was now the only way to relax, and Bea could give me that. And I noticed that when I was deep in thought, she was still there waiting patiently for me to finish my inner deliberations, which didn't actually take as long as I thought they would. I looked at her as if awoken from sleep, and noticed she was smiling at me as though she knew what I needed, and simply said, "Let's make love." And so, we did, and afterwards I felt much better.

Later on, we went for a walk in Hyde Park as we always did after spending a couple of wonderful hours in bed.

We discussed the present situation, which was getting so complicated that I actually couldn't grasp what was really going on.

Then, I suddenly remembered something apparently unrelated to my current issue, and it was the Northern Irish question a friend of mine told me about some time ago. The problem there was one of the most real, so to speak, but its real source was in the way people there were thinking, which was not European by any standards. He called the province a parasite country, that is, one which depended on Westminster money to carry on, the money they wasted on ridiculous projects of theirs, and in the end, of which they were always asking for more. The most corrupt place in this part of the world, my friend called it. Corrupt politicians, police, everyone, and each one of them interested in nothing but money, all obsessed by it. He said he wouldn't advise any foreign business to invest there, for their money could easily be lost due to that enormous corruption. He even urged the still present foreign business to leave the place as soon as possible and find much more reliable countries with which to continue. He said that the EU should have never given them any funds because they were always wasted on ridiculous projects, and not spent on something of essence. And he said it was good news they were leaving the EU, but not Great Britain, for the money wasted there was more needed in other countries, where it could be invested much more reasonably. All in all, the real cause of their troubles was that their thinking was so different from that of any other countries of Europe. They, over there, were actually proud of being provincial, of their ignorance, in fact, because other places in the world were of no interest to them, but only that one bloody godforsaken shithole of theirs. Their thinking lacked integrity, deprived of the ability of abstract thinking which is *sine qua non* of any intellectual achievements, so small wonder they had none of it, and if they had some, that was always imported. Godforsaken dump, intellectual wasteland, these names according to a friend of mine would be the most suitable to describe the Province, yea, a province, for it never deserved to be called a country because it never truly resembled one that existed in any other part of the world. As their thinking resulting in certain actions doesn't, namely both sides having committed outrageous killings of innocent people, shooting them dead in pubs, and some of those killed were as old as ninety, and the killers laughing and bragging about it afterwards. Or shooting at random other religious denominations' people just because of their belonging to the wrong one at the time. And all that was considered normal and right by the perpetrators by their moral standards. Thus, we ask what are their ethical standards which allows them to commit those crimes and be pleased with them having done so afterwards? For as far as one can imagine, no other place in Europe has in its ethical code similar ones, so Northern Ireland is in this respect a very 'distinguished' one. And now, everyone is silent about those atrocities as if they had never happened, and my friend found that very wrong, for that silence justifies all the terrible crimes committed at the time. Moreover, those who did them are still feeling innocent in their opaque scale of values that allowed them to do what they did in the name of their 'holy' war at the time. And most importantly, there are still thousands of their followers whose thinking would consequently be the same once an occasion arose.

Why that conversation with a friend of mine appeared to me now, I couldn't tell. Apparently, it was in relation to that seemingly obvious thing, reality, which *de facto* might be, as the example of Northern Ireland shows, more complicated than black magic. And then, small wonder they could not understand, it either.

But now, after the time I spent remembering that chat with a friend of mine, my thoughts turned to the current situation when Bea, looking straight in my eye, still refused to tell me what she had been doing being away from London. I didn't press her, for I knew perfectly well it would be to no avail. Instead, we tried to visualise our own future after all that turmoil had ended, and we came to the conclusion that we would leave this country for good, moving to France, where we had already found a very nice place in Dordogne to live. But obviously we couldn't leave before we'd accomplished what we were expected to, but the problem was what actually was expected from me? And I meant my conversation with Mr Wahrburg in Zurich and now Lord Hellbridge who had also assigned me a certain task, but never said what exactly he expected me to do. Apparently, he was leaving it to my own initiative. Strangely enough, it seemed to me now that it was my job to find out. But now it was about something else as well, but I couldn't yet comprehend what it was exactly, and because I somehow knew, nobody would tell me that I myself had to find it out. When we got back home from our walk, I sat down in my study, poured my favourite Budvar beer in a glass, took a few sips and began to think. That drink always improved my mood and

347

my ability to think, as it had already done in those very unhappy days of mine.

The first question that came to mind was what should I do first to grasp all that had been happening since I had had my conversation with Mr Wahrburg? And now Lord Hellbridge, who in a way reminded me of the former, apparently too had plans towards my person. Neither of them had ever told me exactly what they expected from me, but I somehow knew they had something in mind. But what exactly it was, I didn't have a clue. Anyway, it would be better, I thought, to leave the question for now and to concentrate on current affairs.

I was to meet the last two of my former friends, Bernard and Justin, and the question was whether to reveal to them my true identity, that one of their former friend, Karl Denker. The only one to whom I had already done so was Jason Goodman, and now I thought it would be to my advantage to let it be known to just another one or two at the most, and I chose Graham and Bernard. I decided to meet both of them at the same time and place, and then to meet Justin separately. So, I rang them and we agreed to meet the next day at 11 am at the Boathouse, which was a good place to have a chat on the terrace with the view of the River Cam.

# PHILOSOPHY AND ART AT THE BOATHOUSE

'Philosophy is to question the obvious.'
'All art is quite useless.'

C.D.

I got there a quarter before the appointed time and shortly afterwards Graham arrived, but Bernard wasn't there yet.

As soon as he sat down, he ordered a pint of his favourite Piddle beer.

"How are things at the university?" I asked.

"Oh, terrible," he said.

"What do you mean?"

"Bah, what I mean, I don't actually know, for I haven't comprehended the stupidity of some of my colleagues yet."

*Aha*, I thought, *the same Graham as ever.*

"You know," he continued, "they think they're in paradise and at the same time they complain about that, so it seems to be contradictory, or they aren't honest enough but just pretend to be rebels of a sort or free spirits who are never pleased with anything. I believe they just want to enhance their own status and that of the university by decreasing their own status, and they think it is very clever of them. They might be good at what they're doing but at the same time they're totally stupid as human beings. Anyway, what is their real worth as such? Almost nil, for if it was tested in true life, especially if they were put in extreme danger, on a battlefield for instance, it would be revealed that their cowardice has no limits."

"You're right. The cat would be out of the bag. But if you're so fed up with them and a couple of other things, why are you still there? You know, some really good academics left," I said.

"Hmm, I'm still with them out of convenience and actually because I like to be with the young, I mean, students. Some of them still have incorrupt minds. I appreciate discussions with them, attend the parties they throw, and the like."

"I do understand you," I said. "If I were you, I would say the same, and actually I often regret leaving university."

"Ah," said Graham, "so, you too used to be one of us?"

"Yes, I was, a long time ago, but often remember the atmosphere, and like you, I liked the students most, especially one of them, a young woman who was my lover, and a very good one for that matter. And I still remember our lovemaking with pleasure. She had no objections at all. I could do with her whatever I wanted and this is what I appreciate in women."

"But you eventually split, didn't you? So, how did it end?"

"It was incredibly stupid of me. I didn't appreciate enough what I had, and one morning, after making love to her all night, I left her in a hotel and let her go. But then, when I tried to meet her again, I found out she was already married and had a child. And years after that night, I stayed on my own this time, at the same hotel, got drunk remembering happy times and had some trouble later on, so I paid for what I'd done before."

"I see, you eventually understood what you really lost," said Graham.

"Oh yes, I did, and bitterly for that matter."

"I, myself, know something about love affairs with young women," said Graham, "and what was your subject in academia?"

"The same as yours."

He looked at me with greater interest now, and asked, "And who of those philosophers was your favourite?"

"Nietzsche and Wittgenstein, but I mean his *Tractatus*, not his *Philosophical Investigations*."

"Oh no, of course not," said Graham, laughing. "Bertrand was right, saying that the author seemed to have grown tired of serious thinking and to have invented a doctrine which would make such an activity unnecessary."

"Know that he got it right. Ludwig entangled himself in his own trap. In his *Tractatus*, warned everybody not to fall in, that's the limits of our language, and then as if he lost his conscience, himself fell in head on."

"That's it," said Graham, "and I wonder how it could have happened, but then we will never know."

"Eh, there might be someone who knows," I said.

"Who do you mean?" he asked and looked at me in surprise.

"The Devil, of course, provided he exists."

"Ah, him," said Graham, "he does exist, believe me."

"Why are you so sure about that?" I enquired.

"For there must be someone who forever denies and not just doubts. And he denies everything, says no to existence as such, because only then may we eventually learn to value it."

"This sounds interesting, but would you care to explain since I don't really catch what you mean by 'there must be someone who denies everything.'"

"It is my belief and hope at the same time, because if there were not someone like him, there would be no hope left for a change in this world," Graham said.

"And what would you like to change?"

"If I were in such a position of supreme power, I would start everything from scratch, for as Nietzsche says, we have incorporated only our errors, and all our consciousness refers to errors. I mean, as he himself said, that all the trouble started with the appearance of God and His metaphysics of the executioner who wants us to suffer, to reject pleasure, for only then we deserve heaven, whereas there is no life without pleasure, and we want it by reason of our nature, so when we say we believe in God, we just pretend to have faith in Him, for in fact we actually deny His existence, don't want Him. And that makes those believers two-faced lying, pretentious rascals, and I mean especially the New Testament.

"By the way, how come, anyway, there are two very different holy scriptures, as if there had been two different Gods or one, but He at some stage changed His mind, demanding, at the start, vindication, a tooth for a tooth, an eye for an eye, and then, later on, something totally different – love your enemy, you should forgive, neither by deeds nor in your heart should you resist him who harms you, etc. The question is why in this respect and many other ones, the Testaments are different, and why should we observe the latter rather than the former? Something is fishy here, and I obviously mean those who were responsible for that switch, so to speak."

At that moment, we saw Bernard enter, and after exchanging a few words with the proprietor of the pub, whom he knew, he didn't come to our table but sat down at the bar counter.

I looked at Graham in surprise and he said, "We recently had an argument regarding art which resulted in a serious quarrel, and now we aren't on speaking terms."

"And what was this about?" I enquired.

"I told him what I thought of the masterpieces he produced, and he called me a philistine," Graham said.

"But what exactly did you tell him?"

"That they're nothing but worthless kitsch."

"And did you really mean that?"

"No," Graham replied.

"So, why did you tell him so?"

"To provoke him so that he would tell me something I wanted to know, namely why he stuck to painting the same theme all over again, that is, painting people who deserve to be mocked for what they're doing. There's nothing positive about his art, just ridicule and condemnation, and I wanted to know why it's so."

"And what did he say?"

"He said that nowadays there's nothing to be proud of or happy about, and all that doth begin should rightly to destruction run, and that's why he's telling the truth in his paintings. What is left in the world, he said, is perfidy, deceit and moral decline."

"What did you say to that?" I asked.

"I said he was right, but to a degree. I meant, there's some hope left to make the world better."

"And what do you exactly mean by making the world better?"

"Hmm, I mean…" Graham hesitated before he said, "…I mean the well-being of the majority of people, which might still be achieved by overcoming the widespread, but not yet fully acknowledged nihilism of modern society. That all started with the death of God, for when He was still alive, people had an ultimate aim in their lives, which is now absent for them."

"I see," I said, "and what would be the way to overcome nihilism?"

"There's only one way, but it's not an easy one, and I don't think it could be pursued by many a man, but I still hope it might be available for some of them in the future when nihilism reaches its climax."

"You use the term nihilism, but I'm still unsure of the precise meaning of it, so tell me, please, your definition of it," I asked Graham.

"You see, nihilism is like an invisible ghost, but being present in everything people do and think. It's an enemy without face which reveals itself in our actions which are its personifications, and people aren't aware of its true physiognomy until it's too late, for instance, as it is in the story of Dorian Grey when he eventually saw his true face.

"Now, once mankind had buried God (who is still present only in very poor countries or where He was reborn, as it is in today's Russia and Ukraine – but for how long will He stay alive?), the questions 'Why?' and 'What for?' couldn't be answered. And material goods available now in plenty, *ex definitio*, cannot replace spiritual ones, for man cannot find the sense of life in them alone. And this is so obvious that it is even a cliché. However, because it's been ignored for so long, its hidden power will reveal itself in its full strength someday in the future. And I mean by that an apocalypse that will be the last attempt of mankind to find God again.

All in all, there are no great values left in this world since God disappeared, and consequently all things are actually permitted. What is left is people subconsciously saying 'no' to existence, and here Bernard is right, but the difference between us is that I am still a dreamer, whereas he believes in nothing."

"You know what, Graham," I said, "I think you should reconcile with him for there's an occasion to do so."

"What do you mean?" he asked.

353

"It's time to reveal another true face of somebody, and I mean myself."

Graham looked at me with curiosity, and said, "Hmm, since I met you, I had the feeling you were actually somebody else, so please go ahead and tell me who art thou?"

"I am Karl Denker, my friend."

Graham looked straight in my eye and nodded. After a minute or so, he eventually said, "And you still call me a friend despite everything that happened to you at the time?"

"Yes, I do, because it wasn't you who did the bad things to me. You had nothing to do with those who did those things."

"No, I didn't, but it doesn't excuse me, for I should have been more observant and then I could have been able to prevent the worst. But I was too lazy to notice, too pleased with my life, too academic, so to speak, to catch the reality of the time."

"But I don't blame you, and there's not even any need to forgive you, for you were who you were, and that's it."

"Thank you for your understanding, my friend, if I can call you that, after all."

"Yes, you can, and now call Bernard. It's time for it, especially as he too had no part in what happened at the time."

"You're right, he was like me. Let's call him then," said Graham, rising to his feet and addressing his friend in a very loud voice. "Bernard, we are here to drink beer, we are here to forget our misunderstandings right now. Come and join us. Our long-lost friend is again with us."

Bernard came to our table, sat down and said, "All right, let bygones be bygones, and whom do you mean, Graham?"

"I mean the gentleman here – Ches Adarsh."

Bernard looked at me and said, "I've heard of you, but how come you might be our long-lost friend?"

"You may recollect a man by the name of Karl Denker," I said to him.

"Certainly, I do, and not just once have I wondered what happened to him since he vanished without a trace," said Bernard.

"I am Karl Denker."

"But you don't look like him, however," and Bernard took a closer look at me, and said, "yes, now I can see there's something familiar, and I mean your eyes, the way you look, that searching curiosity of them, yes, the same as it was with Carl. But your whole appearance, I mean, your face and bearing are very different."

"This is due to my surgery at the clinic and what I've been through since the last time you saw me," I said.

"I see," said Bernard, "and could you tell me what you are doing now, in your new embodiment, so to speak?"

"I'm living in London, and what I do currently… hmm, let's say I investigate the past, so to speak."

"I think I know what you mean," said Bernard, "and yes, there's something to investigate. May I offer you my help with your investigation?"

"Actually, I'd appreciate that, thank you."

"And I, too, might be of assistance if you need me," said Graham.

"Thank you, both, and now I can see that what I thought of you at the time is still there now, and I'm very glad about that," I said.

"So, what can we do for you?" asked Graham.

"I'm thinking about a meeting you suggest to the others in order to discuss some issues you find rather urgent. And because you both have a vivid imagination, you'll think of something that will persuade them to meet and discuss the problem."

"We'll think of something, my friend," said Graham.

"Good, and thanks again."

"All the pleasure's ours, my friend. We owe you one," said Bernard.

"That's it, we do," said Graham, "and let's drink to it." And he said to the table waitress just passing our table, "Susan, love, bring us a few bottles of Budvar, darling. That is the proof that God loves us and wants us to be happy, as the wise Benjamin once said."

And when the beer arrived, he poured it into special mugs which were kept for his personal use at the pub, and when they were filled with beer, we raised them and exclaimed "Prosit!" in unison.

*

At the same time, a very different meeting was taking place, and its nature was very different too, for that matter.

When Mr Dumblodge, the MI6 boss, returned home after a very tedious workday hoping to have a quiet evening, he was to be very disappointed.

First, we must notice that his house in Chelsea was a fortress, or it should be such, as far as he was sure it was. But apparently it wasn't the case, for when he placed himself in a large, comfortable leather armchair with a glass of whisky in his hand, he heard a noise coming from the second floor.

*What's that?* he thought. Usually, his place was very quiet, for he lived alone. There was hardly any traffic in the outside street, and it wasn't the day when his cleaning woman was there doing her job. So, he went upstairs, opened the door to his studio and to his astonishment saw a powerfully built man, who was sitting behind the desk shuffling the papers gathered there.

He opened his mouth to say something, but the unknown man was first to speak. "Where do you keep that report, you bloody moron?"

Now, Mr Dumblodge was so shocked that he forgot what he was going to say. *No, it can't be*, he thought, *"how come? My home is my castle. Am I dreaming? What impertinence! That burglar not only broke in but even dares to ask questions. And how the hell did he get in? All this security is good for nothing, and they assured me there was no way to break in."*

"Are you deaf or don't you understand?" said that cheeky boor. "Where is it?"

Now, Dumblodge was totally lost. He had never felt like this before. His usual self-confidence, acquired at Eton and Oxford, and strengthened by his prominent position, of which he was so proud, somehow disappeared, and he just managed to utter, "And what is it about, sir?"

Now, he was amazed at himself. Instead of throwing the cheeky intruder out of the window, or running downstairs to get his faithful Walther PPK, he called him 'sir'!

"It's about that top secret report you received a week ago from Moscow. Understood?"

"I... I did," the MI6 boss answered meekly.

"If you did, where is it?"

"It should be in the left upper drawer, sir," he hurried to say. He always knew where his papers were, for he was the master of organisation. He was like a Swiss watch, or even better.

"Aha, there it is," said the unknown individuum, looking at a document. And after a while, he announced, "Now, dear Mr Dumblodge, it seems we have here a case of high treason."

"But—" began the other, but the impertinent burglar didn't allow him to finish, saying, "No buts, you're a traitor, and that's that. The document proves beyond doubt you have betrayed your country trying to establish your personal liaison with the Russian secret service behind the Government's back."

"But it was supposed to be in the interest of my country," the accused hurried to say.

"Oh yes, undoubtedly it was, in your and your fellow conspirators' opinions, but to my mind it was a treachery, no doubt about that."

This time, Dumblodge said nothing. He was just standing there with his gaze fixed to the floor.

"Yes, my dear chap, so something must be done about that. Don't you think so?"

"I'm ready to bear full responsibility, but I still refuse to admit I've committed any crime."

"Aha, you say, you're ready to answer for that, and what do you mean by that, dear Mr Dumblodge, if you'd be so kind as to tell me?"

"I'm ready to explain everything to the prime minister, and to answer any questions before any commission if necessary."

"That's very kind of you, dear chap," said the other, "and how would you explain what is shown here in black and white?"

"Yes, I admit, I did that without the Government's knowledge, but in the long run, in was in the best interests of the United Kingdom."

"Your hypocrisy has no limits, my dear fellow. Moreover, it seems you believe what you say, I'm afraid. But your presumed innocence might not be the case here, for your contact with the Russians was established to gain financial benefits, and this is what the document proves, so you'd be prosecuted if it came to light."

Apparently only now, Dumblodge realised it was a serious matter, and there was no excuse for what he had done, so he said, "And what would you suggest, sir?"

"Ah, that's better. At last we can have a reasonable chat, old boy. I suggest, or rather demand, you will first see Lord Hellbridge to discuss the matter in question, and then you both, if of course the lord finds it wise, may see Mr Oddhouse, who will decide how to proceed further."

"I'm fine with that," said Dumblodge.

"I'm happy to hear that, and in this case, I'll arrange a meeting for you with the lord," said the man.

"And do you know him?" asked the chief spy, now totally perplexed, for how in the name of the Devil did a burglar know in person one of *crème de la crème* of the UK establishment?

"Oh yes, I do. Actually, we have known each other for ages, dear Mr Dumblodge, actually forever, so to speak."

Now the spy understood there was something extraordinary about the man. No, he wasn't an ordinary cheeky burglar after all. Oh, no, he was pretty sure now there had to be much more to it, so he said, "I understand you're working for the lord, aren't you?"

"Oh yes, I am, and my job is very responsible and demanding, for I'm one of his Lordship's private assistants."

"You are…" stuttered the other, "his personal…" The MI6 boss was dumbfounded again. A personal assistant to a very eminent man is a burglar. No, it was beyond his comprehension. However, for an unknown reason, for we must say that the chief spy wasn't too well read at all, he somehow remembered now a certain phrase from his great fellow country poet, Shakespeare, that read, 'There are more things in heaven and earth than are dreamt of in your philosophy.'

"So, I'll be going now, and you'll hear soon where and when you'll be meeting the lord, and don't even think of telling your friends about our little chat, for if you do…" The lord's assistant didn't finish but just looked at Dumblodge, and there was something in that gaze that sent a cold shiver down his back, and he closed his eyes and hurried to say, "No, no, of course not, I swear I won't utter a word to anybody. You have my word of honour."

"Your word of honour, you say," the terrible assistant smiled and said, "is of a very doubtful nature, as you yourself know perfectly well, so don't even mention it."

This time, Dumblodge said nothing, as there was nothing to say since the word honour had never been present, so to speak, in his life so far, and he'd never really understood its meaning. And the last time he'd heard the word mentioned was during his time at Eton, and it'd been about something that happened during a war, but which one and where, he couldn't remember.

When the man who had made that unexpected and terrifying visit had left, Dumblodge sat there thinking about what he should do now, and surprised himself, having decided to do nothing at all. He had always been a resourceful man, especially in his life as a chief spy, but now he realised for the first time that there were powers he couldn't challenge, and he even thought of contacting a friend of his, an Anglican pastor, to discuss his sudden realisation, but eventually dropped the idea for he was afraid that the pastor might think he had lost his mind, because as far as he knew the pastor's imagination was somewhat limited. So, in the end, he decided to do nothing but just wait for the summons from the lord, and to console himself a little, he drank a few glasses of whisky at his place, and felt a bit better. Then he went to his favourite pub, the King's Arms, close to Westminster, where he met his lifelong friend, a guy with whom he had been at Oxford, and they both began remembering happy days there, especially the Bullingdon Club, and a few other things. It was pretty late when they parted and Dumblodge couldn't even remember afterwards how he eventually got home.

*

Next day, despite a serious hangover, he was in a better mood and that was due to his newfound view of life. It came as a big surprise to himself to find out he actually wanted to take it easy, having been actually tired of his job and all those intrigues involved in it. Dumblodge had a feeling he should liberate himself not only from that bloody business of snooping, but also from the burden of his legacy, that is, ridiculous snobbery acquired at those prestigious educational institutions he had attended, and people he'd become acquainted with at the time, who now seemed to him a stupid, petty and arrogant gang of useless ignoramuses, in fact like those he'd met during his stretch across the water in that intellectual wasteland of the North-West. The memories from that godforsaken backwater still persecuted him, and now he saw the absurdity of his job over there as well as what he was doing now.

*Enough,* he said to himself, *I'm growing stale and stupid at doing much the same idiotic thing every day. I have a great eagerness for life, and this is not life but just a pretentious existence I must get out of as soon as I can. Otherwise, I will be lost.* And yes, he made up his mind to cooperate with Lord Hellbridge, for he had a premonition that if he didn't, something unpleasant might happen to him, and anyway, it was high time to make amends for all the stupid things he had done before it was too late, but he still didn't have a clue how to go about that. *I'll talk to the lord about that,* he decided. *He will surely tell me what I'm supposed to do.* And now Dumblodge was suddenly dumbstruck by the idea, for it was the first time in his life he intended to ask somebody else for advice, having been so sure of himself until now.

*What's happened to me?* he thought. *How come these ideas have come to my mind out of the blue?* Obviously, he knew what revelation meant, but he actually never believed in it, for until now he had been a calculating and scheming son of a bitch with total self-interest on his mind, so why now did he see everything so differently? Was it due to the visit he had just experienced? *And what actually would I like to do when I leave my job and all these people I know? I must go as far away as possible. Go to a very different place and live a very different sort of life, and get to know very different people, and language too. But where would it be?* He needed help in finding a destination, so he took an atlas of the world from the shelf and opened it at random, placing his forefinger on a page with his eyes closed, and then opening them, he saw the place. It was Tahiti. He'd never been there, but now he was sure that was it. But why he didn't know, and actually he felt no need to know why. He just knew, and it was all he needed to know.

*Am I irrational, crazy perhaps?* he thought. *And even if I am, so what, when I'm so sure and pleased about it.* And now he was very eager to meet Lord Hellbridge soon, very soon for that matter.

*

While the MI6 boss was undergoing that radical metamorphosis, Bernard, Graham and I were still in the Boathouse enjoying our beers, and at some stage of our conversation I decided to be absolutely frank with them and tell them everything I knew about the M7 business. Formally, they were still its members, but they didn't actually belong there since their views were actually very different from those of other members. So, when the right moment came, I said, "You both, I presume, know nothing about the inner workings of your exclusive association which I call the Magnificent Seven."

"A very interesting name you've come up with for our little club," said Graham, "but I assume you mean magnificent in an opaque way, don't you?"

"I do, my friend, and I know you don't really belong there, and know nothing about what your distinguished friends did in the past, I mean, their deliberate false accusations which could have ended for me at court and a pretty long prison sentence."

I could see they were both totally bewildered by what they had just heard, and Bernard was first to say, "No, my friend, we knew nothing at all, and what you say now is shocking."

Looking at their faces, I could see they were both genuinely stunned, and Graham said, "We're terribly sorry, and…" for the first time since I met him here, at the Boathouse, he couldn't finish the sentence, but eventually said, "…we are ashamed of our ignorance at that time and there's no excuse for it."

"No, my friend," I hurried to say, "you are both excused for I always knew you had never been part of the rest, and considering your easy attitude to life, your frequent dwelling in the clouds, so to speak, there is sufficient excuse for you not to be aware of what was happening at the time, so don't you worry, I don't hold a grudge against you."

"Thank you, my friend," said Graham, "we do appreciate that, and now tell us, please, what we can do for you to…" he hesitated "…compensate… sorry, what a silly word. I don't really know how to put it."

"I know what you mean, and yes, there's something you can both do for me," I said.

"Whatever it is, we'll do it," said Bernard.

"Yes, go ahead. We'll do anything," Graham joined his friend.

"Thank you," I said. "I always knew that you were and still are my true friends, so in the first place, you won't tell the others a word about our conversation here. You know that, of course, but considering the frequent absent-mindedness of you both, please always be on your guard while speaking to them."

"We'll do our best, don't we?" said Bernard, looking at Graham.

"We will, so tell us, please, what you expect from us, for we're eager to act," he said.

"Okay, then," I said, "they should obviously pay for what they've done since you should never let anyone who has insulted you get away with it, and they've done more than that. I am biding my time and now want to strike back when actually I don't need to do so, but bearing in mind their evildoing, I can't let it go on principle, because if I did they could do the same to somebody else."

"You're right, we're with you," said Bernard, "and what is it you want us to do?"

"I want you to meet Lord Hellbridge, if you know whom I mean," I said.

"Oh yes, I do. Who doesn't know him!" said Graham, and he smiled. "Meeting him might be a pretty inspirational occasion, especially that to my mind he's much more than just a lord. What do you think, Bernard?"

"Oh, yea, it might be, and I could, if an opportunity arises, paint a picture or two of him afterwards."

"I can't wait to meet the lord, always wanted to have a chat with him, you know, there's something about him I can't put my finger on," said Graham.

"Oh yes," Bernard joined him, "and he's so, hmm, indescribable."

"He is, indeed," said Graham, "especially his black eyes. When you look in them, you feel as if you are falling into an abyss from which you'll never get out. His eyebrows are impressive too, long and black, and the left one is higher than the other. And his sarcastic smile, as if he was mocking everything that he sees and listens to. But then you can also see a deep concern, even sadness, in those black eyes of his, when you look closely. All in all, he's a very impressive man."

"You know what?" Bernard chipped in. "I sometimes have the strange feeling that he isn't actually a man, but then who might he be?"

"Bah," Graham said, "we may never know for that matter, but as for meeting him, where would it take place?"

"I'll speak to him and it's up to him to decide," I said, "and if he likes the idea, he might be so kind as to invite us to his mansion in the country, which is close to Chequers."

"Chequers, you say?" said Bernard, "If so, then the prime minister may well be willing to attend because he goes there as often as he can, for he likes the place."

"That's it," I said, "I'll contact the lord tomorrow when he's back from Moscow."

"Aha, Moscow, you say," said Graham, "and what was he doing there if you happen to know?"

"It's about Jason's connections there, and the lord decided to have a word with a few people about it. Anyway, he's been invited by the Russian president, who wants some advice from him regarding an urgent security matter as the lord's assistant, Mr Wissend, told me," I said.

"Apparently, everybody in the world seeks his advice nowadays," said Graham.

"It seems so," I said, "and his advice is very much appreciated everywhere, but then some countries' leaders, being unreasonable, don't follow it, and obviously bear the consequences afterwards. But Moscow always listens carefully to what the lord says, and follows his guidance to the letter. Dollaria is very different in this respect, and the lord is getting disappointed with its current president, and if he's still reluctant to follow the lord's advice, I wouldn't like to be in his shoes."

"It appears the lord is an éminence grise these days, that secretary of the Cardinal de Richelieu or Prince de Talleyrand of our times," said Bernard.

"I have the impression," I said, "he's much more than that, my friends."

"Yes, he might be," said Bernard, "but then again, who might he be?"

# PART THREE

# THE LIMITS OF REALITY AND HOW THEY WERE CROSSED

'What is thinkable is possible too.'
Ludwig Wittgenstein

'There are more things in heaven and earth
than are dreamt of in your philosophy.'
Shakespeare

'There is nothing more incredible than reality.'
Dostoyevsky

'What is reality?
It is something what we believe in today, and cease to believe tomorrow.
What is fiction today, tomorrow it might be reality.
And vice versa of course.'
C.D.

'If it doesn't agree with reality much the worse for reality.'
Hegel

While our conversation continued until late on that lovely summer's day, some other people happened to be having rather strange or even mysterious adventures, and the first one to experience them was Justin Scornbash who would have never expected to be so thrown off balance in his life, considering his remarkable skills as a barrister QC.

He started his day as usual. After waking up, he looked out of the window to check the weather. He had never watched or listened to the weather report since the day when a TV announcer had reported, 'Tomorrow the day will be bright but the night will be dark.' Justin had not found the information particularly helpful. At first, however, he thought it might have had some cryptic meaning, but when he'd employed his outstanding powers of intellect, had come to the opposite conclusion.

The day in question was neither bright nor dark, which unsettled him because he favoured explicit situations, kind of Kierkegaard's *Either Or*, but of course not in any ethical sense, for in Justin's opinion, ethics and law dwelled as they should, in two totally separate worlds. This was Justin's foremost credo on which was founded his remarkable success as a man of law.

*Hmm,* he thought, after close examination of the skies, *it doesn't look good, there's something wrong with it, as there is with all these people I represent at court. However, I've got some influence on their fate, whereas none regarding the weather.* And Justin was proud of his mastery as a lawyer feared by judges and prosecutors, and was especially glad when one of them suffered health problems, usually cardiac, of course, after confronting him at court. But his clients in turn were almost always extremely pleased and their gratitude was very generous indeed, and they could afford it, anyway. Justin never represented the poor. The first question he asked a client was how much he or she was willing to pay him for his service, and if it didn't meet his expectations, he never took the case. Moreover, he always demanded to be paid substantial money upfront, and because of his fame, none of his clients ever refused. He was actually a legend, and his skills so admired that one Russian billionaire was heard to have said of him, 'That guy performs black magic at court. He's the devil incarnate. I, myself, was frightened by his craft.' And indeed, Justin's virtuosity at the manipulation of facts, witnesses, judges and everybody at court was unsurpassed in this country of the rule of law.

However, Justin had a weakness or two which he couldn't contain, and that was his penchant for playing cards, betting at horse racing and hookers, and considering the fees he charged, he could afford them all. Hookers came first, and his appetite for them was boundless, and their supply in London limitless. He favoured those from the Far East, that is, Chinese and Korean, and had some favourites, whom he frequently invited to his apartment in Kensington. Sometimes there were two of them, for he liked to be fondled all over at the same time and just one wouldn't do.

He also almost always liked to have two differently built partners, for instance, one short and slim, but with big boobs, and the other tall with small ones. He appreciated as well having an athletically built girl, but not fat, while the other petite, especially when he could fuck the latter in the mouth while the other one fucked her using a dildo. Pretty often, he invited one or two of his male friends to perform double or triple penetration on one, especially innocent-looking Asians, and his favourite was a certain petite Chinese whom they fucked for hours on end, taking various sex-stimulating drugs, such as red ginseng, yohimbine and a few others. They literally tortured her, and as she often screamed loudly, one of them would put his cock deep in her mouth.

Very often after a session that sometimes lasted eight or more hours, including a few breaks, the girl couldn't walk, so she would stay at his place when his friends left. When she had recovered a bit, Justin had her anally, ending with deep throat. Afterwards, she told her friends she loved the sessions despite being extremely exhausted after them, for her sexual satisfaction was absolute and she couldn't wait to have another session. Or, Justin had a lot of pleasure with two bisexual girls who made love on themselves, when he meanwhile satisfied himself with either of them. What he loved most was prolonged fellatio performed by two, and then deep throat with both of them. His imagination in the matter in question was infinite, and his performance was much appreciated by all of the women he had sex with.

Justin frequently travelled to the Philippines and Thailand to look for new women, and over there he most liked young ones. These were provided by a Chinese man in Thailand, where actually Justin had a villa at which several very young girls were employed as servants, and they provided full service to him whenever he went there. Usually, he stayed there for a month, and the girls were always very happy to see him. Whereas in Philippines, when he got there he met new sex partners for very rough, even brutal sex, and very often the women were gang-banged by him and his friends. He said the girls over there liked to be humiliated in bed, and he and his male companions often spanked and slapped them while fucking them, or they tied them up and then penetrated their every hole using also big, sophisticated dildos. And some of the girls actually needed medical care afterwards, but they still didn't complain, for their sexual and, of course, financial satisfaction made up for their physical exhaustion. He also had a mother and her two young daughters at his home in Thailand who provided him with every possible kind of sexual gratification. Justin experimented on them with anything that came to his mind; for instance, the mother held one of them from behind while he was fucking her hard, while the other one was fondling him from behind, or the three of them were performing slow fellatio, and in the end swallowed in turns when he came.

All in all, Justin had a very good time when he went there and he said he fully deserved it due to his extremely exhausting and stressful job which he wouldn't be able to carry on if he didn't have proper unwinding holidays of that kind. He also said that he didn't do any harm to those very young girls, for they not only enjoyed sex but had a substantial financial gratification; anyway, he treated them very well and everybody was happy in the end. What is wrong, he said, about fucking a young girl when she is happy about that and has some money for herself afterwards, and especially those being his servants at his home in Thailand would have had miserable lives if they weren't lucky enough to have the opportunity to be his servants? In this respect, Justin mocked and hated the hypocrisy of his home country which took the advantage of the same young girls as half-slaves employed at its overseas company branches talking a lot about human rights, fairness and equality at the same time. Anyway, none of his girls over there were forced to do what she was doing, for it was her voluntary decision to choose that sort of life.

Justin once said that when he retired, he would move to one of those countries, most likely Thailand, because been already tired and disgusted with his own country, he dreamt of a full-time life of pleasure. He did his job only because there was nothing else he could do, and he was very good at what he was doing but hated it at the same time, and his disgust with his own country was so complete that he wouldn't be able to live there. He said that there was no life here but its advertisement, as he put it, for chow, drink and pretence, and nothing else. The country's authorities advertised its deep concern about health matters, having forgotten that man doesn't live by bread alone. There was no spiritual life there. Everything that was left was commerce eventually for commerce's sake in the end. This was, he said, a vicious circle, and in the not-so-remote future, it would end in catastrophe. By reason of his nature, Justin proclaimed, man wouldn't bear this sort of life for long, once he had realised its senselessness, especially the fact that so much advertised freedom was not a genuine one but its substitute. Freedom of gayness and one-sex marriage, for instance, was the evil liberation of a perverted nature that turns against its healthy core, and in this respect, he said, some other countries had a much healthier attitude to that. The aim of the much advertised British utilitarian slogan of the greater good was in fact to make serfs of people by depriving them of individual pride, courage and insight. But then they were still eager to emphasise their own importance and encouraged to do so by the Government's slogans. And that sort of emphasis was typical for the Irish, and Justin asked himself why they did so, and his answer was because they have none. And he said that the freedom of the riff-raff which spread all over Britannia and Eire was to abuse the freedom of their decent fellow countrymen, meaning to abuse their dignity, integrity, privacy and peace. Democracy, he said, was these days a political system where people are being manipulated, not being aware of it. The system protected all kinds of cripples, emphasising their importance because doing so, they were easy to manipulate, feeling themselves important at the same time. The main aim was to gain their support for the Government's internal and foreign policy whatsoever, which always benefited the establishment. Thus, that sort of democracy worked for the advantage of the rich, and those in power, and the rest, were supposed to be happy receiving the scraps. For the majority, it was the freedom of half-witted henchmen, obedient and submissive, being dependent on wages and benefits paid by whoever their employer was. All in all, Justin said, that poor rabble works for their 'own good', so they were made to believe so, against themselves, their value as human beings so decreased that it hardly resembled anything that could be named as an accomplished human being. And therefore, said Justin, Goethe's words, 'All that doth begin should rightly to distraction run,' are so truthful, and sometime in the future they would come true.

He came to the conclusion that all that mumbling about tolerance, equality and diversity was a mask to disguise the true face of the workings of those in power, but as a matter of fact, an ordinary man thinking was actually the same as those who were in power. Yes, certainly, there were a few exceptions, but as always, they just confirmed the rule and had not the slightest influence on the majority whose needs and tastes could be summarised in these few words: 'bread and circus' was all they wanted, as it had been in ancient Rome. And what some good men, but very gullible, in fact, were saying was of no consequence, as it was with Martin Luther King's statement, 'Our scientific power has outrun our spiritual power. We have guided missiles and misguided men,' but we had always been like that, was Justin's view. Or our dear 'cousins' across the ocean… in their opinion, they were 'innocently' air bombing whoever opposed their 'democracy' – and always would – which had ceased to be a genuine one over one hundred years ago. Now, what was left was nothing but democracy of servitude.

Or my own country… and its illusion of grandeur still being inspired *de facto* by the long-gone Empire that enslaved millions, and was still present in those ridiculous noble ranks usually granted to those who delivered money to a party that was actually in power. *Oh yea*, Justin said again to himself, '*all that should rightly to distraction run*,' and he, himself, would, he thought, contribute to that aim. Henry, he thought, was one in very modern times who was of the same opinion, and we must notice here that Justin was a very well-read man. Moreover, very unusually for a man like him, his interests went far beyond his professional activity, for he studied philosophy at a few European universities, at Heidelberg, Bologna and Poitiers. He spoke fluent German, French and Italian, and was now taught Russian by a young, pretty Russian woman he'd already seduced, so tutoring was a pure pleasure.

Justin was an M7 member, but at the same time wasn't too much committed to its activities because they were limited to gain financial profits, and he wanted to go far beyond it. Justin was convinced that his country needed a *coup d'état*, for to his mind there was no other way to save it from decline and certain fall in the near future. Yes, some other members said the same, but they weren't actually particularly interested in the idea except, strangely enough, the MI6 boss, Dumblodge. They had both discussed perspectives of seizure of power but came to the conclusion it wouldn't work because their fellow countrymen lacked the spirit to carry out such a thing, being actually too meek and obedient. Yes, they were adept at making havoc while drunk and yelling, but nothing else. In other words, they felt free to do whatever the Government allowed them to do, and it actually tolerated the drunkenness and many kinds of misbehaviour, regarding it as ways of relieving their feelings of anger, distress, and the like. But as a matter of fact, the dominating trait of the Brits' personality was submission – slave morality, as Friedrich put it. And because they were inclined to simplify everything, they were unable to understand the ideas of individual freedom, that is, the liberty of spirit. All they were able to grasp was mindless, foolish and aimless crowd-liberty. And this is why they had never had any great artistic achievements; they had had some intellectual, but they were limited to everyday practice, and nothing else. And their politeness, of which they were so proud, was the politeness of an overeager shopkeeper to gain the financial benefits of being obliging.

All in all, it seemed to Justin that the only way to change that miserable existence of his country was an intervention from outside, sort of another Norman or Dutch invasion. Or by some supernatural powers so doubted by his limited-in-spirit fellow countrymen, who actually never understood the meaning of the transcendental, eternal deity, for their God never left their stores.

All in all, Justin was a renegade, but somewhere deep inside he still appreciated his home country tradition, which to his mind had gone mostly to the dogs, and wanted England to return to her former grandeur. Now, what he hated most was that his country was overwhelmed by riff-raff vulgarity and had become a coarse place where the principled Englishman was actually out of place. That primitive broadcast rambling, those repulsive idiot-box shows, that crap music and those sickening performers, no, it was more than he could bear anymore. He was certain that something had to be done; otherwise, *hmm, that's it*, he thought, *what might happen if nothing is done about it? What will happen*, he thought, *if we let all that filth spread all over, what then?* And, as a matter of fact, he couldn't answer the question. Was someone out there who could? And then all of a sudden, somebody came to his mind – Lord Hellbridge, yes, but why him? He didn't know.

And exactly then, his telephone rang. Justin answered the call and heard somebody's deep-sounding voice saying, "Dear Mr Dumblodge, this is Lord Hellbridge speaking, and it has come to my attention you want to speak to somebody who would help you to find some answers."

Justin was dumfounded. *How come the lord rang at the moment I was thinking of him?*

"I know," the lord continued, "you're a bit surprised by my call, but, you know, I'm always eager to help those in need, so as soon as I heard about your doubts, I made up my mind to give you a ring. I know it's a bit strange that I would know about your problem, and to clarify that, we would have to meet in person, provided that you're interested. Are you?"

"I… I…" began Justin, still confused by that out-of-the-blue call, "yes, it would be a pleasure, sir. It's very kind of you."

"Great, so let's say eleven o'clock at my place. I presume you know where it is," said the lord.

"Yes, sir, I do. Thank you again, and goodbye," said Dumblodge, who obviously as the head of Her Majesty's formidable intelligence service knew where Lord Hellbridge lived. Anyway, you wouldn't actually have to be a spy to know that because his Lordship's address was available on the internet.

\*

Next morning, the MI6 boss put on his best Savile Row suit and Vass shoes, but it turned out when he was already on his way to see the lord, and it was too late to return home, that he'd forgotten to put on socks, being rather anxious about seeing the lord, but hoped that eccentricity would be forgiven by his Lordship.

When he arrived at the lord's residence in Belgravia, the front door was immediately open for him, but he couldn't see who actually opened it, and the door wasn't automatic, for we must reveal here that the lord hated all things automatic, and he disliked the telephone too, being a very old-fashioned gentleman.

The lord's apartment was a penthouse with a terrace from which you had a very nice view of a park nearby. He loved parks and the woods, and his favourite kind of holiday was a bivouac, wild camping far away from the city, preferably close to a lake or a river. That preference was probably related to his Gothic heritage, his ancestors who had lived in the wild forests of Germania. In the *Almanach de Gotha*, we read that his first ancestors were members of nobility as early as the fourth century, which made him perhaps the oldest nobility in Europe, far older than the Mar or Arundel families, to say nothing of the Queen's, and many other aristocratic families in England, which compared to his were almost *parvenu*. But the lord was actually an unassuming man, as was his apartment.

When Dumblodge entered, and the door again was opened by an invisible hand, he noticed there was hardly any furniture in the reception room. Nevertheless, it had a church atmosphere, but it was hard to say which denomination it was. The lord himself, who warmly greeted him, was clothed rather modestly in a loose black shirt, black trousers and slippers.

"I have long wanted to meet you, dear Mr Dumblodge, and I'm very glad to welcome you at last. Please have a seat."

"Thank you, sir, and I'm also very pleased to have the pleasure of meeting you," said the visitor.

"How are things?" asked the lord.

"Not too bad, but to be honest, I'm a bit tired these days. I mean, my job, you know what recently happened at our headquarters."

"Ah yes, what a story, huh, huh. And who might it have been? Do you already know something?" Hellbridge enquired curiously.

"Nothing, nil, those Special Branch and Scotland Yard useless bunglers have found nothing so far. They're hopeless," said the spy.

"And your own people, they couldn't find out anything either?" asked the lord.

"No, they haven't," Dumblodge admitted sadly. "It's a very mysterious story, and it happened in one of the best guarded places in this country. All these electronic devices are good for nothing, milord. I now have no confidence in them at all."

"I don't, either. I prefer a very traditional means of protection. You know, a solid padlock, German Sheppard, they're the best."

"I agree with you, sir. I have now totally lost my confidence in those bloody – excuse my language – electronics, and all those funny Silicon Valley toys. I too believe now in traditional well-tested security measures, and I am going to introduce them at my job place."

"Very wise of you, dear Mr Dumblodge. High time for a change in the right direction, so to speak. And I mean not only security, for that matter."

"And what else, if I may enquire?" asked the other.

"Ah, my dear chap, I mean all that modernity, the poverty of it I find disgusting, the culture of philistines."

"So do I, dear Lord Hellbridge, so do I."

"It seems we have something in common, and I'm very happy about that," said the lord.

At that moment, a big and beautiful German Shepherd in the company of a huge black cat entered the room, and the lord said, "Let me introduce my faithful companions, Rex the Germanicus and Bulky the Leviathan." The latter was a monster of a cat, and Dumblodge felt uneasy just looking at him. Both animals stared at him for a couple of minutes as if they were scrutinising his worth, and Dumblodge became even more edgy, and in an involuntary attempt to please them, he said something that you normally wouldn't say under the circumstances, that is "Enchanté." But apparently the animals were pleased by his courtesy, and the cat, it seemed to him, was even slightly tickled by it.

"I'm very pleased to see you love animals, and it seems to me that these here reciprocate your feelings, and a man who like animals cannot be thoroughly bad. I, myself, go even further and fully agree with General de

Gaulle's statement, 'The better I get to know men, the more I find myself loving dogs.' But of course, he liked cats too." And now, Dumblodge had the strange impression that both creatures understood what the lord said, for they looked at each other, and in Rex's eyes he noticed something like appraisal of what had just been said.

"I almost never part with them," continued the lord. "Sometimes they act on their own. Bulky especially is a very diligent and extremely efficient individual, and he loves to travel. He's been everywhere, and his travels have always brought a lot of good."

And now, it seemed to Dumblodge, the cat seemed to appreciate the words, for he rubbed himself against Hellbridge's leg.

"And have they been with you long, sir?" asked the boss of spies.

"Oh, they've been my associates forever, dear chap," said Hellbridge.

"How old are they then?"

"Hmm, I don't really know, but mind you, time really doesn't matter here at all. Anyway, I fully agree with Immanuel regarding the matter in question. But now, if you don't mind, let's go *zu dem Sachen selbst*, so to speak."

Dumblodge, who spoke German, and as we have already mentioned, studied philosophy, knew this saying of Edmund's and said, "But of course, milord, as you wish."

"So, Mr Dumblodge, I know that you and your friends have long been scheming against the Government, and some time ago, you and your friends accused Mr Denker of an embezzlement he did not commit. Mr Denker lives now in London under a different name, and obviously wants retribution for what you have done to him, and because he enjoys my protection, I'll support him doing that."

Now, Dumblodge was panic-stricken for he realised perfectly well what might happen to him and his friends if Karl Denker enjoyed Hellbridge's assistance. He opened his mouth to say something, but the lord raised his hand and said, "Please refrain from any comments now and wait until I have finished."

"Yes, of course, sir. I'm sorry."

"I," continued Hellbridge, "am inclined to absolve you and a few other members of your wrongdoing under a certain condition, and I hope

Mr Denker, bearing now the name Adarsh, will accept my offer. The condition is that you and all of your friends will cooperate with us. Do I make myself clear, Mr Dumblodge?"

"Yes, sir, I will, and I'll make sure my friends will too," said the other, perfectly aware of the consequences if he refused.

"Good," said the lord, "so, have a word with them, except messieurs Witmore and Mockingham, who are already with us."

"But sir, what about the former prime ministers? They may not be willing to cooperate."

"Leave it to me, dear Mr Dumblodge. I'll take care of them."

"As you wish, sir."

"That's it, you may go now, and I'll contact you again in due time."

"Thank you, sir, and I'll be waiting for your call."

"Please see the gentleman off, my friends," said the lord, addressing his pets.

Rex and Bulky raised their paws and accompanied Dumblodge to the front door, which again was opened by some invisible hand, and when he came out and was about to descend the staircase, he heard a voice behind his back, saying, "We strongly advise you not to play any tricks, old boy."

Dumblodge was so startled by this unexpected advice, apparently coming from one of the animals, that he stumbled and almost fell downstairs, but somehow managed not to, looked at them and uttered, "No, no, of course I won't." And both of them apparently accepted his assurance, for it seemed to him as if they nodded and even smiled, but of course he was still so confused by the visit, and actually by everything that had been happening over the previous week, that he thought he might have had hallucinations after all.

*

Graham, Bernard and myself at the same time were still at the Boathouse, enjoying our beers and discussing anything possible under the sun.

"Ah, my dear friends," said Graham, "something is rotten in the world, and my country leads in decline because the English have actually always believed that man may live by bread alone, that spiritual life is something needless, in fact. Yes, Henry was right, saying, 'We are at the endpoint of the wrong path, and should change course radically, and to start completely over from scratch.' Let's take, for instance, music nowadays, which with a few exceptions is appalling crap, but what is totally incomprehensible for me is that the majority of people are enjoying it, meaning their taste has gone to the dogs. And the curious thing is that they get excited by their own stupidity, vulgarity and their nihilism, that is, by denial and cynicism, and this is because all great values have lost their value as the great Friedrich rightly observed. Their philosophy is saying 'no', or 'anything goes', and it is about everything, including their own emotions. They are the spirits who, living their lives, forever deny as if they embodied the one who wills forever evil, as is attributed to the Devil himself. And this is the greatest paradox of humanity. They have become the one whom they always blamed for their misery.

"Once, music, I mean classical, was the affirmation of life, and these days music is its negation. For instance, my friends, Pink Floyd, who I still like, but what worries me is that it's the music of the End, and I wonder whether it manifests an acceptance of it or it's a rather awkward attempt to save our hopes as regards the future of the world by making the listeners aware of the hopelessness of their lives. One may say that their music rejects the world in which we live, and yes it does, but the point is what's next and they don't seem to suggest anything positive. Or these songs begging for love, understanding, compassion and the like, and their empty, trivial humanistic appeals – they in fact tell the listeners about things they will never get, especially happiness, that will never come true. Anyway, all these popular slogans concerning humanism are *de facto* a cover-up for the ruthless self-interests of those in charge of finance. But, my friends, the truth is that the man in the street demands to be fed by bread and illusions at the same time, and illusion is nowadays the first of all pleasures, paradoxically, for those who claim to be so pragmatic.

"Now, the point is that a man's needs aren't his conscious decisions, but they are products of his inner thinking of which he isn't aware. In other words, he doesn't know why he wants something, so he can be easily manipulated by those who provide him with goods, the prime goal of which is to satisfy his basic, even vulgar desires, and I have the impression that all scientific progress carries man back to the primordial condition of the caveman, who wanted nothing but chow and drink. And if my feelings are right, then the end of what we call civilisation lies in the not-so-remote future. But the majority doesn't care – easy come easy go, and the philosophy of anything is their credo these days, and the lack of moral principles which have to be more and more enforced by law, and not as they used to be by personal beliefs, and I'm sure mankind will pay dearly in the end. Humankind needs to be shown the way, needs aristocracy of the mind to be led, because man as such doesn't know where he should be heading, and here our friend Friedrich was undoubtedly right, wasn't he?"

I was listening attentively to what Graham was saying, and agreed with him, for my views were very close to his, and when he mentioned Nietzsche, I said, "Certainly he was, but let me tell you that while in der Schweiz, I met a man whose knowledge simply frightened me."

"And who was he?" enquired Bernard.

"Bah, I wish I knew."

"I don't understand. He didn't introduce himself?"

"He did, but until now, I didn't know who he really was, and you know what, Lord Hellbridge is very much like him."

"What do you mean?" asked Graham.

"The lord's appearance, the way he talks, almost everything."

"Hmm, that's interesting. Could they both be the same man?" said Graham.

"How would I know? And I wouldn't dare ask the lord about that, of course," I said.

"We may somehow find out, I think," said Bernard.

"I suggest we visit him if he'd be so kind as to see us," said Graham.

"I like the idea, but how shall we proceed?" said Bernard.

"I'll phone him right now, and ask," I said.

"Okay, do it, why not? Either or," said Bernard.

I hesitated a bit, for the lord may find our request to see him impertinent, but eventually I dialled the number he had given me, and after just one ring my call was answered, but it wasn't him, so I said, "Good evening, Ches Adarsh speaking. Lord Hellbridge, please."

"Ah, it's you, dear Mr Adarsh, the lord's busy at the moment. How can I help you?" said the man.

"I don't want to bother you, I…"

But the man on the other end said, "No bother at all, my friend. This is Wissend speaking. Tell me what it is about and I'll speak to him as soon as he has finished his exercise."

"Ah, Mr Wissend, sorry, I didn't recognise your voice. Yes, we, I mean messieurs Witmore, Mockingham and myself, are here drinking beer at the Boathouse, and we are now a bit confused at not being able to answer some questions. That's why I dare disturb you with my call," I said.

"I like beer myself, and know that the best ideas come to my head when drinking it, and I'm sure the same goes for you, so I'll arrange for you and your friends to meet the lord this very evening."

"That's very kind of you, thank you."

"No bother, and I'll send a car to collect you at the pub. It won't take long, and in the meantime, enjoy your beer."

"That's awfully kind of you, and we'll be waiting. Most obliged and see you soon."

I disconnected and said, "Done, and it was easier than we supposed it to be. His assistant, Wissend, said he would arrange for us to meet the lord, and his car should be here soon to collect us."

"Splendid," said Graham, "nice fellow, that Wissend."

"Oh yes," I said, "he is, and a very clever one for that matter."

*

While we were waiting to see Lord Hellbridge, some very strange things were happening in London, and afterwards all the papers' front pages reported incredible stories which the public could hardly believe. The stories in question were about what a couple of former prime ministers went through, and since the British public was unaccustomed to any incidents which couldn't be explained rationally using common sense, of course, the newspapers' reports deeply shook the readers, stirring hitherto unknown emotions.

The authorities too were surprised, and initially dismissed the reports as being pure inventions made by irresponsible, looking-for-sensationalism reporters. But then when a very confidential investigation confirmed the authenticity of them, the Government, during a very secret meeting at COBRA, decided to act.

The prime minister, Mr Oddhouse, despite much opposition from his cabinet fellows, concluded by seeking the advice of a renowned astrologer, Professor Stern.

The professor's expertise had been sought before by some foreign governments, which had found themselves in trouble having encountered very similar problems, and greatly appreciated his counsel. They'd said that without his invaluable guidance, they would have faced enormous upheaval in their countries, very likely a *coup d'état* or uprising, and since the British government was allergic, so to speak, to that sort of public discontent, which resulted more than once in very serious troubles in their own country, they eventually unanimously agreed to go ahead with the prime minister's motion, but it was in fact only after they had been told about Professor's Stern's accomplishments abroad.

Let's tell the reader about just a few of them.

Thus, for instance, in Russia, the authorities were confronted with an inexplicable phenomenon of what took place in Moscow, called the 'Mystery of Patriarch's Pond'. The incident was investigated by several very experienced agencies, such as the FSB and even the GRU, despite having apparently nothing to do with military. Even the Presidential Security Service took part in the investigation, but they also failed miserably, which so infuriated the president that he fired its bosses.

We should notice, however, that Moscow citizens enjoyed what was happening and were in fact proud of it. Actually, very similar things had happened before and were described in detail in a novel by a writer of incredible imagination. The most powerful man in Russia then had somehow learnt about the book, despite it having not been published, and wondered how the Devil the author could have had such detailed knowledge about what had actually been a state secret at the time. The writer himself had experienced serious difficulties, and once the country's leader had read his novel, he resolved to come to his rescue because he'd been wise enough to imagine what could have happened to him if he had not. He had assumed that the writer's detailed knowledge must have been first hand, and then if his informant would have been displeased with the supreme authority, neither the high walls surrounding the leader's residence nor his numerous guards would have protected him. And once he'd envisioned the danger, he'd spoken to the writer, assuring him of his admiration and eagerness to help, and immediately issued relevant orders.

And now, years later, the Russian president was faced with almost the same problem again. So, let's tell the reader what was actually happening in Moscow that so upset the authorities, and was so enjoyed and even celebrated by so many there.

*

Professor Stern, understandably in total secrecy, was contacted in person by a member of the Presidential Security Council on a sunny June day at his lovely thatched cottage in Dorset. We must notice here that the professor, despite his enormous fame and fees he charged (it was rumoured that the Russian government paid him no less than five million pounds for his advice regarding the so-called Mystery of Patriarch's Pond, when he later on resolved the mystery), was a very unassuming man. He could have easily afforded, if he had retained the money paid to him, to live at any very expensive location in this country or anywhere else for that matter if he chose to do so, but he was living in a very modest house where there were hardly any modern appliances, neither computers nor telephone, and in the kitchen, there was just an old-fashioned wood-burning stove for cooking.

His vacation he invariably spent in the wilderness, sleeping in a tent and cooking on a camp fire. When he was investigating the above-mentioned mystery, he was invited to stay at the Kremlin, but he declined the imperial suite he was offered, sleeping in a tent outside. He never in his life went to a celebrated restaurant, for his tastes were very simple; good self-grown vegetables, full rye bread, eggs and some fish or chicken.

His only weakness was for a good beer, especially Budvar, but no spirits because, as he frankly confessed, of his drinking huge amounts of vodka in the past. He might occasionally drink some good wine while in the company of women who, we must say, adorned his company. And, to tell the truth, it wasn't because of his wealth or fame, for he hardly had any money left, having donated most of it to various charities, but because they found his company so charming and knew he adored theirs, and that was why the Government's emissary who arrived to see him was a lady.

It was Margarita Dubois, a very beautiful woman, tall, with long honey-blonde hair, and she was chosen because of his preference for that kind of beauty.

She arrived at his place at 5 am, for it was known that the professor was a very early bird. Anyway, he couldn't have been contacted in advance because, as we have already noticed, there was neither telephone nor computer at his place. So, Miss Dubois (she was still unmarried despite her beauty, or maybe because of it) knocked on his cottage door, and nothing happened. Nobody answered the door. She was unsure what to do next when she heard a voice calling from somewhere, "Over here, darling", and looking around, she saw something move in the bushes nearby. Being dressed properly for such occasions, she boldly headed for them, and when she walked with some difficulty through those high dense bushes onto a small meadow, she saw him.

The professor was sitting at a camp fire grilling a sausage stuck on a long tree branch, and there was a lovely smell in the air.

"Please have a seat," he said. "I've been expecting this visit, but I'm nicely surprised to see a beautiful woman and not one of these wankers your government offices are full of. Anyway, my best friend, Lord Hellbridge, had already announced to me I might expect a visit by the Cabinet messenger, and here you are. Have you been with them long, *mein Schatz?*"

We must note here that the professor's origins were a mystery, even for himself. He might have had German roots, and therefore he often complemented his speech with German words, but actually nothing was known for sure because there were no records of any of his ancestors at any of the Government's bodies.

"No, I've been appointed just recently," said Margarita, "on the recommendation of your friend, the lord."

"Ah yes, of course. He knows what I like about women, so he apparently told them who should be sent to see me, and that's why they've chosen you. *Enchanté, mademoiselle.* Please have a piece," and Stern gave her a piece of the sausage. Some of his forefathers might also have been French. That's why he used the language of Voltaire too.

Margarita bit on the sausage and said, "*Très delicieux. Merci beaucoup, monsieur.*" She spoke fluent French and German, and that was another reason she got the job.

Professor Stern was a dedicated bachelor, and it was because he'd never met his woman. His kind of woman's looks we already know, but there were other attributes he appreciated, and he was extremely choosy in that respect. In the first place, his woman was supposed to love bivouacking, and that was the *sine qua non* for him. Moreover, she had to be modest, understanding, sweet-tempered and affectionate. His ideal should also be a whore in bed and a lady in a salon. And a good swimmer too. The only criterion not necessary in the list was, she didn't have to love beer, he did so much. Anyway, small wonder then he hadn't found any so far who met those requirements. But now he felt he might eventually have met the one. So, to double-check, he went further, asking Margarita, "What about a swim, *ma chérie.*" Stern was a very good swimmer; however, because he was a heavy smoker, his stamina wasn't too good. Anyway, he swam every day, and his favourite place to grab a swim were lakes, and in Europe, especially those in Poland and Finland.

Margarita loved swimming too, so she said, "Surely, let's go."

After they ate, Stern smoked one of his Gitanes, and they walked towards a rather small pond, and when they got there, he said, "I'm in favour of swimming naked, and what about you?"

It was another double-check. The professor hated prudery and decided to find out whether Margarita suffered from it. He considered prudery a deception, a mask those stupid prudish actors wore, pretending to be modest, shy and humble, at the same time being coarse bumpkins. In a word, they were false. They always had something to hide, whatever it was.

When they arrived at the pond, Professor Stern undressed and Margarita followed suit without the slightest hesitation. Stern had a glimpse of her fantastic body; big, full breasts and long, slim legs.

*Oh yes*, he said to himself, *that's my woman, but I'm much older than her, bloody hell.*

They swam all over the pond for a while, and when they got back to the shore and put on their clothes, they sat down on the grass, and Stern said, "If it wasn't for my good friend Lord Hellbridge, I wouldn't like to have anything to do with these strange, inexplicable things happening now in this country, especially as they concern the former prime ministers, and that, what's his name? Ah, Jobber, yea, he's the best, but upside down, so to speak," and he burst out laughing. "And his nickname's 'The Piggy', I've heard. A very appropriate one, indeed. What's happening in this country to make such morons recognised public figures? Ah, the end of the world is coming fast, first here, anyway, I think. And why was it you decided to join the Government's forces, darling?"

"You know, Professor Stern, it was in fact Lord Hellbridge who not only supported my application but actually persuaded me to join them," said Margarita.

"Ah, if so, I'm not surprised. Knowing him, he would even persuade the Devil himself."

"He said that Mr Oddhouse isn't a bad guy, and therefore he intended to give him assistance," said Miss Dubois.

"No, he's a good man, and that's why I understand my friend's decision," said Stern, "and he knew perfectly well who should ask me for help," and looked at Margarita, smiling.

She returned the smile and said, "So, dear Professor Stern, would you consider helping me?"

"Call me Peter, darling, and yes, I'll give you a hand."

"Thank you, Peter, and by the way, would you be so kind as to tell me about those jobs you were asked to carry out for the Russian and a few other governments. I'm dying of curiosity."

"Ah, those, okay, but in the first place, let me tell you that nothing under the sun happens without the knowledge of that eternal power, whatever it's called. And those incidents you ask me about happened where they happened because those countries deserved them to happen."

"And what do you mean by that?" asked Margarita.

"You know, each country has its own destination, its fate, and a country can do nothing about it. However, sometimes that eternal power may decide to change the course of a country's fate, and I have some skills, so to speak, to talk to that power. But I don't have a clue why it's me, and not somebody else." And Stern looked up in the sky, smiled and said, "Yea, this is something I don't have a clue about."

"But how come you know whether to assist them or not?" asked Margarita.

"I don't know that, either. You know, I've got some knowledge, but there are things I don't know anything about, and this is one of them. Usually, when something very strange and disturbing happens somewhere in the world, and a country's government asks me for help, I have a dream, and in that dream, I am told what to do, and that's it. So, next morning, I begin to carry out what I've been told."

"Hmm, that's interesting indeed," said Margarita, "and what about that mysterious power you mentioned? Do you have a clue what it is?"

"No, I don't, and it always makes me laugh whenever some blockhead claims he knows something about that power, writes a long treatise about it, and there are even some who have claimed to see God in person, and those are the worst and most dangerous, and as a matter of fact, they commit blasphemy according to their own faith principles.

"Now, as for my assistance you mentioned, I'll tell you what I heard before I decided to accept the Russian president's request to carry out an inquiry. Not only Moscow, but it was known in other parts of Russia, and abroad for that matter, that something very unusual, so to speak, was going on at Patriarch's Pond at the time. But it wasn't just about the place, but those incidents had a serious impact on many spheres of life in the country. And it was due to the fact that several eminent people, including politicians, military men, artists, poets and men of literature altogether fell under the spell of a mysterious power while having a stroll in that lovely and popular garden park.

"While they were enjoying their walk, they happened to meet a mysterious man, whose identity is still unknown despite a very intensive investigation, and after having a conversation with him, their behaviour and actions were very unusual, and even irrational, as some people described them.

"For instance, a very famous poet who wrote numerous panegyric lyrics about the current state of affairs in the country, having spoken to that man, began writing very different stuff. Eventually a ban was imposed on his poems. Nevertheless, the damage was done.

"A politician, great patriot and a close associate of the president, after his conversation with the man in question, became something very opposite. In his speeches at the Duma, he revealed his deep outrage at his former friend's politics, and eventually due to some back-door machinations had to resign his mandate. But again, it was done too late, for his stance had a substantial effect on society.

"And the worse was to come. A high-ranking security official, after returning home from his walk in the Patriarch's Ponds, packed his suitcase and went to a very remote monastery to become a monk.

"But what a certain general did was the last straw for the president. The general, a very upright man and a strict disciplinarian, once he was back in his regiment after a stroll in the park, gathered all his soldiers, telling them about the virtues of pacifism and peace, suggesting a one-sided disarmament of the Russian armed forces. After the speech, he was considered mentally unstable and put in a psychiatric hospital. But it wasn't the end of the story. His passionate speech had an enormous impact on his subordinates, and quite a few of them left the army. Moreover, one of the colonels recorded the general's address, which was transcribed and then thousands of copies were effectively published by samizdat.

"All in all, Sodom and Gomorrah, and this time the president came close for the first time in his life to having a heart attack. But with super-human strength he overcame his indisposition, ordering all available security services, the police, whosoever, to begin an urgent investigation, for it was the highest national security matter to find what the Devil had happened to those hitherto trusted and reliable men. The investigation was an enormous affair, and even several very effective spies who were diligently working abroad at the time were immediately called back to Moscow."

And now, let's hear how the investigation proceeded. Only highly experienced FSB officers and other security services were selected for the job, and the first thing to do was to identify what or who caused that terrible havoc. It was assumed the above-mentioned individuals met someone at Patriarch's Pond, and apparently the encounter so traumatised their psyche that they were transformed into their very opposite. It was a Russian version of turning Dr Jekyll into Mr Hyde.

The first thing to do was to put the place under very sophisticated electronic and human surveillance. Helicopters were hovering day and night high above Patriarch's Pond, filming everything on the ground, and numerous agents under deep cover were watching the place. Their disguise was a masterpiece of the art of surveillance. It was simply impossible for anybody to associate them with anything other than they pretended to be.

Thus, for instance, a certain officer disguised himself as a litter bin, and so perfectly that a garbage truck collected it, putting him then into the truck's container, and only the poor guy's ear-tearing shrieks saved him from a terrible end there.

In turn, his colleague, a beefy and muscular man, was disguised as a babushka. However, it didn't convince everybody because of his huge bulk, for nobody had ever seen such a bodybuilder babushka.

Another officer pretended to be a beggar. But then his disguise was so perfect that he was arrested for vagrancy and put under arrest, and nothing, including his ID, persuaded the police officers that he was, in fact, somebody else.

But the mentioned officers' activities brought no results, and it was only a satellite camera that caught something odd. And it was a picture of a tall man wearing a black beret, and despite the day's heat, gloves. It was immediately certain he was a foreigner, and instantly the best of the best, the Alpha troops, were dispatched to catch him. They rushed at tremendous speed to the place where the suspect was spotted, and some of them, being in such a hurry to become the day's heroes, fell into the pond. Anyway, their efforts came to nothing. The foreigner vanished into thin air. And that is why Professor Stern was contacted by the Russian

Embassy and asked to come to Moscow to help the authorities, who were now in total despair. The embassy officials already knew who he was, for his exploits were known all over the world, and knew where Stern was living, but the problem was the lack of any telephone or computer contact with him, and they wouldn't dare disturb him coming in person to his cottage for they knew how he valued privacy.

The problem was mysteriously solved by a telephone call from no other than Lord Hellbridge, who somehow knew about the issue (they tried to find out how the hell he did, because the affair was a state secret, but they failed) and offered his assistance. He told them he was a very good friend of Stern, and ready to give them a hand in contacting the professor. He invited the Russian ambassador to his apartment to discuss the matter in question. The ambassador brought with him a letter from the president, for he was the first to be informed about Lord Hellbridge's offer. In his letter, the president was full of praise for the lord's achievements, begged him to help, and of course invited him to visit Moscow.

Now, a few words about the lord's friendship with Stern, and the latter's other incredible exploits all over the world.

They had known each other forever and very often met to discuss some matters about which we unfortunately never knew too much. However, it was known that the lord was a renowned authority on religion and he travelled the world to study it, his favourite place being Tibet, where his insight was held in great esteem. Not just once had the Dalai Lama himself sought his advice regarding the interpretation of some mysterious passages in the *Book of the Dead*, the *Tripitaka* and *Mahayana Sutras*, and while in Tibet, the lord went for long excursions alone in the mountains. It was considered of course very dangerous, especially in winter, and what was most incredible about it was that Hellbridge never wore proper climber's gear and had no tent. Moreover, he never took any food with him, saying that what he found in nature would do. But nothing bad ever happened to him, and when the Dalai Lama was told about the manner of the lord's escapades, he just smiled, saying that apparently some higher power protected him. Tibet was definitely his favourite place, and he always stayed there as a guest of a remote monastery, what was a bit unusual for he was actually a layperson.

The Chinese government was worried about his travels there, but after the lord had a word with the president of the country, he even didn't need permission to visit Tibet, and already the officials over there were told not to bother him whatever he did.

We must notice here that Hellbridge was a very open-minded man, and always ready to discuss anything as regards religion and faith anywhere and with anyone, for he was not prejudiced at all. For him to be either in the Vatican or a synagogue didn't make any difference. However, both the Pope and the Chief Rabbi were rather disturbed by some of Hellbridge's discoveries, which were numerous contradictions he found in the *Bible* and the *Torah*, and begged the lord not to make them public. He agreed for in his opinion it might lead to unnecessary and unwelcome confusion. Anyway, he never ever took sides, always remaining neutral whatever he dealt with, on principle, saying that to judge is to be unjust.

As we have already mentioned, Tibet was his place to travel. However, it was Zarathustra's teachings he valued most, and his interpretations of Avesta were so amazing that experts didn't rule out that he might have known Friedrich in person, which of course was out of the question. Anyway, what we don't know, we don't, and that's that.

The friendship between the lord and Stern was very firm, despite the differences in their views on certain matters, and actually they quarrelled frequently but this never affected their respect and trust for one another.

The Russian authorities came to the conclusion they would ask Stern for help only after their meticulous inquiry into his previous accomplishments. Initially, they were very reluctant to invite him to investigate the matter in question for they thought their own formidable intelligence service would do, but apparently, they overrated it. However, the service learned, for instance, about the so-called 'Ghost of the Sistine Chapel' that haunted the place, and nothing could be done about it. Neither prayers nor exorcisms had helped, and the ghost had kept disturbing the holy city until the Pope eventually, though very reluctantly, had made the decision to contact Professor Stern, who sorted out the problem in just one day, but how he managed to do so is still a mystery.

Anyway, in recognition of that, he was awarded the Order of the Golden Spur and a special grand Mass was celebrated at which the Pope himself asked God to keep the professor in His care.

When the Russian president was informed about the incident in question, he immediately called the Head of the Russian Orthodox Church, Patriarch Timofyey III, to ask him for advice. The patriarch, during a very long conversation with the president, pointed out irreconcilable differences between Catholicism and their faith, saying that what had worked in the Vatican wouldn't in Moscow, and refused to give his consent to Professor Stern's arrival there. Until then, the cooperation between the patriarch and president had been so good that it had been taken for granted that the president would totally abandon his previous beliefs and wholeheartedly adapt to the Orthodox faith. And actually, it might have been the case, but now facing the stubborn patriarch, he had no choice but to issue a decree that obliged the patriarch to comply.

Another argument in the president's favour for calling Professor Stern was the story of one of the toughest and remorseless leaders of his country who was wise enough to save from troubles a certain author of a novel in which it was proved beyond doubt (it was the so-called Seventh Proof, explained in a manuscript that couldn't have been burnt) that neither high walls nor numerous guards or security services would have protected him from that unknown unearthly power if he had made a wrong decision and let the writer perish.

The president also knew as well about what had happened in Saudi Arabia, also ruled by a hard-hearted sovereign who had had no choice but to call the professor when his country had been tormented by the Ghost of Kaaba, and the monarch's own formidable security could do nothing about it.

Terrible things were happening which had shaken the state to its core. For instance, Saudi Arabian women, who until then had been so submissive and complied with the Sharia Law, had turned into something very opposite. Many of them were seen in public wearing nothing but bikinis, and had held demonstrations demanding equal rights. Nobody had been spared trouble, and the king himself, whose residence had been a fortress, hadn't prevented the ghost from entering, and even in his bedroom the king had no peace. He eventually agreed with his commander-in-chief's idea that two very fit commandos should be stationed under his bed to keep guard, but once they had seen the bedroom door open at midnight by an invisible hand, and a transparent thin silhouette coming into the room, they had immediately fled. For their cowardice, they had been sentenced to death by beheading, but then when the monarch had had a conversation with the Head of the Wahhabi Religion Estate, they had been paroled, because the religious leader had persuaded the monarch to do so, telling him that the death sentence would have made the matter even worse for, as far as he knew, the ghost was not a bloodthirsty individual. And it was he who recommended Professor Stern to the sovereign, and one day he arrived in the country's capital, his only luggage being a rather small rucksack and a tent. A six-star hotel was already booked for him, but he put up his tent instead in the desert, just asking for fresh water, some simple food and Budvar and Weihenstephaner beer, and that appeared to be a serious problem because of the ban on alcohol in the country. But the problem was solved by the same high priest who granted a special dispensation allowing Stern to drink beer while on his mission, and a plane was immediately dispatched to the Czech Republic to fetch the beer, and another one to Freistaat Bayern to get Weihenstephaner. The professor asked as well to pass his best on to the Herzog von Bayern.

In the mentioned case, Professor Stern was rewarded handsomely too. The king awarded him the Order of King Abdul-Aziz and granted him citizenship without the usual compulsory conversion to Islam, and of course once a month a special royal plane arrived in England delivering Budvar and Weihenstephaner for the professor, and thanks to that, he could save some money.

# MOSCOW REVISITED

'The limits of my imagination
mean the limits of my world.'
C.D.

And now back in London, at eleven in the morning, a rather nervous Russian ambassador came to see Lord Hellbridge at his apartment in Kensington, and the lord himself opened the door, inviting him inside. They sat down in rather old but anyway not-antique armchairs, and on the table nearby there already stood a big carafe, filled with Stolichnaya vodka. The ambassador wondered how the hell the lord knew that precisely at this time of the day he was in the habit of drinking it.

The lord poured a good measure of the vodka in large, seemingly unbreakable glasses, for he also knew the other man's habit of smashing a glass on the floor after each toast.

"*Prosit,*" said the lord, raising his glass, and they drank up, and this time the ambassador somehow managed restraining himself from smashing his glass, already knowing the lord's impeccable manners, not wanting to be taken by a yokel just before such an important conversation.

"How are things in Moscow? How is the president?" asked Hellbridge.

"Ah, very good, sir, we work hard to improve things," said the guest.

"Do you?" said the lord, smiling.

The ambassador was immediately taken aback by such an abrupt beginning, but tried his best to keep calm at any cost, for he knew how crucial his visit was for the future of his country. That's why he said, "But of course, however, we sometimes obviously encounter a problem, but considering our boss' efficiency, it is always sorted out at tremendous speed."

"Hmm," began Hellbridge, "but you might be in a hurry going in the wrong direction after all, dear sir, if you know what I mean."

The ambassador was again staggered by such an abrupt conclusion, but with super-human effort, again prevented himself giving any hasty response, saying, "No, I'm very sorry, but I don't understand, sir."

"Let me explain, *dorogoy* Stepan Ivanovich," "everything depends on a criterion we use evaluating our deeds, and yours seems to be, hmm, rather egoistical, so to speak."

*What the Devil!* thought the ambassador. *How come we knew nothing about the lord speaking such impeccable Russian, without the slightest trace of an accent? I must tell the president and suggest him giving a dressing-down to those bloody intelligence agents of ours. How could they miss that information? Those imbeciles! Ah, they used to be far better. Those were happy days!*

"I'm again terribly sorry, milord, but I don't really know—"

He didn't manage to finish, for the lord chipped in, saying, "The point is you do, you do, my dear chap, and now the question is what's next?"

The ambassador was now totally perplexed. Nobody ever called him 'dear chap'. Even his close friends wouldn't dare. Yes, in the past, some had addressed him 'dorogoy tovarisch', but never a chap.

And now he was thinking hard how to respond to the lord's enquiry, but the other saved him from trouble, saying, "Let me put it shortly, for what can be said at all can be said in three words, as a certain philosopher, Ludwig Wittgenstein, rightly observed, so 'divide et impera', this is your criterion. But I suspect you still don't have a clue what I mean because you are of the so-called old guard. I unfortunately have to say now more than just three words.

"You have divided the nation between those who eagerly submit to the power, that's the president, and those who are supposed to submit to his rule. In other words, this is in fact autocracy of a sort, and in the long run, it's not good for your country, but you don't care, for what is important is your own mutual admiration society of like-minded colleagues which forms a caste system based on mutual protection. In consequence, you aim at depriving your people of the individual freedom of spirit and passion, turning them into meek serfs instead. All in all, it makes your country weaker in the long run, but you are so short-sighted, you can't see it, for all you care about is power, not your people's well-being, and you still believe that somehow, miraculously, the power of the state will replace so many citizens' poverty, which was the case under your previous rulers, the tyranny of riff-raff that discarded all moral principles. But remember, no cause whatsoever is worth the spilling of human blood."

If it wasn't for where the ambassador was now, he would do something very different, but now keeping in mind the objective of his mission, he just said, "You know, sir, we do have some, hmm, problems, but there isn't any better solution at the moment. You know, considering our history, our people's thinking, we could hardly do anything else."

"You could if you would, remembering that man doesn't live by bread alone, and that's it. But enough of politics for now, and tell me, what do you expect from my best friend, Professor Stern?"

The ambassador was greatly relieved by that sudden change of topic and hastened to say, "Sir, in the first place, we want to thank you for your kind offer to contact your friend, and we do hope, knowing his incredible skills, he will help us for, to be honest, for the first time during his presidency our leader is rather confused. We would be much obliged if your esteemed friend could spare some of his precious time and visit us as soon as possible. He will, of course, be appropriately rewarded for his priceless expertise, whatever the expense might be. Thank you again, your Lordship, and now I'm impatiently waiting for your kind response."

As we can see, the ambassador was at his possible best, for he knew perfectly well what he might expect back in Moscow if he failed his mission.

"Hmm," began the Lord, "I am after all, inclined to help you for I still believe in your people's innate, that is, truly independent, passion, and I'll contact my friend and I believe he'll agree to come to your country."

The ambassador was greatly relieved and began saying all over again, "Thank you, sir, thank you so much."

So, eventually Hellbridge got tired of it and said, "That's enough, you may thank somebody else, in fact."

"And who's that?" enquired the other.

"You wouldn't know even if I told you, and now if you'll excuse me, I have somebody else waiting to see me. Bulky, see the gentleman off," he called, and in an instant, a big black cat entered the room, and the ambassador froze because at the same moment he remembered a certain novel he'd read years ago in which appeared the very same character, and he thought, *But no, it can't be the same, just a coincidence.*

"Follow my faithful companion," said the Lord, "*i vsego horosheo, dorogoy* Stepan Ivanovich, and keep in mind that there are more things in heaven and earth you could see if you were a bit wiser, and that whatever we see could be other than it is."

The ambassador followed the cat, who opened the door for him and then looked him straight in the eye, and the president's envoy felt a cold shiver run down his spine, and he said to himself, *Pomiluyte, Gospodi! Yes, that's the same one.*

*

Shortly afterwards, Professor Stern arrived in Moscow.

At the Sheremetyevo, he was welcomed by none other than the foreign secretary of the Russian Federation, Victor Stepanovich Razumovsky. That was a bit unusual, for a private visitor had never before been awarded such an honour, but it was the president's idea, who wanted Stern to know how they appreciated his visit.

"Welcome to Russia, dear Professor Stern," said the secretary. "Have you had a nice flight?"

"No, I haven't," said the distinguished guest. "I hate flying on planes. I love flying in my imagination, if you know what I mean."

"Certainly, I do, professor," replied the other. "You will do us a great honour staying at the Kremlin, where a splendid room is awaiting you."

But, as we noticed before, Stern agreed to stay in the Kremlin, not in a room but outside in its grounds.

"First things first," he said to the secretary, "I'd like a sip of Budvar or Weihenstephaner."

"Budvar, Weihenstephaner?" the minister stammered. "Eh, but if you forgive me, what's that?"

Stern looked sternly at him, apparently very upset, and said, "It is something I never work without, for it stimulates my mind, giving me ideas I would have never had without it. And I'm very disappointed you don't know what it is. Your superb intelligence didn't tell you well in advance about that?"

"I… I'm terribly sorry, professor," said his host, and said to himself, *I don't even want to imagine what the president will do to them, those spooks of ours, once he learns about such a blunder, not finding out what those bloody beers are.*

"They're my favourite beers that I can't live without," Stern informed the ignorant official.

"Yes, of course, and I'm certain they are available in our capital, somewhere, anyway."

"I have a feeling we'll get them at a kiosk at Patriarch's Pond. Can we go there?"

"But of course, dear professor, wherever you wish." And he immediately ordered the driver to head for the Pond.

When they got there, this time there was plenty of beer, including the professor's beloved ones.

And the selling woman was very nice to them, and very pretty too. They bought the beer and sat down on a bench not far from the kiosk.

"You see, there must be a reason for that ghost's visit in your country," said Stern, after having a first sip of his beer.

"There might be, but we wouldn't have a clue, to be honest," said Victor Stepanovich.

"No, you wouldn't, and that's the point," Stern said, nodding, and continued, "and before I begin my inquiry, let me tell you something. His visit might be a warning."

"A warning?" exclaimed the official, "but what would it be about, anyway? We don't care much about any warnings."

"I know you don't, but this time I'd suggest you take it very seriously, dear Victor Stepanovich."

"We, of course, highly appreciate your advice, but I don't really know why that – how shall I put it, eh – our unexpected visitor, would need to warn us?"

"Bah," said the professor, "I have some ideas which I'll share with you. So, I presume that ghost, as you call him, might be displeased with some matters in your country, as he is with other places in the world, for as far as I know, he never takes sides, being totally impartial. Now, your current state of affairs compared to some other countries is rather poor regarding the citizens' well-being, their liberties and quality of life. But of course, your country hasn't had as much time as they have to improve the matters in question, and therefore it's not entirely your own fault. However, as your fearless compatriot Mikhail said, without liberty, I cannot imagine anything truly human, and without it there's no life, but you seem not to understand that. You believe in the concentration of all the strength of society in the State. You disregard freedom on principle, and consequently squander that strength in its service. But what is your final aim in the end? Power for power's sake? But this would be a sort of a vicious circle, wouldn't it? And what is the ultimate criterion of everything you do? Certainly not the well-being of your people, for the way you rule it cannot be achieved because your rule turns people into nothing but submissive robots, and as such, they are deprived of humane feelings towards one another, kindness, which is ultimately what man as such needs, and that is the synonym of goodness.

"And that ghost haunting you now has come to point to the misdeeds you do, and in this way, to remind you there is the absolute criterion of our deeds, which lies outside the world and constitutes its sense. Otherwise, there would not be any objective standards of right and wrong, and all things would be permitted, and if so, human life would have no sense at all. That absolute criterion is known under many different names, but in the end, it proves that a human being has needs wherever he lives. However, man's somewhat limited-in-intelligence mind cannot grasp the essence of that power. Ultimately, if he wants to accept himself, to say 'yes' to his existence, he should submit himself to that power even if it is a mere creation of his imagination. This is actually about the very existential questions, about how to solve the problem of life, which is finally solved only when man appreciates it as it is, which is to say 'yes' to it. And even those who apparently ignore these existential questions cannot in fact stop asking them in their innate language. But only then, when we become aware of our inner thoughts, do we become what we are, that is, true human beings. You should remember that a bad man, that is, who does harm to his fellow human beings, in truth acts against himself.

There might be some other issues of which someone somewhere decided to warn you, and remember, nobody knows what will happen to him the next day."

For a good few minutes, Stepan Ivanovich said nothing in response, but eventually somehow managed to overcome this unexpected weakness of his reason, and announced, "All that is pure western propaganda to discredit our government for its tenacious will to maintain our truly independent policy, and not to submit to or be manipulated by Dollaria and its vassals"

"Yes, *dorogoy* Stepan Ivanovich, I did expect such an answer, but facts are really stubborn things, and word-tricks cannot change them at all as you'll see sooner or later. Yes, you are right saying that there's a case of conspiracy of a sort aimed at your country. And it's true that so-called democracy is an overused and therefore an abused word, and their never-ending rambling about that is a pack of trivialities. And I tell you in confidence that the power I mentioned is very likely to pay them a visit too, for they aren't as blameless as they think they are. Oh no, dear Stepan Ivanovich, they aren't, and that's why they will be reminded of it and accordingly receive a well-deserved dressing-down.

"Now, as you know perfectly well, man can imagine anything but..." here Stern gave a pause, and then continued, "...but two things, eternity and infinity. You agree with me of course, don't you?"

Stepan Ivanovich said nothing, just nodded. Anyway, he seemed to be in a rather gloomy mood now, which might have been due to Stern's just delivered lecture on philosophy.

"Yes, these things are mysterious indeed, and at the same time they prove how limited man's intelligence is. However, some men somehow manage to envision them, and that proves that some of them aren't or might not be that stupid after all. And this is of little consolation, isn't it?" And Stern looked at the now visibly depressed Russian Confederation's foreign secretary, who remained silent, so the professor continued, "Yes, it is, but this is not enough to make people happy, that is, to be pleased with themselves. Bah, that longing for happiness, it sometimes turns into a nightmare. You long for it, talking incessantly about it, and in the end, you are empty-handed. And all these stupid lyrics about it, I can't listen to them. You know, in a word, they're about something man will never get. Or that stupid country music, the same tune all over again, and their moaning, the Irish being the worst. And here I must pay you a compliment. You're very good singers, and that proves the strength of your spirit, which is, by the way, a mixture of gentleness and ferocity. Anyway, you don't seem to be just those self-serving English bloody shopkeepers, and obsessed by money as their Irish neighbours are. By the way, the latter blame the former for the misdeeds they suffered under English rule, but now they don't seem to be much better themselves. Anyway, they have incorporated almost all things English into their now seemingly independent country, so what actually is their independence about?

"But I now distract myself talking about matters I'm not really interested in. So, *zu dem Sachen selbst*, as Edmund always reminded us.

"What was I talking about? Ah yes, eternity and infinity. You know, of course, neither of them have anything to do with the facts, do they? No, of course not."

Now, apparently after hearing some compliments about his country, Stepan Ivanovich seemed to recover some optimism, and said, "Of course they don't whatsoever."

"I'm happy you agree with me," said Stern, and continued his consideration, "no, they don't, so we can see that these bloody facts, excuse my language, are just relative, accidental beings we cannot trust at all, and some wiser people, like the immortal Ludwig, can see that the facts all contribute to setting the problem, not to its solution, and that discovery disappoints many a man. But they stick to them after all, those stubborn blockheads. They should be ashamed of themselves, but they aren't. They are actually proud of their stupidity and there's the rub. Yes, I know that ignoring facts seems to be rather strange, but strangeness is my business after all, dear Stepan Ivanovich.

"Anyway, to my mind, everything is strange and I will renounce my opinion under no circumstances. And this is because actually we can't trust facts, you know. They might be very different tomorrow. We should believe in something solid, lasting, that we can rely on, and facts, what use are they in this respect? Nothing, Nil! And all that takes us back to that power again. It seems to value something permanent, even eternal, that is infinite. And I believe the ghost who's visiting you is part of that power."

Stepan Ivanovich now looked petrified, and thought, *What a bloody mess we're in*, but then he overcame his sudden idealistic angle, and thought, *no, what is he talking about? That ghost of ours must be a mere charlatan who has somehow succeeded in hypnotising us, and that's it.* However, he still wasn't too sure of himself, but somehow managed to pull himself together and said, "Yes, we regained our ancient faith, but according to our interpretation of that power, it would have never bothered to visit us in person."

"Ah, all those interpretations," said Stern, "I'm so tired of them, dear Stepan Ivanovich, that I almost stopped believing what is said in the *Bible*, and any other holy scripture for that matter. Anyway, none of them, as my friend Lord Hellbridge says, tell us anything about the true nature of the power."

"Excuse me, professor," interrupted Stepan, "but how would he know that?"

"Bah, an excellent question," Professor Stern said, smiling. "The fact is he knows that first hand."

"First hand?" exclaimed Stepan. "How come? That's impossible."

"Impossible, you say? No, nothing is difficult for him to do, dear Stepan Ivanovich, believe me, and you may find it out yourself someday in the future."

"And how long, may I ask, have you known the lord?"

"I've known him forever," said Stern.

"Forever? What do you mean?"

"I mean that I was already sure of his presence before we met in person."

"Excuse me again, but now I understand nothing."

"Small wonder you don't, for to know that, you would have had to have a revelation, because this is the only way to know something about the powers we are talking about. In other words, you can only grasp them *sub specie aeternitatis*, and not just believing what is written about them. All those wise writings are just words, and nothing but words, and those powers exist beyond words, believe me. Otherwise, they wouldn't be there. And, for instance, all these concepts of evil, calling it the Devil, Satan, Mephistopheles or Lucifer, they're actually ridiculous and useless and tell you nothing. We humans, in our very limited intellectual capacity, know nothing about them unless we are blessed by the ability to see them in a vision that has nothing to do with words. You know, this kind of vision is familiar to me because astrology is my thing. Anyway, to see the world aright is to see it without using words, but man unfortunately for himself believes in them too much, and that's why he's always been in trouble. And this is because he uses so many words. His interpretations never end, and in the end, he knows as much as he knew before. In this respect, his life is a never-ending vicious circle. And the real problem is that he is still so sure of himself. His arrogance has no limits but it may someday in the future make him liable to perish. As Charles put it, 'The problem with the world is that the intelligent people are full of doubts, while the stupid ones full of confidence.' And that's it."

Stepan Ivanovich this time said nothing. He was sitting there thinking, *Damn it all. I understand nothing of that, but I still have a feeling as if I believe it. Strange, it has never happened to me before.*

"You see," the professor said, interrupting Stepan's busy thinking, "it seems you are beginning to understand something because at last you say nothing."

"This is because," said Stepan, "I'm now lost, to be honest."

"Small wonder you are, but don't you worry. Albert himself would be too if he were in your shoes. But now, dear Stepan Ivanovich, I may be speaking in puzzles, and must confess my beloved mother always complained about that, but the point is that we are talking about things which don't belong to reality, which is actually very often unreal. I mean that what we take for reality today might be an illusion tomorrow, and vice versa, of course. Anyway, reality is our own invention through its sense, which we create. In other words, sense is the reality of the world, and not things as such. And now, if you say that something doesn't agree with reality, you in fact disagree with a certain interpretation of what you experience and perceive, don't you? Or, in other words, it isn't as we want it to be. And in this sense, our dear Georg Hegel is right, saying that if something doesn't agree with reality, it is much the worse for reality. You understand and agree, of course?"

Stepan, now even more confused, decided to agree to anything Professor Stern was saying, and he nodded eagerly again.

"I'm very happy you are with me, and now, for instance, let's take history. You know of course how much of it has been invented. History has been just a fable, as Napoleon rightly noticed. And, by the way, how much of your own country's history has been a pure invention? In other words, there are no facts, there are interpretations. And now, *apropos* the problem you want me to deal with, that's the ghost of Patriarch's Pond, you still believe it's an illusion, hypnosis, and all in all you don't want to accept its reality, but its reality, as I just mentioned, is its sense, so that ghost of yours might have come here to make you aware of your actual current state of affairs, so you should appreciate his visit after all. Would you be inclined to do so?"

Stepan Ivanovich, not even trying to grasp the meaning of what his learned conversationalist was saying, nodded again.

"Good, thank you," said Stern, and produced a small sheet of paper out of his pocket. "Here we are." He began looking at it. "This is a note I received just before I boarded the plane for Moscow, and it reads, *Dear friend, I should be most obliged if you could kindly announce my visit at the Kremlin. My visit will obviously be confidential, but you may inform the Russian foreign secretary so he could tell the president about my wish to see him. Your affectionate friend, W."*

And now lastly there was something Stepan Ivanovich could grasp, and he said, "Who's that, I mean, that man who plans to visit my president out of the blue, so to speak? You know, usually, any visitor has to—" but he couldn't finish the sentence because Stern interrupted him.

"That visitor does not have to do anything, believe me, and the president should consider himself lucky that the man is kind enough to announce his visit, for if he hadn't done so, his presence wouldn't be so pleasant. Anyway, I suggest you tell the president immediately about the upcoming visit, which can happen anytime, and nothing, I give you my word of honour, will prevent it from happening."

Now poor Stepan Ivanovich was totally perplexed but somehow

404

managed to stammer, "I… I don't understand. How come? Who's that friend of yours?"

"Ah, this you'll find out in due time, for at the moment I'm not allowed to tell you anything more."

"But, any visit must be announced in advance and accepted by the president himself, otherwise—"

"There isn't any 'otherwise,'" Stern firmly interrupted, "in the matter in question, and I strongly urge you treat the note very seriously."

"But the president will laugh in my face. Moreover, he may fire me on the spot."

"This won't happen, believe me. He's wise enough, as was that other man who too had been informed in advance what might happen to him if he didn't treat some information seriously."

"If you say so," said Ivan, somewhat relieved by the perspective of not losing his prestigious office, and continued, "but how am I to explain all that to the president?"

"There is no need to explain anything. He will understand, for as I've already told you, he's wise enough."

"Very well, I'm going to see him right now. Can I take the note with me to have proof, you know…?"

"But of course, here you are," said Stern, handing him the note.

Stepan Ivanovich thanked him, grabbed the piece of paper and ran to the Kremlin where he demanded to see the president, but was told that the boss was too busy to see him right now. "I understand," he said, "but this is a national security matter, and I need to see him immediately, and please show him this," he said, giving the note to the man. He said so for something convinced him that it was important enough to say so.

"Hmm," said the president's personal secretary, "if you say so. Please wait a moment," and he went to see his boss, but was told that right now a very important national security council was in progress and the president wasn't to be disturbed.

"I see," he said, "but could you at least pass this note on to him? It seems very important."

"If you insist, Igor Bogdanovich, I'll try," said the other man, and entered a grand room where the meeting was being held. All the most important ministers were gathered there discussing certain security matters, and seeing the man, the minister of defence said, "How dare you disturb us!"

But the president said, "It's all right. He wouldn't come here if it wasn't something really important."

"What's the matter?" he asked the man.

"I apologise, but I've been told it's extremely urgent," he said, handing him the note.

The president took the paper and read the message, and then going slightly pale, announced, "Dear comrades, we must unfortunately adjourn our meeting. This is an emergency matter, and I must see the foreign secretary at once."

"But, how..." protested the FSB boss... "can't it wait? I was going to present some crucial information—"

But he couldn't finish for the president said, "This is the most crucial information I just received," he said, pointing to the note on the table, "and believe me, if it wasn't, I wouldn't ask you to postpone our meeting."

Everybody present understood that it had to be something extraordinary. Otherwise, their boss wouldn't interrupt the meeting, so they thanked him and left.

The president said to the man who delivered the note, "Call the secretary now."

Ivan Ivanovich arrived at the double at the now empty, except for the president, meeting room, and said, "I do apologise, but..."

"Sit down, and tell me how you got hold of this note."

"Professor Stern gave it to me."

"Oh yes, I've heard of him, and if it was him... that must be a really serious matter, more serious than you can imagine."

"But this is such an impertinence of that man, whoever he is—."

He couldn't finish because the president chipped in. "Impertinent, you say, a funny expression under the circumstances."

"I don't understand, and I suggest to double or even triple your guards—"

But again he couldn't finish, for the president burst out laughing, saying, "You could put a tank division here and it wouldn't prevent this visitor seeing me, believe me."

"I... I'm really distressed now, and I can think of nothing but lying down to have some sleep. In my long career, I've never experienced anything like this, just a piece a paper from nobody knows whom, and—"

But again, the president didn't allow him to finish, saying, "If you only knew who you're talking about, dear Ivan Ivanovich."

"And who is he?"

"You're better off not knowing. Now go and have a nap. And let me tell you that if I told you who the author of the note is, you wouldn't be sleeping at all for a month or more."

And Ivan Ivanovich went home to have a nap, whereas the president sat down alone in his studio, wondering what the man whom he already knew pretty well expected this time from him. Vladimir Vladimirovich knew perfectly well he couldn't avoid meeting the man and, of course, didn't double or triple the number of his guards because it wouldn't make any sense. Moreover, it would make him a fool in the eyes of his coming quest.

*

Next day, after having some rather uneasy sleep, he was back in his study looking at some papers when his personal secretary knocked on the door.

"Come in," he said, and the secretary, Sasha Pavlovich, entered. It was 11.30 sharp.

"Somebody came to see you," said the secretary, looking a bit baffled, "but he didn't even introduce himself, and I don't really understand how he got in here, you know, all these guards. He was actually seen by them on the grounds before entering the main building, but for some strange reason they didn't stop him. The soldiers were just looking at him, and one of them even saluted as if the stranger was an eminent official he already knew. Crossing the grounds, the man stopped at Professor Stern's tent and had a chat with him. Then he continued to the front door, guarded by two other soldiers, and one of them, you know, that Nikita Sergeyevich, your favourite, didn't even try to stop him but bowed deeply, saluted and, standing to attention, opened the door for him."

"Ah, Nikita," said the president, "yes, he's a very clever chap, and I think he already guessed who the man was. You know, his grandfather had been a priest and taught him a few things. Anyway, let him in, please, and forget the guards or anything else."

Sasha Pavlovich, somewhat puzzled, said nothing in response and held the door open for the visitor who, coming in, said to the president, "It's a pleasure to see you again, dear Vladimir Vladimirovich, and it is very kind of you to allow me to come at such short notice."

"Never mind, sir. Please sit down, and what can I do for you?"

"Hmm, this time, it's about something decisive for you and your country."

"I guessed as much," said the president. "Otherwise, you wouldn't be here."

"No, I wouldn't, and to be honest, I rarely travel these days, you know, that problem with my knee."

"Ah yes! Isn't it getting better? You know, we have excellent specialists here, and if you wish…"

"No, no, thank you for your concern, but I'm already tired of all doctors. Maybe another time."

"As you wish, sir, and I'm listening."

"You know, passing through the grounds outside, I had a word with a very good friend of mine, Professor Stern, who's visiting you regarding a ghost or something."

The president decided to play along, despite knowing that his guest knew perfectly well what it was about, and said, "Ah yes, we had some unexplained incidents in Moscow, but now it's quiet again."

"Quiet, you say, very good, and you don't expect any more disturbances? You know, that's the problem with unexplained phenomena. You never know what comes next."

"No, no, everything's all right, and Professor Stern here was of great help, and we are very thankful to him."

"Oh yes, his knowledge is unsurpassable. Even I myself think that he may know more than I do as regards some matters over there," and the visitor raised his eyes towards the skies.

"More than you?" said Vladimirovich, slightly smiling, "I doubt it, to be honest."

"Maybe not more. Anyway, his expertise on the Constellation of Stars is amazing, and I'm pretty sure he gave you some precious advice regarding that ghost among other things."

"Oh yes, he did," replied the president.

"And, if I may enquire, what did he say?"

"The professor said just one thing: 'When you don't understand something, do nothing at all', and this was *apropos* that ghost on Patriarch's Pond."

"Very wise of him. This is exactly what I would expect from him, and I must congratulate him again. Yes, that's it, if you deal with some unexplained phenomena, say and do nothing, then you may understand their nature. In other words, the rest is silence. You know, people talk too much, as if they were trying to talk themselves down. And what makes things even worse, they talk but say nothing. A tautology is first of all pleasures these days as our wise Soren remarked. Ah, he was such an authority on religion, and a discussion with him about the subject is always a pure delight."

"I'm sure it is," said the president, but your knowledge of the subject…"

"Yes, yes, of course, not to boast myself, I know something about this or that, and by the way, what about you, dear Vladimir Vladimirovich? Are you still interested in the subject in question?"

"Oh yes, more and more, and I visit some monasteries quite often, and have begun to understand that story, even if it's not true, about one of the tsars who renounced his power and went to live in a monastery."

"Oh yes, I too understand him and admire his decision. And what about yourself? Have you ever considered following in his footsteps and settling down, for instance, at that beautiful Valaam Monastery?"

The president exclaimed in his mind, *Pomiluyte gospodi, this is the reason he's come to see* me!

"You know, before coming here, I had a consultation with somebody, but unfortunately can't tell you who it was for he wished to remain anonymous, and we fully agreed on a certain point, that is that you don't deserve light but you actually deserve peace, and you will never get it unless you leave this place," and the president's guest looked around, and said, "yes, a very impressive place, indeed."

"Yes, I see," said Vladimir Vladimirovich, "but I have a mission, my country needs me."

"Hmm, it might have needed you a while back under the circumstances, which as always are neglected in that ridiculous propaganda in some other countries, but now, old man, it's time to quit. You want it yourself deep in your heart, don't you?"

The president was deep in thought, now seeing himself in the wilderness he loved so much, its peace and quiet, and those little wooden churches and monasteries hidden there, and said to himself, *He might be right after all.*

"You seem to agree with me, dear friend, and I'm happy about that, so are you ready?"

"I think I am, but, of course, I have to put some things in order first."

"But of course, *obezatyelno*, and actually I, myself, would be most grateful if you could help me regarding a small issue."

"Whatever you wish, sir, I'm at your service," and saying this was another proof of the president's wisdom.

"Most obliged, and it is a rather small matter, but still a bit annoying. It concerns an association of a sort called M7, and you've actually heard of them. You remember my consultants' visit a while ago, don't you?"

"Of course I do, how could I forget them? And thank you again for that magnificent present, that wonderful machine, sir."

"Has it been of any use, dear friend?"

"Oh yes, it has, and we still benefit having it."

"Great, but please remember not to overuse it, as my assistant already cautioned you."

"But of course, I would never dare contradict your kind counsel," Mikhail Vladimirovich said eagerly. "But tell me, please," he continued, "what about my counterpart? You know who I mean."

"Ah yes, you mean, 'The Trumpet', or 'The Twit' as he's called, Dollaria's president. Don't you worry, be assured you won't be disappointed with him, and he will eventually fulfil his life's dream soon."

"And what is it if I may enquire?" asked the president.

"Ah, he will soon become the Salvation Army general, and a renowned trumpeter. I've just signed his promotion papers."

"How wonderful and very kind of you, sir, and I'm sure he'll be very happy."

"Maybe not at the very beginning, but eventually he will, I'll see to it."

"That's very generous of you, sir, and I wish him my best."

"I'll pass your wishes on to him, and I'm glad you, yourself, are so magnanimous."

"All the pleasure's mine, but please tell me, what about his obliging cousins?"

"Ah, those shopkeepers across the ocean. Hmm, I'll deal with them accordingly. In the end, everyone gets what they deserve. And what annoys me most is their ignorance as regards black magic, which by the way, is not so black, because it metes out justice, if you know what I mean."

"I certainly do, sir, and actually always understand it."

"Yes, I know you do, but they, unfortunately for themselves, don't, and that's why they'll get what they deserve. And it is related to the aforementioned M7. They, as a matter of fact, make me laugh, thinking they can even deceive the Devil himself. What short-sighted people they are, unbelievable!"

"Oh yes, they are. I know something about that, looking back at our own history," exclaimed the president. "Nothing counts for them but money, and for it, they'd proverbially sell their own mothers, something we, ourselves, would never do."

"I know that, and appreciate it. You aren't short of the spirit, and they are, and that's why they've never had great composers or painters, for they aren't able to understand, to envision eternity and infinity, which are actually one and the same. And that politeness of theirs, of which they are so proud… it is in fact a way to deceive you, to hide their true motive, which is their financial interest in anything they touch. But it is a madness of sorts, isn't it? You know, money for money's sake, that's ridiculous! Money – what for? They say it is needed to be happy in their sick thinking. This is upside-down logic, so to speak, isn't it? And this is because by reason of his nature, man cannot be happy unless he's altruistic, self-denying and self-sacrificing, for only then can he be trusted, reliable and noble. Otherwise, he will always betray you when it comes to money. And their nobility is a fake, a mask, as is their happiness, and therefore they talk so much about it, as if they knew they will never get it, the main reason being that they lack the ability to think abstractly, and as you know perfectly well, *non in solo pane vivit homo*, and I mean not exactly the religious sense of it. You Russians possess that ability and the other Slavs do, and therefore the author I admire, our dear Albert, says that on the scale of nations' ranking, you come second to the Mediterranean peoples, and they come last. They have never had great composers, philosophers or painters, which proves their lack of spirit that is the soul of civilisation's worth, and which actually makes them unable to believe in God. They have no other ethic but money, and they're actually proud of that, as they are in fact proud of their perfidy. And you know what? We could in fact paraphrase that *Bible*'s passage about the rich being unable to go through a needle, and say the same about them. They admire what their ex-PM, what was his name, ah, that Palmerston, said about the permanent interests of his country, by which he meant money. But at the same time, they consider themselves Christian, as 'The Preacher', another ex-PM has always boasted. As far as I know, their addressee, so to speak, isn't too happy about that, and actually asked me to do something about that, and I obviously will, on principle, dear Mikhail Vladimirovich."

"Yes, certainly on principle, because you're a man of principle, sir."

"Thank you, dear friend, and to say a few words more, ah yes, almost forgotten, that Christianity of theirs, a laughing stock, they don't believe in the Devil, either, which makes everything even worse. And when they eventually find out he does exist, they'll be very disappointed, I guarantee that. As will be their neighbours, but I don't mean France, of course. Those neighbours, despite having been on such bad terms with the English in their troubled past, have finally became almost like them, and therefore they both now enjoy mutual understanding, especially in economic matters.

"Ah, enough of that. It's a tiresome business to talk about the subject. It always makes me tired, you know," said the president's visitor.

"Certainly, it does, and that's why I kindly suggest we switch to something different."

"Yes, high time to consider something else," said Mr W. "However, there's something else regarding your country's international relations that bothers me, and therefore let me say a few words about that.

412

"Now, I want to put some things clearly, and not hide them in quasi-clever rambling, these word-tricks of their learned impostors who do their best to cover up the actual state of affairs, I mean, the West's constant mumbling about democracy, humanism and human rights. Fortunately, I own neither a TV set nor a radio, so I'm spared most of that rambling. However, willy-nilly, so to speak, I can't avoid being disturbed by those trivialities of theirs. Thus, for instance, they find fault with almost everything in your country but appear not to see what's happening in their own territories. And I especially mean here the pride and glory of the UK's democracy, which to my mind looks rather gloomy these days. For what kind of a democratic country is it where such income inequality occurs, where there are the greatest numbers of CCTV cameras existing anywhere in the world, a justification for it being their security and safety? That's total rubbish, and their hypocrisy is well-known, for the cameras are actually for something very different, and I mean their psychological effect on the public. You, a supposed free citizen of the country, have the feeling of being watched all the time, thus, involuntarily, it turns you into something very opposite – an obedient, meek fellow, whose only freedom consists in quasi-clever relentless useless mumbling, of saying tautologies all over again. And that ceaseless talking is the only consolation of the so-called free citizen, and our dear Soren had already noticed the beginning of that a long time ago. All in all, people over there have no ideas of their own. They just repeat what they're told by their idiot-boxes. But they're still bragging of being free, and yes, they are, but free-serfs, in a word, for the only freedom I know is liberty of spirit, independence of the mind, self-responsibility, insight, courage and pride, which is everything they lack themselves. Moreover, I'm not sure whether they still understand the meaning of these words, probably not.

"Another kind of boasting is their claimed unprejudiced views on anything under the sun, but I, myself, am sure that that sun of theirs has already set for good. They live in a darkness they seem not to notice – the darkness of ignorance, clichés and trivialities. And it concerns, among other things, your country, dear Vladimir Vladimirovich. Thus, all they would like to do is to exploit your motherland, to treat you as an inferior country which can be subdued to their business, you being a vassal of a kind. But they have failed, and knowing that makes them very disappointed. And by the way, you may remember a certain matter mentioned to you by my assistants visiting your country some time ago?"

"Yes," said the president, "I know what you mean."

"Then, I'd be grateful if you could do something about that conspiracy of the so-called M7. You know, their dealings harm your economy, and not only yours for that matter. I've had a word with Mr Oddhouse regarding that, and he might also do something about it."

"Yes, I know you've spoken to him, and I'll do what I can and can assure you they won't be happy about that."

"Thank you very much, and now let me return to our main topic of conversation, that is your retirement."

"I'm still not sure about that," said the president.

"But, my dear friend, there's nothing to worry about, believe me. You've done what you were supposed to do and it's time to have a rest, peace and quiet. You know, you actually don't deserve the light. You deserve peace, which is something that just a few are lucky enough to enjoy, and I can grant it to you."

"Thank you, I know you can, and perhaps I'll accept your kind offer, but not right now if you don't mind since there are a few more matters I'm supposed to deal with, yours being one of them."

"But of course, dear Vladimir Vladimirovich, take it easy, step by step, so to speak. I, myself, have something to do at the moment. Normally, I wouldn't bother, but because it's about a man I care about, and who was once harmed by their actions, I'll do my best to make them regret their actions."

"If you," said the president, "take the trouble to deal with it, I'm sure they'll make honest amends. Anyway, I know there's nothing difficult for you to do."

"Thank you for your confidence in me, and as you may know, the matter in question is related to the much bigger picture of their own country. I may not be so severe dealing with their problems, depending on their own willingness to change a few things. The problem is, among others, they talk too much, whereas they should be thinking more, and doing this, they should think over their so much-loved ethic, and I mean utilitarianism, of course, of that blockhead, as Friedrich called him, John Stuart. You know, his ethics are not a foundation but only a theory of consequences, and absolutely cannot be made obligatory for everyone, for in the first place, each man may have a different view of the outcome of his doing, but does one know his actions have consequences in advance? Of course, he doesn't have a clue about that. And in any case, we must first know what is useful, but again we cannot know that in advance.

"And now, *dorogoy* Mikhail Vladimirovich, I've got to go, and thank you once again for your hospitality, which I always appreciate. There is nothing like Russian and also Polish ways to entertain guests, and not the Limeys' dry, superficial welcome which makes you feel as if you were attending an office meeting. Thank you again, and goodbye." And Mr W. left the president.

Outside, a car was waiting for him, and the driver asked, "Where do you wish to go first, *vashe blogorodye?*"

"Ah, go to Patriarch's Pond first. I'm to meet somebody there."

"As you wish, sir," and the car sped towards the Pond accompanied by several police motorbikes. Once they got there, Mr W. thanked the driver, wishing him and his family best, suggesting more frequent visits to that beautiful city of Kiev where the driver was born. Afterwards, the man wondered how the hell the gentleman knew that, and as a trusted president's man, even dared to ask Mikhail Vladimirovich. The president just smiled and said, "My dear boy, if you knew who he was, you wouldn't ask stupid questions."

At Patriarch's Pond, Mr W. entered the main alley and walked under the lindens where on one of the benches there, Professor Stern was sitting. Mr W. greeted him warmly, sitting down next to him.

"How did it go?" the professor asked.

"Pretty well, as I expected, as a matter of fact. Anyway, I actually find him a pleasant man, not like his counterpart, that buffoon of Dollaria."

"Ah, 'The Trumpet', what a yokel he is," agreed Stern, "and you know what a brilliant and famous actor suggested at an important cultural gathering?"

"Ah yes, Robert, but fortunately that blockhead is leaving office soon," said Mr W.

"The sooner the better, and you've already decided his fate, I suppose."

"Yes, I have."

"He'll finally have a chance to do what he's made for, I guess, I mean his alias."

"Exactly, my friend, this is the only thing he might be good at. And now as for more important matters, are you going back to England?"

"Yes, I am," said the professor, "there's something going on over there and the Government have asked for my assistance."

"Uh, uh, did they? Then it seems they've got miraculously wiser. Anyway, I, myself, am going to England as well. Shall I give you a lift? The president was so kind as to let me use one of the Government's planes," said Mr W.

"That's very kind of you, thank you, and we'll have the opportunity to continue our conversation," said Stern.

"That's it, so at five today at the Sheremetyevo. The president's car will get you there."

"See you later, my friend," said Stern.

"Bye now," said Mr W., and left.

# THE CONVERSATION

'I am not a man, I am dynamite.'
Nietzsche


'He whose task it is to produce
a corrective idea, has only to study,
precisely and deeply, the rotten parts of the
existing order – and then, in the most partial
way possible, to stress the opposite of it.'
Kierkegaard


The lord's mansion was a very cosy eighteenth century former rectory, and Bea and I were the first there to arrive. On that day, it was the first time I saw her again, because until then she had been away again and as usual had told me nothing about her journey. I was rather upset by her persistent silence regarding her travelling, but could do nothing about it. She simply said I would find out more, myself, in due time. As a matter of fact, her frequent absence only strengthened my love and I couldn't imagine her leaving me; therefore, I made up my mind not to bother her with any questions and just wait for that 'due time'.

"Nice place, and somewhat mysterious, isn't it?" she said.

"Yes, indeed," I agreed, "anyway, there is something mysterious about its owner too."

Bea smiled but said nothing.

Nobody was there to welcome us outside, so I pulled the ancient bell-string and could hear a church-bell like tone inside the house. We waited a couple of minutes, and since nobody came to answer the door, we eventually entered on our own.

"Follow me," said Bea, apparently familiar with the place.

I followed her into a very spacious reception room, where there was nobody waiting for us, either.

*Hmm,* I said to myself, *maybe we are here on the wrong day,* but then a huge black cat in the company of a beautiful German Shepherd came in and placed themselves on a large sofa, looking at us but saying nothing, of course.

After a while, our host, Lord Hellbridge, entered, sitting down next to them.

"I'm terribly sorry about keeping you waiting, but I had to answer an urgent telephone call from a friend of mine, Professor Stern."

I had already heard of the professor since his exploits were reported by the media, and he was a kind of celebrity now.

"I perfectly understand, sir," I said. "You're a very busy man. Anyway, we aren't in a hurry."

"And very good, *festina lente.* It's a very wise saying we should all respect. And you're," turning to Bea, he said, "more beautiful than ever, isn't she?" and he looked at me.

*But how come he's saying that?* I thought. *I've never introduced her to him.*

"I know that you're a bit surprised," said Hellbridge, "thinking of how I could already know your charming partner. And I think it's the right time now to reveal that mystery, isn't it, my dear?" He turned to Bea.

"It's up to you, milord," she answered.

"Very well, and now let me," the lord said, addressing me, "introduce my faithful assistant, *Signorina* Sforza, who's been with me for..." he paused, then continued, "...I don't actually remember. Remind me, please." He turned to Beatrice.

"A very long time," said Bea.

"That's it," said the lord, "a very correct answer. Anyway, time doesn't exist, and here I've always agreed with Immanuel, but not on many other

418

issues. He's a very stubborn fellow, that Koenigsberger. Not just once have I almost lost my patience talking to him, and it took place every time we were discussing the existence of God. I'm not sure if I'll visit him again, for next time, our conversation might end in a sort of apocalypse."

I must have had a very stupid-looking face, hearing the lord's confessions, for Bea was giggling, looking at me.

"You're a bit surprised, my friend," he said, looking at me too.

"I… yes, I am because—"

I couldn't finish, for the lord said, "Never mind, you'll know in due time what I mean now. And now, for instance," the lord continued, "in this country, I have never watched TV. I simply can't listen to their ceaseless rambling, the worst place being the House of Commons, and that talking barrel organ, what's his name? Aha, that Igor Jobber. If I were his fellow house member, I don't know what I would do to him. I can't even look at him without being put out. That hair of his… does he see anything through it? Anyway, he's dog-like… eh, what's the name of it…?"

"Schnauzer," said Bea.

"Oh, that's it. Thank you, my dear, but he's too fat, and a Schnauzer is a rather slim dog, and I actually prefer black ones." said Hellbridge. "Aye, aye, something should be done about that, my friends. Would you suggest anything?" he asked, turning to me.

I had been so perplexed since the very beginning, listening to all he'd said, that I just managed to stammer, "I'm not really sure… you know your—"

But the Lord chipped in, "Oh, that's it, to say 'I'm not sure' I find much better-sounding than 'because'. Do you agree with me, *mia carissima signora?*"

"As always, milord," said Beatrice.

"Ah, I do appreciate that. At least one woman agrees with me, and such a beauty for that matter. When do you plan to get married, and by the way, may I consider myself lucky enough to be invited to your wedding?" asked the lord.

"I… I…" I began again, now completely perplexed, for Bea and I had never discussed marriage.

"Pretty soon," said Bea, "and of course you are. I couldn't imagine it without you, your Lordship."

"Splendid, thank you, and what kind of a present would you like to have?"

"Just your blessing, sir," she replied.

"But of course, my dearest, but I'll think of something in addition as well," said Hellbridge, apparently very pleased with her reply.

"But now unfortunately, this splendid occasion has to be postponed a bit because there are some issues that need to be sorted out, and you, my friend, know what I'm talking about, don't you?" he said, turning to me.

"Yes, sir, I do. It's about that unfinished M7 business."

"That's it, and you are still willing to go ahead with it?"

"Yes, I am, for everyone should get what one deserves."

"Precisely! Otherwise, there wouldn't be order in the world. You remember what your beloved mother told you about your father's batman?"

"Yes, I do remember, the man, a simple fellow but possessing that priceless folk's wisdom, said that order must be because it is for." And I wondered how the lord could know about that, but then I just thought, *But yes, of course.*

"That's it, and it means that some things should be put in order, for order rules the world, doesn't it?"

"As a matter of fact," chipped in Bea, "there are a couple of other things, as well."

"*Naturalmente, la mia bella signora,*" agreed Hellbridge, "but you Italians always overrate these other things, and you know what I mean, don't you?"

Bea chuckled and said, "*Sì, signor,* we do, and we do that for a good reason, that is enjoyment of life, which is impossible without good food, wine and love."

"Yes, yes, I agree, and I, myself, am in favour of your great art of living, but sometimes regrettably we must put aside all that fun and mend a few things. Otherwise, we wouldn't be able to enjoy those good things in life."

"As usual, you're right, milord," said Bea, smiling.

Hellbridge returned her smile, apparently not insulted by that rather frivolous affirmation of his wisdom. I could see he liked her very much, and was ready to forgive her things he wouldn't if confronted by other people.

"So, now, after that introduction, so to speak, I suggest we move to that rather unpleasant task we have in mind. Yes, that M7 business is still unfinished, but what about those who as a matter of fact are close to it? I obviously mean those former prime ministers, and I propose to deal with them first. Do we have agreement?"

"I'm not against, sir," I said, "and you, Bea?"

"I am in," she said.

"Splendid," said the lord, "but hold on, what time is it? Aha, almost eleven, strange, why does everything usually start at this time? Bah! – we may never know. Anyway, everything is strange and that's why anything is possible, my friends. But now we're expecting somebody to come, aren't we?"

"Yes, sir," I said, "my friends Graham and Bernard are coming."

"Ah yes, them. I like the men and may even agree to let Mr Mockingham paint a portrait of my insignificant person. However, I am a bit afraid, to be honest." And I wondered how the hell he knew about Bernard's intention, but again, I thought, *How bloody stupid of me to think he wouldn't know.*

"And why are you afraid, milord?" enquired Beatrice.

"Bah, good question. You know, painting you would be a pure pleasure, and painting me could end in disaster. I'm not photogenic at all, my friends, and besides, Mr Mockingham may be skilled enough to grasp in his portrait the very innermost side of me, as unforgettable Stanislaw Ignacy could, I mean, his so-called psychological portraits. And then what? Everybody would know who I really am. And actually, Stasiu wanted to paint me, but I refused." And I was startled again – yes, the lord had even known Witkacy, and not even for that matter because it had been a good thing to know him.

"As far as I know, milord," said Bea, "nobody will ever know who you are, so I'd suggest letting him."

"Yes, that might be true that nobody ever..." the lord paused here, "... and it might be better for everybody. I don't really know, you know, pretty often, too much knowledge is not advisable at all. Pretty often, there is nothing like ignorance. You know, it gives us peace of mind. It could be a getaway from the world so full of human tragedy. It may allow you to escape from worries, ah! I don't really know what to think of it."

At that very moment, the lord's assistant, Mr Wissend, entered the room in which we were sitting.

"We've been waiting for you," said Hellbridge. "Where have you been?"

"Ah, this morning, there was the Parliament session I decided to attend."

"And was it interesting?"

"In a way, it was, milord. As usual, they tried again to break down the boundaries of language."

"Ah yes, yes, apparently most of them never read Ludwig's *Tractatus*," said Hellbridge.

"I wonder whether they read anything at all," said his assistant, "at any rate, I find them first-class philistines."

"That's it, and if they do any reading, it is the same nonsensical rambling as theirs, but at the same time they love to be interviewed, don't they?" said the lord.

"Oh yes, very much so, because this way they can muddle everything even more, but then they think that doing it, they prove themselves to be open-minded, you know, very democratic," replied his assistant.

"Ah yes, yes, and they feel the need to prove it all over again. Otherwise, it wouldn't exist. I, myself, never give any interviews, you know, I could have a slip of the tongue, and then what? Everybody would learn more about me that I want to keep private. But among friends, as it is now, I feel free to say anything, and to mention Ludwig again, let me paraphrase his famous proposition and say that 'the limits of my language mean the limits of my intelligence', and many of those so talkative MPs, they are able to cross them both, and I'm afraid it might be schizophrenia of a kind. What do you think?"

"Oh, oh, that's it," said Graham, who in the company of Bernard had come in and overheard his favourite philosopher's name mentioned. "It certainly is. Anyway, anything is possible with them, except opening an umbrella in the cunt, if you'll excuse my language, madam," and he bowed to Beatrice.

"I don't mind, for what matters is to say things clearly, to be *expressis verbis*, and I'm not prudish at all for that matter," said Bea.

"*Bravo, bravissimo*, I, myself, couldn't put it better," said Graham, visibly impressed by Bea's statement. "Fortunately, you aren't one of those unbearable, priggish English ladies I can't stand anymore."

"Thank you, but now, that Parliament session you mentioned, Mr Wissend," she turned to Hellbridge's assistant, "did you see our Casanova?"

Wissend, slightly surprised, said, "Excuse me, but who do you mean, *signora?*"

"Who? Igor Jobber, of course," said Bea.

"Ah, him, yes. I had the pleasure I was not too pleased about, so to speak. But I've never heard that alias of him, Casanova. It's a new one, I suppose."

"It's my own invention," said Bea, "and you know what I mean by that, don't you?"

"Oh yes, I do. He's famous for his amorous conquests, for apparently many ladies think him harmless, very boyish, almost a child, so he can't actually, they believe, do them any harm. And he might seem to be pastor-like to them, you know, so they would confess to him almost everything, looking for consolation."

And now another guest arrived, Mr Oddhouse, our very disillusioned prime minister. He entered, saw the cat sitting next to the lord and exclaimed, "Bulky, is it you?"

The cat gave him a sympathetic look, saying nothing of course, but his master, Hellbridge, said, "Yes, the same, indeed."

"You wouldn't believe how I missed him, sir," said the prime minister.

"Bah, I would too. He's an exceptional companion. Was he of any assistance while with you at 10 Downing Street?" the lord enquired.

"You can't overestimate his help," and in a pleading voice, added, "would you be so kind as to allow him to stay with me for a couple of days from time to time?"

"I don't mind if he's willing," graciously agreed the lord.

"Thank you, sir, I'm most grateful," said the prime minister.

"Don't mention it, and you," said the lord, addressing the cat, "what do you think of it?"

The cat seemed to be pleased with the idea and came over to Mr Oddhouse, sat in front of him and did something very unusual for cats, namely, stretched his paw to him, and the prime minister shook it gratefully. And everybody present could see how moved he was.

"And they say there are no feelings left in this world," said Hellbridge, "but unfortunately, we were just talking about some unpleasant things, and what was it? Remind me, please," he said, turning to Wissend.

"We were talking about Mr Jobber," said the assistant.

"Ah yes, him," and looking at Oddhouse, he asked him, "and you, if I may enquire, what do you think of him?"

"I don't like him at all," said the other, "as I don't that sidekick of his, that clown Fooltone, also a great friend of Dollaria's chief prat. Have you noticed the appearance resemblance between the three of them? Their mugs are very similar, and hair too, and of course their mumbling. All in all, they could be brothers."

"In a way, they are, dear Mr Oddhouse," said Hellbridge, "and by the way, we must consider what to do with them. What would you suggest?"

"Hmm," the prime minister took some time to answer and then said, "I would send them to hell if I could."

"What an excellent idea!" exclaimed the lord, and turning to Wissend, said, "would you be so kind as to take care of it?"

"I'm always at your service, milord. You may consider it done."

"Splendid, I know I can always rely on you," said Hellbridge. "But then," he continued, "what about the others? I mean 'The Grin', 'The Preacher' and 'The Duck' as you call them."

"They're a slightly different matter," said Wissend, "but because they too conspired against the Holy Spirit, if I may use this expression, they deserve a little something as well."

"Yes, they do, "agreed the lord, "and do you have any ideas what to do with them?"

"Yes, I do, milord, but first, if you'll allow me, I'd like to introduce them, so to speak, to all present here, to justify the further action."

"Please do," said the lord.

"Thank you, so" Wissend began, "I'll allow myself to give a short presentation of them, and at the same time try to show a bigger picture."

"Certainly," said Hellbridge, "we must always think of the context, for without it we wouldn't have the right Weltanschauung, would we?"

"We wouldn't," eagerly agreed Wissend. "Thus, first I'll say why I don't find them likeable, and then I'll draw that bigger picture.

"So, as for 'The Grin', his alias is *nomen omen*, and as such says a lot about his personality. Whatever it is he grins about, good or bad news, his grinning is there, and he might do that in his sleep too, I presume. And I think he believes his grinning makes this country and even the whole world a better place. Everything, whatever it is, should be nice, even if it is downright nasty. In other words, it's the famous English 'think positive' which actually means to beautify everything, that is in fact to conceal or falsify. Therefore, lies are permitted and even obligatory, and the same goes for treachery and any other wrongdoings which are *de facto* not such in that sort of opaque ethic. All in all, this world is the best of all possible ones under the sun, and here we can see the influence of a philosopher. However, The Grin's reasoning isn't so refined, but it doesn't have to be, for if it were, his fellow countrymen wouldn't understand anything.

"Enough of him, and let's move to 'The Preacher'. In some respects, he's like the other one. But instead of grinning, he loves to lecture on morality, which always comes first whatever the problem. If there was mad cow disease or frozen pipes for that matter, a plumber should first, of course, find a relevant gospel and only then set to work. Otherwise, he wouldn't succeed.

"But now, as we know, there are two holy Christian scriptures, the Old and the New Testament, and our Preacher in definitely in favour of the former. An eye for an eye, a tooth for a tooth, so he's rather an orthodox believer. When the country suffered from widespread riots, the most important matter was to punish the guilty, so Mr Camelot is also a sort of a Christian, but not one of those forgiving ones. But for him his country has always been Christian whatever it has done. Let it be invading poor unarmed countries, enslaving their people, selling opium to China, England has always done everything in the name of Jesus Christ, and I wish I had an opportunity to ask him what he thinks of it. Who knows? I may, after all – 'there are more things in heaven and earth...' gentlemen, aren't there?"

"You've put it right, to the point, and you, Mr Oddhouse," said Hellbridge, turning his attention to the prime minister, "wouldn't, I presume, agree with my assistant?"

"Hmm," said the other, apparently embarrassed by Wissend's words, "I'm not sure what to say, but it might be true to some degree, after all."

"I like what you say, especially that 'to some degree', for in this world everything is to some degree, if you know what I mean. By the way, in a part of your country, I mean the Province, that quasi-question is one of their favourites. They're convinced, I assume, that if they didn't ask it, the person who they're talking to wouldn't know what it was about."

"Ah, them, yes," said Oddhouse, "their thinking is the source of all the troubles."

"That's it, for everything starts there, in thinking, where else? But now let my assistant finish his resumé as regards your fellow politicians. I believe you want to say a few more words , don't you?" the lord said to Wissend.

"Yes, indeed. So the next in the queue is John Snobbery, 'The Duck', but with your permission, milord, I would leave him alone, for he isn't that bad after all."

"I agree," said Hellbridge, "he isn't, so let's leave him in peace."

We all noticed how pleased Oddhouse was with the idea, because I already knew he was a friend of 'The Duck', valued his advice, and didn't want to bother him at all.

"Thank you, sir," Wissend went on, "and now, if you don't mind, I'll make a short resumé of my observations regarding our guests' fatherland. They, of course, never use this word or motherland either, as the Russians do, and the word fatherland in turn is preferred by the Germans and Polish.

"The English don't use them, either, because they value a kind of neutrality towards their own country. They believe that an absence of these words in their vocabulary grants them independence of judgement and emphasises their individualism. But, the truth is, they're terrible nationalists and racists, of course. Moreover, they consider themselves the guardians and arbiters of morality and manners in the world. So, as we can see, this is another example of their double-thinking, which actually has no limits, and I wonder what our philosopher friend," turning to Graham, "thinks of it?"

Now, I myself wondered what my friend may say in response to such a straightforward description, for his response mattered to me. It would show his true beliefs regarding his country, and in the first place, his philosophical stance.

Graham took a moment to reply, and eventually said, addressing Wissend, "I wholly agree with what you've just told us. And my philosophical integrity wouldn't allow me to say otherwise. It is harsh but truthful, and it has to be said."

"I appreciate your objectivity," said Wissend, "and what do you, Mr Mockingham," he asked, "think of it?"

"Well, I, as an artist, am obliged to have a totally independent view on everything under the sun, and therefore on my own country too. And it wholly deserves your opinion, Mr Wissend. I'm a painter, as you know, but let me say a few words about literature, because it's obviously an art as well and as such belongs to my world.

"And here we come across more than a couple of amazing accounts. For instance, George, hmm, he indeed undoubtedly made some valuable observations, but at the same time terrible blunders. And I don't really know the reason for making them. He, I presume, must have suffered a temporary intellectual blackout, or something like that. Otherwise, he would have never said that this country's predominant feature is its gentleness. Unfortunately, we can no longer ask him about that…"

"Excuse me for interrupting you," said Wissend, "but I actually know someone who could ask him."

"Really, then please do, and let me know what that person finds out," said Bernard, not offended by the interruption at all.

"You're very welcome, and I certainly will, and now please continue."

"Thus, considering the mentioned gentleness, George failed miserably to grasp the essence of it. And here I don't really understand his interpretation of the word in respect to his country's policy. Did he mean that Britain was allowed to enslave other peoples as long as it was done gentlemanly, that is, observing the principle that manners maketh man? If so, that it didn't really matter how many people died in the course of all those gentle actions in Ireland during the big famine, or in any other country under British rule, provided it was carried out gently? Whereas, those countries which applied a more direct, so to speak, approach, were guilty of outrageous crimes, let it be Germany, Russia and a good couple of others we know, studying history? And consequently, we spot a very different interpretation of the world's events.

In other words, as Friedrich observed, there are no facts, there are only interpretations, and obviously the English ways of interpretations are superior to all others. And because I'm really confused by the problem, please do ask George what he had in mind here if the opportunity arises, Mr Wissend."

"No worries, I will, and I'll let you know, and pretty soon for that matter. And please carry on with that very penetrating analysis of yours."

"Thank you again, and I'll be waiting anxiously for the news. And now, let's mention another writer, I mean, James, who wasn't an Englishman, but since he wrote in my country's language, he actually thought, partially at least, in English.

"So, to continue, it's said he broke down the boundaries of language, and yes, he did in a way, for some of his writing is unreadable indeed. And here we would need the priceless help of dear Ludwig in an attempt to find out what our James really meant. But I am not sure at all that even Ludwig could be of assistance. But I still believe he could be after all, and then our unfortunate James would have himself broken down. But to be sure, if you could ask him too, I'd be most grateful, Mr Wissend."

"No problem at all. I promise I will."

"Thank you again, and now, let's be honest and say that I never liked him as a person, either. That James sponged on almost every fellow writer of his, giving nothing in return but never-ending rambling. And in many aspects, I'd even compare him to a leech, a nasty word indeed, but I can't resist using it. He received a small fortune from a very generous English spinster but couldn't even afford a pair of shoes, but he eventually got them, but not by himself, for it was Ezra who, in spite of being short of money himself, bought for him that indispensable article.

"Anyway, their breaking the boundaries of anything ended in nothing. It never posed any threat to the existing order, and in reality, was welcomed by authorities because they provided a sort of safety valve for that order. And on the whole, we have here another example of Vladimir's '*pust' govopyat*' or 'let them talk', and the more they do, the better for us, those in power. Thus, their quasi-liberating mumbling is another mere façade protecting the system. And their constant mumbling about democracy. That overused word, which has been abused by saying it all over again.

Anyway, democracies vary, depending which country we have in mind. Moreover, it's not so much about the system but what people are like, their customs and character, their culture in toto. And these things often matter more than the system they are living in. And what is there to appreciate in this inhospitable, pokey, stultifying country of Britain? What's more, this country seems to live by fault-finding as regards other countries, as if it were a Delphic oracle, whatever it is, to be evaluated. And underneath all that, I can sense some dangerous trait, a hidden, furtive need for another war, which may seem to be a way to protect its system. And to support this view, we have, for instance, an intellectual masterpiece produced by a wise army general, and I mean *War with Russia*, in which it's assumed, of course, that victory will be ours, says the prophet. But I think he's more than stupid. He suffers from a mental breakdown presuming such a thing, which is obviously beyond any assumption. Yea, it is indeed, for I'd like to see what they would be assuming when 'Tsar Bomba' was dropped on their stupid heads.

"All in all, I believe it's time for a certain person's visit again, but this time not in Moscow, but in London."

"And who might that be?" asked Bernard, interrupting Wissend's narration.

"Bah, good question, my friend, but you yourself must find the answer, trying to identify him. You may start your thinking by asking yourself the question, 'Who is he whose whereabouts are totally unknown?' as in the lyrics, '*Nobody knows where you are, how near or how far…*'"

"I know that piece," I said, "it used to be one of my favourites."

"Good for you, Ches," said Wissend. "Moreover, you may try to write an essay about your feelings as regards that piece, as you say."

"I'll think about it," I said.

"Oh yes, do that, and the sooner you give it a try, the better for you, believe me."

"May I say something?" Beatrice said, interrupting our philosophical thoughts.

"But of course, *mia cara signora*," said Wissend, always a gentleman.

"I'd like to say something about our benevolent hosts, and please excuse my frankness in advance, Mr Oddhouse."

"You're very welcome, and if I understand correctly, you're going to say something about us, the English, or some say British. I, myself, am one of them, but this word-trick always makes me laugh."

"Thank you, sir, and what I intend to say won't be pleasant, but at the same time, I must emphasise that it doesn't apply to all of your compatriots, but regrettably to many of them, too many for that matter.

"So, it's about a certain characteristic, I mean, these protruding teeth and love for pink, and I have in mind many of your men, and that's why I have my own name for them – pink rabbits, it is."

"Aha," and here the prime minister cleared his throat and said, "yes, I've noticed that."

"But fortunately, you aren't one of them," said Bea.

"Yes, madam, I am very fortunate indeed not to be," agreed Oddhouse.

"I, as a woman," Bea went on, "can hardly imagine kissing one of those pink rabbits, for I'd find that repulsive. Yes, I could kiss a real rabbit, a very nice creature, but not a pink one."

"*La mia bella e saggia signora*," said Wissend, "what an accurate description, isn't it, and I must remember it." And for some unknown reason, he looked at the sitting cat, as if looking for his approval.

Then Bulky seemed to agree, raising his right paw and scratching his head. And Wissend, apparently pleased by Bulky's reaction, bowed slightly to him.

"And now," Wissend went on, "let me say something more about the matter in question. The English call a certain group of foreigners, and plenty of them are living in this country, vermin. Hmm, as a matter of fact, they're such themselves, creeping in every possible place, contaminating it with their perfidy, deceit and hypocrisy. And it had already been noticed by the father of that famous spy, who himself was one of them."

"You mean the man whose first name sounded Korean, don't you?" asked Graham.

"That's him. And I wonder all over again, what is the ultimate aim of those pink rabbits, as our wise lady calls them? That is, what do they want to achieve in the end? And I still can't fathom it," and saying that, Wissend looked at his boss.

430

"I may be of some assistance to you, my loyal companion," said Lord Hellbridge.

"If you'd be so kind, milord," said the assistant.

"But first I'd like to ask Signora Sforza about something that bothers me," said the lord, smiling at her.

"Please do, sir" said Bea, smiling too.

"You've been with Mr Adarsh for some time now, and I presume it will continue."

"It will, and I'm sure about it," said Bea.

"I'm pleased to hear that, for I like him," and Hellbridge looked at me and smiled again. "But," he went on, "I'd be grateful if you could tell me why, if I may ask this personal question, you've chosen him, for having known you a pretty long time, I know you're very choosy with regards to men in general."

I was listening to what they were saying, and I thought I had eventually answered the question that had bothered me for some time now. That was why she had been away from me all over again – she actually worked for Hellbridge, but in what capacity? I wondered.

"I know what you are thinking now," said the lord to me, "and it's time to answer your question. *Signora* Sforza has been my assistant for years now, and at some stage of our cooperation, I decided she would be the right woman for you, that only one, and I believe I've been right making that decision, haven't I?"

"Yes, sir," I said, "you haven't been mistaken. She's the one."

"And now," continued the lord, turning to Bea, "please tell us, if you don't mind saying it in the presence of those gathered here, why have you chosen Mr Adarsh as this only one?"

"When I first met him," Bea began, "it wasn't love at first glance, as they say, and I actually don't know why I made up my mind to start the relationship. Moreover, it was me, not him, who made the first step. I think, and it was and still is Ches' thinking, that meeting the one doesn't occur by chance. It's a fate, that is, something beyond our control. And this is because we can't explain it, can't put it into words. However, we're also mistaken in thinking that whatever we can put into language, we understand the reason for doing so. Not at all, as not just once I've found out. Actually, it is the other way around, our best decisions we make when we use no words, when there's no reason to explain why we make them. We know what we shall do, I mean, meeting a person, not thinking at all, this knowledge is beyond the world of language. We meet a person, I mean, a woman meeting a man and vice versa, and we simply know. How come we do? I don't know, and if you press me on answering, I'd say I see that man in my mind's eye, and nobody else can see him but me. And that's it, milord, and this is the answer to your question as to why I've chosen Ches."

"And this is the right answer, *mia cara* Beatrice, and the only one, and the rest is silence, for there are no words needed to answer the question 'Why?' here. And now," said Hellbridge, addressing Wissend, "I may help you answer your question as to what is the ultimate aim, what do they, the English or British, want to achieve in the end? And my answer is that they don't have a clue, for they don't actually have any final aim of their actions because they're unable to have it since they cannot see anything in their mind's eye because they lack the ability of that perception. And to see the world in your mind's eye is to see it *sub specie aeternitatis,* which is to see the world aright, so curiously enough they cannot see it as it is, and that's why they've always wanted to subdue the world to their own needs, but eventually failed miserably, for no man can ever do it, and that's it.

"Moreover, in order to see the world this way. you have to question the obvious, and they are incapable of doing it. In other words, you must be able to say 'no' to what you perceive in order to say eventually 'yes'. And they have a slavish submissive belief in reality. Therefore, they cannot go beyond it in their thinking. In consequence, they aren't free. They just suffer from the illusion of being such. They are just free to do what they are permitted to by their government, and *basta.*

"For them, God has always been dead, for to believe in Him you must go beyond a world of appearances, beyond reality in order to find greatness in Him, and as our good friend says, he who does not find greatness in God finds it nowhere. He must either deny it or create it. But these pink rabbits, in their plebeian, slavish spirit, are incapable of creating any greatness. And the Irish also, because of having been subjected to hundreds of years of schooling by the former. They're the only nation, in

432

Europe at least, that doesn't speak their own language. In consequence, they think English, to some degree of course, thus being deprived, as their former masters are, of the ability of abstract thinking.

"Anyway, many of the Irish are more English that the English themselves, but being, many of them, at any rate, more vulgar, simplify everything they touch.

"Other nations, to mention just a few, the Russians and Germans perhaps, despite Friedrich's harsh criticism of his fellow countrymen, and the Mediterranean people too, have the right spirit to see it. Let's just remind ourselves of what Henry said, that is, 'Greece made me free.' The Chinese, despite being unbelievers in a supreme being like God, are somehow capable of seeing beyond the world, as can small nations, just to mention the Armenians or Georgians.

"And the greatness of God is in Him being the only objective standard of right and wrong we may think of. Otherwise, all things would be permitted. That has already been seen by some thinkers, including that dark genius Fyodor, as his fellow writer, Vladimir, called him. Those objective standards are the only way to see the world from the perspective of the eternal, and you need imagination to see the world this way. And those objective standards are the only basis of the sense of the world, for reality being relative and accidental cannot provide them. In addition to that, the solution of the problem of life can be achieved only by seeing the world from that perspective, namely, *sub specie aeternitatis*, which is the only way to see it aright. Man might be capable of seeing the world this way in his inner language, that is, the language of his soul, as some call that sort of vision, which is the puzzle of all puzzles, and Ludwig was close to solving its mystery. The problem is that once he sees this way, he can't put the experience of that experience into words. Anyway, people usually put too much trust in words and therefore become victims of their seduction. A true philosopher is suspicious of words, and that's why his philosophy is the task, and not its solution. As for imagination again, Albert was very right in saying that imagination is more important than knowledge, for knowledge is limited, whereas imagination embraces the entire world. And Albert proved the truth of his statement by demolishing the theory of that poor slave of reality, Isaac.

"To be capable of seeing greatness, you must perhaps have experienced suffering and be able to not to be affected by it, be capable of resistance to misfortunes and be ready to sacrifice oneself and others.

"The English just suffer from the illusion of being free, for they mean a freedom of the open society which is not free at all because it is limited just to the rule of law which itself limits the freedom of the spirit by countless restrictions and regulations. *Corruptissima republica plurimae leges*, and I mean the corruption of the spirit of the individual, that is, his own unique independence of ideas. And to be such is the only way to be self-responsible, brave, proud, to have insight and sympathy for his fellow human beings, and only such a man can be trustworthy.

"We," Lord Hellbridge turned to me, "we may meet each other sometime in the future to discuss further the subject in question, but not in this country, for I presume you are tired of living here, aren't you?"

"Yes, sir, I am. And it is mostly because of its stultifying atmosphere, the stuffy air of its affected bearing, hypocrisy, perfidy and deceit. And those acclaimed good manners of the English, what in fact are they, when that politeness is actually lined with meanness? And it is in fact a way to patronise, to show their alleged superiority. And then their alleged impartiality, the love of diversity? These qualities are pretence, in fact, and they are to pull the wool over your eyes and to satisfy those not clever enough to see what is underneath that masquerade. All in all, their democracy is a joke. Great Britain, which has always been seen in its aristocratic 'shape', at its core is very plebeian, being one of the best examples of plebeianism of the modern spirit. Where are, in this country, the greatest Christian values? The answer is – they vanished into the shops. Yes, a shopkeeper mentality replaced them in full. Now the greatest values of this country are conformity, uniformity and selfishness on a scale unheard of in any of the other European countries. Moreover, the British democracy is strictly limited to freedom of having the right to say 'no' within the limits of the system and nothing beyond it. They are actually incapable of true rebellion, that is, the liberty of the spirit, and that's why they are incapable of having great art and faith too. And this is an inherited incapability which implicates self-censorship of anything they think or do. All in all, they have reduced whatever they do and think to temporary self-interest, which makes them deprived of honour, principles and goodness.

"Anyway, it seems that plebs have conquered a pretty large part of the earth. But then it will result in their own extinction. And that reminds us of Faust's Mephistopheles' words: 'All that doth begin should rightly to destruction run.' And actually, the last book of the *New Testament, the Apocalypse* confirms that.

Yes, I said then to myself, I asked myself the question not once, that is why I came to this country, what actually was the reason for living here? It wasn't a conscious decision to do so, because when I came here, I wasn't aware of the consequences of my arrival, and it took a good couple of years to grasp their impact on my consciousness. Anyway, how can you predict what will happen to you the next day, to say nothing of after one year or longer? However, in our stubborn ignorance, vanity and arrogance, we often think that we can.

Now, speaking of those consequences, I'd say I've lived here to possess eventually the courage for what I really know in order to become what I am. To find out what I really need, and thus want. To think over the past and imagine the future. To discover the truth in the appreciation of suffering, not being crushed by it. To learn the value of resisting misfortunes, to fully grasp the meaning of Friedrich's 'what doesn't kill me makes me stronger.'

And yes, to triumph over my nihilism, my hitherto denial of life, that is, my saying 'no' to everything around me.

All in all, I eventually realised that my stay here, and in many other places, was to toughen up and due to my newfound strength to say lastly 'yes', for to be able to say eventually 'yes' to existence is victory, and victory is the only reality.

And during that time, I did remember how, paradoxically, I used to comfort myself with the distress and misery of my life at the time.

The moment I had finished thinking all that, Hellbridge said, "Yes, isn't it strange to begin to think positive through denying any goodness in existence? It seems that negative power might do some good after all. But the problems of living by that power are countless, actually unanswerable questions you ask, so you can't live long like that. I, myself, never ask any questions except a very few formal ones, and that's why I am never mistaken and nothing is difficult for me to do."

Everybody present, except Wissend and me, looked at the lord in amazement, having heard his statement, but I didn't because I already knew who the lord was.

"And now, my friends," the lord continued, "we'll try to prove in the near future the truthfulness of that already mentioned by me, that apparently ludicrous supposition that negative power might do good after all, and we'll do that in practice. "And now I thank you for coming to see me and contributing so much to our fruitful conversation.

"Thank you again, and see you sometime in the future." We too thanked the Lord and left. The very next day, some very strange incidents began to happen in England.

# AFTERMATH

'...I am the spirit that forever denies!
And rightly too; for all that doth
begin should rightly to destruction run.'
Goethe, Faust


'Eventually, everyone gets what one deserves.'
C.D.


Igor Jobber, 'The Piggy', began his day as usual. He looked at himself in the mirror, and as always was very pleased with what he saw. Arranged his hair in its customary sophisticated configuration readying himself for another difficult battle.

We owe here some explanation as regards his alias. He was called 'The Piggy' behind his back, by his most bitchy critics, while the others called him 'The Heap' in relation to his unruly mass of hair. He knew about that nickname and disapproved of it because the word insinuated a phrase, a 'heap of rubbish'. Moreover, some had the very bad habit of exclaiming, 'Hip, hip, hooray' once they caught sight of him. In relation to that first rather vulgar, we must admit, nickname, his favourite animal was actually a pig, a pedigree one, of course.

So, today's battle was again about the continuous threat coming from terrorism hidden behind every tree in his beloved country. However, luckily enough, there weren't too many of them in this country. There weren't too many trees left there, but political foresight could always plant as many as was needed on any chosen day of the year. And one of these trees, which had always been in place, so to speak, was an ageless and a very tall one for that matter, of Northern Ireland, and the countless attempts to uproot it had been fruitless so far. And our dear Igor, like his like-minded fellow politicians, couldn't really grasp its nature. Why, they asked themselves all over again, was it still there? Why were those bloody dissidents never pleased with all our hard efforts to satisfy them, those generous grants they had been receiving for so many years? Why, they repeatedly asked themselves, was there no end to those troubles despite the most benevolent approaches made all over again by our charitable government?

*All they want is money, and we give it to them, but they are never happy enough, so is there anything else underneath their insatiable greed? We work hard laundering money in the City of London to provide it for them, but they have never enough. There must be something else underneath, but what's that? Bloody hell!* And if there is anything else, Igor thought, I cannot imagine it, for once you have money you have everything you may reasonably want in this life. And even if you can't get something of what you want then you can blame yourself because apparently you wanted something that you didn't actually need it. And if you're still dissatisfied, you can always imagine having it, listening, for instance, to one of our so beautiful songs, dreaming of love and happiness. Or you can beautify whatever you aren't happy about. And you may admire one or two of our world-famous celebrities, and to be one of them in your dream. All in all, you have everything having money.

*Perhaps*, he thought, *I should contact that impossible philosopher Witmore, whom I don't like too much because his ideas are packed with totally impracticable rubbish, and practice is everything, even if it sometimes doesn't work. But he might advise me on something,* Igor pondered the idea again. Hmm, he wasn't that stupid after all. *Anyway, our James Bond, Dumblodge, says that that cloud-dweller is quite admired in academic circles. Moreover, he's respected, curiously enough, by the Russian president for that matter. Maybe he's another specimen of reborn Cambridge five or even six or seven? Yes, I'll contact him after all.*

*Ah*, Igor sighed again, *enough of that! They're waiting for me in our impregnable fortress of democracy, COBRA, and it's time to get there on my little wonderful thing.*

That wonder he was going to mount was of course his bicycle, a state-of-the-art little thing he was so proud of. Specially strengthened for him (after checking his weight, they advised him so) by a German company, which he never mentioned because of his deep patriotism.

Before mounting his wonder, Igor took a small pocket mirror out of the pocket to check his appearance again. *Not bad*, he thought, *small wonder I'm so popular with the ladies*. And then he set off in the direction of the Government bunker, which he was to reach in a few minutes considering his incredible body fitness. But it wasn't to happen on that fateful day.

At this point, we should mention a certain trait in Igor's view on human character. It was namely his deep conviction that man essentially, by reason of his nature, is bad in the conventional meaning of the word. That cheating, perfidy and greed are those traits which are leading motives which dominate his life, and that they actually aren't bad *per se* because they stimulate progress, giving birth to evolution, and as such should be appreciated. His favourite book was 'Vanity Fair', and he firmly believed that in that masterpiece the author actually praised arrogance, narcissism and egotism, and so did Igor. So, as we can see, it was a complete reversal of the hitherto recognised system of moral values. Igor said of himself that his philosophy went much further than that of Friedrich, and that in his spare time he did his best to put it in a treatise provisionally entitled *Homines stulti non olet*, or *Human stupidity does not stink*, with the subtitle, *Homo Non Est Bonum*, or *Man is not good*. A part of that monumental work had already been submitted to the Oxford University Press, whose opinion of Igor's *Tractatus* we won't mention here for so-called diplomatic reasons. But his work had been widely discussed at a meeting of a club Igor used to be a member of, and highly praised for its revolutionary approach to the problems of ethics. However, some scholars, among them professor Graham Witmore, were of a very different opinion, calling it a half-wit's product. And it had been rumoured that Witmore was going to present his opinion to Jobber in a rather unconventional way, very different from that normally accepted in those highly intellectual circles of which Great Britain was so proud. However, we're certain that Professor Witmore didn't carry out his intention, for if he did, we obviously would have heard of Igor's stay in hospital.

And now, our Igor on his way to the meeting was already thinking of putting those ethical ideas into practice. A lot of people would be surprised if they only knew about his simply phenomenal skill of doing at the same time such extremely different activities as riding a bicycle at tremendous speed and thinking, but it was still nothing in comparison to another proof of his fitness we certainly won't mention here because of its very personal character. However, later on, we will say a couple of words related to some particular feat of his, for it had already been reported by a very inquisitive journalist in an article under the title *The Dark Side of the Moon*. By the way, we may notice here that the musicians who were the authors of those famous, or infamous as some prefer to value it, lyrics, protested and were even about to take legal action against the journalist, but fortunately for him (we presume so, because if they did, he would be left in the proverbial stocks after a trial), a certain philosophy professor whose name had not been mentioned, but it could have been our Graham Witmore as far as we know now, managed to calm down the opposite parties by writing a highly sophisticated essay in which he proved beyond doubt they were both actually right and therefore shouldn't argue about the matter, and become friends instead, as they actually did, perhaps due to the fact that the aforementioned essay was so complex that even his author couldn't in fact explain its essence at a conference especially called at the University of Cambridge to discuss the work. Professor Koczkodan from Poland said that only Ludwig would be able to explain the meaning of Graham's paper, but added that perhaps fortunately for them Ludwig couldn't attend for the obvious reason, for if he did, they would know even less afterwards, as had happened once in his native country when a renowned metaphysician, Franz, worthy of attending Plato's Symposium, described his friend's arrival, a poet called Lesmian, at the famous restaurant, Ziemianska, in that way, 'An empty horse-cart arrived and Lesmian got off.' Or, when a much less famous philosopher, another of Koczkodan's compatriots who preferred to be anonymous, said in his paper after having lived on the green island, 'The Centre of the Intellectual Wasteland and the Irish Question', and those both metaphysician statements were understood by no one but a few.

Let us say a few more words about Professor Koczkodan. In the first place, his name was the *nomen est omen* of his appearance, but we'll spare the reader its description so as not to frighten him. It was reported that on his visit to Yellowstone Park, he met a monstrous grizzly bear, and his appearance frightened the poor animal so much that it began to run away, and according to the latest news, it's still running and has been seen recently in Alaska. However, some say it already reached Siberia, which seems rather unlikely because how would it swim across a pretty wide Bering Strait?

Anyway, he never ever carried any weapons with him wherever he went, whether it be the Amazon jungle or some African wilderness, and a good friend of his, Professor Stern, can confirm that. He wasn't afraid of sharks or any other dangerous sea creatures, either. On his trip to Florida and its waters full of sharks, but they never disturbed his swimming. It was reported to the US president, who then contacted the Navy Seals commander, urging him to offer a permanent contract to the professor so that he could give the famous sea warriors his invaluable advice, but to their great disappointment, Professor Koczkodan wasn't interested.

Professor Koczkodan was also a highly qualified scholar in other fields, be it psychiatry and psychology. His achievements in the latter were often favourably compared to the so penetrating unmasking psychology of Nietzsche and Kierkegaard. As regards the latter thinker, the professor was once invited by the king of Denmark to attend a symposium dedicated to that famous and frequently misunderstood philosopher. The symposium took place of course at Kronborg Castle, and Koczkodan began his lecture quoting the famous William's words, 'To be or not to be, that's the question,' and then he said that actually the question was wrong, for the second part of it should be 'that was the question', and that was it, for he left then and after waiting an hour in vain for him to return, the other attendants left too.

On another occasion, at a conference in Oxford, his lecture's theme was the existence of Satan, already thoroughly analysed in his book *If*

*There Is no Devil*, first published in Moscow, and then translated into sixty-six languages, with the total of ninety-nine million copies sold worldwide.

The conference brought rather unfortunate consequences for more than a few participants. Several female professors fainted during it, while their male equivalents had to undergo medical examination by psychiatry consultants who fortunately were available at the time due to the vice-chancellor's foreseeing wisdom.

Among the casualties was Professor Dullard from St Andrews, whose fate was decided once he stated that the discussion on the existence of that presumed, as he put it, individuum, was pointless unless a proof of his existence was given. Professor Koczkodan said he would present proof, but only at a private conversation with his colleague. And shortly afterwards, that conversation took place, and afterwards, Professor Dullard reported at his own will at the nearest psychiatric hospital and asked to be locked up in a steel-plated room. His request was granted, and as far as we know, he's still there.

There were other responses to the Jobber's paper as well. A friend of Professor Koczkodan, professor Niedowiarski, well known for his expertise in aesthetics, wrote a paper entitled *Homo non solum pecuniae*, or *Man is not only the money*, which pointed out some essential mistakes in Jobber's reasoning. Money, said Niedowiarski, is *de facto* a crime, and love for money is the love of evil, and that love was instituted in people by the Devil. Once his paper was published, the professor received a phone call suggesting he withdraw the thesis; otherwise, he would have another surrealistic experience, but this time much worse than the one he had on his return to Poland after many years abroad. The experience in question began when nostalgic Niedowiarski was walking down the streets of Warsaw recalling happy days of the past. A man in a military uniform approached him asking for a favour; namely, he wanted to have a drink with him, and the professor was willing to grant the soldier his request, because the soldier said he hated drinking alone. Then the military man invited Niedowiarski into an arched gate of a big pre-war building, produced a bottle of vodka out of his coat pocket, drank it up and said, 'Thank you, sir. I do hate drinking alone.'

442

Another reaction to Jobber's article came from Professor Caramba of the University of Barcelona. In his paper, the professor compared Piggy's reasoning to a cholera plague and suggested imposing a quarantine on him.

All in all, the academic milieu all over the world was very much dissatisfied with Jobber's revelations, and I, myself, also wrote an essay in which I did my best to renounce Jobber's thesis, and now let me present the main points of my work.

First of all, I'd like to emphasise that what a human being really needs to be worthy of being called a human, are certain attributes which are given to him at birth, but other ones can be acquired due to his own effort. At his birth, he isn't either good or bad, he's beyond good and evil, and he may become either only much later. In other words, he possesses some inherited qualities which can predispose him to be either good or bad later on. But then how could we tell goodness from evil? "Do you think you can tell heaven from hell, blue sky from pain?" as David and his friends ask. How to learn the difference when the knowledge is not given to you? This is the most puzzling questions of all questions, and we may never find out the right answer. And, as a matter of fact, we never know for sure, for to doubt is to be human. It is a paradox of life itself, the ceaseless scepticism and mistrust and the everlasting need for certainty. The paradox of all paradoxes, with which everything of the utmost importance begins. Consequently, a man must find his own belief, to choose what he should believe in, and this choice will implicate all of his future actions, his own future life.

But to choose, in the first place he must study himself and only then the others, and in this meaning *vita sine litteris mors est*, his own death as a human being.

And then, that task is about finding the right set of principles for yourself, for they will determine that life, and here is the very start of everything that comes further. Should a man choose the Christian values and make them his own? Is humility and compassion the right choice for his all further deeds, or rather pride, the will to power and courage? But then it very often happens that those Christian values serve to achieve the same goals as those of a man who does not consider himself a Christian. And then a man who claims to be a Christian may have on his mind the same goals, of which the most crucial one is to dominate, to carry out his will to power.

But it might be helpful to know that the choice of what to believe in is a true one only when we aren't followers, believers in somebody's else ideas and directives. But the freedom of choice might be, and usually is, the most difficult task ever. Too often that freedom is just an illusion or a façade, or both.

But the burden of that freedom is terrible, for we never know whether our choice is right until we have already made it, never before. So, we must be tough enough to keep on searching for it, and this toughness is the quality of a few, and is not surely of the followers of others' commands, that is not slave morality which is the prison of a follower, the believer. You should not be believers to find your own choice, for if you are, you will never find it. And if you really want and can achieve that aim, then your philosophy of life is to be suspicious first towards yourself and only then toward others. You must question the obvious forced on you by them; otherwise, you have no right to call yourself free. And what you should keep in your mind is that your right choice can be found only on your own, for only then it is truly yours.

How would one know all this is true? To answer the question, let's think over Ludwig's enquiry: what is the reason why those who have eventually found the sense of life are unable to say what constituted that sense? And the only answer possible seems to be that the solution of the problem of life is seen in the vanishing of the problem. And that's it, either you're willing and able to begin your search for the sense of life or you aren't. But keep in mind that your search is the most crucial and difficult one of all of your life's tasks, and also duties I believe, but then not everyone is worthy of attending Plato's Symposium.

While I was pondering all that, Igor was on his way to the meeting at COBRA. He was a bit late but being confident in his incredible skill of riding his bike, he was sure he would arrive in time.

He had just emerged from around the corner of Oxford Street when he noticed a huge black cat sitting at some distance from him on his usual path of his bicycle race. Igor rang the bike's bell furiously, but the cat paid no attention, still sitting there and looking at him. *"What a cheeky bastard,"* Igor thought, *like that Bismarck's mascot, Oscar, which brought bad luck not only to her but also to a couple of our own ships. However,* he admitted reluctantly, *that bloody cat did bring luck to his ship, enabling her to sink our Hood that was even bigger than Bismarck.*

And now, the one who might have been Oscar's descendant didn't even move, showing total indifference to Igor's political eminence. So, he came to a halt in front of the cat and shouted, "Get out of my way, you bloody monster!"

A few pedestrians looked at him with disgust, and a policeman appeared on the scene out of nowhere. The policeman was a very thin, tall man sporting a thin moustache and wearing small round glasses. All in all, he didn't look police-like at all, but he acted like a very professional one, coming up to Igor and saying, "Sir, you should be ashamed of yourself. Your behaviour suggests you're a cat-hater and perhaps even an animal-hater for that matter."

"But I'm not," exclaimed the accused. "I love them all."

"I'm not so sure, sir, and what's your name by the way?"

"You don't know who I am?" asked Igor in surprise.

"No, never seen you before," replied the policeman.

"You don't watch TV then?" asked the famous politician, slightly confused now.

"No, I've never had a TV set. I hate it," said that apparently antisocial law-enforcement member.

Now Igor, already bewildered, became even more so because he noticed a trace of a strange accent in the policeman's voice.

"I'm Igor Jobber MP," he said, "and I'm already late for an extremely important cabinet meeting chaired today exceptionally by none other than the prime minister himself."

"I perfectly understand, sir, but first things first," the policeman said, not too impressed by Igor's statement.

"And," he went on, "we must first sort out the current issue, the problem of the cat, and more precisely what are you going to do to about it?"

"Excuse me," said Jobber, "but I don't understand, and what should I do about it? Nothing happened, so let's forget it."

"Oh, no," said the policeman, "you should compensate him for your inappropriate behaviour."

"Are you off your rocker?" exclaimed Igor. "Compensate? What are you talking about?"

"I might be off my rocker, as you say. Anyway, who isn't these days? But since you actually breached this poor animal's rights, you should compensate him somehow."

Igor looked at the policeman and said to himself, *He's nuts, how the hell did he make it into the force?*

"They were very reluctant to take me, but then someone contacted them, and here I am," said the crazy policeman.

Now Jobber, hearing that, was really stunned, something that never happened before, and he was famous for his cool. *Can he read my thoughts?" No, out of the question, just an incident.*

The policeman was now saying nothing. He was just looking at Igor, who noticed sparks of amusement and mockery in his small round eyes.

In the meantime, he who was the cause of that unpleasant incident, namely the cat, was just sitting there looking at them and moving his head from one man to the other one, as if he was following their conversation.

The policeman eventually broke the silence, saying, "I suggest the following solution to our little problem."

"I'm listening," said Jobber, who was now eager to conclude the matter in question amiably and quickly, for he was now really late for the meeting and had just remembered an unpleasant incident involving a close aide to his colleague, Daniel Camelot, 'The Preacher', that had occurred at the entrance to Downing Street some time ago.

"So," continued the officer, "I suggest you take the cat with you, adopt him, so to speak, and look after him from now on."

"Oh no," Igor exclaimed, "never ever in my life. Anyway, a gentleman doesn't own a cat."

"A gentleman maybe doesn't," said the guardian of the peace, grinning. "However, as a matter of fact, there are some exceptions to the matter in question."

"And if I refuse, what then?" said Igor.

"If you do, then I'll follow a relevant legal procedure which may oblige you to comply."

"And what procedure do you mean?" asked Jobber.

"I suppose that you as an MP, should know what I mean," said the officer, smiling.

Now, Igor, seeing how stubborn that fellow was, was willing to end that bizarre situation as soon as possible, and said, "Okay then, I'll take him," and thought at the same time, *and will leave him at the first opportunity.*

"And I, of course," continued the officer, "will check on him from time to time. But everything depends on what our dear object of our dispute says to our wee agreement." And he looked at the object, namely the cat, as if he was asking him to decide.

Igor too looked at him, and it seemed to him that judging by his expression, the animal was rather pleased with the outcome and, what must have been a hallucination, was approving of the outcome by nodding.

In the end, to cut a long story short, Igor was back on his way to the meeting in the company of the cat, whom he placed on the back of his bike. When they arrived at the bunker, they both dismounted and entered the meeting room where a debate was already well in progress, but once all present in the room saw the pair coming in, they immediately stopped talking, just looking at the pair coming in.

"Is it your extraordinary aide?" General Sir Trevor Battleberg asked Igor.

"I..." he began, clearing his throat, "met him by chance just this morning and took an immediate liking to him, so decided to take him along. You know, he seemed to be so alone, vulnerable, lost in our big city."

"Ah, how good of you!" said the general. "Who would think of you being so sensitive?"

There were a few smiles around and a chuckle, and someone apparently not being a cat sympathiser, said, "Are cats actually allowed here?" But one man seemed very interested in Igor's new companion, and that man was John Oddhouse, the PM himself.

He was looking intensely at the animal thinking, *Gosh, that's Bulky, but how come he found himself in the company of that...?* He stopped thinking for lack of an appropriate word. Anyway, he didn't want to reveal to the others that he already knew the cat, and pretty well for that matter, so he just announced, "I have nothing against him joining us. He's very welcome. What do you say, gentlemen?"

The gentlemen looked at each other, and there were several approving nods, so the prime minister said, "If so, let's continue what was temporarily interrupted by the arrival of our new friend, I mean the cat of course."

Now there were still more smiles and chuckles, and John Oddhouse said, "Thank you, gentlemen, for your understanding, and now let's resume the subject we were discussing." And the subject in question was the usual one, namely the Northern Irish question. And we know perfectly well that they're as false as their weather is. Genius, as Friedrich put it, is conditioned by dry air, and their only genius lies in their deceitful nature which is something inherited, conditioned, among others, by that weather.

The foreign secretary began, "It's a never-ending discussion leading to nowhere, as usual. They, over there, think they live in the centre of the universe, and everything rotates round their problems and that will continue like that forever. Anyway, their concept of time is even more difficult to grasp than that of Albert Einstein."

"I'm inclined to agree," said somebody there, "as Einstein himself would, I presume."

"To say nothing of Immanuel Kant," somebody else contributed.

"That's it," another voice was heard, "the vicious circle is nothing compared to it."

"Yes, yes, gentlemen," interrupted Oddhouse, "but we have to reach some resolution, after all."

"I think," Igor Jobber chipped in, "I've found it, and to my mind it could be the final solution to our problems we have over there."

"The final, you say," said the prime minister, "I can hardly imagine something like that, but we're listening."

"Gentlemen," began Igor, "just recently, I've spoken to the president..."

"You mean 'The Trumpet'?" Somebody asked that rather rhetorical question.

"I disapprove of calling him that," Jobber said, raising his voice. "He's our great friend, perhaps the only one we have nowadays, and he's deeply concerned about an eternal, if I may use the word, peaceful solution to the problem of Northern Ireland."

"I'm sure that even in eternal heaven, they wouldn't agree with you," somebody commented.

"Anyway, but Mr President, and I share his point of view, has an idea I believe would eventually allow us to sort out the problem for good."

"And what does that genius have on his mind?" the same voice enquired.

"The president being a visionary, as I see him, came up with the idea so close to his heart, and which he has forever wished for, for the good of his own country. That's a wall."

"Do you mean a wall parting genius from stupidity?" again the same persistent voice asked.

"I don't understand," said Igor.

"Small wonder," said somebody else.

"He means," the unperturbed Igor went on, "a wall between those who are for a full, true reconciliation and those who still oppose that. And the opponents, the bad, would be resettled to a specially designed zone, and a wall will be built, separating them from those peaceful and good."

"And what about technical matters here?" asked MI6 boss, Boris Dumblodge. "How would we tell the good from the bad?"

"Ah, this shouldn't be a problem," replied Igor, "our country has always had a clear understanding as to how to distinguish those contradictions, so to speak."

"So to speak, it's a ridiculous idea, a nonsense," said the foreign secretary.

"Not at all, I find it an idea of a genius, and I'm certain it'll work. However, I suggested another solution during the conversation with my friend, the president."

"Another work of a genius," somebody chipped in.

"I wouldn't go that far," replied Igor, "but still it might be a good one."

"We're listening to a Delphic oracle proclamation," a voice was heard.

"The solution, I mean, would be about resettling, but much faraway or that matter, that is Alaska, up to some 100,000 bad souls, and I asked my friend if he would consider the option. And to my great joy he said he would think it over.

"Then I had an even better idea. I asked him what about contacting the president of Russia and suggesting he accept some 30,000 of those very bad into Siberia if he'd be so kind as to cooperate."

"You should both go over there," somebody suggested.

"That's it, they belong there," somebody else added.

"And never return," another voice complemented.

"Gentlemen, gentlemen, please," exclaimed Igor, "treat that idea seriously for the lack of any other reasonable ones."

"The only serious statement about our dear cousin I've heard so far," said Andrew Sharp, "was made by Robert at a ceremony in New York City, and it was one of the most consistent, to the point, speeches I've ever heard, as it followed Ludwig's invaluable canon, 'Whatever a man knows, whatever is not mere rumbling and roaring that he has heard, can be said in three words.'" And apparently those gathered there were wise enough to understand what he meant, for he received a standing ovation.

"Anyway," Andrew went on, "Dollaria's duce seems to be above any lengthy scribbling, and says his position doesn't allow him to waste words and therefore twitting is the best way to announce his great ideas. Poetry, to his mind, should be banned and here his genius is close to the greatness of Plato."

"And does he read anything for that matter, except, of course, some memos and the like?" asked Steven Peep, the intelligence expert.

"He doesn't, as far as I know," said Andrew, "and back to poetry, his opinion of it is the same as that of Michael in one of his films, namely that those poets are simply dead men, and that's it."

"If we forget literature for now," chipped in the foreign secretary, "what worries me most is his constant change of opinion regarding our country."

"I don't know what you're talking about," said Igor.

"I'm hardly surprised," said the secretary, "you seldom ever do."

"I'd like you very much to consider that idea for the final solution for the troubles in the Province, for it might be our last hope to end the problem," said Igor.

"If you insist, let's have it," said the foreign secretary, "for it might have some sense after all. But what about the Russian president? Would he be really willing to come forward?

"And as a matter of fact, I'm not sure about Dollaria, either. They may be our cousins, but at the same time they're so distant. You know, we should always keep in mind their Read Plan, for who knows? They might have another one on their mind."

"Oh no, no, no," exclaimed Igor, "never ever again, I unreservedly trust them."

"You'd better believe in their trust in the dollar," said Joanne Miser, the Chancellor of the Exchequer.

"Oh yes," she was joined by Paul Blackstone, a Navy expert, exceptionally invited today by the PM for some reason as yet unknown to the other participants. "For the factual inscription on the dollar," he went on, "is a mere metaphor."

"Ladies and gentlemen, please, it appears our discussion has become a bit chaotic…"

But he couldn't finish the sentence because somebody said, "You shouldn't complain. Chaos is your thing, dear chap."

"In a way, it is indeed. Anyway, we live in a chaotic world where nothing is certain anymore," said Igor.

"Except for the chaos," the same voice said.

"I wouldn't say so," said Igor, "for God is still there."

"God, you say?" General Battleberg joined the discussion again. "You never mentioned Him before."

"There wasn't any occasion for it, but now considering the problem we're looking at, the time's come to mention Him, moreover, to turn to Him with our problem."

"Very interesting," said the general, "and how do you suggest proceeding?"

"Hmm, to be honest, I'm not so sure," admitted Igor.

"And do you have any idea how to establish contact with Him?"

"We may ask the Archbishop of Canterbury how to go about that," suggested Igor.

"Why not, provided he would be willing to talk to you?" the MI6 boss said.

"You'll ask him."

"Me?" the now perplexed Dumblodge exclaimed. "Yes, you. Don't tell me you don't have any material on him," said Igor.

"I may have something after all."

"And what is that?" enquired Igor.

"That I won't tell you. You're a politician, and politicians come and go, whereas we're always there, at Her Majesty's service. Anyway, I don't think you believe in God, and He of course knows that, so any attempt to contact Him will be futile."

At that very moment, the cat, who seemed to be asleep on the chair next to the prime minister, woke up and jumped onto the table they were sitting at. Then he slowly came up to Igor and sat in front of him, looking him straight in the eye.

"What does he want?" Igor said, slightly perplexed.

"I don't know," said Oddhouse, "ask him."

"But how? He wouldn't understand, he doesn't speak."

"How would you know, anyway? You may try telepathy," suggested the prime minister.

"Telepathy? I don't believe in it," firmly declared Jobber.

"That's the problem with you, for if you did, you would understand perhaps more than you do now," said Oddhouse.

And because the cat was still there looking at him, Igor became slightly nervous and eventually asked Oddhouse, "would you please call him back?"

"No," said Oddhouse. "I wouldn't, it's a free country and cats have their rights too."

Jobber was getting more and more uneasy facing the cat's hypnotic stare, and eventually being not able to stand it anymore, closed his eyes and a thought crossed his mind, *I'm actually tired of all that all, of that politics, never-ending conversations, unsolved problems. It'd be a good idea to leave it all and go to spring waters, perhaps Kislovodsk, as the Russian foreign secretary recommended to me.*

And once his thoughts came to an end, the cat returned to his chair and lay there again.

"You see," said Oddhouse, "he perhaps told you something after all, anyway, and you say you don't believe in telepathy. You know, believing in telepathy is the same thing as believing in God, for it's the only way to contact him, or somebody else for that matter."

452

Jobber, back from his vision, said, "Who do you mean?"

"You don't really want to know, but a day will come when you'll find out yourself," said Oddhouse, smiling. "And now, ladies and gentlemen, since, as usual, we have come to no conclusion with regard to the Northern Irish question, and other issues , I suggest we end our meeting now, for the only conclusion that seems to be reasonable is to leave to God the matter in question. He's our only hope… here he paused, and then said, "…or it might be somebody else."

"Thank you all, and see you at the Parliament session tomorrow. Goodbye."

And they left, along with the cat, who now accompanied the prime minister.


Jobber was deeply dissatisfied with the outcome of their gathering, but at least he was relieved to be able to get rid of that annoying creature, the cat.

When he was back at his apartment, all his thoughts were now with his new girlfriend, Susan Flattery, not a real beauty, but then not that ugly that she couldn't be shown in public. What he liked most about her was her affection for him, showed among other ways in her apparent admiration of his looks, and in this respect, she compared him with Gregory Peck, despite the very different colour of his hair, and a few other features, for that matter.

She was due to come to see him shortly, so he was getting ready for meeting her. He changed into sports pants and put trainers on his feet. Once he'd done that, he thought, *Maybe it would be a good idea to take up some other sport activity besides cycling. Swimming perhaps? But where?* A swimming pool didn't seem too good because he would have to show himself in swimming pants alone. *The sea? Hmm, yes, why not?* I may try blue waters. But because he wasn't any Phelps for that matter, and as a matter of fact was afraid of water, he thought of some precautions before he submerged into the cold waters of the English Channel. A life jacket? But how to swim with it on? No, it should be something else, but what then? Aha, yes, Susan might accompany him in a boat. *I'll ask her,* he decided.

So, when she came, he revealed that idea to her. "But Igor, darling, I'm not good with boats at all, so be a good boy and try on your own."

And Igor, eager not to disappoint his admirer, said, "Yes, of course. You're right, my love. I'll do it on my own."

"How brave of you," she said, and gave him a kiss.

Thus, once the matter of security, or rather lack of any, was decided, they set off in the direction of the sea in Susan's rather battered Toyota.

They arrived in Brighton, where they checked into the very same hotel where Margaret once almost met her fate. And where by a strange coincidence none other than Lord Hellbridge was now staying along ,with a cat very similar to the one Igor met before.

Igor, still eager to impress Suzan, changed quickly into his swimming gear and they both set off. Once they reached the famous Brighton beach, Igor to his horror, saw very big waves crushing there, but decided to give it a try after all.

"Darling," Suzan said, "I think you better try another day, look at these waves."

"No, now or never, we never surrender."

"Hmm, if you say so, but please be careful."

He just nodded and marched bravely to meet the sea, whistling *Rule Britannia*.

Igor jumped bravely into the water, and using some hitherto unknown technique, as bystanders said later on, began his heroic swim. But it didn't last long, and he felt his strength was leaving him as he fought those huge waves, and after a while, he was in serious trouble, and realising that, he exclaimed desperately, 'God help me!'

But it wasn't our Lord who saved his life on that fateful day. However, we will never know.

Anyway, it was Lord Hellbridge who, on hearing the shouting coming from the beach because people gathered there noticed Igor's trouble, asked the cat, "What's going on out there?"

"Igor Jobber's drowning, mon sire," said the cat.

"Get him out. we're humanists after all."

And the cat set off with enormously long jumps towards the sea to accomplish one more of his already many humanistic missions. The people who were later interviewed by journalists and the police said that the cat was simply flying at supersonic speed through the air, and a former

Tornado pilot who happened to be there, confirmed that.

It was later reported that gathered bystanders claimed that once the cat hit the waters, his technique and speed was far better than that of Phelps.

Once the cat reached Jobber, who had almost drowned by then, he grabbed him professionally and towed him quickly towards the shore, where the cat left him and then disappeared from view.

Once safe on mother earth, Igor, totally exhausted, began moving on all fours towards a brightly painted kiosk and, reaching it, asked for water in a hoarse voice.

"You haven't had enough yet?" asked the soulless proprietor.

"Yes, I have, but it was salty," Igor replied in a weak voice.

"I'll give you some Guinness Special for strength," said the owner, handing him a bottle.

"Thank you," said Igor, and greedily drank it in two gulps.

"Feel much better now," he said, and only now Susan, who had been away shopping, came up to her miraculously saved lover.

"I've only now been told that someone was drowning, but I was pretty sure it wasn't you, being so sure of your incredible stamina," she said.

"Bah," exclaimed Igor, "it wasn't about my stamina. Something got hold of my leg, pulling me into the depths, and it might have been that Brighton monster, if you know what I mean." As we can see, he tried his best to blame something else for his hopelessly tragic lack of swimming fitness.

"Never heard of it," she said.

"Bah," he exclaimed again, "of course you haven't, it is a state secret."

"Ah, I see, and who came to your rescue? I've heard it was a cat. Was it?"

He knew perfectly well it was a cat, for he actually hadn't lost consciousness, but still wanting to shift responsibility on something else, said, "Nonsense, cats cannot swim."

Anyway, by now, Igor had had enough of cats, for even his dreams were full of them. And here we'd like to inform the reader that if he or she has had enough of them reading this novel, then they are kindly advised to be aware that one of them may visit you anytime and anywhere you happen to be.

455

"Whatever!" she said. "Luckily, darling, the most important thing is you are safe now, and thank God I have you back."

*Yes,* Igor thought, *who knows? It could have been He himself who saved me.*

Just after the incident, the police issued the following appeal through the media, *The cat who saved the life of the Right Hon. Igor Jobber, MP, is kindly asked to come to Scotland Yard Headquarters, London at his earliest convenience. We would like very much to interview him in relation to an incident that occurred in Brighton on 10 July, 2013, but in the first place, profoundly thank him on behalf of the Metropolitan Police Commissioner and Mr Jobber's fellow*

*members of the House of Commons. Thank you for your cooperation.*

After a week or so, a cat of enormous proportions appeared at Scotland Yard. The receptionist was so frightened that once he saw it, he hid somewhere, and the cat had to press the desk bell countless times until eventually, scared to death, the poor fellow dared to come back. Then he directed the cat to the fifth floor, room 10A, to see Inspector Ronald Smarty, who greeted him with opened arms, thanked him for coming, offered tea and biscuits, and they had a very pleasant chat. One might be curious how the hell the inspector had no doubts he was speaking to the real cat, for nobody ever heard them speak. But Inspector Smarty possessed almost visionary insight, and had already assumed that there had been something more behind the story, that in the first place, it wasn't of course a cat who had saved Mr Jobber's life, but someone else pretending to be, and the question was who the Devil might it have been? And he shared his suspicions with Sir Omar Salomon, the Met Commissioner, an equally wise man, who too was of the opinion that there must be much more in the story in question. Thus, they both decided to investigate thoroughly the problem at any cost. And now Inspector Smarty on behalf of his fellow policeman offered his guest a week-long stay at the Dorchester Hotel, all expenses paid by the police. In the meantime, they gave the case the highest priority to examine it thoroughly. Their guest was kind enough to accept the offer, and stayed there, enjoying the hotel's splendours in full. All expenses, we want to underline, included everything, indeed, Havana cigars which he puffed on day and night, and so many that you could hang a proverbial axe in the blue air of his smoking room, so dense that once, a waiter who delivered a lobster (£180) at 2 am, almost fainted on entering the place. The guest was enjoying wines as well, especially Chateau Margaux (£500 a bottle) and Krug Champagne (£1000 a bottle). And, apparently being a man of various needs, invited more than once very pretty girls (£2,000 per night) provided by the London Prive agency, famous for its high-quality service. It seemed that in this respect he was in disagreement with a famous philosopher Immanuel, who called the movements required while performing that activity farcical and unworthy of a philosopher.

All in all, his stay at the hotel was rather costly, and the police's thorough investigation, for which Scotland Yard were famous, didn't reveal anything other than what had already been suspected, namely, that it wasn't of course a cat but a cleverly disguised minuteman who played his role marvellously.

Sir Omar wanted him to be questioned again, but unfortunately, he disappeared into thin air and couldn't be found anywhere despite enormous police efforts on a scale never heard of before. Apparently, he'd already found his wide-range needs satisfied.

Yes, some suspiciously big cats were denounced to the police, and anti-terrorist units, including some so famous that the SAS forced them to surrender, but they turned out to be the real things after all.

A special committee was established to examine the matter in question and found the expenses mentioned before too high, so Sir Omar, who in his wisdom had approved the operation, code name 'Leviathan', number 352764/129450/111/222/000/, as the newspaper The Moon found out, was asked to pay half of its cost. Sir Omar, by now a very distressed man, had to ask his bank for a substantial loan. Rather reluctantly, they gave it to him, and the same paper says he's still paying it back after all those years.

Inspector Smarty isn't with Scotland Yard anymore because of his transfer to some faraway place, so far in fact, that even The Moon hasn't been able to find him.

While all that was going on, our Igor, safely back at his home, was getting ready for a decisive Parliament battle that was to take place the day after his adventurous weekend in Brighton.

The battle in question was crucial for his political career, and requested all his political expertise to succeed. It was in fact not just one, but actually several battles, and not on just one but more than a couple fronts simultaneously. So many in fact that only such a strategic genius (even Field Marshal Erich von Manstein himself, wouldn't have been a match for him) as his could expect victory, of which he of course was sure, for he had never ever lost faith in himself. And his great hero, Sir Walter Cardinal, 'The Toad', would have been proud of Igor if he could only have heard of his incredible exploits.

Those battlefronts were actually a war, and almost a total one for that matter. It was about the Russian question, the Irish question (yes, once again, for it hadn't ended yet, and would never end as some pessimists claimed) and a good few more questions, so Igor was now working really hard and nobody, not even his lovely Susan, was allowed to disturb him.

But Igor was clever enough to realise that he might encounter opposition, and therefore he was readying himself in earnest to fight and never surrender as did his greatest hero, his beloved Sir Walter. Those who dared to deny his greatness were about to be crushed, especially those who in relation to the present situation of the country, denied his great concern about the unfortunate, the poor, saying that on the whole, shame on them, he was very much an overrated statesman.

There were other urgent issues, among others, that of the Russian Federation, which was perceived by him as a real threat to his cherished country, and he strongly condemned those who were impertinent enough to remind that their own ancestors had helped to give birth to the genesis of a new system under the red banner, which was still very much intact in Igor's opinion. The interpretation professing that the help had been motivated by greed was certainly false and unjust. And here he was supported by his faithful ally, Mr Foolstone, despite some disagreements between them.

Other issues concerned national defence, social security, the usual nightmare of the NHS and obviously the relationship with the cousins. Fortunately, Dollaria's president liked him, as much as he could like somebody but himself.

As for the defence of the country, which was said not to be accustomed to losing wars, except some unessential ones, Igor was going to press his demand for increasing substantially its strength. British infantry, he asserted, was still the finest, and if some events proved it otherwise, much the worse for the events. And here, at least for once he was in full agreement with George, criticising him in all other respects, especially that of the free spirit.

Social security, he said, was far too generous, for too many who were receiving it were losing their will to power, perhaps the most important attribute of the Englishman. We, he maintained, never wasted it unnecessarily as did the fellow countrymen of Friedrich. Igor didn't admire him too much, but found some passages good enough, however, never admitting that because of his unlimited love for his country.

He wasn't very eager to sacrifice too much of his precious time on the NHS question. British people are essentially of sound health, and even if they had some problems, again Friedrich was at hand, meaning his 'what doesn't kill me makes me stronger' recipe.

The eternal friendship with Dollaria was *sine qua non* of the country's foreign policy, and nobody, whatever happened, should ever doubt it.

The day before that important Parliament session at which he was sure to prevail, Igor was almost ready for a fight when he heard his telephone ring. It was Monday, the 21st of November, a day he would never forget, and at the memory of which he still trembles with cold.

The reader is obviously curious to know what could frighten such a brave, full-of-fighting-will man, so we're willing to satisfy his curiosity and tell him a story that happened on that fateful day.

Thus, nine o'clock on Thursday morning, Igor answered when that telephone rang. "We want to remind you that you have an appointment at ten," the voice said.

"What appointment?" he asked. "I haven't made any." We must say here that on that fateful and terrible day, as it would turn out to be later, Igor wasn't feeling good. On the previous day, he drank a bit too much, his biggest mistake having been to drink some exotic alcoholic mixtures served to him by a friend of his, a Russian aristocrat Venedict Yakovlev. The man was the only child of a couple who had left the Soviet Union under some unspecified circumstances, and came to live in England. There were some rumours they might be spies; otherwise, how would they have been able not only to leave the country but afford buying property in Mayfair for that matter? That had been investigated by MI5, supported by precious knowledge of Boris Dumblodge, but nothing suspicious had ever been uncovered. As a matter of fact, the MI6 boss studied at Oxford, and some resentful individuals claimed that at the time he might have belonged to an Oxford six or seven (nobody was sure about the number) which was suspected to exist then.

Our Igor met Venedict at Oxford where they were both members of the Bullingdon Club, and shared lovely memories of innumerable festivities they'd attended. And at the time, young Venedict had already been famous for his ingenious cocktails, after which their mutual friends could hardly remember what they had said.

Back to the matter in question, that is the telephone call Igor received. The voice on his telephone went on, "An appointment at your doctor's, of course. You aren't well, are you?"

"And how would you know that? Anyway, who am I talking to?"

"It's Wissend, Lord Hellbridge's personal assistant," the voice said.

"Ah," said Igor, and thought at the same time that under the circumstances, it was better to be on good terms with his lordship, so he said to the man, "ah yes, I haven't had the pleasure of meeting you yet, sir."

"I haven't, either, but we'll soon make up for it since the lord would like very much to see you today."

"But of course," Igor said, "and so would I."

"Thank you very much, and what time would be convenient for you, dear Mr Jobber?"

"Let's see, it's ten past nine now, so let's say 5 pm?"

"Oh, no, rather not, the lord is always at his best for important meetings in the morning, so I suggest eleven o'clock if it wouldn't be a trouble."

Igor was rather reluctant to see the lord at such an early hour. He was still unwell. Besides, he was never at his best in the morning, but now he knew it'd be better for him (he hoped so, anyway) to be accommodating and to accept. Thus, he said, "Fine, I await you at eleven then."

"Most obliged, see you then. Goodbye," said the lord's assistant, and hung up.

When Big Ben was striking eleven, Igor heard someone knocking on the door. He wondered how for the Devil's sake someone could slip through that very secure, steel-plated front door downstairs. He came to the door, peeped through the spyhole and saw nothing, but the knocking continued. *All these safety devices,* he thought, *are useless. Anyone can sneak in as if there weren't any, and the same is true for those CCTV cameras all over the country, waste of money, and the crime rate has even increased, and London is now perhaps the most dangerous city in Europe. On the other hand, however, it is not, for we aren't a European country, we are...* He couldn't finish his thought because another knock was so powerful that a crack appeared on the wall close to the door's frame. *I'd better open that damned door,* Igor thought, and he did. Before him stood a very short man, even shorter than him, but as powerfully built as the unforgettable Anderson, who could lift up a 170 kg dumbbell with one hand. Next to him stood a totally different individual, who frightened Igor with his pale, death-like face and very dark spectacles.

"We've come," announced the strongman, "in the name of Lord Hellbridge to apologise on behalf of him for being a bit late since he's still busy training his cat."

*Those bloody cats again,* Igor said to himself.

"But," continued the Anderson-like man, "it shouldn't take much longer for him to arrive. Could we in the meantime wait for him in your apartment?"

"I...I..." began Igor, "I'm not sure..."

"No need to worry," said the strongman. "We won't disturb you."

Igor still hesitated, for he felt very much ill at ease in the company of these two messengers of the lord, but then it would be a *faux pas* not to let them in. So he eventually said, "Well, yes, please come in."

"My name's Fortis," said the weightlifter as soon as they sat down on an antique sofa, "and my friend here is D'Amort."

"My pleasure," said Igor. "Is your friend French?" he enquired.

"Hmm," as if he wasn't sure what to say, said Fortis. "I don't actually know. Are you?" he asked, turning to his companion.

"Yes, I am," said the death-like fellow. "Actually, I'm a Gascon, from the Gave de Pau valley. My family has been living there since the times of the Roman Empire, and my father was a close friend of D'Artagnan."

461

"But," said Igor, ever a realist, "D'Artagnan was a fictitious character."

"Bah," said the Gascon, "you never know how to tell fiction from reality, you know, what is fiction today, is reality tomorrow."

*What a weird reasoning*, Igor thought, and said, "if it were so, how the hell would we tell them apart?"

"The point is that you actually cannot," said the Gascon philosopher, "for if you could, the world would be a much better place. You know, the more inconceivable something is, the more truthful it might be. Anyway, what is easy to understand is worth nothing."

By now, Igor had already lost track of the Gascon's logic, but he was trying his best to put together his somewhat confused thoughts.

"What was it we were talking about?" asked Fortis, and answered himself, "aha, the world as a better place, so I wonder what in your mind would make the world better, dear Mr Jobber."

"It is my strong belief," began Igor, who for some reason felt more assured of himself now, "that it is our compassion, understanding each other, diversity and…" he stopped as if unsure of choosing the right word, "…and respect for each other. Yes, that's it," he eventually said, now feeling proud of himself.

"Do you really think so?" said the Gascon, looking at Igor through his dark glasses.

"Yes, I do," decisively stated the advocate of those humanistic virtues.

"Hmm," the Frenchman said, still looking at him, "but these cherished values of yours haven't done much good for humanity so far, have they?"

"No, you're right, they haven't because there are sadly some dark forces at work," said Igor the humanist, nodding thoughtfully.

"And what might these forces be in your thoughtful opinion?" asked the other man.

"To be honest, it's rather difficult to identify them, but I think the reason might be…" Igor hesitated a second, "…that still too many people haven't understood the value of those noble virtues of man."

"I see," said the Gascon, "but it might be that they have, and that's why they rejected them. What would you say to that?"

Now, Igor became slightly confused again, but not wanting to appear indecisive, shook his head, and said, "No, those who rejected these great values are wrong. They simply haven't understood their worth."

"But it might be," began D'Amort, apparently a conversationalist, "that those noble values aren't good for man, after all."

"What is then good for him?" asked Igor, slightly annoyed now.

"Power, this is what is good for them, and what they really want!" firmly announced the Gascon, "and that compassion, modesty, integrity and humility are for those who lack the will to power, and these noble values were invented by those who, possessing that power, are able to console the former, to deceive them, to pull the wool over their faces and doing so to exert control over them, to manipulate. But the truth is that even the weak, those of slave morality deep at heart, consider Socrates and all his followers, all those humanists incorrigible gullible fantasists.

"And your own country and a few others, as a matter of fact, are good examples of the fact that manipulation, propaganda and façade are everything they employ to deceive the naïve, and the greater good, a democracy which *de facto* isn't there. But you've chosen to console the underdogs by that ridiculous kitsch of your songs and quasi-literature, that crap of yours, you bloody hypocrites. And as a result of your lies and deception, people have given up serious thinking, which is the only way not only to liberate themselves from the slavery of stupidity, but also to live a good life, which is to see it from the perspective of the eternal.

"And due to your never-ending duplicity and cunning, the majority of people got tired of serious thinking as I say, for you yourself convinced them of the uselessness of such an activity, and they focussed themselves on those vulgar earthly pleasures.

"Oh, oh, that's it," chipped in Fortis, nodding eagerly.

"In the past," continued the Gascon, "you were at least a bit more honest ruling your colonies, the best example being Ireland, where, when the great famine broke out, your faithful civil servants said that it was the judgement of God, who sent the calamity to teach the Irish a lesson, and the famine was an effective mechanism for reducing surplus population.

"But then, according to what He himself says, your deeds were actually deadly sins and therefore you would deserve punishment for what you had done."

"That's it, I think they do," said Fortis looking ominously at Igor, who was now truly scared.

"But," D'Amort resumed his devastating reasoning, "there might still be a chance left for you and your country."

"Would you please tell me what you mean by that?" enquired Jobber in a very weak voice.

"I may tell you, but I'm afraid you won't understand, being the slave of reality, of your wretched facts, and therefore you cannot afford the liberty of imagination.

"But I will tell you, after all. There is someone out there, who as you say wills forever evil, but you aren't willing to accept that he in fact is able to do eternal good. And that he may do so, in agreement with somebody else, for that matter."

At that very moment, Lord Hellbridge, accompanied by apparently the very same cat that had caused Igor so much trouble the other day, and his assistant, Wissend, came into the room where the discussion was taking place.

Seeing them, Igor closed his eyes and said to himself, *That cat again, God help me!*

"Don't call Him when you don't really need His help. Anyway, He won't help you," said the lord, and the cat nodded as if he was agreeing.

"How's the conversation going?" Hellbridge asked the new friends of Igor.

"Ah," replied D'Amort, "so far, we haven't arrived at any final conclusion, mon sire."

"To be honest, I wouldn't expect anything else, but it is our duty at least to try, after all," said the lord.

"I'd rather meet him in the boxing or wrestling ring," said Fortis, giving Igor a quick glance.

"In that case, a conversation wouldn't last long, if there would be any," Hellbridge replied, smiling, "but we are here to reach some conclusions, so let us be patient."

"Yes, sire," said the other. "Unfortunately, we must be."

"Anyway," Hellbridge said, "you've made some progress, I presume."

"As a matter of fact," commented D'Amort, "we've hardly made a start."

"What we can do," replied the lord, "it takes time, but I'm pretty sure, we'll move forward sooner or later. And I've come here to assist you in your efforts to find out some truth."

"Thank you, sire," said D'Amort, "you'll be, as usual, of great help."

"And now tell me, please, what were you discussing? I'm particularly interested in some conclusions, if there are any," Hellbridge asked his assistants.

"We were talking about the deadly sins in general and particularly whether there's any chance left for England to make amends for her wrongdoings in the past."

"Huh, huh, that's a very difficult subject, and I find it hard to envision any chances, for that matter," said the lord, shaking his head. "But," he went on, "we may try to explore the matter in question after all. But first of all, my friends, I think we should identify what or who is responsible for such a bad situation in this world in general, and only then may we have a chance to examine whether there are any chances left."

"Yes, of course, sire," agreed D'Amort. "This is the only way to deal with the problem at hand."

"But I, myself," said Fortis, "am already tired just thinking of our task, and think that challenging Zbyszko or Winfried would be a much easier task."

"But, my friends," said Hellbridge, "shouldn't we continue to get somewhere, after all?"

"At your command, sire," both the lord's assistants said in unison.

"Thank you, gentlemen. So, *primo*, let me make a digression as regards the human search for good and beauty in this world. In my humble opinion, there is hardly any of that there, and the search for them might be quite futile as it was in the case of that poor Icarus, the son of Daedalus. Recently, Mr Adarsh told me about an acquaintance of his, Declan, who was very much inclined to find these goods almost everywhere, and that reminds us, putting it metaphorically, of Icarus himself. I mean his flight, during which he flew too near the sun so that the wax that fastened his artificial wings melted and he fell into the sea and drowned. The sun in the metaphor represents, of course, the search for good and beauty, which are supposed to make us happy. Now, if we tend to find them at any cost, then in fact we're liable to catch very dangerous diseases called gullibility and hypocrisy and, as a result, are disposed to beautify anything on earth, that is, in truth to falsify things. We instead have a tendency to see things as they are, for only then are we convinced we can make them better.

"Icarus' flight ended badly, and so will end any attempt to make the world better through falsification. And I asked Mr Adarsh to tell Declan about that, to warn him of the consequences of his futile and actually irresponsible approach to some problems he deals with. But he told me that it would be hard to persuade somebody who was educated as a mathematician, for such a man tends to forget that a proposition of mathematics does not express a thought, as our dear Ludwig rightly observed.

"Now, we've already asked whether there are any chances left to save the world, and now, to be more precise, I suggest making that question more specific, that is, to ask whether this world might be saved from an apocalypse which, as we know, was foretold rather a long time ago.

"I discussed the matter in question with somebody else a few days back, and he said he would be rather reluctant to change his mind as regards the problem. He said that if he changed his mind regarding the issue in question, it would disappoint some of his associates, his co-workers, who had laboured so hard and so long to reach the final conclusion. But, at the end of our conversation, he was kind enough to leave the matter with me because he said it was me in point of fact who would deal with the problem in future.

"So now, to consider any options we might think of, I propose we examine the core of the matter in question, and I mean those stubborn facts people are so obsessed with, and those facts in relation to the matter of good and evil."

Igor, who was listening attentively to the lord, felt his horror increase, and his only hope was that Hellbridge was just theorising, that it was just academic speculation with no connection whatsoever to reality. Alas, as he would find out, that apparently scholastic analysis would concern himself, and pretty soon for that matter.

"And to begin," the lord resumed his learned reasoning, "I will take the liberty of quoting a short verse written down by a man, known as

Witkacy, whom I acknowledge as having really impressive insight. I spoke to him yesterday and he graciously permitted me to quote him.

"Please listen carefully, and then we'll interpret carefully what our dear Stas had to say. Here you are, 'Those petty, insignificant facts!

In the infinity of those dark desires of ours;

How wretched are deeds of men, who swagger being so meek!'

"And that's it, my friends. And as you may guess, it is actually, I mean, the problem we now discussing, about men who are responsible for those petty facts our Stas is telling us about. And unless we get rid of such men, nothing will change for the better.

"You know, too much good is not good for the world at all, for a shade is a very powerful stimulation, being actually the drive to reach a place which is in fact beyond good and evil which, I believe, should be the final objective for man. But, huh, huh, it's not so easy to get there, and just a few chosen people may eventually arrive at the destination where finally there are no questions left, and consequently no answers are needed.

"You know that rather stupid saying, I mean, the show must go on, don't you? And I always wonder what it actually means, especially what kind of show it is, and where it is going, which direction. It reminds me of our unforgettable Franz, who was enjoying dinner with a friend at a restaurant when a famous runner came in, and the friend said, 'Look, this is that famous runner,' and Franz said, 'A runner? And in which direction does he run?'

"You see, it is all about direction, my friends, and as far as I can see, this world is going in the wrong direction, but apparently people don't give a damn about that, for they say 'carpe diem', don't they? And yes, of course, but the question is what that 'carpe diem' of theirs is like, and I, myself, have a rather dim view of it. A man mentioned before, that obstinate Bakunin, said, 'Today's slaves are called wage earners,' and that is their carpe diem. There've been some who suggested starting everything from scratch, precisely because the direction has been wrong from the very beginning, and who is in fact responsible for that grave mistake?" said Hellbridge, looking at Igor, who now seemed to be on the verge of a breakdown, "and we'll try to answer the question why the world is going in the wrong direction. Do you have any suggestions?" The lord turned to Wissend.

467

"Yes, mon sire, I have a few."

"So, please share with us the results of your acclaimed powers of observation," the lord encouraged him.

"With your kind permission, I will, sire, but first I must say that my investigation into the matter at hand isn't finished yet. However, I did arrive at some conclusions I hope you all will appreciate, perhaps with the exception of..." and here Wissend looked at Igor.

"But, let's begin after all. So, first of all, we must ask again who's responsible for that wretched state of affairs, for they created a system which prevails in some parts of the world and benefits just its inventors. Yes, the system aims at making the majority happy, they say, but we ask, what is the quality of this happiness? And we actually find it shabby. So-called happiness today is nothing but chow, drink and a few other very basic pleasures which the makers of the system consider sufficient to fulfil the needs of the majority, but we aren't Marxists, so we aren't convinced that quantity is everything.

"That majority is pretty satisfied having those few pleasures, but I don't think they will be so in the long run, and sometime in the future they may wake up and say, 'We need more to live.' But then they would require new values. And what I say now was already fully understood by our good friend Friedrich, and we owe him a profound debt of gratitude. You, mon sire," Wissend addressed the Lord, "spoke to him recently and as far as I know, he was pleased to hear we agreed with him."

"Yes," said Hellbridge, "he was indeed, and he too expressed his pleasure at not dwelling at a place where all interesting people are missing, and thanked me again."

And only now did a thought cross Igor's mind, and he said to himself, *Gosh, he is there after all!*

Hellbridge looked at him, smiled and said, "Yes, dear Mr Jobber, 'after all' as you say. And now, there's something we want to make clear before moving further to get to the essence of our visit here. You may not be able to understand it, but we'll do our best to emphasise our point of view.

So, to my mind, and I believe my assistants will agree with me, man isn't born wise, and only the right education, if anything else, may make him wiser, and in your country, dear Mr Jobber, this sort of education is accessible to not many a man. But this looks very different in some other countries, where education is within reach of the vast majority, provided that applicants eager to acquire such schooling are intelligent enough to begin their study. By the way, what I find funny here is that those unprivileged financially are proud of those educational facilities they can't afford. Even those in rags boast of their rich compatriots and their financial establishments, as if they have already lost their sense of reality and became total nuts. Moreover, the poorer their background, the stronger their support for the money aristocracy. On the whole, it seems that 'rags to riches' is the highest moral obligation. As far as I know, that kind of mental disease is not yet of interest to psychiatry as it should be, but I do hope that someday in the future it will be.

"Now, those lucky ones educating themselves find sooner or later that their tuition isn't actually knowledge as such, not at all, for it is about the art of manipulation of those unlucky enough to be educated at all. As a matter of fact, the curriculum of your schools is of a lower quality than it is at totally unknown teaching facilities in countries poorer than yours. But schooling in manipulation, deceit and perfidy is here, I must admit, very high indeed. But I won't congratulate you on this matter. Actually, I'll do the opposite, and someday, pretty soon in fact, you'll see what I mean."

Wissend, along with the cat, nodded, and Igor thought not for the first time, *I must be dreaming.*

"No, no," said Hellbridge, "you aren't, and you'll be better readying yourself for something even worse than today's little chat."

Igor said nothing in response. He was about to call God again in his mind but realised He wouldn't respond to his call.

"So," Lord Hellbridge resumed his reasoning, "those poor wretches can do nothing but admire those privileged, which is of course very much appreciated by them."

Igor said nothing again. He was sitting still, his eyes shut, as if half-paralysed.

"Are you okay, Mr Jobber?" asked Hellbridge. "You don't look well. Wissend, give him something for strength. You know, that elixir of yours. I heard it does wonders."

The lord's assistant produced a green bottle out of his pocket and poured some of its contents into a glass that he handed to Igor, saying, "Drink up, it'll help you."

"Thank you," said the beneficiary in a hardly audible voice, swallowing the fluid in a gulp. And then he saw nothing but complete darkness in which one star after another began to appear. He couldn't catch his breath for a good couple of minutes, but then he felt bliss within, and thought, *Am I already there, in heaven?*

"Not yet, my old chap," said Hellbridge. "Anyway, it hasn't been decided yet where you'll get to."

Jobber, who wasn't that stupid after all, resolved now to agree with everything the lord told him, so he just nodded in response.

"What were we talking about?" Hellbridge asked nobody in particular. "Aha, education and its capabilities, yes, that's it.

"Not to dwell too long on the subject," he continued, "I'd just say that those who aren't lucky enough to get it don't actually live. I believe they merely exist. *Vita sine litteris mors est,* I've already heard somebody mention it. And it's very much a true, but to my great disappointment, almost commonly disregarded credo. And now please note that if we censure here our hosts or their neighbours, the Irish, whosoever for that matter, we don't do it out of malicious pleasure. No, not at all, on the contrary, we feel sorry for them and want as far as we can to come to their relief. But the problem is, they aren't too eager to believe in our good intentions, so we must take some necessary precautions to succeed eventually in persuading them to accept our point of view. Otherwise, they won't understand our noble assignment. They won't be capable of grasping the importance of saying 'no' in this world, to deny in order to finally say 'yes'. In other words, saying 'no' serves to purify things. It is a catharsis that is needed urgently, and if it doesn't come, I see no future ahead.

"And now, let's have a look at our guest's achievements, if we may call them so, and then we'll consider a precaution or two to put in order a few matters.

"Let's look first at his domain, that's politics, and here we have a few issues which are puzzling for his fellow countrymen. However, quite a few of them say that his ideas are brilliant or even the work of a genius."

"Perhaps, mon sire," went on Wissend, "we should analyse his ideas with the help of Ludwig's second philosophy?"

"Oh, no, no, no, anything but that, for we would get nowhere and eventually end up left with his word games, which haven't achieved anything at all. And by the way, I wonder why his analytical philosophy became so popular in Britain."

"If I may offer my humble opinion, sire," said Wissend, "this is because the Brits have never understood his first one, and they actually love those games because it makes it possible for them to hide their true intentions in word tricks."

"Yes, precisely," said Hellbridge, "you've got it right, and you obviously remember what Ludwig said to Bertrand with regard to the *Tractatus*, don't you?"

"Oh yes, how could I forget? He said. 'Don't worry, you will never understand it.'"

"That's it," said Hellbridge, "and Bertrand and his fellow countrymen have never understood because they lack the innate capability of doing so, and this is where the rub is, and we should never forget it when dealing with them, if you know what I mean."

"But of course, sire, I do, and this is about a very different kind of inner capability, I mean, their tendency we have already mentioned to confuse you with incoherent mumbling to deceive, to conceal their real intentions."

"As usual, you haven't failed my expectations, my dear friend, and now talking to our reverend host," said the lord, looking at Igor, "we have here the perfect example of what we've just said, and accordingly we should proceed never forgetting that."

"Thank you, sire," said Wissend, "and just now something dawned on me, I mean, a letter that comes after 'B', that's 'C', and I think that in fact it might rather be about a letter game. But if I could stay with 'B' for a while, then just recently listening to the BBC, I heard a conversation, an analytical one, of course, regarding a once extremely popular band whose name starts with 'B'. And what they said was an example of analytical philosophy of the highest degree, really amazing. They essentially came to the conclusion that the band's musical artistic sophistication surpassed by far the music of a man whose surname also starts with 'B', and his first name is by a strange coincidence Ludwig. But then, I remembered an English composer's opinion of that former B's music, and all he had to say was 'that crap.'"

"You see," said Hellbridge, "that composer went even further than our Ludwig of the *Tractatus*, who recommended three words to deal with anything, and here we have just one. Anyway, I, myself, am a bit confused by all these games, whatever they might be, and fed up with words in general."

"If I may venture my opinion, sire, you're simply overworked. Everybody round the globe seeks your advice. For instance, just this morning, I again took telephone calls from three presidents asking me if you would be available soon for counsel on very urgent matters. All that you need now, mon sire, is a rest, and I'd suggest a long vacation, in France or Italy, of course."

"Thank you for your consideration, my faithful comrade. I think you're right. Yes, a sabbatical seems to be the right solution, and these lovely countries are the perfect choice, for a vacation in this country would make me feel even worse.

"But, fortunately or not, we're still here and we have to deal with the problem at hand and a couple of others for that matter. And in relation to those damn letters, another one just came to mind, and I mean 'C'. And here we have a rather particular case which would be even hard to understand using analytical philosophy. Yes, it would be useless, for I mean the word 'cousin', and the word, apparently so simple, turns out to be very mysterious, for it denotes something whose existence defies all plausible reality. On the other hand, small wonder it does so because it is used within the realm of politics, and the British, being faithful disciples of Ludwig's second philosophy, apply the word 'cousin' to every citizen of Dollaria, whatever his or her ethnicity might be. Let it be a black man, or Italian, Polish, Irish, whosoever, they are all their cousins. And you can see now how mysterious the interpretation of blood relations might be, simply astounding, and I'm sure that Ludwig himself would go pale if he had the chance to learn about that, and perhaps fortunately for him he doesn't have it any longer."

"Yes, mon sire," Wissend chipped in, "and because I still care about him, I won't mention that to him during our next meeting."

"That's very considerate of you, and I appreciate it," said Hellbridge, "and now let's go back to the heart of the matter or as Joseph would have said, the *Heart of Darkness*, for it is indeed something very disturbing, and I mean people's ignorance. And, as a matter of fact, I wouldn't be willing to blame them for being so, and let me say what I have on my mind, and you, old chap," the lord addressed Igor, "please listen carefully, for it actually concerns you as well."

By now, our poor Igor was still listening to what was being said, but he had the feeling that it wasn't really happening, that it was a dream, and being an incorrigible realist, he did his best to deny the reality of the experience, but alas in vain.

"So," continued Hellbridge, "whom shall we hold responsible for that darkness? And to my mind, it isn't an ordinary man but the system, which we may describe as an organised rape of incredible strength and efficiency. But that man in the street must find the way out of it on his own, for all we can do is show him the direction. Anyway, we aren't politicians, God forbid."

The cat was apparently listening attentively to his master, either nodding or shaking his head, and anticipating future events, we want to say that our Igor's first question, whenever later on he was invited to visit somebody, was, "Do you own a cat?" As we can see, he will still be unaccustomed to supernatural phenomena, and shame on him, for if he'd managed to abandon his mistrust in them, his political career could have been far more successful.

"And," Lord Hellbridge continued his resumé, "and sadly enough, what our ordinary man takes for the reality of his existence is actually a fiction because it is a substitute of life, an ersatz of being, for there's nothing genuine about it. It is like those commercials which advertise goods, praising their quality to excess, and they're actually worth nothing. Eventually, he cannot tell good from evil, heaven from hell, as a certain band were singing. All in all, the system has created a fiction and wants our poor man to accept it as reality, but as it happens, such a swindle can't last forever."

"If I may express my point of view," said Wissend, "that system, sire, you just so precisely described in a few words, totally denies another system, that is the system of Christian values and principles they still pretend to observe."

"Ah," exclaimed Hellbridge, "don't even mention it. What a shame and disappointment for its author, who may never forgive them. But actually, He'd predicted it long before all that circus began, hadn't He? There's a relevant gospel that confirms His foresight, isn't there?"

"But of course, mon sire," said his wise assistant. "The problem is our man seems not to be very much disturbed by that bad news, I mean, that gospel, and I fully understand him, for why should he care about something that is supposed to happen in the unspecified future? Anyway, as far as I know, he doesn't give a damn about it, and in point of fact he doesn't believe in that prophecy."

"That's it," said Hellbridge, nodding, "he doesn't anymore. And this is where the rub is, for if he did, his life could have been very different. Who knows? Anyway, it's too late now to ponder on that, for our man has already gone too far, but I, being an optimist, still believe there's a chance left for him, an almost invisible light in the dark tunnel, so to speak."

"Do you really think, sire, he still has a chance?"

"Yes, I do, and this is exactly why I am here."

"But yes, of course, forgive me. I'd almost forgotten what we've come here for," said Wissend.

"No need to apologise, my friend. My memory fails me too. Oh no, it isn't as good as it used to be. And this is, I believe, because I want to forget so much, so many unpleasant things happening all over this poor earth. And to have a little rest at last. Ah, our job is so hard, and I don't really know how long I'll manage to keep on doing it.

"But because we still have a job to do, let's rethink some other matters, and in the first place, let's emphasise we've come here to benefit those who need our assistance, not being even aware of it. I stress this once again. We're here to do good, contrary to so-called common opinion. Anyway, common sense is not so common, as our clever friend Francois Marie already noticed.

"And our first priority to carry out our duty is no tolerance for stupidity, because this tolerance is nowadays something to please all kinds of half-witted in order to keep them under control, and not to express any humanistic respect for them, as advertised by the Government's policy. Anyway, tolerance has never taught anyone to be better. The only way to make a man better is to educate him, and I mean of course humanities, which should be taught at every stage of his education. And this is the only hope for humanity to survive. Otherwise, an apocalypse will surely come. What kind of catastrophe, one may ask, might it be? Hmm, let's pass over the answer in silence for the time being.

"Now, I notice a curious paradox, and because I've always been very keen on studying paradoxes as such, which I consider so essential in human life, which is a paradox in itself, the paradox I mean now is a very odd and quite common kind of taking pleasure in the hopeless misery of modern life. As if, paradoxically, people want to console themselves by all those doubtful kinds of gratification. It may work for a while, but I'm pretty sure it won't for too long.

"As for the so common word, that is 'common', I, myself, have a deep distrust of it, and I don't actually know what it is supposed to mean for the majority. Anyway, I'd recommend limiting its use, and this is because life as such is the task of a single man which has nothing to do with the lives of others, contrary to that idiotic common opinion."

Igor was trying his best to follow Hellbridge's reasoning, but without much success, but at the same time he noticed the cat was apparently very interested in it, and now when the lord took a short pause, he nodded his agreement and emphasised it with a loud meow. And right now, he decided to make a draft of a bill limiting the number of cats in his country, and to do it, he thought that a special licence to possess one should be required by law.

At that very moment, Hellbridge looked at him, shaking his head as if with regret and said, "Your ideas are getting stupider than ever, and we must do something about that. I suggest that you try to understand what I'm saying, for you may need to grasp the meaning of it someday.

"To resume, what it is all about, I mean, our visit in this country of all places, which I believe leads the world in decline. Now let's point out some other characteristics to make clear what I mean by that.

"What was it I was saying? Aha, tolerance, fiction and consolation among others. Yes, it's difficult to comprehend the complexity of interrelations between them, and I, myself, can hardly understand them, but I promise I'll make them as clear as I can, and my learned assistant," Hellbridge nodded to Wissend, "will give me a hand, won't you? And you too, I trust?" said the lord, looking at the cat.

"But of course, mon sire, I'll do my best," said Wissend, and the cat bowed.

"Then, *et voilà*, and now, to my mind, tolerance for stupidity increases evil on this earth, and by the way, it might be perhaps unreasonable to believe that hell is the capital of it. Anyway, I wonder," said Hellbridge, addressing Igor, "have you ever listened to that wonderful performance of *Dance with the Devil* by 'Cosy' Powell, for if you have, then you would better understand me, have you?"

Igor just shook his head and said nothing.

"What a shame!" the lord went on, "so, let's first have a look at consolation, and what we see here is again the system in this country, and a few other places, of course, that does its best to please people, providing them with the essentials and expecting them to be happy. And, as a matter of fact, they are, but unfortunately it is a very crude sort of happiness. And if that were all they could experience in their lives, then I would feel sorry for them. At any rate, a modern man, especially in English-speaking countries, for some reason, and I tend to think the reason is him being a mongrel, is nothing but a meek creature unable to resist, to take arms against the sea of trouble he's in. He has lost the power to rebel, to resist, and all that is left for him is to submit, to accept the existence of wage-earner serfs, and paradoxically to find pleasure in the decline, finding consolation in the most primitive joys of life. But I'm certain that men, deep in their hearts, need more than that. What would you say to that, my friend?" Hellbridge asked, looking at Wissend.

"I certainly believe they need more, mon sire," said the lord's assistant, "but the problem is how could they achieve that more as you put it, especially when in this country the establishment is working on creating, furtively of course, a police state? And it is being done by introducing more and more laws, especially all kinds of restrictions, bans, and the like. This is a good example of that Roman saying, '*corruptissima re publica plurimae leges*', and by corruption in relation to the present situation, I mean, the corruption of the spirit. And since the English has always ignored it, or even denied the existence of such a thing, it's much easier to subdue the citizens. The spirit I mean is the spirit of life, that is, the spirit of freedom, but I'm afraid that neither our host," and now Wissend looked sternly at Igor, "nor too many of his fellow countrymen, for that matter, would understand what I mean because the condition of that spirit has always been extremely poor here, and that's why their arts and philosophy have always been of such a poor quality.

"And now I take the liberty of saying what you, mon sire, have already emphasised, which is that our censure of their acts is not aimed at condemning them, but to help them to escape the consequences of their wrongdoings, and if they don't notice the danger in time they will pay dearly for it, and very soon for that matter."

"Yes," said the lord, "imagination, so closely related to the spirit, ah, it is in such poor health nowadays, and that's why the fate of the world looks so dim. Moreover, I'm afraid that the one who somewhat overestimated his ability in creating man, if you know whom I mean, is very likely to administer justice to him. Anyway, he said some time ago, 'My punishment will be horrific, and you will prostrate before my sword.' Didn't he say that?" asked Hellbridge, looking at Igor.

"I'm afraid I don't know what you mean, sir."

"You don't, you say? That's much the worse for you because ignorance doesn't excuse," said the lord, "as you'll find out yourself pretty soon.

"But let's go back to the main leitmotiv of our reflexions today, and what we want to stress again is how we appreciate the liberty of the spirit. We're even, contrary to common opinion, the guardians of it, for it is the only chance left for man to avoid that punishment.

"But no, our host and his limited-in-imagination fellow countrymen decided to fight that spirit of life. They even attempted to get rid of it for good. And that's why they are stealthily introducing all kinds of restrictions and bans for which they're infamous.

"But at the same time, in their renowned hypocrisy, they are eager to criticise other countries, Russia, for instance, and a couple of others.

"Anyway, they may, deep in their hearts, not being aware of it, long for an apocalypse. And it may come. I'm inclined to wait a while, but then

I'm not that patient, and besides, I'm rather sure that my words will reach deaf ears. But they're so proud of their matter-of-fact view of the world, not being wise enough to comprehend that it is as unpredictable as the financial markets, as George proved a few years back. And what about their deep-rooted prejudice towards other countries? Let's just mention our delightful France, which by comparison makes this country look like a godforsaken backwater in more than one respect. It is, I assume, a sort of inferiority complex that pink rabbits have been suffering for centuries now.

"And what about that famous politeness of which they're so proud? In fact, it is nothing but a routine, habitual and unfeeling reaction. It should rather put us on alert because behind it there's nothing but ruthless self-interest, but how many gullible enough people have been taken in by that?

"Ah, I'm already tired of myself giving this lecture, but please understand that I consider it my duty to clear up some matters before I turn to action. Otherwise, nobody but a few would understand why I am doing what I do. But I promise it won't take much longer, and then..." and here Hellbridge interrupted himself, looked at Igor, and went on, "... perhaps even some bigots will eventually understand why I've come here."

Igor Jobber said nothing in response, just looking blankly ahead as if he were half-conscious. But he had the feeling there was something in store for him and began to feel uneasy, but decided to hold on for he was certain he would survive after all as he had already done before, but this time it wouldn't be the case. And relatively soon we'll witness some events which will prove Hellbridge's promise came true.

"So," the lord resumed his address, "all in all, I'm going to make an offer that you can't really refuse, for if you do..." he suspended his voice for a moment and then continued, "...it'll make everything even worse for you, so be reasonable and accept it.

"Now, the main reason I'm talking to you is my will to do good, and because you might understand what I mean only when you voluntary give up your current position, forget politics and start doing things which *de facto* better suit your disposition.

"There's little need to say that everything I've just said about your country and your compatriots applies of course to yourself.

"Anyway, we're now leaving you, thanking you for your hospitality, and good luck. You'll need it, and maybe something else too. That's it for now, and you'll soon see things from a different perspective, so to speak, and you may even appreciate it.

"Goodbye, Mr Jobber," said Lord Hellbridge, standing up and leaving Igor's apartment with his assistants in tow. Just before leaving, the cat looked back at Igor and winked, and then all of them were gone.

Igor kept sitting down for a good while, thinking and repeatedly asking himself, *What shall I do?* The situation he'd just experienced seemed not to be from this world. He tried his best to shake off all he'd just heard but somehow couldn't. Suddenly he made up his mind and decided to seek advice from a minister at the Church of England parish not far away from where he lived.

He got there in five minutes, introduced himself and said he needed to speak to the Reverend Heavenbrook, whom he'd already met before.

That pastor was a well-known personage, and many a man sought the advice he was always ready to give. Some of Igor's associates had done so, as a matter of fact, more than once, and were always extremely grateful for it. They'd done so in secrecy but Igor had learned about it from Mr Dumblodge, who was curiously interested in where and whom some politicians were visiting, including the minister's office. The MI6 boss even tried to find out something more about the visits from the reverend, but to no avail. The minister firmly refused to divulge anything. We see here that in fact Dumblodge worked in truth outside his territory, for internal business was not his by law, but that overeager fellow had somehow forgotten that.

"To what do I owe the honour of welcoming you at my humble abode?" the minister said, seeing Igor.

"I'm here," said Igor, "to ask for your opinion, Reverend Heavenbrook, on a, hmm, how shall I put it, delicate matter."

"This is what I'm here for, so, please, tell me what it's about. You can speak frankly, and I assure you nobody will learn the subject of our conversation. I take some special precautions to keep this place free of anything that could put in danger the confidentiality of my conversations. I mean some over-curious individuals, among others, your friend…" and here the minister smiled at Jobber, "…Dumblodge, who would spy on himself if he noticed some, let's say, irregularities. Actually, he should, I mean his imbecility that put this country in continuous danger. He has no respect even for this sacred place, and recently, with the help of some specialists, of course, I found some of his devises. Nobody else but him could have put them here, so I rang him and gave him a dressing-down, but he denied of course any wrongdoing. That dimwit would spy even on his mother if he found it necessary. To be honest, I don't understand how he can be a friend of yours, Mr Jobber."

"I… I don't understand that myself, dear Reverend Heavenbrook."

"If you don't, then you're partially excused. Anyway, please tell me what I can do for you. This must be some unusual matter, I assume, for you don't look your usual self. Something must have seriously disturbed you, so tell me what it's about."

"Yes, indeed, there's some rather stressful matter, you know, I've just had a visitor accompanied by a couple of assistants, and what he told me left me rather anxious, to be honest."

"I see," said the minister, "and who was it, Mr Jobber?"

"It was Lord Hellbridge, Reverend Heavenbrook."

"Ah, him, yes, there's something unearthly about him that I can't put my finger on. And what did he say to you?"

"He said I should give up doing what I do now and occupy myself with something that will suit me better, as he put it himself."

"Aha, and did he say what that would be?" asked the minister.

"No, he didn't."

"So, how could you find out what it would be?"

"I don't have a clue, and that's why I'm here."

"Hmm, I'm not sure if I can be of any help, dear Mr Jobber, and why didn't you ask him yourself?"

"You know, I was distressed by what he said, and didn't want that conversation to last longer, so actually I was just listening to him."

"I perfectly understand, but tell me, what was it he said to you?"

"In the first place, he was very critical about a great number of things in our country, and apparently would be willing to make them better, as he put it."

"Ah, that was it. And you know what? I, myself, am of the same mind, dear Mr Jobber. High time to make some necessary changes, and very soon for that matter."

"Really?" said Igor, taken aback by the pastor's words, being now not so sure if he had arrived at the right address to seek advice.

"But you know what?" Heavenbrook paused now as if he wasn't sure of what to say further, and then continued, this time in a much lower voice, "I actually think we should ask someone to advise us what to do in the near future."

"Do you have somebody particular in mind?" asked Igor.

"Yes, I do," said the minister, "but I'm still not sure it would be appropriate to contact him under the circumstances."

"And who might it be?" said Igor, curious now and wanting to resolve the problem as soon as possible.

"I'm thinking of asking Father O'Godley, whose knowledge of spiritual matters, I must admit, is much more impressive than mine."

Igor glared at him in surprise and said, "But he's a Catholic priest."

"So what? said Heavenbrook sternly. "These matters are very different these days, and we could get in touch even with the Devil if it were possible."

"With the Devil? exclaimed Igor, truly astounded now. And would it be appropriate?"

"Why not? Now we are allowed to speak to whoever we want. So, shall I give him a ring?"

Since Igor was desperate for advice, he said, "Yes, please. Go ahead."

Heavenbrook went to make his call, and after a mere few minutes was back, but with a very different expression on his face.

"How did it go?" asked a curious Igor.

"Hmm," started the reverend, looking rather puzzled, "my conversation with Father O'Godley wasn't long, and all I heard from him after describing your experience was, 'Tell him just this, do as you were told,' and then he hung up. So, it's now up to you how to proceed, dear Mr Jobber."

Igor thanked Heavenbrook for his assistance, and on his way back home, he thought, "*There was something missing in the behaviour of both the clergymen. Heavenbrook, contrary to his normal self, seemed to be very* unsure of himself, and the other one acted as if he wanted to have nothing to do with the problem, limiting his advice to just a couple of words. Thus, the question is, what was it that made them both so elusive, and as far as I could see, rather frightened, or something? Anyway, why should I follow Hellbridge's words? His range of influence is rather wide, but as a matter of fact, not strong enough to pose a real threat to my position. Anyway, he didn't express himself precisely. Ah, let's forget the problem, and I'll proceed as if nothing has happened.

We forgot to mention that Igor arrived to see the reverend on his bike, and now, as he was mounting his technological wonder, he felt his usual self-confidence was back. And he was soon on his way to Westminster.

He boldly joined the traffic and was soon speeding, overtaking other bikers. He was just emerging from behind the corner entering Oxford Street when he saw something he hoped never to see again, namely, a big black cat.

The animal seemed to be even bigger than the one owned by Hellbridge. The cat blocked the cyclists' path, sitting on it, licking his paws with philosophic calmness, paying no attention to anything around him. And what greatly astonished Igor was the fact that a policeman passing by seemed not to be bothered by the cat's impertinence, for he did something quite the opposite. He smiled at him, raising his hand in greeting, and the cheeky animal responded likewise. *As soon as I get to my destination, I'll immediately contact the police commissioner and tell him how irresponsible his subordinates are*, thought Igor, not knowing yet that he would never again get a chance to speak to the commissioner.

Not wanting to be anywhere close to the cat, Igor now decided to change his route, which now wasn't easy, even for such an experienced cyclist as him, for the street was packed with cars. But being as always so sure of himself (perhaps with the exception of what he experienced during his recent visit), he turned abruptly to the right, but now it was already too late to avoid a head-on collision with a vintage Bentley Continental Drophead of 1986, a truly beautiful car, which appeared out of nowhere before him. Just before bumping into her, in a flash of reminiscence, he realised that Lord Hellbridge was being driven in the same model, and then everything went dark.

When Igor regained consciousness, but still with his eyes shut, he felt that someone or something was licking his face, and he actually liked the feeling. But when he eventually opened his eyes, he was rather surprised to see the huge head of a pig still licking his face. *Am I dreaming? Or maybe I'm no longer on this earth,* he asked himself. But apparently, he was still there, for the licking continued. He didn't have a clue how he had arrived at this place and how one should behave in such a situation.

Then he saw an unshaved man wearing dirty overalls and wellingtons, who was staring at him and smoking a fat roller, and Igor, who hadn't fully recovered his strength yet, somehow managed to ask him in a very weak voice, "Excuse me sir, but what am I doing here?"

"I, myself, was going to ask you the same thing," said the man.

"Yes, of course, but I don't really know how come I'm here. All I remember is a cat, a car, and then everything went blank."

"I see, and that cat and car, where had they been?"

"In London, as far as I remember," said Igor, not being sure of anything now.

"London, you say? But you're now in Ballyleny."

"Ballyleny?" Igor repeated, bewildered. "And where is that?"

"You don't know that, either?" asked the man angrily, apparently insulted by Igor's ignorance.

"I'm terribly sorry, sir, but I'm still not well, so my memory…"

"Yes, of course, that probably excuses your poor knowledge of geography. Ballyleny is in Northern Ireland, County Armagh."

*Oh my God!* thought Igor, and felt that remnants of his strength were now leaving him. Especially as he just remembered his extremely harsh exposé about the Province at the House of Commons he delivered just a week ago. *And now, what happens if they saw me on TV, which seems to be very likely, considering people's love of it anywhere in the world, including even Ballyleny. And now, given that county's bad reputation –* it was actually called bandit country, as he remembered – *if they find out it was me who gave the speech, I'm finished.*

And now he noticed with horror that the smoker was regarding him suspiciously, as if he already knew that, and then said, "You know, your face rings a bell. You know, you look very similar to a politician, you know,

483

that fucking Igor Jobber…" he paused, and then asked straightaway, "are you him?"

"Oh, no, no, of course not, just a coincidental resemblance," cried a horrified Igor, feeling he might pass out any moment now.

"If you aren't him," said the man, still regarding him sceptically, "you may consider yourself lucky, for if we had a chance to get hold of that son of a bitch, then…" The man didn't finish, but Igor guessed what the man meant, and a cold shiver run down his spine.

"And tell me," the man continued, "what are you doing over there, in London? What's your line of work?"

"I…" Igor hesitantly began, frantically thinking of something that would please the man of Ballyleny, and eventually uttered, "I work for the City Council."

"Aha, and in what capacity?" the man kept enquiring.

"I…" Igor started in the same manner, searching his mind for the name of an occupation, and finally said, "it's the Animal Care Department, and my specialty is to ensure the well-being of cats. But I like pigs too," he added hastily.

"Aha," said the man, apparently pleased with Igor's noble line of work, "but tell me, what about London pigs?"

"We don't have many of them in London," Igor informed the man.

"Oh, what a shame," said the man. This time, he seemed to be rather disappointed.

"Apart from…" Igor began, and as if by a miracle, he felt, hitherto unknown to him, a sense of sincerity, and said, "politicians, of course."

"Ah, them," shouted the man, glancing at him so furiously that Igor felt another wave of weakness encompassing him. "If I only could… (words not to be printed)" the man continued, further revealing his opinion about that particular kind of human being. "We too here aren't short of them, either, believe me. They're coming in an ever-growing supply, and every next one is always worse than his predecessor."

"To tell you the truth, we in London have the same problem," said Igor.

"Aha, I already suspected that," said the man, nodding. "But tell me," he went on, "are you going to stay here for a while?"

"I may, after all," said Igor, who had no desire to go back where that nasty Hellbridge was, and in the first place, didn't want to encounter his terrible cat again.

"Good," said the man, "for I actually need a partner to expand my pig farm, and you seem to be sent here by an act of providence at the right time. But, may I ask you, do you have any financial means to contribute if we decide to do it together?"

"Hmm," Igor, who liked the idea, began carefully, but he didn't know the man so wasn't sure he could trust him. But at the same time, he thought it was a chance, that is, to escape Hellbridge, the cat and a couple of other things he now realised he was thoroughly fed up with. So, after a short hesitation, he said, "I think I could contribute a couple of thousand."

"Grand," said the man, "you won't regret it, and now because we're about to be partners in business, let's introduce ourselves properly to each other. My name's O'Bogey, Darren O'Bogey, and yours?"

Igor thought for a split second and blurted out, "Brian McHeap." The name came to him in a sudden inspiration, but was still a part of his old self because he knew perfectly well what his enemies back in London called him behind his back.

So now, Igor felt, having been properly introduced, that he could ask the man something, and the first thing he was curious about was Darren's accent and then his background and other matters.

Igor decided to proceed carefully, one question at a time. He started like that, "Darren, your accent seems not to be from around here."

"I'm from around here, but I used to live in England long enough and that's why my accent isn't local anymore."

"I see," said Igor and went on, "and where was it, and what were you doing if I may enquire?"

"I actually lived in London, so I'm your compatriot in a way. And what did I do? Hmm, I had a couple of very different jobs. Among others, I was a dog trainer."

"Ah, very interesting. We may use your skills right here for, you know, I have a couple of ideas since you kindly offered me a partnership in running your pig farm."

"And what do you actually mean?"

"Bah," began Igor, "something, you know, rather unusual, I mean a sophisticated pig training programme. But it must be just between you and me because it should be strictly confidential. Otherwise, you know, we might encounter competition that may steal our ideas, and the like. So, let me ask you first, are you close to the local community?"

"No," Darren said, "not at all. On the contrary, they regard me suspiciously, you know, because I lived in England that long, and they, I presume, suspect me," and Darren lowered his voice and glanced left and right, and only then went on, "of not being in favour of their political ideas, if you know what I mean. And, to tell you the truth, I'm not."

*That's good,* Igor thought. *I'm a lucky man, after all, for what might have happened if I'd come across one of those dissidents?* And now the idea of working with Darren seemed to be even more promising, so he said to him, "I appreciate that, you seem to be a very reasonable man.

"Anyway, let's stay away from politics. It's very unhealthy to be too close to it," and he shook his head a couple of times and then looked at the sky for a good while, as if he was thanking someone up there for sparing him more serious troubles after his landing in Northern Ireland.

"And," Darren in turn asked Igor, "could you tell me more about that sophisticated programme of yours?"

"Since we're partners now, or we're about to be, for you know, we must go and see a solicitor first, anyway, I can now tell you a few details."

"Thank you, I appreciate it," said Darren, the anti-dissident.

"First of all," Igor began, "they, I mean, the pigs, must be trained for a special purpose, thus, we have to teach them a couple of, uncommon for them, so to speak, crafts. One of them would be," and now it was his turn to lower his voice and to look carefully around, "to teach them to speak."

Darren, now looking totally perplexed, thought, *That Englishman must be nuts. Talking pigs! I've never heard such rubbish.*

"I know," Igor said, apparently unperturbed by Darren's amazement, "you find the idea absurd enough, but I believe it can be done after all."

"And on what basis are you so sure about that?" said Darren, who decided to continue the conversation after all, for he was curious to find out what proportions his partner's madness might reach.

486

"The basis, my friend, is man's unlimited ability to do almost anything on this earth."

"Aha," Darren nodded, but said nothing in response to that rather vague explanation. "And that ability," he asked, after a pause, "involves, according to you, the possibility of breeding talking pigs."

"I know you find my idea rather fantastic and even ridiculous, but as I say, I'm convinced we'll succeed."

"If you're so sure about that," said Darren, who didn't think so, but not wanting to lose his would-be benefactor, for he was in desperate need of cash because his farm was in debt, was willing to accept Igor's idea after all. He might have some other ones in his so imaginative mind, he thought. That's why he asked, "And do you have any other plans for them, the pigs?"

"Oh, certainly, I have…" enthusiastically exclaimed Brian (as we'll call Igor from now on) "…and several of them, for that matter. One of them is to train some of them as search pigs. Do you know that German customs used to have one, and a very efficient one for that matter?

Then, perhaps we may even try to breed a police attack pig as well. Anyway, you never know what they might be able to do, but as you know, they are generally underrated, and we'll try to change that opinion. But my main aim – and I hope you'll join me here – is to teach a couple of them, I mean the most intelligent ones, to talk."

"Here we go again!" exclaimed Darren.

"Yes, it might seem to be a crazy idea, but I believe it can be done after all," Brian stated firmly.

*That Englishman*, thought Darren, *must have always been crazy or became so after arriving in Northern Ireland, which is often the case.*

But Darren wanted Brian to stay with him, so he just nodded and said, "We may try after all, for I too believe in them having a lot of capabilities."

"That's it," said Brian, "and we'll exploit them to the extreme. And I think that black pigs should be the most suitable for fulfilling our expectations in the project."

"Why?" asked Darren.

"Hmm," Brian hesitated, "I don't really know, but the colour black seems to me to be a sign of good, contrary to common opinion, which always associates it with evil. I used to be of the same opinion but changed my mind due to some experience I had."

And here we notice a substantial change in Brian's thinking, a very unusual one, for who the Devil would expect it after such a distressing experience, which now seemed to him a gift sent from… that's it, where from, he still wasn't sure about that.

*

Anyway, they began to work in earnest, and it wasn't an easy job. Pigs turned out to be very insubordinate, but due to the partners' patience and determination, they achieved some positive results.

It was relatively easy to train some of the pigs as search and rescue ones, but the most serious challenge was to teach them to talk. Brian devoted almost all of his time to the task. He worked hard, day and night, and apparently his students appreciated that, and one day, one of them, a black one, of course, named 'The Colossus', eventually uttered some mutterings resembling human speech. Brian was overjoyed, and even Darren, who had remained sceptical all the time, joined him in cheering the success. However, there was still a little problem, namely the way 'The Colossus' spoke. Apparently, it took after Brian in its manner of speaking, that is, the rather incoherent, hardly comprehensible speech for which Brian, the former politician, had been known.

Anyway, the success was celebrated at a local pub, the Paddy's Arms, and a lot of Irish whisky and beer was drunk. The locals still regarded Brian with suspicion, but they were proud too, having such an experimenter among them, and soon enough, news of his success reached famous universities of England, and even some abroad, among others, Harvard and MIT.

Also, pretty soon, our experimenters were receiving distinguished visitors. Even some of the royal family members were kind enough to honour them by coming over to admire that unbelievable intellectual achievement. And, due to very close cooperation between the UK and Dollaria intelligence services, the president himself heard the news, and one day, Ballyleny was swarmed with Secret Service agents, who inspected thoroughly our heroes' farm, but some of their pupils didn't seem to be happy with it. When the Service boss, Jerry Phantomas, was poking his nose in every hole, 'The Colossus' lost his temper and charged at him. Having been cornered, Jerry reached for his Glock, but fortunately Brian was nearby and rushed to his pupil's rescue, sheltering him with his own body. Later, he complained to the president about Jerry's overreaction, and Jerry was assigned a different job, which was at Washington Zoo, where he was supposed to learn a proper attitude toward animals. It took him five years to learn enough and be back with the Service, no longer as the boss but as an animal relations officer.

The president was over the moon being there. The pigs all seemed to be very pleased with his visit, mainly thanks to his apparent delight in their company. He even had a chat with 'The Colossus', but since its content is still classified, we aren't able to disclose what they talked about.

At the end of his visit, in the evening, the president entertained the animals by playing the trumpet. It was a special composition written by him especially for the occasion. It was slightly reminiscent of the polka dance due to Johan Strauss' influence on 'The Trumpet', and some of the pigs charmed him with their hopes, which were similar to what is called St Vitus' dance.

On the whole, the visit was a great success and was crucial in improving the relationship between both countries.

We should also mention the visits of eminent scientists, one of whom was the aforementioned Professor Koczkodan, who this time arrived in the company of his cousin, Privat Dozent Lynas Kockodanus from the Lithuanian branch of the family. Previously, recounting the professor's incredible ability to drive away the most terrifying animals (he could also easily frighten people if he wanted), we failed to say that actually, day to day, Koczkodan's features weren't scary at all; he was actually a very innocent-looking man. His features changed at his will, and only when he needed them to scare the chosen objects. He could transform them without any particular drugs, as Dr Jekyll had to. And the Koczkodan family had had this ability for centuries, and its legendary predecessor, Vitalis Kockodanus, gained his fame at the Battle of Grunwald, where he scared to death even the bravest knights of the Teutonic Order, and in doing so greatly contributed to the victory of Polish-Lithuanian forces, which was recognised by King Jagiello, who knighted him and bestowed him with a coat of arms whose motto is, '*Veni, Vidi, Terrebis*' or 'I came, I saw, I scared'. But we'll restrain ourselves from showing the crest here so as not to scare the reader.

The cousins came on the invitation of the MOD to evaluate the pigs' potential to scare the enemy, and their own resistance to being driven out by fright. Regretfully, their report disappointed the Ministry and both breeders too, of course, for they found them brave enough but not enough to challenge the sight of the cousins once they'd transformed their appearance. By the way, we may mention also here the cousins' previous visit to Australia, where they arrived, invited by their good friend, Professor Sexton, a world-renowned expert on animals' sexuality. He, of course, went there to conduct his research on kangaroos, but he was also curious about their other character traits, and that's why the cousins were asked to come. The Australian government greatly regretted allowing the professor to be joined by the cousins, because when the poor animals saw them, they ran away as far as Perth, and the experiment took place close to Brisbane, so thousands of miles away.

The Australian prime minister dismissed later those responsible for the experts' arrival, mainly because of their substantial honorariums which amounted to five hundred thousand dollars. Anyway, they charged £2,000 per hour while an English writer was given £3,000 at the University of Manchester for something that wasn't, as some said, value for money. Thus, considering the invaluable expertise of both Koczkodans, we don't find their pay too excessive.

Another expert to arrive was Professor Wunderberg from Germany. His name accidentally corresponded to what had been called Wunderwaffe during World War 2. The story of his presence at the pigs' farm is still classified under the Official Secrets Act, but we learned some details after Mr Dumblodge's escape to Peking for a change, so to speak, because it used to be always Moscow where he went. But we'll reveal some details about that later on. He claimed to know for sure that the MOD (again them) and American general staff invited the professor to assess the pigs' capability in case of total war. And the former MI6 director general said that yes, Wunderberg found them quite useful and recommended their use, however, not against all enemies of both countries at the same time, for there were too many of them, considering the number of properly trained pigs available for both countries.

Professor Wunderberg was the inventor of the so-called invisible rays, a kind of laser weapon recently introduced on one of the German Navy ships.

The rays proved to be a very powerful means of modern warfare, but to the disappointment of generals, seemed to be, let's say, unprejudiced in their choice of destruction, and that was the case during the NATO exercise in Poland. Two groups of troops confronting each other, the Reds and the Whites, were both destroyed before they even had a chance to prove their individual combat worthiness. Fortunately, the only casualties were both troops' equipment, and not soldiers, for the rays were designed to annihilate just material objects, and not human or any other living creatures. And this was a great advantage of the rays because they were the opposite of neutron bombs, which destroy life but not property, and the generals wanted it the other way around.

But all in all, Brian and Darren's great experiments were widely recognised, and they were awarded several distinctions for their hard work for the good of their country. The government minister for work and pensions even suggested bestowing on them both a knighthood or the rank of baron, even some higher one, but the proposal didn't find enough supporters to be presented to the Queen for acceptance. Instead, they were both awarded an OBE and a newly created order of the Hero of Farming.

There were, of course, some sceptical opinions regarding the true value of their work, and not wanting to diminish their merits in the service of the country, we'll mention just one given by our dear, unforgettable Franz, which read, *Mr Jobber and his colleague in creating their wonders somehow managed to cross the limits of nonsense.*

And that's about all the story of Igor Jobber OBE, and the recipient of the order of the Hero of Farming.

Now, it's time to tell the stories of those people we talked about before, some of the Magnificent Seven and also of 'The Grin' and 'The Preacher'.

But this time we'll try not to be so talkative, so as not to bore our readers, who by now might be a wee bit tired or even outraged and disgusted by some parts of our story. But if they are so, we urge them to try to rethink their views and in doing this to ask themselves the obvious question: why have they found the story so displeasing? For it might be so because they actually know it is true. And they would prefer to stick to something very different, and of their own invention, and proclaim that to be true, as is usually the case with our views, that is, convictions which, as Friedrich so rightly says, are worse enemies of truth than lies.

Anyway, after all, we'll be satisfied more by their outrage and disgust than by indifference, for it is very true that a man does his reporting well only when people start to hate him.

So, all in all, let's wait and see.

And now to those who also think themselves in particular to be right about everything under the sun, and in the first place about themselves, of course.

And first, here comes Daniel Camelot, 'The Preacher', the moralist possessed by the mission of his country to do good anywhere on earth, being convinced that Britain is the guardian of justice and fairness, which are guaranteed by her high standards of morality. At the same time, those who disagreed with him should be brought into line. So, in point of fact, he wasn't the forgiving Christian he claimed to be.

Anyway, one day, 'The Preacher' found himself under attack, for it makes people happy to find their own faults in somebody else, and here the papers are especially delighted to do so. Moreover, his relationships with the M7 were uncovered and so the cat was out of the bag. Chiefly, the press slammed him, and he was thoroughly lashed by them day after day, and eventually saw no other way out but to leave politics for good, and therefore one day he appeared at a village church somewhere in Dorset and had a chat with its minister.

We found out about the conversation due to the minister's exaggerated concern for security, namely, he was in the habit of recording all of his conversations with anybody he talked to because, in his opinion, ill-founded accusations were too much 'in fashion' as he put it. Therefore, if anybody attributed to him a wrongdoing, he would be able to prove it to be undeserved. Since he, like 'The Preacher', had no doubts about his high ethical standards, their conversation went smoothly. The minister agreed with Daniel that all accusations against him had been fabricated by envious and treacherous enemies, especially those of a different denomination, and therefore they should support each other, for together they stand, divided they fall. Apart from that, the minister, being in favour of John's opinion that every man was able to start his life from scratch at any time in his life since (and here he went much further than John) his mind is in fact *tabula rasa* all the time, urged Daniel to renew his own, as he put it, and actually made an offer on the spot. Under the circumstances, the minister said, it would be the best solution to leave those cursed politics for good and start doing something noble instead, something that would benefit people on a small but actual scale.

"And what do you mean?" Daniel asked him.

"I mean you'll stay here in my parish and you'll be a sexton at my church."

"Hmm," began Tobias, still undecided, "it's tempting, but do you really see me doing that?"

"Oh yes, I do," firmly stated the minister, "because I believe you've talked enough in your life, and now it's time for silence, no words but the bell tolling, and in this silence, you'll find serenity and contentment, peace of the soul."

As we can see, the minister, whose name was Archibald Dreamshipper, was an insightful man and at the same time a very pragmatic one, for he knew perfectly well that Daniel, deep in his heart, hated what he'd previously done, and politics had never been his true calling, so sooner or later he would have had to leave it, and now fortunately for him he was finished there, and his true vocation might be at last fulfilled. And Daniel himself could see that Archibald's offer was perhaps his last chance to get what he had always needed, that is, seclusion and tranquillity.

So, he was deeply grateful to Archibald for giving him that chance, and accepted the offer on the spot, and from then on, he was a happy man, for he was still preaching but nowhere else but in his mind.

And now let's say a few words about somebody else, who wasn't that dissimilar to the man we have just described. And by the likeness between them, we mean their shared something that was their inborn inclination to feign tolerance, impartiality, fairness and the like. All of this was a sham and the objective was to pull the wool over somebody's eyes, to deceive him in order to benefit themselves.

And Tobias Bubble, 'The Grin', was one of those who distinguished themselves doing that.

Let's begin with his political stance, that is, his apparent socialistic beliefs which were fake through and through. He, himself, didn't believe in them, as nobody else did, but in official propaganda they were still there. But he didn't care, for he knew perfectly well that his people never think. It is the system that thinks for them.

In his earthly stance, his prime aim was to enrich himself, and he was pretty successful here and acquired very substantial capital. As we can see, Tobias' concept of socialism was not the same as Marx's, for it was nothing else but to make of his country a semi-police state, and in doing so, he made some progress still present there considering the country's countless laws, bans and regulations, to say nothing of other innumerable means which were all there to watch everyone, everywhere. And all that made him happy, with his grin present anywhere he went.

He also loved peace in his own way, so to speak, and that's why he lied so much, as if he had replaced the famous 'si vis pacem para bellum' with 'si vis pacem, ut supra, et tune ipse mendacem iacentem' or 'if you want peace, keep on lying and smiling'. One of those clever, but not clever enough, as it turned out, English linguistic creations.

Tobias represented an international organisation, being an envoy in some areas where wars had never ended, and was paid handsomely for his work, but he actually achieved nothing there. And this is exactly the usual outcome of those organisations' activities. In other words, the more they talked about peace, the more wars were going on.

But Tobias knew perfectly well how those organisations work, and what they are for, that is, keeping up appearances of doing something that can never be achieved, but substantial sums of money can be earned, and that was it, the money that he loved to spend, especially on properties.

And there were several of them, and everyone wondered why he needed them all. Possibly just to invest his money which now, curiously enough, replaced his passion for the socialistic meaning of justice. We actually don't know that, but he might have read some of Friedrich's works where socialism was defined as the tyranny of the dumbest and the least, and he arrived at the same conclusion, and in consequence, replaced his former passion for social justice by the one that is money, which he now considered the only genuine one of humankind.

As we know, passion for money is useless unless we know how to make use of it, that is, where and how to invest the money we have. In other words, our passion can only be satisfied by making more money even if we don't really need more of it; otherwise, our passion is in danger of disappearing.

Tobias himself wasn't too skilled in performing that activity on his own, so he had a couple of advisers who did the job for him, but he had the impression their efforts could have been better. Actually, he suspected them of cheating on him, which was probably true, as had been the case with a rock band that was named 'rolling something', until they found a man who made them multi-millionaires. And because of his well-founded suspicions, Tobias was now looking for such a man.

And he found his man in a very particular individual by the name of Bemot Colossus, already famous for his financial feats, especially the one which earned him the nickname, 'The man who broke the Bank of Ireland'. His feat wasn't as exceptional as George's in England, but still serious enough for him to be respected and hated at the same time in both countries.

Bemot was presumably of Greek origin, and his surname curiously corresponded with the one we know from Henry's book that he himself thought to be his best. The first name in turn personified his main character traits, that is, of being an efficient, determined, unique and creative man who tended to resent authority. There were some rumours he respected an authority, but what exactly that was had never been found out. Actually, he was suspected to be a member of a Satanist congregation based in Switzerland, but the Swiss authorities firmly rejected the accusation and never investigated the matter in question, claiming that Satan would have never bothered them for that matter.

Anyway, in the field of finance, he was an artiste, as good as the unforgettable Prince Rupert, notorious for having made a rock band very rich, as we've already mentioned. However, he never actually liked them too much, for his choice was always classical music and not that incomprehensible noise of rocking everything.

When Tobias met that hero of the Stock Exchange, he was rather disappointed. Bemot had nothing of Prince Rupert's charisma and aristocratic bearing. On the contrary, he was short, plump and strangely cat-like, and his clothes surely weren't tailored in Savile Row.

They never met in Bemot's office (as a matter of fact, nobody never knew where his office was, and never put their foot in there, for that matter) but always at a pub, for the Black Magus, as some envious characters called him, said that while discussing money, he had to strengthen his reasoning with the help of beer, preferably Budvar, Weihenstephaner or Wolters pilsner from Braunschweig.

The pub they met in a few times ordered the beers especially for him, delivered by those brewery trucks at discounted prices in recognition of the financial services Bemot had done for them.

So, as we've already mentioned, Tobias wasn't impressed with meeting Bemot until the latter began one of his famous lectures on the philosophy of evil, as he curiously enough called money.

After the first lecture, which was actually the only one, Tobias was so perplexed that he even considered seeing a psychiatrist, but somehow eventually came to his senses, mainly due to Bemot's advice to drink a couple of beers. But, the man insisted, never ever touch any ales; those 'slops' as he called them.

So, they were drinking beer, and Tobias hardly uttered a word during the meeting. All he said was in answer to Bemot's question to him, "What do you need more money for?"

Tobias found the question ridiculous but didn't dare to say anything, of course. All he said in reply was, "Hmm, I find it normal," to which Bemot said, "Normal, you say, so what's abnormal then?" Understandably, Tobias couldn't answer the question.

Anyway, Bemot promised to do his best. And here we come to the very crucial stage of the story. Nobody ever suspected Bemot of his true motive in becoming a financier (they found his philosophy of evil merely a joke of his) which was in fact to punish the greedy. Yes, he did make more than a few *nouveau riches,* which made them walk on air, but then in the twinkle of an eye, later on, they mysteriously lost the money. And it was the destiny of Tobias himself, but how the Devil would he have ever thought of it when in just a month Bemot enriched him by five million pounds? How could he have known that this money, all of his money, in fact, would disappear two months later?

Now, let us inform the curious reader that in doing all that, Bemot was kindly enough to accept a very polite request that came from the president of the Russian Federation, who one day telephoned him asking for a favour, that was to make 'The Grin' poor. After a very short hesitation, all the Black Magus told the president was *"Net problem, dorogoy* Mikhail Vladimirovich."

What is very important to mention now, as regards Bemot's stance towards the money question, is in truth his great respect for liberty of the spirit. And not just once did he say that some people would never understand the importance of that spirit, the only one that can make people free, for which his Greece had always been famous. And not the bloody shopkeepers of England, those slaves of a materialistic view of life. Bemot said, he was convinced, that sooner or later someone (he never mentioned his name) would come, and then, as he put it, the sound of silence would reign everywhere.

Bemot believed that the freedom of the spirit and integrity are one and the same. At the same time, he was convinced that only when a person has sufficient brains is he able to act ethically, for ethics are inseparable from reason. Ethical behaviour, that is, to be capable of telling good from evil, is based on reason, so a person who has no brains cannot be good.

And here we come to the most crucial part of his reasoning, which was his belief that nothing in this world is higher than any human individual.

Back to Bemot's dealings with 'The Grin'– he found Tobias guilty of possessing no good qualities at all. The man's main drive in life was greed, and therefore Bemot decided to punish him using Tobias' motivation to his own disadvantage and suggesting to him an apparently good business deal abroad. 'The Grin' was, of course, eager to go ahead, for the business in question seemed to be very profitable, and profit was the first of his pleasures.

The business negotiations were to take place in Russia, and Tobias thought them easy enough, especially due to his rather poor opinion of the country. More than once he had said that yes, Russia may be a vast country, rich in everything, but since her GDP was even lower than that of New York state, then there was no reason to worry about the Russians' business acumen. And here he made his worst blunder, the blunder rather typical of western thinking of Russia, which was the opinion that the strength of a country can be estimated just in terms of the money it possessed. He forgot, or rather wasn't clever enough to know, that money alone doesn't make a country strong and capable of worthy achievements, especially those of intellectual and artistic value.

Bemot wasn't a military expert, but he knew enough to reason correctly that military power isn't just about the money. His good friend Wissend was even surprised to find out that Bemot knew something about such things after all, and during one of their countless intellectual disputes, Bemot astonished Wissend by saying, "You know, there are a few very rich countries which spend incredible amounts of money on their defence, and at the same time, their armed forces are good for nothing. Whereas a few others, such as Confederatio Helvetica, Sweden and Finland, just to mention a few, those who are neutral, peaceful and rich too, are very capable of defending themselves."

Anyway, Bemot's interpretation of 'Vive gladio peri gladio' went much further than its literal meaning. More than once he told his friends that the saying refers accurately to the money question itself. And that's why those obsessed by money will be persecuted by their own weapons, and once the friends had learned about Bemot's view on the matter in question, they understood why he'd chosen to break the Bank of Ireland. "They," he said, "might appreciate what I've done someday in the future, unless it's too late. Anyway, we'll never know, for time concepts are very vague in nature."

And now, we feel it necessary to say that Lord Hellbridge, once he'd learned from Wissend about Bemot's activities, was quite impressed by his philosophical reasoning regarding the money question, and in his letter to Bemot, the lord congratulated him and encouraged him to keep on doing that, as he put it, good job for as long as possible.

Now, back to the story of the business in Russia. 'The Grin', driven by his obsession, went too far despite Bemot's quite honest warnings to be careful. In Russia, Tobias obviously found people like himself, and they went ahead with all the money schemes possible. But then, one day, the president, Mikhail Vladimirovich, had enough, and it didn't take long and their business was finished. Anyway, Tobias was lucky enough not to land in the slammer. Anyway, he was back in England, penniless, and wondered what to do next.

One day, he came again to a pub, the Bubbly Chappie, which had been his favourite watering hole for some time now, and saw a man whom he'd never seen before. The man was thin as a rake, sported a moustache and wearing John Lennon-style spectacles, but in the man's glasses, one lens was black while the other one was normal. On his head there was a Garibaldi-style cap.

The moment Tobias sat down at his usual place, the man stood up and 'The Grin' saw the man was unusually tall, about seven feet perhaps. *He could play basketball*, Tobias thought, *but he's too thin, so supposedly not strong enough.*

Once he'd thought this, the man unexpectedly came to him and said, "No, I've never actually played the game. My favourite sport is of a very different kind."

*Can he read my thoughts?* 'The Grin' asked himself.

"And it is," the man went on, "four times one hundred."

"Metres?" asked Tobias.

"No, millilitres," said the man.

Tobias, slightly bewildered, said, "What do you mean?"

"I mean one hundred millilitres of vodka in four schnapps."

Tobias had obviously never heard of that kind of sport and was going to ask for some details but didn't manage, for the man said, "Excuse me, but in the fervour of our sport choice preference, I forgot to introduce myself. My name's Alexander Kuropatkin. Alex will do."

*Aha*, thought 'The Grin', who'd already noticed the man's foreign accent, *a Russian*, and at the same time felt his throat going dry because a thought crossed his mind: *is he an SVR agent sent after me, so wasn't it enough what I went through over there, in Russia?* And he asked the man, "Are you Russian?"

"Yes, I think I'm Russian," said the man.

"You think you're Russian? What do you mean by that? Do you have some doubts about being Russian?"

"No, no, but there have been so many different nationals among my ancestors that..." He didn't finish the sentence, asking instead, "And you, aren't you that former politician, what was his name...?"

"Yes, I am. Tobias Bubble. Pleased to meet you."

"Ah, that's it, Mr Bubble. Sorry, I'd forgotten the name."

"No need to apologise," said Tobias, "and have you been living here for long?"

"Don't remember exactly," said the man. "Anyway, long enough to know a thing or two about this country. And, if I may ask, are you still in politics?"

"Oh no, I left it for good and will never return," said 'The Grin'.

"And rightly so too, it is a wretched occupation," Alex announced, shaking his head.

"That's it, but I found it out too late."

"Better late than never, as they say," said the other man. "And what are you doing now, if I may enquire?"

"I... I..." began Tobias, "actually, I'm doing nothing at the moment, and what about you?"

"I'm in retail," said Alex.

"In retail? And what exactly is it?"

"Ah, we sell mainly literature, rather light, so to speak, but very entertaining," said Alex, smiling.

"Entertaining, you say? Do you mean porn?" asked Tobias, glancing at Alex.

"Oh, no, God forbid, nothing like that. No, we're against that filth. And what about you? Are you looking for a job at the moment?"

"Actually," said Tobias, "I've already tried here and there, but there aren't many jobs for me around."

"Oh no, there aren't, we live in rather hard times in this respect. But I may have something for you, after all."

"Really?" asked Tobias, raising his eyebrows, "and what would it be?"

"What about joining my small enterprise?"

"Hmm, I'm not sure, but I may after all," said 'The Grin'.

"And do you have, after all, any other options?" asked Alex.

"No, I don't, I'm afraid."

"So, join us, you're very welcome!" Alex enthusiastically invited him.

"I think I will, but could you tell me some details about the nature of your entertainment business?"

"But of course, my partner. We mainly sell comics which as a matter of fact are rather serious in their nature, about which you are so curious. And this is because they reveal, please listen carefully now, the true face of politics."

'The Grin' raised his eyebrows on hearing that and said, "The true nature, you say? But nothing is true about the subject in question, and I know something about that."

"No, no, no," exclaimed Alex, "there is a lot of truth, my friend, and it is paradoxically the truth of lies, or we may say, the truth behind lies, but it doesn't really matter which one we prefer. You know, lying is lying, and that's that."

"What?" asked Tobias, staring uncomprehendingly at his new business friend.

"Yes, yes, my friend, the truth and nothing but the truth. And our aim is to reveal the truth, the truth of how something can be taken for being true when actually it isn't."

"I don't follow, to be honest," uttered Tobias.

"Bah, small wonder you don't, for you used to be one of them. But now you're with us, and your opinion of the matter in question will obviously be different pretty soon, very different, for that matter," Alex announced firmly.

"Hmm, yes, it might be, but I still don't grasp the essence of that..." he hesitated "...what you call, the truth of lies or the truth behind lies."

"Let me explain then, and don't you worry, you will like it," said Alex, smiling, and went on, "and what I'll tell you will rejuvenate you. You'll feel much younger, more willing to live, my friend, you'll see, believe me. And now please listen carefully, for what I'm going to say is not easy to understand, and I suppose that even such a great analyst and synthetyst, of course, if I may use such a neologism, as Immanuel would have trouble understanding it.

"Now, as regards truth or rather the truth about the truth of lies, an ordinary man would not endure truth itself, for he actually isn't prepared to face the truth of his and his fellow men's lives. That's why the truth about their lives must be transformed, so to speak, before it reaches him, otherwise he would land… Alex hesitated, and then shot "…in a loony bin, or it might be even worse."

"So," Tobias chipped in, "you think truth might be so dangerous."

"Oh yes, my friend, it is the most dangerous thing ever, and there's nothing more dangerous than that in this world," Alex Kuropatkin announced firmly. "And," he continued, "there used to be some philosophers too scared to analyse the word, for they realised the danger of knowing truth in itself, if I may use Immanuel's favourite phrase."

"Sorry," said The Grin', feeling totally perplexed, "but I still don't—"

"Don't worry," Alex interrupted him, "I'll make everything clear for you in a minute, and you'll instantly grasp the heart of the matter."

"If you say so," Tobias agreed, rather hesitantly.

"Wait and you'll see, anyway, I'm not going to disappoint you, my friend. So, what was I talking about? Aha, the danger of knowing the truth, that's it. As you understand perfectly well, the problem at hand is not just of a linguistic nature. It is actually, how shall I put it… the matter of to be or not to be of humankind, and the rub is whether man is really ready for truth in this world."

From now on, Tobias was totally unable to follow Alex' trail of reasoning, and was just stupidly grinning at him, but Alex didn't seem to worry about that and carried on his Immanuel-like analysis.

"Yes, my friend," he continued, "actually, truth is something not from this world. It resides in a kingdom unreachable for a human being, I'd say, and here one day I reached complete agreement with Ludwig, you know, that Austrian philosopher, but some say he was a British one as well, but you know what, if he were one of those islanders, he wouldn't even be able to utter a word about the matter in question, because for them truth is no problem at all because they don't care about such trivial matters like truth. But now the time has come, they eventually have to deal with the problem, and this is because truth is something, let's say, a very stubborn thing that never gives up. It fights to the end, but not on its own, if you know what I mean.

"And now, my friend, we come closer to comprehending the main problem we're now dealing with. I mean the practicality, so to speak, of truth when we face our day-to-day problems, and the problems of a more general nature but close to them, I mean politics and all related to it. But who the Devil invented the word that nobody really understands? Yea, it's of Greek origin, but they, the Greeks, had a clear meaning of it, but now nobody has the slightest idea what politics means, do they, I mean your fellow country citizens?"

Tobias said nothing in reply. He just nodded, as if he was agreeing with Alex.

"You see," Alex carried on, "you yourself don't seem to make anything out of that bloody word. You know what? It should be abolished by law, of course. You know, anything is possible in law in your country, isn't it? Because it is a country that boasts of and takes pride in the rule of law. Thus, they may, for instance, hmm, abolish or ban the right to use the word 'truth' in public, except religious gatherings, because the word there is safe, no harm at all using it, if you know what I mean. Do you?"

"No," Tobias said curtly.

"And good for you, my friend, for I, my God, how much I've suffered trying to understand that cursed word. Ah, if you only knew! But now, old chap, we must somehow come to a conclusion, for by now even Immanuel and Ludwig, of course, or even Friedrich, would have gone pale if they had only had a chance to listen to us, but who knows, they might be listening after all. What do you think?"

"I'm not sure," said Tobias.

"I'm not, either, but I'll ask them later on when we've finished this tiresome business of the truth."

"You what…" stuttered 'The Grin', "…but they're all dead."

"Bah, it doesn't really matter, my friend, and if I were you, I wouldn't worry about that. We have much more important things at hand."

Tobias began to feel more and more uneasy now, for he suspected that learned in dialectic, man was unpredictable not only in what he said, but he might also be so in what he could do.

"Anyway, take it easy. We're now coming closer to the earth, so to speak, and you'll soon be able to relax. However, some say you can actually relax only in the afterlife."

Now Tobias, hearing that, was really scared and was about to stand up and run, but where to, he thought.

"Yes, I, myself," said Alex, "have a strong urge to fly, but I've got nowhere to fly to. You know the feeling of course, don't you?" he asked.

"Yes," Tobias said, for by some miracle, a very unusual thing for him, he remembered that existential question asked by, that's it, who was it, some psychedelic rock band, or someone.

"But," Alex went on, unperturbed by Tobias' dilemma, "at the same time I've got amazing powers of observation, and that's why from now on we'll leave that shaky ground of philosophy and look at things from the perspective of our beloved ordinary man.

"*Et voilà!* Our average fellow human being seems to be, hmm, worried about his existence, but at the same time he wants to trust the future, and here he willy-nilly accepts what is said in parliament, in broadcasting, watching the idiot-box and reading those marvellous stories in the papers.

"And in them, he paradoxically finds a sort of serenity, and this is…" Alex suspended his voice "…due to what we said at the very beginning, that is, the truth behind the lies."

Now Tobias felt much more assured that he wasn't in immediate danger anymore, because of his familiarity with the vocabulary Alex was using. It was at last his well-known territory; lying, cheating, pulling the wool over one person's, or two, even a thousand or more, eyes. Numbers don't count here, anyway, so he began to feel safe and was eager to listen attentively to his would-be partner. *Yes,* he said to himself, *I might be his partner after all, for now he seems to be a down-to-earth man, pragmatic, so, yes, I might join him.*

After a short pause, Alex resumed his speech and said, "Yes, the truth and nothing but the truth. And in our business, the truth will be brought to light through laughter, mocking our adversaries, those who deserve punishment, and they will prostrate before our sword."

"Excuse me," chipped in Tobias, "but what do you mean exactly by sword?"

"Our sword is our comics we publish. And they are the most powerful weapon available these days, days of the poverty of modernity, that is, perfidy, deceit and the moral decline of humankind."

"Aha," said Tobias, "I begin to understand, and you want me to be a part of your enterprise."

"That's it, and the job will make you happy, old chap, very happy indeed. You'll see how much pleasure you'll get out of doing our noble business. In the name of truth, through the power of words, we'll make this world a better place. *Calamus gladio fortior*, my friend, its power is invincible, as my boss says."

"And who's your boss, if I may enquire?"

Alex looked gravely at Tobias and said, "My boss is none other than the Grand Master of Black Magic."

"Who?" stuttered 'The Grin'. "I... I've never heard of—"

"But you will," Alex interrupted him, "and pretty soon for that matter."

"If you say so," Tobias reluctantly agreed.

"Now," Alex continued, "we're going to declare war on that cursed United Kingdom of Bureaucracy." He now raised his voice, jumped to his feet and yelled, "Down with it, now!" And then he began singing the *Marseillaise*, "'*Aux armes, citoyens, formez vos bataillons. Marchons, marchons!*'"

And the stunned Tobias saw other patrons of the pub stand up and join Alex in singing the French national anthem.

*My God*, he thought, *republicans! As if we didn't have enough of them in Northern Ireland. They're even here, in my beloved England. This is the end, yes, we're finished.*

Alex didn't pay the slightest attention to his perplexed future partner now, and when he and his fellow republicans had finished the *Marseillaise*, he, stretching his imposing height, cried out, "*Lunga vita a Giuseppe!*" Apparently, the Italians too were going to join his crusade.

*Ah*, Tobias said to himself, *caro Giuseppe Garibaldi, yes, in the olden days, 500,000 of my compatriots welcomed you in London, but now there would be hardly anybody in the streets. That fellow Alex might be right, after all, but up to a point, of course.*

Alex was now shaking hands with his fellow singers, thanking them warmly for their support in his struggle. When he had finished, he sat down in his chair and announced, "And now, old chap, we'll have a bottle or two of Budvar to celebrate our victory."

Tobias looked at him and said, "How come? Our campaign isn't finished yet."

"Bah," exclaimed the man, "actually, it is, for whenever my boss makes up his mind, then whatever it is, it's done, and I'd suggest you believe it, otherwise…" He didn't finish the sentence but just smiled at Tobias and shook his head.

And he went on, "You know, it's far better to believe that nothing is too difficult for him to do. Oh yes, my friend, much better." He looked straight into Tobias' eyes, and nodded.

"It might be so," said Tobias, "but sorry, you know, I haven't had the pleasure of…"

"But you will, and as a matter of fact you have already had the pleasure as you say, but of a slightly different kind, so to speak."

*I understand nothing of this*, thought Tobias.

"But again," Alex went on, "you will, and pretty soon, don't you worry. Be patient and take it easy," and he smiled again. "Perhaps you won't be lucky enough to meet him in person, but you'll meet him, anyway, through his doing, my friend, and then you may eventually understand something. Hopefully, you will, for your own good.

"Ah, here we go. Budvar, my love!" he cried, and Tobias saw a very pretty woman coming to their table, carrying a large tray full of beer bottles. She had raven black hair, and when she looked at Tobias who looked back, and for a split second he caught a glimpse of an abyss-like image in her eyes, a shiver run down his spine. But he somehow managed to say, "Thank you," and the woman smiled at him and put the tray on the table.

"Gorgeous creature she is, isn't she?" said Alex. "Her name's Beatrice, but I must disappoint you, you wouldn't stand a chance. Anyway, she's already very seriously engaged with a man, his name's Adarsh, Ches Adarsh. He's a rather peaceful man, but if you tried something, you know, inappropriate, then he may see red, to say nothing of what some of his friends would do. A mere look at them would leave you terrified to death. Ah, if you could only see one of them, that Fortis fellow, heavens, bison-like, and perhaps even stronger than it. With one hand, he would throw you out of the window and you would fly to... you don't really want to know where to, my friend. Oh no, better not. But now, let's go back to our partnership, and you haven't said yes or no to it, so what's your decision?"

"Hmm," Tobias hesitated, "I don't really know, but could you give me some more details? What do you expect me to do?"

"But of course, my friend, and you'll see how advantageous it would be for you to start the job. *Primo*, you can be fully free in saying and writing whatever you want. You know, that apparent freedom of speech in this country is just a sham. In fact, there is hardly any freedom about it, for those whose job is to publish anything censor themselves, and very strictly for that matter. The censorship is in their way of thinking, and they wouldn't accept anything which crosses the limits of that. And you, in turn, will have no bounds whatsoever. You can do what you what, I mean, you picture the reality as it really is in what you write or show in the drawings in our comics. By the way, you know what honesty means?"

Tobias, who had a rather vague notion of the word, for he had never actually had a chance to check its value in practice, didn't really know what to say.

"You see, old chap, such a simple word, one of the few that form the very basis of so-called democracy, and you're already having trouble defining it. So, let me tell you what I, myself, understand by it.

"Honesty means frankness, or honesty and frankness are one and the same, and that's it. You know yourself how much both words are used, or rather overused, that is, abused in this country, aren't they?"

That was something Tobias understood perfectly, so he said, "Oh yes, they are, and very much so."

"You see," said Alex," "you're beginning to grasp what I say about our little business, and this way we've made a start. And now, these days, people are like automatons. They don't really think. Others, those in charge of affairs, think for them. The establishment thinks for them, and they are pretty happy about that for now, but somewhere inside them there is a doubt about the sense of what is going on in this world, in the world of politics and, of course, in the world of culture of our times – literature, music, movies, etc., etc. Almost every day, without really being aware of it, they ask themselves what they are actually doing on this earth, and we, my friend, will grab the chance and will turn that small flame of their doubt into fire, inferno, in fact, and thus passion, which will turn their meaningless lives into full, meaningful ones."

"That sounds good," agreed Tobias, "but how do we go about that?"

"Bah!" exclaimed Alex, "I have precise, and strict, to be honest, guidelines and instructions how to proceed. Don't you worry, we're very well organised, even better than the Swiss, as a matter of fact."

"And where do these instructions come from if I may enquire?" asked Tobias, somewhat curious now.

"Directly from my boss, my friend. He's commander-in-chief of our operation and whatever he says, we obey. His word is our law and duty."

"But you've just said I would have total freedom of—"

"But of course, my dear friend," interrupted Alex, "you will have freedom of saying, writing, etc. But at the same time you must respect and follow what he says."

"How come then I'll have freedom—" began Tobias, but his companion interrupted him again.

"First of all, freedom, my friend, is something you have no clue about, do you?"

"No, I don't." Honesty prevailed, and Tobias was frank here.

"You see, so let me tell you what my boss and I after him understand by freedom. Freedom is not something from this world, the world of relative and accidental happenings, contemptible facts, oh no, for it is something transcendental, something that lies outside the world, but at the same time it is within our reach, however, within the reach of a few, only those who understand that life is a task, a challenge, and not the solution. In other words, you shouldn't live your life as if it were a tiresome, dull business, a mere duty to perform, but as a challenge to your thoughts and soul, knowing that all facts contribute only to setting the problem of life, and not to its solution. For only then will you see the world and your life under the aspect of eternity, and only then will you be free, for only then will you see truth, and the truth will set you free, free from the relativity and accidentality of this meaningless existence of your everyday life. And this view of life, the life seen *sub specie aeternitatis* or from the perspective of the eternal, is to see it aright, but this cannot be put into words, so you can either experience this or you cannot, *enten eller* or either or, as our dear Soren says.

"And now, you must believe what our Grand Master says, for only he, himself, knows what is really there, beyond words, that is, beyond good and evil, and therefore you should trust him *a priori*, and obey his orders. There is nothing either good or bad, as William says, but thinking makes it so, I mean, thinking about accidental, worthless facts. But this seems to be senseless, for someone would ask how come those facts have no value? And thus, our deeds don't, either, but then they constitute facts, don't they?

"And yes," Alex continued his high-flying lecture that even Ludwig would envy, "of course, the facts do, but from facts alone only facts arise, and nothing else, for facts are only a matter of interpretation, and whatever your fellow human beings' interpretation might be, it's usually a different one to yours, and therefore the only rightful interpretation is, paradoxically, no interpretation at all. But to understand that, you must accept the truth of what I say *a priori*, and you do that only by living your life as a challenge, a task or a question, that is, you question whatever you think and do, for you assume you may always be wrong. And a human being, unless he questions himself, cannot be good and do good on this earth. Meaningful life, that is, a worthwhile one, is to live knowing all the time that you might be wrong, and only then can you respect another human being. Only then can you treat him or her as equal, recognise him as your brother or sister. Are you with me, my friend?"

Tobias was silent, for the philosophy of Alex had hitherto been totally strange to him, so he was totally dumbfounded and unable to say anything. However, he sensed that something was right about what he'd just heard. He wasn't sure what it was, but some unknown power urged him to believe it, and therefore he eventually said, "I think I begin to grasp what you mean, but I cannot put it into words yet so—"

He couldn't finish, for Alex chipped in, "And very good, thus you've just made a start. And now for a change, to have a little rest from these

Kant-like considerations, let's move to some practical aspects of your job, shall we?"

Tobias was actually grateful for the proposal, so he said nothing but nodded.

"*Et voilà*! Partner, here we go," said Alex.

"First, doing your job, you'll be able to relieve yourself from all your discomfort and stagnation and, more importantly, all worries. It'll be a unique opportunity to start afresh your life, to see your country from a very different angle and so your own life. The job will be fun, a lot of it, because you'll be able to see what is hidden underneath, all those appearances that hitherto blurred your vision and made it impossible to see things as they really are.

"Let's have a look at a few specific examples. I once went to a place where anything you touch is considered legendary by the natives. Legendary food, drink, culture, even the sun that is almost never there, but legendary rain surely is. Now, my friend, under all those legendary things, there is, legendary too, but with a different meaning, sham and stupidity, the legendary godforsaken backwater of ignorance, an intellectual wasteland. And here we come to the things themselves, for only when you see what is underneath can you make things better, but apparently, they up there don't want any change for the better, and the question is why, Because they are so used to lies? Are they so accustomed to falsifying things around them? I don't really know and they don't, either. They simply keep on doing it, for they seemingly feel the need to live by illusions and impose them on strangers, because they actually know there's nothing legendary about anything there, so they keep up appearances, and to do so, they have to beautify things, that is, to falsify.

"In your country, which is not too far from that legendary one, things are slightly different but similar in a way.

"Let's take, for instance, your country's legendary freedom, liberties you're proud of. Are they really there? Hmm, yea, a few of them, but on the whole, there isn't much freedom and there are not many liberties there at all. But then, in order to impress foreigners, to feel superior, you have to claim there are, and in abundance for that matter. You see, it's a matter of long-standing tradition. I mean, they've been taught how things should be for so long that they eventually believe they really are there. In a word, your beliefs make reality, what you believe must exist.

And we are here, doing our job decently means to reveal all these appearances, that sham of all shams, and we do so by laughing at them. For only by our merciless mockery are we able to cure your fellow countrymen from the disease they suffer, that is, their inclination to deceive, to falsify, to be perfidious and first of all to be so sure of themselves, so self-centred and self-assertive. But you know what? They still think that whatever they do, they're right, that they are arbiters of all that happens under the sun, and they'll try to ignore our job, but our boss will make sure they won't succeed in trying that. Oh yes, he will, and if they don't come to their senses in time then I wouldn't like to be in their shoes."

Tobias was listening to that very informative – he had to agree – lecture, but at the same time he still had some doubts, for his old convictions were still there. Thus, all he said was, "But it seems to be a Herculean task, that job of ours, and to be frank, I'm not sure you and I will succeed."

"I appreciate your uncertainty, of course," replied Alex, "but want to assure you again that nothing our boss is doing will remain unfinished. Nothing at all, trust me, you can take it for granted, and it'll be better for you to believe it without delay."

"And why?" Tobias asked curtly

"You don't really want to know why. And let me tell you something. Hasn't your recent experience taught you anything?"

"My..." started Tobias, but somehow understood what was beneath the question, and said to himself, *what the Devil, it was them—*

But he couldn't finish his thought for Alex said, "Better you don't think too hard now. It won't do any good. It's much better for you to accept my offer, and the rest will come on its own. Deal?"

Tobias, who wasn't that stupid, realised that he couldn't refuse the offer. Too many things had already proved he'd been dealing with some... he wasn't sure of the word... perhaps mysterious, unknown hitherto, or... bloody hell, that black magic may really exist after all. All in all, he was now sure of nothing.

"Bravo, my friend," said Alex. "You've eventually got there, my congratulations."

*

And Tobias Bubble, 'The Grin', began his work, and he did it with such enthusiasm and sacrifice that pretty soon a circulation of their comics reached an incredible five million copies. Now he had the chance he was so eager to have to slash people he despised. Those bloody prigs, bigots and puritans (we must note here that he converted to Catholicism doing his job) of all kinds. The paper was read by all strata of society, by the poor and the rich alike, and its influence was so enormous that the Government found it very wise to seek their editors' advice every time it was about to make an important decision.

Tobias was now a very content and gratified man, and he understood that only a man who enjoys the good things in life is able to love his fellow human beings.

# REVENGE IS THE DELIGHT OF GODS

## And not only theirs for that matter

'Never let anyone who has insulted you
get away with it. Bide your time and strike
back when you are in a position of strength –
even if you no longer need to strike back.'
Stieg Larsson, *The Girl with the Dragon Tattoo*

They say you should forgive your enemies. It is one of countless clichés that no one actually respects, but they're still there, living their independent lives, comforting people by telling them what they should be like if they only might be. In fact, they're hardly ever ready for that. On the contrary – they, by reason of their nature that they cannot overcome, always tend to seek revenge for the wrong that has been done to them. And Ches wasn't an exception here. For he knew now that the order of this world depends on values which aren't readily adopted by the majority of people, and if so, good will never prevail. It may happen after all, but only when that majority is taught a lesson may they understand the value of doing good. And what the good really was he was about to find out, because he, himself, was not sure yet what it actually meant.

On the 30th of June, Beatrice was back from one of her numerable journeys and, as agreed, he wasn't too inquisitive this time.

They had an evening meal, one of his favourites, which was a few simple potato pancakes. He enjoyed them very much and hardly anybody knew why he loved them so much. But then, how could they have known what was so special about them? They would only have known if they had had the same recollection of happiness as he had.

'There is no greater sorrow than to remember happiness while in misery.' These words of Dante were perfectly understood by him, and Bea, being Italian, understood them too, so she now joined his delight in savouring the pancakes.

There was still something missing in Ches' happiness. He knew he should have been a fully satisfied man for he apparently had everything a man needs: a loving woman, respectable status and money, but there was still something missing, and the question was, what was it? Thus, he kept on looking for it. His search was not yet complete.

But now there were a couple of things to be dealt with. There was the unfinished business of his former friends, those of the Magnificent Seven, he had to complete. And just when he was thinking of it once again, his telephone rang. And it was the assistant of Lord Hellbridge, Mr Wissend, who – apparently being an early riser, it was only 4.30 am – was calling him. But Ches, an early bird too, didn't mind at all. Besides, he was curious what business the man had calling so early and after a considerable space of time; the last time Ches had seen him was a month or so ago.

Bea was already awake too, and was preparing his usual breakfast, the same as ever, two soft-boiled eggs and two slices of rye bread. "Who is it?" she asked. Ches made a victory sign with his two fingers, which meant, in their agreed code, that either the lord himself or one of his assistants was in touch.

"I'm ringing so early, hoping you're already up, to tell you I have some news for you," said the man.

"You know, I'm almost always up at this time, so no problem at all, and what is it?" Ches asked.

"It would be better to tell you that in person. Anyway, you know I hate telephones. Would eleven o'clock suit you?"

"Surely," he said, and asked himself, *why must it almost always be eleven for them to come?*

"Thank you," said Wissend, "so, see you then."

"See you later," replied Ches, and hung up.

"Wissend is coming to see us," he said to Bea. "Apparently, he's got some news for us."

"At eleven, I suppose," she said.

"Yes, the usual eleven, *mia cara* Beatrice. Eleven is their time as we know."

"I wonder why," she said, but he already knew she knew perfectly well it was Hellbridge's favourite time of the day to start his business.

And right then he remembered why it was eleven. *That's it,* he thought, *I remember now, he's like that professor in the novel I like so much. What a coincidence!*

And at eleven sharp, Wissend entered their apartment in Queen's Gate, and sitting down, announced, "Beertime, my friends. We're here to drink beer. No beer, no business, so to speak."

Ches already knew that as well, so the beer was waiting in the fridge. He fetched two bottles of Budvar for Wissend and himself, because beer wasn't Bea's favourite drink; she as an Italian obviously preferred wine, but curiously enough, German Riesling.

"*Prosit!*" said Wissend, raising his glass.

"*Zum Wohl,*" replied Ches.

*Why does he like raising toasts in German?* Ches asked himself. *However, I, myself, am the same. Maybe it's because it sounds better? But then,* he thought, *the Czech and Polish languages would do as well.*

"Ah, there's nothing in the world like that first sip of beer," said Wissend, "but now *zu dem Sachen selbst, meine Freunde.*

"I'm here to tell you, dear Ches, some interesting news as regards your former brothers in arms, so to speak. And it might be interesting for you too, *mia cara* Beatrice," he said, smiling at her. Bea returned his smile, and judging by her expression, I had the strange impression that she already knew what he was going to tell us.

"I'm listening, *mein Freund,*" said Ches, "it must be something important you've come so early to tell us about."

"It certainly is. However, there are still some much more significant

515

matters in your life, as you know, for you to deal with."

It was as if he was referring to what I'd been thinking that morning, right after waking up.

"Anyway," Wissend went on, "you, I presume, have been wondering what might have happened to the men who have done much harm to you. But not all of them, of course, as you've already found out. On the other hand, their wrongdoings have taught you something you might have needed; however, it doesn't mean you owe them anything because what they did wasn't motivated by good will towards you. They hadn't wished you well. The opposite is true, they'd wanted you, let's say, to go to hell, but strangely enough, they landed there themselves. Not literary, obviously, not yet anyway. By hell, I mean the total reversal of their once high standing and affluence."

"So," I said, "if I may interrupt you, in a way, they got what they wished me to get."

"Yes, my friend, they did, in a way, as you say."

"If I may say something," Bea chipped in, "it seems you shouldn't wish somebody evil, for that evil might happen to you."

"Precisely, *mia bella signorina*, you actually shouldn't, and by the way, my master, the lord, always emphasises that you shouldn't wish someone anything that you, yourself, wouldn't wish for yourself."

"*Naturalmente, signor Wissend*, you should never do that, and Lord Hellbridge as always is right," said Bea.

"Bah, he's seldom ever wrong. In truth, he never is. It's his job anyway to make difficult decisions so, considering his enormous responsibilities, he's not supposed to make mistakes. If, as happens sometimes, he's in doubt, he may discuss with somebody else some difficult matter, but in reality, it almost never happens.

"And now, if I may," said Wissend, "allow me to return to the leitmotif of our conversation."

"Yes, please do," Bea and I said in unison.

"Then, *voilà*, my friends. All the pleasure's mine.

"Let's begin with, hmm, ah, let him go first, I mean, that leading swine, so to speak, Jason. He's of swine breed indeed, and unlucky enough not to be a genuine pig, for if he were, he would be forgiven.

"Yea, Jason Goodman, alias 'The Duck', and *nomen omen*, in a way, he did duck, but this time for good. I mean, once we found out that his goodness is good for nothing, we decided, sorry, I mean the lord did, that he should be treated accordingly. In others words, everyone gets what one deserves. Justice comes first. This is, obviously, not the justice of English common law, which is often very far from being just, due perhaps to the fact of the difficulty in saying what the word really means. Anyway, all those phrases including the words common and just, always arise suspicion in the lord's reasoning. He tends to think that there's something dishonest about them, even something perfidious. And as you know, he's a very principled person, and the clarity of semantics is of the utmost importance to him. He actually quite recently had another chat with Ludwig with regards to the matter in question, and they agreed that if you don't make yourself clear, that is, if you fail to give a meaning to certain signs in your propositions, then whatever you say is senseless, that is, lacks sense, or even worse, it's nonsensical, i.e., of no value at all, which means we cannot give any answer to questions of this kind, but can only point out that they're nonsensical.

"And now, back to that scoundrel Jason. For him, life didn't have any sense unless you're rich, and now, he's as poor as the proverbial church mouse, and he somehow carries on living, so he might have eventually found some different sense to keep himself going."

"So, what is happening to him now?" I asked Wissend.

"Ah, a good question, and it took a while for the lord to decide his destiny, because the lord, as usual, is very careful about the measures he takes. He's never in a hurry about that."

"That's it," said Bea, "and I do appreciate that."

"I won't fail to mention that to him, and I'm sure he'll be very glad to hear about your kind appraisal."

"Please do, and now if you could tell us a few details as regards that ***** ****," said Bea (words not to be printed).

"*Certo, mia cara signora*," said Wissend, always a gentleman. And he started the story of 'that man', whose more accurate description shouldn't be put into words.

"As you both know," he said, "Mr Goodman had never been good in the proper sense of the word. However, he always considered himself to be such a man, but this is of course a matter of personal opinion that usually has nothing to do with reality. For who in the history of mankind, I mean, even the worst tyrants, would have called themselves bad men? I'm sure none of them. And our Jason here isn't an exception.

"One day, apparently after he'd rethought a few financial matters of his own, he came to the conclusion he wasn't yet that rich at all, so he was sure he had to do something about that. And he started to consider all options he envisioned at that moment.

"The first one that came to mind was a very clever, and he was sure about that, financial deal with a couple of Russian oligarchs he had just met, and they'd been introduced to him by those he already knew. At the same time, a new character had arrived at the scene of Jason's business domain, and was a man by the name of Stepan Plohodelayet, who'd appeared in fact out of nowhere, so to speak. We, I mean, the lord, myself and a couple of our other fellow workers, knew where he'd actually come from, but because," and here Wissend cleared his throat, coughed twice, said "excuse me," and then went on, "it's still a personal matter, I unfortunately can't say anything more. Anyway, that Stepan seemed to be a financial virtuoso, a magician, whose money-making schemes so impressed Jason, and he offered the man a position in his company. But unfortunately for him, he didn't realise – because despite being so good at finance, his imagination had always been rather poor – what kind of magic Stepan represented. But I'm pretty sure that you," and our guest smiled at us, "yourselves already know what the true nature of that magic is."

Bea and I returned his smile, and Wissend resumed his story. "Yes, my friends, everything is strange, even in the domain of finance, but here, as it is everywhere else, you need imagination to know that. Anyway, imagination, as *mon maître* says, is everything. Moreover, curiously enough, it is very often the only reality. And again, you already know that yourselves, don't you?"

Hearing that, we said nothing, but nodded.

"*Voilà*, my friends," continued our visitor, "and as it happens, however strange it may seem, when you lack imagination, you can't really grasp the essence of reality. And this is exactly the situation our Jason, a man always

518

so sure about his capacity for understanding nothing but reality, found himself in. And thereafter he couldn't actually comfort, in a way, of course, himself by saying '*grustno i zhalko i nikomu mordy bit*,' but all he could say was '*vsyo ne tak rebyata, vsyo na plevat*.'

"And," Wissend went on, "so it happened that Stepan suggested to our wise realist, Jason, a couple of financial deals here and there, I mean, Russia, the UK and a few other places. The future financial rewards that were to come seemed so attractive, so irresistible to Jason, that his usual realism somehow significantly got smaller. And it was a paradoxical example of how a man may lose his whole capacity for realistic reasoning when a vision of enriching himself is so tempting. And Jason wasn't here an exception, and following Stepan's advice, he rushed forward. But as it turned out, he went a bit too far, and to spare you those rather boring financial details of his journey, I'll just tell you of their consequences.

"So, our Jason's capacity for realistic thinking curiously vanished as a result, a paradox again, of his lack of imagination. Anyway, he'd never even been close to someone like George in this respect, and you know what I mean.

"Afterwards, when it was in fact too late, Jason regained his ability for rational, sober reasoning, which was now enriched by some imagination he'd acquired while bearing the consequences of his going too far, which meant for him a spell dwelling, package holidays of a sort, in rather faraway places, and as far as I know, it was Kamchatka or somewhere like that. In our beloved Britain, he was also in trouble, for Mr Oddhouse, acting on information received from his Russian counterpart, issued relevant instructions after parliament's decision to take some harsher measures against those compatriots who, like Jason, went too far. So, Jason wasn't eager to return to his dearest England and decided to stay in Russia, where strangely enough he was granted a sort of asylum.

"Initially, he wanted to find out for himself why the Devil all that had happened to him, for he still considered himself innocent. But there was now no other way for him to get any explanation in his position but to have a chat with a priest. And one day he had a rather long one, and once Jason had told him everything, the *batiushka* advised him to visit Patriarch's Pond, but why there he didn't say. But Jason was brave enough to follow the advice, drank some apricot juice there upon arrival, sat on a bench, and shortly afterwards, because it was a very hot day, he fell asleep. In his dream, he witnessed a conversation between a couple of men who were discussing good and evil in relation, of course, to the destiny of man. One of the men maintained that whatever happens to a human being is due to his own sovereign actions, while the other one held the opposite view, saying that on the contrary, a man is good for nothing planning his life, the future and the like, for he cannot know anything for sure, especially what may happen to him the very next day. And initially, Jason, listening to the conversation, unreservedly supported the first man's opinion, but once the other man mentioned some kind of proof (Jason couldn't exactly catch what it was because of the man's heavy foreign accent), strangely enough, Jason had a vision, a revelation of a kind. And in his vision, there were no words spoken. A total silence reigned, and in that silence, Jason understood at last the meaning of the man's proof.

Afterwards, our Jason was a very different man. He became very religious, and first of all he went to see the same priest again and profoundly thanked him for his invaluable advice. And then he started a business very dissimilar to his previous one, namely, begging outside the Cathedral of Christ the Saviour. As you know, it is very close to the Kremlin. And now his imagination reached levels previously unimaginable for him, and I mean his very original enterprise.

In order to supplement the rather modest income he got from his everyday activity outside the cathedral, he started the production of something that had always been held in esteem over there, that is, spirits. But it wasn't obviously an official, so to speak, distillery but just a small, very private business that supplied the thirsty with – very high quality, we must say in Jason's favour – *samogon* or moonshine as it is called somewhere else. He's still in business, and there are three kinds of it, all from Jason's unique recipe, and each one under a different name.

The first is called 'The Jolly Beggar', very popular among his fellow co-workers. Another one, 'The Black Magus', is highly valued by the experts and in very high demand, and it is said that a high-ranking Kremlin official (acting in disguise of course) regularly purchases it, handsomely paying Jason in recognition of the truly magnificent (even miraculous, some say) effects of the drink. And lastly, 'Homo Britannicus', a joy of British Embassy personnel and of the professors at Moscow University's Faculty of Humanities. It is said that the ambassador alone purchases two bottles a week, but it is still not much compared to what the military chargé d'affaires buys, which is five or even more sometimes. And if we were to believe in rumours, the chairman of the faculty asks for even more.

All in all, everything now looks pretty good, after all, for our Jason. Yes, to be honest, he's missing England, as do some of those who years ago preferred, for so-called obvious reasons, to remain in Russia, but he doesn't complain too much, for after all, he's back in business and pretty respected due to the quality of his product (he has even considered some foreign deals) and his newfound faith in human destiny, which is now, and he's very much convinced about that, not based solely on what a man thinks he can do.

We should also note that for some unknown reason, the authorities, despite being fully aware of Jason's enterprise, tolerate his small industry. He has never been disturbed by the taxman, or whoever else for that matter. It's not easy to explain why it is, so we'll leave it alone.

We must emphasise as well that Jason, as much as he can, supports all kinds of charities there, in Russia, and abroad too, including Oxfam. Not that long ago, the organisation's representative met Jason to thank him profoundly for his generous donations. He also tasted all kinds of the product, and again, if we are to believe what people say, he was so overjoyed that he was determined to stay in Moscow for good. And it was only the intervention of high-ranking British officials that persuaded him to return to England.

And this is everything at the moment we know about Jason, whom we wish well after all, mainly because of his newborn beliefs, which we appreciate much more that those he had so mistakenly held in his previous life.

Bea and I were listening intently to what Wissend was telling us about Jason's adventures, and together came to the conclusion that what he'd gone through had been enough, and anything further wouldn't be necessary.

Now, we all, drinking Budvar (Bea had wine, of course), were talking about other things, and then Wissend told us another story whose hero was Shaun Swindley, 'The Elephant Toad' as he was called by his malicious fellow politicians.

He was an Irishman, and many of his fellow countrymen still observe a very unique ethical code which might be defined in an even shorter way than that of Ludwig's, that is, what can be said at all can be said clearly. They have made it even clearer, for just one word is required to spell it out, and the word is 'he'. However, it is repeated three times to underline its meaning. So, 'he, he, he' may be used to express your views, on very different matters, in fact, precisely, to the point. What that point actually is, is a mystery for anyone but the Irish. It must be said that even some renowned linguists have tried but failed to grasp the meaning of that extraordinary ethic.

Shaun, himself, was also a strict believer in that mysterious moral philosophy, but unfortunately for him, his belief wasn't shared by too many of his fellow MPs.

What made matters even worse for him was that he tried as far as he could to implement the ethic into almost every kind of parliamentary debate.

Thus, for instance, when it came to discussing the defence budget, Shaun's proposals not only surprised almost every one of his colleagues, but actually shocked the public. But what should be mentioned here was that Shaun made of that 'he, he, he,' a much more refined political tool, making his propositions funny enough to amuse even those who hardly ever had a reason to laugh.

"The liberating power of laughter, yes," Wissend began, "is indeed a kind of relief we need so much, but when you lose control over it then you may expect no understanding for it among your fellow human beings. Anyway, understanding is not the best characteristic of a politician. And it was precisely the lack of it in the case of Shaun that brought about rather serious consequences for him. Still, understanding, to say nothing of recognition of his ideas, was hardly to be expected on account of their extraordinary nature which I'm going to describe to you.

"One of his rather weird designs presented at parliament was to abolish all the armed forces of this country. In favour of such a resolution was, he argued, to prove this country's true wish for world peace, and once that move was implemented, its potential enemies would have no reason to attack it. Moreover, Great Britain's allies might follow its honest display of good will and do the same, so the universal longing for peace may eventually come true.

"The only thing that may remain in place, he suggested, would be a special automatic telephone service which would repeatedly, just in case, as he put it, tell a potential aggressor, *We surrender, we surrender*, for ten minutes or so.

"At first, his fellow parliamentarians thought he was joking, but when it turned out that he was very serious about the idea, they began to worry, especially when he found quite a number of various institutions and also individuals who were willing to support such a move. There were even demonstrations outside parliament. Some newspapers joined the movement. The Internet was full of messages in favour of it. All in all, such a mess and chaos spread all over the country that something had to be done. But the question was what could be done in a democratic country like this one?

"Countless meetings behind closed doors, of course, took place and finally a decision was made to somehow persuade Shaun to change his mind about his proposal. But his answer was a simple 'no', no chance he would back off, and what made everything even worse was his other incredible motions which were continually coming.

"The next one of those was a carefully elaborated plan to redesign the current foreign policy. It was wrong, Shaun firmly declared, to treat as a potential enemy the Russian Federation, or whoever else for that matter. All those newspaper articles, he maintained, were full of rubbish about the matter in question. Such a threat had never been real, he stated, having been merely a pure invention of those whose true aim was to benefit from armaments sale and to implement measures which would result in even stricter control over society. Their dream, Shaun specified, was George's *1984*, and this should be avoided at all costs.

"And his insights were going even further. All schemes for leaving the European Community should be abandoned, for the claim of British uniqueness was unfounded, simply false, and everything should be done to have even closer relations with the rest of Europe. But then, as for the eternal friendship with Dollaria, the policy should be thoroughly modified, for it had actually never benefited this country.

"As we can see, it was all becoming really serious, and a worry for many who had never envisaged a day on which something like this could have posed a serious threat to the well-established order of their country.

"But the last straw was yet to come. And it did when Shaun, whose appetite for change was apparently growing even bigger, said that the sooner Great Britain leaves Northern Ireland in peace, as he put it, the better.

"Once he'd announced his idea, Shaun was warmly welcomed in some parts of the Province, and of course in Dublin, where a great number of people gathered at the airport to welcome him. Then, of course, several meetings took place, not only in Dublin, but all over Eire, and Shaun was declared a hero, another Parnell, or someone even grander.

"At the same time in Britain, nobody of those in or close to power knew what they could actually do about all that cock-up. There was freedom of speech, after all, and even a politician was entitled to it. So, what eventually could be done?

And actually, nobody knew, until one day when a rather oddly looking citizen came to see Sir Herbert Grey, whose name was true *nomen omen* since he was an *éminence grise* of politics. His influence was enormous, but understandably, true to his position, he remained in the shadows.

Sir Herbert was rather reluctant to see the citizen, for he, anyway, never appreciated any visits, but this time, however, he was of a different mind because as it happened he'd had a dream the previous night, and the dream had unsettled him very much. He had seen himself in a park, totally unfamiliar to him, especially as it looked very foreign, but where it had been exactly, he hadn't the slightest idea, and in that park, he'd met a man, also looking very foreign, with whom he'd had a conversation. And it had been the conversation that made him very anxious, and so much so that afterwards he could never forget it.

"We don't know all the peculiarities of the conversation, but what we do know was its main theme, which was the destiny of man in general, but in that case, particularly the destiny of a politician.

"The strange foreigner pointed out that all politics and its servants are in fact useless, dispensable, a pain in the arse, and that they are only there because the majority of people don't know what to do when they are in a group. Separately, each of them does know, but once they're together, they don't have a clue what to do with themselves, where to go, what for, and the like. And all that obviously poses serious problems, especially because when they are together, they tend to behave like 'homo homini lupus est'. So, a decision must be made about that, but again not by any one of them, but by an outsider. And the outsider is out there, but nobody actually knows who he is and where he came from. Nevertheless, his decisions are final and irreversible. Moreover, he who disobeys him bears the consequences.

"But then Sir Herbert asked the foreigner who that mysterious decision-maker was, and what kind of proof existed of his power of such enormity.

"The stranger smiled in response and advised him to read carefully the history of mankind and its leaders, whose power was once so absolute but who, all of a sudden, in the twinkle of an eye, lost it. And that, he said, was sufficient proof of the outsider's power. That outsider, the strange foreigner added, was in the habit of sending his representative anywhere in the world, and it was rather wise to listen to his advice. Otherwise, something unpleasant might happen out of the blue, anywhere, even here in the park right now.

"Sir Herbert followed the advice and read some stories, and found out that there had been more than one of such unfortunate men, who could do anything they wanted, but then one day all their enormous prerogatives had inexplicably ended. And that was it, he thought, sufficient proof did exist, and on the day when that odd-looking visitor arrived, Sir Herbert, remembering the discussion in the park, welcomed him and they had a chat.

"All the peculiarities of the conversation still remain unknown," Wissend said, "but what was decided then, on the suggestion of the visitor, was that the only solution to the Shaun question, as it was called, was to arrange for him a stay at a psychiatric hospital. And there he went after several obligatory medical examinations organised for him by his fellow politicians.

"As far as I know," said Wissend, "he's still there, apparently happy enough, because as he himself says, happiness is where there is no politics."

Bea and I found the story very engaging, and at the same time, informative, and profoundly thanked Wissend for telling it. He was cheered up by our gratitude and offered to tell us another one, and this time it was the story of James Serfield, 'The Rat' or 'The Shovel', as he was called by his sardonic co-workers.

He, as we previously said, was a civil servant, and a very obedient one for that matter. He was actually a perfect servant because his intellectual capacity wasn't too great. But, after all, what he was doing and how he was doing his job was valued at the place he worked, which was the Department for Work and Pensions.

The story Wissend told us wasn't as engaging as others he had told us, and it was due to the unremarkable character of James' work. His responsibilities were of a very mediocre kind, but anyway, he was supposed to do something after all. The most crucial trait of James' predisposition was above all to please his superiors, but also everybody else who had some relation to his reports. But one day he went too far with his eagerness to satisfy everybody, far too far, in his immediate superior's opinion.

James was asked to produce a draft of benefits project for the unemployed, estimate their essential needs, and on that basis, their money allowance.

Usually, such projects promised much more than was actually offered in terms of money. In theory, you could get quite a lot, but in practice very little was paid. And here was the fatal mistake James committed, when one day he decided to make those benefits recipients' dream-like expectations come true.

The project he elaborated had somehow escaped the attention of Mr Miserly, the immediate supervisor of James, mainly because Mr Miserly spent a month in hospital due to an accident. A black cat was crossing the road when he was driving his car, and he, as a man who disliked cats, almost ran it over, but shortly afterwards he himself crashed his car against the lamp post, and because it was actually his fault, he suffered unpleasant consequences. And that chain of events in consequence benefitted those day-dreamers, whose prayers finally became long-awaited reality.

Those unfortunates were overjoyed, and when they somehow learned to whom they owed their unexpected wealth, James received hundreds of complimentary letters praising his unbelievable generosity. In some of them there were invitations asking him to come to celebrate the occasion, dating offers from several women, and even marriage proposals.

James was over the moon, but his boss, Mr Miserly, wasn't when he was back in the office. And he himself was in trouble because of insufficient supervision, he was told, resulting in incredible sums of money paid in benefits. He tried his best to excuse himself by blaming the cat, but it wasn't a well-grounded excuse for his superiors, especially the ministry secretary, who actually suffered a heart attack once he got wind of the blunder. All in all, all hell broke loose.

James' unheard-of generosity resulted in him being accused of sabotage, and appropriate measures were immediately taken to find out what actually motivated him to produce such a princely gift of money paid to people who had been a pain in the neck of the Government for years, and it'd always been believed they should have been left in the cold, for a welfare state was in fact something very un-British. Eventually, the decision was made to relieve him of his job, but something else apart from his grand magnanimity was also needed to make the decision justified.

James' career and also his private life were thoroughly investigated, and to the great satisfaction and relief of his superiors, something they were hoping for was finally found. And it was his association with Mr Dumblodge, who by now was dwelling in Peking. That was what they needed so much, and accordingly, they began to draw up a plan of action against our overgenerous fellow.

But what they didn't know, yet at least, was that Dumblodge, who was always eager to benefit more from his outstanding qualities as a spy, and a traitor for that matter, was thinking of something more than just living his life as a mere retired spymaster. But he had no opportunity to do anything more until one day in June when he was taking a leisurely stroll across Tiananmen Square, he was approached by an unhealthy-looking pale man wearing very dark glasses.

When the man came up to Dumblodge, his first thought was, *Why is he so pale?*

"Sorry for disturbing you, sir," said the man in impeccable English, "but it's my first day in the capital, and I'm not too sure what my first point of interest in the city should be. And since you seem to look like a man who could help me, I have taken the liberty of disturbing you."

"Not at all, you aren't disturbing me," said Dumblodge, being happy in fact to meet one of his, as he presumed, fellow countrymen, but to be sure, he asked, "Are you English?"

"Hmm," the man seemed to hesitate, but finally said, "yes, but to some extent."

*What does he bloody mean*, our James Bond asked himself, '*but to some extent*', what's that? But still being eager to make the acquaintance of somebody from outside his current milieu, he ignored the problem. So, he said, "The first thing to see, would be, of course, the Forbidden City."

"Ah yes, how stupid I am," said the unknown Englishman of 'some extent', and continued, "but of course you yourself have already been there. Anyway, I find the word 'forbidden' very attractive."

"So, do I," replied his 'to some extent' compatriot, "so do I. In fact, I find anything forbidden of interest."

"Very interesting approach to the matter in question you have, sir, very. But may I ask why it is so?"

"Hmm, old chap," said Dumblodge, "I," he went on, "am always curious what is beyond that wall of appearances, what's inside."

"Ah, you're like me. I too take a great interest in anything invisible, so to speak," said the man. "And apologies, in the fervour of our most interesting conversation, I forgot to introduce myself. My name's Carnage, Apollonius Carnage."

*What a strange name he has*, thought Dumblodge.

"Boris Dumblodge, nice to meet you," he said, shaking the already outstretched hand of Apollonius.

"All the pleasure's mine. And if you don't mind me asking you, what's your *métier*?"

"Ah," began Boris, not too sure what to say, "I'm actually a pensioner."

"Oh, are you?" said Apollonius, apparently surprised. "How come, at your age?"

"Ah, you know, certain circumstances, and the like…"

"I see, circumstances, yes, they always matter. But what is it you occupy yourself with these days, if I may enquire?"

Boris, whose main occupation at the moment was being questioned day and night by the Chinese intelligence officers, curious to know everything about his pre-retirement activity, didn't actually know what to say, but eventually in lack of any other reply, blurted out, "I'm very much interested in religion as such, you know, faith, what it really means, and so on."

"Ah," Apollonius said, visibly impressed, "yes, of course, and what religion in particular?"

"Hinduism," replied Boris, because that was the only thing that came to his mind at that moment.

"Oh yes," Apollonius seemed to be impressed again, and went on, "this is exactly what I, myself, study now. And, by the way, have you ever been to India, or rather Hindustan, as I prefer to call the country?"

"No, never," said Boris, who as a matter of fact knew nothing of India or Hindustan as his new friend called it, and the only thing that interested him about the country was its women, that is, their kind of beauty, which he liked very much. And he often imagined himself being with a stunningly gorgeous Madhuri at his side, taking a stroll on the beach in Goa. But in reality he had never met any Hindu women. Anyway, he had never had much luck with any Hindu women, or any other representatives of the opposite sex for that matter, because his looks weren't even remotely like, let's say, Gregory Peck.

Anyway, he was still dreaming after all. Madhuri's image still persecuted him in his dreams.

"Yes, my friend," continued Apollonius, "if I may call you so, due to our common interest, Hindustan, that's something, and its women, huh, huh, what beauties they are!"

"Ah," Boris now began to take more interest in his new friend, "and what about yourself, have you ever—"

He didn't manage to finish the question, for his friend chipped in, "Oh yes, countless times I've been there, and apart from Hinduism and its very engaging particularities, another field of my studies there is women."

"Oh," Boris was now showing even more interest in Apollonius, "and, hmm, are you... how shall I put it... more familiar with them, so to speak?"

"To some extent," said the other man, the expression apparently being his favourite, "yes, I am, and in fact I'm engaged to one of them. Ah, how lucky I am, I can hardly believe my luck."

"Yes, yes, of course," Boris was now more than happy to listen to what Apollonius was telling him, "and…" he hesitated "…is it difficult to, let's say, become acquainted with any of them?"

"Not at all, old boy," said Apollonius, who now felt it right to call his new friend by a more familiar name. "They're easy-going creatures, very straightforward, and as for other matters, you're in paradise, if you know what I mean."

And that paradise was what mainly occupied Boris' mind whenever he dreamt of his walks in Goa, so his interest was now rising. "And what about if I take a trip there, and hmm, would you be so kind as to give me a hand during my journey if I take it sometime in the future?"

"But of course, my dear Boris, all the pleasure will be mine. And are you going to visit the country soon?"

Boris, who actually could hardly move anywhere, being watched by his new employers all the time, didn't know what to say, but eventually uttered, "I'm not sure, you know, under the circumstances, and the like, it would be…"

"But if you really want to go there, I might be of some help regarding what you call circumstances, no problem at all, dear chap. Say the word and I am at your service. And now back to religious matters, if you don't mind. You would find so much there, such sophisticated gods they have, and I, myself, take a particular interest in Shiva, you know, the god of destruction."

"Ah yes, I've heard of him," said Boris, who *de facto* knew nothing about Hinduism, or any other religion for that matter.

"Bah," exclaimed Apollonius, "he's something to study, believe me. I've actually been studying him for years, and it still seems to me I still know nothing about him. You know, I mean, whether he's good or bad, really hard to say. Does he do good or evil in this world? Nobody knows, in point of fact, and so it is about him. A very mysterious personage, if I may call him that. The magic mountain, to paraphrase his actions, a pure black magic. You never know what to expect of him, what's coming next, never."

Boris, whose main motive for carrying on the conversation with

Shiva's disciple of a sort was Indian women, asked, "And, let's suppose I get there, but you know, I know nobody…"

"For God's sake, my friend, I've already offered my services. Shoot, what do you want me to do for you? Don't hesitate at all. I'll do anything, and in fact I have some resources at my disposal, believe me."

"Ah, that's great to know, for I may in fact be considering a trip there pretty soon," said Boris, who was now taking an earnest interest in everything his new friend was saying.

"If so, I'd be glad to help as I just said. Shall I make some arrangements right away?"

"Hmm," Boris still hesitated, but then Madhuri showed herself again in his mind, and he said, "please, do, and thank you very much."

"No problem at all, dear friend, we'll be ready to go soon, very soon, next week at the latest."

And to tell the truth, it wasn't that difficult for Apollonius to organise the trip, for he as a matter of fact was in touch with the Indian Intelligence Service. However, during an investigation afterwards, the Chinese counterpart wasn't able to establish for sure whether he actually worked for them or for any other business, for that matter.

Anyway, next day, when they met again, he jubilantly announced, "Everything's ready. We can leave next Monday. I've already got the plane tickets and booked hotels, so, my friend, we're going. Hope you haven't changed your mind."

"Not at all," said Boris, who was by now so preoccupied with his dreams about the Indian women's delights that nothing, even the potential risk of taking the trip, mattered to him. And the risk, actually a serious danger, was that because those two intelligence services had never had a good relationship, quite the opposite, he wasn't allowed to travel to India because, as already mentioned, he worked for the Chinese. Yes, he could dream as much as he wanted but nothing else. But now those dreams prevailed, the reality ceased to exist for our Boris, and he said to his most obliging friend, "That's great! Next Monday, you say. I'll get ready by then, and many thanks again."

"It's a pleasure, old chap. I'll see you on Monday, 6 am at the… airport. Bye now."

And on the Monday, they went. Later, during the interrogation back in China, Boris was honest enough to confess he hadn't met over there any Madhuris, or any other good-looking women. He did meet a couple of prostitutes instead, for his looks hadn't attracted the attention of any beautiful Indian women for that matter. And that might have been due to something other than just the way he looked, for in fact he wasn't as ugly as our Professor Koczkodan, whom, curiously enough, some very attractive women found interesting, but it was about something else, but what exactly it was, we would never know. All in all, Boris was rather disappointed with his trip. However, we must recognise his flexibility in this kind of expertise, for while in the country of Mahatma, he'd had talks not only with Indian Intelligence officers, but also their Russian counterparts, so it could be said that during his pursuits as a spy he had actually surpassed the world-famous sophistication of MI6, for now our Boris had become not only a double agent, but a triple one, or perhaps even more than that, and only a few of his fellow countrymen had reached a higher level in this area of activity before him.

After his spell in India, he was supposed to spy on China, and he did so for a couple of months until it came suddenly to an unexpected and disappointing end. He was found guilty of betraying his Chinese hosts and landed in a place far away from Madhuri-likes and the similar delights of this world. It was, as far as we know, somewhere in or close to Tibet, and his stay turned out to be rather long, and of a rather boring everyday routine. However, fortunately for him, a chance for a change appeared when he and his fellow dwellers were allowed to engage themselves in a hobby of their choice, but under strict supervision, of course. And our Boris' choice astonished everybody, including the governor himself. And it was nothing else but the Yeti, its habits, exact whereabouts and the like. And in his newfound vocation, Boris showed remarkable, hidden and unknown to himself, skills.

First, he read all the available literature on the subject; and in doing so, he was understandably required to learn Chinese and the languages spoken in Tibet. And it came as a big surprise to himself, because he, being an Englishman, never ever suspected himself of any ability to learn a foreign language. After his theoretical knowledge was considered sufficient by his supervisors, he was allowed to pursue his hobby outside the place, which presumably he didn't enjoy very much. In the company of his guardian, of course, he made several trips on foot all over the wilds under extreme, especially in winter understandably, weather conditions. Boris' courage and determination were recognised and highly praised by the governor himself, and he was awarded an additional bowl of rice every day. He was most grateful for that because during his expeditions he obviously lost a few pounds, and he found climbing particularly difficult, for his already over-sized baggy trousers were falling down. But, all in all, he was good and most importantly became a very different man, a man who finally found his vocation, a man of courage and purpose, and thus he actually benefitted from his stay there. Moreover, when he eventually returned to his native country, he was frequently invited by several universities and other institutions, not only in England for that matter, to give lectures on the subject he mastered while in Tibet.

His previous favourite kind of leisure was long forgotten, and his once beloved Oxford club made the mistake, having overlooked that, of inviting him to join them in their very popular 'wrecking everything' pastime. In his written reply, he ridiculed them, calling them a stupid, crazy gang of useless bums who actually deserved to be expelled and sent to Tibet, yes, that's it, he emphasised that, or at least to Siberia where they belonged, as he put it. Boris sent the vice-chancellor a copy of his letter and urged him to put into practice his evaluation of the 'gang', but the addressee was rather reluctant to follow the now-wise man's advice.

Nowadays, Boris hardly ever has a prolonged stay in his once beloved England. Most of the time, he travels all over the world in pursuit of other Yeti-like creatures. And he found the Andes to be a place they may inhabit, and now, his astonishing climbing skills allow him to rich the rugged and hitherto unexploited territories up there in those high mountains.

And this is all we know for now about Boris, and we're inclined to wish him well after all, for his blunders eventually resulted in him becoming a better man. So, goodbye, and lot of luck, Boris.

Bea and I liked the story, and as a matter of fact were quite impressed by the totally changed Boris whom we would have never expected to become anything but one of those quasi-clever James Bond-like schmaltzy characters.

And now back to James, once 'The Shovel' and his 'adventures' and the relationship with Dumblodge became known to his bosses, they finally found what they were hoping for, and he was made redundant, for it was seen unwise to make his leave too pronounced by firing him.

Now he was unemployed, with no chance of getting any decent job, and had to live on benefits, but fortunately not for too long, for as it turned out, our James was an industrious man after all. Moreover, it was thanks to the dismissal that he eventually had the opportunity to put into practice his true vocation, that is, to keep everything clean. He always hated dirt and now declared total war on it.

The beginnings were rather modest, but in the course of time, his cleaning business expanded, but not in terms of people joining his company, for James always worked alone, single-handedly fighting the enemy. The lonely, he said, are the brave. The company he founded was named 'The Conqueror', and pretty soon established itself in that quite competitive market, for as we know, there are thousands of cleaners in London. What made his enterprise so successful was his attention to detail and incredible meticulousness of the job. The quality was checked more than once by world-class British experts in the field; even powerful electronic microscopes didn't find a speck of dirt once James had declared everything clean.

He obtained several certificates which he proudly displayed in his office that was in fact based in his own, now very modest flat. The certificates came from famous universities, namely their departments of chemistry and biology. But the crucial thing about the business was the cleaning stuff, that is, the weapons with which James fought his enemy. He didn't trust mass-produced cleaning products, once calling them horse piss when interviewed on BBC2. After the interview, several international companies contacted him, in secrecy of course, offering very substantial sums of money to prevent such interviews in future, but to his credit, James declined the offer which, rumour has it, was in millions of pounds sterling.

What was important about his work was not only James' perfectionism, but what he actually used to fight his sworn enemy. The formula of his cleaning stuff was a well-guarded secret, so well guarded that even some renowned intelligence services failed in trying to discover it. In protecting the mysterious formula, James was later joined by his friend, Boris Dumblodge, after his release from that remote place in Tibet. And here, we must admit frankly, the former spy performed miracles defending the secrecy of the job, and until this day the formula remains unknown to anybody but James.

The strength of his product simply performed miracles; even the most stubborn dirt vanished once just a few drops were used, and James understandably always put on a special military outfit while doing his job, normally used only in the event of nuclear war. And in truth, the uniform wasn't the British army one, because he asked them for it more than once, as he did their American counterpart, but they both refused to issue it to him. It was a shame, a terrible disgrace, and the reasons for turning down his request were brought to light when a special royal commission learned that some high-ranking officers had been bribed by those multinational companies who obviously wished James to die by his own weapon, such bastards they are. And as a result, some officers were dishonourably dismissed when the scandal came to public attention thanks to the ever-curious paper, The *Shadow Behind*. It is said that its reporters' investigative skills were far better than those of the Secret Intelligence Service and its CIA friends.

As we've already mentioned, James was always on his own while performing the miracles of his job. As happened more than once during a thorough cleaning of Buckingham Palace, the Queen herself wanted to glance upon our hero performing miracles, but James very politely but sternly barred her from entering the premises within which he was working. In his letter to Her Majesty afterwards, after apologising again, he explained his refusal by saying that he could have allowed her inspection only provided she was wearing the same overall as he was, which was out of the question, for his gear was of unmatched quality (it was rumoured it arrived from Russia), and if she was wearing the home-produced version, she would be in danger.

It didn't take long, and James' local fame attracted the attention of overseas countries. The invitations and very substantial honoraria came from all over the world. We should note here that James didn't charge any fixed prices for his job; instead, he followed that very well-tested way some churches had employed forever, that is, of telling the receivers of their services, when they enquired about the costs, that extremely well-working formula, "Up to your Grace," and it was assumed that grace was expected to be as vast as that of God's Himself. The invitations came from rich individuals, institutions (from the Pentagon, for instance, despite the aforementioned blunder of theirs) of various kinds, and even governments. Those were, among others, the Saudi Arabian (it's said James' honorarium matched the cost of a state-of-the-art weapon), the Israeli (it was agreed it would be paid in instalments), and lastly, from the British one, and James' invoice almost emptied its special budget.

Thus, James became a very wealthy man, but he was, for unknown reasons, still living at the same rundown accommodation guarded (because of his top-secret lab) surprisingly not by a vicious dog or sophisticated electronic device, but by the Tibetan cat presented to him by his now best friend, Boris. As expected, there were attempts to enter it, but all failed. Moreover, once, the unsuccessful perpetrators landed afterwards in a psychiatric hospital where they were reported to be recovering from extremely severe shock caused by the mere horrifying sight of the cat. We should mention here that James didn't spare any cost on his precious animal, feeding it salmon and sturgeon, and it drunk nothing but beer, occasionally a schnapps for strength.

Because of his well-deserved fame, James was a sought-after guest at countless social gatherings, and became very successful with women. He changed his female companions like the proverbial gloves, but it wasn't actually their fault it never lasted long, for it was due to his unbelievable thriftiness that they left him. He never invited them to any high-class restaurants, despite his wealth, but always to the cheapest facilities that served nothing but crap processed food. Anyway, he paid no attention to any luxuries and didn't drive a Rolls-Royce and the like, but his old Fiat which hardly moved.

So, as we can see, James remained to his credit a very humble, unassuming man. Only that bloody thriftiness of his was annoying, and at the same time, people asked, what was actually the cause of it? And it took a long time to reveal the secret, and the discovery left many a man astonished.

It turned out that almost all the money he earned, and there were very substantial amounts of it, went to support an organisation called 'Cleaners International' whose motto was 'Purity is everything', and accordingly the credos were 'Cleanliness must be', 'Purity will prevail', and lastly, 'Spotlessness is the only virtue'.

The organisation's headquarters were based in Poland, close to a mountain called Lysa Gora or the 'Bald Mountain', and legend said that it had once been a place where every year the most important conference of witches had been held. They'd come from all parts of the world to discuss their issues and policies, and the organisation had been led by the witch-in-chief, who'd been known just by the initial, 'M'.

As we know perfectly well, witches travel on their brooms; unsurprisingly, the coat of arms of the organisation had been a broom.

And now, after centuries had passed, it turned out that the organisation was still intact, and the conferences still took place on the same mountain, and that again, a woman in charge still acted under a simple 'M', and the honorary chairman was none other than that terrible cat of James'.

The news of all that didn't come from any of the formidable intelligence services which were actually responsible for gathering information on any suspicious activities around the world, but again from the already-known-to-us newspaper, The *Shadow Behind*. And it was only after its publication of an article that all the spooks of the world got ready for action because the organisation was suspected of planning a *coup d'état*, in fact, a worldwide revolution. However, it was still unknown what its aims actually were, and how it was to carry out the revolution.

Anyway, all available resources were used to gather as much information as possible about the organisation.

And here all the secret services cooperated in unison for once, and all their satellites, planes, helicopters, whatsoever, were used to find out everything about that assumed rebellion, *coup d'état*, revolution, whatsoever – nobody in fact was sure what in truth the organisation was up to, and still very little is known about it. Millions were spent on the aforementioned allied action, all state-of-the-art spying equipment used, but a lot of it, for an unknown reason, broke down during the operation. Anyway, all their efforts were in vain, and they learned nothing.

Lord Hellbridge, who at the time of that allied action was present in Poland, attending a seminar at Jagiellonian University, had been aware of the planned action long before it started, despite its super classified nature, and shared his opinion about its failure with his Polish friends, and all we know is that they went to celebrate the failure (but why they did so, we don't really know) at U Havelka restaurant and had mountains of its delicious *pierogi z miesem*, Tyskie beer and a few schnapps, of course. And again, all we know about their celebration is that they were laughing till the small hours.

Yes, an attempt to know something about the celebration was actually made, curiously enough, not by a Polish intelligence officer, as we would have been expected, but by his Israeli counterpart. And ditto, it was another blunder of the famed spooks. And this time, their top agent, a man, tried to sneak into U Havelka, disguised as one of the Cracovian women selling flowers on the main square, but a cat, Lord Hellbridge's bodyguard, spotted him at once, and again all we know about the encounter is that the spy underwent very intensive and long courses of psychological and psychiatric interviews afterwards, but we don't know whether they proved to be successful.

"And now to tell you a few final words about James' adventures, he's still doing his job and has received several awards for its outstanding quality, among others, 'Golden Broom' in England and 'Cleaner of the Year' in Dollaria, and also *'Sauber Muss Sein'* in Germany. It's also very likely he'll receive the CPE – Commander of the Purity Empire – created especially for him, and it seems possible he'll be nominated for a knighthood, the first-ever nomination for this kind of excellence.

"Yes, my friends," concluded Wissend, "strange things happen on earth, but what might be actually happening in heaven, you would never imagine, but then, unfortunately for them of course, there are people who claim they do. Ah, I feel sorry for them, I mean, they would be very disappointed if they really knew what's happening there. People in general seem to be very unreasonable in their opinions as regards things they cannot know, and these opinions lead them so often astray, they commit horrible blunders, but they carry on as if nothing has happened. They hardly ever learn from their mistakes.

"You know, the truth is quite simple, in fact, anything is possible on earth because you don't really know what may be possible. You don't even know what's going to happen in an hour or two, to say nothing of next day or next year. On the whole, you cannot predict the future, and then you put far too much trust in technology as if it alone would provide you with all the solutions, whereas, it doesn't actually answer your most important problem, the problem of life, which is constant denial, that saying 'no' all over again. And in truth the solution of the problem of life cannot be found in technology, or any science for that matter. Here, Ludwig is right in saying that even when all possible scientific questions have been answered, the problems of life remain completely untouched. Ah, these computers, they just unlearn people of the individual, independent ability to think, to have ideas of their own, but they seem not to care, clicking on them all the time as if all the answers were there. But then, when it turns out that there aren't any answers, you may land in an asylum, and small wonder so many people are there, in highly technologically developed countries. And these are apparently responsible, prudent people, whereas in fact they are like infantile children who keep on making the same mistakes, expecting at the same time to find the answers, which cannot be found there. Their stupidity has no limits because they put too much trust in their intellectual powers. They actually think they're infallible whatever opinions they have at the moment, and if later these opinions are proved to be false, they simply replace them with other ones, saying they were mistaken and, feeling no remorse whatsoever, replace them with other ones which turn out to be false again. And it goes on like that *ad infinitum*. Or rather they believe it will be so, but actually how would they know when, as we have just noticed, they don't even know what may happen to them on the very same day? Yes, that's the hyperbolic naivety of man positing himself as the meaning and measure of the value of things, as our dear friend Friedrich says, man as judge of the world. Such monstrous stupidity results in fact in committing an infinite series of blunders, and there is no end of them because of that naïve, overpowering stupidity of his. But then, one day, not unsurprisingly, disappointment, or even contempt, but again not for himself, that is, for his naiveté, but for the world, because man still feels it has not all been his fault. He remains not guilty, innocent, and there is a certain pathology in this thinking; some inborn faulty mechanism he is subdued to. And it seems that our poor creature, man, can do nothing about that. But we're still trying to teach him something after all, to show him a different path, but I often have the impression that our efforts are in vain, a waste of time and our health of course.

"I, myself, am at the end of my tether, and don't really know how come *mon maître*, the lord, has such patience to carry on his task to start teaching them all over again. And he is on his own doing that job, that is, persuading man in the first place that he shouldn't be so sure of himself, and his complaints should be addressed to himself, for this is the only right beginning of knowing something in the end. To question himself is the only way to change things for the better for him and his fellow men. And there is no other way, believe me.

"But then, in this country, and its neighbouring countries, but not those across the Channel, you should, people say, think positive after all, and if so, there very likely might be, I believe, an apocalypse after all. And by the way, I don't really know the reason for the lord's infinite patience. I think he should retire for he needs some rest and peace, but unfortunately, no, I don't think he ever will. For him, duty comes first. But what is likely to happen is that one day he may finally lose that limitless patience of his, and say, all that doth begin should rightly to destruction run, and then it will, for there is nothing too difficult for him to do, believe me.

"But then again and again, people seem to ignore him and his well-wishing advice, but they might eventually believe it when, yes, it is already too late. Too late to find the solution to the problem of life, which is to be or not to be for man on this earth.

"In the meantime, in some countries as it is here, people and their politicians try to cheer themselves up by all means available, by that crap music they play all over again, by those artificial, primitive pleasures of theirs, and they believe their freedom lives on in all of that. And yes, it does, but it's the freedom of stupidity. And you know what, all that crap is, curiously enough, typical for English-speaking countries. Yes, it is, and the reason is, I believe, their natives are actually mongrels, especially in

540

Great Britain. And it is typical for a mongrel to be satisfied with crap, for quality is not their cup of tea. They wouldn't even be able to enjoy it. Yes, there are a few among them who may, but the majority, their cities packed with riff-raff, would not bear any good things, for they wouldn't digest them, so to speak. Fortunately, the future is not in their hands, and as for the struggle of the species, they will lose, says *mon maître*, and he will be the last to laugh.

"One of these places, where that crap grows in abundance, was visited recently by a friend of mine who after his return resumed his experience in Russian, for he said that the essence of the subject would be better told in the language. Thus, he said, '*Na khuy nam svoboda etogo naroda, kogda nichego interesnova i nikogo umnogo ne mozhna nayti. Nichego nibut' krome travy i svobody gluposti.*' And consequently, he added, '*Grustno i zhalko i nikomu mordy bit*,' which is a rather specific Russian way to illustrate disappointment.

"But, we, I believe," continued Wissend, "shouldn't be tolerant towards stupidity, and therefore," he glanced at me and smiled, "I approve of the harshness of your views on some places, and especially the way you portray that so-called 'north-west' where dumbness has reached its summit. I regard brainlessness as the main threat to the existence of humankind, to say nothing of its devastating impact on its quality of living and thinking for that matter. And quality means civilisation in its true meaning, that is, the principles we observe and values we cherish and implement practically in the way we live.

"And that's it, what can be said at all can be said clearly, but there are exceptions, as was the case of a former Polish president who said, 'I'm for and even against' with the intention, presumably, of satisfying everybody. And probably for that reason his German counterpart called him 'an incredible phenomenon of nature'.

"You know of course that such phenomena, quite common especially among politicians, tend to confuse everyone, and they do so on purpose, of course, so that nobody could blame them afterwards whichever way things go. In other words, they tend to be in the middle, that is, in fact, nowhere.

"But fortunately, we aren't them, and neither is our language. We are very careful here, because we know that the way you use words is the way

541

you are. They actually say who you are. You know that the purest art is the art of music, and this is because even if some words accompany it, as it is in operas and symphonies, the message is still in music. It prevails, and the best one takes you beyond this world of relativity and accidentality. Listen to our *caro* Pietro and his Cavalleria Rusticana, and where are you then? In heaven, for the only one is where no words exist. And then, and only then, you might be beyond good and evil. And here our William, the only Englishman so far who seems to have understood anything of philosophy, grasped the essence of the problem, saying, 'There is nothing either good or bad, but thinking makes it so.' You see, thinking is the way we use words, which so oft-times leads humans nowhere. And that's why my master, the lord, always insists on me speaking as clearly as possible. He even allows me to be rude, harsh with words, for he says that truth outweighs them, even if they seemingly insult someone. And to say something about a writer so easily with words, I mean, Jean-Paul, he got what he well deserved from one of his fellow philosophers when he eventually dropped any niceties, calling Jean-Paul a 'filthy creature', and some of his fellow writers found those words very adequate. Anyway, people who tend to be excessively polite aren't honest. In fact, they're actually two-faced, and that kind of duplicity is so characteristic for some nations, as is the case of this country. And that's exactly why *mon maître* decided to visit it in his well-meaning attempt to teach them something, and still hopes his lesson might be appreciated after all, and if it isn't, bah, I'll be very sorry for them. And their famous positive thinking won't help them once he has decided they've flunked the exam. And, their now best friends, the Irish, are supposed to learn as well, for it seems that that very long-lasting bad influence of their good friends (previously they weren't good at all, quite the opposite) has led them astray.

Yes, my friends, something is rotten, as William says, but this time not in Denmark, which is by the way, a very friendly country, moreover, in terms of that bloody money, that crime, as Roger and his friends called it, the country is just with it (if we may mention any justice regarding money), I mean, income equality, which is not the case with Eire or Anglia. Oh no, quite the opposite.

"Yes, now that rottenness has spread all over the globe, and to say more, we can – and he would, I believe, give us his kind permission to do that – say after him, quote Stanislaw Ignacy, that is, 'My writings won't get under any thatched roofs, for then, fortunately, there won't be any left, and my scripts won't cheer up anyone any more, for only filth will spread everywhere.'

"And now, where are you, people? It seems you are where the aforementioned confused language of yours, the seduction of words, has led you, as Friedrich so rightly foretold. It seems you have finally arrived where the questions, 'What for?' and 'Why?' find no answers.

"'*Da, vse ne tak, rebyata, vse ne tak,*' to quote Vladimir, but you, yourself," and now Wissend smiled and looked at me, "seem to be a wee bit confused. Your own writings appear not to have arrived anywhere yet. What would you say to that, my friend?"

"Yes, you're right of course," I said, "but you know, I'm still in doubt, not sure of myself what to say, I mean, some final conclusions, provided that there are any for that matter."

"No, no, no, my friend, *keine Sorge*, don't worry about that, and actually it's good you're still in doubt, for if someone isn't then he's neither learnt anything nor got anywhere. Thinking, as life itself, is a task not a solution, for as regards both, there aren't any final solutions, and this is simply because you should never stop thinking, for you can do that only when you've already left this world. There aren't any final solutions or conclusions whatsoever, regarding thinking and life, my friend. Man is incapable of finding out what he calls truth. The absolute truth, truth *an sich*, as that stubborn Immanuel says, or truth in itself, huh, huh, never ever try to get there. Remember my good advice, my friend. But then, you, humans, want to get there, even if you aren't aware of your pursuit. It seems to be an irrational drive of yours to get there, but then do you think you can really tell rational from irrational? Anyway, that quasi-sophistication and subtleness, that flowery, wordy language of some intellectuals only blurs the matter in question, as was the case, among a few others, of our Jean-Paul, who consequently got so confused by his own way of thinking, his views, that he didn't have any idea where he stood himself. In a word, one day he was for something, and the week after, against it, or vice versa. All in all, it seems he said nothing of value, anything you could follow to comprehend life and the world. On the whole, we can call his confused style pathological, and consequently damaging to the readers of his scribbling. Yes, there are some exceptions, for some of his writings are good, but those transmitting his political views are good for nothing.

"But then, there are others whose language is, huh, huh, very complicated indeed, but at the same time worth reading, as is the case of our dear Immanuel. Ah, what a terrible martinet and formalist he was, but then even if he was wrong, and he was so, and still is, it was in grand style, because great philosophers make great mistakes. It was Edmund who said that, as far as I remember, and we can paradoxically learn a lot from mistakes; trying to correct them is our own way of doing that.

"Anyway, you may say you actually know nothing but you can still rely on God, for he being almighty and omnipotent knows everything, but then how can you claim to know that? Isn't it a blasphemy of those who call themselves Christian? Whatsoever, all in all, to say you're one of them proves nothing. But to say 'I believe' is very common, especially for those bad ones, because for them Christianity means freehand in doing anything since God will always forgive them after all.

"And back to your unforgiving way of writing, don't you worry, for I don't think that truth is ever insulting because it always outweighs rudeness which is, anyway, something relative, a matter of interpretation. An interesting thing is that it's them, those dimwits, who so often remind you about it in their own defence, don't they? Small wonder, for they always, at all costs, want to excuse themselves from any wrongdoing. As the inhabitants of that north-west do, especially in one particular place which, they say, is just one step from worldwide recognition of their cultural achievement, and yes, it is indeed, but upside-down, so to speak.

"Ah, my dear friends, I'm getting tired of this sort of analysis, and I feel envious of Immanuel, who is now dwelling in a very pleasant place, peace and quiet, no worries at all, arranged for him by the maître in recognition of his hard and, in truth, productive thinking. But what can I do? I, myself, am not allowed to put my feet up, to lie down and do nothing. No, the lord would never allow me, for he says duty comes first, and it is our duty to maintain the order of this world. Order must be because it is for, he says. You see, what can be said at all, can be said clearly."

"May I say something?" asked Bea, who, like me, was listening attentively to Wissend, who now, I could see, expected us to say something.

"But of course, *mein Schatz*, you're very welcome," he said, always a gentleman.

"Yes," Bea began, "that is all very interesting, but then how is it supposed to lead us somewhere in the future? I mean a place where eventually we may be at peace, as Immanuel is now."

"Very good question, *mia cara signora*, which I in fact expected from such a wise and beautiful lady. And I'll satisfy your curiosity straightaway, being pretty sure at the same time you already know the answer," said Wissend, and smiled.

"I may know, but I would still appreciate your answer first," said Bea.

"All right then," said Wissend, "I will if you insist. However, I'm sorry to say but your question is somewhat, hmm, general in nature, so please tell me what you mean by 'to lead us somewhere in the future.'"

"I mean how to get there, where we may finally find peace."

"Aha, yes, now I can see clearly what is on your mind, and let me put my reply in the briefest way possible.

"You see, an interesting story, as you say, can be of value for us only when thanks to it we may start to rethink the story of our own life, when we can know it as if for the first time, to arrive where we started, and begin our life from scratch in a way. If we don't experience such a need to go back to our own beginning, any stories we have heard are worthless for us, for they don't stimulate us enough to start the journey of our own life once again. In other words, your journey back into your life may lead you to a place where tranquillity resides, and you've found peace at last."

"You put it in a very philosophical way, *Lieber* Herr Wissend, but I think I know what you mean."

"I'm very glad to hear that, and as for putting anything in a philosophical way, as you say, it is to put it as a challenge, a task, to somebody else, and if that challenge results in his motivation to rethink his own experience, then, and only then, have we succeeded.

"We should never ever," Wissend carried on, "provide another man with ready, wise advice of ours, any final, so to speak, solutions, because if we do that, he will never succeed in finding his own particular way to understand the problem of life, his own life. His life is his own task, and nobody else can accomplish it for him. And only when he, on his own, has finally resolved his problem of life, does he find peace and quiet. The problem of life cannot be put into any words because it is a very innate matter, our problem, and nobody else's. That's why we wouldn't be able to explain what the problem is about, for to explain means to put our answer into words, and the words are our own words, because it is our own thinking, that is, our inner thinking in which its ideas think for us, and only for us, and no one else can access that domain, for it is our own domain and nobody's else."

"Yes, I see clearly now what you mean, Herr Wissend, and what about you?" Bea looked at me and smiled.

"Yes, darling, the same here. I think I know what our friend means by saying that you already known what he means by finding peace and quiet, that is, to solve the problem of life. He means yours and my life."

"Yes, darling, I have, for your life and mine are one and the same."

I said nothing to that, just nodded and said to myself, *At last I got there. It's been a long journey, but finally I've reached the destination.*

"So, my friends," said Wissend, "we've just found out that words may help lead people to their destination, but they alone cannot explain the experience of others because this is their own destination and nobody's else.

"And to go back to the problem of that flowery, wordy language of some authors, they actually abuse the things they describe, making them look artificial. They create fictitious worlds that don't exist. They seem to have found the final solutions to the problems, whereas in real life, there aren't any final ones in words, and to claim there are is a mere stupidity. And here, the difference between genius and stupidity truly proves that the latter has no limits.

"Yes, we may be under that specific charm of their intellectual brilliance with words, that masquerade of them, but as a matter of fact, such an abundance of words says nothing, actually hiding the meaning. There is no message left for the reader. We may marvel at their mastery with words, but in truth it leads us nowhere. Reading them, you arrive nowhere. In their mastery, they cannot formulate any conclusions from which the reader might benefit, and finally no direction is shown to him. Finally, he knows even less than he knew before.

"We're the opposite of them. We believe we should slash the reader with words, even insult him, and not falsely console him using them, for only then may what we say have an effect on him. For only when we are harsh saying our message, then and only then, may he wake up from his illusions and get rid of his wrong beliefs. And if he has been awoken, we in turn have proven the truth that once he started to hate us, our job actually benefitted him. Otherwise, he would remain indifferent. He wouldn't give a damn about what has been said. But when our words insult him, he, paradoxically, out of hatred, begins to understand us.

"And when, for instance, he reads some incredible stories he doesn't understand, actually laughing at them, it might be of even bigger help because then he's even more eager to hate us and then, curiously enough, his understanding increases, his awareness grows. And only then does he begin to live, for to live, as Henry tells us, is to be aware; joyously, drunkenly, serenely, divinely aware. And that's it. That's life."

We should in our writing tell the reader about his own doubts, his reluctance to understand, his fears. He must be shocked by our message to understand it. And in this sense, writing might be a psychoanalytical analysis of a sort, and consequently a therapy.

"And now," continued Wissend, "let me tell you another story whose hero was Simon Prigstone, 'The Evangelist', as he was called by his brothers and sisters in Christ, but what He, himself, that noblest human being ever, as Friedrich called him, would say about our Simon, I can't really imagine. So, shall I begin?"

"Yes, please do," we both, Bea and I, said in unison.

"All right then. As we already knew, Simon was an avid lecturer, so to speak, at his congregation gatherings. His sermons were listened to, and his word seemed to be law, anyway, in his parishioners' view. But, as a matter of fact, he himself was never sure whether it was the case for himself. Yes, he thought his lectures useful for others, but not so much for himself because he felt he was always in doubt as regards his own life and what to do with it. He couldn't see the future, that is, couldn't envisage any final destination where he would eventually find the solution to his own life problem, which is, as we know now, asking questions all over again and not being able to find any answers. This is what I call the problem of life – that infinite stream of questioning. In other words, the sense of life is found only when we have ceased to ask questions about it. The rest, that is, the answer, is silence.

"Let's now see his way to get there. And again, our Simon would never have made his journey if there had not been help from outside. Where it came from exactly, he afterwards didn't actually know. He might have just guessed, but every guess is usually a disappointment when reality comes and proves our guess wrong.

"And then eventually a day came when our Simon started to doubt the sense of his job. Why, he asked himself, am I doing this when my flock doesn't change at all? They remain the same creatures of slave morality. For them, God has never existed because to believe in Him, Simon arrived at the conclusion only after several years of service, is to go beyond your own self, that is, beyond your self-serving motives and opportunism. My parishioners, Simon thought, have never actually been on the way to know God, for to know Him is nothing but to respect His commandments, and they never have. Not faith but actions prove your belief. That Friedrich, Simon now knew, was ultimately right here. He thought that actually no human could claim to know absolute, that is, divine truth, or to hope he might ever know it, for that is reserved for God alone, and He, Simon was convinced now, would not be willing to share His knowledge with us. People say, bah, God might still be there, but since we cannot go beyond our own nature to follow him, what is left for us is to gain pleasures of our own choice. And there are so many of them for that matter. Eventually, Simon came to the conclusion he was in truth one of them, and as such wasn't able to observe any longer what he thought he believed in, and accordingly he changed his lifestyle. And the feeling of being liberated, to do whatever he wanted, urged him to enjoy life to the full.

"And when he realised his newfound liberation, his sermons began to be very different. He was making his parishioners aware of what they really were – a gang of egocentric, ruthless prigs who claimed to believe in God while carrying the Devil under their shirts, as the saying goes. He didn't spare them anything. He was like the Grand Inquisitor, with no mercy for the sinners. If he could, he would have reintroduced *auto-da-fé*, but fortunately for them he couldn't.

"Furthermore, Simon wrote a letter to his bishop calling him names, and he thought himself right doing that since he knew almost everything about the bishop. The bishop's second shadow life was known to him thanks to his friend, Dumblodge, who, for some uncertain reason, was spying on Simon's superior. He knew what his Excellency was doing while visiting African and Latin American countries, his liking for very young girls and boys where there were plenty of them, easy to get almost for free.

"Simon called him a filthy bastard no less, a bloody prick, a swine in human disguise. All in all, it proved to be enough for his dismissal to be considered, which is never easily done in that mutual admiration society of the church fraternity. But because Simon went far too far, it was decided to go ahead with it and he left the holy congregation one day in May, and a bright sunny day perfectly matched his newfound liberation.

The bishop, Eugene Dickman, 'The Prissyhole', as he was nicknamed, was still eager to go further with Simon's condemnation, for he considered it wasn't enough just to strip Simon of his priesthood, so he petitioned the Pope to have him excommunicated. But his holiness wasn't of the same mind because he actually knew about the bishop's escapades and disapproved of them. But at the same time, he was very forgiving, and during his numerous visits abroad, his forgiving attitude was shown. Even in countries where human rights abuse had gone beyond imagination, he never ever said anything bad about their bloodthirsty leaders. When he visited the north-west peripheries of Europe, the place still a godforsaken backwater, and was told by his advisers that the place might in truth benefit from some criticism, he disagreed. In his limitless compassion, he went even further than the voice of centuries ago which had established the holy institution. When one of his aides mentioned bottomless stupidity as one of the deadly sins, he said his interpretation of it was different. When they said that even the father of the Church would have lost patience with them, his own interpretation of their nature was different.

"So, in comparison, it was relatively easy for his holiness to forgive Simon, for whom now the first objective was to find a woman willing to

549

submit to the desires he had already tasted once or twice, but currently he was eager to satisfy them as often as possible, if possible six days a week, for Sunday, he thought, he should still sacrifice a few moments for his former master, God.

"But since it wasn't that easy to find such a woman, he started visiting brothels, and could afford it because he'd saved some money doing his previous job, due mainly to his travels on charitable missions to countries of the so-called emerging, developing economies.

"The visits to brothels weren't enough. Something was still missing, and it was children, for Simon now wanted to have some of his own. Why, he couldn't tell, but that newfound need urged him to look for a woman fit to provide him with a couple of them. *Five will do*, he thought, *hmm, maybe one or two more.*

"And he found such a woman and immediately got to work, and proved himself to be a very efficient worker, producing ten in the end. In the meantime, he kept on visiting brothels because they were places where he could find a large variety of women willing to satisfy his various likings, and there were plenty of them. As a matter of fact, so many that no woman alone would meet the requirements.

"But in the end, Simon's savings proved to be insufficient to keep on living like that. He now needed an extra income, and the only thing he could think of was to acquire a more business-like approach to his adventurous pleasures. And one day he visited the managers of those establishments and suggested his cooperation in running them. And they agreed because they had heard of and highly valued his acumen in the matters of business which he had already proved, leading his parish flock. Now, the place that he'd run so efficiently was actually bankrupt, but during his time, it had been the richest in the country, and the managers knew perfectly well he would be as efficient in their domain.

"And, as far as I know," Wissend said, "he's still there, and now his new business appears to be very successful and is considered the richest of this sort in England. So good, that some open-minded people suggested naming him 'Businessman of the Year', but some reluctant voices prevailed that it wouldn't be appropriate to award him that prestigious title. They said that even in business some ethical issues still mattered."

"Yes," I said, "even in business, for there are places where it is common to regard the matter as the most important, whatever we would think. Anything can be brought down to the level of business, and in truth nothing is above it, for business is the only reality. It is everything that matters. There's nothing like business. Whatever we touch, whatever we do and feel, business comes first. But the question is what's left of life then? Business as such, business in itself? But then, businessmen can't answer the question because they have already gone beyond such questions. For them, there's nothing either good or bad, for business is the absolute judge of all matters because its value is established *per se*, so it's beyond good and evil, being *de facto* transcendental, and this is so because these days nobody can say what business values consist of. It has been considered a dogma for some time now, something given *a priori*, something like Immanuel's categorical imperative, even, curiously enough, a moral imperative in practice. And as such is beyond any reasoning, so it seems to be not from this world where paradoxically it actually rules, being at the same time close to heaven or even already there, as if business and heaven were one and the same. And many a man believe that, since the word 'business' has for them magical power on which the will to power in based. Money, apparently being something easy to estimate in numbers, turns out to be priceless. The value of something that would seemingly be easy to size up cannot be in point of fact calculated. So, the question is, what actually happened to the human mind to come up with such an amazing, actually incomprehensible idea? And the problem is that the question is still to be answered. Yea, there are indeed more things in heaven and earth… even in terms of money."

"You've got it right." Wissend turned to me, "I, myself, couldn't put it better. But then, there might be someone who could answer the question. What do you think, my friend?"

"Yes, by now, I'm more and more convinced there's someone who can tell me what it's all about, and to answer a lot of other questions as well."

"Precisely, and other questions too, for you still have quite a few to answer, and as far as I know, you'll have a chance to meet that person pretty soon for that matter. Anyway, you've already met him, and more than once, which you'll now get to realise. I mean, that you know he isn't easily recognised by the average man, only by those who are thinking hard, trying to answer their own questions, the questions of the problem of life. And these men know perfectly well they cannot answer these questions themselves. They need somebody else to help them in doing this.

"You see, not everyone is worthy of having a very personal chat with that man, but you apparently have been chosen to have that privilege, and why do you think you've been granted it?"

"I'm not sure yet, but I presume it might be due to my previous naivety and, at the same time, my eagerness to find answers that aren't actually asked by the majority of people. And then, of course, I've always been eager to find the truth about things that bothered me in their complexity. But, at the same time, I've been more and more convinced I won't be able to find the answers on my own, and more importantly to get rid of my gullibility without help. But then, I'm still certain my credulity has been of some advantage, for it's always allowed me to see the things of my attention in many different aspects, their very different faces, their truths and facades. I somehow always knew that something that seems to be so obvious and clear isn't so in its nature. That much too often it proves to be the opposite. The more convinced we are about something, the less we know about it. And, as a matter of fact, it's already been said by somebody else in a different way, 'Convictions are worse enemies of truth than lies.' Anyway, I still believe that naivety proves man's honesty, that is, his enormous curiosity and simultaneously his concern about his fellow man, and the world as a whole."

"Yes, Ches, my friend, this is exactly the reason you've got a chance to have a chat with that person, and not just once for that matter, and you'll have, as I've already told you, another one. And, who knows, it's not up to me to decide, perhaps even more than one in the future. Are you ready for that?"

"Yes, Mr Wissend, I am, and I think I've always been."

"Good, and now let us consider a few matters related to what we've just been talking about.

"So, man's ignorance regarding some judgements he pronounces seems to be infinite, as if they were not his own, I mean, he appears not to foresee the actual bad effect they actually have on him, but he still maintains he's right. And it is a paradox of his nature that he seems to act against himself, to hold on to something that may destroy him in the future, and as a matter of fact this future may be just around the corner, so to speak. In other words, this sort of stupidity is incapable of the ability to envisage the harmful effects of your own views on yourself and your fellow man. And anybody may be stupid in this respect, no matter how wise he may be in his area of expertise. In other words, many a man seems not to care as regards the matters of their future. They believe the *carpe diem* of today's reality is enough to secure their future."

"I, myself, can't answer these questions, Mr Wissend. "Not right now anyway."

"I know you can't, and that's why you need to meet that person again, and as for now, let us look at a couple of other matters. There've been philosophers, like, let's say, our stubborn Immanuel, who have maintained that a man can actually predict, or rather secure, the outcome of his future actions by setting and respecting a certain ethical code whose principle is a moral imperative based on the maxim which at the same time can be universal law. For then and only then will your actions equally serve all the people, whereby they can avoid doing anything that would harm any of them, and then and only then is the future secured.

"But then how, *zum Teufel*, could our single man correctly predict all consequences of any principle for that matter, and in the first place, how could all the people be willing to observe it voluntarily? I can't imagine it, can you?"

"No, I can't, either, considering their very different personal needs."

"That's it, so different are they that the only way to introduce that moral imperative would be to make it obligatory by force, the force of law," said Wissend.

"Yes," I said, "this would be the only way, but then what about those different needs? They would be ignored by introducing just one code of behaviour for all the people. And how could it make all of them happy? Moreover, our Immanuel thinks that that moral imperative should be an independent, intentional decision of your own, and not something enforced from the outside. But I can't really imagine people *en masse* adopting such an imperative that in fact would prevent them carrying out the egoistical desires of each one of them.

"On the whole, it seems to me that people cannot establish a universal law which would be voluntarily observed by each of them, for it wouldn't, certainly, make each of them happy."

"You've got it right, dear Ches. "All in all, it seems that man cannot establish, just by himself, any universal laws that would satisfy all his fellow men. He tries, but then those laws are very imperfect, and the majority of people consider them a mere burden, nothing but a pain in the arse.

"Ah, you know, I suggest we leave the subject and let's focus on some more familiar matters.

"As we have concluded, man is unable to foresee all the future effects of his actions. What makes things even worse is that all that he has on his mind is how to please himself. And here, especially in some zones on this earth, that poor wretch exceeds himself in inventing the means of his pleasure. And these pleasures of his are far away from any humane intentions. For here he acts on his own egocentric motives, and restrains himself only because of the fear that he might be punished if he went too far in pleasing himself.

"Ah, that freedom people long for! You know what, it often turns out to be freedom of stupidity, bungling and shambles, as it is in those peripheries of Western Europe. You know that saying, 'I see red', but it seems as if there was also another one, I mean, 'I see green', and then what do you see? Nothing but your own arse. So, can you really have a serious conversation with such a man? No, you can't, all you can do is to follow Stas' advice and say, 'It doesn't make sense to talk to prats, so button up your faces and please sit down.' We have already given some examples of that sort of idiocy, as you have yourself in your notes.

"And now, one may denounce us for having been slanderers who dare to lecture all others on anything under the sun, but it is not the case, since in our notes we just invite everyone else to join us in a dialogue, an exchange of ideas. And shame on you, dear reader, if you have failed to notice that. Anyway, on the whole, we aren't as bad as we seem to be. Appearances, as usual, deceive. We might be, however, misanthropes, but then if you have never been one of them, then you have never cared about humankind as a whole.

"People often ask a rather silly question, 'Who's to blame?', and it is a very stupid question because this question should be asked by each of them, himself, because there isn't any collective responsibility in this respect. There's always an individual who might be held responsible, and not all the people, for all of them in this respect are a mere statistic, an artificial, schematised entity, and as such cannot be blamed for anything.

"Ah, and the problem of freedom again. There's nothing like freedom, people say, but I don't think they really know what they're talking about. They talk and talk about something about which they don't have a clue, for they mumble about freedom for all, but such freedom doesn't exist because freedom for all is nothing but an abstract, a phantasy, a Fata Morgana for that matter. There's only freedom of the individual and therefore no one but an individual can be held responsible for his own actions.

"You know, that talking has made me thirsty, so let's drink some Franziskaner.

"Oh yes, that's it," said Wissend, having taken his first sip. "Oh yea, that John was a wise man, and that's why he's now with us and not on the other side of the wall, so to speak, where, by the way, beer is not allowed. Can you imagine them being happy? I can't."

And now, apparently in a much better condition, Wissend resumed his exposé.

"Yea, how many words are wasted on this earth, and almost all of them in vain? So many chatterboxes and nothing changes for the better. They may kill you with their mumbling, and themselves as a matter of fact, and they will if they don't stop in time. We do talk as well, but our talk concerns important, that is, difficult matters, the things themselves, I dare say, and they, what are they talking about? What their neighbours are doing at night, or who won a match? Is it so important anyway? Apparently, they don't have the slightest idea what's important, having lost touch, curiously enough, with reality they appreciate so much. All they have are convictions, and they are nothing but proof of how they're even worse enemies of truth than lies, aren't they? And let us here remember again that cute observation of Charles: 'The problem with the world is that the intelligent people are full of doubts, while the stupid ones full of confidence.'

555

"And, as a matter of fact, truth has never been important enough for the majority of people, who in fact value lies much more, especially the ones that make them happy, disregarding what is true about their own actions. But this, I believe, cannot go on forever like that, for there's someone out there who might lose his patience with it. And, as far as I know, he will, for he doesn't appreciate the way he's portrayed by those who claim to believe in his existence, actually knowing nothing of what it is truly like. And we here, in our outspokenness, are trying to be as close as possible to his true image, and therefore, our bluntness depicts the truth about the things that others want to dismiss or be silent about. And the harsher our picture, the more truthful it is, for frankness and truth are one and the same.

"Anyway, it's not easy to find out what is underneath the façade, and that's why our words might confuse the reader, but then his very own thinking is usually confused in seeking the truth, provided he's eager to reach it. And it is all about what we call inner thinking, which is in fact almost impossible to be aware of, but at the same time, it is where what we really know resides.

"But then, one may accuse us of being offensive in our ways of description, even vulgar and rude, and we are in truth often like that on purpose because we share Ralph Waldo's belief that truly speaking, it is not instruction but provocation that we can receive from another soul. In other words, it is necessary and important to be offensive, for it is to set a challenge for the reader because only then will he look for answers on his own. Otherwise, he would never bother to search for them. In other words, he must deny what he's told and in doing so he isn't a mere unthinking believer, a follower. And we do hope it'll be appreciated in the end, but if it is not, he'll keep on making the same blunders which will lead him towards a very unpleasant end, which is the usual destination for those who believe themselves to be the masters of the world. They aren't. Somebody or something else is.

"Whenever they manage to notice something's not right, people often ask that ridiculous rhetorical question, 'Who's to blame?' We believe that the only way to answer this is to ask yourselves. Each of you should ask the question over and over again, and then it might finally be answered. All in all, people cannot be judged collectively, but just one at a time. And not exactly judged for that matter but described, more specifically, someone's own actions should be portrayed, for this is actually a true testimony of who one really is, that is, what one is worth.

"Ah, how tiresome all this theorising might be, and in fact I don't expect many a man to follow it, but then it is, as usual, addressed to those who may, for in them lies our last hope of putting things in the right direction.

"For the majority of people, reasoning is a kind of illusion, a Fata Morgana which they dismiss, believing just what they can see with their own eyes. But then, what we see is not everything that actually exists, and in the first place we see things the way we perceive and interpret them because meaning is the reality of the world. Reality is accessible only through its meaning, which is the way people understand what they see and experience.

"But now it's time, I believe, to move forward in our story, for the reader might be already fed up with all that philosophy, and be more than eager to hear what's happening in our story. And, by the way, I'd like to remind the reader that our aim here is not to please him, but provoke, that is, to rock him. Otherwise, he might not understand the message.

"And writing like this proves that we in truth value the reader's opinion of our story, because telling him a pack of banalities and clichés would be testimony to our underestimation of his capacity for understanding.

"And now it's time to move forward, and to deal with another hero of ours, who is now Justin Scornbash, known as 'The Casanova'.

"So, as we've already noticed, Justin was always eager to get hold of more funds, and he certainly knew how to go about it, but then some particular sources of extra income were beyond the legal limits he was supposed to observe.

"But then a certain opportunity appeared and was so tempting that Justin couldn't help himself when it came. And it was when a certain businessman from Latin America came to his office one day in July. The sun was shining, the air was already hot early that day, and Justin was dreaming of leaving London as he always did at that time of year, but not on this occasion because of that particular meeting.

557

"Actually, he knew before it started what it would be about, for his visitor wasn't an anonymous individual but somebody very well known in the mysterious circle of justice which in truth had been eager to get hold of him for several years but couldn't because of people like Justin, skilled at moulding the law as easily as Plasticine. And the gentleman who came to see him knew perfectly well that Justin was one of the most talented men in London in this respect.

Jose Rodrigo Emmanuel Carlos Bonaventura de Monte Christo y Salamanca was the man, better known as 'Son Eminence'. He preferred to be known by his French name and was a very cultivated, extremely well-educated man who would have been welcome at every royal court if it hadn't been for his particular profession, which was drugs. But then who would expect that someone could distinguish himself by producing several scientific articles on the subject, two or three of them published by National Geographic, others for the Humboldt Foundation, and several others in France, Russia and elsewhere too? And it was he who wrote them, and they were all written in the original language of the publisher, for 'Son Eminence' actually spoke every civilised language in the world.

"The articles in question proved the benefits of cocaine in such a well-documented way that law enforcement all over the world, but especially in the US, found itself in trouble making their actions ethically justified, and that was so because Son Eminence didn't limit his writing just to prove the pure physical benefits of using cocaine, but also its enormous potential, he proved beyond doubt, to stimulate the mind's capability for creativity. He actually said that if it wasn't for the drug, hardly any masterpiece of art would have ever been produced, and culture itself could have very well disappeared from the face of the earth. There hadn't ever been another Shakespeare or Goethe without it, neither Scorsese nor Lang, nor Einstein, either, for scientific discoveries too required cocaine's miraculous stimulation.

"It must also be said that the *senor* was actually a very modest man, totally free from pretence, mild-mannered, every inch a gentleman. Nothing was known about him collecting ocean-going boats or huge airplanes nor very expensive vintage cars. Very often he was in fact seen riding an old-fashioned bicycle, and his only cars were a 1960s Warszawa and Volga. He never ever stayed at any luxurious hotels, either, but pretty often in self-made – as it was one of his hobbies – tents. And, as for his other habits, he never drank any expensive wines or champagne but beer, preferably Weihenstephaner, sipping it very often at Nymphenburg in the company of Herzog von Bayern, or Franziskaner, in the company of the General of the Order, and Budvar, Wolters and Tyskie. As for Budvar, his favourite place for drinking it was Praha, and its magnificent Stare Mesto. But he liked other Czech beers too, and at U Fleku he felt very much at home. And in Praha he often attended concerts at which Smetana's and Dvorak's great music was played. Apart from beer, he occasionally had a few schnapps or Stolichnaya, and he smoked too. His favourites were either Schwarzer Krauser Tabak or Gauloises and Gitanes. And the curious thing was that despite his rather heavy smoking, he was an excellent swimmer, and more than once beat none other than the great Yannick, who then toyed with the idea of smoking himself. As regards Son Eminence's other activities, he donated huge sums of money to charities, the so-called targeted ones, of course, as was the case with John D. Rockefeller and George Soros donations.

"And on the day when he entered Justin's premises, the latter was obviously aware of all that and getting ready for the challenge.

"Son Eminence was tall, slim and of rather pale complexion, his eyes adorned by very dark glasses, not because they were in fashion among drug barons but because he preferred to see everything in shadow, in the shade of shadow, as he put it himself.

"Justin welcomed him warmly, and before discussing business, they drank some Budvar and smoked a couple of Schwarzer Krauser rollers. These articles were already available at Justin's office, for he knew his guest's choice.

"They were to discuss business options in a couple of countries, among others, Dollaria and Russia.

"Son Eminence had always had a poor opinion of the former, considering its rather insane mentality, their culture of crafty crap, and junk food consumed in huge quantities that resulted in many citizens having become elephantine dimwits. And all that done in the disguise of democracy which, curiously enough, severely punished those opposing those great achievements. To say nothing of invading any other country whenever it suited its interests. However, some of those invasions ended in disaster, Dollaria ending up having been beaten by much smaller countries.

"With regard to the country being a kind of psychiatric asylum, as its famous poet Ezra Pound once called it, Son Eminence explained the phenomenon as follows: 'Dollaria's follies reside in the conviction that the value of life can be estimated in terms of money, whereas, paradoxically, its value cannot be estimated at all.'

"And what about your opinion as regards the matter in question, my friends?" asked Wissend.

"Oh yes," said Bea, "we do agree with Son Eminence, and it is, I'd say, one of the most accurate definitions of Dollaria's way of thinking I've ever heard. When you, Mr Wissend, have a chance to see him again, please assure him of our esteem and pass on to him our best wishes."

"I certainly will, *mia cara signora*, and yes, I'll see him, for in fact Son Eminence is a close friend of Lord Hellbridge, and let me tell you that their views on almost every matter are actually very similar."

"Good to hear that," I said. "It seems the lord's friends are wise men, having amazing powers of observation."

"Oh yes," agreed Wissend, "and second sight too for that matter."

"That's it. I wish I had it," I said, "but now, please continue your story that sounds so interesting."

And Mr Wissend, the lord's right hand went on.

"So back to our Justin and his conversation with Son Eminence. I should stress that the former wasn't of the same opinion of Dollaria, for as a British subject, he felt he was obliged to appreciate its significance, even if his country was merely a vassal of the latter.

"Political views aside, Son Eminence came to see Justin due to the latter's familiarity with London City banks to carry out his own scheme.

"Justin knew, of course, where the money came from, but was sure the banks would appreciate having it, despite its suspicious origin, for *pecunia non olet* was their gold maxim after all. And the same was a credo of Justin's, so they both quickly agreed to make a deal in which Justin would become a middleman and would soon benefit enormously from doing the job. It didn't take long for him to become a millionaire, and he enjoyed life on an even grander scale than before.

"He was supposed to travel to Dollaria from time to time, and Latin America too, in order to facilitate the business in question. In those hot countries, full of plenty of hot and easy, available women, he found a paradise like many before him. He predicted, quite reasonably, that demand for drugs might only increase, so the business may last as long as mankind on this earth.

"During one of his numerous visits to Bolivia, he met a woman, but this time it wasn't an easy conquest as usual. In truth, for the first time, Justin had to admit he was defeated by a woman.

"Her name was Marguerite de Rohan, and she was actually born in France, and once Justin found this out, he wondered what the Devil had brought her to Bolivia of all places. Her name rang a bell, but Justin's ignorance prevented him from identifying its origin, and only when he Googled it did he learn that the name de Rohan was one of the most illustrious aristocratic names of her home country. He met Marguerite at a charity event supported lavishly by Son Eminence, and there she told Justin she had been working for charities all over the world and had been to practically every corner of the globe. Russia, China, India, Nepal; in a word, the world was her home, and anywhere she went, it felt like home. Everywhere, she was welcomed with reverence, and Justin was slightly shocked when on YouTube he saw her taking a stroll on Nevsky Prospect in the company of none other than the president of Russia. And when another video showed her together with the president of China on the beach on Hainan Island, both of them wearing just swimming gear, Justin had to lie down to recover his mental balance. But it wasn't just her highly placed acquaintances which threatened to damage the balance, for her looks were so stunning that his famous oratory skills left him for good. Anyway, he didn't even try to employ them because he wasn't that stupid after all. He knew perfectly well they would only have made him look foolish in Margot's eyes.

"But the most astonishing things he experienced was when they both went travelling to very remote parts of the country, and also its neighbours, Brazil, Colombia and Peru, and places there inhabited by Indian tribes untouched by civilisation. Every time they entered a village where in fact she had never been before, its chief, along with the shaman and the elders, greeted her with warship-like respect, and when the chief of a tribe in Peru fell to his knees once he saw her, Justin, in order to recover his mental balance, felt compelled to drink a large bowl of the locally produced liquor and to smoke several pipes filled with an unidentified substance, but that resulted in losing whatever was left of the balance, and falling asleep for twenty-four hours. When he eventually came to his senses, he still couldn't believe what he'd witnessed before. Such reverence paid by those men to a woman was unheard-of in those places, among those peoples; that much he knew. They treated her as if she was a goddess, but then they had never seen her before, so what was the reason for their enormous reverence?

Justin couldn't help wondering about that and eventually summoned the courage to ask Margot, but in reply she just smiled and said, "If you wish to know, ask them, not me," but he obviously declined the proposition because how the hell would he ask them, not speaking a word of their language? And that itself was another mystery, for Margot, wherever they went, any country or tribe they visited, spoke their own dialect with ease. When Justin asked where she'd mustered the knowledge, she said it had been private tutoring organised for her by Lord Hellbridge.

"I see, apparently the lord can organise anything he wants," Justin remarked.

"Oh yes," Margot said, "if you only knew what he can do."

Eventually, Justin let it go, for he didn't want to appear inquisitive, but most of all wouldn't dare risk losing the opportunity of standing a chance with her, especially as he felt he was falling in love with her, and it would be the first time in his life that such a thing was happening.

"But then he didn't have a clue how to go about conquering her, but one day he was at the end of his tether, so desperate in his feelings that he knelt before her like that Indians' chief did, and confessed his love to her. Margot listened patiently to his incomprehensible, in fact, declaration of love and said she would think it over but only after he underwent some sort of purgatory trial. She said she knew about his previous exploits (how she was aware of them, she didn't tell him), and if he passed the test then perhaps she would be willing to accept his feelings. He must, she demanded, purify his soul by abandoning his hitherto wicked sort of life, his love of money and privilege, and become someone very different. And he must also tell Son Eminence everything he knew about his M7 friends' dodgy business.

"Justin readily accepted these conditions, for now his friends and everything else except her didn't really matter. So, when he met Son Eminence, he told him everything without a second thought during a session at the gentleman's chateau in Dordogne.

It took Justin several hours to tell everything he knew in detail because of the enormous quantity of what they had been doing, but he was amazed that despite the bulk of information he was providing, Son Eminence didn't take any notes. There was also something else that seemed to be quite exceptional, namely, that nobody witnessed Justin's confessions but a huge, black-as-tar cat that obviously said nothing but seemed (such was Justin's impression) to understand every word. And, when the conversation ended, it was the behemoth of a cat that saw him off to the waiting vintage Bentley driven by such a wide-shouldered man that Justin wondered how he could squeeze himself into the car. And when the Bentley was about to pull off, the cat raised his left paw in a farewell greeting, but then Justin thought it must have been a Fata Morgana because of that day's exceptional heat.

"Shortly afterwards, he was back in Bolivia, where Margot listened to his account of the meeting and graciously gave her consent to Justin's next step in the mentioned purgatory test.

Now, our Casanova was obliged to spend some time among the Indians, living their lifestyle in every detail, including the way they dressed, namely, in nothing but a rather narrow strip of cloth. Initially, Justin found it difficult to adapt to his new outfit because of his long-life habit of wearing nothing but Savile Row's suits, but after a while he was happy enough and even felt a sort of liberation. Anyway, all old habits had soon been forgotten, and he came to enjoy his new life, especially when Margot said she didn't mind his relationship with an Indian woman.

"The Casanova was most grateful for her benevolence, and soon found his new territory a paradise in that respect, and now he became almost as good as his namesake in that field of expertise. Eventually, he found that only one; however, he never ceased dreaming of Margot, and children began arriving in this world, one, two, then three, and even more were to come.

All in all, Justin not only fully adapted to his new life, but he felt he was really happy for the first time in his life, and once, when his fellow countryman, an Oxford University anthropologist, Professor Balthasar Bones, arrived in the village where Justin was living a happy life, and was somewhat surprised to find the once-famous barrister QC here of all places, and asked whether he missed all London pleasures, the ex-lawyer said that even if he was now offered a wing at Buckingham Palace ,he wouldn't even think of moving back. Moreover, he said his previous life was a senseless existence and urged the professor to join him now and then. But the academician was reluctant to accept the offer, quoted the great Samuel and his praise of London's delights, and every day of his stay in the village bothered Justin with all possible doubts about the alleged merits of living there. Finally, the ex-barrister lost his patience and threatened Bones with shooting him (he had become an expert shooter and won the all-Latin America shooting competition) with a curare projectile if he didn't leave the village immediately. Horrified, the professor left in a hurry, and soon after, in his very cosy study at Oxford, wrote a book entitled *The Incredible Anthropological Transformation of an Englishman*. The book became hugely popular among his fellow academics, and these days, a tenth edition is being published. But the British government didn't share the high esteem of it, considering it a serious threat to all best things English, and mulled over banning it because of its apparent threat to national security.

"But Professor Bones earned such high recognition not only in his home country, but also in Dollaria (it's said that even the president read his book with interest; however, this hasn't been confirmed) that the British government felt compelled to abandon the idea of banning the book.

"There would be much more to say about the book's merits and Justin's new brave world," said Wissend, "but because of the need to move on with telling you other things, let me just say that the once-so-admired hero of the British courts is still living there, in Bolivia, still dreaming of Margot, but without the slightest desire to return to his previous wasteful and senseless life, as he put it, in civilised Britain.

"And now, let me tell you about Son Eminence, and the truth that so unexpectedly emerged as to his real personage, and so his deeds.

"It was groundbreaking news when the notorious drug baron turned out to be in fact the man who brought that filthy business to its knees. Moreover, he did it single-handedly, and no law enforcement had a part in it. It was revealed during an interview with his assistants, for he himself was unavailable to journalists, that he actually had a very low opinion of the so-called war on drugs operations which were, particularly DEA, good for nothing (a laughing stock, he called them), the assistants, quoting his words, told reporters.

After what he had done so efficiently, journalists all over the world wanted to meet him, and of course the very same guardians of law, but he'd vanished without a trace. It was reported he was allegedly seen in such diverse places of the globe that people wondered how he could move with such ease without being noticed by the police, customs, intelligence services, whatsoever.

"Superintendent Boris Barmy from Scotland Yard suggested he might even have been on the moon, after a conversation reluctantly granted him by none other, but known already to us, than the famous Professor Koczkodan, who said that in fact nothing was impossible for Son Eminence. After hearing that, the superintendent assumed that the moon should be taken into consideration too, when the search for him proved to be fruitless on earth. So, the superintendent suggested the Home Office contact the American authorities and ask them to lend a spaceship which would fly there to look for the fugitive. But the Home Office Secretary considered Barmy's supposition rather exaggerated after all, and in the first place too costly to carry out, so he refused.

"While the search for Son Eminence continued, massive manifestations took place all over the world to express people's gratitude and, of course, *Te Deum* was heard in churches, starting with the one at Saint Peter's Basilica in Rome, celebrated by the Pope himself. But those celebrations were happening exclusively at Catholic and Orthodox Churches, for their Protestant counterparts stuck to the opinion that whatever people do, it was business as usual, and the money, wherever it came from, was confirmation of the Lord's blessing. They said that it was sufficiently demonstrated by Max Weber in his analysis of the relationship between the Protestant ethic and the spirit of capitalism. As regards his famous book *The Protestant Ethic and the Spirit of Capitalism*, there were Protestants who suggested that the Holy Spirit might reside in money. And once that was known to the Archbishop of York, he said he wished after all that the Grand Inquisition had still been there to deal with such perverts. 'I am a Protestant,' he said, 'but then there are matters where there is no other solution but *auto-da-fé* to take care of such deviants.' And the Archbishop of New York City said he wished Max were a Catholic, but then if he were, he would surely be excommunicated.

At the Cathedral of Christ the Saviour in Moscow, Mass too was celebrated, and next to Mikhail Vladimirovich stood an unidentified tall brunette who, afterwards, *Novaya Gazeta* reported, was seen taking a stroll at Patriarch's Pond, but when its journalist enquired of FSB as to the man's identity, they said it was a *secret d'état*.

"And now," said Wissend, "back to Justin and his new life in Bolivia. He's still there, happily living in a hut with his Indian wife and children, very fit now due to his daily exploits in the jungle, and it's even likely he will be the next chief of the tribe he's living with. He understands perfectly now how stupid his former life was, and how Lord Byron had been right condemning the alleged benefits of civilisation.

"But he's still dreaming of Margot de Rohan, and at the same time is most grateful to her for showing him the right direction, for making him aware of his true needs, for the courage to know what he's really known.

"So, my friend," Wissend said to me, "these are stories of your former friends who actually should be grateful to... but to whom? Hmm, let's pass the question over in silence, because they have finally become what they are. Strange, isn't it? Anyway, it takes courage after all to be what you are, and those who lack that courage must be helped by someone else who knows their true identity, and does his best it will come true.

"Anyway, their final destinations could have been much worse, but apparently, he who is in charge of them seems to be a benevolent person, someone who does good after all, contrary to the opinions of those narrow-minded and lacking-in-imagination self-rightness prigs, who say something very different. But then, they will never know who that person really is, and this is because of their arrogant self-assumed right to know everything, when in fact they know nothing. And then, of course, they will never know where he is, how near or how far.

"Whereas you, Ches," Wissend continued, "might be lucky enough to know him better, for you seem to deserve that privilege. And by the way, what are you and Bea going to do now, when the stories of those men have already arrived at the final stage?"

"We've decided," said Beatrice, "to leave London and England altogether."

"Yes," said Wissend, "I find it a very good idea. It's high time to leave this place, where nothing interesting will ever happen anyway. Terribly stultifying spot, and its stuffy air, simply unbearable. One may suffocate sooner or later. Anyway, not everyone is free to live everywhere, and you two don't seem to fit here. And where are you moving to?"

"First Zurich, and then we'll see," I said.

"Confederatio Helvetica," said Wissend, "in more than one respect, it's a good place to live. Very orderly country, perhaps too much order after all, but it's the right place to put your thoughts in order, and this is what matters. *Nicht wahr?*"

"*Stimmt,*" I said, "order must be because this is for."

"I do like it," said Wissend, "that batman of your father was a wise guy, such a simple saying, and it says so much. Moreover, it follows exactly the Husserl's principle, '*Zuruck zu dem Sachen selbst.*' And then and only then may we finally have everything in order, and only then peace and quiet.

"Do you think you have earned peace after all, for surely you don't deserve light?"

"I agree," said Bea, "Ches hasn't earned the latter."

"And you, Ches," enquired Wissend further, "what are you going to do in Zurich?"

"First, I'd very much like to meet the man I met before, for I still have some questions to ask him."

"I see," said Wissend, "and who is that man?"

"I'm still not sure, and that's exactly why I want to see him again."

"Hmm, you are not sure, you say. You know, as a matter of fact, it sounds good that you aren't sure, for I wouldn't recommend too much confidence, especially as regards difficult questions, and this might be one of them. Anyway, you might answer your question, and I wish you luck in this respect, my friend."

"Thank you. And you, if I may ask, what are your plans?"

"Ah, here I'm in a far better position than you are, Ches, for my plans are the plans of my boss. It's up to him to decide what they are."

"You mean Lord Hellbridge, of course."

"Yes, him, but you know, he's a convertible man, so to speak. You never actually know what he could be the next day. But then, you can always rely on him because he's a person of high principle."

"And what is it?"

"It's simple, nothing but truth."

"So, he seems to be a philosopher."

"Oh yes, indeed, he is a philosopher, and a very inquisitive one, for that matter. He never stops wondering what things are like in this world, and even hereafter, for that matter."

"Then he asks very difficult questions, I mean, especially the latter."

"Oh yes, indeed, the latter is a particularly difficult one, but he's indefatigable, believe me."

"Hmm, if so, he's like the man I met in Rieterpark."

"Ah, that one in Zurich, where you're going now."

"Yes, the very same. Have you ever been there?"

"Oh yes, where haven't I been together with *mon maître*! We've been travelling all over this planet, and we may never stop, for that matter, for our travelling is the search for truth as it is, I presume, for the man you met in the Zurich park."

"Yes, and it seems they're alike."

"Yes, they are, and very much so, my friend."

"That's it, I've noticed a certain similarity between Lord Hellbridge and the man, and I have the strange impression that they are the same person."

"Bah, but then, there are more things in heaven and earth than are dreamt of in your philosophy. And then, how little you seem to know about anyone, after all, especially about yourself. Yea, it seems to be the most difficult question of all to answer – what in truth am I? But if you're lucky enough, you may meet someone who'll help to answer it, for very often you wouldn't answer it by yourself alone. And that man you met in the park might be the one you need to finally answer the question.

"All my best to you and you, *mia cara*, and please look after him, for now he needs that more than ever."

"I certainly will, don't you worry," said Bea.

"I beg your pardon, *mia bellissima signora*, but to worry is my business, after all."

Bea chuckled and said, "Yes, I know that, and not just since yesterday."

Wissend smiled at her and said, "*Arrivederci e buona fortuna*, my friends."

"*Bis dann*, and I mean that," I said.

"I do hope so," said Wissend, and left.

The next day, we left London and headed for Zurich.

# THE PARK REVISITED

'It is only late that one musters the courage
for what one really knows.'
Nietzsche

'The more I know the less I am
inclined to say anything.'
C. D.

It was a hot, sunny day when we arrived in Zurich, where all that had
started, and I wondered whether anything more was waiting for Bea
and me. She was happy to be closer to her beloved Italy, and I too much
preferred the place, especially because it wasn't far away from my favourite
spots in Europe, cities of France, Italy, Germany and a few other countries.
Anyway, I'd become tired of living in that pokey England and its capital,
pretending to be cosmopolitan, but actually provincial due to the insular,
prejudiced, narrow-minded mentality of its inhabitants. And it is precisely
this kind of thinking that makes them so sure of their uniqueness and
greatness. Anyway, as Friedrich put it, strength of character is conditioned
by the bound views.

We had arranged our accommodation here well before our arrival,
and we went there straight from the airport. It was an apartment in
Mythenquai, stuffed with rather modern furniture and conveniently

close to the city centre. And the view of Zürichsee was magnificent, and I enjoyed it very much since I'd always been so fond of lakes. And we actually purchased a log cottage in Finland, a country of thousands of lakes, and were going to stay there in summer and winter too, for a month or so, rowing, sailing and fishing. And of course, chopping wood, my favourite, and perhaps the only manual activity I liked, and was good at. The cottage wasn't too big, but spacious enough, especially the ground floor with a large combined sitting room- kitchen area with a big fireplace built of stones, and a traditional wood and coal-burning oven.

Bea liked Finland too, for she like me loved lakes and forests, and the country is perfect for bivouacking, one of our most loved forms of recreation. And we did that not only there, but in many other countries, which were also great places for doing it, especially Poland, the Baltic countries and Russia. We had a G500 Wagon, so there was no problem whatsoever getting anywhere we wanted, along with a Francois Vivier sail-and-oar boat. And now we were both eager to get to our place in Finland, but there was still something else that awaited me here in Zurich before we could leave for Suomi. And I somehow knew what it was, and was getting ready to meet the challenge, being, curiously enough, aware of how important it would be. For there was still something unfinished about my travelling, something that constituted the essence of everything that had already happened. And I also knew that there were some important answers I couldn't get on my own. I needed someone else to help me to get them.

It was another hot spring day when, not knowing exactly why, I headed for Rieterpark. And it had there where actually all things had begun, and where they, I felt, might come to their conclusion.

I was strolling rather absentmindedly through the alleys and eventually entered the one where I'd previously met the man who had directed the route of my life when I'd been cast out by everybody else.

And now he was there again, sitting on the same bench, dressed as usual in his well-tailored three-piece suit, and a black beret on his head.

I came up to the bench he was sitting on and said, "Good morning, sir."

"Welcome back, dear Mr Adarsh. How are things?"

"They're much better now than they had been when we saw each other some time ago."

"Glad to hear that. And how's *Signora* Sforza?"

"She's good too, and thank you again, Mr Wahrburg, for if you weren't…"

"Don't mention it, because I don't actually appreciate any thanks. Have a seat, and tell me about your… I mean, both of your plans for the future, for now you can have a plan, can't you?"

"Yes, now at last I can, which was out of the question not that long ago."

"Good, it's always of advantage to have a plan, but to be honest I, myself, never plan. All of my plans come to me on their own, so to speak."

"Yes, sir, but then you're in a different position if I may say that."

"Yes, somewhat different, I agree, but then my position shouldn't be envied too much, believe me."

"Yes, Mr Wahrburg, I think I know what you mean, but I still have some questions to answer, and—"

"But of course," he interrupted me, "people usually have many questions, and too many for that matter. But then they can't help it. It seems they cannot live without questions, and that causes a serious problem, which may be called the problem of life. But now, the question is how to solve the problem in question. And many a man almost always tends to think that the problem can be solved by talking alone, by ceaseless reasoning, but then they're very surprised at not being able to come to any reasonable solutions. A vicious circle their thinking is, like their lives are. I feel sorry for them, but this is their own fault after all, I mean, they're so sure of finding all answers in words alone, whereas they are somewhere else, but it's not that easy to know that, not at all. And now, my friend, I assume you're finally ready to share my opinion, aren't you?"

"Yes, I am, and it is high time for me to do so," I said.

"But as a matter of fact, it isn't about time at all, my friend," said Mr Wahrburg.

"Yes, you're right, sir, it isn't. Just a figure of speech of mine, out of habit, so to speak."

"I thought so, ah, all these figures of speech, and so many of them. Small wonder people get lost."

"I, myself, used to be one of them."

"But now, fortunately, you aren't anymore. And as regards time and a couple of other things, let me tell you about my recent conversation with Immanuel. I, of course, met him more than once, and on every occasion, he proved to be so stubborn in his beliefs that if it wasn't for my extraordinary patience, I really don't know what might have happened. We disagreed on almost every subject, including that regarding time, which he perceived as a *priori* form of intuition, but I still don't really know what he meant by that. I told him more than once that such things as time, and space, for that matter, are actually governed by something much more superior to man, and his very limited sensual forms of intuition and categories of reason. But no, that obstinate, stiff-necked martinet stuck to his prejudiced views and nothing, absolutely nothing, could have changed his opinion. He's like that cow in a Polish anecdote. You tell it not to do something, but that bloody animal will always do it after all. He's just the same and perhaps even worse. And that critique of practical reason of his, that's a pure nonsense, totally useless, and has nothing to do with any genuine practice for that matter. But tell him that, try to persuade him. No, no chance! Such an obstinate bore he is.

But, you know, I still respect him, for he's a great philosopher after all, despite his unbelievable stubbornness. You know, great philosophers make great mistakes, and that's that.

"But now let's forget him and his mania and turn to something far more important, and something that currently matters, and I mean your writings. Hmm, I'm sorry to say but there's something still missing there.

"I mean, you've failed to emphasise certain important issues so crucial in the lives of humans, and now let me tell you what I mean by that.

"I believe that, all in all, man cannot know anything about what he, himself, calls truth. He invented the concept because of his longing for the eternal, absolute, ideal, but these concepts are and always will be beyond his means of comprehension. However, they play an enormous role in his life, here on earth, where he's yearning for something infinite, transcendental, in that very limited life of his. And in this sense, these concepts are realities for him because of their impact on his life. They have all been invented out of the innate, unconscious need for them, and have accompanied lives of humans forever. But then, the individual interpretation of them is different and always causes a problem, dividing people, and so making them enemies of one another.

"On the other hand, without these ideas, man would be nothing but an automaton, an unthinking, unfeeling robot. And those who wanted to abolish those concepts established *de facto* hell on earth, for to tell you the truth, there is no other one at all.

"Another great ideal is God, and as Friedrich rightly says, 'He who does not find greatness in God finds it nowhere. He must either deny it or create it.' However, at the same time, there is a problem regarding that greatness. I mean, the way people understand it, or more precisely what concept of God they mean and believe in. You see, a god of petty people's morality doesn't seem to be a good choice, because it results in a disgusting degeneration of culture. That kind of culture means hatred for the privileged in body and soul, revolt, as Friedrich says, of the ugly against the beautiful, proud and joyous. But that kind of culture perfectly suits riff-raff, those who are unfair, impudent, envious, cowardly and false, pretending at the same time to be virtuous. Such a culture will certainly end in an apocalypse, which as we know has already been foretold, hasn't it? So, all in all, there is a strange logic in the matter in question.

"Anyway, as regards the aforementioned dilemma, and as regards many other subjects, Friedrich and I agree, and it's always been a pleasure to talk to him. And you know why it actually is so? Because he's never ever tried to please, to flatter anybody, and only those like him are honest, the only ones you can call good men. All the others are mere philistines, and to hell with them, where they belong." And here Wahrburg laughed and said, "Yes, they actually belong there, those neatly scribbling intellectual impostors."

"But now," Wahrburg carried on, "back to God, bah, terrible things happen, and they could have easily been avoided if some quasi-theologians hadn't perverted His concept. But they have, and why? Because it suited them for their own ends. And they've done that so many times that a poor believer doesn't know anymore who He is with whom he is dealing. Who is He then? he asks, and finding no answer becomes a nihilist, that is, a man who judges of the world as it is that it ought not to be, and of the world as it ought to be that it does not exist, as our dear Friedrich says. And consequently, your existence, whatever you do, has no meaning.

574

"Anyway, to my mind, the God question is and will remain in truth incomprehensible for man, but now let's forget the problem for a while and let me mention something that you said more than once in your writings.

"I mean," and here Wahrburg chuckled, "your harsh depiction of the English and the Irish. Why *zum Teufel* if I may say so," he chuckled again, "have you done that? Anyway, is that all there is to say about them?"

"Hmm," I began, "no, there would be more to say, they obviously have some good traits I haven't mentioned, but I've done that on purpose."

"On purpose?" exclaimed Wahrburg, "and what the hell do you mean?"

"You know, sir, if I said anything about their better side then it would be an attempt to flatter them after all, to absolve, to appease and please, and I wanted to emphasise something they might not be aware of, I mean, those sickening character traits."

"Ah, I see now. Then you were right, I believe, but leave them in peace, so to speak, and may they forgive you. Anyway, I appreciate you've chosen those wise words as one of your mottos, I mean, that a man is doing his reporting well only when people start to hate him.

"And now, back to those concepts of God, the ideals. As I've already said, they have caused a lot of trouble for their own inventors and their followers. And, as a matter of fact, it's been a never-ending story, and I wonder if it will ever end. No, I tend to think it may never end unless man in his arrogance, and at the same time hyperbolic naivety, ceases to believe he's the measure of all things, and the meaning and the value of them. Doing that, he positions himself above the world as if he were God himself, but he obviously isn't and never will be, being in fact so limited in his capacity for understanding things that actually surpass the limits of his reason.

"And I must admit, you haven't neglected the subject in question in your writings, and to say something more about that monstrous stupidity of man, that, despite suffering from it, it has finally dawned on him he knows nothing regarding the concepts he invented, and that have bred the opposite – pessimism, even contempt for existence, as our dear Friedrich rightly noticed. Ah, our Friedrich is so perceptive, I can't praise him enough, and I, myself, wouldn't have done that better. He seems to have second sight, and you know, he never ever takes any hallucinogenic drugs for that matter, so I wonder how the Devil he has such amazing powers of observation? And, to be honest, I don't really know.

"Anyway, I believe that if man doesn't come to his senses soon enough, his stay on this planet may end, as another friend of mine, Wolfgang, warns, in cataclysm. You know what I mean, don't you, that 'all that doth begin should rightly to destruction run.'

"Now, back again to that troublesome question of God, let me again quote our dear but troublesome Friedrich. Yes, all in all, he's nothing but trouble, but as a matter of fact trouble is a philosopher's business, isn't it?

"So, let's say that again. 'He who does not find greatness in God finds it nowhere – he must either deny it or create it.'

"That's it, to create greatness, here we go, but where to? So far, it seems that you, people, have gone nowhere. Have you, for instance, successfully replaced God with another greatness, matching Him? With yourselves, for instance? You've tried but failed miserably, haven't you? Thus, what's left, my friend? Is there another something, so to speak, you can use? Doesn't seem so. Back to God, then? But I'm not sure if He would welcome you again, for you've already disappointed Him too much. Anyway, modern man doesn't seem to be able to create any greatness. Modernity lacks greatness because integrity is missing there, and it means truth, because honesty and truth are one and the same. Modernity has become decadent, and there is nothing left but denial. And in this way, humanity has turned unconsciously against itself, for by destroying greatness, it's destroyed authority and the hierarchy of values. And now man is fully exposed to any influence coming from outside, and this 'outside', the system, is an organised rape of enormous power and effectiveness, isn't it? The modern man willy-nilly obeys commands coming from outside, doesn't he?

"All in all, slave morality prevails, for the less someone knows how to command, the more urgently he desires someone who commands, who commands severely. Once a human arrives at the basic conviction that he must be commanded, he becomes a 'believer'. And as such he personifies the plebeian spirit of modernity. Yes, it's a very sad story, my friend, for it appears that the system has replaced God, and this is the end of Him.

You've killed Him. He's dead. For you, anyway, and then you're dead too, I mean, your spiritual life. And God's next resurrection seems very unlikely under the circumstances.

"And I won't say another word, for the matter in question is between you and Him, and I have no right to interfere. I've just suggested something to consider.

"Anyway, the question of God remains open, and if I were to give you some advice, I would suggest pondering the problem very carefully because a lot depends on it, I mean, the future of man, if there's any left for that matter, due to the unbearable abundance of words he uses that gets him nowhere, for as a matter of fact, truth lies in silence, my friend. The more you talk, the less you know. Truth can be understood nowhere but in silence, remember that. But then, look how many words we had to say to come to that conclusion, how many questions had been asked before you finally understood that truth is where there are no questions left, which means when there is finally no difference between your thoughts and Being. And only then the world is your world. Yes, Ludwig had some good ideas about the matter in question, and showed the right direction, but then for some unknown reason went astray afterwards. Hmm, a sad story it was, indeed. And I tend to think that it was due to him living in that mumbling, rambling England, I mean, their inhabitants' unhealthy – mentally of course – inclination to profess integrity and doing something very opposite. That's why they may deserve punishment, but then what kind might it be…?

"You know now that I am the fortress of truth, and it is up to me what happens to you on this earth, and believe me, no one else will come to help you unless you change the way you see the world and life, and if you still believe there might be someone else who would forgive the errors you are still committing, you're nothing but an incorrigible fantasist.

"So, what would you say to all that, dear Mr Adarsh?"

"Hmm, I'm not sure, to be honest."

"Small wonder, and good for you for that matter, but try anyway."

"I will if you insist. So, the first question that comes to mind is how to see the world and life aright."

"Very good question, go ahead."

"It seems to me that in order to see them aright, that is, as one and the same, I should refrain myself from presenting any statements, I mean, any final conclusions for that matter."

"Good start, carry on."

"I'm pretty sure that once we see something aright, we should remain silent, as you said, for words would confuse everything, blur our understanding.

"And when I see it aright, I see it in my mind's eye and cannot really share my views with anybody else, and then cannot impose them on anyone else. All that I can actually do is show them something, just hint a direction and the rest belongs to them.

"And then, when I say nothing, there's nothing either good or bad, for these are creations of our words. And only then is the Being beyond good and evil, is it finally innocent, and so are we, at last."

"That's it, you've got there, and you actually made a start in your writings, and now it's time to come to some final conclusions, if there are any, of course."

"Yes, Mr Wahrburg, if there are any. That's the question. And I tend to think there is one at least, I mean, to be aware that the question as to whether to say something or to be silent is actually the question of to be or not to be."

"Yes, that's it, carry on."

"Hmm, I think that the question, 'To be or not to be?' isn't actually the question we ask in words, in language. The question comes from within, and as such is wordless. Thus, the answer must be the same. Otherwise, it wouldn't be the right one."

"Oh, oh, Ludwig would have liked it. Carry on, my friend."

"Yes, truth, as you have already observed, resides in silence, because it has nothing to do with facts. It lies outside the world, that's beyond the facts, and in words we can express nothing but facts. And as long as we keep on using words, we come nowhere near truth. We are trapped in the vicious circle of them.

"The rest is silence. I mean that the final answer to the problem of life is to be silent, for the problem can be answered, curiously enough, only in silence. Otherwise, we get lost in a never-ending chain of words.

"And only then, in silence, you've solved your problem of life, your very own, the sense of your life has become clear to you. And as a matter of fact, the sense of the world, your world in fact, becomes clear to you. That all I say here I say in words, for there is no other way to say that, but my words just show the way. They are that Ludwig's ladder, and not the solution that lies beyond them.

"And, by the way, de Lamartine's 'I never think, my ideas think for me' occurs only when translated into man's capability for individual, independent thinking, having ideas of your own, will and conviction of your own, and this never happens as long as you just follow someone else's ideas, being merely a believer. And that freedom of thinking that seems to be so cherished at an academy almost never, curiously enough, happens there. Those academics' elaborated writings are crafty enough, but often say nothing at all. They are nothing but flowery, crafty crap. The higher the ranking of a university, the less understandable are its professors' long treaties. Those gurus of truth actually have nothing to say, and that's why Ludwig says that an honest and serious man should never work at university."

"You know what, my friend," Wahrburg chipped in, and gave a short burst of laughter, "sometimes it seems to me that Goethe's Mephistopheles does good mainly because he aims at destroying that endless stupidity of mumbling.

"But now," he continued, "the problem of truth we are pondering seems to be the question of you being at peace with yourself. And this is because only then, having finally found truth, your own truth, in fact, you may finally say 'yes' to existence, but it doesn't actually mean you agree with everything that happens. And all this we are now talking about reminds me of a story of our unforgettable Franz, who, when asked what 'those metaphysicians do', said, 'they do nothing at all,' and when his adversary doubted the merit of doing nothing, Franz pointed out that 'you cannot demand such a difficult thing from everybody.' And this is where the rub is, my friend, for apparently pointless wasting of time might be, paradoxically, of great value and is a way to achieve something that matters in your life. Anyway, whatever you do, thinking should come first, shouldn't it?

"And then, yes, that liberating power of imagination while holding a pen. Otherwise, his writing is like a 'says-nothing' routine, boring his readers to death. And you, my friend," Wahrburg smiled at me, "possess that power of imagination, but then you tend to overuse it sometimes. However, all in all, your piece of work isn't too bad, for you, partially at least, have accomplished what our unforgettable Soren advises, that he whose task it is to produce a corrective idea has only to study, precisely and deeply, the rotten parts of the existing order – and then, in the most impartial way possible, to stress the opposite of it.

"Anyway, what's the good of any writing if it doesn't produce anything useful in life?

"That's all done, my friend, my play is done for now. But then, who knows, we may see each other again, for you may come up with some new ideas in the future.

*

And here Ches' manuscript ended, and I asked myself, *Did* it all really happen?

At that very moment, my telephone rang, and when I answered it, a deep male voice speaking with an unidentified foreign accent said, "It did happen, my friend."

"Who art thou?" I asked.

But the man had already hung up.